The
Collected Papers
of
Sherlock
Holmes
Volume VI – Muniments
(21 Holmes Adventures)

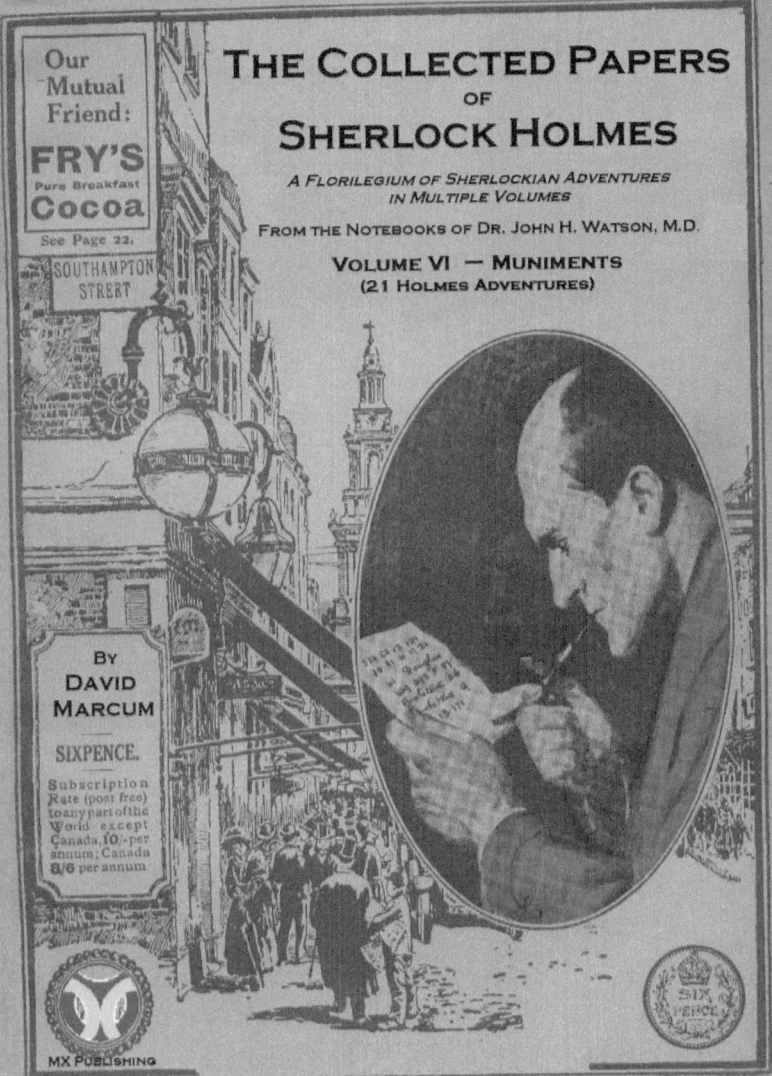

New Sherlock Holmes

THE COLLECTED PAPERS
OF
SHERLOCK HOLMES

*A Florilegium of Sherlockian Adventures
in Multiple Volumes*

FROM THE NOTEBOOKS OF DR. JOHN H. WATSON, M.D.

VOLUME VI — MUNIMENTS
(21 HOLMES ADVENTURES)

By
DAVID
MARCUM

MX PUBLISHING

Published by MX PUBLISHING, 335 PRINCESS PARK MANOR, London, England.

ISBN Hardback 978-1-80424-188-2
ISBN Paperback 978-1-80424-189-9
AUK ePub ISBN 978-1-80424-190-5
AUK PDF ISBN 978-1-80424-191-2

Published in the UK by
MX Publishing
335 Princess Park Manor, Royal Drive,
London, N11 3GX
www.mxpublishing.co.uk

David Marcum can be reached at:
thepapersofsherlockholmes@gmail.com

Cover design by Brian Belanger
www.belangerbooks.com and *www.redbubble.com/people/zhahadun*

Internal illustrations by Sidney Paget

CONTENTS

Forewords

Muniments

Sources

"The Fashionably Dressed Girl" **Sherlock Holmes: A Year of Mystery 1881**, *Belanger Books, 2021*

"The Christmas Ghost of Crailloch Taigh" **The MX Book of New Sherlock Holmes Stories – Part XXVIII: More Christmas Adventures (1869-1888)** *MX Publishing, 2021*

"The Curious Affair of the Temporal Traveler" **Sherlock Holmes: Further Adventures in the Realms of H.G. Wells – Volume Two**, *Belanger Books, 2021*

"The Father Christmas Brigade" **The MX Book of New Sherlock Holmes Stories – Part XXIX: More Christmas Adventures (1889-1896)** *MX Publishing, 2021*

"Some Additional Notes Regarding Mr. Melas" – *Previously Unpublished*

"The *Vodou* Drum" **The MX Book of New Sherlock Holmes Stories – Part XXXVI: "However Improbable . . . ." (1897-1919)** *MX Publishing, 2022*

"The Tragic Affair at the Millennium Manor" **Sherlock Holmes: A Detective's Life**, *Titan Books, 2022*

"The Canterbury Manifesto" **The MX Book of New Sherlock Holmes Stories – Part XXX: More Christmas Adventures (1897-1928)** *MX Publishing, 2021*

"The Noel Street Oracle" **Sherlock Holmes: A Year of Mystery 1882**, *Belanger Books, 2021*

"The Well-Lit Séance" **The MX Book of New Sherlock Holmes Stories – Part XXXV: "However Improbable . . . ." (1889-1896)** *MX Publishing, 2022*

"The Templarian Tattoo" – *Previously Unpublished*

"The Betrayer Moon" **Sherlock Holmes and the Occult Detectives III**, *Belanger Books, 2022*

"The Distasteful Affair of the Minatory Messages" **The MX Book of New Sherlock Holmes Stories – Part XXXII: 2022 Annual (1888-1895)** *MX Publishing, 2022*

"The First Spivey Encounter" **Sherlock Holmes and Dr. Watson: Medical Mysteries Volume One** *Belanger Books, 2021*

"Jonathan Sparler, Resurrectionist" **The Book of Carnacki the Ghost-Finder** *Belanger Books, 2022*

"The Sethian Messiah" **The MX Book of New Sherlock Holmes Stories – Part XXXI: 2022 Annual (1875-1887)** *MX Publishing, 2022*

"The Outpost Incident" – *Previously Unpublished*

"Kindred Spirits" **The Nefarious Villains of Sherlock Holmes – Volume I** *Belanger Books, 2021*

"Enquiry in Conduit Street" **The Nefarious Villains of Sherlock Holmes – Volume II** *Belanger Books, 2021*

"The Gillette Play's the Thing!" **The MX Book of New Sherlock Holmes Stories – Part XXXIII: 2022 Annual (1896-1919)** *MX Publishing, 2022*

"The Mediobogdum Sword" **The MX Book of New Sherlock Holmes Stories – Part XXXIV: "However Improbable . . . ." (1878-1888)** *MX Publishing, 2022*

These additional adventures are contained in
The Collected Papers of Sherlock Holmes

Volume I – Tales
(9 Short Stories and a Novel)

The Papers of Sherlock Holmes (9 Short Stories)
The Adventure of the Least Winning Woman
The Adventure of the Treacherous Tea
The Singular Affair at Sissinghurst Castle
The Adventure of the Second Chance
The Haunting of Sutton House
The Adventure of the Missing Missing Link
The Affair of The Brother's Request
The Adventure of the Madman's Ceremony
The Adventure of the Other Brother
and
Sherlock Holmes and A Quantity of Debt (A Novel)

Volume II – Records
(5 Short Stories and a Novel)

Sherlock Holmes – Tangled Skeins
The Mystery at Kerrett's Rood
The Curious Incident of the Goat-Cart Man
The Matter of Boz's Last Letter
The Tangled Skein at Birling Gap
The Gower Street Murder
and
Sherlock Holmes and The Eye of Heka (A Novel)

Volume III – Accounts
(22 Holmes Adventures)

The Adventure of the Pawnbroker's Daughter
The Problem of the Holy Oil
The Trusted Advisor
An Actor and a Rare One
The Unnerved Estate Agent
The Cat's Meat Lady of Cavendish Square

(Continued on the next page . . . .)

(Continued on the next page . . . .)

Volume V – Chronicles
(20 Holmes Adventures)
The Stolen Relic
The Helverton Inheritance
The Carroun Document
The Reappearance of Mr. James Phillimore
The Keadby Cross
The Rhayader Affair
The Cliddesden Questions
The Affair of the Mother's Return
The Painting in the Parlour
The Two Bullets
The Coombs Contrivance
The True Account of the Bushell Street Killing
The Polmayne Puzzles
The Curious Cardboard Boxes
The Bizarre Affair of the Octagon House
The Peculiar Persecution of Mr. Druitt
The Service for the American Colonel
The Rescue at Ypres
The Problem of the Hindhead Minister
The Edinburgh Bankers

ALSO BY DAVID MARCUM

As author. . . .

- *The Papers of Sherlock Holmes* (Volumes I and II)
- *Sherlock Holmes and A Quantity of Debt*
- *Sherlock Holmes – Tangled Skeins*
- *Sherlock Holmes and The Eye of Heka*
- *The Complete Papers of Solar Pons* (Volumes I-VI - More forthcoming)
- *The Papers of Solar Pons*
- *The Further Papers of Solar Pons*

As editor . . . .

- *The MX Book of New Sherlock Holmes Stories* (Volumes I-XXXIX – and counting!)
- *Sherlock Holmes: Before Baker Street*
- *Holmes Away From Home: Adventures from The Great Hiatus* (Volumes I and II)
- *Sherlock Holmes and Doctor Watson: The Early Adventures* (Volumes I, II, and III)
- *Sherlock Holmes: Adventures Beyond the Canon* (Volumes I, II, and III)
- *After the East Wind Blows: World War I and Roaring Twenties Adventures of Sherlock Holmes* (Volumes I, II, and III)
- *The New Adventures of Solar Pons*
- *The Meeting of the Minds: The Cases of Sherlock Holmes and Solar Pons* (Volumes I and II)
- *The Nefarious Villains of Sherlock Holmes* (Volumes I and II)
- *The Complete Solar Pons* (by August Derleth – Volumes I-VIII)
- *The Complete Dr. Thorndyke* (by R. Austin Freeman – Volumes I-IX)
- *Sherlock Holmes in Montague Street* (by Arthur Morrison – Volumes I, II, and III. Martin Hewitt stories retold as early Sherlock Holmes Adventures)
- *A Proofreader's Adventures of Sherlock Holmes* (by Nick Dunn-Meynell)
- *The Rediscovered Annals of Sherlock Holmes* (by Terry Golledge)
- *Sherlock Holmes is Everywhere!* (co-edited with Sonia Fetherston and Derrick Belanger)
- *The Detective and the Clergyman: The Adventures of Sherlock Holmes and Father Brown* (Forthcoming)

As always, this is for Rebecca and Dan, with all my love

"It's all one case."
by David Marcum

It's all about playing *The Game*.

That's the bottom-line reason behind these stories. And what is *The Game*? For those who don't know, it's reading the Sherlock Holmes stories with the firm belief that he and Watson were *real historical figures*. That Dr. Watson *wrote* the stories, and Sir Arthur Conan Doyle was his *Literary Agent*. That Our Heroes actually *lived* in Baker Street (for a couple of decades, off and on, and *not* forever) and solved real cases for real people, even if names and places and dates were changed and obfuscated to protect the innocent, or maybe because Watson's handwriting was bad, or because of some hidden agenda that the Literary Agent needed to fulfill.

By acknowledging that Holmes and Watson were real, living, breathing, functioning people, then it's a given that were born, lived, and died. (No magic immortal detectives need apply!) And if they were born and lived and died, then these lives occurred across a fixed period. These men aren't Time Lords who can be picked up and dropped into other eras, or supernaturally gifted monster hunters in a world where such things exist, and they cannot be remade into a plethora of completely different people to fit whatever agenda some current reader needs to project upon them.

No, the stories in these books are about the same Sherlock Holmes and Dr. Watson that one finds in the original Canon – those pitifully few sixty stories that were published from 1887 to 1927.

I've enjoyed the notion that Mr. Sherlock Holmes was real from nearly the same time that I discovered him – as a boy of ten in 1975. Before I'd even read many of the Canonical adventures, I found two other books that reinforced this idea: William S. Baring-Gould's biography *Sherlock Holmes of Baker Street* (1962), with its chronology of the events in Holmes's long and amazing life (1854-1957), and also Nicholas Meyer's *The Seven-Per-Cent Solution* (1974), in which Holmes meets historical figures such as Sigmund Freud. How could one read those books, especially at that age, and not be convinced that Holmes was real?

In the decades that have passed since then, my interest in Mr. Holmes has only grown. While I read and collect a great many volumes about my other "book friends", as my son called them when he was small – and there are a great lot of them besides Holmes – I've always had a special interest in the consulting detective in Baker Street and his Boswell. Since obtaining my first Holmes book in 1975, I've managed to collect and read (and create a massively dense chronology for) literally thousands of traditional Canonical adventures. I've worn a deerstalker as my only hat, all year long and everywhere since age nineteen. I've been able to make three extensive Holmes Pilgrimages to England and Scotland (so far), wherein I pretty much visited only Holmes-related sites. So it was probably inevitable that, in 2008, I started writing Holmes adventures.

I'd always wanted to write, all the way back to when I was eight years old and intensely reading about The Three Investigators and The Hardy Boys. Not satisfied with just the official publications, I wanted more new stories too. I spent quite a few Saturdays of my young boyhood tapping away on my dad's typewriter to create new "books".

As I grew, I dabbled with writing little short pieces, mostly humorous, just intended to make family members laugh, because I loved to write, and it always came easily to me. By the late 1980's, I was a U.S. Federal Investigator employed by an obscure government agency, often sent away from home for long periods, conducting investigations that lasted anywhere from five weeks to three months. Once, when I was sent to Albuquerque for several months to conduct extensive field investigations, I impulsively stopped at a local Walmart and bought a hundred-dollar typewriter and a big pack of paper with some of my *per diem* money. (This was the early 1990's – a long time before personal computers or laptops.)

It was there that I sat down for my first real effort at being a writer – and before I departed I'd finished most of a 600-plus page Ludlumesque novel. (One can get a lot of writing done night after night in a bleak hotel room.) The book was coincidentally about a heroic federal investigator – not unlike myself – who stumbled into a vast Russian-led conspiracy in the American southeast where I'm from. I still have that book – *Civil Servants* – stored in my old federal investigator briefcase, pushed underneath my bed. Its plot is mired in the early 1990's when it was written, locked to the aftermath of the Cold War, but it isn't half bad, and it taught me the valuable lesson that other writers also know: *The secret to writing is to put your butt in the chair and do it.*

After that particular trip, I went back home, finished up what was left of my epic adventure novel, and then settled back into writing the occasional short piece for our private amusement – but it was inevitable that at some point I would write a Holmes adventure.

In the mid-1990's, the federal agency where I'd been employed was abruptly eliminated, a victim of the end of the Cold War and a move to reduce the size of government. (After all, the higher-up wise men thought, who needs security now? We won!) Over the next few years, I went back to school and obtained a second degree in Civil Engineering. Then, in 2008 at the start of the Great Recession, I was unexpectedly laid off from my engineering job. With time on my hands, and a desire to try my hand at Sherlockian pastichery, I began writing each morning after the daily job searching was finished.

I ended up with nine Holmes pastiches, written over several weeks, and then . . . I did nothing with them. That's right. Simply satisfied that I'd written them and that they existed, I put them in a binder labeled *The Papers of Sherlock Holmes* and shelved them with the rest of my Holmes Collection, happy with my secret collector's item.

But eventually I began to wish for other Sherlockians to see them. I shared one with a Sherlockian friend here and another one there, and the response was very positive. Finally I became bolder and wanted more people to see them, asking myself: *Why not put them in a real book of my own?*

I communicated about it with a Sherlockian publisher from whom I'd bought books in the past. He immediately offered to publish *The Papers*, and after a great deal of back-and-forth, my first book eventually appeared. For those who have had that experience – Opening the newly delivered carton to see *your book!* – there is nothing like it. It's a satisfaction that cannot easily be described.

That was in 2011. Over the next couple of years, I became aware of MX Publishing. I saw that an acquaintance of mine who'd also had his first book published with the same original publisher as mine had switched to MX, and I reached out to him. He informed me that he was happy to have switched to MX. With that in mind, I sent an email to Steve Emecz, Sherlockian Publisher Extraordinaire – and that was truly life-changing and improving decision.

In 2013, Steve republished my first book, *The Papers of Sherlock Holmes*, and he made the whole experience so painless that I set about writing a Holmes novel, *Sherlock Holmes and A Quantity of Debt*. That same fall, I was making my long-planned first Holmes Pilgrimage to London, and Steve arranged for me to have a book-signing in The Sherlock Holmes Hotel in Baker Street, where I was staying (when not traveling about to Dartmoor, the Sussex Coast, Edinburgh, and other locations). I was able to meet Steve for the first time on that trip, and found him to be one of the nicest, most supportive, and most thoughtful people around – and that hasn't changed a bit.

Jump ahead a little bit: In early 2015, I woke up early from a dream in which I'd edited a Holmes anthology. Instead of rolling over and forgetting the idea, I arose and started thinking about authors whom I admired and that I might want to invite to write stories. I ran the idea by Steve, and he was willing to publish it, so I began sending invitations. I hoped that I might get a dozen stories (at best) for a modest paperback volume. Fearing a lack of response, I kept sending invitations to everyone that I could think of – and then, amazingly, people started signing up. New Sherlock Holmes stories started to arrive in my email in-box – which quickly becomes addictive. More and more authors heard about it – some that I didn't even know about yet – and before we knew it, the little idea had grown into a three-volume hardcover behemoth of over 60 new Holmes stories – *Parts I, II*, and *III* of *The MX Book of New Sherlock Holmes Stories*, the largest collection of its kind ever produced to that point.

Early on, Steve and I had decided that the royalties from the project would go to support the Stepping Stones School for special needs children, located at Undershaw, one of Sir Arthur Conan Doyle's former homes. The books were a smashing success and received a lot of attention, and I was able to go to London in the fall of 2015 for the release party – what turned out to be Holmes Pilgrimage No. 2. There I was able to meet a number of the contributing authors in person – and to my everlasting regret, I was so thrilled that I barely remembered to take any photos!

After I returned home, I began to receive more emails, now asking when the next book was planned – *Good grief! A next book?!?* – and also stating that many authors (both returning and new) wanted to contribute.

I'd had no plans to do any more books, thinking that the first three were lightning in a bottle that couldn't be recaptured . . . but then I realized that the heavy-lifting in terms of decision-making and set-up and formatting and process-building had already occurred, so Steve and I decided to keep going. (I think I said to him "Let's do one more . . . .")

Part IV came out in the spring of 2016 – and after that, more people kept sending stories for *the next books* and wanting to join the party. We came up with the plan to have yearly books. But we received so many stories that it grew to twice a year. We now have an un-themed spring collection – the yearly *Annual* – and also a fall collection with a specific theme, such as Christmas adventures, seemingly impossible crimes, Untold Cases, etc. As more and more stories kept rolling in, it became necessary for each season's particular set to grow to multiple simultaneously published volumes. That's how, in just a few short years, we're now up to *Parts XXXVII, XXXVIII*, and *XXXIX*, (to be published in Spring 2023), and as I write this, I'm already receiving stories for *Further Untold Cases – Part XL* (and *XLI* and *XLII* too . . . ?)

So far the books have raised over $100,000 for the school, and that will just keep going up!

4

As part of editing these books, I couldn't let them pass by without adding my own stories – editor's prerogative. Thus, that helped to motivate me to sit my butt in the chair and write more about Mr. Holmes. By way of these books, I've met some really incredible people, including the incomparable Belanger Brothers, Derrick and Brian. Derrick initially contributed short stories, while Brian – a truly gifted artist – became the MX cover artist after the original artist passed away.

At one point, the two Belangers wrote a series of Holmes books for children. Eventually they formed Belanger Books – another amazing Sherlockian publishing venture. Between MX and Belanger Books – both of which cooperate beautifully with one another – the Sherlockian publishing field is amazingly well covered, providing an opportunity for so many people to be Sherlockian pasticheurs when they would otherwise be excluded by those who happily and aggressively seek to squash that aspect of the Sherlockian experience.

In 2016, the Belangers asked me to assemble and edit a Holmes story collection for them. I did, and as it also consisted of traditional and Canonical adventures, and had many of the same authors as in the MX anthologies, I formatted it the same way. After that, I edited another one for them, and another, and those also grew to simultaneously published multiple volumes. This extra editing also served to motivate me to write more Holmes stories for each of those collections as well – because I didn't want those trains leaving without me being on them.

From there, I began to receive invitations to write still more stories for other editors' anthologies and magazines. Along the way I published a couple more of my own books – *Sherlock Holmes – Tangled Skeins* (2015) and *Sherlock Holmes and The Eye of Heka* (2021) – but most of my stories that I wrote over those years remained uncollected within the various anthologies and magazines in which they had originally appeared. All along, I stayed too busy with real life and family and my dream job (as a civil engineer working for my home town's public works department), along with writing more stories and editing various books, to take the time to properly collect them all into my own books.

At some point, I ended up writing my 100th pastiche, (along with 28 pastiches about Solar Pons, "The Sherlock Holmes of Baker Street" – but that's another story and another hero.) In 2021, I had the idea of collecting my uncollected Holmes stories.

The initial five books of *The Complete Papers*, published in 2021, contained 77 of those stories. This book contains 21 more of them. Others are still in the pipeline to be published elsewhere. I have a number of other pastiched planned and promised for 2023, so Volume 7 of *The Complete Papers* will hopefully appear in the next year or so . . . *Fingers crossed!*

Many people have sports figures or musicians or actors or (curiously) politicians as heroes. My heroes have always been my book friends and authors – all the way back to when I was eight or nine and wondering about why I couldn't track down satisfying biographical information concerning the brilliant and prolific and mysterious author Franklin W. Dixon. I've always admired writers for what they accomplish and create while spending great chunks of their lives self-imposed isolation – something which I now understand. And at least if I had to set aside all that time to put my butt in the chair, I've been very fortunate that all of these stories almost told themselves. I almost never outline or plan. Instead, when I write – when I find that it's time for another story – I simply open a blank Word document on the computer and then wait for Watson to begin whispering to me. It's scary, but I trust the process now, and when it works – and it always has so far – there's no feeling quite like it.

Through these stories, I've achieved two important personal goals: In my own small way, I've become a writer, and I've also added to *The Great Holmes Tapestry*, a phrase I coined several years ago to describe the massive collection of narratives about the *true* Holmes and Watson – novels, short stories, radio and television episodes, movies and scripts, comics and fan-fiction, and unpublished manuscripts – that tell the complete and entire course of their lives from beginning to end. The Canon serves as the supporting structure – the wire core of the rope, the heavy steel girders of the skyscraper – but the thousands of traditional post-Canonical pastiches provide essential depth and color, filling in all the spaces around The Canon, and adding important information about The Whole Lives of Our Heroes.

I've long described myself as a missionary for The Church of the Traditional Canonical Holmes, preaching that the bigger picture of both Canon and the traditional pastiches should be seen and supported. This means giving respect and value to additional Holmes adventures, and not just those original sixty because they were the ones that came across the first Literary Agent's desk.

Ross MacDonald – (Real Name: Kenneth Millar, another of my authorial heroes because of his incredible private eye, Lew Archer) – said *"It's all one case."* In other words, a *Great Tapestry*. He meant that even though he'd written eighteen Archer novels and a number of short stories from the 1940's to the 1970's, they were never meant to stand alone. They were all part of one overall arching story – Lew Archer's story – spanning across multiple narratives.

6

It's the same with the Holmes adventures – *all* of them, Canon and traditional pastiche, mine and everyone else's. They fit together to tell the *entire* story of Sherlock Holmes, and with the stories in this collection, I'm incredibly proud to have added my own contribution.

* * * * *

"Of course, I could only stammer out my thanks."
– *The unhappy John Hector McFarlane, "The Norwood Builder"*

At some point during the foreword-writing for the various MX anthologies, I began to use the quote shown above from Mr. McFarlane in regard to *Thank You*'s. It's fitting – I can only stammer out thanks, and never adequately express how grateful I am for all the help and encouragement I've received over the years in all aspects of my life – not just the writing and editing of Sherlock Holmes stories.

First and foremost, I am always overwhelmed at how incredibly fortunate I am to have my wife and son in my life. In all aspects, my wife – nearly 35 years as I write this – is the kindest and wisest and most beautiful person inside and out I know, and she has been there throughout with complete support and encouragement when we went through such things as some terrible jobs and the grind of my returning to school to be an engineer. We have pushed through together, and anything that I can ever accomplish I owe to her. And equally amazing is our son, so incredibly funny and smart, and truly an amazing person in every way. I enjoy every minute spent with him, and it only gets better. I love you both, and you are everything to me!

Then there are my parents and sister, who put up with me during those first couple of decades – I probably don't even realize how bad that was for them. My parents did everything to encourage me – music lessons leading to a piano scholarship in college, all the books that I could read, and generally anything to help me grow as a person, so that it never occurred to me that I couldn't do whatever I wanted. And my sister was my best friend then, patiently listening as I rambled about whatever interested me. Even then, she probably heard more about Sherlock Holmes than she'd ever bargained for!

There is a group that exchanges emails with me when we have the time – and time is a valuable commodity for all of us these days! As the years have gone by, we've gotten busier and busier, and I don't get to write as often as I'd like, but I really enjoy catching up whenever we get the chance. These people are all wonderful writers, and I recommend them highly as both friends and authors: Mark Mower, Denis Smith, Tom Turley, Dan Victor, and Marcia Wilson.

Next, I wish to send several huge *Thank You*'s to the following:

- *Steve Emecz* – When I first emailed Steve from out of the blue back in 2013 – *Ten years? So much in ten years!* – I was interested in MX re-publishing my first book. Even then, as a guy who works to accumulate *all* traditional Sherlockian pastiches, I could see that MX (under Steve's leadership) was *the* fast-rising superstar of the Sherlockian publishing world.

  The re-publication of my first book with MX was an amazing life-changing event for me, leading to writing many more stories and then editing books, along with unexpected additional Holmes Pilgrimages to England. By way of that first email with Steve, I've had the chance to make some incredible Sherlockian friends and play in the Holmesian Sandbox in ways that I'd never before dreamed possible.

  Through all of it, Steve has been one of the most positive and supportive people that I've ever known. He works far more than a full-time week at his day job, and he still finds time to take care of all aspects of MX Publishing, with the help of his wife Sharon Emecz, and cousin, Timi Emecz. (That's right – MX is just the three of them who get all of this done!)

  Many who just buy books and have a vague idea of how the publishing industry works now might not realize that MX, a non-profit which supports several important charities, consists of simply these three people. Between them, they take care of running the entire business, including the production, marketing, and shipping – all in their precious spare time, in and around their real lives.

  With incredible hard work, they have made MX into a world-wide Sherlockian publishing phenomenon, providing opportunities for authors who would never have them otherwise. There are some like me who return more than once to Watson's Tin Dispatch Box, and there are others who only find one or two stories there – but they get the chance to publish their books, and then they can point with pride at this accomplishment, and how they too have added to The Great Holmes Tapestry.

From the beginning, Steve has let me explore various Sherlockian projects and open up my own personal possibilities in ways that otherwise would have never happened. Thank you, Steve, for every opportunity!

- *Derrick Belanger* and *Brian Belanger* – I first "met" Derrick Belanger when he graciously reviewed one of my early books, and we quickly became friends. Then he interviewed me several times for his online blog, and when I had the idea for the first MX Holmes anthology in 2015, he quickly joined the party and contributed a fine pastiche. From there he's written a number of others, and then he formed Belanger Books with his brother, Brian. It's turned into a Sherlockian powerhouse, working in tandem with MX Publishing, supporting each other to produce more and more wonderful Holmes adventures. I've very grateful to have had this additional opportunity to further contribute to The Great Holmes Tapestry by editing and writing stories for their different anthologies. Derrick continues to write, but he also stays quite busy as a noted aware-winning teacher, husband, and father, as well as running Belanger Books with Brian.

Over the last few years, my amazement at Brian Belanger's ever-increasing talent has only grown. I initially became acquainted with him when he took over the duties of creating the covers for MX Books following the untimely death of their previous graphic artist. I found Brian to be a great collaborator, very easy-going and stress-free in his approach and willingness to work with authors, and wonderfully creative and positive too. His skills became most apparent to me when he created the cover for my 2017 book, *The Papers of Solar Pons*, which was one of the most striking covers that I've ever seen. Later, when the Belangers and I began reissuing the original Pons books in new editions, and then new Pons anthologies, Brian's similarly themed covers continued to astound me. He truly deserves an award for these.

In the meantime, he has become busier and busier, continuing to provide covers for MX Books, and now for

Belanger Books as well, along with editing and occasionally writing.

I finally met both Brian and Derrick in person in early (pre-pandemic) 2020 at the annual Sherlock Holmes Birthday Celebration in New York City, and they're just as great in person as they were by way of email. I immediately felt like I'd known them both forever. I cannot express to either one of you just how grateful I am.

- *Roger Johnson* – I had known of Roger for quite a while, having seen his name connected with the "District Messenger" newsletter of *The Sherlock Holmes Society of London Journal*. I could tell, even then, that he represented the finest kind of Sherlockian. When I wrote my first Holmes book, I sent him a copy – out of the blue, as he had no idea who I was – as a thank you, and with the timid and dim spark of a hope that he would review it, because having him do so would mean (to me) that what I had written was legitimized. He did write a great review, and we began to correspond. When I was able to get to England for my first Holmes Pilgrimage in 2013, I made arrangements to meet with Roger and his wonderful wife, Jean Upton, in person, and I discovered that what I'd already known by email was true: They are both the very best people!

Later, in 2015 on Holmes Pilgrimage No. 2, they invited me to stay with them for several days in their home, and that was one of the best parts of all the trips. They gave me tours, they showed me their incredible collection, they let me see life in a real British household and not just from a hotel room, and we had some wonderful conversations along the way. I was able to see them again in 2016, Holmes Pilgrimage No. 3, when we attended the Grand Opening of the Stepping Stones School at Undershaw.

I'm more grateful than I can say that I know Roger. His Sherlockian knowledge is exceptional, as is the work that he does to further the cause of The Master. But even more than that, both Roger and his wonderful wife, Jean, are simply the finest and best, and I'm very lucky to know both of them – even though I don't get to see them nearly as often as I'd like, and especially in these crazy

10

days! In so many ways, Roger, I can't thank you enough, and I can't imagine these books without you.

- *Nicholas Meyer* – I started reading Nick Meyer's Holmes books before I'd even read all of The Canon, and for that I'm eternally grateful. It was through his first two books, *The Seven-Per-Cent Solution* and *The West End Horror* (the latter of which is still one of my favorite pastiches to this very day) that I firmly understood that The Canon wasn't the be-all end-all of Sherlockian story-telling. I obtained Nick's first book as part of a free book give-away at school, and I found the second not long after when my mother took my sister and me to buy school clothes and I spotted it in the mall bookstore. (I sat cross-legged along an out-of-the-way wall in a Sears while my mother and sister shopped and started reading *The West End Horror* straight out of the bag.)

    After those first two books, Nick went on to have a very successful career in film. (More about that in a minute.) But he has continued to dip in an out of Sherlockian pastichery with *The Canary Trainer* (1993), *The Adventure of the Peculiar Protocols* (2019), and *The Return of the Pharaoh* (2021). He is a Sherlockian legend, and it's an indisputable fact that the publication in 1974 of *The Seven-Per-Cent Solution* – a *pastiche*, mind you! – was the beginning of the Sherlockian Golden Age when has grown and grown, and has never stopped, all the way to today.

    If it was just that, Sherlockians – and especially pasticheurs – would owe him an unpayable debt. But then there's *Star Trek*, which he also saved. As mentioned above, I have lots of interests besides Mr. Holmes, although he does demand more and more attention as my years pass. But I've been a Trekkie (or Trekker, or whatever the correct term is) since I was a wee lad in the late 1960's, when my babysitter happened to watch one of the original prime-time episodes. After that, I grew up seeing the original series in re-reruns, and then I was among those who saw the first Star Trek film in 1979 (and truthfully felt mightily disappointed. I do like it better now.) But it was Nick Meyer's *Star Trek: The Wrath of Khan* (1982) which electrified the Trek Universe, jump-starting it into motion in a way that – like the Holmes Golden Age – has only grown. And how it's grown! Hundreds and hundreds of Star Trek novels and comic books, multiple films and television shows, with more in planning and production all the time, and fan interest around the world at an all-time high. As a nearly life-long Star Trek fan, who loves it nearly as much as The World of Sherlock Holmes, I credit the origin of this original escalation entirely to Nick Meyer.

I generally despise social media, but it's a very useful way for Sherlockians to connect. Imagine my thrill when I began to see occasional online posts from Nick Meyer – and when I dared to respond, sometimes he would respond back! I've learned that if you don't ask, you'll never know, so I connected with him a bit more often, and eventually I boldly asked him to write a foreword to one of the MX anthologies that I edit, and he most-generously agreed. After that, we've stayed in touch off-and-on, and that still never ceases to amaze me.

I met him in person at the 2011 *From Gillette to Brett* conference in Bloomington, Indiana, where he was the featured guest. I took my Holmes book, asked him to autograph them, and asked – like everyone does – when he'd write his next Holmes book. He certainly doesn't remember that, but he was the main reason I chose to attend that event.

One of my greatest regrets is that, while attending the 2020 Sherlock Holmes Birthday Celebration in New York, I was almost able to meet him in person again – and this time he'd know who I was – but I didn't get to speak with him, and it was my own fault. We had emailed ahead of time, planning to meet, and that day I entered the famed dealer's room and saw him seated at a table near the door, surrounded by many fans. I wandered away, intending to return in a just a very few minutes and dive into the crowd, hoping that it might have thinned a bit. But when I got back over there, he'd already left! Hopefully I'll get another chance, sooner rather than later, where I can thank him in person for so many things . . .

. . . including generously writing a foreword for this ongoing series of volumes. When I was considering who could write a foreword, I couldn't think of anyone more

12

fitting. Through Nicholas Meyer I found pastiches, which have been so important to me over the years. Nick, thanks from the bottom of my heart for taking the time to be part of these books!

And finally, last but certainly *not* least, thanks to **Sir Arthur Conan Doyle**: Author, doctor, adventurer, and the Founder of the Sherlockian Feast. Honored, and present in spirit.

As I always note when putting together a collection of Holmes stories, the effort has been a labor of love. This time the labor and love have been mine. These adventures are more tiny threads woven into the ongoing *Great Holmes Tapestry*, continuing to grow and grow, for there can *never* be enough stories about the man whom Watson described as *"the best and wisest . . . whom I have ever known."*

David Marcum
Originally written September 8th, 2021
Revised February 11th, 2023

Questions, comments, or story submissions
may be addressed to David Marcum at

thepapersofsherlockholmes@gmail.com

13

A Note on the
Modern Publishing Paradigm

For the longest time, publishing something was mostly impossible for most people. The Great Publishing Houses – which sounds like something from *Dune* – are giant machines, with carefully calculated formulas to know just how many books they need to sell to make a profit. It's no different than selling cereal: Many of the boxes of cereal on grocery store shelves won't be sold, and they were never meant to be sold, and the manufacturers are okay with that, because they've calculated the amount that they do need to actually sell in order to stay profitable while figuring in just how much can be discarded.

It used to be the same with books. Publishers would create a print run of a certain number of copies, sending out so many of them to bookstores across the country. Some would be sold – enough, hopefully, to cover costs – while many copies would just sit there, unsold, forever. Then, after a certain amount of time, they would be removed – either destroyed, or "remaindered", to be sold at rock-bottom prices in bargain bins.

It's an investment by the publishers to go to the trouble and expense to create all of those physical books, hoping to make their money back on enough of them to justify the waste of the others. That's why they're so restrictive about what they publish: They must meet the razor-thin edge of profit. But that makes the path to being published a very narrow needle's eye.

Several years ago, the paradigm began to shift. Online sales began to disrupt the physical bookstore model. And as people ordered online, some publishers figured out that they didn't have to have back rooms and warehouses jammed full of physical books sitting around waiting for a physical customer to enter a store or a dealer's room, examine it, and possibly buy it. Instead, when an online order arrived, the manufacturing of the book could commence right then, only as needed, and not months or years earlier.

This print-on-demand idea had been around for a while. (When I was going back to school for my second degree in civil engineering, the campus print shop did the same thing for certain locally produced textbooks, printing them as they were purchased on fancy copying machines.) Publishers and authors began to take advantage of technological advances to produce their own books – straight from author to reader, happily eliminating the giant publishing middlemen.

Steve Emecz of MX Publishing brilliantly took advantage of this, building his business and allowing authors who would have never had a chance otherwise – like me – to create and connect.

But there are certain legitimate complaints.

In the olden days, the giant publishers slow-walked books through the process, so that it sometimes took literally years for a book to actually be published. Authors could actually die before ever seeing their work excreted at the far end of the giant publisher's process. The print-on-demand process, by comparison, is nearly immediate. As part of the large publishers' slow walk, there were battalions of editors who went through books forwards, backwards, and upside down. With the new technology, where a file can be loaded with the book manufacturer with very little effort and time spent, there is clearly less editing . . . and mistakes slip through.

Some readers continue to expect flawless and perfect works, as if legions of editors were behind the curtain as in days of old, still involved in the process. For this type of reader/consumer, the new format of publishing will always be pain they just can't ease. That's why, with this set of my stories, I want to apologize up front to those who will find typos – *because in spite of every effort, there will be some typos.*

In my own case, I love to write and edit, and I spend a sizeable amount of time doing both, but I also have a very busy and rich life doing other things. I spend time with my family, and I work more-than-full time as a civil engineer, fitting in these Sherlockian writing and editing projects during lunch hours, evenings, and weekends. It's a high wire act with no safety net. I'm the writer and sole editor of the stories in this collection. My wife, with a Bachelor's Degree in Journalism and two Master's Degrees in English Literature and Library Science, and with a first job as a copy editor, used to go through my stories and catch what I missed – because you never *ever* see your own mistakes – but she works way more than full time at her own job, and she just doesn't have any extra time to spare for playing uncredited editor on these projects. So they're all on me.

It's the same with the anthologies that I edit – any mistake that slips through in the end is my fault, because there are no other editors. When assembling a Holmes anthology, I receive the stories, format them to the "house style", print them on 8½ x 11-inch paper, edit and revise with a red pen, go back and forth with emails to the author – sometimes a lot of emails – and then plug them into a giant Word document for more editing and revision. But from the time I get the story until I send the final file to the publisher, there isn't anyone else to do additional editing or proofreading, and no time to work someone into the process. It's the new publishing paradigm.

16

As a print-on-demand publisher, MX does not have squadrons of editors. The business consists of three part-time people who also have busy lives elsewhere – so the editing effort largely falls on the contributors. Some readers and consumers out there in the world absolutely despise this – They foam at the mouth in rage, apparently forgetting about all those self-produced Holmes stories and volumes from decades ago with awkward self-published formatting and loads of errors that are now prized as collector's items.

These critics should recall that every one of these new volumes by various authors – even those that have typographic and formatting errors – are the very best efforts that can be produced by very sincere people who don't have professional full-time editors to help, and who would never ever have had the opportunity to publish otherwise, and because of these authors, there is thankfully more Sherlockian content in the world.

I'm personally mortified when errors slip through – ironically, there will probably be errors in this essay – and I apologize now, but without a regiment of editors looking over my shoulder, this is as good as it gets. Real life is more important than writing and editing, and only so much time can be spent preparing these books before they are released into the wild. I hope that you can look past any errors, small or huge, and simply enjoy these stories, and appreciate the effort involved, and the sincere desire to add to The Great Holmes Tapestry.

And in spite of any errors here, there are more Sherlock Holmes stories than there were before, and that's a good thing.

David Marcum

Watson's Descendants
by Nicholas Meyer

It is generally felt that the short story was Sherlock Holmes's best venue. The novellas, by contrast, are judged to be . . . lesser. Even the fabled *The Hound of the Baskervilles* suffers from the detective's absence for many pages. Though *A Study in Scarlet*, *The Sign of the Four*, and *The Valley of Fear* remain deliciously absorbing, it is in the short stories that Holmes and Watson truly flourish.

As Michael Chabon has observed, all fiction is fan fiction. Almost from the beginning, Sherlock Holmes has prompted imitators of his creator's creation. Arthur Conan Doyle wrote sixty Holmes cases in all – fifty-six short stories and four novellas. When they ended, boys and girls, men and women of all ages mourned Watson's silence and the series' cessation. But it wasn't long before others took up – or attempted to take up – Sir Arthur's pen.

Writing a full-length Holmes novel has always posed a challenge, even for Doyle himself, to say nothing of generations of later writers and filmmakers. Short stories, on the other hand, pose problems of their own. A good short story must compress action and character. It must – obviously – be short. The gift of writing compelling short fiction remains in a class by itself. Poe, Doyle of course, Twain, Saki, and Hawthorne are among the masters of the form from the Victorian and Edwardian eras, but over the years, the short story has produced many masters.

I alas am not among them. Even as a kid in art class, my paintings were so huge the murals I attempted had to be unfurled in the hall, not the studio. And so it comes as no surprise that writing a short Holmes story does not come easily to me. In fact, it does not come at all.

I retain nothing but admiration for those writers who *can* create short fiction, and a special respect for those who can bring off simulacra of Doyle's charming and distinctive Holmes tales. There many practitioners, including some whose efforts, unfortunately, resemble nothing so much as taxidermy. But among the best I must number David Marcum, who, by this point has written more Holmes stories than Doyle himself. Characterized by unflagging imagination and ceaseless ingenuity, along with felicitous prose, these tales continue to provide what we all crave: More Sherlock.

All Sherlock Holmes stories, (except Doyle's), are of course forgeries. And it's the rare forger who can resist signing his own work. See if you can spot David Marcum's fine Italian hand.
Enjoy.

Nicholas Meyer
Los Angeles, 2021

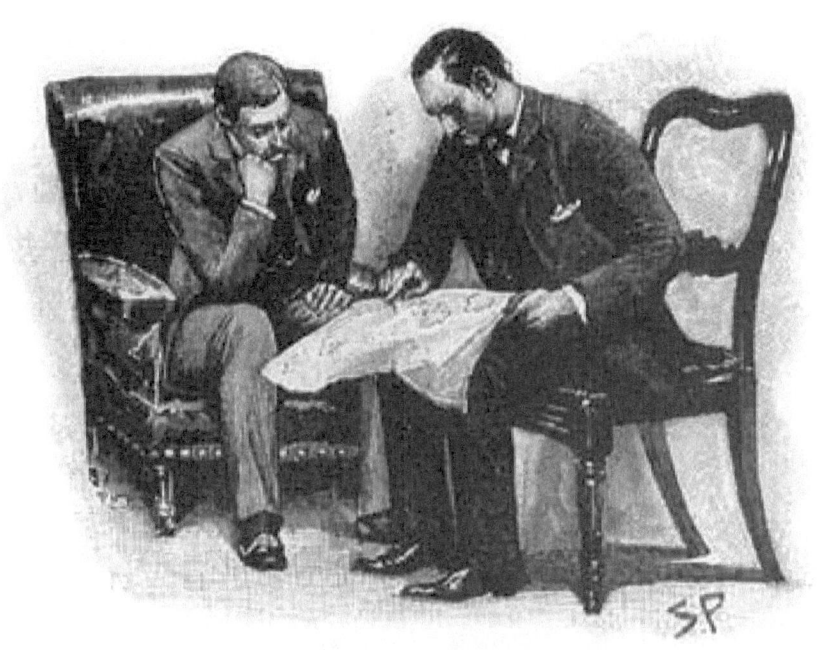

Sherlock Holmes (1854-1957) was born in Yorkshire, England, on 6 January, 1854. In the mid-1870's, he moved to 24 Montague Street, London, where he established himself as the world's first Consulting Detective. After meeting Dr. John H. Watson in early 1881, he and Watson moved to rooms at 221b Baker Street, where his reputation as the world's greatest detective grew for several decades. He was presumed to have died battling noted criminal Professor James Moriarty on 4 May, 1891, but he returned to London on 5 April, 1894, resuming his consulting practice in Baker Street. Retiring to the Sussex coast near Beachy Head in October 1903, he continued to be associated in various private and government investigations while giving the impression of being a reclusive apiarist. He was very involved in the events encompassing World War I, and to a lesser degree those of World War II. He passed away peacefully upon the cliffs above his Sussex home on his 103rd birthday, 6 January, 1957.

Dr. John Hamish Watson (1852-1929) was born in Stranraer, Scotland on 7 August, 1852. In 1878, he took his Doctor of Medicine Degree from the University of London, and later joined the army as a surgeon. Wounded at the Battle of Maiwand in Afghanistan (27 July, 1880), he returned to London late that same year. On New Year's Day, 1881, he was introduced to Sherlock Holmes in the chemical laboratory at Barts. Agreeing to share rooms with Holmes in Baker Street, Watson became invaluable to Holmes's consulting detective practice. Watson was married and widowed three times, and from the late 1880's onward, in addition to his participation in Holmes's investigations and his medical practice, he chronicled Holmes's adventures, with the assistance of his literary agent, Sir Arthur Conan Doyle, in a series of popular narratives, most of which were first published in *The Strand* magazine. Watson's later years were spent preparing a vast number of his notes of Holmes's cases for future publication. Following a final important investigation with Holmes, Watson contracted pneumonia and passed away on 24 July, 1929.

Photos of Sherlock Holmes and Dr. John H. Watson courtesy of Roger Johnson

The
Collected Papers
of
Sherlock
Holmes
Volume VI - Muniments
(21 Holmes Adventures)

The Fashionably Dressed Girl

Editor's Note: As mentioned in the Foreword of my book Sherlock Holmes and The Eye of Heka, *I was fortunate to stumble across a vast cache of Watsonian Manuscripts while in London my second Holmes Pilgrimage, having boldly knocked on the door of Watson's former Queen Anne Street lodgings and finding a distant descendant living within. This person, assured of my sincerity by my deerstalker hat and knowledge of Watson's life, has since given me access to these various accounts – of which I've only scratched the surface. Among those papers were a number of Holmes's documents as well, and presented here are selected entries from both his and Watson's journals in early 1881, during those early days when they first met, but knew nothing of one another, and had no idea that theirs would be any more than a temporary acquaintance at best . . . .*

1 January, 1881 – From the Journals of Dr. John H. Watson

*T*he colonel calls my name, but I ignore him. He says it again, angry now – and this time there is a pleading note too. With a snarl, I turn from the body laid out in front of me. Ten minutes ago this had been a soldier, bravely doing his best. A minute ago he'd been someone's child, screaming for his mother. Now he was a lump of inert materials, meat and water and minerals and worse, all held together for just a very few years by . . . something . . . something indefinable, that let him walk and talk and breath and laugh and cry. For a time, he'd had a favorite color, a favorite taste, a favorite place.

Someone had probably loved him. Perhaps he'd even been fortunate enough to truly love someone else. Now that something that had bound him together was gone as if it had never been, yesterday's smoke, and this bloody thing was taking up space urgently needed for others. What had been a brave young man – no one in the field tent even knew his name – would soon return to the earth, his water seeping in or evaporating away to somewhere else, with the rest of him slowly dispersing all around this small dusty hell – for I knew he'd never return home and he'd never have a proper grave – and maybe one day a tiny piece of him would once again be part of something else, here in this Afghan wasteland, that was alive. But that piece of him then wouldn't remember this piece now, and no one would ever know what had happened here. To him or to me.

I want to curse as I turn to face the colonel. I had *cursed him the first time I'd turned, on that day. But now I cannot speak. It's as if I can barely move at all.*

The colonel is there, as he always is, standing close, a box in his hand. That part is always the same. He holds the box out to me, and I can see what it contains – bullets.

"The Ghazis are almost here," he says, gesturing for me to take the box. "There's nothing we can do, John. There's no way to move them. And we can't let these lads fall into the enemy's hands – not while they're still alive."

I can't raise my hand to take the box. That was real – to the bottom of my soul I hadn't wanted to take that box, because I knew what it meant. I had sworn an oath to protect life. This act – this very place – was a violation of all that was Holy. But somehow I did take the box – I take it, and then I nearly drop it as my blood-slicked hand loses its grip.

Sometimes it's different – the dream is never the same way twice. If I'm lucky, I awaken right then, when I take the box. That happens enough for me to think that I won't be cursed with this dream forever, night after night. But at other times, the colonel keeps talking, and I cease to understand what he says. What's he's telling me blends into the cacophony all around us. In that version of the dream, I can't understand his words, but his face never changes, and the terrible expression upon it – equal parts fear and sadness at what both he and I must do next.

But in most versions of the dream – such as the one last night –

I'm in front of the unsteady surgeon's table, trying to save another soldier as the screams and gunfire rage around me. I can't look up, as my attention is on the opened man in front of me. I don't know why I bother – Wouldn't it be better to let them go now, perhaps just slipping away from shock and blood loss, instead of in a few minutes, when in their terror they see me approaching, one after another, walking from injured soldier to injured soldier, matching the colonel's steps on the opposite side of the tent as we work our way toward the middle, making sure to save one bullet each for ourselves?

Then I am walking along the soldiers. They are mostly on the ground, as we only had a few cots. Behind me I hear a gunshot – not the rifle fire of the Ghazis, but that of a service revolver, identical to the one in my own hand. The men on the ground are whimpering and crying. One behind me begins to repeat "No, no!" over and over. A pistol fires, and he stops.

The young fellow looking up at me arrived just an hour or so ago – one of the first of the wounded to stumble in when the shooting started. We were a well-ordered hospital tent then, and the gunshot to his leg had been stabilized. It was a terrible wound, and in any London hospital it would

30

have been something awful and unusual, but now – seeing the other wounds that came after his – one would have thought him lucky. Until this moment.

"Doctor?" he says, his eyes cutting between my face and the revolver that I'm lifting. He is confused, but there is no sign of fear. He doesn't understand.

I'm on the ground, face down, my body curled. How did I get here? It's dark – I cannot see, except for a perception of light somewhere to my left. I can see from my left eye, but not my right. The right side of my head is pressed to the earth. I can taste dirt in my mouth. Tiny flakes of stone rest on my tongue. I try to scrape it against my teeth to remove them, and then the pain hits. The light vanishes. My shoulder feels as if it's on fire. I scream, but there is no sound. I'm in my own grave, covered by countless feet of soil above me. I scream, but there is no sound. I can't move. I scream, but there is no sound . . . .

The dream came again last night, and yet I awakened as I always do, on the other side of the world from where it happened. I am one of the lucky ones, I suppose. So said one of the sailors to me as we were docking after the long journey home.

Now, however, in spite of being alive and here, it's with more regret than I would have imagined that I consider leaving my snug little nest, my refuge since my return to England on the *Orontes* a couple of months ago.

Since arriving in London by way of Portsmouth last November, this small room has been where I could hide from the world, leaving only when I must, and always anxious to return. Here I don't have to face the glances of pity from those that I pass on the street who see my emaciated condition, or become impatient as my impaired gait impedes them, forcing them to slow with a grunt of annoyance when they suddenly come upon me before dodging quickly around to vanish into the crowds.

But at the same time, I have come to curse this room. A bed, a small wardrobe, a table and ladder-back chair, and another more-plush chair for reclining and smoking and thinking: This is what one would expect of a small private hotel just off the Strand, and there is nothing objectionable about it, and yet, many has been the night when I cannot sleep, recalling what I have seen – the butchery and horrors of Maiwand, just a little over five months ago – or the pain which seems to worsen at night, refusing to abate. I suppose that I could drink it away, but my brother's sad state is lesson enough to avoid that dangerous path. Instead, I will continue to keep my journals, as writing both helps me to forget for a while, and also strangely enough, seats me in a position that eases the pain of my shoulder wound.

31

In any case, it seems as if I might be shifting to new rooms in Baker Street, pending their inspection tomorrow morning – and also dependent upon what I am to make of the man who will be my fellow lodger.

I had almost forgotten that today was New Year's Day when I set out this morning for my forced constitutional. It never occurred to me why the streets were so quiet until I entered Trafalgar Square and was suddenly struck by the date. Here's hoping that 1881 will be better than the previous one!

I was standing in the Criterion, considering the ridiculous cost of living in London on my temporary wound pension of eleven-shillings-and-sixpence-a-day, when I felt a tap on the shoulder – my uninjured one, thank heavens. It was Stamford, my old dresser at Barts. I suppose that I was a bit too happy to see him, but I was in something of a brown study when he said hello, and I latched onto him like a drowning man brushing against a rope. I said something about him being the first familiar face I'd seen since my return, and he gave a funny look, pointing out that all my old friends were still to be found at Barts. The gist of our conversation was that he insisted that we go around there after lunch – his treat – and find some of them. Further conversation brought forth my unhappy living arrangements, which suggested to him a solution – namely, sharing digs with someone that he'd heard just that morning expressing a desire to share expenses on what sounded like much better rooms than my current bivouac.

After our meal – for which I was quite grateful, as shekels are running rather lean at the moment – we set off for Barts. I found that I was grateful when Stamford turned away from the hospital itself – and the possibility of seeing my old acquaintances – and instead entered through the Henry Gate and so around to the old familiar door, topped with the motto *"Whatsoever thy hand findeth to do, do it with thy might."* How many times had I passed this way, not even considering what that was trying to tell me?

Inside, we passed the entrance to the old medical library, and then up the flights of gray steps to the laboratory where we found Mr. Sherlock Holmes.

Stamford's acquaintance is rather unique – a tall thin fellow about my age with a most enthusiastic nature and an ebullient laugh – and perhaps rather braggadocious in nature. He had just completed some experiment that I gathered involved forcing blood to crystalize and fall to the bottom of a large container of water. He indicated that it would have far-reaching forensic effects, but to be honest, I wasn't listening too closely, as I had already been out far longer than I'd intended, and my shoulder pain was becoming intolerable. I was impressed that the fellow somehow perceived

32

that I had served in the military – and specifically Afghanistan – and as it seems that we'll be sharing lodgings soon, I'll ask him to explain how he knew.

He's found what sounds like rather comfortable lodgings at No. 221b Baker Street – a couple of bedrooms and a large furnished sitting room – with board provided at reasonable rates (if two split the costs). We plan to meet there in the morning and, if there is nothing drastically objectionable, I will plan on vacating my current room, which is feeling more and more like a temporary cell where I await the next inevitable slide into despair.

After we left Holmes, Stamford wanted to drag me around to re-visit some former cronies, but I begged off, explaining some about my wound, and that I had already expended far more energy that day than normal. That was the truth, but I found that it was more than that – the mass of Barts itself loomed over me like a great suffocating weight. I found that my memories of the place, and in fact those of my profession, revulsed me.

I'm tempted to pull out the bottle of brandy and ease the pain in that way, but I will resist. Tomorrow will be here soon enough.

1 January, 1881 – From the Journals of Sherlock Holmes

I may have been too enthusiastic in my belief that the reagent to precipitate haemoglobin was a success. I must avoid such enthusiastic outbursts in the future, and proceed only upon the logical presentation of facts.

In any case, my experiments have likely produced enough corroboration for Inspector Plummer and Constable Miller to effect an arrest of Kincaid – there is more than enough evidence without the proof of the dried blood stains on his waistcoat.

I am still considering conducting my experiments at Barts at night, when I can work in peace. I was rather irritated this morning when Stamford pulled up a stool and wanted to chat, but my casual mention of discovering rooms in Baker Street beyond my means may have had hidden benefits after all, as later in the day he ran across a fellow in similar straits. I have some memory of this Watson fellow from several years ago – I believe he was studying medicine at the University of London, and I encountered him a few times at the Alpha Inn, around the corner from my rooms in Montague Street, or sometimes in passing along the streets. I believe that he even set up a practice for a very short time in Southampton Street – I recall seeing his name on the door when I would walk by while heading to the Holborn, but he closed up shop after a short period and I lost track of him.

I perceived that he had been in Afghanistan, even before I remembered him from earlier (He is of the medical type, with the air of a military man. Clearly an army doctor, just come from the tropics, for his face is dark – not the natural tint of his skin, for his wrists are fair. He has undergone hardship and sickness in the last few months, as his haggard face says clearly. His left arm has been injured. He holds it in a stiff and unnatural manner. Where in the tropics could an English army doctor have seen much hardship and had his arm wounded? Clearly in Afghanistan – likely Maiwand, considering his condition of recovery and the implied time elapsed, and how he carries himself.)

If he's the same fellow that I knew before, he is much changed. Before, he'd been athletic, with the build of a rugby player. Now is as thin as a rail, and clearly recovering from a subsequent illness beyond his war wound – enteric fever, perhaps? He will be an interesting study for the time that we room together. I hope that my continuing success will allow me at some point in the future – sooner rather than later – to pay for the Baker Street rooms on my own, without need of a fellow lodger, and I suspect that this doctor chap will soon be on his way. (He indicated as much, fully expecting to return to service in a few months when he's healed and fit.)

A thought for further investigation on the morrow: Could Amos Ritchie have had *two* illegitimate children? That would explain the vague language in his holographic will. It is late, but I believe that I'll be able to find Philip Cable at the slaughterhouse around 6 a.m. in time to get an answer.

2 January, 1881 – From the Journals of Dr. John Watson

I take a moment from my labors to record my thoughts regarding these new lodgings.

221 Baker Street is located near Regent's Park – I can already picture myself walking there with greater pleasure than my recent days poking about the riverfront or avoiding hurrying pedestrians along the Strand. The house itself is four stories, but unlike other similar lodging houses, the landlady, Mrs. Hudson, has means enough that she only intends to keep two lodgers – Holmes and myself – reserving the rest of the house for her own use. Likewise, the ground floor is part of her residence, and not converted into a shop like so many of her neighbors.

Holmes and I met this morning – and strangely, his shoes had marks of blood on them. I asked if he'd been involved in a procedure at Barts, but he vaguely indicated that he'd been at an East End slaughterhouse before dawn. (Curious.) So desirable in every way were the prospective

34

apartments, and so moderate did the terms seem when divided between us, that the bargain was concluded upon the spot, and we at once entered into possession. I've already moved my meagre possessions from the hotel, and Holmes threatens to do so tomorrow. I put it in those terms, as he already seems to have laid a greater claim to the rooms, simply by right of finding them first. Without apparently giving any thought to the fact that I'm rather injured, he has assumed possession of the bedroom immediately adjacent to the sitting room, while mine is located one flight up, directly over his, looking over a barren and bleak little rear yard, it's grayness broken only by a solitary plane tree.

I was able to bring my own few possessions – some personal items and books, and the little clothing that I own – in one cab ride, while Holmes informed me that the movers would "begin" to move his belongings from his current rooms near the British Museum tomorrow – the word "begin" implying that it will not be accomplished immediately, and further implying that his personal accoutrements and appurtenances far outnumber mine.

In any case, it may not matter – I suspect this arrangement will be temporary at best. While I find these rooms pleasing in every way, I hope that my health will improve and that, after the nine-month recuperative period ends this summer, I'll be declared once again fit for duty. And yet, I continue to have doubts about returning to the medical profession. In quiet moments, the memories return, just as vivid as the day when they were made.

6 January, 1881 – From the Journals of Sherlock Holmes

Lunch with Mycroft today. I believe that this may be the first time when he hasn't tried to talk me out of my profession – which would be rather hypocritical, as a number of my recent cases have come my way based on his recommendations. (Perhaps he chose not to bring up the unpleasant and ongoing discussion of my chosen career so as not to spoil the modest celebration of my birth anniversary.) He did mention that he'd had "good reports" from Scotland Yard regarding my recent solution of the Trethaway Entanglement. (It made me some friends there, I'll wager, but it was the mere child's play of deduction.)

I confess that I had fully expected to receive the usual speech about returning to Oxford to finish my engineering degree – I can almost hear Father's voice speaking through Mycroft every time I'm forced to endure it – but he seemed to realize that, as I've now turned twenty-seven and have been earning my bread and cheese at this for over five years (and doing it for free for a lot longer), I'm unlikely to be cajoled into abandoning my career.

He seemed surprised that I'd moved from my long-time Montague Street rooms, and we were both amused at how relieved our erstwhile aunt-by-marriage – Mrs. Holmes – would be, as now she, the lease-holder of the property, would no longer be vexed by my comings and goings.

Mycroft appeared to be pleased – as much as one can tell – when I described my new rooms, and also mildly intrigued regarding my fellow lodger – a graduate of the University of London, a veteran who served with distinction and bravery at Maiwand, and someone now recovering his health with dignity and patience from grievous wounds and terrible set-backs. I didn't mention how the poor fellow cannot sleep – I hear him moving around above me in the night, or slipping down to the sitting room, where he obviously writes through the long dark hours. And when he does sleep, he sometimes cries out.

I would like to help in some way, but I know of nothing that I could offer. We keep to ourselves, two polite strangers. During the day he takes long walks, mostly to the Park I think, and we take our meals together at night, where our conversation ranges over a wide variety of topics. He has the grand gift of silence, and is quite patient to entertain himself when I'm not in the mood to talk, or when I'm puzzling out a problem or conducting a chemical investigation. And most of all, he has asked no questions regarding my profession.

12 January, 1881 – From the Journals of Dr. John H. Watson

I ranged further afield today. The weather was pleasant enough, and instead of turning north toward the Park, I set out to the east, walking slowly but steadily. I was breathing deeply, and felt better than I had in some days. Whenever a voice in my head told me I'd gone far enough, and to veer back toward my comfortable nest, I instead pressed on, walking more than I had in months. My route took me around Russell Square, and then through the Inns of Court. Before I knew it, I was nearing Barts – it seemed to have drawn me unaware like a magnet – and with a start I drew myself up, awash with a sudden undefined anxiety.

As is typical when this occurs, I try to understand it. Of course, the reason is obvious, but still, this fellow that I've become, tarrying on the pavement before a place which has only ever been a home to me, makes no sense whatsoever, and it must be addressed. Within a few months, I will be standing before a review board, charged with evaluating my recovery and fitness to return to duty. I will be of no use whatsoever if I'm marked down as gun-shy. I must come to some understanding of the problem to work my way toward a solution.

It isn't a fear of blood, or even death. After my years of training – after what happened at Maiwand – these have no power over me. Rather, I think, it is a fear of *responsibility* – taking on the duty of preserving life and health, and seeing the trust in patients' – in *soldiers'* – eyes, hoping that I will be able to rescue them, and make things the way they were, even when this is impossible. When I think of those last minutes at Maiwand, before I myself was shot down, and we knew that the enemy was nearly upon us – when we knew that the only humane thing left to do was to –

I turned away from Barts and started back toward Baker Street, now in pain from pushing myself too far, a grim and frightening look no doubt upon my face and my brow beaded with sweat, even in the January cold. I tried to make it the entire way, but in the end, I was forced to spend preciously hoarded capital to hire a hansom.

17 January, 1881 – From the Journals of Sherlock Holmes

Mycroft summoned me to his office this morning, in relation to the bombing of the fourteenth, at a military barracks in Salford, Lancashire. A young boy was killed.

"We've expected something like this for some time," he said. "You pretend to ignore politics, Sherlock, but surely you're aware of the revolutionary insistence in recent years to establish an independent Irish Republic."

"Fenianism," I replied. "I'm careful about what I put in my brain attic, but not to the point of ridiculous exclusion of facts and incidents like this, which may have importance in my work. I've heard talk around the docks for the last few months concerning the rising tide of Irish nationalism."

"And yet you've kept this knowledge to yourself?"

"I've heard nothing that matters," I replied. "Nothing that you didn't know. Angry and drunken sailors in a dank pub, listing old grievances with one another until they're too inebriated to do much more than shamble back to their ships. These common folk have no knowledge of plots, or specific plans to foment terror and rebellion. When it happens, they will only stand to one side and cheer as the true Fenians do the heavy lifting." I crossed my legs and took a sip of Mycroft's excellent port. "I take it that there is something I can do to help in your investigation?"

He closed his eyes and pursed his lips in an out several times, as if this, requesting my assistance in yet another matter, was simply one more step along the slippery slope of his acceptance of my profession.

"Facts are scarce, but I have my eye on a secretary in the Irish Division, Brian Mullingar, as a likely source of inside information for the bombers. As you know, I keep my eye on many areas, and that includes a number of people who work in positions of responsibilities – Mullingar being one of them. In short, he appears to be living beyond his means. I instituted some discreet inquiries with an agent whom I trust and found that Mullingar has relatives – close relatives – with a great deal of sympathy for the Irish Republican Brotherhood – or the Fenian Brotherhood, or *Clan na Gael*, or whatever they choose to call themselves this year. At that point I terminated the efforts of my official inquiry, preferring to operate from here on out within a much smaller loop. Should we determine that Mullingar is innocent, then no harm will come to his reputation and the investigation can be forgotten. And conversely, should he be found guilty by association with these treasonous acts – well, the less who are officially involved the better, when a solution is required."

Mycroft informed me that Mullingar lives with his young wife on the northeast corner of Smith Square, and apparently walks to and from his office in Whitehall on most days. It's a modest house, and the man's official story of how he can afford it is that his income is supplemented by a vague inheritance, as well as money brought to the marriage by his wife. Mycroft showed me several financial records indicating that neither of these can explain Mullingar's actual expenditures. It didn't take me long at all to see in Mycroft's other assembled documents exactly how Mullingar was indeed living beyond his means – quite the betrayal of his young wife – and also that Mullingar's relatives, who according to Mycroft had "a great deal of sympathy" for the Irish revolutionaries, were in fact very angry sympathizers indeed, with strong ties to the Fenian groups.

Another interesting fact is that Mullingar's wife, from all accounts, appears to be quite unhappy. I foresee that I'll need to find a way to meet her and, if possible, gain her trust. (When I mentioned this possibility, Mycroft called me a fool to attempt to turn a man's wife against him. In this case, I think that turning will be unnecessary. From what I see in the confidential report, she has been cruelly used.)

I shall enjoy this little case. It's good to be out and about – too often lately my clients have all been mere consultations, each arriving in the mornings to climb the stairs, share their stories, and then pay my fee when I've managed to set them on the right path. Watson has been most gracious – agreeing to allow me the use of the sitting room to conduct these interviews without complaint, either going upstairs to his room with a book, or bundling up for a walk. I can see that he's bursting with questions,

38

but he's too much of a gentleman to ask – and no doubt as a medical professional, he's learned how to keep a secret or two, and knows not to pry about other people's.

17 January, 1881 – From the Journals of Dr. John H. Watson

Holmes was gone when I came down this morning. Perhaps he wanted to get out and walk in the snow – the newspaper says that in the counties south of London, it is a veritable blizzard. I'm glad to be safe inside – a spill on the ice would not be advisable, and I'm still too rickety to be navigating around or across snowbanks and ice.

As I sat in my chair, looking at the sitting room around me, I realized just how little my own personality has impressed itself here. I have my own desk, of course, and a small shelf of books in addition to those that I keep in my bedroom upstairs. But Holmes has quite taken over the corner between the fireplace and the front window for his chemical corner, which may be used to produce vomitous odors at any time. On the other side of the fireplace, a set of sturdy bookshelves are mounted to the wall between the mantel and Holmes's bedroom door. When I first saw them, on the day we examined the apartment, I had thought that we might share them, but my flatmate quickly claimed them for his "scrapbooks", which seem to contain clippings and puzzling annotations regarding the most disparate range of topics. (I only know this because he left one open once on the dining table – I would not presume to take one down and peruse it without an invitation.)

I find myself again and again wondering about this strange man – I started to write "young" man, as in some ways – particularly in his enthusiasms – he seems much younger than me, but in fact I'm only about a year-and-a-half older than him. (A worn-out veteran at age twenty-eight!) His appearance is quite striking, and he's always quite neat and tidy. In height he is rather over six feet, and so excessively lean that he seems to be considerably taller. His eyes are sharp and piercing, and his thin, hawk-like nose gives his whole expression an air of alertness and decision. His chin, too, has the prominence and squareness which mark the man of determination. His hands are invariably blotted with ink and stained with chemicals, yet he possesses an extraordinary delicacy of touch, as I frequently have occasion to observe when I watch him manipulating his fragile philosophical instruments or his violin – for he is a violin player of some skill indeed.

He seems to have enough income to get by, although he isn't extravagant by any means. (It's too soon to know if he'll have any problems with his half of the rent – I'm already carefully conserving my own pennies.) He has some sort of consulting service, as our rooms are visited regularly by a most diverse array of people – ranging from high-born and wealthy to those in the lowest circumstances. They often arrive in the mornings, during what seem to be his visiting hours, and Holmes asks (always politely) if he can have use of the sitting room to meet with them. I always acquiesce, and I feel like he's waiting for me to ask why, but I refuse to do so. (Petulant, I know, but I don't want to appear to be too curious.)

I do wonder, though. I don't think that he's studying medicine, although he does regularly visit Barts, as well as conducting those terrible chemical experiments. He seems to be ignorant about the most basic of topics – literature, and astronomical physics – but sometimes I suspect that he has a deeply buried sense of humor, and that when he pretends ignorance of such things, he's only tweaking me. He has spoken of his "brain attic", and that he is concerned that every new fact he puts there will push out some other. Again, I don't believe that he really espouses this philosophy, but it is an atypical approach to life.

After my ponderings reached their typical conclusion of determining that I really knew nothing, I pulled out a piece of paper and attempted to list Holmes's Limits. It was an odd document, but ultimately frustrating, and in the end I threw it into the fire in despair.

Some hours later, Holmes arrived to discover me asleep in my chair. The fire had been built up while I dreamed – certainly by Mrs. Hudson – and the room was quite cozy. Holmes told me tales of what he'd seen in the snow-covered capital that seemed to be from a Dickens narrative, so vivid and unusual were they. He acted out some of the parts, and I commented that he could have been an actor. He only smiled.

19 January, 1881 – From the Journals of Sherlock Holmes

After several days of ongoing efforts on my part, Mrs. Mullingar visited Baker Street this morning.

I don't think that she would have come at all, except that I exerted a modicum of influence by way of her friend, Mrs. Judith Denton, who was most willing to pass along my message requesting a meeting. (Mrs. Denton's son is now four years old, and appears to have entirely recovered from the events of his kidnapping in '79. I was more lucky than I'd care to admit to find him alive, and I learned a valuable lesson about whom I can and cannot trust.)

Luckily Watson was departing on one of his walks as she arrived, feeling that the snow had retreated enough for him to make his way safely to the Park. Mrs. Mullingar seated herself in the basket chair by the fire, but chose to retain her coat, ostensibly because she was cold, but more likely so she could bolt at the first sign of something distressful – which turned out to be the case.

I frankly explained that the situation between her and her husband was well known – his drinking, and the abuse that she received from him. I did it with cold precision – there is no other way – in order to get past any unnecessary embarrassment or denials. She sat and listened while I explained what I knew, a single tear tracking down her cheek. In order to present my case more forcefully, I then pivoted immediately to what we – the government and I – suspected: That her husband had supplied information to the Fenian bombers, a few of whom were known to be associated with his relatives, leading to the explosion at the barracks which had killed a young boy. I then asked if she, as the youngest daughter of a patriotic Englishman, Lord Moreton, would provide information to assure that justice was done.

She made no comment, and no movement either, and I – fearing that she remained unconvinced – hurried to explain that the government – and I – understood the shame that her husband's exposure would bring, and that everything possible would be managed to salvage the situation for her.

She gave a small sad smile. "And for my child as well?" she asked quietly.

This changed things, and she confirmed that she carried Mullingar's unborn issue. While I still pondered what she'd said and the implications to my request, she stood. "I know that you tell me is true," she said. "I know he's a traitor. But I cannot help you. I'm . . . I'm sorry." And she turned to go.

"Please," I added. "If you reconsider, you can trust me to help you, or you can discuss it with my brother, Mycroft Holmes. A message for him at the Diogenes Club in Pall Mall will reach me as well."

When she had departed, I sat for several minutes, pulling my ear and considering what to do next. With no other options, I could at least report to Mycroft her statement of semi-confirmation – without tangible proof – that her husband was indeed the man we sought. If nothing else, we could consider how to best manipulate events and settle this situation for the good of all concerned.

19 January, 1881 – From the Journals of Dr. John H. Watson

As I returned from my walk, having been able to tolerate the cold for only half-an-hour or so, I saw – in the distance – Holmes stepping away from our rooms, heading in the other direction. He had only gone fifty feet or so before hailing a hansom, and then he was off to the south.

41

He is always quite distinguishable, and there is no mistaking him for someone else. His tall lean figure, his confident movement, and his striking Inverness and fore-and-aft cap cause him to stand out wherever he goes.

I had just reached our door when a fashionably-dressed lady – no more than a girl, really – suddenly joined me at our front step. I recognized her as the same girl who had arrived just as I'd departed. She was quite breathless, and indicated that she needed to speak Holmes once again.

"I'm sorry," I replied. "I saw him leaving just as I was walking this way."

She bit her lip in frustration, and then, with a cry of despair, her eyes rolled up in her head and she collapsed at my feet!

A surge of adrenalin coursed through me – a feeling that hadn't manifested itself in many months – and even as she fell, I dropped with her, cushioning her as she reached the ground. A small crowd formed, and I instructed one of the men nearby – the tobacconist from across the road – to knock on the door and summon Mrs. Hudson. Before he could do so, however, the landlady was beside me, having just walked up after a return from a nearby merchant's shop. I asked if she had any information about the unconscious young lady, but she could provide nothing of use, not even a name.

In the meantime, I had been examining the girl as best I could, while discreetly trying to protect her dignity as she lay sprawled before the gaping strangers, happy to have this free and serendipitous entertainment. I considered whether I ought to take her inside, but decided that might be improper. Instead, I asked the tobacconist summon a cab, and within minutes the girl and I were sitting in a hansom, me supporting her while her head rested upon my shoulder.

It would have been quickest to take her to St. Mary's in Praed Street, but they didn't know me. It wasn't much farther in the other direction, to Barts, and that's where I instructed the cabbie to go, balancing my rising and inexplicable dread about our destination with the knowledge that once we arrived, I knew exactly where to take her, and that I'd have a much stronger argument for remaining with her while she received treatment.

I tried to deduce what I could about her as we rode along. The day was dark, and it was darker still within the cab. Additionally, I could only see so much from our awkward positioning, so my conclusions were minimal. Her clothing and coat were of very good quality. She wore a modest but expensive-looking wedding band. She was fair-haired and petite, almost bird-like. Yet beyond that, she seemed abnormally thin, much more than under normal circumstances. Her hair was thinning and there were dark circles under her eyes. She had the ketonish smell of starvation. A small blue vein was under the pale skin along her temple, and the flesh there was so thin that her face appeared skeletal. The vein pulsed steadily, however, and I felt that under her temporarily deprived condition was someone of essential good health who could recover from whatever had caused the manifestation of these obvious physical indicators. Still, there was no telling what else might be the matter.

As we neared the hospital, I instructed the cabbie as to which entrance we should approach. When we pulled to a stop, a couple of orderlies came out – one named Willis that I recognized from the old days. Without too much fuss, we transported the girl to an examination area, and within minutes old Dr. Thurlow entered.

I remembered being quite intimidated by him in my younger days, but now I saw that he was just a middle-aged fellow, aged prematurely, with an air of overworked and weary distraction that I'd previously taken for impatience. He recognized me, and seemed glad to see me. "What's this then, Watson? Have you rescued a fair damsel in distress?"

I explained that she was a stranger to me, and how our paths had crossed. As she was unconscious, we could not ask questions or even confirm that she wanted treatment – we could only try and help.

It wasn't long before two things were determined: She was with child, a possible explanation for her faint – especially when combined with her apparent starved state – and that someone had hurt her. There were bruises across her body – her wrists and arms, where strong fingers of a large hand had grasped her, and on her torso, where dark spots of varying colors and degrees of recovery, some old and some fresh, indicated that she had been hit with a fist. I had to turn away to control my anger.

After her initial care, there was nothing to be done except wait for her to awaken. I decided to wander the halls for a time, attempting to diminish my growing anxiety.

I realized that when I'd arrived with the injured girl, my recent distaste for my profession, haunting me so for the last several months, had faded for a while. I had been focused on the situation at hand, and my training had left no room for unimportant distractions or doubts. Now, with time on my hands, I felt the unease creeping back. I had to resist the urge to retrieve my coat, hat, and stick, and flee as quickly as I could, back to my fireside chair, my books, and the comforting and restorative meals provided by my new and motherly landlady.

I passed along one corridor to the next, pausing to look in this ward or that, all the while avoiding any human interaction. When I saw someone coming toward me, I would randomly turn a different direction, or wait in a nearby empty hallway until he or she had passed. But the unavoidable eventually occurred: I turned a corner to find a group of doctors and nurses congregated in quiet conversation, and there was no way to go forward or backward without acknowledging them.

I recognized several faces – some I'd known quite well in the old days – and despite my inclination to retreat, I stepped forward when I was hailed with an enthusiasm that surprised me. Stamford, I saw, was there amongst them, and I think he'd realized from our meeting a few weeks before that I was uncomfortable trying to fit back into my old skin. He took the lead, relating where I'd been and what had happened to me, but without too much detail or embarrassment. Several of my old friends asked questions, and were genuinely glad to see me back and – as far as they were concerned – healthy. It was only when Stamford went on to say that I was now sharing rooms with that curious gentleman, Sherlock Holmes – and in doing so, presenting Holmes with a whiff of ridicule and with the idea that I deserved some sort of sympathy – that I frowned. Before I could rise in defense of my fellow lodger, Stamford perceptively saw my irritation and changed the subject. I did note, however, that several of those around me, apparently aware of Holmes's peculiarities, had been prepared to add their own anecdotes to the shared experience before they were abruptly prevented from doing so.

I eventually disengaged from the group and walked back to the patients' ward with somewhat more ease than I'd felt during my initial tour of the hospital. I found that while I was gone, the girl had awakened. "You're the man at Mr. Holmes's front door."

I acknowledged it. "How are you feeling?" I queried.

Her lips tightened. "All right, I suppose. I haven't fainted like that since I was young. I know better – I left without eating this morning."

I pulled up a stool. "I suspect," I said with the well-earned gravitas of a physician, "that you've missed more than just one meal. Is there a reason?"

She closed her eyes and simply shook her head.

"You must care for yourself," I added. "And for your unborn child."

Her eyes opened abruptly, a small flash in them as her brows lowered slightly. "You know?"

"We do. The signs were obvious as we began to treat you. That . . . and other things as well. You have been abused."

She simply continued to look my way, the expression on her face unchanging, but her focus drifting past me and slightly to my right, as if seeing something, an unpleasant memory. Or more likely, many of them.

"Is it your husband?" I asked softly, glancing at the modest ring on her left hand. Something in my tone apparently reached her, for she finally nodded.

44

"This cannot be tolerated," I continued in the same tone. "It's not only you that is in danger now."

"I know," she whispered. "But what can I do? He is my husband . . . ."

"We must do something," I countered. "How long – ?"

"Since the day that we married," she interrupted, tears now rimming her lower eyelids. "He became angry soon after the ceremony, when we were alone. He said . . . he said that I needed to understand who was the master. He . . . he lets me eat when I've been good." Seeing how near starvation she was, I doubted that he found her so very often.

I swallowed. "How long have you been married?"

"Not quite two years."

I looked around. We were quite alone. "Do you have somewhere that you can go? Someplace safe?"

She shook her head, barely at all, and then with more vehemence. "I've thought of it, but it's no use. He is my husband. There is no choice!"

She began to pluck and pull at the blankets covering her, as if she'd suddenly decided to flee – not to safety, but back to the man who had helped put her here. I leaned forward and laid a hand across hers. She started as if I'd also hit her, but then, realizing that this wasn't my intent, she relaxed and settled back with a sob.

I talked to her for quite a while – assuring her that all would be well, and that she didn't need to live in this manner. I entreated her to have faith that things would improve. At times she looked at me with an expression that wanted to believe, before her eyes would again fill with tears.

One of the nurses across the room had noticed her agitation and started our way. I squeezed the back of the girl's hand. "There is a solution. There must be. Stay here for a while, and we will find it. I promise that you don't have to remain in this kind of danger."

Her eyes were shut then, but as the tears leaked and ran down to the pillow, she nodded. With another squeeze, I stood and left the room.

I made the rounds of several offices throughout the facility, renewing acquaintances, telling my story to those that were interested and wanted to hear it, and then getting to the reason for my visit: To find out what options there were for protecting the woman from her abusive husband. I had already been aware that the prospective for a good solution was bleak, but I had hopes. Still, as I went from one place to another, I heard nothing but indifferent recitations of the lady's standing under the law and a husband's rights. It was with a heavy heart that I turned back toward the ward where she was recovering, dreading reporting my lack of good news, but still intending to reassure her.

I found that she had left while I was gone, rising and dressing and walking out of her own accord without even leaving a name or address.

I went back to Baker Street.

20 January, 1881 – From the Journals of Sherlock Holmes

I was called away yesterday soon after Mrs. Mullingar's departure, and was gone the rest of the day and all night as well. I had only returned to Baker Street early this morning when I was met on the front step, when I was about to enter, by one of Mycroft's agents, bearing an urgent summons to join him immediately. Within fifteen minutes, we had maneuvered our way south to Pall Mall and I was entering that curious establishment, the Diogenes Club, a refuge for some of the most anti-social men in London. My brother had arranged a membership for me quite a while ago, and though I rarely take advantage of it, I have on occasion enjoyed the absolute tomblike quiet, the comfortable chairs, and the latest periodicals – it has a very soothing atmosphere. Since I'm known there to a certain degree, I was passed through the entryway unhindered, and within moments found myself in the Stranger's Room, the only location within the building where talking is permitted. (I must say, however, that this statement may not entirely be accurate. At some point, I need to investigate those places below-stairs where the servants congregate, and the kitchens, as I cannot imagine that anything can be accomplished there without some noise or conversation.)

I expected that Mycroft's message to join him related to the Fenian bombings, but I was more than surprised to see that he was in the company of Mrs. Mullingar. She still looked thin and ill, but something was different. There was a new core of resolve about her that hadn't been there before. She nodded in my direction.

"Mrs. Mullingar has decided upon the side of patriotism," said Mycroft, with the tone he takes when he believes he's known that something would turn out as he'd predicted all along. He held up a heavy leather book. "She has provided the latest volume of her husband's journal. He has been most . . . careless."

He handed me the book, which was filled with close neat handwriting, was more than careless – it was damning. It began in early 1880, and was filled with a curious regularity of grievances, rants, diatribes, and threats, all directed toward the British Government, the Queen, and a number of his fellow employees. I glanced up at my brother. "Was any of this obvious to those who work with him?"

"Not at all," he replied. "He has been quite cunning – keeping his head down and apparently listening to whatever he could hear, before passing it on to where it can do the most damage."

"To what level of information has he been privy?"

"Too much. There are indications there that it isn't just the Fenians who have benefited from his treachery. The Germans, the French. There are even indications that he's tried to attract the interest of the Belgians and the Dutch."

I looked at his wife. "He seems to be an inveterate chronicler of his own thoughts. I take it that there are other, similar, journals to be found."

She nodded. "I thought one was enough to relate what you needed to know."

I looked back at the end of the book, specifically the entries for the most recent weeks. It was all there – his contacts within the Fenians, their plans that had led to the bomb at the barracks in Salford, and details about further planned atrocities in upcoming months.

"You put yourself at great risk to take this," I said.

"I'm not going back to him," was her quiet reply. "Our . . . *my* child must be protected from him."

"And you both shall be," said Mycroft. He looked at me. "He is already in custody, as are his other journals. It was done quietly – his fellow conspirators will have no knowledge, as yet, as to his arrest. There is hope that we can turn that to our advantage."

The young woman sat quietly, looking from one to the other of us without expression, her hands folded quietly across her stomach. "What changed your mind?" I asked. "Yesterday in Baker Street, you were afraid. You seemed adamant. I had no hope for a solution from this direction."

She lowered her head for a moment, and then looked back at me. "After I departed, I came back to ask if you could keep me safe – if I were to betray my husband. But you had already gone. I was filled with despair. I – But then, later, I had a chance to speak with someone else. He was very . . . a very decent man. I haven't met anyone like him before. He was trustworthy, and genuinely worried about me. Just after we talked, he leapt into motion, telling me that he'd find a way to . . . to rescue me. But I became afraid again, and left before he could tell me what he'd learned."

I wondered who such a fellow could be, to have inspired such trust and confidence. I had been unable to convince her during our initial discussion, and even if I'd still been at home when she returned, I suspect that I still wouldn't have been able to win her confidence in the manner that this unknown man had done. Whomever he is, he has a skill that eludes me.

47

"I went home," continued the lady, "and my husband was still at work. I left a message with the servants that I had a headache and locked myself in my room. I couldn't face him. But I thought about the words of the man I'd recently seen, that decent man, and realized that I didn't have to put myself in such danger – nor my child. I had no right to place my child in such a position. So this morning, I looked through my husband's journals, saw the one that would tell you what you needed, and came here, per your instructions, as it was closer, and also because I felt safer disappearing into a club than being seen again at your lodgings. If I am to vanish and begin a new life, let it begin now, and here."

"I don't think that vanishing will be necessary," rumbled Mycroft. "We'll stage-manage things so that you will be taken care of. But in the meantime – " He hoisted himself to his feet with an involuntary grunt and pulled the nearby bell-rope. " – it will be a good idea for you to remain in my protective care, until such time as things are settled."

The door opened and a fellow of about thirty leaned in, lean and sunburnt, one of those typical agents who carry out my brother's bidding. "Go with Sykes here – he'll put you into a house of safety. I'll be in touch in a few days when the matter is resolved. And, Mrs. Mullingar," he said as she turned to follow the dangerous-looking Sykes, "your government very sincerely thanks you."

I nodded. "As do I."

When she had gone, I laid the book aside and poured us each a brandy. "'Until such time as things are settled'," I quoted, dropping back into my seat while Mycroft repositioned himself in the massive red-leather chair that I suspected had been specially constructed for him. "You make it sound rather easy."

"It will be. A shooting accident would be best, of course, but if he chooses suicide, we'll take that as well."

I raised an eyebrow. My brother deals in harsh realities. "All too embarrassing for the Government if he lives, I take it."

"Indeed. The trial will be private, the evidence incontrovertible, and the sentence certain. He will, of course, be allowed the option to carry it out for himself. If it's to be a firing squad, then we'll be somewhat inconvenienced arranging an unplanned hunting trip for the subsequent discovery and display of the corpse, but hopefully he'll choose to step off in his own drawing room." He pinched his lower lip. "Yes, perhaps that is the better option."

"And his wife?" I asked. "You promised her that things would be 'stage-managed'."

"They will. I'll make sure that their combined wealth remains with her, and there is a good, decent man, a widower and peer from the West Country, who has two young children and will make her a fine husband."

I took a sip of brandy. "And she will go along with this? Because you have written it in the script?"

He scowled. "It will work, and they will be happy with one another. It is the most satisfactory solution." He nodded, repeated, "Satisfactory,", and then shifted, as if preparing to stand and depart. "I appreciate your efforts."

"Such as they were," I responded. "I only confirmed the easily obtained information that her husband was abusing her, and then tried to drive a wedge – and failed. It was this mystery man who talked to her of decency that did the trick."

"Then I would thank him as well, if I could," said my brother, standing up. "He sounds like someone we could use on our side – if we only knew who he is." He walked to the door. "Follow me. The cutlets promise to be excellent today, and while it's a bit early for lunch, I suspect that we shall nevertheless be served."

20 January, 1881 – From the Journals of Dr. John H. Watson

I awoke with an energy this morning that I haven't felt for quite some time. I attribute it to a great deal of thought that I've given lately to my recent visit to Barts. While I still feel some of the anxiousness that has crippled me over the last several months, I also realize that, following the unexpected care provided for the mysterious young woman, I am still a physician.

It was with this thought in mind that I made my way across the city, presenting myself at the office of Dr. Thurlow before I had the chance to talk myself out of it.

He wasn't surprised to see me – in fact, he seemed to be expecting it. I explained my injuries in clinical terms, as well as my limitations. I indicated that I fully expect to be returning to active service later this year, when I have healed sufficiently and present myself before the Review Board. "But in the meantime, as I am able, I would like to assist, if you can find a place for me. Making rounds, working shifts when I can, serving as a *locum* when such need is identified."

He nodded. "Will tomorrow morning suit you?"

"Today would be better." And thus, I helped where I could throughout much of today.

I was weary when I settled back in my armchair by the fire this evening, but in a most satisfying way. A whisky in hand – in a moderate amount – my feet stretched toward the flames, and the day's late-edition newspaper open before me. I glanced at the stories of the day: The south was still digging out from the blizzard of a few days before, a Ministry employee named Mullingar had blown his head off earlier that afternoon with a loaded shotgun while cleaning it in his Smith Square townhouse, and British forces had been defeated by the Boers a few days earlier at the Battle of Laing's Nek.

That last story gave me pause. Images of Maiwand washed over me – the dirt and noise, the smells, the blood and screams, the agony when the Jezail bullet in my shoulder had thrown me to the ground, scrabbling through the dirt and offal on the surgical tent floor like a stepped-on insect – but I closed my eyes and reopened them to look around the sitting room. I am *here* now, and that was the past. I tried to fix this moment in time, and gradually, the sound of carriages passing continuously up and down the street outside our windows calmed me.

I considered where I might be posted when I rejoin the Army. Wherever I go will be quite different from this tame Baker Street sitting room, where very little happens, except for those times when Holmes's "clients" consult with him. I was reminded of the fashionably dressed visitor of the day before. I wonder who she was, and where she has gone. I worry for her. Possibly she is one of Holmes's clients – when I met her, she was walking up asking for him. I should ask him who she is, and see about getting her some help. And yet – how can I violate her confidence in that manner, now that I know of her situation, and how too can I ask Holmes to do the same thing, for him to share with me information that isn't any of my business? Still, the matter is unresolved, and I know that I'll be pondering a solution until some good outcome is found.

Holmes, whom I haven't seen for a day or so, arrived just in time for dinner, climbing the steps with Mrs. Hudson and holding the door for her as she set our evening meal upon the dining room table. As she turned to go, she looked my way and reached into her pocket.

"I just remembered, Doctor – this note was pushed through the slot for you. It hasn't been mailed."

I was curious – no one should be sending me any notes. I could tell that Holmes was interested, but too polite to ask as he sat down and looked to determine the nature of the entrée.

He checked to see that the sitting room door was shut, and then murmured, "Cutlets – I was afraid so. I had them for lunch. Ah well, they'll do, I suppose. After all, this is simply fuel for my mind. I don't require variety."

"Mrs. Hudson is an excellent cook," I countered, only half paying attention. I was reading the note.

Dear Dr. Watson, [it read]

Thank you for rescuing me the yesterday, and accompanying me to the hospital, and for your good advice. It has helped me more than you will ever know. I had the strength following our talk to do what must be done, and I think that my life is going to be better now.

I wish you the very best.

It wasn't signed. I looked to see if any clue might reveal itself about the writer, but there was nothing. Perhaps a detective – one of those chaps like Dupin or Lecoq who made such a study of thing – might see something that I was missing, but where to find such a fellow? And after all, those types are only in books.

At least I am relieved of the responsibility of awkwardly asking Holmes about who she is.

I put the note back in the envelope and then put both in my current book, *A Sailor's Sweetheart* by Clark Russell. Then I heaved myself upright and joined Holmes at the table.

He was in fine fettle, and our conversation ranged from art – his opinions are really most uninformed – to discoveries related to the Neanderthal, to recidivism in the criminal justice system. He was genuinely happy when I shared the news regarding my new position at Barts. Later, while he played me some of Mendelssohn's *Lieder* and other favorites on his violin, I re-read the mysterious note from the young lady who had seemed so full of despair. Her life, whoever she is, now seems to have the promise of a brighter future. It makes me believe that mine will as well.

> "One morning a young girl called, fashionably dressed,
> and stayed for half an hour or more."
> – Dr. John H. Watson
> *A Study in Scarlet*

The Christmas Ghost
of Crailloch Taigh

Although I would have wagered that being alone was the best medicine after the day I'd just experienced, Holmes knew better, and insisted that I join him downstairs in the inn's small bar.

We had journeyed to Stranraer the day before, traveling north across a cold and bleak landscape that looked blasted in the weak December light. I knew that come spring, the land would awaken as it always did, and these blue-gray empty fields, dotted with barren leafless trees and scattered black buildings under a low metallic sky, would again be filled with color and life and ever-renewing vitality. But for now, this emptied and grim terrain matched the mood of the task which called me back to the town of my birth.

Just days before Christmas, I'd been summoned there to take care a bit of long-delayed business that had suddenly become urgent and then final. I don't propose to recount it here – it's not my story to tell. I simply reference its unpleasant nature so that one might understand how Holmes and I came to be there, and my perspective as we tarried overnight before returning to London on the following morning's train.

A couple of hours before, our business finished, we had entered the inn, located on the southern outskirts of town. It was far too late to start the journey home, though I didn't fancy staying any longer that I had too. In the closed carriage on the way to our temporary lodgings, I tried to both thank Holmes, who had offered to accompany me on my unpleasant journey, and to apologize for him being there, so far from Baker Street just before the holidays. He would have none of it, attempting to distract me with an amusing anecdote concerning one of the old ladies he'd encountered earlier in the day while I was otherwise occupied. I appreciated the effort, but I simply didn't want to hear it, and he soon fell silent.

I would have been content to sit upstairs, brooding in my room, but after I'd retreated there for a few minutes, Holmes knocked and reminded me that I hadn't eaten at all that day, and the whisky I'd carried upstairs would sit better on a full stomach. So we went down and found a table at the back of the low-ceilinged room. The young missus whose husband owned the inn approached our table and heard our choices from the night's menu. I found that I had an appetite after all and favored the roast pork, crisped along the fatty side, while Holmes ordered some of the local seafood – caught fresh by fisherman who didn't rest simply because of inclement seasonal weather.

The mood in the bar was subdued but not unpleasant, and I found myself beginning to thaw. After all, this Stranraer business wasn't unexpected, and finally I could draw a line under it, for good or ill. Holmes perceived that my attitude had shifted, and when he tentatively asked a few questions about how things had been resolved, I was able to answer with objectivity.

The food was excellent and the local whisky tolerable. The fire was warm, and the modest but sincere Christmas decorations scattered around the room helped to further ease my tension. During a lull in our conversation, I looked more closely at our surroundings. There were half-a-dozen or so locals, sitting in small groups, talking softly and comfortably, and not put out at all by the presence of a pair of London strangers. These men themselves showed no indication that this night, with Christmas just days away, was any different from any other that they might spend here, but there was still something festive about the place. The owner's wife, a beautiful lass in her twenties with thick dark hair and the glow of a woman who was obviously expecting her first in just a couple of months, still moved with a dancer's grace, and hummed various Christmas carols in soft tones as she went about her tasks.

Her husband held station behind the bar. Introduced to us as William Fraser, he was a tall fellow with black hair and broad shoulders, and his outlook matched that of his wife. He clearly had pride in his establishment, and a joyful satisfied expression as he watched his wife and child-to-be moving about the room, or carrying meals from the kitchen.

I had settled lower in my seat, feeling the unpleasantness of the day finally sloughing away, when the front door opened abruptly, flying back and lowering the room's temperature by twenty or more degrees almost immediately. Most of the men sitting around had the same reaction as the womb-like warmth of the room was stripped away in an instant, causing them to jerk upright in their chairs as one while making raucous complaints and grumbles toward the figure who stood in the doorway.

Realizing what he'd done, the new visitor bent to push the door shut, but too late – the damage was already done.

The grumping men settled back, attempting to regain their warmth and comfortable leisure. I glanced at our hosts. Fraser was looking at the newcomer with sudden ill-concealed distaste – unexpected, as he'd been quite genial to this point – while in turn his wife watched her husband, a troubled expression upon her face.

"Mr. Holmes?" said the man in a strident voice with an unmistakable Dartmoor accent. He looked around for half-a-second after speaking before seeing us at the back of the room. As we apparently looked different enough to stand out as strangers, he moved with decision in our direction. He stopped on Holmes's side of the table, clearly having been told the appearance of the man he sought. "I bring a note from Mr. Bloom."

The name meant nothing to me, and I could see that Holmes was in the dark as well. Instead of taking the envelope thrust in his direction, Holmes asked, "And who might that be?"

The room had grown silent as all those present made no secret about listening to this conversation. Behind the bar, Fraser gave a small but dark chuckle when Bloom's messenger seemed taken aback at Holmes's ignorance of his master. "Lucius Bloom," he answered, his voice a bit less confident now. "He's one of the men associated with the waterfront properties – a most important man, you know. He helped to form the harbor syndicate." He shook the envelope again, as if it were a lure on a line. "He heard that you were here, in Stranraer, and needs to engage your services."

Holmes nodded in my direction. "Dr. Watson and I plan on returning to London in the morning. Christmas will be here soon, you know."

I nearly laughed aloud, in spite of my day. The idea that Holmes might turn down a case because of a holiday was unthinkable. But I didn't openly express this thought. Clearly Holmes was fishing his own line here, nudging further information from the messenger with his apparent indifference. And he still did not take the note. "Tell us more of Mr. Bloom. I'm afraid that his reputation hasn't made it to London quite yet – and in fact, he hasn't been mentioned to us since our arrival in Stranraer either, Mr. . . . ?"

This seemed incomprehensible to the man standing before us. While I'm not Sherlock Holmes, I have managed to successfully learn some of his methods during the time that I've known him. I could see that the man holding the note was in his early thirties, and was likely unmarried. He was well-dressed and looked as if kept himself in good physical condition. He was thin, but not in an unhealthy way, and there were no blemishes on his skin that might indicate unhealthy habits. His nails were quite short, and in places appeared to have been bitten to the quick. He appeared to have a certain amount of nervous energy as he shifted from one foot to the other. The creases in his well-polished shoes indicated that he moved about quite a bit, and that his duties didn't keep him behind a desk too often. What wasn't obvious from his appearance, but was already quite clear otherwise, was his unappealing awe for Lucius Bloom.

"My name is Grayson," was the reply to Holmes's question, "but that isn't important. As you will read if you'll accept this note, Mr. Bloom requests your presence at the manor immediately. Tonight! He won't tolerate another day of this . . . this abuse!" His voice had risen, and he took another step closer to Holmes. If my friend hadn't taken the envelope at that moment, I expect that Grayson would have thrown it at him.

I looked past him. The other occupants of the room seemed to have returned to their own business, as our conversation was too low for them to hear. Still, glances were often turned our way.

With a neutral smile, Holmes accepted the note, looked at the front and back of the envelope, and then pulled out a folded sheet. The paper of both was cream-colored, appearing thick and expensive – facts that I verified just a moment later when Holmes handed both to me.

Mr. Sherlock Holmes, [it read]

> *I've learned that you're in the area and am writing to avail myself of your services. I'm disappointed in myself that doing so hadn't occurred to me earlier. I would have hesitated to request that you be inconvenienced to travel all this way from London, but things have reached the point that I might have considered it, in spite of the distance.*
>
> *I apologize for writing so late in the evening, and requesting that you leave the comfort of your temporary lodgings, but as the events seem to occur only at night, and only at this time of year, possibly you can conduct a quick investigation now before the next manifestation occurs.*
>
> *I've asked my man, Grayson, to deliver this note discreetly,* [I raised an eyebrow at how that had turned out.] *for what is happening is no one's business beyond these walls. If you'll agree to accompany him back to the manor, he can explain what's been taking place as you travel, so you'll be ready to begin upon your arrival.*
>
> *Again, I apologize for the abrupt and inconvenient invitation, but I'd be a fool not to seek your help while it's available.*

Very Best,
Lucius Bloom

I looked up and met Holmes's gaze. Clearly the tone meant to be conveyed in Bloom's note had been missed by his rather enthusiastic and demanding employee.

"Have you read this?" asked Holmes, his voice even lower than before.

"I have not!" replied Grayson, missing the cue to speak more softly, and outraged that such might be suspected of him. "I have no need. I'm fully aware of everything that has taken place, from – "

"If you have not read it," Holmes interrupted, frowning and lowering a hand, advising Grayson to be quiet, "then apparently you do not know that your employer hoped for your discretion in the matter. Now is not the time to explain." He looked my way and I nodded. "We will accompany you. Give us five minutes to ready ourselves and get our coats. We'll join you outside."

"Very good," said Grayson with a sharp nod. The matter was done, the mission accomplished, and without further interaction, he spun, walked to the door, opened it with much less force than before, and then departed.

As Holmes and I stood, our landlord spoke, his voice cutting through the low murmur of conversation. "Once again, the high and mighty Mr. Lucius Bloom – " There was a definite contemptuous sneer that slid into his voice. " – thinks that he can just send his toady into the night and order people to do his bidding." His tone was surprising – bitter and scathing, and nothing like what I'd heard from the man in the short time I'd known him. Looking quickly around the room, I could see that the other patrons were also rather surprised at this was unexpected behavior.

"William – " began his wife, but he raised a hand.

"I'll be silent, Em. But you and I both know what I think of that man. He'll get what he deserves someday. Mark my words."

I could tell that Holmes would have liked to question William Fraser a bit before we left the inn, but it was impossible with so many strangers sitting about and our transportation awaiting us outside. We both went upstairs to make ready for the journey, and soon I was stepping into the narrow dark hallway and pulling my bedroom door shut behind me. I'd already heard Holmes move along the passage and go downstairs, so I was surprised to find the landlord's wife standing silently in the corridor when I turned.

"Don't mind William," she whispered glancing toward the back stairs as if fearing she would soon be caught. "He . . . he's a good man. But he has some ideas – about rich folk – that he'd be better off forgetting. And certainly never mentioning aloud."

"Do you know anything about Bloom's household that might be of use to us?" I whispered. "I've never heard of the man before now, and I'm sure that the same is true for Mr. Holmes. Anything at all might be useful."

She shook her head. "He's an Englishman who moved here and bought the old manor many years ago. I've heard that he's hard but fair. But – " Then she looked again toward the stairs. "You must go! Your friend is waiting. And William thinks that I'm in the kitchen." With that, she turned toward the back of the building, and within seconds she'd started carefully down the steep rear stairs.

I wanted to share this small exchange with Holmes, but it would have to wait. Insignificant as it was, it was no business of Grayson's.

Downstairs, I crossed the room toward the door even as I saw Mrs. Fraser entering by way of the kitchen, conspicuously wiping her hands with a towel. Her husband watched me with a scowl on his face as I joined Holmes at the front door and he didn't glance toward his wife, apparently having no idea that she had slipped upstairs to speak with me.

The sudden shock from the warm room to the dark night made me instantly pull my heavy coat tighter. The temperature had dropped quite a bit from just a few hours earlier, and there was a fresh breeze coming from the direction of Loch Ryan that carried a dampness that made my eyes sting and my throat ache with each freezing inhalation. The particular sensation made me recall very faint memories of my youngest years.

There was a hint of snow, and the sky had that peculiar pinkish look which indicated that more was on the way. As little protection as it was, I was glad to be in the closed carriage with the door shut and the shades tied down over the windows. I knew that Holmes would have wished to see what we passed on our way to Bloom's manor house, but that would have been nearly impossible on that dark night. At best, we might have observed a few lit windows in distant houses. Nothing else would have been visible.

"Now," said Holmes as we settled ourselves and the carriage rolled forward, "Mr. Bloom's note said that you would discreetly explain what has been occurring." His voice was low, as if he didn't want the driver to hear what was being discussed.

"I'm aware that Mr. Bloom wants me to brief you," was Grayson's rather haughty reply, "but I only know so much myself. His daughter is being terrorized by a Christmas ghost."

That statement hung unanswered between us for a long moment. I was curious by what it implied, but also wondering what Holmes's reaction might be. He had often said that a foundational tenet of his practice was that "No ghosts need apply." I half-wondered if he would bang on the carriage roof with his stick before ordering the driver to turn us around. And yet he surprised me. "How?" he asked simply.

"Mr. Bloom's daughter is now eight years old," Grayson replied. "For the last five years, at Christmas-time, she has received mysterious gifts – treats, or small toys. Sometimes picture books. They are wrapped in bright festive paper and ribbons, and usually left in her bedroom – on the bedside table, or on the mantel, or on a chair. On occasion they are found in other parts of the house."

57

"And they are discovered on Christmas morning, when she awakens?"

"Oh, not just then. There are a dozen of them each year, as if counting down the Twelve Days of Christmas, leading up to the twenty-fifth. They start appearing in mid-December, culminating with the nicest gift on Christmas Day."

"Do they have a theme?" I asked, thinking of the unique and increasing series of gifts described in that old carol – and how tedious it would be to receive flocks of birds and maids and lords and drummers, especially for a small girl, year after year.

"Not at all – except they are something that a child would appreciate. They have remained appropriate to her age. When she was quite young, the books were those that are read to small children. The same for the toys. As she has aged, they have become more elaborate."

"The girl's name?" asked Holmes.

"Elsbeth."

"And her parents are naturally concerned."

"Just Mr. Bloom," was the reply. "His wife died a year or so after Elsbeth was born. I'm told that she had a weak heart."

"Today is the twenty-third," I said. "The gifts have been appearing this year as usual? Then tonight should be the tenth of this series."

"That's correct. No matter what precautions are taken, the gifts are delivered, one way or another, to some part of the house."

"And I'm sure that efforts have been made to stop this from occurring," said Holmes. "Or to discover and catch whomever is responsible."

"Of course," replied Grayson with a bit of disdain, as if even asking the question was foolish. "This has been occurring for five years now – with a total of nearly sixty gifts. Often Mr. Bloom has stayed in the bedroom himself to see who is coming in and leaving gifts. He's had staff do the same – I've spent my share of sleepless nights there without any success. On the nights that one of us stays in Elsbeth's room, a gift is left there if we fall asleep while on watch, and elsewhere in the house if we remain alert. He's had Elsbeth sleep in other rooms, but she protests this, and so he always lets her return. If she were my child, I'd have no hesitation about moving her to another room entirely – or at least for the month of December! I might even leave Stranraer for the entire time – " Then he shut his mouth abruptly, as if voicing aloud any implied criticism of his liege, particularly before strangers who were an unknown factor and might betray him, was a very foolish thing indeed.

At that point, the carriage took a decided lurch to the right, and I could feel that the nature of the roadway had changed beneath us. Soon we were slowing. "Where are we?" asked Holmes.

"Crailloch Taigh," was the reply. "Mr. Bloom's manor house. Just a few miles west of the inn, not far from where Crailloch Burn joins Pilanton. It's a fine old house, neatly restored. It's a pity you can't see the approach in daylight."

"Perhaps we will," said Holmes.

The carriage pulled to a stop and we climbed down underneath a large *porte cochere*, extending from what seemed to be a very large house. It was too dark to get a full sense of the place, being so close as we were to the front door, but the walls on either side extended for quite a ways before vanishing into the night. Looking beyond the carriage, I could see that the curved drive behind us similarly stretched beyond vision toward the road and the distant lights of Stranraer. I turned back toward the house in time to see the door open. I joined Holmes and Grayson as we stepped inside.

We were met by a tall cadaverous fellow, apparently the butler, in formal clothing who offered to take our hats and coats. As he did so, I examined our surroundings. The entry hall was a wide room with a high ceiling, running back nearly forty feet toward a substantial staircase, ascending into darkness. Although the room was dimly lit, I could see that the walls were covered with a number of striking paintings. One seemed to be in the style of Whistler, and I wondered if it was an original. However, before I could step over and examine it further, we heard the sound of rapidly approaching footsteps, and in a moment, a big heavy-set man with thick iron-gray hair and a wide moustache joined us.

"Gentlemen," he said, thrusting out a hand, "I'm Lucius Bloom."

I was surprised to hear his American accent. "This way," he said, holding out an arm toward a nearby doorway. "Would you care for something to drink? Whisky? Port? Something hot?"

"A cup of coffee," said Holmes. "If it isn't too much trouble. It has been a long day, and your note was unexpected."

I nodded in agreement. "Something hot would be welcome."

"Of course." Bloom turned to the cadaverous man. "Blair, if you please?"

The butler nodded and departed. As we entered a tasteful sitting room, with Bloom behind us, our host turned. "That will be all Grayson," he said, moving to shut the door in the face of the man who had brought us there before he could cross the threshold. The last I saw of our summoner was a stoic expression, punctuated by disappointed eyes.

"So," said Bloom, rubbing his hands and indicating seats before a blazing fire, "how much did Grayson tell you?"

As we settled, I had a chance to further study the American. He was older than I had initially believed – at least sixty – and seemed to exude a great vitality and strength. I suppose that I had been expecting someone much more unpleasant, based on both the initial attitude evinced by Grayson, and also by our landlord's comments, indicating that he didn't have much respect for Bloom at best. But his note had been humble enough – a request rather than an arrogant demand as we saw so often from the wealthy – and I found the man to pleasant and seemingly forthright. However, he was clearly rather worried as his eyes cut back and forth between Holmes and me.

"The gist of his statement was that for the past five years, Christmas gifts have been left for your daughter, usually in her bedroom, whether or not she is there, and even if someone has remained in the room to guard it."

"That's right – somehow the next morning, the gifts are there. If it's only Elsbeth sleeping there, then they're placed in obvious locations. On the table beside her bed, for instance. The thought that someone approaches her so closely in her sleep . . . ."

He closed his eyes, overcome at the thought. Then he swallowed. "But if someone is on guard, and unfortunately falls asleep, then the gift will be discovered later: Behind a chair, perhaps, or underneath a tossed-aside piece of clothing. If the watcher remains awake – and I can assure you that I have remained awake many times – then the gifts are found elsewhere in the house, even if there are other guards on duty in the other rooms as well."

"It sounds as if you have made quite the effort to catch this ghost," I said. "Knowing that the visits will occur must surely oppress any holiday cheer."

Holmes then glanced pointedly around the room. "Our sample is very small in terms of what we've so far seen of your home, but I haven't observed any Christmas decorations."

For the first time since meeting him shortly before, Bloom's countenance hardened, and I saw the man who was responsible for his success in life. His eyes narrowed, and his mouth tightened. "That's right. I'll have none of it. I find the whole season to be most unpleasant."

"Indeed," Holmes replied. "I understand that your wife died five years ago. Might I venture a shot to state that her passing occurred at Christmastime?"

Bloom's mouth twitched as his lips tightened, and then he took a sharp breath, as if to make a quick retort. But then he stopped and swallowed. "That is correct. Thus, I have no use for such frippery."

60

"And your daughter?" I asked. "She has never had a Christmas celebration then?"

"She has not," Bloom replied shortly. I could see that he was becoming more defensive, but I raised a placating hand.

"Not everyone does," I said. "I was born here in Stranraer, and spent my early years not far from here. We didn't observe Christmas. My father was strict Church of Scotland, which has no use for Christ's Mass – 'Too Popish!' he would always say. I only learned of the traditional British Christmas on those few occasions when we traveled south to visit my Grandfather on my mother's side."

I didn't mention that there were many others who didn't celebrate because they were unable – living in terribly deprived conditions where simply finding their daily bread was the most blessing that could be hoped for. I knew that there was far too much of that all around us, often within mere blocks of great wealth. In fact, I had no doubt that, not far in any direction from Bloom's fine home, I could locate any number of individuals and families to whom the idea of a Christmas celebration was somewhere between altogether unknown and tragically laughable.

"May we examine your daughter's room?" asked Holmes.

"Of course. This way."

Bloom stood and led us into the hallway, where we met Blair returning with a tray containing a pot of coffee and three cups. He was expressionless as we passed him, but I thought I could see sympathy in his eyes nonetheless as we walked past him toward the wide stairway and he saw how my gaze lingered on the pot. "I'll keep it hot for you, sir," he said softly.

We went up one floor and wound along the back of the building to the east wing. "The manor is quite old," Bloom explained, "with records about the original foundations dating back over four-hundred years. It was in ruins when I bought it, nearly thirty years ago when I came here from Philadelphia to expand my business. I found that I loved Scotland, and stayed. I hope that you can see it in daylight – I'm quite proud of how it's turned out. I brought in the finest architects and builders."

He paused before a wide door made of dark oak – possibly in place since the building was first constructed. He knocked, and a girl's voice answered. Bloom opened the door, well-maintained and silent, to reveal a most cozy room, well-lit, and tastefully decorated to suit a young girl.

Seated near the fireplace was Bloom's daughter, a girl of about eight, alongside a matronly lady who was holding a book. They had apparently been reading before putting the girl to bed, as she was attired in a nightgown and slippers. With a look toward Holmes and me, the girl slid forward on the settee to place her feet upon the floor and then ran to her father, who bent to receive her enthusiastic hug.

"Oh, Papa," the girl cried, releasing him and glancing again our way, "please don't let them stop the Ghost from visiting! It's so much fun!"

The hint of a frown appeared between Bloom's eyebrows, but it vanished in an instant. "You know that I'm concerned that someone can get in here so easily," he said. "If someone wants to send you gifts, why can't they have them delivered by post?"

A good question, I thought, and indicative that there was more to this than simply getting a gift into the girl's hands.

Meanwhile, the elderly woman stood. "This," explained Bloom, "is Mrs. Treathaway. She's been Elsbeth's nurse since the passing of her mother six years ago."

The woman nodded. "Nice to meet you both."

"Mr. Holmes and Dr. Watson are going to see what they can determine about our ghost," added Bloom. He turned toward my friend. "How would you like to begin?"

"I understand," Holmes answered, "that on occasion Elsbeth sleeps elsewhere during this season. Perhaps this would be possible tonight as well?"

"Certainly." Bloom turned to Mrs. Treathaway. "Can you gather her things?"

The woman nodded. "After Elsbeth is settled," added Holmes to the nurse, "may we speak?" He received an acknowledgement, and then Mrs. Treathaway began assembling a few items to carry away, including the book she had just been holding.

Holmes knelt down and faced Elsbeth. "So you aren't afraid of the ghost?" he asked.

She shook her head. "He always brings me gifts, for as long as I can remember."

"'He'? Are you sure that the ghost is a 'he'?"

She nodded, and glanced toward her father. "I've seen him."

At this, her father sputtered in surprise. "What? You've never mentioned *that*!"

The girl nodded and took her father's hand – seeming to instinctively know that doing so would calm him a bit. "Just this year. I've pretended to be asleep. I didn't know he was here until he was setting one of the presents beside my bed. I tried to breathe normally and kept my eyes almost closed, but I could see him. He isn't a ghost at all – he's *Father Christmas*!"

"And how do you know what Father Christmas looks like?" asked her father. The question surprised me for an instant before I remembered that Bloom hadn't allowed Christmas into his house since his wife died.

The little girl gave a wise smile, older than her years. "I know you don't like Christmas because of Mama, Papa, but I still know about it. I see the decorations when I'm in town, and I know about it from the other girls. I know Mama died then, and that's why you don't want to be reminded of it, but it doesn't bother me that way. That's why I'm so happy that Father Christmas has found a way to help me celebrate . . . ."

Bloom swallowed, as if rocked by unexpected emotions. After a moment, he dropped to one knee and pulled her closer, even as Holmes rose to both feet. "You are getting older, my girl. Perhaps we should talk more often about . . . about these things." Then he released her and stood. "But still, I can't have anyone – even Father Christmas – entering and leaving the house uninvited." He looked toward us. "Gentlemen – if you can help us learn the truth . . . ?"

I nodded, and Holmes answered. "I will examine the room, and then one of us will stay in here tonight, with a suitable false Elsbeth constructed in the bed. Hopefully the fact that strangers to the household are here won't disrupt the good Father's generous inclinations. I suspect that someone who has been so consistent for five years won't be dissuaded by a couple of visitors from London."

With that we said goodnight to Elsbeth, who was led away by Mrs. Treathaway. Then, Holmes requested that Bloom and I wait in the hallway while he made his investigation alone.

Outside, I could see that Bloom was becoming rather nervous. I mentioned it to him, and he laughed. "It's the same every night leading up to Christmas – wondering how he'll get in, despite our precautions, and if this is the night we'll catch him."

"What precautions have you taken?"

"Anything from elaborate to nearly giving up in defeat. When this started, I initially accused the staff – of one or all of them of being responsible. At the time, Mrs. Treathaway was quite critical of my . . . my avoidance of anything to do with Christmas. I thought that she was the one providing the gifts to get around my wishes. But I could tell that her concern regarding an intruder in the house was sincere, and was stronger than any desire to expose Elsbeth to aspects of the holiday.

"During the first year, and the first twelve gifts, each night became increasingly worrisome. No matter where we watched or waited, somehow the gifts appeared. The next year, I didn't believe that it would continue, but it did, and I arranged for a number of local men to supplement the staff, watching much of the inside, and outside as well. It did no good. The same for the third year. By last Christmas, I was ready to give up and just get through the days as best we could."

"It sounds as if you allow Elsbeth to spend some nights in the room alone – even knowing that a stranger is entering."

"She has never been alone. On those nights when no one is in the room, I stand guard in the hall with the door cracked. But even then, there are times when I have turned away for a short period, or my spirit momentarily weakens, and I assume that's when this 'Father Christmas' finds his way inside. I would move her out of the room entirely, as we've done tonight, but she does love it there so, and whether she's in there or elsewhere, the intruder gets inside."

At that moment, Holmes opened the door and joined us. "I've made my examination and found a few points of interest." He held up a hand. "Watson will tell you, Mr. Bloom, that I like to hold my cards close at this stage of an investigation. I propose that, after we speak with Mrs. Treathaway, we prepare for the rest of the night." He looked toward me. "Watson, would you mind taking the shift in the rather comfortable looking chair in Elsbeth's room, somewhat disguised as Mr. Bloom here, while I take up a post in the hallway? Feel free to sleep – you will be safe enough – and if you do wake up, make no effort to disturb Father Christmas's work. I propose to let him come and go unopposed tonight, in order to learn more about him so that we can bring this to a conclusion tomorrow night. Agreed?"

It was, and we then went in search of the nurse.

She had little to tell us. A very quiet woman, she answered mostly in one-word responses, but one had the sense that she had secrets to keep. Perhaps, however, it was simply the cast of her face, with a small upturn at one side of her mouth that seemed to imply hidden knowledge that amused her. She confirmed Bloom's introduction that she'd been the girl's nurse for six years, and that she had been a part of the household staff before then – quite a few years back in fact. "Since the time of the master's first wife," she explained. We glanced toward Bloom.

"Elsbeth's mother was my second wife," he explained shortly. "My first wife came with me from America. She died a quarter-century ago. A year or so after that, I met my second wife. On a trip to the Continent. She was . . . she was quite a bit younger than me. We'd been married for quite a while before Elsbeth came along. She was . . . something of a surprise, and by then my wife had . . . weakened. She never quite recovered from giving birth. Since her passing, it's just been the two of us – Elsbeth and me. I don't plan to remarry a third time."

"And did you have any children from our first marriage."

Bloom shook his head. "Sadly, no. My first wife was unable to bear children. My second wife and I believed that to be true in her case as well. That's why my girl was such a blessing."

Mrs. Treathaway had nothing further of importance to add, stating only that she had no idea who the ghost – or Father Christmas – might be, and while she disagreed with the ghost's methods – and here she looked pointedly at her employer – she admired his motivations.

"Motivations?" asked Holmes. "You understand them, then?"

"Certainly," she said with her secret and possibly unintended smile. "He wants that girl to have her Christmases."

We left her where we'd spoken, in the hallway outside Elsbeth's temporary bedroom. Bloom went in to say good night one more time, and Holmes and returned to the girl's regular room.

Inside, Holmes set about constructing a false Elsbeth in the girl's bed, made from pillows artfully bunched under her sheets and blankets. Meanwhile, I related my short conversation with Mrs. Fraser while I arranged the chair where I would sleep, setting it according to Holmes's instructions at a certain location facing the bed. I asked if this placement was in relation to something he'd seen during his examination while Bloom and I waited in the hallway, and he grunted in agreement without elaboration.

"What Mrs. Fraser told me . . ." I said. "Is it important?"

"Initially, everything is important," was his cryptic reply.

When all was arranged in the room, Holmes wished me a good night and stepped into the hallway, pulling the door closed behind him. I settled into the chair, turned down the table lamp, and settled in the darkness, only dimly lit by the dying embers in the tidy little fireplace. After the day I'd had, it wasn't long before I was fast asleep. My last thought was that I'd forgotten to tell Blair that I no longer needed the coffee.

The chair was comfortable, and when I awoke to morning light, I had no particular aches to complain of. I was surprised to have slept the whole night through, and had no difficulties in remembering where I was. I thought that nothing must have happened, because I'd been aware of no visitors in the night. Throwing aside the heavy quilt in which I'd wrapped myself, I stood, noticing the shape in the bed remained as Holmes had arranged it. There was nothing different about the bedside table.

Then I turned and saw, on the small settee behind my chair where Mrs. Treathaway had been reading to Elsbeth, a large box wrapped in red paper and a green ribbon.

Father Christmas had been here, just feet away from me, while I slept in ignorance. I felt a chill run up my back.

The fire was out, and after being wrapped in the quilt all night, I was suddenly cold. I checked watch and saw that it was early, not long after six a.m. I left the bedroom, looking for Holmes. Unsurprisingly, he wasn't still on duty in the hallway. I found him downstairs, in the room where we'd first spoken with Bloom, sitting quietly with his pipe and a cup of coffee. He stood and nodded my way, passing without speaking toward the hallway and then the rear of the house. Soon he returned with a second cup. As he handed it to me, I said, "Did you see him?"

"I did."

"Who is it?"

He shook his head. "I'm not ready to reveal that quite yet. I need to understand a few more things first – motivations and history."

I took a sip. "I expect that it's Grayson, although I don't know what would motivate him so."

"You simply don't like him."

"That's true. I wonder if he's been here long enough to have started this five years ago."

"He has. I found the cook, Mrs. Ames, to be most gregarious when I spoke with her earlier this morning."

"Well, let's wake Bloom and haul Grayson in front of him and be done with it then."

Holmes shook his head and smiled. "Ever the man of action. No, as I said, I'm not ready yet for the dramatic *denouement* that you so crave. In truth, the only reason to awaken Bloom is to have him arrange for our transportation back to the inn.

But our host was already awake. He wasn't surprised at all to learn that there had been another visitation and another gift, and while he also wanted to know what – and whom – Holmes had seen, he was satisfied that the matter would be wrapped up within another day. He left to arrange for the carriage, and within a short while we were headed back toward Stranraer.

It had snowed some more during the night – not an excessive amount, but enough to re-whiten the landscape and cover the trees in a sugary dusting of white. As we drove away, I looked back at the manor, as did Holmes, and saw that it was quite large indeed. Although there were a number of more modern features tacked onto it here and there, the overall ancientness of the structure was unmistakable.

The roads were safe enough, and we were conveyed without incident to the inn door. By daylight, I could see that it was only a few miles' journey, and would be quite beautiful during the warmer months. Thanking our driver, we turned to go inside. However, Holmes stopped me for a moment, seeming to be in thought as he pinched his ear while staring at the ground outside the main door. Finally, he nodded to himself and we continued inside. As it was still quite early, the main room was empty, although I could hear sounds of activity in the kitchen beyond the bar.

We went upstairs to freshen up for the day, and when I was finished, I walked down the hall to knock on Holmes's door. He was ready to go downstairs as well, but beforehand he gave me instructions.

"I intend to throw a small party," he said. "A little Christmas celebration for the locals we met last night, and the Frasers. If you could let them know that I'll be buying drinks and refreshments for whomever wants to attend this afternoon, it would be much appreciated. Around three o'clock, I think – the more, the merrier."

I smiled and accepted that I would understand the reason for this at some point. "Anything else?"

"Yes," Holmes said. "There's no need for you to venture forth today. Spend time downstairs, talking and listening and asking questions. See if you can get Mrs. Fraser to tell you about the locals. Start by asking about her and her husband – people always like to talk about themselves, and it will be a good point from which to pivot to the wider community."

"And you?" I asked. "While I stay in, I expect that you'll go out."

"An accurate assumption. After breakfast, I want to visit and ask some questions of my own. Perhaps I'll spend time with the local vicar at the nearby church. What better way to acknowledge the approach of Christmas than in the presence of a holy man?"

I laughed and Holmes smiled, and we ventured downstairs to request some breakfast.

Much of that day passed in a rather dreamlike haze. We arranged to stay for another night beyond what we'd originally requested – not a difficulty, as we were the inn's only guests – and then Holmes departed while I settled myself into a cozy corner of the bar. I began with coffee in the morning, resisting the temptation to begin too early with beverages that would have the opposite effect. I had a book to read, and made great progress through it, but I also engaged in conversations and became acclimated to the flow of the place as various patrons arrived and departed, all on their own schedules.

Toward midday I ordered a meal, and when Mrs. Fraser placed it before me, I took the opportunity to start a conversation. As there were no other visitors needing her just then, she accepted my offer to join me. Easing into her chair across the table, she explained that as her delivery date approached, she found it harder to get through the days, and she indicated that soon she would desist and they would hire a replacement. They would have done so sooner, she said, as her husband was most insistent that she not exert herself, but she hated to concede that she needed to go easier.

The pub, she explained, was a family affair which her husband had inherited from his widowed mother. She had opened it with some inherited money when he was a very small boy, and he'd grown up here. He had gone away for a while to serve in the military, but there was never any intention that he make a career of it, and after receiving a slight wound, he'd returned home. Soon after that they had married, and not much later after that his mother had passed. Now, after several years of patient waiting, they were to have a child of their own. I congratulated her again on their good fortune.

Our talk turned to the local area, and she commented on how this location south of the town and the loch had changed during her lifetime. I heard the stories and gossip about several of the more colorful locals, but she conspicuously deflected my attempts to steer the conversation toward the Bloom household. When I did so, she glanced nervously toward the bar, where her husband sat on a stool, reading a newspaper. Soon after, seeing that I had finished eating, she stood and took my plate. I wasn't able to question her again as more people drifted in through the passing afternoon.

Mrs. Fraser had been pleased but frankly puzzled about Holmes's idea of throwing a small Christmas party, but she allowed that it would be a welcome event. Holmes himself returned a little before three o'clock, a Pied Piper leading a number of locals inside to mingle with those who had already heard about it. Within a short time, the room, which I'd already grown accustomed to being a quiet and peaceful sort of place, was full of a loud and raucous but good-natured celebration.

I spent time moving from group to group, and I heard a number of interesting tales, along with unexpectedly meeting several old-timers who had known my father. In spite of whatever they remembered about him in truth – for he had been a difficult man at times, with a grim outlook – they were quite willing to only refer to him in the best possible terms.

I lost track of Holmes rather quickly, in spite of my attempts to see what he was up to – for he would have never suggested such a gathering without having another purpose in mind. I only noticed him again when the party started to thin and die an hour or so later. Three or four men seemed inclined to stay and try and keep it going, but when Holmes signaled to Fraser that he was done buying drinks, their interest quickly flagged. In another hour, the scene was very similar to how we'd found it the night before when returning from my very difficult day – the same regulars in their typical places, and Holmes and me at our table in the back, having chosen to repeat our previous menu choices. Why seek after something new when satisfaction is already established?

As we ate, Holmes explained that we would go upstairs after a suitable time and then wait until a man that he'd met the previous day when involved in my business, a local who now owed him a favor, would enter by way of the front door. He would ask to speak to the Frasers, delivering a meaningless message, while Holmes and I surreptitiously departed by way of the back stairs and out through the kitchen. Then we would return to the manor, where with any luck, the matter of the false Father Christmas would be explained.

I still had no idea what to expect, but that wasn't unusual. Holmes had the twin aspects of preferring a dramatic revelation, for which I always made a perfect audience, and also that he preferred to keep as much information to himself as he could, in case his interpretation of the facts somehow went awry. I had once been frustrated by it, but no longer. Additionally, I was a doctor and a former soldier, and in each capacity, I was trained to accept and carry out orders when needed – the former during surgeries when one rarely second-guessed a senior surgeon during a procedure, and the latter when following instructions might mean the difference between life and death.

All went according to plan. We rose and wished everyone good night. Then we went upstairs. I sat smoking in my room, reading further in my book, while Holmes waited in his down the hall, watching out the window toward the front of the inn. In about an hour, he softly knocked on my door, indicating that the distraction had arrived. I pulled on my coat and hat, and we slipped along the hall and down the back steps, which Holmes had already ascertained could be descended quietly. The cook having long since departed, we were able to exit while both Frasers were out front. A walk of five minutes brought us to an alley where a hansom cab stood waiting. Holmes spoke softly to the driver, and then we were in transit to the manor house.

Bloom met us outside the front door, where he'd apparently been waiting impatiently for some time, if the amount of cigar ash at his feet was any indication. Of Grayson or the staff there was no sign. "I've sent them away, as instructed," Bloom explained. "Do you really know who it is?"

"I do," said Holmes. "All will be revealed – later tonight."

"Good, good. Where do you want me to hide?"

"In your own bedroom," announced Holmes, raising his hand as Bloom started to protest. "I assure you that we'll call as soon as we have him – but nothing must occur beforehand to spook him." He indicated that we should go inside. "Shall we get into place?"

Bloom accompanied us upstairs toward his daughter's room. "I did as you asked," he said. "I had everyone loaded up and sent north, to a smaller house that I keep near Ballantrae. No one had time or opportunity to send word that they would be away – I made sure of that. I . . . I told them that we would have a Christmas celebration there." He swallowed. "I . . . I didn't want to, but you should have seen . . . seen how pleased Elsbeth was. Perhaps . . . perhaps I've made a mistake. Keeping Christmas from her. If nothing else, perhaps . . . this whole business has softened my heart, just a bit."

"You won't regret it," I said as we reached his daughter's doorway. "I grew up without Christmas. I'm glad now that I celebrate it. I can't imagine not doing so."

He nodded, and then asked if we needed anything. Hearing that we didn't, he said good night and retreated down the hall. When he'd vanished around the corner, I asked softly, "Will he stay away?"

"I expect so. In any case, I'll be here in the hallway to wave him away should he come creeping back."

"And I'll be back in my chair?" I asked, wondering if I'd sleep as well tonight as before, especially after spending such a tranquil, warm, and untaxing afternoon.

"No, not at all. I have a different spot picked out for you."

Inside, the room was as we'd left it that morning, although there were some small signs that Elsbeth had retrieved a few items since then for her journey. The bed still contained its false figure curled in supposed sleep. Holmes stepped that way, rearranged the pose somewhat, and then nodded in satisfaction. "And now for your station."

I looked around. There was no obvious place in here to hide – no bureaus or cabinets to step behind. I wondered if I'd be standing behind the drapes all night when Holmes inexplicably moved to the wall beside the fireplace. With a bend and flick of his fingers, he stepped back to allow a segment of the wall room to swing silently open, revealing a black passage behind.

"Behold: One of the remnants of the original manor – with the works oiled, guaranteeing unhindered and undetected passage by Father Christmas."

I moved forward with a wondrous look. This wasn't the first such passage that I'd seen, but I always reacted the same way – as if I were a boy reading of such things in adventure books about knights and pirates, castles and treasures, and exciting deeds both noble and otherwise.

"I spoke at length today with the vicar. When I'd gained his trust and explained what was occurring, he told me some of the house's history – how such passages were necessary for the original owner of this building

– a merchant who often ran afoul of enemies or thieves, and also those of opposing religions who used their beliefs to justify their attempts at his murder."

"And did he tell you where to find this doorway, and how to open it as well?"

"No, I learned that for myself last night when I initially examined the room while you and Bloom waited in the hallway."

"So you already knew how Father Christmas would enter."

"I did. And I saw him do so from my place at the cracked doorway while you slept. He was dressed as Elsbeth said – in the traditional costume. He never approached the bed, or even stepped near your chair. I suppose on those nights that he finds a guard, he waits for his chance and then enters no further than necessary. He simply left the gift on the settee and returned to the passage, closing the door behind him without a single sound."

"And you know who he is. You saw his face."

"As clearly as I see you – and yes, in spite of his false beard, he was unmistakable."

"Then why wait another day? Why didn't you confront him this morning?"

"Because the vicar told me other stories besides the history of the house. I think that by waiting, and catching him tonight when he least suspects it, we can help mend something that has been broken for too long."

Holmes lit his dark lantern and then led me into the passage. Immediately after entering, he paused to point out a boot mark in the dust. "This passage was swept clean when I first examined it last night – obviously kept that way to avoid any indications being tracked into the bedroom. I scattered just a bit of ash here during my inspection to show footprints, if possible, and I was successful. You didn't observe, but there were some new prints in the bedroom – although they weren't easily noticed on the wooden floor."

He walked on, and we had to keep our heads ducked and our shoulders tucked to avoid the low ceiling and narrow stone walls. I wondered just how far the passage went, and if there were others. Seemingly reading my thoughts, Holmes replied, "There are openings to other rooms – which is how, I expect, Father Christmas has been able to leave gifts elsewhere when Elsbeth's bedroom was too well guarded. I was also able to backtrack through this passage to find the exit – several hundred yards behind the house, well-hidden behind a thick and ancient growth of yew trees lying next to a rocky embankment."

He stopped before a small turning to our left, about fifty feet from where we'd entered the manor's walls. I could see that it went about ten feet or so before turning out of sight to the right.

"This leads down to a wall behind the kitchen. You'll hide here until our visitor passes. By the time he reaches the bedroom, you will have come along behind, bottling him up while I enter from the hallway. Tonight, with no guard in the room, he will fully enter to leave a gift beside the bed. It's nearly eleven now. If he keeps the same schedule as last night, we shouldn't have to wait very long – even Father Christmas wants to finish up and get home earlier rather than later."

I wanted to ask who to expect, and whether there would be any danger. It has been my experience that even the most tame creature can turn and fight when surprised or threatened. But Holmes seemed to expect no danger – he hadn't warned me or asked if I had my service revolver, although of course he knew that I did, as I'd learned long ago to never, ever travel without it.

With a nod, as he considered that all that I needed to know was explained, he handed me the dark lantern and retreated down the black passageway.

I looked around, made sure that there was a comfortable place to stand without any nails or other intrusions that might snag my coat, and settled to pass the time. With a sigh, as this wasn't my first occasion in this type of situation, I lowered the flame and closed the lantern's doors. Except for the comforting smell of hot metal, ready to illuminate the passage when needed, there was no indication that I was here.

I was always curious to see how much time passed during those periods on Holmes's investigations when I waited in darkness before something happened. Generally my internal clock wasn't too disappointing. It was never as long as I thought, but then again it wasn't as if I were off by hours. I had time to recall a great many things, including past Christmases, and times before that as a boy in Stranraer. This latter was no doubt related to the sad business that had called me back to the town of my birth just a few days before. My mind wandered eventually to those more tedious things – the lists of things to do and accomplish that eat up one's day-to-day life and cannot be avoided by those making an effort to function as successful adults – when I heard the faintest shuffle in the passageway beyond where I hid.

I began to perceive a small glow as Father Christmas approached – for who else could it be? Apparently he brought his own dark lantern, not caring to cross the untold distances within the walls without some sort of assistance. I couldn't blame him. If the spaces were as Holmes described, with branches going here and there to multiple rooms, there was lot of opportunity to become lost. And who could say that the other routes were as well-kept as the small segment that I had I witnessed?

It occurred to me to wonder just how Father Christmas knew about these lost passages. I supposed that the answer would be forthcoming.

When the light had reached its peak at the junction of the narrow corridor where I hid and then started to dim, I knew that he had passed, and I slowly allowed the smallest amount of light to escape my own lantern. Unlike Holmes, I didn't trust my own ability to navigate my way back to the main house in the dark. After standing in the blackness for nearly two hours, even the small amount of light from the lantern seemed extraordinarily bright, and was more than sufficient. I silently stepped out of my spot and moved back toward Elsbeth's bedroom.

Turning into the main passageway, I could see the crack ahead where the bedroom entrance was already opened. I quickly covered the remaining distance, pausing just inside the doorway, and holding my breath, while hoping that the intruder couldn't hear the pounding of my heart which seemed deafening in my own years. Then, I had to wait no longer. The light in the room grew much brighter, causing me to suddenly squint, and I heard Holmes stating that the game was up. I surged forward.

Father Christmas had his back to me, facing Holmes, who stood in the bedroom doorway. He was a tall fellow with broad shoulders, and underneath his white wig, I could see that he had black hair. I glanced down at his boots, which had tracked ash from the passageway across the floor, much as he would have done the previous night.

He wasn't aware of me yet and, ignoring Holmes's command, he quickly pivoted back toward my direction and his escape. He was carrying a package – this one much smaller than that of the night before – and when he saw me, it slipped from his fingers. There was a small tinkling of broken glass, and he lurched to a stop, looking down at the gift. He gave a small groan, looked back in my direction, and then knelt almost without thought to pick it up.

"You can get her another one, Mr. Fraser," said Holmes softly, stepping in and pushing the bedroom door shut behind him. "Although perhaps meeting you – properly, if you haven't already met her otherwise – would be a greater gift."

Holmes took another step forward, and just after he did so, the door behind him reopened to reveal Bloom, still in the clothes in which we'd last seen him – and carrying an ugly revolver.

"So you have him, then," he said, his eyes cold. "Didn't take long. Thank you, Mr. Holmes. I can take it from here."

"I think not, Mr. Bloom," said Holmes, turning and stepping between the two men. I shifted as I withdrew my own service revolver, revealing it to our client and covering him so that there was no doubt that Fraser was – at least for now – under my protection. Fraser might have bolted for the passage at that point, as I was no longer in his way, but he simply turned and faced Bloom as well, a frown on his face as he reached up to pull off the white beard and attached wig.

"Don't worry, Mr. Holmes," said Bloom. "You misunderstand. I won't shoot him – unless he tries to flee. But I will see him arrested and put away. Five years of intrusions! Five years of ruining my peace of mind, invading my home, and destroying any sense of security. And the threat to my daughter – "

"There is no threat to Elsbeth," said Fraser, his voice low.

"What?" asked Bloom. "You know her name?"

"He does," said Holmes. "She is his half-sister. Mr. Fraser is your son."

My surprise was only equaled by that of Bloom himself. He took a step back as if pushed, the gun lowering in his hand toward the floor. He stumbled against a chair and dropped into it. I saw him uncurl his finger from the trigger.

Looking at them both, I could now see a resemblance, and was angry with myself for not noticing it before. I had known Holmes long enough by then that I should have done as he always advised and looked beyond surface appearances. I had been lulled when looking at Bloom's features by his heftiness and aged features, as well as his grey hair. Now that I'd been told, I could see that their relationship was undoubtedly true.

"His son?" I asked. "Did you learn this from the vicar?"

"I did," replied Holmes. "He's been remarkably discreet, considering what he has known all of these years. I verified it from the baptism records – where it has rested unnoticed for all of these years simply because no one here has ever cared enough to examine them. Mr. Fraser's mother felt the need to have the child's father recorded accurately and honestly, in spite of the fact that she could have shown her late husband, Mr. Fraser, as the father."

"But – " I gestured to Bloom. "He obviously didn't know. How did that happen?"

Fraser took a step forward, looking rather disconcerting with his big frame garbed in the Father Christmas attire, which I could see now had the aspect of a cheap seasonal costume. "He didn't know. My mother never told him, and after he sent her away, he never bothered to check on her."

"I didn't know," breathed Bloom in agreement, his eyes on his son. "She led me to understand that our . . . *relationship*, such as it had been, would best be kept secret. For her own reputation, more than my own."

Fraser looked back at Bloom, and one could almost see him rethinking whatever beliefs had sustained him for so long. I recalled his comments the night before, when Grayson had arrived at the inn to request our presence – how he seemed to have no use for Bloom, and no respect either. And then, a few moments later, Mrs. Fraser had tried to make excuses for him when she'd spoken to me in confidence.

"My mother and father worked here, at the manor," explained Fraser. "My father – Silas Fraser – was apparently a bad man, but what could a woman do? From what she told me, Mrs. Bloom – the first Mrs. Bloom – was something of a cold harridan. She made his life – " He jerked a thumb at the seated man. " – a living hell. They . . . they . . . It's difficult to speak of one's mother this way. But she and . . . this man . . . found one another. Comforted one another, here in this house. Even after his first wife died – especially then. But after several years more of that, he sent her away. She and my father both. Turned them out."

"I didn't know," muttered Bloom. "I had met my wife – my second wife – and I knew that having your mother remain here . . . so close . . . would never work out. I . . . I cared for her. Seeing her every day, and given how we'd felt about each other, while my first wife . . . I didn't just turn them out. I gave them money. That's what they – she and Fraser – used to buy the inn. And I didn't communicate with her afterwards. I thought that's what she – your mother – wanted. And I was newly married. I loved my wife, you see. I couldn't hurt her that way, or be dishonest to our vows. I made a clean break of it."

"Which is why," countered Fraser, rather coldly, "you never knew that she was with child – with *me* – by the time you sent her and my father away. He died soon after, and people believed that I was his son."

Bloom looked up at him then. "But how do you know that I am your father, and not him?" Then he blinked and shook his head, a sad smile upon his face. "But no, I can see the resemblance between us. There is no doubt." He raised a hand to his eyes. "So close. So close, and I never knew. I remember when she . . . when your mother died, and I knew of you, of course, but I always thought that you were Fraser's son." He looked up again. "But there is no doubt."

"None," agreed Fraser. "And in any case, my mother was certain that it was you – and she would certainly know, wouldn't she? Not long after they bought the inn, my father died – a drunken accident, from what I was told – and several months after that, I was born. No one questioned who my father was – but she told me the truth when I was old enough. My mother had good help, and ran the place well until she died. She brought me up right, and it's mine now, and I run it right too."

75

"I'm sure you do," said Bloom softly. Only then did he notice that he still held the gun in his hand. He placed it quickly on a nearby table, as if he were hot and burning his hand.

"But why this business with Father Christmas?" I asked. "What has that accomplished?"

"I knew that I had a sister. From all I've heard, she's happy and well cared for. But for some reason, this man – my . . . father – refused to let her celebrate the holiday. A girl should be able to celebrate Christmas! How dare he keep that from her? Maybe what I'd heard wasn't true – maybe she wasn't as happy as everyone believed. I decided that I would celebrate for her – and in doing so be the brother she didn't know she had."

"And you knew of the passageways into the manor that allowed your access?" Holmes asked.

Fraser nodded. "Some of us who have grown up here know them. It's a secret that gets passed along. Not everyone who knew ever used them, obviously, but we would sometimes sneak inside when I was younger, my friends and I. But during the occasions when I've entered over the last five years, I haven't seen any signs that anyone else has been in or out in a long time. Maybe they're forgotten now – possibly all of the others who knew of them kept it to themselves, rather than tell their own children. Some of them aren't safe. The passageways are old – far older than the building that stands here now."

"As the vicar confirmed for me earlier today," confirmed Holmes.

"I suppose that you visited last night and again tonight," I said to Fraser, "because you refused to be stopped this close to Christmas, even knowing that a trap might be set."

"I wasn't sure," replied the innkeeper. "I knew that Grayson had summoned you here last night, but I didn't know why. I thought that it might simply be related to business."

"Then you don't know that Holmes is a detective?" I asked, glancing at my friend. "You haven't heard of him?"

Fraser shook his head. "No. Should I have?"

I smiled. This would be a point of discussion on the train back to London. It was always good to have a few examples such as these for those occasions when Sherlock Holmes needed to be humbled a bit.

"The affair at the inn this afternoon," I asked Holmes. "What did that accomplish?"

"I knew from watching last night who Father Christmas was." He pointed toward the doorway into the walls. "As you can see, Mr. Fraser, I had left some ash on the passage floor to record your footprints. Although I knew who you were when we returned to the inn early this morning, I saw those same footprints in the inn doorway, left in the newly fallen

76

snow. I spent the day asking questions, confirming that Mr. Bloom is well thought-of in the community, by both current and former employees from the house, as well as those at his various businesses, and local merchants, and even his business competitors. Only your negative comments last night seemed out of place. It was the vicar who confirmed why."

"But the Christmas party – " I prompted.

"Ah, yes. That little distraction kept Mr. and Mrs. Fraser busy long enough for me to search their quarters and find the Father Christmas costume. You can see my mark that I placed there on the right knee – something that looks rather like an *H.*"

"And of course Mrs. Fraser knows," I added.

"She does – and how could she not? For twelve nights at Christmas, for the last five years, her husband has stepped out not long after midnight." He looked at Fraser. "Has she tried to discourage you?"

Fraser nodded. "She has. But I'd already been doing it for two years when we married, and I didn't want to stop."

"She has been very supportive, I'm sure, but I believe that she'll be pleased that this matter will now be resolved."

Fraser looked surprised – we all did – as Holmes spoke louder. "You may come in now, Mrs. Fraser."

The door to the hall opened and the innkeeper's wife stepped through. Walking beside her and holding her hand was young Elsbeth Bloom, her eyes wide as they fixed on the tall dark-haired man wearing the Father Christmas costume.

"It's you," she breathed. "It's really you."

"Not Father Christmas," said Bloom, finally pulling himself to his feet. "This is . . . this is your brother, William Fraser." He looked from his daughter to the tall young man standing beside him. Then, tentatively, he took a step toward his son, and then another. He put out his hand as if to shake, but then with a choked sob, he lurched forward and pulled Fraser into an embrace.

The younger man seemed surprised, and his chest inflated for a second as he inhaled deeply, as if in preparation to pulling loose and stepping back. Then – and one could see him meet his wife's steady smiling gaze as the conscious decision to relent washed across his features – he relaxed and raised his arms, returning his father's hug.

Mrs. Fraser nodded to Elsbeth, who released her hand and ran forward, throwing her arms around both men – each of whom freed an arm in turn to pull her closer. Mrs. Fraser looked toward Holmes, her eyes rimmed with tears, and silently whispered, "Thank you."

As other members of the household slipped into the now-crowded bedroom – Grayson, Mrs. Treathaway, Blair, and others that I hadn't met

– Holmes tapped my arm and nodded toward the hallway. We slipped past the last of the staff entering the room, went downstairs, and retrieved our hats and coats.

Outside, Holmes tugged his wool fore-and-aft cap tighter on his head, pulled his coat close, and asked, "Are you up for a night walk?"

It was cold but clear, and I found it – at least for the moment – quite bracing. I had mixed emotions about departing from the house at such a moving moment, but it belonged to the Blooms and the Frasers, and not us. I might regret it before we had walked the few miles back to the inn through the cold darkness, but for then I agreed.

"You've had a busy day," I said as we set out, moving slowly but steadily to avoid any unseen patches of ice on the otherwise cleared road.

"It was simply dotting *I*'s and crossing *T*'s," he replied. "Once I saw who the visitor was, the rest was just frosting."

"And you made the assumption that there would be a happy ending. You summoned back Elsbeth and the staff from Ballantrae, knowing what time to have them arrive, based on last night's Father Christmas visit."

"It seemed logical. And Bloom really does have an excellent reputation as a good man. Additionally, the vicar confirmed that he had strong feelings for Fraser's mother. It was only circumstances and societal expectations that kept them apart. I knew that when Bloom understood the truth, he would be pleased. And likewise, a good man like William Fraser – and he must be good to have won such a fine lady as his wife – would not hold onto his bitterness."

"And you took Mrs. Fraser into your confidence. Nothing that I heard from her and related to you gave any indication that she wouldn't simply tell her husband of the trap, causing him to stay home tonight."

"Ah, that was a bit more of a gamble, but from what you told me, she didn't seem comfortable with what was going on, and a person of her character, based on the small bit that we witnessed, would certainly wish to see things open and aboveboard, and a family mended, rather than let it continue along the same course."

We walked on in silence for a while, and I found myself scanning the skies for a large star. It was something that I did every year – never with any success, but still I did it – looking for some signs of a Biblical miracle in these less-than-miraculous modern times.

Once again, as if reading my mind, but probably just noticing where my gaze remained directed, Holmes said, "There are many theories as to the true nature of the Bethlehem star. A comet, perhaps? The nova of some distant star? Possibly two or more planets that came into alignment at just the right time to glow particularly bright."

He began to explain the thinking about the latter, raising both hands to illustrate the motions of the planets. He was still doing so when we reached the inn, and he continued as we entered and I stepped behind the bar to retrieve a bottle of the local whisky. We built up the fire and settled at our usual table, neither of a mind to go to sleep.

From that topic we progressed to a number of others, including me finally discussing my true thoughts as to our visit to Stranraer. We were still talking in the early morning when the Frasers returned, their faces glowing. We stood as Fraser silently crossed the room to shake our hands, while Mrs. Fraser waited her turn to hug us both on that bright Christmas morning.

The Curious Affair of the Temporal Traveler

I have found one of the trials of getting older, in the same way that aches and pains become unwanted company upon life's journey, is that some friends whom we admired in our younger days become tedious, querulous, and unpleasant.

Such was the case in the summer of 1902, as the date of my marriage approached. I had located and subsequently purchased an established medical practice at No. 9 Queen Anne Street, within the Harley Street medical district. It was a fine four-story brick building, in many ways mirroring the layout of 221 Baker Street, where I had resided off-and-on since January 1881, and most recently from the spring of 1894, when Sherlock Holmes had returned to London after his three-years of presumed death.

By early July, I was deeply involved in the planning and execution of my new enterprise, as well as spending time with my bride-to-be as we made preparations for our upcoming wedding. I was also recovering from an irritating but not dangerous gunshot wound to the leg which had been inflicted upon me (during the course of one of Holmes's recent investigations) by an American criminal with the curious sobriquet of "Killer" Evans. As one might imagine, my future wife was not overly thrilled with the idea that such wounds were possible when associating with my detective friend. While we did not openly argue about it, and despite my assurances that this was not typical, there was a definite frostiness when the topic was approached.

In the meantime, I continued to be associated with those various investigations which had been so much a part of my life for the better part of the previous two decades. Most recently, Holmes and I had been of valuable service when defeating a band of rag-tag revolutionaries who had adopted the long-deceased and unlamented Oliver Cromwell as their symbolic leader.

It was in the middle of this small tempest of criminal intersections, impending marriage, and establishment of a medical practice, that I received a note on the morning of Friday, July 11th, from Bertie Wells.

Curiously, it arrived at the Queen Anne Street address, and not Baker Street, where I was still residing – at least for the next few weeks until my marriage. It was delivered by a messenger who waited for a reply. After reading it, I realized that I could only tell the boy to return with the statement that I would do my best. Then, as I had been alone in the house, simply adjusting books and various medically connected impedimenta and accoutrements, I locked up and set off for my lodgings in order to confer with Sherlock Holmes.

Normally I would have made the relatively short trip between Queen Anne Street and Baker Street on foot, but the pain my leg due to the recent gunshot wound was a reminder that I wasn't quite healed enough to undertake that effort. In any case, the urgency of Bertie's message indicated that I should make haste to see if Holmes was to be found, or if he was otherwise engaged. If the latter, then I would continue on to the address provided by Bertie, offering whatever assistance I could provide.

As was usually the case, I had my best luck at obtaining a hansom around the corner in Cavendish Square, and within a few moments we were rattling up Harley Street. I had a bit of time to ponder my friendship with Bertie, which had progressed from initial good will to the point that I generally dreaded seeing or hearing from him – which by definition is not really much of a friendship at all.

We had first met in late 1894, when he had approached me while I was signing copies of my books and old *Strand* magazines at a shop near Baker Street. He was seeking assistance in recovering the stolen manuscript of a fantastic sort of novel that he'd written involving pointed social commentary, rather like *Gulliver's Travels* but without any sense of fun. The story related the adventures of a fellow who jumps forward and backwards in time in a contraption of his own construction. While I found it entertaining in its own way, I felt that the attempts to convey pointed jabs at aspects of our modern society were rather heavy-handed. Still, the book had become quite popular, and in spite of my earlier impressions of Bertie as a rather brittle and pompous young man – then just in his late-twenties – we continued to run into one another by way of mutual friends until I might have considered him something of a friend as well – although at more than a dozen years younger than me, he was never the sort of close companion that I might invite to my club or to arrange spending an afternoon at billiards.

Bertie, or "H.G" as he was sometimes called, seemed to run hot and cold, evincing optimism or pessimism in equally measurable extremes, but never resting comfortably on the middle ground between them. One never new which Bertie would be encountered, but over the course of 1902, another version of him had seemed to take precedence over the other two – a rather arrogant H.G. Wells.

The previous January, Bertie had presented a philosophical speech to the Royal Institution entitled *The Discovery of the Future: A Discourse*. Holmes and I had both been invited to attend, but I went alone, as Holmes chose to remain hunched over his chemical table, filling our rooms with the choking fumes from a coal tar derivative. "I have no interest in hearing Wells preen," he stated, "yet again, about his speculative fiction, or any other topic. The world as we find it is strange enough. No . . . whatever-it-is that he espouses this time need not apply." I tended to agree, having been in the presence of some of Bertie's rather boastful pronouncements, but nevertheless I felt that I ought to attend – and in doing so, I found myself greatly surprised, for he seemed to have completely moved on from writing the type of novels which had made his fame, involving previously unimagined scientific speculations, to that of a socialist proselytizer.

I knew that Bertie's background, flirting with poverty and serving unsuccessfully as an apprentice for several different professions, had given him rather socialistic ideas, but it seemed, after his successful talk to the Royal Institution, that his new calling was to spread the word of evenly distributed resources to the masses. In decades past, such talk would have painted him as a radical. (It was fear of socialistic uprisings, especially after Bloody Sunday, that had, in part, led to the horrible Ripper Murders – and another painful wound that I received during the course of one of Holmes's investigations.) But now, in the new Twentieth Century, such talk – especially from recognized intellectuals such as Bertie – was becoming more and more common.

Following the success of his speech, the man had become rather more proud of himself than he already had been. I discussed it once with our mutual friend, Conan Doyle – soon to be "Sir Arthur" in a few months. He was much more tolerant of Bertie's ideas, as he himself had something of a socialistic bent. In his case, this took the form of an interest in providing for better conditions for British workers, and adequate medical care and education for those who couldn't afford it – very worthy goals indeed. I was in agreement with him there, but some of the more radical thinkers – those with whom Bertie now apparently associated – tended to make it more difficult for middle-of-the-roaders like myself with good intentions to get things done.

Doyle admired Bertie for making a stand. "He is a prophet, Watson," he told me. "A 'sociologist'. Like a surgeon who spies the cancer and cleanly cuts it away, he has his eye clearly on the problem, and with his authorial skills, he'll be able to reveal it in new ways that make it obvious to all, and in doing so, no other interpretation will be possible."

I hoped that Doyle was correct, for there was much work to be done and suffering to be alleviated – but I wasn't sure that Bertie was the right man for the job. Besides his somewhat objectionable personality, he tended to charge into new interests with great enthusiasm before losing steam a short time later. The novels that had made his fame – with tales of traveling through time, and strange man-beasts or gigantic mutated creatures, or even invaders from another planet – had given way to a period when he eagerly wrote stories of typical modern-day British life and manners. I was with him in a group not long after the publication of one of them, *Love and Mr. Lewisham*, when a mutual acquaintance asked when his next science-gone-wrong story would be published, slyly suggesting that he instead ought to write something else about another planet – possible a sequel to the Martian invasion, but instead where Mankind launched a counter-expeditionary force.

"Why the h--- have you joined the conspiracy to restrict me to one particular type of story?" Bertie had exploded in reply to the young man. "I want to write novels and before God *I will write novels!*" He took a step forward, his high voice even more querulous than before. "They are the proper stuff for my everyday work – a methodical careful distillation of one's thoughts and sentiments and experiences and impressions." With that, he had turned and departed in a huff, leaving the rest of us in an awkward silence. I suppose that it was from that point on that I began to see him in a new light, and to distance myself from him when possible.

But now he had sent a message to Queen Anne Street, requesting my assistance, and more importantly that of Sherlock Holmes – for a dead man had been left upon his front doorstep with a warning pinned to his coat. And apparently, although no details were provided, that was the least unusual aspect of the problem.

Baker Street was relatively quiet at that time of morning as the cabbie pulled to a stop before 221. I waved or nodded to several long-time acquaintances as I paid him and then stepped across to the familiar doorway. Through the open window one floor above, I could hear the sound of a violin. Tempting as it might have been to assume that it was Holmes, I knew that the music might very well be produced by his gramophone. Still, calling it "music" was something of an exaggeration, as it resembled something along the lines of atonal scales instead of anything that might have been recorded for posterity, so it was much more likely that it was actually Holmes.

Without bothering to knock, I let myself in with my key. I knew that Mrs. Hudson was almost certainly out at this time of morning, and there was no sign of her when I stepped inside. I proceeded up the stairs, allowing the fifth from the top to creak (instead of stepping over it) so that my presence would be announced. The violin music ceased.

When I opened the door, Holmes was replacing his violin in its case. Over his shoulder, he said, "Did you know that some of the musical church modes, occasionally called the ecclesiastical modes, were thought by the medieval theorists who derived them to cause a man to commit murder?"

I took a few steps across the room to my old chair. "I did know that," I said. "Surely you haven't forgotten the Rigby death, back in '95, when that parish minister – what was his name?"

"Father McKenzie."

"That's him. When he called us in after that poor old widow was murdered. Her nephew, the music professor, tried to foist that story upon us about how she'd been done to death by a phantom fiddler haunting the church cemetery beside her sad cottage, playing grim tunes in Aeolion and Dorion modes, when in fact she had killed by way of poison rice."

"As I recall," replied Holmes, "you spent half-a-day following that that pointless thread, when the nephew's prosaic bank records told the whole story. In any case, that knowledge may prove useful in another case that has recently come my way."

I feared that my quest to seek his aid with Bertie's problem would be unsuccessful if he'd taken on a new client. "You are currently engaged, then?"

Without answering my question, he turned and looked out the window, pulling back the curtain. "Ah, my dear Watson, look at all the lonely people. Where do they all come from?" Then he looked back with a smile. "Perhaps from the future, by way of Wells's time machine, to clutter up our pathways more and more each year?"

I knew by then that surprise was wasted. There was only one explanation for him having that bit of knowledge, as there was nothing about my person, in spite of Holmes's amazing skill, that could have otherwise specifically told him my reason for visiting. "You also received a message from Bertie," I stated. "He neglected to mention that."

He reached into his coat and pulled forth a sheet of paper, seemingly identical to the one in my own possession. "I knew that you would be here shortly. A body left on the fellow's doorstep, and Friend Lestrade in charge of the investigation? I believe that the matter of this new church mode murder can wait for a day or so. Shall we make our way to St. John's Wood?"

And so minutes later we were rattling northwest around the Park. Holmes glanced at me. "You find this matter distasteful?"

I paused for a moment before replying. Then, "I suppose that Bertie is something of a friend, but not top tier. And I know that he recently constructed a family mansion overlooking Sandgate near Folkestone, so our destination isn't his actual home. I've heard that he rents a number of houses in London for his mistresses. Yes, *houses* – plural. Likely this is one of those establishments."

"I see. Yet another example of a public hero having feet of clay. Well, we've certainly encountered enough of those over the years. Still, it's likely that the poor victim deserves some sort of investigation and justice, even if assisting Wells isn't a satisfying reason."

With that I agreed, and my attitude lightened somewhat. We discussed other unrelated matters as the cab made good time. We stayed on Grove End Road until the split to the west and so into Abbey Road, and almost immediately we pulled up across from a small home on the left, one of several tucked between a large white home, not quite a mansion, and Hill Road. The cabbie had been forced to stop on the right side of the street, as a crowd was standing on the pavement in front of a small house under the watchful eyes of a pair of constables. Holmes tossed a coin to the driver, and then we crossed Abbey Road in front of the white house, passing through the crowd to the small house where the body had been discovered. The constables recognized us and cleared a path through the masses, and within moments we were inside the ironwork fence and approaching the front door, where two more officers were posted.

Holmes glanced at their feet, standing in the spot where Bertie's letter indicated that the body had been found. His eyes narrowed in irritation, and I could almost hear him aloud, railing as to how the official force would never learn, and that a herd of yaks could have done no worse to trample the evidence than did the constables' heavy boots.

We passed inside and followed the sound of voices down a rather plain and undecorated hallway to a barely furnished sitting room on the right. There we found Lestrade, standing patiently as Bertie pontificated about the way the common man was often mistreated by officers of the law. They both glanced our way, Lestrade with an expression of relief and Bertie with a look of surprise, in spite of him having sent us both requests for our assistance. It was as if his thoughts had to physically draw to a halt so that they could then be dragged across to move along on new tracks in a different direction.

"Watson!" he then cried. "Mr. Holmes. Thank you both for coming." He scowled at Lestrade. "I have no faith that this specimen is going to arrive at the truth anytime soon."

Lestrade gave a tight but weary smile. "Mr. Wells has apparently been reading your chronicles, Doctor. It was such a pleasant reminder yet again to be referred to as 'rat-faced'."

I blushed with shame. When I first described Lestrade in that manner, in my journals of early March 1881, I had only known him for a few months, just one of the many mysterious visitors who regularly called upon my new flatmate, Sherlock Holmes. I had no idea who the inspector was, or why he sought out Holmes's advice. It was only in the matter of the Stangerson and Drebber murders that I learned of Lestrade's profession – "the best of the Yarders" Holmes had called him and Gregson.

At the conclusion of the matter, when the policemen had received all of the credit for Holmes's solution, I had fiercely vowed that someday the truth would be told.

It took many years before I completed my task. Based on my impressions of that long-ago investigation, I had finally managed to have the story published, with the assistance of my friend Conan Doyle. He had served as an agent, finding a journal of sorts willing to publish it, and also writing a lengthy middle section offering some of the story of the events of decades earlier that had led to the present murders. It was he who had, upon reading my journals, insisted on leaving in certain negative phrasing, including the aforementioned reference to *genus rattus*. By the time that first story was published, in late 1887, I had actually become friends with Lestrade and a number of other officers, and during the time of Holmes's supposed death in 1891, and the slow illness and passing of my wife, Mary, a couple of years later, these men had been my best friends, standing by me in those great stretches of anguish and emptiness. Hearing that my initial impressions, recorded for all to see, were still being batted about caused me no end of pain.

I saw that Lestrade knew my thoughts, and he gave a little shake of his head to show that it meant nothing to him. But I was still ashamed.

"Mr. Holmes," said Lestrade. "Doctor. I – "

"This is intolerable!" interrupted Bertie, his voice shrill and tense. "I will not be threatened – and not in such a . . . a *ridiculous fashion*! My work – my message – it's all too important to be suppressed. I refuse to be brow-beaten from making my thoughts known. I *will* be in Manchester tomorrow night to give that speech, and I defy anyone to stop me. There is no devil in Hell who will prevent me from going! I – "

"Your message mentioned a note, Mr. Wells," interrupted Holmes. Again, Bertie seemed to be thrown off his game as he was prevented from completing his rant. Lestrade held up a sheet of paper.

"This is it – pinned to the body."

"Which I notice is no longer located where it was discovered – on the front step."

Lestrade shook his head. "The body was discovered nearly three hours ago. We couldn't leave it there – you see what a crowd has formed. And – " He held up a hand to forestall Holmes's next comment. " – I know that we should have left the location where the body was found undisturbed until you had a chance to examine it – except that we didn't know that you would *be* examining it. There were no plans to consult you until Mr. Wells lost patience with the official force and sent each of you messages requesting your presence."

Holmes nodded, accepting the situation as it was, instead of how he wished it to be. "May I see the note?"

Lestrade passed it to him, and while he examined it, walking over to the window to catch some of the weak northern light, I turned to Bertie.

"This isn't your actual house," I said softly.

He nodded his head cautiously, suddenly quiet.

"Bertie, I've heard . . . ." I stopped myself, and then asked, "Is your wife still in Sandgate with the children?"

"She is," he murmured. "I need somewhere to stay when I come up to town. I leased this property a few months ago from the men in the big white house at No. 3 Abbey Road, just down the street. Four brothers. Quite rich. They own the whole block."

"I've heard that you keep . . . *other* houses in London as well."

His eyes, which had been roaming to focus on various points around the room, suddenly darted my way. He only met my gaze for an instant before they dropped, but rarely have I seen a guiltier look.

"I . . . I need companionship – someone who can understand me."

More than one someone, I thought, based on the gossip I'd heard for quite a while.

"I'm a writer, Watson," he continued, a whine entering his high-pitched whisper. "I'm different – I can't be tied down to one tedious existence. How will I ever be able to create? I have to get away – up to London. I have to set aside the shackles of everyday responsibilities and an unvaried routine, broken only by household tempests that serve to distract me. I need more – someone who has an interest in me beyond making sure that the bills get paid." He had been looking to one side, as if envisioning the life that he had built in Sandgate, and the alternatives he found here in the capital. Then he turned back toward me, this time with confidence instead of guilt, and a smug little smile, as if he had convinced me of something. "Surely you understand?"

"No," I said coldly. "No, I do not."

He sagged a little, but he started to say something else, no doubt convinced that if he explained it a different way I would certainly understand. But he was interrupted by Holmes, who asked, "Who discovered the body?"

"I did," replied Bertie in a louder tone. "I came down this morning to . . . to let out a visitor, and it . . . he was there, lying near the door. It . . . the body was completely covered in a tarpaulin, and at first we . . . I didn't know what it was. My . . . guest was in a hurry. She . . . she stepped around it and walked back toward Grove End Road. She can . . . catch a cab there."

He glanced back toward me and observed my expression – at what I thought about him letting a woman find her way alone at that type of morning, after such a rendezvous, to seek her own transport. He dropped his eyes and continued.

"We . . . I had noticed the . . . *object*, of course. She . . . one had to step around it, you see. So after she . . . after I was alone, I bent down and pulled at a loose end. I could already . . . could already smell it."

"Smell it?" I asked.

"The body was partially burned, Doctor," interrupted Lestrade. "Likely he perished in a fire. But his face was left mostly intact."

"*My* face," murmured Bertie.

"Hmm?" said Holmes. "Your face? As alluded to in the letter?"

Suddenly I was all at sea. Taking pity upon me, Holmes handed me the sheet.

"It was pinned to the body," repeated the inspector.

Nodding, I lifted it for a closer examination. It was a quarto-sized page, unfolded except for some wrinkling around the two small holes near the top where the pin had been placed. It was typewritten, with a very even depth and shade to the characters, indicating that the typist was skilled, applying even pressure to the keys, and without any mistakes. There was nothing too special about it – or so I thought, until I read the message.

> *Dear Bertie,* [it said]
>
> *I write this as a warning, with the hopes that I can convince you to change your destiny, and that of England as well. You must heed these words, for both our sakes.*
>
> *You are due to speak in Manchester on the 12th. I warn you and beg you: DO NOT GO! Your speech will enthuse the wrong sorts of people, and England will follow a path that will only lead to destruction.*
>
> *The socialistic programs that you espouse are good in and of themselves, but they will be subsumed into the greater schemes of evil grasping men with their own agendas. Your speech will make England weak, and the challenges of the coming years need for her to remain strong – for there are wars looming on the horizon, and what you start in Manchester, should you make that speech, will be the undoing of us all.*
>
> *You are asking how I know this. I know it for I AM YOU! I too am Herbert Wells, and I have been part of a group of scientists and thinkers from far beyond 1902 – 1942 to be exact – who, using our initial concept – yours and mine – have constructed a time machine. It isn't like the device that we*

described in that dreadful book of ours, but the notion was enough to suggest certain ideas to knowledgeable men at the Cavendish Laboratory in Cambridge.

Using various theoretical ideas associated with the very nature of the atom, along with notes obtained from the late James Moriarty's files, the question of superposition has been answered. As only you and I know, this was an idea that initially gave us pause when writing the book, for the planet is in constant motion around the sun, and the sun itself is in motion through the galaxy, and surely the galaxy itself moves as well in relation to other positions. When traveling through time, how can one compensate for that? To use a time machine and travel from the present to one million years in the past, one would rematerialize in the vast emptiness of space, for the earth from where we left would be in a completely different spot from that of one million years ago. To leave from a certain fixed point means reappearing in that same certain fixed point – wherever it is, but at a different time.

It was for such a problem that the calculus was derived: If the velocity of an object is measured, then the position of the moving object cannot be determined. If the fixed point is located, then there is no velocity to measure. If position is given by a function of X, then the velocity is the first derivative of that function, and the acceleration is the second derivative. But how to apply this to time travel, and the device which we imagined?

After being stymied with an answer to such a problem for far too long, we – you and I – chose to ignore the question when constructing the story, hoping that no one would notice the issue. However, after decades of thought, the Moriarty equations allowed the physicists at Cambridge to compensate for the difference in position, as they posited a link between certain atomic aspects relating to connectivity across great distances that would allow position and velocity to be determined and located, as well as a certain point in time.

By now I am an old man, and I have seen the terrible future that awaits Britain. It has been determined that there are certain points in history where a single event can affect the future – you know this to be true. We both recall reading of when the Roman Empire finally fell, on 4 September, 476, as Odoacer led a successful revolt against Romulus Augustulus, then the Emperor. Likewise, historians in my time

89

have shown that it was your – our – speech that changed history.

Do not be proud of this, even in your most secret thoughts, for you should rue that day! Instead of perpetuating this disaster, you must resist. You must not give that speech in Manchester on the 12th!

I write this in case something goes wrong, so that you will at least have my words, if I do not survive and cannot reason with you in person. This is not our first attempt to reach you, and each repetition becomes more dangerous for both my companion and me. I can tell you no more, for knowing too much of the future is also a risk, but if I am successful, the future that I describe, and from whence I have traveled, will not even exist. I fear that, as I continue to exist now, with my memories intact of what has occurred and the terrible future that awaits you and me and our nation, my mission is ordained to be a failure, and history cannot be changed. What has happened has happened. But still I must try, in spite of this paradox which my journey will create.

I hope that you will make the correct decision – the right decision. For all our sakes.

And although it is strangely self-serving, I wish you well.

Herbert George Wells

I continued to look at the paper for a moment before raising my eyes to those of my companions.

"Ineffeble twaddle," Holmes snorted.

"Did the body look like you?" I asked Bertie.

He shook his head. "No. Not at all. Well, yes, in the sense that we had the same facial features and general build, from what I could tell. But he was bald, and while he had a moustache, it wasn't shaped the same as I wear mine. And he was old. Frail. He had to be in his seventies. I . . . I couldn't . . . I didn't notice much more than that. It was . . . it was too terrible. The smell . . . ."

"He was thin and quite old looking, whatever his age," added Lestrade. "The body is at the mortuary when you want to examine him. Except for the burns, which likely killed him, there's no other sign of violence. The police surgeon found no violent wounds or bruises. Of course, the autopsy will show whether there's anything more subtle involved – an injection site, for instance, or the possibility of ingested poison before the fire. "

90

"What about – what about those things mentioned in the letter that only you would know?" I asked. "About the questions you raised concerning the problems with time travel and . . . 'positioning'."

Bertie shook his head. "It's true that when I was writing the book, I became sidetracked for a while as I tried to think of answers to questions that someone might ask. One of them was about where you would reappear if you traveled in a time machine – how would you make it not only journey to a certain *time*, but also be able to find a specific *spot*? In the end, I chose to let it be implied that the machine somehow had the ability to compensate for this question. Who knows – I may have told someone at the time, or asked advice from some other writer. I probably did – it was no secret, and people are always interested in what I'm doing. But I don't know any scientists that I could have queried – and certainly not any interested in traveling to the past! No, this is some cheap attempt to scare me, that's all."

Holmes tapped his lip and then asked, "The handwritten signature – does it match yours?"

Bertie sniffed. "It looks like mine, yes – but it's an obvious forgery."

"Lestrade." Holmes shifted his gaze to the inspector. "What's your impression of this?"

"A threat?" replied the inspector. "A terrible prank? For some reason, someone has gone to a lot of trouble one way or the other to try and warn Mr. Wells away from Manchester tomorrow."

Holmes nodded. "Mr. Wells, do you have any enemies?"

"Certainly. What author doesn't?"

Quite a few don't, I thought. Most authors, actually, live quiet peaceful lives without generating any animus. I wondered if Bertie had made his own enemies because of his writings, or by way of his rather arrogant attitude as he passed through life. And of course one couldn't discount the existence of jealous and unforgiving husbands.

"Can you think of anyone who would make this effort to keep you from speaking in Manchester?"

"Absolutely not! Well, perhaps the Government. Or the Crown. It's no secret what they did back in '88 to suppress the rise of the socialistic effort to improve the lives of the people that the ruling class which wish to keep in chains." His voice became strident as he settled into a well-rehearsed litany of typical clap-trap. While I agreed wholeheartedly that the poor and downtrodden needed every opportunity for better lives – how could I not after what I have seen? – the methods of Bertie and his cronies was not the way to achieve it. They had no real plan other than to look upon themselves as modern-day Robin Hoods, advocating taking from the rich by whatever means to distribute to the poor. And while the rich could certainly stand to have a vast amount taken away without ever feeling its loss, the lack of an intelligent method to turn around and make use of those redistributed funds – to provide education, medical care, and good jobs and housing – accomplished nothing. Bertie's clever speeches were nothing more than a path to anarchy. I found myself agreeing with this fictional future man's reasoning.

We let Bertie fulminate for another couple of complex and layered sentences, filled with long clauses and parenthetical statements that were fit in cleverly throughout before Holmes abruptly lost patience and turned away, heading for the doorway. Lestrade and I followed. Bertie abruptly shut his mouth as his audience abandoned him, and he gave me a look as if he'd been somehow betrayed.

On the front steps, we took leave of the man of the house, assuring him that he would be informed of any progress. He stood there as we turned away, looking like a boy in a man's suit between the two massive constables.

At the street, Lestrade offered to convey us to the mortuary in his growler, and we accepted gratefully. As we began the slow trip south, Lestrade laughed.

"I've read that book," he said. "*The Time Machine*. It had its moments, but I can't say that I enjoyed it. I'm too much of a practical man. I don't suppose that you've read it, Mr. Holmes?"

"No, but Watson has."

Lestrade glanced at me with a raised eyebrow. "Not my favorite," I answered. "Give me a good Clark Russell sea adventure any day, or something by Stevenson, or even one of Doyle's histories. But when it was published, I felt that I ought to read Bertie's book, and a few others by him, since we've been friendly acquaintances and have run into each other quite a bit over the years."

"I'm leaning more toward the prank theory," said Lestrade, looking back at Holmes. "Someone is trying to prevent Wells from giving that speech – someone that certainly knows him. Somehow he obtained a body and left it there to provide the man with a good scare – and tailored that ridiculous note to fit the circumstances."

Holmes nodded. "I expect that we'll know more when we examine the dead man. Have you made inquiries to see if there were any recent fires where he could have died?"

"I have, but it's too soon to hear back from anyone."

"Have you only queried here in London?"

Lestrade nodded.

"You might expand your search a bit. There's no reason why he couldn't have died elsewhere and been brought here. Except for the age difference, how much does this dead man look like Wells?"

"There's quite a bit of superficial resemblance, I suppose, but then again, Mr. Wells is an average-looking fellow, and so was this man. If you look at the two of them in one way, they are similar – in build, and the shape of the eyes and skull. But to look more closely, about all they have in common is a moustache – and the dead man's is much more ragged and fully white."

"What about the ears?"

Lestrade shook his head. "Burned off." His mouth was tight. "The flames seemed to have consumed him from the back – there was quite a bit of smoldering of the clothing and flesh there, but the front is essentially untouched."

"His hands?" Holmes asked. "As you know, I've been involved with some of the work classifying finger marks. We could examine those of the dead man and compare them to those of Wells."

"No good," said Lestrade. "The flesh of the hands is scorched as well. And in any case, that sounds as if you give credence to the idea that this old man is Wells, back from the future."

"Not at all – but such a comparison would provide an absolute argument to shut down those who might want to believe otherwise. Any crack might allow that kind of idiocy room to take root, and should this story get about . . . ."

Holmes stared from the window for a moment at the passing London scenes. Then, "The typewritten message was composed on a Remington, not more than a year old – so nothing from the future there. There is no sign of excessive wear of the various letters as might be expected, nor of any build-up of grime within the small cavities of the striking faces of the letter keys which would make the letters look unclear." He looked at me. "You will have noticed, of course, the skill of the typist."

I nodded, and we all fell silent and into our own thoughts and speculations for the remaining time, with nothing left to discuss until we reached the mortuary. Inside, in spite of the July heat, it was quite a bit cooler, in that unusual way that all such buildings seem to have. We followed the inspector along that well-remembered route that we'd traveled so often before, until we were at last led to the table where the unfortunate man was resting.

His clothes were stacked neatly on an adjacent ledge, and Holmes spent quite a bit of time looking through them. Other than announcing that they were comfortably worn but not shabby, that there were indications of time spent near the southern coast (as based on bits of chalk, quartz, and other sea-related detritus found in the cuffs), and that they were clearly of present-day manufacture and not from the future, he provided no other facts. Then he turned his attention to the body.

One of the police surgeons, Dr. Leighton, stepped across, explaining that the autopsy was scheduled for later that day. "But as you can see," he added, "we can make a few good assumptions beforehand. The soot in his mouth indicates that he has likely inhaled a great deal of smoke, and mostly likely died of smoke inhalation. The burns appear to have occurred *post mortem*. His hands and limbs are relaxed, so the heat wasn't enough to cause the characteristic contraction of a burned body, and the expression on his face peaceful. He likely passed out before he felt any pain."

Holmes verified the presence of the soot in the mouth, turning the head this way and that to see the back of the dead man's throat. Then he asked, "What do you think, Watson? His face. You know Wells best. Is there a resemblance?"

I had already been studying the corpse's visage, and couldn't provide any more of an opinion than Lestrade's. "There is some similarity, but then again, this fellow is considerably older than Bertie. The ears would have told us much. Perhaps a comparison of Bertie's teeth to this man's – although these are much worn and damaged, as one would expect based on his age. But again, Holmes – you aren't seriously considering that this might *be* Bertie, are you?"

"Of course not. But I'm wondering if he's a distant relative with a slight resemblance, or possibly he's just some stranger who died, and as Lestrade theorized, whomever wished to stop Wells from making his speech saw enough of a resemblance to this dead man that he concocted that outrageous letter."

There wasn't much else to learn, and we thanked Leighton and walked out. Lestrade accompanied us back to the street, indicating that he'd keep us informed of anything that we learned.

"Be sure to include Watson in any messages," Holmes said. "I may be called suddenly to Liverpool in the next couple of days – you'll have read of that murder involving the curious music."

"Ah," replied Lestrade, "so you've been pulled into that one. I'm glad that it's their problem and not ours." And with a wave, he turned back inside.

I hailed a hansom, but Holmes chose not to accompany me. "I have some other inquiries afoot, related to different cases, so I'll leave you here. If it isn't too distasteful, you might check in with further Wells to see if he's had any other thoughts. This may not amount to anything at all, but if he intends to continue with his speech tomorrow, in spite of the warning, things might take a more grim turn."

"More grim than leaving a burned corpse upon his doorstep?" I asked, but with a wave, Holmes had already turned and walked away, vanishing quickly into the thick foot traffic.

In fact, when I spoke to Bertie that afternoon on the telephone, he had reconsidered his earlier adamant declarations that nothing would keep him from traveling to Manchester the next day. "After all," he said, "it's just one speech. I can always make it again – as many times as I'd like. But going to Manchester now, after someone has taken the trouble to warn me – well, that seems rather like waving a red cape in front of a bull. There's no need to make things worse than they are already, you know." He would have rationalized further, but I thanked him when I was able to slip in a word or too and disconnected the call.

Holmes arrived not long after, and I informed him of Bertie's decision. He shook his head. "Do you know if he's actually notified the theatre of his change of plans?"

"He didn't say."

"Please telephone him again and, if it isn't too late, have him keep his decision to himself until we can discuss it with him further."

I did so and confirmed that Bertie hadn't yet canceled his appearance. When I told him not to do so, he wished to know why, but all that I could truthfully reply was that Holmes asked me let him know, and that I would share more with him more later.

After the conversation ended, I turned back to Holmes, expecting an explanation for my unspoken question, which was the same as Bertie's.

"Because," he replied, "we can't be sure that there isn't more to this than we've seen so far. Time is moving quickly, and if we don't take this opportunity, when we can be in control of events, then another occasion might arise under less favorable conditions, and then we would be hopelessly behind. No, the speech must go forward."

"I'm not sure that you'll convince Bertie of that. He agreed to delay his announcement to the Manchester people, but he now seems set on staying home."

"He won't be going there tomorrow – to the theatre. You will."

I stared at him, and he smiled. "There is just the barest resemblance between the two of you, Watson, but it should suffice. You are a bigger and stronger man – how was it Lestrade once described you? 'Middle-sized, strongly-built man – square jaw, thick neck, moustache'. Well, at least Wells has the moustache, even if his is so much bigger than your tidy military version, and physically he is quite the shrimp – nearly half-a-foot shorter than you are. Nevertheless, I can fix up the rest."

"You want me to go in his place, as some sort of staked goat."

"We've done something similar before."

"Many times," I agreed. "I just wanted to ascertain that was your intent in this particular case. But regardless of my role, I have no intention of delivering his speech."

"He wouldn't want you to. The only sticking point is that by continuing to allow the public to believe that the speech will occur, only to be canceled at the last minute, Wells might feel that it reflects more poorly on his reputation than if he canceled the event today."

And in truth that was Bertie's reaction. However, when I explained Holmes's reasoning, and that it was better to use this opportunity while we could, while we currently held a few threads, he agreed that it would be better than starting from scratch the next time a speech was scheduled and another threat was made.

No further immediate progress was accomplished – the body remained unidentified, despite Lestrade's queries beyond London, and no further warnings were sent. Holmes made time to help me prepare for my disguised appearance in Manchester. We discussed the best techniques for making myself look like the quite-a-bit smaller Bertie, including how I should stand. I spent an hour in a second-hand shop purchasing some baggy clothing. A false moustache of the walrus variety was constructed to fit over my own more sensible growth.

Early on the morning of Saturday the 12th, Bertie sent to me (unasked) a copy of his speech, with some sort of rambling explanation that I ought to become familiar with it, should I be asked a question from an enthusiastic reporter – "so that I don't look the fool trying to come up with an answer" he wrote. I looked it over for a moment before becoming bogged down and losing interest. He began by distinguishing between *"two divergent types of mind"* – one that judges and attaches importance principally to what has happened in the past, and the other that does the same to what will happen in the future. He wrote that these two minds reach *"divergent and incompatible consequences"* in the spheres of morality and public affairs. From there, he spiraled into a discussion of the use of generalizations when determining human destiny. I tried to read further, but I found my eyes dropping. This was certainly a far cry from the thought-provoking concepts of his speculative novels, and I wondered for which he would be eventually remembered.

We arrived at the Manchester theatre about an hour before the event was scheduled to occur. Holmes went his own way to see what he might see, and I slipped down a side alley and into the backstage area, taking care to mimic Bertie as closely as I could. A small dressing room was set aside for him, and I installed myself in it, prepared to wait and see what would occur, now that the elaborate and fantastic warning had clearly been ignored.

I sat in a small chair in front of the dressing table and a speckled mirror. I'd quickly observed that the room was featureless and rather unattractive. It was lit by a single electric bulb, which cast harsh shadows into the empty corners.

I placed myself where I could keep an eye on the door behind me, as reflected in the mirror. I'd brought a small book to read, as I felt that such an action wouldn't be out of character for Bertie himself, but I found as I sat there that instead of distracting myself with the sea story, I was intrigued by the distant and curious sounds of the theatre, and that time was passing quickly toward that point when the speech was scheduled to begin. I pulled Bertie's notes from my pocket and onto the much-abused old makeup table before me, as if I were studying them, and kept my attention focused on the sound of approaching and passing footsteps outside the closed door, and the door-knob itself, watching for any movement.

It seemed inevitable and anticlimactic when the knob actually began to turn. I doubted that it was Holmes. There had been no indication from outside of any excitement having occurred, and he wouldn't enter at this point in the plan. By this time, he would have told the theatre manager what was happening, and no one would be entering to tell me it was time to begin. It was almost certainly someone related to the curious body found in Bertie's doorway just the previous morning.

Strangely, as the door opened, there was a bright glow. The hallway outside the dressing room had been dark. It seemed that whomever was pushing open the door was also carrying some sort of lamp.

I watched as the doorway opened further, and then a man stepped through. He looked to be around forty years of age, and solidly built. I couldn't tell very much in the old mirror, but he seemed rather unkempt, as if his heavy coat – much too thick for this time of year – didn't quite fit, and his receding hair needed a trim. But what I saw most was the intensity of his gaze. It found mine, and I could see the white rim of his eyes, completely visible around his pupils. I had long ago learned that when someone carries that expression, they are in a state of unpredictability, their emotions running high, and with the possibility of becoming dangerous without any notice whatsoever.

"You ignored our warning, then," he croaked, while I slowly turned in the chair to face him. I didn't want to stand yet – in spite of the clothing that Holmes had found, I knew that I was a much bigger man than Bertie, and rising to my full height would reveal it. Instead, trying to match Bertie's high-pitched voice – and feeling ridiculous while doing so – I said, "I really have no choice. My argument is too important to be suppressed."

He took a small step forward. He snarled. "You selfish b-----d! You would throw away the future, when there's a chance to change it! You would crucify all of us on the altar of your arrogance! How dare you! How dare you, sir! I know you well in this future you will create – the wars, the destruction, the death. England will fall – it will be the Germans, always the Germans! – and it will be *your* fault – what you do here today! I know you – I *know* the H.G. Wells of the future. We were friends, once – before I learned that what you do here today will cause the eventual death of my family.

"We were friends, you and I," he repeated, "but I can never forgive you – and I cannot leave you be, for you are the only one who can repair what you caused. *Will* cause!" He clenched his teeth and closed his eyes as if in pain. He pressed his free hand to his forehead and made a keening sound, high and faint, while the lantern swung crazily in his other hand, causing the shadows at the edges and corners of the room to rise and fall like black waves.

"The man you become is a broken man," he continued. "*He* knew. *He* was willing to help do *anything* that he could to correct the mistake you will make here today – even risk traveling through time to stop you. Ah, if only he – *you* – had survived our last attempt to come back and warn you! We were so close – we only missed by a couple of days! But the fire! You were too old and weak. Your heart – ! You – you're older self – would have been standing here with me now, if only you had been stronger.

"Having you here – the *older* you – here now – Ah, that would have convinced you! But you died in our last crossing through time. It was becoming too dangerous, they said. Too many trips back to change the path. And we arrived too late – instead of today, we appeared here on Monday – two days from now. And you died then – in the fire. But I still saw a way. I took your body. I'd hoped that seeing it – your *future* self – left on your doorstep with the note that that *you* had written would convince you. But your arrogance is too great! Or perhaps it's as we feared – the future cannot be undone. What has happened has happened!"

That phrase had been in the letter – a fear that the mad plan to change the future by altering the past would fail because of the inevitability of time's path. It was more than I could comprehend, especially with a madman swaying in front of me.

"I made the crossing once more – this time with your burned body. Finally I arrived in time – before the speech. In the night, I followed you – found where you were staying. I left it on your doorstep as a warning – but in spite of everything, you're still here. You refuse to turn away from this terrible path!"

98

"Why not simply approach me then – to tell me all of this yourself?" I asked, my voice a poor imitation of Bertie's querulous tone. "You could have made an appointment. Stated your case. Instead, you left the mutilated body of an elderly indigent upon my doorstep, with a fantastic piece of fiction pinned to it. How is that supposed to convince any man of reason?"

"I couldn't tell you!" he whined. His voice dropped to a whisper. "Not that way. You might have had me arrested . . . as a *madman*. I might have been held *captive*. What if they thought actually believed me to be mad? I could not take that chance! *I'm not mad!* I had to convince you. I had to remain free, hoping that my warning and your dead body as undeniable evidence would convince you. If not, I had to be prepared to take further action – to be free to travel again. As many times as I could survive it. And here we are now – I have arrived at the correct time – in time to stop you. I'm sorry, Wells. It was my mistake that killed you in the crossing through time. I should have been more precise in my settings, and known that you weren't strong enough. And now I have to kill you again!"

With that, he tossed the lamp toward me, almost with a sob. Instinctively, I rose and batted it aside.

"He burned too!" he cried. "It seems that destiny cannot be avoided! He burned on our last attempt, and now you will burn too!"

I moved toward the blazing lantern where it had crashed and broken against the wall. The oil inside had splashed from floor to ceiling, and the old wood was immediately ignited.

It was then that the door burst open behind the man, revealing Holmes and a thicket of constables. They poured in, some downing the shrieking man before he could even turn or understand what had happened, and the others acting quickly to suppress the fire before it was able to do much more than blacken that one wall.

After the man was taken away, I changed into my own clothes, brought from London in a carpetbag. As I did so, Holmes explained that he'd waited outside, spotting the assailant quite easily as he approached the theatre, mingling with the very few people that had showed up to hear the speech. Then, when the man had entered the building's back door, it had been easy enough to follow behind without his knowledge, for he seemed quite oblivious to anything but penetrating the deeper recesses in an effort to complete his mission.

At the main Manchester police station, Inspector Givens, whom Holmes and I had met previously on a number of occasions, led us down to the cellars where the mysterious man was being interrogated. Along the way, he handed a thin folder to Holmes, stating, "Graham Merryman. Here's what we know of him so far. We obtained his name and address from a bill in his coat. His landlord said he showed up just a few weeks ago and took a room near a mission where he has a job, helping out and sweeping. We sent a man 'round there, but they have nothing to tell. He was very quiet and thorough. Often late to work – never quite on time, they said – but not bad enough yet to sack him. They need all the help they can get, after all. He kept to himself, except for sometimes when an older fellow would meet him after work."

"This other man?" Holmes asked. "Thin? With a moustache?"

Givens nodded, and Holmes looked my way. "Possibly our dead indigent."

The inspector continued. "Apparently something recent made him completely lose his sanity today – perhaps seeing that Mr. Wells was coming to town. Seems to have a grudge against him, from his ramblings. In any case, he apparently came up with this convoluted warning, and all that he claims along with it."

"You've heard his story, then?" I asked.

"I was in the Maria with him as we drove in," the inspector related. "He couldn't stop talking – begging us to free him so that he could go back kill Wells while we had the chance. Or he begged us to do it for him. He only calmed down when I told him that Wells wasn't there – the speech was canceled. He settled back then with a sigh and a smile. 'It worked,' he said.

"'What worked?' I asked him.

"'The plan,' was his answer. 'History has been changed. It all turned on today, you see, and now today is different than it was before.' I couldn't get anything out of him after that."

We saw Merryman again in a basement room with stone walls, a plain deal table, and four or five uncomfortable chairs. He didn't seem as satisfied as he'd been in the Black Maria, based on Givens' description. Now he was agitated once more, and rocking back and forth. "Why?" he kept repeating. "Why?"

I stepped closer, pulled over one of the chairs, and sat down near him. One of the constables stepped a bit closer, I suppose to protect me if the shackled prisoner made some effort to attack. "What is the problem, Mr. Merryman?" I asked. "I understood that you were pleased how things turned out – that the speech never occurred. The events that you sought to prevent will now never happen."

"No, no," he muttered. "It's driving me mad. If history was changed, then the history that *was* to occur has *never* occurred. But yet – I have memories of it – from when I was there."

"Where, Mr. Merryman?" I asked.

"My name isn't Merryman!" he snarled. "I took that name when we escaped here – to the past."

"Who . . . escaped?"

"My family – to flee the wars. We came through time, but it did no good. I still remember – they *died*. Both of them. Wells's speech took place, and the future happened. *It happened!*"

I glanced around at Holmes, but he was expressionless. The inspector's face was somewhere between pity and disgust.

"I knew about the wars," continued Merryman, "and the deaths, and . . . and worse. So much worse! If it's all been prevented – if he never gave the speech – then it never happened. But I remember it! All of it! *How can I remember it if it didn't happen?*" he sobbed. "I remember every bit of it! They all died. My sweet Audrey – she *died*! And . . . and our daughter as well. This was supposed to save them – I came back to *save them*, but I still remember them dying. Oh, what is to become of me? Have I failed? Will it happen again anyway? Are they alive, or will they still die? Has it happened? Will it happen? Oh! Oh!"

And he began to weep. Nothing more of any sense was ever spoken by him again, and he ended the rest of his few days in a sanitarium.

Holmes and I returned to London and resumed our normal routines – which is to say that I picked up building my new (and rather dull) practice in Queen Anne Street, while helping Holmes with his investigations as time permitted. Holmes himself – whose routine was never dull – continued to be involved in an always-fascinating and continuing series of activities. I wasn't surprised a few days later to read in the newspapers that he'd brought the Church Mode Murders to a successful conclusion. I only hoped that I'd be able to get the true story out of him one day, although he was often reluctant – or too stubborn – to relate details about his past adventures.

A few weeks later, my fiancé and I, having neither close family nor interest in an excessive and expensive ceremony, were married in a quiet ceremony at the Registry Office. Holmes served as my best man, as he had twice before in '86 and '89, and then he returned to Baker Street, while my new wife and I, after a short trip to the Continent, settled together in Queen Anne Street.

I knew that Holmes remained curious as to the unresolved identity of the dead man, as he hated loose ends, but he conceded that the fellow might never be identified. (Holmes had been unable to find anything specific about the old man that might indicate a place of origin or a profession, and in fact, no satisfactory background was ever established for Merryman either.) Bertie Wells had also wondered about the corpse's identity and where he came from, and we discussed it when I stopped by his rented house on the Sunday following the trip to Manchester. I'd been leery of again visiting that house on Abbey Road, not knowing what – or whom – I might find there, but Bertie had been alone that afternoon, sitting in his downstairs study and working on another speech. I'd told him about Merryman's arrest and the startling and rambling declarations that he'd subsequently made, and Bertie was fascinated.

"So this Merryman chap was the one who typed the letter, pretending that it was written by a version of me from the future, and then he pinned it to that old man's body," he stated. "And somehow he'd developed this *idée fixe* that I was – or *will be* – responsible for some dark future, and that was all tied to his loss of reason following the death of his family."

I replied that such was as likely an explanation as we might find, but the exact details of what had occurred would probably never be determined. Some cases were like that, despite the nice and tidy versions that I wrote up for *The Strand*. After a few more points were discussed, we fell into an awkward silence, and I departed soon afterwards. Although we continued to encounter one another over the subsequent years, I never thought of Bertie Wells as a friend after that weekend – and as in truth I hadn't thought of him too much that way beforehand, it wasn't a difficult cessation.

A few weeks later, I was passing through Baker Street and stopped in to return a volume that I had borrowed. Holmes wasn't there, and as I laid the book upon his desk, I noticed an opened letter to him from the police in Stockport, on the outskirts of Manchester. It was in response to Lestrade's inquiry about the identity of the burned old man. They knew of such a man, and the description within exactly matched that of the body we'd found in terms of clothing and appearance. The letter indicated that the body had been discovered inside a burned building before it could be completely consumed, having apparently succumbed to smoke inhalation. His identity was unknown, and there was no record of him those parts. Not long after the dead man was discovered and brought to the morgue, the body had disappeared – taken with no indications as to whom was responsible. Could Holmes provide any further information, *etcetera* and *etcetera*.

I was about to toss it aside, much as Holmes has probably done after reading it, when I happened to notice that a date had been given for the fire and the body's discovery – the 14th, the Monday two days *after* the speech.

I found that a moment or two had passed, and I was still standing beside Holmes's desk, my brow contracted in a frown, as I tried to work out this inconsistency. If the body was found in London on the early morning of Friday the 11th, not long dead, how could it be the same one as that found freshly dead on Monday the 14th in the remains of a fire which occurred on that date? Clearly the police had made a mistake, asking for information about the wrong corpse. Surely it was another body – another man entirely – and the one found on Bertie's doorstep remained unidentified.

But I recalled that Merryman had raved about additional journeys through time, and missed temporal destinations, and retrieval of the body in order to send his warning. He'd said that the man had died when they arrived two days late during one of their trips through time. What if – ?

What if, indeed? *Ineffable twaddle!* I could hear Holmes declare. I saw why he had tossed the letter aside – for he would surely have also seen the date and known that it couldn't be the same dead man, so why waste his time?

But had he understood what it implied? He'd been outside during Merryman's ramblings, and while I'd assumed that he'd heard all of what was said, we hadn't fully discussed it. I knew that he would have no more use for such speculation than I should have. And yet . . . an unidentified body, dead under specific circumstances and matching a specific description, had been found and then lost. An unknown body of the same description had turned up and had been used to warn Bertie Wells not to give a speech. In fact, he hadn't given that speech, so whatever might have happened – whatever future might have unfolded – from that moment, that crossroads in time, had been prevented.

Or had it?

I feared that if I followed this rabbit trail for much longer, I would still be standing beside Holmes's desk when he arrived, ready to join Merryman in the asylum.

"Ineffable twaddle!" I muttered aloud for myself, sounding very much like my friend as I turned to leave.

The Father Christmas Brigade
for Marcia Wilson

"**M**r. Holmes," said the young man, taking a sip of whisky and smiling, "if I'd had any sense, I would have asked you last Christmas to help me, but I tried to do it myself and muffed it, and I've had to wait a whole year for a second chance."

I considered this statement, and who he was, and hoped that he would soon explain what he meant.

I had stopped by about an hour earlier, late one afternoon, to wish my friend Sherlock Holmes the Compliments of the Season, and to catch up on those cases which were currently holding his attention. While I hadn't lost touch with him by any means after my marriage in the middle of the preceding year – my masses of notes and strained casebooks for 1889 and 1890 would easily attest to that – I had found that after the events of the recent autumn, as his ongoing campaign against Professor Moriarty's organization escalated, and also after an unexpected trip to Vienna in connection with Holmes's health which had threatened to shatter from the strain, it was a good idea to check on him, making certain that he was taking care of his body as well as his great mind.

I had been there some three-quarters of an hour, and our talk had ranged from his sincere interest in my growing practice and my wife's health to curious questions about aspects of my Paddington neighborhood, not far to the west (as he always wished to improve his encyclopedic knowledge of London). Finally we had caught up on a few of his more interesting investigations, and he smiled tolerantly as I jotted a few notes concerning the events connected to the Chamber Faith Swindle (of which I had read in the newspapers, not realizing Holmes's involvement), and the much more grim Healeyfield murders, where his examination of the murder weapon, an iron spike of ancient manufacture accidentally dropped by the killer, had led to a terrible confrontation in the Derwent Gorge with the man whom the newspapers called "The Writhing Watcher". I was sincerely disappointed that I had been unable to join him.

It was at that point in my visit that I began to think of departure, and of course Holmes noticed it. On past occasions when this point was reached, and he was in a garrulous mood, he might mention some other case, perhaps from his Montague Street days, tossed out as a conversational lure so that I might tarry just a bit longer. It was on such times as this that I'd heard of the last and most fatal disappearance of Able

King of Crewe, and also the Seven Smiling Sisters – not pleasant women, as one might expect, but instead a series of seven turns and traps in a previously unmapped Yorkshire Cavern, where a Viking horde had been hidden long ago, and more importantly, where the two enterprising but ill-equipped brothers who had entered the earth to retrieve it had been rescued at nearly the last moment.

But today Holmes didn't tease any earlier cases, and I was preparing to rise with an eye toward walking back to Paddington when the doorbell rang. With a smile, I continued to my feet, crossing the room and refilling my glass at the sideboard. Holmes laughed and declined.

We both recognized Holmes's visitor, as he had been featured off-and-on in the newspapers for well over a year. It was John Oersted, the young heir to the Gravens fortune. It was a story that had captivated the public – and rightly so. Oersted had been an orphan, living on the streets of London after his parents had emigrated from Denmark to England in 1879 to obtain work, both sadly dying soon afterwards in a rail accident.

"They would sometimes leave me with a neighbor here in London," explained Oersted as he settled back in his seat with a comfortable measure of whisky, "while they traveled elsewhere, looking for work that suited them. Needless to say," he added with a sad smile, "we hadn't found the success we'd expected when we came here. Unfortunately, my parents had failed to carry out the necessary research before deciding to change countries. But we had no relatives left in Denmark, and they were seduced by the reports coming from England regarding the ever-increasing industrial successes."

His accent was a curious thing – more of a flat and featureless English than anything that reflected his original Danish upbringing, his years in London, both as a child and now, and the considerable time he'd more recently spent in America. It was as if he consciously and carefully monitored his speech so as to give no clue to his background. And yet, his story was so well known that it would certainly be rare that he might meet someone who didn't know who he was.

"It was on one such trip, to Liverpool and the surrounding areas, that my parents were killed – in the Burscough Junction collision, when the train to Ormskirk hit the Liverpool-to-Preston line. From what I've been able to learn, they died immediately. However, it was a number of days before I learned about it, as they weren't expected back home for a week or more. It was only when a man from the railway came to our lodgings that I heard anything. I was able to discover in later years that my parents weren't immediately identified, and by the time they were, they had already been buried in Burscough.

"The family who had been watching out for me was generally sympathetic, but the father – a hard and dark-tempered man – made it clear that he couldn't afford to feed another mouth, so I was turned out of both his home, and my parents' rooms as well, only able to carry a change of clothes. I watched as the landlord locked the door behind me, with all that we had brought with us from Denmark. He planned to retain it to pay the back rent – or so he claimed, but my parents had never been late with the rent. So at age eleven, I found myself living on the streets of the East End."

It was a fascinating story, especially knowing as we did what happened next, but I was unsure why he felt the need to explain it to us, instead of immediately telling Holmes why he was there. However, as Oersted continued to speak, it gradually became clear.

"In those days, as both you gentlemen know, the East End was not quite as terrible as it became – and fortunately I was long gone before the Autumn of Terror a couple of years ago. As you can imagine, I followed the story very much in the American newspapers, and when I was able to return to England, that area became the focus of my work." By which he meant his altruistic charitable efforts where he used his inherited fortune to try and improve the abominable conditions facing the residents of the East End. Some had tried to say that this was as fruitless as Canute attempting to command the waves of the sea, but in fact young Oersted was making a difference, his wealth and resources having arrived at a time when there was a sincere interest in improvement in that district, following the awareness that came because of the Ripper Murders.

"As a young boy living by his wits, I didn't do half badly. I worked small jobs throughout the East End when I could find them – unloading for the merchants, running errands and messages, and so on. Once or twice, Mr. Holmes, I was on the periphery of a couple of your investigations – Oh, we never met, but I was friends with one of your Irregulars, and he recruited me as something of a day laborer. His name was Joe Mancot. I believe that he died in the mid-eighties, after I'd gone to America."

Holmes nodded, his expression grim. I'm afraid that I'd never heard of that particular lad, but I suspected that there was some tragic story related to the boy's passing which Holmes might or might not ever share.

"It was through Joe that my life changed, gentlemen – and that's also the reason that I'm here tonight."

He finished the last sip of whisky, declined a refill, and continued.

"It was Christmas 1883, and by then I was fourteen, and not doing too badly. I had a room in the back of a small mission for the poor, run by a brother and sister. I had a friend – Joe – whom I'd met that fall, and there was talk that I could join him again at some point on one of your investigations, Mr. Holmes – possibly even become one of the Irregulars – although truth be told, I kept myself busy enough with the small jobs that I found and what help I gave around the mission.

"It was seemingly like any other day, but Joe asked if I was going that night to the Father Christmas party, held at the back of The White Hart. I'd never heard anything about it, but he insisted that I accompany him. He explained that we were a little old to attend, but that it would be good fun. And fun, gentlemen, was rare enough in that quarter that I was willing to go out of my way to find a little.

"As you both certainly know, a walk through the East End at Christmas-time looks nothing like a similar stroll down Oxford Street. The decorations in the West End, and the efforts that the stores make – the window displays, the foods, the ostentatious gifts! – Why, it's enough to make a man wonder if some of us will ever recognize the random inequities that are visited upon each of us. When I see the difference between the two Londons, so different and jammed side-by-side, I am amazed and dismayed. 'There, but for the Grace of God' I want to tell everyone – for I have seen both sides, and I know."

His voice drifted off for a moment, as if the work that he had taken on, in trying to help the downtrodden of the capital, was sometimes overwhelming and discouraging. But then he returned to his tale.

"Joe and I went to the pub, and it was a break in the daily routine that we each faced. The front was filled with its usual patrons, but at the back were crowded about two-dozen children, all quite poor, and many of them immigrants, as I had been – some looking frightened, and a number of others having no idea what was happening, as I doubt that they could even speak English. Around the periphery were their parents, some adding to the forced festivity of the moment, and others looking suspicious, or as confused as their own offspring.

"A man – I took him to be the owner of the pub – made a little speech, and then he called forth from a back room a tall man dressed as Father Christmas, who lumbered out, laughing loudly and crying 'Happy Christmas! Happy Christmas to all!' Then he set down a heavy sack which had been slung over his shoulder, bent over, and began to distribute little wrapped gifts to the children surrounding him.

"It was all sincerely for the best, but of course the children were more puzzled than anything, and a few looked as if they might cry. But after the gifts were distributed – and not a child made an effort to open his or hers just then – Father Christmas again delved into the sack and brought forth a number of treats, consisting of candies of all colors and flavors. This the children understood, and from their initial tentative response, they quickly progressed to smiles and laughter, having more of that type of thing in their hands that night than they'd probably ever held before in their entire lives.

"Joe and I were too old for such things, and we stayed at the edge, just watching and enjoying what was happening. I wanted to remember what I'd seen so as to tell Mr. and Mrs. Mullingar, who ran the mission, all about it, thinking that if a few spare coins could be saved back, something similar might be done for the children that we saw on a regular basis.

"Although we hadn't intended to do anything but watch, Father Christmas came our way and pressed a few pieces of candy into our hands as well. I felt that he gave me something of an extra look then, but thought nothing about it. Then, seeing as things were winding down, Joe and I stepped outside, where we stood under the gas-lamp and continued to eat the treats while we talked about what we'd seen. As you may remember, Mr. Holmes, Joe had a good heart, and if he hadn't been killed, I wonder if he might not have found a way into the ministry.

"'Oersted,' he said, for he always called me by my last name, 'tell me the truth – aren't you glad that you joined me?'

"Before I could answer, however, someone behind me said, 'Oersted? What's your first name, lad?'

"I turned to find that Father Christmas had come up behind us without our knowledge. I strangely felt no threat, and by then my instincts were quite good, so I answered his question.

"'John, sir. Originally Johannes, before my parents brought me here. To England.'

"'Would that have been in '79?'

"'Yes,' I replied, now becoming a bit puzzled, if not outright suspicious.

"'Were your parents Agner and Lise Oersted?'

"This time I simply nodded.

"'Then,' Father Christmas said, 'Some friends of your parents have been trying to find you, lad. After their deaths, you vanished. Do you have any objection to meeting them?'

"Dumbly I shook my head, and when asked, I informed him that I could be found at the Mullingar's mission, near the Boy's and Girl's School in Hanbury Street. Father Christmas said he knew of the place, and he would let my parents' friends know where to find me.

"Well, gentlemen, you probably know what happened next – it has been featured enough in the newspapers. The next day, Erling Gravens and his wife, Vada, came to the mission. They were a childless couple who had long before gone to America, where Erling made a fortune. They had no living relatives – except for me, the child of Erling's distant cousin, the late Agner Oersted. They wished to adopt me. And so, with the amazed encouragement of the Mullingar's, I barely had time to pack my meager possessions before I was in a room at the Langham and being outfitted with clothes for the journey to the United States. I never had a chance to see or say goodbye to Joe, and within days we were at the coast, and just a few weeks later, I was installed in their home along Fifth Avenue in Manhattan.

"To make a long story short, Erling had no hesitation at fully accepting me as his heir and adopted son. Both he and Vada were as good to me as they could be, and I loved them nearly as much as the true parents that I'd lost. Erling set about involving me in all the aspects of the management of his fortune, and it turned out that I had an aptitude for it. And when they were both unexpectedly killed two years ago in the Tariffville train disaster, terribly mimicking the type of tragedy that took my parents, I unexpectedly found myself as the heir to the Gravens fortune, and all that went with it.

"I had been trained well, and in truth with good managers, much of the affairs take care of themselves. During my time in America, I realized that many of the great fortunes were maintained and curated in this way, with the rich allowing a pilot to steer their financial ship while they lived off the proceeds in all sorts of manners, ranging from essentially harmless to detrimental and dissipated. As my life there seemed to be fencing me into such an existence as well, my thoughts turned more and more to the work of the Mullingars, and others like them. So in the middle of last year, I returned to England.

"It's nothing for the owners of the great American fortunes to jump up and travel the world, so I haven't been missed over there. But while the rest of them rotate between their main New York residences and similar gargantuan palaces scattered elsewhere in the United States, or make grand tours of the European capitals, I've rather vanished from their circles, staying quite busy here in London.

"I have been in the newspapers more than I'd like, but it's been useful enough in its own way, calling attention a bit to the charitable work that we're hoping to accomplish. And I must report that so far, things have been moving along quite well. But there is one thing that I've wanted to accomplish, and last year when I tried, I failed."

"You wished to identify Father Christmas," said Holmes.

"Exactly, and to do so in a way that will not spoil what he is doing by throwing bright light on it before I understand who and what it's all about."

"And he is still up to the same business as before you left?"

"He is, as I confirmed before I went looking for him last Christmas. When I returned to England in the middle of '89, I stayed busy setting up the various programs that I'd been planning, but as the weather turned colder, I began to recall that Christmas of 1883, and how the unexpected intervention of Father Christmas had so changed my life. Naturally I was curious as to his true identity – I've never stopped wondering about that. But I also recalled that little gathering in the back of the dark pub, and those small children who had no idea what was happening, somewhere between confusion and fear, and then the shared joy on their faces when the good Father started distributing candy. I want to help his work, small in scale as it is, but I can't just burst in and unmask him, and offer a vast amount of money for him to buy more and more candy. That would spoil it somehow, and that's the last thing I want to occur. No, this is a small but precious thing, and I want to do it right – or, if I learn what I can and determine that my involvement would ruin it, I want to slip away and allow it to continue without it ever being known that I have any interest."

"And you said that your efforts didn't go as planned last year," said Holmes, crossing his legs.

"I did." Oersted smiled. "Last year, my first Christmas back. A few weeks before Christmas, I went alone to The White Hart, to ask if Father Christmas still gave gifts to the children a few days before the holiday. Of course, I've learned to disguise myself somewhat as I go about the East end, as a man wearing the habiliments of the Graven fortune's heir attracts too much attention.

"I learned that indeed Father Christmas did still visit each year, and the word had already started to spread for the parents to have their children there on the twenty-first – but the pub owner became reticent when I seemed too curious, particularly about the man's true identity. Next I asked around amongst some of the people that I've met since my return, and some were aware of Father Christmas's visits to the pub, and others were not. Curiously, I also learned that there are a few other pubs in the district that also have visits by Father Christmas on the same night.

"Last year, on the night of the twenty-first, I was at The White Hart when the children and their parents began to arrive. As they gathered in the back, I drifted that way too. To those watching, I might have been a curious patron, or a relative. After a few minutes, the scene played out almost exactly as it had in 1883 – Father Christmas arrived, and there was some suspicion and confusion. Gifts were passed around, and then candy and treats, which seemed to be the universal language wherein any concerns were removed. I found that my eyes had filled with tears as I looked to the wall where Joe and I had stood then. I was filled with regret that I'd never had the chance to see him again, or let him know what his friendship had meant to me, or that he'd been unable to fulfill his own potential – for he always had a good heart.

110

"I said that the scene was almost exactly like the small party I'd attended before my own life changed, but there was one difference: Where before Father Christmas had been a tall man, he was now much shorter, but no less jolly. From what I've heard and read, Mr. Holmes, I have no doubt that you could have identified much from him that I missed, but all I could see was a man in a costume, his face thoroughly obscured by a thick, white, false beard.

"When Joe and I had attended the affair in '83, we had left before it was entirely over, but this time I stayed to the end, as Father Christmas displayed his empty sack to the children, wished a Happy Christmas to everyone, and then retreated to the rear room from whence he'd initially appeared. I finished my beer and stepped outside to wait for Father Christmas, but when he didn't appear – either in costume, or as a man of the same height who might likely be him – I realized that he must have gone out the back entrance. I made my way quickly around the block into the mews in time to see him, still in costume, making good time along Osborn Street. I tried to follow him for a few minutes, but I lost him. I wondered afterwards if he suspected that he was being followed and intentionally took turns down side streets and alleys in order to disappear.

"In the following days, I asked more questions, both at The White Hart and other Whitechapel pubs where I'd heard that Father Christmas also gives gifts to children. Nothing could be determined. Either they don't know who the fellow is, or they're deliberately obfuscating his identity.

"As my daily tasks continued to take up my time, I gradually stopped trying to track him down – and then the weather turned cool again, and eventually as thoughts turned to Christmas, so too did my interest in identifying Father Christmas, both to assist in his work if possible, and also to thank him for the intervention in my own life that led me to where I am now."

"But you said that it was a different man last year," I said. "Do you intend to thank him, whomever he might be? Before he was tall, and now he is short."

"That's true – or I believe it to be true. But then again, I was much shorter myself in 1883, so perhaps my perspective changed. The only way to know is to speak with him, but to do that he must be found, and then I must decide if my asking and potential involvement will perhaps spoil something good that should not be spoiled."

He looked back toward Holmes. "As I said, Mr. Holmes, I was one of your irregular Irregulars on a couple of instances – Oh, we never met, but I knew from Joe that the man we were following was important to one of your investigations. That's why, when I returned to London, I remained interested and aware of the work that you do, and have followed what mention there is of you and your investigations in the newspaper. It was with great enjoyment, then, that I read of your investigation into the stolen Indian treasure and the river chase, which was published earlier this year."

I glanced at Holmes to see his reaction, as he hadn't been overly pleased with either that volume, *The Sign of the Four*, or the previous narrative that had been published in late 1887, *A Study in Scarlet*. However, in spite of the comments that he regularly shared with me, the author, about his dim views on the subject, he chose to withhold them while conferring with his client.

"I especially enjoyed the segment," continued Oersted, "where you and the doctor, along with the dog, trailed the one-legged man across London and down to the boat-yard. Recalling that, I realized that you were both exactly whom I needed to follow Father Christmas, hopefully identifying him to the point where I can speak to him and see if I can provide any assistance."

Holmes shifted in his seat. "And it is your intention to assist this Father Christmas in his work?"

"I assure you that is my purpose, should that prove to be the best help to him," Oersted replied. "But first he must be found – and I'm convinced that you should do it instead of me."

"What additional information have you gleaned? I cannot imagine that a man of your resources simply gave up after last year's attempt."

"All that I've been able to ascertain is that Father Christmas meets the poor children at a half-dozen pubs throughout the East End – here is a list . . . ." And he fished a folded sheet from his pocket, handing it to Holmes, who glanced at it and placed it on the small octagonal table beside his chair.

"And the next meeting?" Holmes asked.

"It will be tomorrow night – the twenty-first, as it always seems to be, based on my limited experience. I've confirmed that date with the different pub owners, but they – all of them – become quite cagy and reticent when I press as to who is playing the part of Father Christmas. Most of them don't recognize me, but one of them does know who I am, and he's as secretive on the subject as the others."

Holmes glanced my way. "What say you, Doctor? Shall we be at The White Hart tomorrow night at – ?"

"Seven o'clock," replied Oersted.

I nodded. "I wouldn't miss it." What I didn't mention was that I would certainly have my service revolver with me, as I had long ago learned never to leave home without it. I felt its comforting presence in my coat pocket even then as I was sitting there, pressed between me and the arm of my old chair. While this sounded like a story of good Christmas cheer,

I knew that, when joining Holmes on one of his investigations, anything might happen before things were settled. For instance, once he and I had been taken captive by a cabal of deaf men soon after buying a Christmas present for Mrs. Hudson.

Oersted seemed satisfied and provided us with an address in Holborn where he might be reached with our findings. Then he stood, shook our hands, and departed.

We listened until we heard the front door shut. Then we conversed, while still keeping our voices low – for just a few weeks before, a man had supposedly departed before slipping quietly back up the stairs, attempting to hear our discussion from the landing outside the sitting room door. We'd since verified that, with the transom shut as it usually was, nothing of a normal conversation could be heard through the thick door and walls, but it had still made us more careful.

As I sat back down, Holmes rose and stepped across to the shelves where his scrapbooks were placed. These commonplace volumes contained a mass of clippings, notes, and other curious ephemera, often exhaustively cross-referenced, providing very useful information about individuals and incidents related to Holmes's work. He devoted a significant amount of time toward their upkeep, but it had proven worthwhile upon countless occasions. At this time, however, nothing further was learned.

"I have no additional notes about Oersted's personal story – the death of his parents and the transformation into a fabulously rich young man – beyond what is already popularly known," Holmes explained. "That was certainly him – I've seen him in passing more than once – although I have no memory of ever hearing of him before he went to America in connection with any old cases. Since his return last year, he has done exactly as we've heard – devoted himself to bettering the conditions of those in the East End, and using his substantial funds in responsible and effective ways."

"Then his efforts to find Father Christmas are mostly likely sincere."

"Almost certainly. I can't imagine that we'll lead Oersted to the man's true residence and introduce them, only to have our client pull a pistol from his pocket while crying aloud about some grievance of a decade past which has culminated in this moment of vengeance."

"He doesn't seem the Count of Monte Cristo type," I confirmed. In earlier years, I might have withheld that comment and its literary reference, literally believing Holmes's statement not long after we met that he had no use for such references in his "brain attic", but I had since learned that he had been misrepresenting himself to a certain degree when we first met, and that in fact he was much more knowledgeable about things, including literature, than I had first credited him, believing then that his knowledge about such was "*Nil*". (And I specifically knew that he was aware of the Monte Cristo reference after one of our early cases when a very old man, whom we later identified as one Edmond Dantès, sought Holmes's help to rescue his great-granddaughter from the influence of a particularly vile lesser member of the Royal Family.)

After replacing the scrapbook, Holmes remained standing. "You see the obvious question, no doubt?" he asked.

I nodded. "How did the Father Christmas of 1883 so easily recognize Johannes Oersted."

"Indeed. Perhaps learning that will help us discover the true nature of *this* Father Christmas, or possibly we'll learn it at the other end, when we've unmasked him."

I smiled. "Now you sound as if he's a villain in a music hall drama."

"One never knows – as you well know yourself." He took a step forward. "I know that you need to get home to your good wife. Shall we meet here tomorrow at five o'clock? Of course, wear something shabby."

I stood and agreed, and then walked home, crossing into Paddington and arriving on time for dinner, where Mary was quite interested to hear of my encounter with the famed young heir whose reputation was rising every day as the public's fascination with his history was matched only by their admiration of his charitable endeavors.

The next day was carried out like many others since I had married and gone back into active practice. My offices took up the ground floor of our modest building, but in spite of the general separation between the rooms where I saw patients and our quarters upstairs, Mary had gone out of our way to give the practice a sense of Christmas celebration, decorating the tabletops, windows, mantels, and other such places as she could find with colorful and seasonal ribbons and trimmings. When I went upstairs for lunch, I could hear that she was humming a lively carol, but she stopped when she heard me approach, and then ordered that I remain waiting on the stairs until such time as she accomplished some mysterious task – most likely the wrapping a gift. I had been forced to be just as careful downstairs several days earlier when taking pains to prepare *her* gifts, so I completely understood.

Although dealing with some of my patients' sad situations tended to dampen the good feelings associated with the season, in general there was a sense of joy and anticipation in the house that marveled me, and I was very happy indeed to count my blessings.

As the day passed and I completed my tasks, my thoughts were more and more occupied with thoughts of Oersted's request that we locate and identify the mysterious benefactor of the East End children. The previous night, Mary and I had discussed it from several angles, and like me, she couldn't perceive any way that the situation might turn out badly – but experience had taught me that absolute prediction of the path to any conclusion was impossible, and that it was better to be safe than full of later regret, so as usual, I made sure that I had my service revolver as I departed for Baker Street.

Mrs. Hudson was just returning from a shopping excursion, and I complimented her regarding the fine wreath upon the door. We stood outside for a moment, reminiscing about past Christmases when I had been one of her two tenants. We laughed at some of Holmes's adamant frustrations about how decorations would not be tolerated, for she had simply ignored him as one would a petulant child who issued ultimatums while stamping his feet and holding his breath as she went about the business of fixing up the sitting room nearly as nicely as her own festively adorned rooms. She'd had somewhat less success now that I'd moved away, but she hadn't given up.

We were still discussing her latest campaign when Holmes joined us, and I told her goodbye when he'd secured a hansom. Then we were off to Whitechapel.

I was in the worn clothing that I saved for such occasions, having learned to keep a few sets of such for these expeditions. The entire outfit probably wasn't as filthy as it should have been, but Mary, with a wary eye, refused to let anything truly dirty hang in the allotted space in my closet. But perhaps, I thought, the grime and sourness emanating from Holmes's own much-more-authentic disguise would suffice to mask my unhelpful cleanliness.

Our route found us working south and then east, along Oxford Street, and then through Holborn and into the City. Although I was already aware of the drastic differences in wealth and privilege between the residences of different parts of the capital, I saw what Oersted had meant about decorations. Most of the shops and houses that we passed had something of the sort, ranging from a simple sprig of holly to a fully contrived window display. And all around us, people seemed to step along with a great deal of bounce and good cheer. Yet I knew that in just a few miles, all of this would vanish as we entered the area with much less reason or opportunity to celebrate.

As we progressed, I debated whether to mention something that I'd wondered about since yesterday, during Oersted's visit. Finally I did so, knowing that Holmes would either answer, or he wouldn't.

"Yesterday," I began. "There seemed to be something tragic about your former Irregular, Joe Mancot. If you don't mind, might I ask what occurred?"

Holmes's eyes tightened, but not angrily. "I expected that you would ask. It's an unfortunate situation. As Oersted said, Joe was a good lad who was trapped in bad circumstances – an orphan living with a true rogue of an uncle. One night, this uncle had been drinking even more than usual and, having been thwarted in his attempts to start trouble at a nearby pub, he returned home to try the same on his family. Joe was there, and when his young cousin, a boy of just four, was the target of the father's cruelty, Joe intervened. While it was certainly an accident, the uncle swung a great sweeping blow toward Joe, who ducked away. But his feet slipped and he crashed to the floor, breaking his head open upon the hearth. He died immediately. The uncle was sent to Pentonville, where in less than a year he had a seizure in his isolated cell and passed unnoticed and unmissed."

Strangely at that moment, we rounded a corner where a street musician was playing "God Rest Ye Merry, Gentlemen" upon his fiddle to an appreciative crowd.

"I'd had hopes," continued Holmes, "that Joe would soon be able to begin studies that I'd arranged for him with a clergyman for whom I'd recently performed a modest service – locating a misplaced vital document. I greatly regret that I didn't make the effort sooner, to remove Joe from that house."

He sighed. "Such disappointments are part of my trade, Watson – or so I've come to believe. Because of that, I need some good news. Too often lately I've encountered various setbacks – losing ground for every step forward. I do wish that the solution to this Father Christmas business falls on the pleasant side of the scales."

"I'm sure that it will." And in truth, I hoped that it would, for I knew that of late he'd been using himself up quite too freely in his escalating efforts to place various counter-moves in answer to each of Moriarty's actions, gradually fencing in the wily academic and criminal – but I hadn't realized until then that his spirit was being so affected. I would need to make a better effort to assist him when possible as the situation reached a crisis.

But it was not at that point yet, and I turned the conversation to less grim shadings. I asked questions about locations that we passed, or made comments about people going about their business, allowing him to elaborate – or correct me – based upon his own observations. He knew what I was doing, but he was in better spirits by the time we disembarked in Whitechapel Road.

We walked the short distance to The White Hart, a small building not more than twelve or fifteen feet wide, and only four stories high. I had no idea what occurred upstairs – if there were rooms to let, or if the owner himself lived there, or if those upper floors served as meeting space for bar

116

patrons. I'd been inside the ground floor on any number of occasions, one way or another, and most recently during the autumn of 1888, when I'd been summoned from a patrol through some of the more evil nearby streets and alleys and passages to sew up a gash on a constable's wounded forehead, the result of a false accusation from one drunk to another that the latter was most certainly The Ripper – a charge which he most vociferously denied, with the aid of a broken bottle.

As I had improved my ability to change my appearance over the years, as taught by Holmes, I was certain that we wouldn't be recognized. We slipped inside the dark and poorly lit room, the winter sun having long-since set. Ordering a brace of beers, we found a pair of stools along the right-hand wall and waited to see what happened next.

As seven o'clock approached, more and more small families tentatively entered the building. The pub's landlord, Mr. Bledsoe, met them at the door with a gruff sort of bonhomie and shepherded them toward the back. A few extra lanterns had been lit there to augment the normal dim gaslight. At five or so minutes after the top of the hour, about two-dozen children were seated in a circle on the filthy floor while their parents were layered around and behind them. Then, without further delay, Bledsoe danced his way across the crowded floor to a door at the rear, opened it, and ushered in Father Christmas.

The fellow was rather short – around five-and-a-half-feet tall – and dressed as one might expect in the typical costume of the holiday's patron saint. His robe was green in the old style, and he had a matching cap which held in place an apparently wig of long white hair – the same too-white shade as the heavy false beard which hung rather awkwardly and sideways upon his face.

He had a large and bulky brown Hessian sack across his right shoulder, held by both hands. However, it seemed more awkward than heavy, and he swung it rather easily to the floor when he stopped to face the children.

The events were carried out as described to us by Oersted during his visit to Baker Street the night before: The wishes of holiday cheer in a falsely deepened and hearty voice, followed by the dispersal of the contents of the sack, consisting of a number of small but festively wrapped gifts, and finally the distribution of quite a bit of candy – which successfully served to brighten the spirits of both the children and the parents. Then, after only a few minutes more, the garbed figure waved a gloved hand, boomed "Happy Holidays!" and slipped away through the back door. Holmes, having left most of his beer untouched on the shelf where we had leaned, was already out the front door, and I was close behind.

117

By that time, I had known Holmes for almost ten years, and he had managed to teach me, a rather slow pupil at first, a number of useful skills that enabled me to more effectively assist him in his work. While we were good friends – in many ways he was much more my brother than the disappointing fellow who was actually my blood kin – I don't believe that he would have tolerated me quite so much or for so long if I'd been completely ineffectual at assisting him. After working together for so long, we functioned in some similarity to the way that a wolf pack can slowly approach and then gradually get around and in front of its prey. Without discussion, we separated outside the pub, Holmes more directly following Father Christmas while I moved ahead on a side street, picking up the trail while Holmes took the opportunity to advance to his next location farther ahead. Thus, we stayed with our subject as we crossed a good-sized piece of London.

The festively attired man didn't make it difficult. He first led us along the Aldgate High Street, moving at a steady even pace with his empty sack hanging at one side. On occasion he would stop and speak with a random passer-by, and several times he fished in his pocket to give a less fortunate figure a coin or two. Once, I saw from a distance when a drunk began to yell something his way in a mocking tone, but Father Christmas simply changed direction and went directly up to the man, who then abruptly changed his tone and slunk away. Then the green-garbed fellow resumed his previous pace.

I was beginning to have suspicions about the true identity of the man I followed, and wished that I could have conferred with Holmes, but he and I were taking separated routes so that one or the other of us wouldn't be spotted, and our thoughts would have to remain unshared for the present.

Down Leadenhall Street, and then along Cheapside we went. By the time we were passing through Newgate Street and then into Holborn, I would have bet a hundred pounds that I knew our destination – and I was sure that Holmes knew as well, although he had been there far fewer times than I had. By the time we veered left from High Holborn into the Little Turnstile, I felt that I could have gone on ahead and been waiting for Father Christmas when he arrived at the doorway his destination – the Ship's Tavern in Gates Street, just to the northwest of Lincoln's Inn Fields. In truth, as I emerged from the narrow passage, Holmes was already waiting at the door, alone.

"I let him go inside," he explained.

"When did you realize who it was? I think that I knew from the first time I saw the way he walked."

Holmes smiled. "Yes, that left foot of his with its inward twist is unmistakable. Shall we?" And with that, he held the door for me to enter.

Unexpectedly, for it was still rather early, the pub appeared to be closed, except for a small private gathering at some tables about midway back. I was rather amazed to see that the group, consisting a dozen men, were all frozen in some sort of curious *tableau*, looking in our direction. Some sat, while others were standing. Some held drinks, and a few were in the process of pouring their own. The most unique feature of the group was that all were dressed, in some form or fashion, in traditional green or more modern red, as Father Christmas. There were tall ones and short, thick and thin. And to a man they were turned to face us. Standing in front of them was the shorter fellow whom we had just followed from Whitechapel, and he was the first to break the illusion and step our way.

"Welcome, Mr. Holmes, Doctor Watson. I thought about stopping and inviting you to walk with me when I realized that you were both following, but as we would all get here in any case, it was more fun to draw you along."

"Good evening, Inspector," said Holmes, stepping forward into the better-lit part of the room. "*Inspectors*, I should say. Season's Greetings to all of you."

"And to you!" came their hearty reply, in tones high and low, from various parts of the island.

The shorter man stepped further forward, peeling off his white wig and beard. "I suppose it was young Mr. Oersted who hired you," commented Inspector Lestrade of Scotland Yard.

We nodded. "Yesterday," I said. "He knows something of your charitable work, and wishes to learn more."

A taller Father Christmas broke from the group and approached us, revealing himself to be our old friend, Inspector Bradstreet. "We knew he'd keep after it – several of the pub owners who help arrange this each year said that someone was asking questions, and Bill Parrott at The Boar knew that it was him."

"Was it you, Bradstreet, that identified Oersted back in '83 at The White Hart and directed Mr. and Mrs. Gravens to find him?"

Bradstreet nodded. "It was. The Gravens had come to London just a few days before. I was one of the officers who met with them. It was just coincidence – or a Christmas miracle, I suppose – that I noticed he matched the description, and not long after I heard the boy's name spoken outside the pub, and I was able to make the connection."

"But you didn't reveal yourself then," I said, "because you didn't want to explain the connection between Father Christmas and the Force."

119

"That's it," Bradstreet explained. "This is something that we do, and it's between us – for us. We don't even tell our colleagues about it – constables or superintendents. If I'd identified myself to Oersted that night, he would have either mentioned that Father Christmas was an inspector, or if I'd have taken him to the station while still in my Christmas suit, I would have had to explain to the lads on duty. Better to send the Gravens to find him at the mission the next day."

By this point, the other Father Christmases had joined us: Lanner, and the Jones brothers – Athelney and Peter. There was MacDonald and Youghal and Morton, and of course Gregson, standing at the rear, with a silent nod in my direction.

"Oersted wants to help what you're doing," I explained.

"I have no doubt of it," said Lestrade. "But as Bradstreet explained, this is something just for us. Of course, we trust you two, as friends, to keep our secret."

"Certainly," agreed Holmes. "We will not report a word of what we found here tonight – and hopefully it will be explained in such a way that Mr. Oersted will stop trying to discover who you all are. But perhaps you might agree to his financial support, even if he remains unaware of who is receiving it?"

The question remained open-ended at that point, but as the evening progressed, it was discussed several times, and by the end of the festivities, the inspectors' secret Christmas party, it was decided that if John Oersted wished to donate funds to their cause, they would gratefully accept them.

It was a jolly time, and I cannot remember when I had so much actual fun in the company of the Yard's inspectors. I was honored, as I know Holmes was as well, to be included in the party, and it was a most unique experience to be surrounded by a dozen or more Father Christmases.

Later, after Holmes and I had shared a cab as far as Baker Street, and then I rode on alone in the gaslit darkness to my Praed Street home in Paddington, it all began to feel like a distant Christmas dream, and even more so when I described it to Mary before falling into a deep sleep.

The next year was one of great emotion. As 1891 commenced, Holmes's struggles with Professor Moriarty escalated as he was finally able to head off the criminal's schemes, in one direction after another, leaving the only path forward one toward inevitable destruction of the illegal organization – but not without great cost.

On the fourth of May, Holmes was thought to have perished at the Reichenbach Falls, locked in combat with the Professor as both tumbled to their terrible deaths at the base of the nearly nine-hundred-feet tall cascade into the raging torrent below. I returned to London in despair, and it was Mary who reminded me of how fortunate that I still was. I had a wonderful wife, a growing practice, and friends, many of whom were inspectors with the Yard. I was more honored than I could express when they invited me to be a part of their Father Christmas Brigade the following December.

I had been taking on work throughout those months as a police surgeon, and my ties and friendship with the inspectors continued to grow. It was to them that I turned for strength when Mary, never in the best of health, had passed away in the spring of 1893. It nearly broke me then, but they were my firm and fast friends and they made sure that I survived.

In April 1894, Holmes returned to London, having never, in fact, gone over the Falls to his death. Instead, he had roamed the world for three years, carrying out a number of delicate tasks for his brother Mycroft, and also looking for the opportunity to bring Moriarty's prime henchman finally to justice. After that task was complete, I – having no reason to stay there by then – sold my practice and moved back to Baker Street. What followed were many months of investigations and adventures, keeping us both extremely busy as the year passed.

As Christmas approached, we had visitors – Lestrade, Gregson, and Bradstreet. They ranged themselves throughout our sitting room in a loose semi-circle in front of the fireplace, with the mantel very much decorated for the holiday, courtesy of our landlady.

"We really won't take no for an answer," explained Lestrade. "Through the financial arrangement you worked out with Mr. Oersted, and his happy willingness to let us remain anonymous – even to him – the amount of good that we've been able to accomplish at Christmas – with Dr. Watson's assistance – has grown ten-fold in just a few years. Now it's that time of year again, Mr. Holmes, and we want you to join us. To be part of the Brigade, as the Doctor started calling us."

Holmes started to speak, but Gregson cut him off, raising one of his large hands and leaving my friend sitting there speechless for one of those rare occasions in his life, his mouth open for a moment like that of a codfish.

"There will be no debate, Mr. Holmes," said the flaxen-haired detective, his fingers wide. "Your suit has been ordered, and it will be delivered tomorrow. The day after that we'll gather at The Ships and spread out across the city. The doctor can explain further. Afterwards will be the celebration. You've been there before. You know what to expect."

After that, there was really nothing that Holmes could do to say no, and so he didn't. He and I were there at the pub two nights later, where we separated to give out toys and treats to the young children in some of the worst parts of the city who didn't have much else to look forward to. Later, as we returned to the small bar for the policeman's own celebration, I don't think that anyone enjoyed it more than Sherlock Holmes – and he has continued to do so in all the years since, right up to the time that I've set this account down on paper. He's returning to London tonight from his retirement villa in Sussex, and as he told me when I confirmed his attendance the other day on the telephone, "I wouldn't miss it for the world!"

JHW
21 December, 1909

Some Additional Notes Regarding Mr. Melas

Part I – Early September 1903

"This is unusual," I said by way of greeting as I pulled off my coat, and then made my way over to the sideboard for something refreshing. It was a bit early, but I was not sure what to expect, and felt the need for extra fortification. "Why here, and not the usual summons to the Diogenes Club?"

Holmes, seated in his chair by the fire and sorting a stack of papers into two different boxes on the floor before him, replied, "Everything with Mycroft has some calculated meaning. It may only make sense to him, and we may never understand. In any case, I'm sorry that you had to interrupt your morning, but it does make it more convenient for me as I try to categorize a quarter-century of documents accumulated since moving here."

It wasn't quite that long, I thought to myself, but close – although one might not count the nearly three years when Holmes was presumed dead and away from London as time spent in these Baker Street rooms.

Settling into my old chair across from him, which had already been used when I'd bought it in early January 1881, and it was showing every one of its years, I sighed with both comfort and a feeling of sadness. It wasn't imminent, but Sherlock Holmes's retirement was fast approaching, and I had many feelings about that, none of them good.

I gestured toward the two boxes, one of which had quite a bit more papers than the other. "Which is going to Sussex, and which will be burned?"

He tapped the more-full box with his right foot. "This one for the fire. I'll admit that the reason for keeping some of these pages has passed beyond my memory." He leaned forward and retrieved one of the discarded sheets. "For instance, I have some recollection that this related to that business in Cheadle and the cache of Roman coins, but I'm now uncertain why I constructed it."

He displayed a graph, bars drawn in multiple colors, of which red was the tallest – or widest, depending on if the sheet was turned sideways. There was no labeling to identify any meanings, except for one word written in Holmes's fist, placed the lower right corner (when held so that the sheet was longer from top to bottom): *Tenebrous*.

He dropped it back into the discard box and resumed examining the papers still in his hands. I took the opportunity to glance around the room.

Holmes was never the tidiest of men, but he always seemed to know where to find a document or object when needed. He maintained his own peculiar order of arrangement, whether it be pieces of evidence that found their way to the Baker Street rooms, weapons and poisons and pieces of victims, or documents such as what he was currently culling, or those clippings and souvenirs that ended up in his voluminous scrapbooks. Over the years, I had somewhat learned his methods, so that when required, I could generally locate something more often than not. I understood, for instance, that the ongoing biographical sketch he maintained of Lord Funt would not be found in the commonplace volume labeled "*F*", as one might suppose. Rather, it was located in "*S*" for "*Slapping*", due to the nobleman's propensity for applying his open-palmed hand regularly across the faces of his enemies, with force, to be immediately followed by substantial pecuniary compensation as offered by his trusted aide and harried nephew, Digby Broadheath.

In some ways, the sitting room did not look much changed from previous days, and much of the regular clutter was still in place. There was no chance at the chemical corner, and the bookshelves were still as packed as they had been for years. But perhaps the mantel was a bit thinned from its usual disorder, and there were certainly less stacks of papers ranged along the back of the dining table – some of which had likely already been separated into two boxes like the ones now between us.

I heard the sound of a carriage stop out front – It was a warm day, even for early September and the windows were open – and then the ringing of a bell indicated that a visitor had arrived. I glanced at the mantel clock. Mycroft was punctual, as would be expected.

I had seen Holmes's older brother many times over the years since meeting him in the late summer of 1888, that tempestuous year when the Kingdom, and we personally as well, had faced such peril. I was surprised when first learning of that most unusual fellow, as I'd been friends with Sherlock Holmes for nearly eight years before learning that he even had a brother. By that time, I'd long assumed that he had no relatives at all. When he announced one September evening that he had a brother, while making the point that "Art in the blood is liable to take the strangest forms," I was quite surprised, to say the least. To prove his assertion, we had then set out on a leisurely stroll, ending up at No. 78, Pall Mall – the location of the little-known and most unusual Diogenes Club. My first meeting with Mycroft Holmes had been quite dramatic, as we became involved in the curious affairs and subsequent rescue of a Greek gentleman and the discovery of a dead man who had been much less fortunate.

At the time, I'd believed that Mycroft Holmes was some obscure government functionary, an accountant in an unimportant department who tallied his books all day before shuffling around to his club, but I soon learned of his immense involvement and importance within the shadowy halls of power. In the fifteen years since I'd first met him, I had seen him and worked with him countless times, even during those years when Holmes was away from London and thought to have died at the Reichenbach Falls. The vast majority of our meetings had occurred in the Stranger's Room at the Diogenes Club, or less frequently in either Mycroft's Whitehall office or his lodgings across from the Club. Thus, his request to visit us in Baker Street set the tone for something a bit more unusual.

Mycroft's lumbering climb up the stairs was steady. I'd long-ago learned from Holmes to listen as visitors ascended – whether they had an energetic pace, or if they paused on the landing to catch a breath before continuing. Certain footsteps, such as Inspectors Lestrade or Bradstreet, were quite distinctive. Others would stop on the landing just outside the door, as if collecting their thoughts or their courage before entering Holmes's presence.

Mycroft Holmes was indifferent to any of that. He simply climbed the stairs with the same forward-facing determination that a dreadnought would use when leaving the harbor.

After he had settled himself on the settee – the basket chair generally reserved for visitors had never been an option – he declined the offer of a restorative, asked after our health and that of my wife, and then nodded toward Holmes's current activity.

"At this rate," he stated, "you'll still be in Baker Street after the New Year."

"You should be satisfied that I'm making forward progress of any sort," Holmes replied, a bit sourly.

It had long been a bone of contention between the two of them. As foreign threats against Great Britain grew by the day, some still only recognized by Mycroft Holmes, and by way of him Holmes and me, Mycroft had pressed his younger brother to abandon his work as a consulting detective – "Petty," as he often called it – and return to being a full-time government agent, as he had been from 1891 to 1894, during that time when he was believed to be dead. Then, he had been Mycroft's trusted man in the field, using his supposed demise as a cloak for all that he was able to accomplish, ceaselessly traveling here and there over six continents. In the nine years since Holmes's return, Mycroft had missed having his own personal "man of action", as he called Holmes, and he had regularly pressed for Holmes's return to service.

125

As the threat of war became more certain, at some unknown point in the future, Sherlock Holmes had come around more and more to his brother's way of thinking – and so he had finally agreed to once again work for his brother. But this time he would not fake his own death. Rather, he would fake his retirement.

Years before, Holmes had acquired, by way of an investigation, a small house and farm in Sussex, just west of Birling Gap, at the base of Beachy Head, the highest cliff in England. It was there that he would "retire", giving the impression that he was abandoning London for the new life of a reclusive apiarist. In fact, he planned to retain the lease on the Baker Street rooms for use when he needed to return to the city, and after establishing himself in Sussex, he would be able to come and go in secret, hopefully to work nearly as effectively as when the world had thought him to be dead.

Mycroft shifted his attention from Holmes to me. "Doctor, how is your practice? Successful, I hope."

I nodded, replying, "It's as busy as I want it to be. My wife is pleased, although in truth I'm somewhat weary of the number of patients who make appointments simply to say that they've met me." I glanced toward Holmes, who was studying a yellowed map. As he refolded it and dropped it into the left box, which would go with him to Sussex, I added, "I believe that a number of those who visit are also hoping that we'll be interrupted by a summons from your brother, calling me away to some urgent investigation."

Mycroft nodded, as if I'd confirmed what he expected to hear. Then, he continued. "And your writing? You have continued that as always – for your own enjoyment, and to keep records of Sherlock's investigations."

"I have. I've kept extensive journals since I was a lad, and writing was very therapeutic as I recovered from my war wounds."

"Good, good. That makes things easier. We wish for you to resume publication of your stories in *The Strand* – next month, if possible."

I was nonplussed, to say the least, and I believe that Holmes was surprised as well. He lowered the papers in his hand and looked at Mycroft with a twist of his head.

In the past, I'd had the sense that the publication of my writings about Holmes's cases had generally met with disapproval from both Holmes himself, and other quarters as well. I'd initially published the story of how Holmes and I met, and the first investigation in which I'd participated, because I wished for people to know of my friend's gifts, and for him to receive credit that was due. When the matter had occurred in early March of '81, I'd only known Holmes for a couple of months, and was rather negatively incensed that the newspapers had given credit for the solution to the official police – and that the officials seemed quite willing to go along with it. I'd promised then that the truth would be known, and that I would relate what actually occurred. Holmes had seemed indifferent, and it was only later that I realized he would have preferred that I not relate the story at all.

That first story, fancifully titled *A Study in Scarlet*, didn't actually appear in print until late 1887, and by then Holmes's fame had grown considerably, as had his much friendlier relations with the police. In hindsight, I regretted some of the negative comments about a few of the inspectors and officers that I'd initially included when I wrote the matter up in 1881, as they seemed quite harsh in hindsight. However, I tried to keep in mind that my feelings were historically accurate in light of how I'd felt then, as a recovering and rather fragile twenty-eight-year-old wounded war veteran.

After that, I'd published another longer piece in 1890, relating how I'd met my late wife Mary by way of one of Holmes's more notable investigations, and then, during the first two years when Holmes was missing, two-dozen more shorter works. These had concluded with the narrative explaining how Holmes was believed to have died atop the Swiss waterfall near Meiringen. After his return to London, Holmes had been quite dismayed to see just how many tales about him had been published, and in a manner that he found rather disagreeable. (He argued that these case studies should have been written in a clinical fashion and published in a respected journal, in spite of how they ended up making him much better known to the general public, leading to more clients arriving at his door.)

Most recently, my sometime-literary agent, knighted less than a year earlier as "Sir Arthur" Conan Doyle, had pushed for the publication of the Dartmoor investigation into deaths related to the Baskerville's family curse. That had brought a certain amount of renewed interest in the previous stories, resulting in an increase in sales – which was not unwelcome as I purchased a medical practice in Queen Anne Street in mid-1902, prior to my marriage.

All of this raced through my mind as I pondered Mycroft's curious statement. "'We'?" I asked. "Who is the 'We' to whom you refer?"

Holmes gave a small laugh. "Mycroft is referring to himself, although his use of 'We' is less in the royal sense, and more to simply give the impression that blame for this idea can be spread to additional people."

Mycroft frowned. "It's true that I conceived the notion, but others with whom I've discussed it have been in accord."

"And what purpose would this serve?" asked Holmes before I could ask it myself, although with a bit less rancor in my tone.

127

"An extra decoration on top of the cake," replied Mycroft. "It will be another way for us to spread the word that you are retiring. A line dropped here or there into the narratives will be quite effective for those in the various embassies who will be combing through the stories to read between the lines. For example, Doctor, you might casually mention that my brother's restriction on publishing the stories has been lifted, intriguing those who are reading it. *'Why has it been lifted?'* will be asked. Later, you might mention that Sherlock is no longer in actual professional practice – that he has definitely retired from London and betaken himself to study and bee-farming on the Sussex Downs. You can give the impression that he's become a hermit, and that notoriety has become hateful to him, and he has peremptorily requested that his wishes in the matter of his privacy and seclusion should be strictly observed. It can only help further the impression that he's ensconced in Sussex, rusticating permanently on his little plot until such time as he shuffles off."

Holmes snorted. "It sounds as if you should be writing them yourself, Mycroft. *'Ensconsed'*. *'Rusticating'*. Cut the poetry. What else do you mean?"

Mycroft nodded. "We . . . that is, *I* – would ask to have some editorial review. Not – " he added, raising one of his flipper-like hands, " – to interfere with which stories you choose, or to argue with you over choices of phrasing or choice of words. Rather, on occasion, I would wish – With your consent! – to add a word or phrase here or there, which might further give the impression of Sherlock's retirement, or to convey a coded message to an agent in such an unexpected way that it would go unnoticed by our enemies. Related to that, I might ask that something be added – never to the detriment of the story – that would confuse the enemy when they understand its meaning, or even serve as an oblique warning."

I was silent for a moment as they both looked at me, Mycroft patiently waiting for a response, and Sherlock Holmes with an amused expression. I could think of several ways in which this might go wrong, and even though I believed that Mycroft would honor his statement of relative noninterference, I also knew that he might also find ways around the actual words of his pledge to some other interpretation if he felt the need.

Still, on the whole, I could find no objections, and the added funds would certainly be of use. But that suddenly caused me to remember my wife, who would also appreciate the augmented income, but at the price of further association with Holmes by way of my stories.

My first wife, Constance, had very little interaction with Holmes, as her steadily worsening illness had meant that she and her mother were forced to travel away from London for much of our marriage, while I stayed behind, earning money for her recuperative trips while also hoping to bank enough funds to purchase a practice in the countryside far away from the unhealthy capital. Three-quarters-of-a-year after Constance's passing, I met my second wife, Mary, by way of Holmes's investigation into the Sholto murder. She and Holmes had much more contact with one another, and she cared for and worried after him like a sister – and he appreciated the attention and cared for her as well, in his own fashion. She passed away in 1893, while Holmes was missing. I had remarried again in the fall of 1902, just a year before this meeting with Mycroft, and my new wife was somewhat less enthused regarding my friendship with Holmes and my assistance with his investigations. I still made time to assist him, nonetheless, but I was uncertain as to her reaction when she found out that more stories would be appearing in *The Strand*. She had been pleased when she'd heard that Holmes was retiring and moving to the south coast, possibly believing that phase of my life was coming to a close. In reality, it was not.

With an inward sigh, as if I were crossing another Rubicon in my life, and uncertain as to what my commitment might actually involve, I nodded my agreement. Mycroft smiled, as if he'd known the outcome all along – but now the deed was done.

Over the next few minutes, we worked out a few early details: Mycroft would make the arrangements with *The Strand*, and likely an American periodical as well, probably *Collier's*, to begin publication as soon as possible, helping spread the word quickly of Holmes's retirement.

"We should begin with a narrative of how Sherlock actually survived at the Reichenbach," Mycroft explained. "I don't believe that you've explained that in print before, have you?"

I shook my head. "No. 'The Final Problem' was published in December of '93, in response to Colonel Moriarty's scurrilous and libelous attacks. Then, there was nothing until *The Hound* appeared in *The Strand* from the late summer of 1901 to the following spring. That made no mention of Holmes's return – it simply told the story of what happened in the fall of 1888. I understand that a number of people believed that the narrative was posthumous."

"You've always insisted that your stories generated clients," Holmes muttered, almost to himself. "How so, if these readers to whom you refer still believed me to be dead?"

I chose to ignore him, as was always best when he was trending toward a disputatious mood.

When it was all fixed up, Mycroft put his hands upon his knees, preparatory to levering himself upward to his feet. "I believe that should do it. I assume that you have a number of manuscripts ready – or nearly so – for publication?"

"I do."

"Good."

"How long do you expect this performance to run?" asked Holmes.

Mycroft was quick to answer. "To be effective, probably a year – one-dozen stories between now and late 1904, I think. That should be enough to cement the notion of your retirement in the public mind, and for you to have settled into your own routines of living as Sherlock Holmes in your little cottage, and also slipping away to carry out your other tasks. You can even work in the occasional investigation as yourself if you wish."

"Quite generous of you," murmured Holmes.

Mycroft rose. "If you can send around the manuscript describing Sherlock's return, and the solution of the Adair murder, I'll get things moving quickly. I believe that, with any luck, we can have it published in America by the end of the month."

"But today is only the third of September!" I said with surprise. "Surely it takes much longer than that."

"Possibly it would have, just a few years ago, but the publishing paradigm is much quicker now. Plus," he added, "I have means and methods beyond the typical publisher."

"And apparently beyond the typical literary agent, as well," added Holmes. "You have neglected to account for Doyle's part of this scheme."

"Sir Arthur," replied Mycroft, pointedly using our old friend's new title, "will do what's expected. He always has. Hence the knighthood that he's coveted for so long." He glanced at the clock. His entire visit had actually taken less than a quarter-hour. It seemed much longer. "And now, if you will excuse me, I must return to my office. Last month's move by the Second Congress of the Russian Social Democratic Labour Party from Brussels to London has not been handled smoothly, to say the least. The Belgians kicked them out, and I suspect we should do the same. Perhaps, Sherlock, when you're 'retired', you will be able to look into them a bit more."

Holmes, whose attention had been pulled back to the sheaf of papers in his hand, nodded absently without looking up. I rose and shook Mycroft's hand, indicating that I'd be by in the next day or so with some stories. Then he turned toward the door, moving – as always – with much more grace than one would expect from such a large man. After we heard the downstairs door shut, Holmes said, "I suspect that he'll want further control of your stories than he's admitting – especially after how you published the tale of Mr. Melas, the interpreter. But you already knew that."

I nodded, remembering that particularly unpleasant encounter. "The Greek Interpreter" had been published in September 1893 – nearly ten

130

years to the day before Mycroft's visit that morning to Baker Street – and by then, perhaps, I was getting a bit careless, but not without good reason. Mary had passed away the previous April, and for a time, I was a man outside myself. I know that my friends were quite worried for me then. In the meantime, I was torn between continuing to provide monthly manuscripts to *The Strand* for their hungry readers, as writing was sometimes all that motivated me on any given day, and simply giving up.

Doyle, who was acting as my literary agent, was always encouraging, at least on the surface, and yet it became more and more clear that he was tiring of the whole effort as well, anxious to turn his attentions to writing the historical romances that had always interested him, and fearful that further continued association with the recounting of Holmes's cases would somehow darken his ambitious literary reputation and become the work with which he was most associated. When Colonel Moriarty began to defend his dead brother in the press, acting as if the Professor was a wronged innocent victim who had been hounded by a mad or criminal Sherlock Holmes, I knew that I must respond and publish the truth – and aiming for that particular story to be told became something of an end-point in my mind, a goal to reach, with blissful nothingness beyond. There would be no more writing, and no more deadlines. Just one foggy day passing into the next.

On the day after "The Greek Interpreter", telling the story of my first meeting with Mycroft Holmes, was published, I received terse note summoning me to the Diogenes Club. Having no idea why, I rearranged my schedule and decided to walk, crossing from my home and practice in Vicarage Gate, Kensington (where I had lived and worked while married to Constance, and which I had repurchased a year or so before,) through Hyde Park and alongside Green Park, arriving at the Diogenes by the appointed hour. I stood in front of the building for a moment, thinking of all the times that I had been there with Holmes, and then without him. I had come here in mid-May of 1891, upon my return to England after the events at Reichenbach, to apologize for how I had failed Sherlock Holmes – how I had been lured away, leaving him to face Professor Moriarty alone. Mycroft Holmes had gruffly told me not to hold myself responsible – which he could do easily enough, already knowing by that point that his brother was actually still alive – a fact that was kept from me for a variety of reasons.

Now, as I made the single step up onto the portico and then opened the door of No. 78, I wondered again why I'd been summoned. Perhaps some bit of business related to one of Holmes's old cases – it wouldn't be the first time – or possibly some new affair in which I could be of assistance.

But I soon learned, upon being shown to the Stranger's Room, that I was being called onto the carpet for a serious breach I didn't know I'd committed.

Mycroft expressed his dismay, his disbelief, that I would have written about him without his consent. While I hadn't revealed in the story anything regarding his true skills or profession, or the work he did for the Government, and even *as* the Government, the mere acknowledgement of his existence was something that had not been encouraged, and now it was on everyone's lips – for, he pointed out, it could not be denied that in death, his brother was far more known and popularized than he had been in life.

"I don't know if you're aware, Doctor, that a *mythology* is growing up around Sherlock's legacy. He's gaining the stature of legend – like Robin Hood and King Arthur. Many who knew him realize that they only had an inkling of the larger truth about what he did, and others are now convinced that he's a fictional character – a larger-than-life hero! And now I, who by necessity functions in the shadows, have been dragged into the light – written into Sherlock's story like one of the other Arthurian characters. It will not do, Doctor."

I had seven separate responses that all struggled for simultaneous expression. Some were irrelevant, such as a reminder to Mycroft that Holmes's recovery of the Mediobogdum Sword ten years earlier had more than confirmed Arthur to be a man and not a myth. About how I, as a free citizen of good standing, could publish what I wanted, when I wanted. As I struggled for a response, and as he waited for one, I did something that I had never done before, and never have since: I angrily turned without speaking and walked out on Mycroft Holmes.

I had already sensed that my writings were coming to an end – that was one of the things I might have mentioned to Mycroft that day – but instead I returned home, feeling angry, and also a bit betrayed. I had been writing these stories to let people know more about my heroic friend, and to make sure that he received credit where it was due, and I supposed that some part of me also wanted to please Mycroft as I honored his brother – especially since he himself didn't seem to be doing so. Now, in the first time the series of stories had been mentioned between us since their initial publication in mid-1891, I'd heard only criticism. I suppose that's why, to express my anger and independence, I next chose as the penultimate publication "The Naval Treaty" – a great triumph for Holmes, and also a previously unknown embarrassment for the Government. When that story was published, across October and November of 1893, I never heard a word from Mycroft, and a month or so later, when I re-encountered him on another matter, nothing was mentioned again of his appearance in "The

Greek Interpreter", nor the revelations exposed in the matter of the stolen treaty.

Mycroft Holmes's plans were always wheels within discs within hoops, and the person enmeshed in them was often unaware of how complex the arrangement might become. And now he was asking me to publish anew.

Holmes was watching me, no doubt reading a great deal of my thoughts as I recalled those events of a decade before. I nodded.

"In truth," I said, "Mycroft was quite unhappy about being mentioned in the story. I suppose one might say it's been our only argument."

"That was only half of it," said Holmes. "Oh, he was upset about the revelation of his existence to the wider world, no doubt. But he was also afraid that you might tell the rest of the story."

I raised an eyebrow. "There's more? What was left to tell? As you'll recall, months after the Greek man, Paul Katrides, was killed, we received a newspaper cutting from Buda-Pesth, telling how two Englishmen, travelling with a woman, had each been stabbed to death. While the police thought that they killed one another, you and I both agreed that Paul's sister, Sophy, executed both of them – Wilson Kemp and Harold Latimer."

"I don't refer to the resolution of the affair that we investigated at The Myrtles in Beckenham, where Katrides was held captive and then died. I mean the truth about Mr. Melas, the interpreter."

I simply looked at him for a moment, and then decided that I needed some more whisky, despite the fact that it was still a half-hour before lunchtime.

Returning to my seat, I simply waited and sipped. I knew that Holmes wouldn't have mentioned the matter if he didn't intend to expound upon it.

For most of the years that I've known Holmes, he has been reticent about considering past cases – even those that are very recently past. Something that he and I have just completed might or might not be discussed after the fact, and I have often had to work quite hard to get an explanation from him for my notes. Once an investigation is complete, it is filed away in his mental lumber room, there if he needs to recall some detail as it related to something that occurred later. Otherwise, he considers it nothing to waste time upon.

But there seemed to be one sure way to unlock his memory, leaving him in the mood to relate his past adventures – and that was to set him cleaning up his old papers and mementos. In year's past, I had heard some fine tales when he started sorting the tin box that he kept under his bed. The Tarleton murders, or the peculiar activities of the old Russian woman, or the young phantom mother of Skye. The strange reckoning of the five hoary bottles, or the events surrounding the *Gloria Scott*. The murdered man left in his Montague Street rooms, which so nearly cost him his freedom. The case of Vamberry, the wine merchant. The theft from the British Museum of the Eye of Heka. The aluminium crutch, and the club-footed man's wife, and the truth of Wade's Stone in East Barnby.

Now, Sherlock Holmes had been sorting papers all morning, and he was in the mood to tell a story – apparently a sequel or addendum to one that I thought that I already knew quite well. I settled back as he began to speak . . . .

Part II – The Truth About the Greek Interpreter

"You must remember that when you first met Mycroft, he was a bit leery of you. Oh, he'd heard of you from the earliest days, but there had never been any reason to introduce the two of you. In any case, as you've gathered, he values his privacy – and as you'd published your first story in late 1887, he knew that you wrote things in a frank manner – look at the way you described Lestrade, for instance – and there was always the threat that once you'd had a taste of having something published, you might do so again. If you didn't know who Mycroft was, you couldn't mention him – and he knew that I hadn't mentioned him to you."

I took a sip and didn't say anything. I had wondered why it took so many years for me to learn of Mycroft's existence. This was not the time to ask distracting questions as to Holmes's own motivations.

"When necessary," he continued, "I consulted Mycroft, and his armchair perspective was often quite useful to help me eliminate extraneous data and identify the one fact that I needed to find a solution. Occasionally, my willingness to get about and see things was of similar use to Mycroft, and he would direct a case my way which involved more effort than he was willing to expend.

"On the morning of the day that we've been discussing, he sent 'round a note requesting that I drop by soon to discuss just such a case. That evening, when you and I had the conversation that led me to reveal Mycroft's existence, it seemed like a good time for the two of you to meet, and so we walked to Pall Mall and you were introduced. Then Mycroft, without going into too much detail because you were unexpectedly present, explained the matter that he'd intended to refer to me: Mr. Melas' curious encounter with the two Englishmen who were holding poor Paul Katrides captive.

"As you'll recall, Mycroft sent a note across the street to summon Melas, who was an interpreter working around the law courts, and assisting foreign visitors at the various Northumberland hotels. He had taken rooms one floor above Mycroft's, and so they knew each other in passing. The previous day – a Tuesday – Melas had told Mycroft the curious story about how he'd been taken to a mysterious house just the night before and forced to converse with a Greek prisoner regarding the matter of signing over an inheritance."

I nodded. "It was fifteen years ago, but I still recall it quite clearly. Melas hadn't known where he was taken, and upon arrival, he was forced to interpret for the two Englishmen, Kemp and Latimer, while they tried to bully Katrides into signing some papers. Apparently Katrides had arrived in England from Greece, looking for his sister, Sophy, who was involved with one of the two men. Melas began inserting extra sentences during his conversation with Katrides and was on his way to figuring out the whole business when Sophy entered the room, shocked to see her brother being so mistreated."

"Exactly. At which point Melas was removed and subsequently dumped out at Wandsworth Common, from which he had to make his way back to London. The next morning, he told Mycroft about it, and Mycroft placed an advertisement in *The Daily News* and all the other daily papers of note, seeking further information about either the Greek prisoner or his sister."

"I wondered about that," I said. "It seemed rather careless of Mycroft to alert Kemp and Latimer that Melas had ignored their warnings to be silent, and that the affair was being advertised in the newspaper."

"Mycroft had his reasons, which I'll explain in a moment. What do you recall about the rest of the affair?"

"Well, the advertisement ran on Tuesday, and we met with Mycroft and Melas the next day. After we returned to Baker Street, we found Mycroft here – he'd beaten us back because we walked and he took a cab. I remember being surprised, as you had been at great pains to describe how he ran on fixed rails, and less than an hour after we'd left him, he'd run off in a completely unexpected direction."

"Because he'd had an answer to his advertisement."

"Exactly. Some man in Lower Brixton – Debenham? Davenport? I'd have to look it up – had written to say that he knew this Sophy Katrides, who lived at The Myrtles in Beckenham, and that he'd be happy to provide further details if we'd call upon him. Instead of going there, you indicated that it was more important to go directly to Beckenham. I suggested that we pick up Mr. Melas on the way, in case we needed an interpreter."

"And I thought that to be an excellent idea," added Holmes. "If you hadn't suggested it, I would have – but for an entirely different reason."

I turned my head with curiosity, but Holmes replied, "More about that in a moment as well. You'll recall that when we returned to Pall Mall, and climbed up to Melas' rooms, one floor above Mycroft's flat. The door was answered by a woman who told us that the interpreter had just left with a man who was likely Wilson Kemp. Thus motivated, we then went to Scotland Yard to retrieve an inspector, and had the misfortune to encounter Gregson, whose by-the-book attitude cost us an hour. I would have much preferred to recruit Lestrade, or even Athelney Jones – and in truth we should have gone to Beckenham without any officer with us at all. We might have been in time to interrupt the guilty party."

"Parties," I corrected.

"As you say," Holmes replied. "In any case, when we arrived, the house was dark, and all indications were that they occupants had flown, but we entered anyway, only to hear a moaning coming from one of the upstairs rooms, where we found Katrides dead, the room filled with poisonous charcoal smoke, and Melas there with him, seemingly at Death's Door."

"Seemingly?" I asked. "I'm beginning to vaguely see what you're driving at."

Holmes nodded. "As I've said, one can encounter a construct head-on, meant to convey a specific story, and just taking a step to one side or the other will reveal an unsuspected supporting structure, entirely unseen from the front, which then tells an entirely different tale."

I took another sip of whisky and then set my glass aside. "Let me see if I understand," I said. "Mr. Melas took rooms one floor above Mycroft's. Might I assume that he had done so not long before these events?"

Holmes smiled. "Correct."

"Something about Melas made Mycroft suspicious. And then, on the Tuesday before Katrides' death, Melas approached Mycroft, whom he barely knew – certainly one would suppose that he knew nothing of Mycroft's position with the government, considering Mycroft's discretion – and told him the strange tale of the summons to Beckenham and the mistreated Greek prisoner." I had been seeing it all again in my mind, and then I turned my focus back toward Holmes. "Melas was some sort of spy."

"Exactly. And he was trying to get close to Mycroft – first by moving into the same building where Mycroft resides, across from the Diogenes Club, and then by attempting to intrigue him with the story of his night trip to The Myrtles."

"But what was the purpose? Simply to forcefully accelerate some kind of acquaintance by way of the mysterious event? Or did they plan to lure Mycroft to Beckenham to kidnap or kill him?"

"Nothing so drastic as that," Holmes answered. "Melas had actually come across Kemp and Latimer by way of his work as an interpreter, which was his cover. He was a Russian agent, having realized that placing himself around Whitehall in such a position meant that he could involve himself in all sorts of matters that might otherwise be none of his business. People will confide in a doctor or a lawyer – but they will also reveal, without hesitation, the most personal things through an interpreter. Consider: You are in a foreign country with no knowledge of the language, and in situations that are bound to generate some degree of anxiety. Just as Melas said he worked in extra questions while interpreting for the Englishmen and Katrides, he could do the same for his other clients. An official might ask a normal routine question – place of residence, perhaps – and Melas could then add something about how much currency was the person carrying, where was it kept, and so on. In the course of his work, he was bound to come across agents of foreign governments, and in doing so, he could ask them the same sort extra personal and sensitive questions, but this time in relation to their nation's interests. It wouldn't always produce fruit – but it would often enough."

"So did the events described by Melas with the Englishmen and Katrides actually occur? Was the Greek man truly interrogated as we were told, in order to force him to sign the papers giving over the inheritance?"

"That part of the story was true."

"How do you know this?"

Holmes sighed. "It came out during Melas' interrogation. But I see that we're pecking at this from all different directions. I shall tell what happened in order, so you understand what occurred.

"Mycroft is a suspicious man – and rightly so. He would be cautious regarding anyone who moves into his building. When Melas arrived just a week or so earlier, he noted that the man was gregarious and friendly – and while that might be normal behavior, it was off-putting to a cautious introvert like my brother.

"Mycroft noted that Melas kept trying to find ways to instigate conversations. For instance, on occasion they would meet in the lobby, and it seemed as if Melas had been loitering just a bit too long – looking at his mail, or tying a shoe. As Mycroft is very fixed in his movements, it would be easy for someone creating an opportunity to talk with him to know when he would be arriving or departing.

"It was during such a forced and awkward and artificial meeting on Tuesday morning, in the lobby of their building, that Melas had related the details of his curious journey the night before. Mycroft found it most strange that Melas would choose him, a near stranger, to tell such a tale – particularly after the interpreter had been warned to keep the matter confidential."

"So to force the issue," I said, "Mycroft placed the advertisement in *The Daily Mail* and the other newspapers"

"He did. He didn't tell Melas that he would do so, either waiting to see the man's reaction when he read it for himself, or if nothing was said, Mycroft would contrive to bring it to his attention – especially if a response was received.

"In the meantime, Mycroft instituted a cursory investigation of Melas with his own resources, and he sent a message to me, asking that I come by when convenient to check into the matter of Paul Katrides. Although he didn't let us know at the time, he had verified that the two men, Kemp and Latimer, were traveling with a young Greek lady, so that seemed to give some credence to the story – and to imply that Melas was no more than an indiscreet and verbose neighbor. It was quite possible, Mycroft realized, that Melas had been telling anyone he barely knew the same story about his Monday night adventure. And so it stood when you and I dropped by the Diogenes Club on Wednesday evening. Mycroft was still waiting for developments, and Melas had said nothing about the advertisement.

"Mycroft found it intriguing that Melas, who learned about the advertisement when we did, and also that Mycroft had taken the additional steps of querying the Greek Legation, made no comment, and indeed displayed no reaction at all. One might expect that he would be concerned – Melas had been warned to keep his mouth shut, and the next morning, the business was being advertised in all of the capital's major newspapers. Surely if Melas was innocent, he would realize that he was in danger. Then, later, for him to actually willingly depart with Kemp, was quite unbelievable.

"The events of that Wednesday night moved quite quickly. If they had been more spread out, you would have needed to telescope them into a single night when you came to write it up – but fortunately it played out rapidly. Mycroft received a reply to his advertisement – almost immediately after we and Melas had departed from the Diogenes Club. It advised us that the solution was in Beckenham. We then learned that Melas had been taken to Beckenham, and we rushed there, to find Katrides dead, and Melas himself in nearly the same state – or so we were led to believe.

"In actuality, as soon as he left the Diogenes, Melas sent a wire to Mycroft, supposedly from J. Davenport in Lower Brixton, setting us in motion. It worked out well for Melas that Mycroft went to Baker Street while we meandered in that same direction. Then we spent more time returning to Pall Mall, where the woman who answered Melas' door gave us the important news that he had inexplicably returned with one of the

138

villains to Beckenham. Finally, we gave Melas even more time to carry out his plan by making a long detour by way of Scotland Yard.

"Later, during his interrogation, Melas confirmed all of this. Working for the Russians, he had come across information regarding Mycroft and his unique position, and he had set about getting closer to him, without realizing just who he was up against. He had been legitimately approached by Harold Latimer at his Pall Mall rooms on Monday night, and taken mysteriously to The Myrtles, where his interrogation of Paul Katrides occurred as described. But Latimer didn't realize that when hiring an interpreter, he'd also found a trained Russian agent, and Melas wasn't as helpless or confused as he implied. He knew, or worked out, where he'd been taken. The next morning, he realized that this curious story might be a way to open a door with Mycroft, and so he told him the story, setting in motion the events that eventually involved us.

"Melas was quite surprised on Wednesday evening when a note arrived, inviting him across the street to the Diogenes – and even more so to find us there. He had no choice but to tell his story and see which way the wind was blowing. Realizing that Mycroft had already initiated the investigation, and that I would carry it further, he decided to take control of the story. When he sent the wire to Mycroft from J. Davenport of Lower Brixton, he also sent one to Harold Latimer at The Myrtles, supposedly from another member of Sophy Kratides family, indicating that a number of Kratides would be there in the morning for a reckoning. Then he left for Beckenham.

"As expected, Latimer, Kemp, and Sophy had already departed, getting away ahead of the falsely arriving relative. But Melas was surprised to find that they had left Paul behind, in a room with a charcoal brazier. Paul was already dead, and Melas decided to wait and see if we took the bait, and he was beginning to despair that we would show up when finally we arrived in the cab, having made the final half-mile dash from the Beckenham Station. He waited upstairs, hidden, while we searched below. Then he began to moan, attracting our attention. When he was sure we were coming up, he slipped into the poisonous chamber where we found him, and by the time we 'rescued' him, he was showing symptoms of carbon monoxide poisoning, although not to a fatal level.

"When Melas had recovered, he told the false story of how Kemp had arrived in Pall Mall earlier that night and threatened him into accompanying him. He also told the fiction of how he'd had a second interview with Katrides before being shown one of the newspaper advertisements and condemned for his treachery. Mycroft and I both understood that he was lying. If he'd been in the same poisoned room as

Katrides for so long – even considering the Greek's weakened condition – he would also have been long-dead by the time we arrived."

"I should have thought of that," I said.

"You were simply trying to save a man's life," countered Holmes. "You didn't know that he wasn't really dying."

"You spoke of an interrogation?" I asked. "Where all this was revealed, I presume. Was that the next day?"

"Not at all. In fact, as far as I was concerned, other than to satisfy a few minor points with Mycroft about our interpretation of the events, I was out of it. Mycroft viewed this as a golden opportunity. Here was a Russian agent who had gone to a great deal of effort to get in Mycroft's good graces – apparently successfully. They had shared an adventure with one another. Mycroft worked out with his superiors a great deal of false and misleading information to feed back to Russia by way of the little interpreter. All the while, he was gathering information about him – his background, his contacts, and so on – so that there was nothing unknown about him, or how he would react in any given situation.

"This went on for a number of years – until September 1893, as a matter of fact, when you published your account of 'The Greek Interpreter' in *The Strand*."

This caused me to sit a bit straighter. "Ah. So Mycroft was perhaps less worried that I'd revealed his existence, and instead that I'd drawn attention to one of his ongoing plots."

"I expect so. I only heard about it some months later, after I'd returned to London and was catching up on what I'd missed. I'd long known that Mycroft was making use of Melas, and I asked if that was still the case following your exposure of those earlier events."

"And that's when Melas was interrogated? After the story was published?"

"It was. Melas' usefulness had been declining for a while, and it was decided to bring an end to the matter, in a useful way. You'll recall the woman we met at Melas' rooms in Pall Mall?"

"I assumed she was some sort of housekeeper."

"No. She was actually his mistress – and something of a minder, set in place by his superiors. When it was decided to stop using Mr. Melas, Mycroft saw to it that the mistress – who went under the name Mrs. Burnside – learned of Melas' other mistresses. All three of them. Apparently she had feelings for the man that were beyond professional. She was already disposed to be angry with him when further word reached her that he had been turned by the British and was now a double agent."

"Holmes," I said, somewhat shocked. "You marked that man for death."

"Not me, Watson," he said. "I was out of the country then. And as I've told you before – in Mycroft's world, there are no nice Rules of Engagement. His work isn't a cricket game. Melas was a spy, and as such, he deserved to be treated like one. He had thought he was clever, but he vastly underestimated his opponent, and he was completely outplayed. Just before the Russians were about to kill him, at the direction of his mistress, he was 'rescued' by Mycroft – leading to the interrogation I mentioned. That's when Melas explained the entire sequence of events on that September night in 1888. Then, he was returned to his flat – right to the front door and the custody of Mrs. Burnside – by two well-known British agents. I imagine that he declared his innocence to her, but how could he explain that he'd just spent two days in British custody without telling her why? In any case, his body was found in the Serpentine the next morning. I don't believe that it received much attention in the press, so it's not surprising that you missed seeing any mention of it.

I sat quietly, considering what I'd heard and the questions that surfaced in my thoughts. Rather than ask them, however, I thought back to other times when Holmes had hinted about his own activities while abroad during his Hiatus, acting for Mycroft. He'd spoken once about how, during those times, he occasionally had to leave behind the skills of consulting detective and, working as an agent of the British Government, he'd had to function much more coldly as a "blunt instrument". I realized that, with all of my curiosity regarding Holmes's past cases, there were some that I never wanted to know.

I cleared my throat. "Mycroft mentioned that he thinks we should publish a dozen cases in the next year or so. I think – " I caught Holmes's eye as I said it. "I think that I'll be certain not to select any of them where Mycroft had any involvement – because what I think that I know about it might be completely incorrect."

Holmes smiled and nodded. "That's a wise sentiment. The only difficulty lies in being certain that Mycroft didn't actually have any involvement. You might be surprised."

That gave me pause. "Don't say that, Holmes. I might be forced to reevaluate everything that I've ever thought that I knew. Good Lord!" I added with a *faux* worried expression. "Do you think that Grimesby Roylott was actually one of Mycroft's men, living in seclusion so that he could keep watch on the Japanese Ambassador, who was himself living secretly near Stoke Moran so that he could dig a tunnel to invade the Aldershot Garrison?"

"Close, Watson," Holmes replied, a twinkle in his eye. "But Roylott was actually a Fenian Freemason who was going to fill the Devil's

Punchbowl with dynamite, with the intent of blowing it into space on the Queen's next birthday."

I laughed and reached for my whisky. I knew that I'd consider further the curious affairs of Mr. Melas at a later time, but for now, Holmes resumed sorting his documents, and we continued to reminisce about past events. I glanced around at the long-familiar room, still looking much the same as it always had. I knew that Holmes planned to retain it when he departed for Sussex, but it would never be the same, and I had to wonder how I would feel the first time I came back when it was no longer his home, but simply another of his hidey-holes, those hidden places dotted around London where he could change his disguises or lurk unseen when he didn't want to be found. These rooms somehow deserved better than that – but time marched on, and nothing lasts forever.

Just a few weeks later, on the eighth of October, a tragic event hundreds of miles away (which I don't propose to further explain here) set in motion a series of events which accelerated Holmes's retirement and departure quite abruptly. Holmes had to leave early for Sussex to make sure that his new home – his "villa" as he called it – was fully prepared, and I went to Baker Street to finish some of his packing for him. The sitting room was emptier than when I'd recently visited, and there were a number of boxes already sealed and ready for shipping. One was still open, and as I set about closing it up, I saw laying on top an old brown copy of *The Daily News* – containing Mycroft's advertisement of 11 September, 1888, asking for information about Paul Kratides.

I'd recently met with Mycroft several times to discuss the new publication of additional stories, and the first had already appeared in America, with hurried illustrations completed there by an artist named Steele, and likewise in Britain by my old friend, Sidney Page. Several times I'd wanted to ask Mycroft about the additional events concerning Mr. Melas, but I'd refrained, as it felt that, once cracking open that door, I would be unable to stop from going further – asking about other cases, and possibly finding out things that I did not want to know.

I dropped the old newspaper into the box and closed it up. Some things are better sealed away and sent on to another place. I could be satisfied with that.

The *Vodou* Drum

Chapter I – The Curse

I folded my stethoscope and stood upright, looking down at the man in the basket chair. "I'm not telling you anything that you don't already know."

He nodded and looked rather embarrassed. "You are correct, Doctor. I'm afraid that I'm not the best patient."

"Do you take your prescribed medication?"

"I do, but my current condition isn't simply due to my heart. It's become worse, for I must admit: I am living in fear." He lowered his gaze. "Terror, actually. I'm normally not one to seek help, but I don't know what else to do."

"Hopefully we can be of assistance," said Alton Peake, the noted consulting spiritualist – invited as I had been to Baker Street in order to hear the visitor's curious story. Peake was a good-natured and sympathetic man, and his presence would certainly go a long way as a calming influence.

I glanced over at Sherlock Holmes, seated in his favorite chair near the chemical table, with one of the windows overlooking Baker Street behind him. The afternoon light limned his outline, leaving his face in shadow except for the sharp expression of his eyes. He had watched with great interest as Mr. Clayton Enderby had paused almost as soon as he'd begun to relate his story, asking for a moment while his heart calmed itself.

As I'd risen from my own chair and begun to examine him, grateful that I had brought my medical bag with me, I had a chance to evaluate the famed author. I had read all of his books, insightful tales blending the harsh truths of everyday life with notable characters and mysterious happenings, all presented in a way so as to pull the reader ever-forward. Some critics had compared him to a modern Mr. Dickens, and there was always talk in some quarters that Enderby should be recruited to write a continuation and conclusion of Dickens' unfinished final novel, *The Mystery of Edwin Druid.* I hoped that someday he'd be convinced to undertake the endeavor.

Enderby was a solid fellow in his mid-fifties, just a few years older than Holmes, Peake, and me. His hair was cut short, as was his beard, and though both had once been dark, there were now sprinkled with white threads. He wore square bifocals, and there were squint-lines rising vertically over the bridge of his nose. I knew that he'd begun his working career as a government employee before shifting to finance. All the while, he'd been writing during his spare time, and when finally he'd been bold enough to share one of his works with a friend, the enthusiastic encouragement he'd received had been enough to prompt him to submit it for publication. After that, one book followed another, with his novels becoming something of a vast tapestry – the main character in one story appearing as a background character in the next, while similarly someone of only passing interest in this year's book would soon become a fascinating featured protagonist, showing how everyone is interconnected, and everyone's life is a fascinating story in some sense.

From all that I'd heard, Clayton Enderby was a well-respected, intelligent, and jovial individual, popular and confident in all aspects of his life. While he was a successful author, he'd continued with his modest regular employment, regularly turning out new works composed in his spare time. It was hard to reconcile that successful and steady image with the frightened man who had chosen that afternoon to visit Sherlock Holmes, full of apologies for immediately collapsing back into his chair in fear and pain.

After receiving a note from Holmes that morning, I'd rearranged my schedule to attend this appointment. I'd planned to stop by that afternoon in any case to see how Holmes was recovering, as he'd recently been in a scuffle while retrieving some documents related to the fiasco connected with Joseph Chamberlain's resignation as Colonial Secretary, ostensibly due to trade policy disagreements with the Prime Minister, but actually because of far grimmer issues. A number of other Cabinet ministers had ended up resigning as well, and the uncertainty was making the Government nervous. Holmes's brother, Mycroft, from his curious position at the center of the Government's web, had sniffed out the real reason – a nasty bit of blackmail.

Sherlock Holmes never had any use for blackmailers, and Mycroft less so. Together the two of them had set about correcting the course of the Ship of State as best they could, but their plans hadn't taken into account the fact that politicians cannot be trusted to follow directions or take matters on faith that appropriate steps were being taken, and when two of them decided to make their own separate arrangements with the blackmailer, cracks appeared in the Holmes Brothers' plan. Only by swift action, and with the unexpected assistance by a formerly discredited Freemason, was Sherlock Holmes able to avert a far greater crisis – although he would carry the aches and bruises of his encounter with the blackmailing brute, Vickers Natterson, for several more weeks.

I was initially unaware of that investigation, as my practice in Queen Anne Street, where I'd been for nearly a year following my remarriage, took up much more time than I would have liked – although my wife was pleased enough with my new success. Too often, I found that patients invented reasons to visit – a false cough isn't difficult to spot – so that they could say they'd met Dr. Watson, the friend of the famed detective. (Some even spent their time looking around, as if they expected to see Holmes dramatically burst into the consulting room, seeking my assistance.) It was a far different sort of practice than those which I'd maintained years before in Kensington and Paddington – seeing patients and making rounds. Now I spent most of my time indoors, and I felt more like one of the "celebrity" doctors I'd secretly despised for so long as they built their practices in Harley and Devonshire Streets, becoming some sort of personality cult for the upper class rather than actually practicing medicine.

Still, I was actually able to act as a physician more often than not, seeing people with real illnesses who needed my real help. And I did enjoy when my wife and I often walked the few hundred feet or so east to the Langham for afternoon tea –even though it wasn't as often as I would have liked. I also found time to drop by Baker Street to visit with my old friend and join him regularly on his investigations. He reciprocated by visiting Queen Anne Street to recruit me when he needed assistance – sometimes vexing my typically tolerant wife.

I had managed to get out and go on rounds that morning, and had been in Bickenhall Street after eating a quick lunch and then visiting my last patient. I arrived as planned at 221b just before one o'clock. Using my old key, I let myself in as I often did, greeted Mrs. Hudson, and climbed upstairs to the sitting room, where Holmes was sitting in his chair and discussing a pair of photographs – one of a man ostensibly dead since the 1860's, and the other of what seemed to be the same fellow from just a week before – with Peake. I knew the details of that curious inquiry, and Holmes was stating while nodding my way, "Politicians are never to be trusted, Peake – but there's no need to belabor that point to you, after what we saw during the affair of the lighthouse and the *Phalacrocoracidae* – " when the doorbell rang.

In the years that I'd either lived in or visited those rooms, I'd had the chance to listen to thousands of individuals ascend from the hallway below, first a rise of nine steps, turning at the landing, and then eight more to the space outside the sitting room door. Some visitors bounded up, while others climbed steadily. Others paused – sometimes on the landing to catch his or her breath while looking out the window at the plane tree in the rear yard, and occasionally elsewhere along the climb. Some tarried on nearly every step, which was useful when deducing that they were in poor physical condition, but not so helpful when listening for an indicative limp, or a telling squeaky shoe, or a left foot with an inward twist.

We had no more than introduced ourselves and settled in to hear Enderby's story than he expressed the need to pause for a moment, leading to my examination. Now complete, I replaced my stethoscope in my bag and remarked, "I trust that your regular physician is aware of these symptoms, and that you're receiving proper treatment?"

He nodded. "I've had the symptoms for several months. My doctor has prescribed nitroglycerin."

"And do you take it as directed?" I asked.

He lowered his head. "When I can. Sometimes I'm rather busy and lose track of things . . . ."

"Mr. Enderby," I said, with all the stern physician *gravitas* that I could muster. "tachycardia and atrial fibrillation cannot be ignored. Untreated, they can lead to apoplexy, and you wouldn't want your gifts snuffed so needlessly."

He nodded, and then added, "But it's only become worse in the last few days, Doctor. Since I've fallen under the curse. Before then, the condition was so insignificant that I barely paid attention to it."

I had my doubts whether a curse, as he believed, could only recently cause the racing and lurching heartbeat that I'd just heard, but before I could query him further about his medical history and what might have caused such a dramatic presentation, Holmes – the man with whom Clayton Enderby had journeyed to consult – took over the conversation.

"You mentioned in your note that you were the victim of a curse, and now you suggest that it's affecting your health. I must inform you that I have no patience for supernatural explanations, but in deference to your reputation, and that you might not be as gullible as such a belief would imply, I've asked our friend, Alton Peake, to join us."

He nodded toward Peake, seated to the side on the settee. "Mr. Peake is a noted investigator of this type of thing," Holmes continued, "and, while we don't always see eye to eye, he has specialized knowledge which could be of great use."

"Holmes mentioned your belief in a Haitian *vodou* curse," explained Peake. "I'll admit that's something that I've had less experience with than some of our homegrown manifestations, but I have read a great deal. There was the Liveson affair of '79, when the family of eight was found dead in their sitting room in Camberwell, all staring in terror at a small doll lying on the table, an effigy of the father, pierced through the heart with a pin." He glanced at Holmes. "You'll recall that we disagreed on that one – I speculated that it did have an effect, functioning as something of a substitute golem for the victim, while you showed that the married daughter was responsible, but in the end, I was still proven – "

146

Enderby shook his head and interrupted. "I'm afraid that I haven't heard of that one, Mr. Peake. And after my youthful visit to Haiti, I've done quite a bit of research, and know of these *vodou* dolls, although I never saw one for myself. No, my curse has taken the form of a drum – the same rhythm I heard so many years ago."

Peake sat back. "I know something of these drums. Fascinating."

"This curse," interrupted Holmes, resuming control of the conversation. "Why do you believe such a thing is occurring?"

"I have no idea. I traveled to Haiti when I was nineteen – thirty-nine years ago – and I heard the drums then, on one terrible night. Since then, I've lived my life here in relative normalcy and only studied Haiti occasionally, as having been there, I found that it interested me. I know a bit more about the country than when I went, but I'm no expert. Over the years, I've occasionally recalled the drums – after all, it's an interesting anecdote to tell people that I've heard *vodou* drums – but I have no idea why they recently began sounding outside my own home."

"When?" asked Holmes, leaning forward and reaching for his pipe.

"Six days ago. It was at night, actually, as one would expect. I live in a small home with a bit of ground around it, in Hampstead. The house is on Hampstead Lane, situated in the southern portion of Bishop's Wood. My writing has provided me with extra income, allowing us to purchase the property over ten years ago. We're quiet people, my wife and I, and it's just the two of us – our son is grown and gone – and we have no servants. Our routine is quiet as well. I return home from my work each night, we eat the meal prepared by my wife, and then we adjourn to the study, where I write while my wife occupies herself nearby with her book, or sewing, or whatever other interest she has at the moment.

"It was just such a night last Thursday – six days ago, as I said. It was getting late, near the time when we go to bed, that it began – softly at first, no louder than the sounds of the traffic that we now hear through the windows. I wouldn't have given it any thought at all, except we're well back from the road, and typically we near no noises at all, except for those of nature – wind, birds, thunder, and rain. We were quite fortunate to find such a little sanctuary so near London, but now after nearly a week of the drums, I realize just how remote we are – only a hundred yards from the road or our nearest neighbors, yet if we're in danger, it might as well be a hundred miles.

"It was actually my wife who noticed it first, thinking that something was rattling in the wind – a loose gutter, perhaps – although there was no wind to speak of that night. We tarried for a moment as I also heard it, and it was a moment longer before I realized that I knew what it was – a peculiar and regularly repeated syncopation that I hadn't heard in nearly forty years – a Haitian *vodou* drum.

"The rhythm is unmistakable – " And here he paused to tap out an odd and rather unnerving beat upon his chair arm, the thumps lurching and then hurried, and not following the typical expected regularity of those we know and absorb in our Western music. The pattern would at times seem disjointed and irregular, but then it would begin anew, and one could see that there was a plan to it, a meaning that eluded understanding. In spite of our setting – a warm sitting room in the heart of London in autumn 1903 – I felt the hairs raise on my neck, as if the beat itself could somehow summon the attention of a creature or some other entity that had ignored us until now, but upon the repetition of the rhythm, it had *heard* . . . and it was coming.

I glanced at Peake, who was leaning forward with great interest, and he was trying to mimic the pattern with a finger upon his leg. Holmes, meanwhile, had his eyes shut, clearly committing the sequence to memory.

"Was it just the one drum – with one tonality," he asked, "or were there multiple drums of different sizes, so that the beats almost had a musical quality, playing different notes?"

"Just the one," answered Enderby, finally ceasing the skin-crawling thumping. I could only wonder if the sound had travelled down the chair and into the floor, and thus through the ceiling of Mrs. Hudson's parlour just below. I wondered if she, not knowing what the patterns represented, had felt the same unease that had just gripped me.

"I have read," added the client, "of different types of *vodou* drumming – with multiple drums, as you describe, and also of faster rhythms with increasing speed, wherein those listening are prompted into some sort of ecstatic frenzy. But this was the steady beat I've demonstrated, not much faster than a resting heartbeat."

In fact, I thought, it resembled something of the man's lurching tachycardia that I had just heard through my stethoscope.

"And this was the beat you heard as a young man in Haiti?" asked Peake.

"It was. It once played incessantly throughout one long terrible night, worming its way into our minds, and thus I when I heard it again last week, I recognized it instantly."

"You said it remained steady in tempo," asked Holmes, rising and reaching for his violin. "Did it increase in volume?"

Enderby simply shook his head, watching curiously as Holmes raised the violin and began to pluck the E-string, accurately reproducing the rhythm the older man had just demonstrated. Somehow, this was even more unsettling – as if the pattern had been given a voice. He then shifted to the higher A, D, and G strings, repeating the pizzicato upon each until I felt my teeth clenching. Then, suddenly having satisfied himself, Holmes stopped, replaced the violin against the mantel, and reseated himself.

"You went outside to investigate?" he asked.

Enderby nodded. "I was unnerved, and concerned about someone trespassing upon my property, so I told my wife to wait and went rushing outside without further thought – and without arming myself. I went through the back door, as the rear of the property was where the drums seemed to originate, and it's also the most wooded part, adjoining the larger forest to the northwest.

"The drums were louder outside, and coming from the trees that grow beyond the house. I had no light with me, and as my eyes adjusted, I only saw various shades of darkness. But as I stepped in that direction, the drumming ceased. I went back inside, retrieved a lantern and a heavy stick, and returned to the woods, entering by one of the walking paths that cut through there. I looked around for several minutes, seeing and hearing nothing, and suddenly I thought that perhaps that this had been some sort of method to decoy me away from the house, where I'd left my wife alone and defenseless. Abandoning my search, I fled back to the building and up the steps, only to find her, frightened, and no intruders. I returned to lock the back door, and that's when I saw the note, left lying on the outside steps. I had missed it during my initial race to get back inside."

He reached into a pocket and pulled out a folded page, which he handed to Holmes.

I could see that it was a quarto-sized sheet, yellowed with age. "This has been dampened at some point," said Holmes. "It has old stains and ripples. Is this the way you found it?"

Enderby nodded. "It was also folded that way."

Holmes opened it and examined front and back. "'*Leave your Haiti journal on the step – Tell not that story.*'" He read it aloud and then looked up. "Written with a thick pencil in block letters, straight across the page – no rises or dips – and well-spaced. What is this journal?" He reached across to hand the note to me, and when I'd looked it over, I passed it along to Peake.

"When I went to Haiti, I kept a journal – it was encouraged, and I was glad that I did it, as it's my memento of the trip, full of daily descriptions of the events and people, as well as sketches of scenes that I observed."

"'*Tell not that story* – ' Is it your intent to write a book about your Haitian adventure?

"It is – I'm in the preliminary planning stages – outlining and researching and so on. This reference in the warning is another mysterious feature of this whole business. I've kept the knowledge of the next book to myself – even my wife never knows what I'm writing about until I've finished – so I don't know how this intruder knew my plans."

"And did you leave the journal on the steps?"

"I did not. The idea of capitulating to the demands never even crossed my mind."

"Demands? You've said that the drums have played each night. Have you also received additional sheets?"

"I have. I'd hoped that this was a one-time thing, so I wasn't prepared when the drums began again on the second night. My lantern and stick were still by the back door, however, so I went out, only this time to find a note on the steps before I descended." He reached into another pocket and pulled a small folded sheaf of papers. "These are all of the rest of them."

Holmes also looked at these before commenting, "Same paper and pencil, and the exact same message. There are no threats, and no escalation of urgency. Why did you keep the first separate?"

"I've read of your methods. I suppose I thought that it might have some different significance – as if he wrote it, thinking that one warning would be enough, and then he was forced to write more, and the repetition would show some clue that he took time to avoid in the first."

"Unfortunately, he was remarkably consistent – each is equivalent to the first. But that also indicates that it's the same person, and the chore of writing new notes isn't being passed from one person to another. Did you go forth to examine the woods?"

"I did, and the drumming ceased when I reached the tree line. The next day, I asked my only close neighbor if he had heard the sound, and he replied negatively, but gave me a queer look, as if I was losing part of my mind – so I haven't asked him again.

"It was much the same on the next nights. On the third, I watched from the back window near the door to see who left a note, but no one approached. Later, when the drumming started, I found the note on the path to the woods. On the fourth, I left the lantern outside, far enough back from the house that it illuminated both the steps and the path. When the drums started, I rushed out to the woods, and it stopped, and I found no note – until this morning, when I discovered it on the front steps, on the opposite side of the house. On the fifth night, I wanted to wait outside in the darkness, to see if I could sense anyone moving about as he approached the house, but my wife begged me to stay indoors. I must add that she is becoming more and more terrified as this affair progresses, as she vaguely understands the nature of the drums and their connection to my Haitian voyage. I relented and stayed inside, and this morning I required that she go to visit her sister in Hornsey until the matter is resolved.

"Then, as I had the house to myself, I waited outside, as I'd intended for the night before. But my efforts were wasted. The drums began and I moved about in the darkness looking and listening for any signs of someone going by me to the house. But I heard nothing, and after a few minutes, the drums stopped. I lit my lantern, explored the woods without any success, and returned to the house. The most recent note was lying by the back door, the same as the first had been. It was then, Mr. Holmes, that I decided to seek your help. My wife can't remain at her sister's forever, and I have no intention of relinquishing my journal. I am acquainted with the Hendons of Thornton Heath, and know what you were able to do for their unfortunate daughter. It was with this in mind that I sought your time."

"The journal?" asked Holmes. "Is it still at your house?"

"It is. Perhaps I should have taken it with me to-and-from my employment, but I feared that I might be waylaid – for whomever wants it seems quite intent on getting it, and a violent attack probably isn't beyond the realms of possibility. But I've hidden it quite well at home – no one will find it very easily."

"Good. It's not long after midday, so we have time to make plans before this evening's performance – and there will almost certainly be one. It's unlikely that after six days your persecutor will stop for the seventh."

At this point, Peake cleared his throat. "I'm sure that we'll resolve this matter tonight – Holmes is very good at what he does, and the fellow behind this will certainly be caught – but I would be interested in hearing about your Haitian voyage, and how you first came to hear these drums so long ago."

Enderby nodded, and looked toward Holmes, as if to seek permission. My friend nodded. Having traveled quite a bit myself, and having once passed through that part of the world in my youth, I was quite interested as well, and I felt that we needed to know the historical background to understand what was occurring now at the lonely house in Hampstead.

I stood and asked if anyone wanted something to drink. After serving each of us with something from the sideboard, we settled in to hear Enderby's tale. Alton Peake sat forward the entire time, alert and fascinated at hearing of a visit to another land and culture. At times I think Holmes became impatient, but he listened intently nonetheless throughout to pick out the relevant threads as the author wove his tapestry.

Chapter II – The Recollection

"For you to understand the drums," Enderby explained, "and why this current experience makes so little sense to me, I must tell you how I journeyed to Haiti, and my naïve perspective as a young man. In 1863, I was but eighteen years old, and in my first year of University. Like so many, I attended because it was expected, but I had no true idea of what I wanted to do with my life. I had read a great deal, but felt that I'd seen very little of the world. It was then that I learned of an opportunity to serve as a missionary to Haiti on a short-term basis. It seemed like the perfect way to expand my horizons.

"I was raised in one of the churches belonging to the Baptist Union of Great Britain, and I continued to attend while in school. I had been vaguely aware that my church had a strong sense of mission, donating to the less-fortunate in other countries, and even sending members overseas. When it was discussed that the next trip being planned was a return to Haiti, where they had been twice before, I was suddenly interested and set about seeing if I could volunteer.

"I was only doing it because of the promise of adventure, but I believe the members of the church felt that I'd been called to life-long religious service. I wasn't truly aware of that at the time, but in hindsight, I'm sure that's the only reason why I was allowed to go. On two previous occasions, a group of eight men had taken a substantial portion of their time and sailed to Haiti to do God's work. The entire idea of the church's support of Haiti, and of sending men there to provide physical and financial assistance, had come about because a career-long Haitian missionary, Jack Hedford, had come to England and spoken to our church, along with a number of others, seeking support.

"At first my participation was discouraged, but I stuck to my guns, and they relented, making arrangements for nine of us to make the journey this time instead of eight. Throughout the winter, we met in their homes every few weeks, getting to know one another, and planning for the trip. It was strange in a way – I was not much more than a boy, and the youngest of these other men were in their forties, with the oldest over seventy. One of them, Mr. Birch, had been a former teacher of mine, and it was odd now be interacting with him as an adult. In truth, I felt like I was playing a role, trying to be an adult when I often felt like a child inside, but I've learned that many feel the same way throughout their entire lives.

"Curiously, my parents were unexpectedly supportive of the trip. Perhaps they also mistakenly believed that I wanted to be a missionary, but I suspect that my father admired my desire to see the world and wished a bit that he could have gone too. They, along with my sister, were both

152

there at the dock to see us off in the spring of '64, along with the wives and families of the other eight men. I had just turned nineteen a few weeks earlier, but I was old enough to appreciate that I was actually setting off on a great adventure – an opportunity that many would never have.

"If you sailed anywhere in the 1860's, then you recall just how unpleasant it was. The journeys were long and dangerous. With today's steamships, able to steadily make the crossing to America in little more than a week, the age of the great sailing ships is already a memory, only to be experienced vicariously in novels. But it's something that I'll never forget, and I'm proud to say that I tolerated the voyage well enough. Some of the other eight men suffered. Able Welsh, the oldest of us, was seasick the entire time. I truly feared that he might die, and I'd never seen a man with purely blue lips before. Another of the men, Lawson Roberts, was a doctor, and he spent a great deal of time helping Old Welsh pull through.

"We finally docked in Virginia – and recall, this was in the middle of the American Civil War. The harbor was filled with the Confederate traitors' warships, but we were only there long enough to shift our meagre belongings to another vessel that had been arranged to meet us. We then sailed south along the coast, and it was early in hurricane season, but fortunately we had clear weather. I stood day after day watching to the west, occasionally catching glimpses of the American coastline. The air became warmer and more tropical, and one of the sailors told me that within a few days we'd be docking in Port-au-Prince. When we finally saw it, however, I was still amazed, watching our destination grow larger and larger on the horizon.

"The next day or so was a blur. We were met at the docks by the missionary, Jack Hedford, who helped us get our supplies loaded onto wagons. By the time we were finished, it was evening, and we still had ten miles to travel north along the bay to where we'd sleep for the night. As we traveled, I couldn't see anything in the dark, but the smells were overpowering, and both terrible and wonderful at the same time – damp jungle odors overlain with rot, and a constant smokiness that settled in my raw throat. We finally came to an inn, lit only by a couple of dim lanterns, and we gratefully tumbled into our waiting beds, assured by Jack that he'd guard our supplies through the night.

"The next morning, I walked down to the dock, wondering just what I'd gotten myself into. There was a small wooden boat, no more than fifteen or twenty feet in length, already piled with our supplies – including our heavy wooden crates of construction tools. There was no true mast. Instead, where one should have stood was a great upright tree-limb, tacked into place with supporting boards. With the supplies, three or four sailors, the nine of us from England, and Jack Hedford, it seemed that the boat was dangerously overloaded – and yet a number of other locals standing on the dock tried to climb aboard as well until Jack chased them away. Finally, with great but unexpressed trepidation on my part, we untied the ropes and set sail for La Gonave, just a hazy bump on the horizon.

"The excitement quickly overcame any uneasiness that I might have felt. We were nothing more than a cork bobbing on the vast sea, riding unimaginably blue waves up and over that were taller than our little boat. I had wisely placed myself on the stern, so that as we rocked from side-to-side to climb and drop along the waves, my motion was considerably less than the others – many of whom became quite seasick before we were done.

"After several long hours, we docked at Anse-à-Galets, a little village on La Gonave, situated around a tiny bay that was more tidal flat than deep water. We jumped into the task unloading the boat and shifting our cargo to wagons. The we climbed aboard, fitting in as best we could around the boxes, for the final push into the interior of the island, leaving the sea behind as we began a hot and tedious climb along barren and sandy hills, switching back and forth along 'roads' that were little more than eroded pathways. Often we had to climb down and push, as the slope and weight were more than the little donkeys pulling the wagons could overcome. Finally by late afternoon, we reached our remote destination: Petite Source, a tiny village of only three buildings – if one could call them that – resting at the foot of one of the larger mountains on the island, Morne Petite Source. This, then, would be our home for the next few months, and where we would build a church.

"It wasn't long after our arrival that I felt guilty, as it seemed that our presence was already a sore drain upon their resources, and more than whatever value we could provide to them by our labors. The main building was a four-room house made of wattle and daub, wherein a wooden lattice is constructed – the wattle – to form the walls. This is then daubed with a sticky material usually made of some combination of wet soil, clay, sand, animal dung, and straw. The building had been set aside for our use. I was later to learn that the family that lived there had moved out to give us the space, and that they had bartered dearly for the new sheet-metal roof which reflected brightly every day in the hot Haitian sun. A couple of other wattle buildings were on either side, and these had doors with shiny padlocks on the rough doors. It was here that the village kept their valuables – namely, their meagre supplies of grain, doled out each day for making bread. Close behind the main building was a cistern, and the narrow door on top had a lock on it as well.

"Jack Hedford introduced us to the four people with whom we would have the most dealings over the next months – I say four, but in reality, one of them proved to be rather sadly insignificant. He was a small man, the owner of the main house vacated for our stay, and the theoretical leader of the village. He looked to be ancient, but I was later to learn that he was just in his mid-forties, his figure wasted away by a lifetime of hard work and terrible conditions. He stepped forward and shook each of our hands with a very grave and sincere welcome, speaking some words in the Haitian Creole that conveyed welcome, even if their exact meaning was unknown.

"We next met his wife, a big stout woman in a white shirt, gray skirt, and blue kerchief on her head. We would come to learn that she, in truth, was the matriarch who ran the village and the immediate surrounding countryside. I never learned her name, unfortunately, but I've never forgotten her. She was grim, as one would expect in that life, but it wasn't long before she betrayed flashes of humor.

"Next was their daughter, Marulla, a beautiful girl of twenty-five or so, as I later found through my limited conversations with her. She had moved to Port-au-Prince several years before to work and obtain money for her family, but during the course of our stay, she'd returned to Petite Source to help do any extra work that we might generate, such as assisting in the preparation of meals, and dealing with our laundry.

"Finally, standing to one side, was a tall and lanky young man, also brought over from the capital by Jack Hedford to act as a translator – as Marulla's English was quite limited. His name was Daniel – pronounced *Dan-yell*, in the French way – and he was twenty-one. Over the weeks that we were there, I made friends with him as best as I could, considering the language barrier – he wasn't that good of a translator – and the vast differences in our backgrounds.

"That night, countless Haitians gathered around as we settled in, and I understood how creatures in the zoo feel. They were lined up a dozen deep all around the little porch in front of the main building where we sat or prepared our evening meal or readied our tools for the morrow's work. As the sun went down, more and more of them arrived, lining up around us deeper and deeper, but never making a sound. The night was soon as dark as a mine pit, and I had no idea how many were watching, waiting for us to do . . . something. Anything. But eventually, and probably to their disappointment, we went inside and settled in to sleep.

"We quickly settled into a routine that remained mostly unbroken day after day. I was amazed at how small our world became. Petite Source was probably no more than six or eight miles inland as the crow flies from Anse-à-Galets at the sea, but the distance had to have been twice that when traveled by trail to climb into the mountains. By the following daylight, and with a bit of time to look around, I could see the mountain rising to

155

the west of us behind the main house – Morne Petite Source – and that on the opposite side, far away down a long slope to the east and barely visible in the haze, was Anse-à-Galets. As we discovered, beginning in the middle of each night and lasting until mid-morning the next day, a stiff and steady wind would arise from the sea and up along this miles-long slope to our village, often becoming quite cold. La Gonave, in spite of being a Caribbean island, is very much like a desert, with the drastic daily changes in temperature that one finds in such places. We froze at night, and roasted in sunlight.

"Across the road from the main house was a wide field, stripped of vegetation by roaming goats. It was here that the church would be built. Our own church back in England, along with supplying missionaries, had provided funds to construct the new building. Additionally, Jack Hedford had hired local crews to come do much of the actual skilled work, while we provided assistance and more technical skills as necessary. Not long after sunrise of our first full day there, Jack's crew came walking down the road, carrying tools and whistling some local song. I had seen where a number of timbers had been previously brought in and stacked behind one of the side sheds – these would be used for building roof joists. There were also bags of cement to be used in construction of concrete blocks that would form the walls.

"I've since learned that the construction methods used for that church were dodgy at best, and would make an engineer cry. The locals began mixing up the cement with local sand and stones, and then putting the mixture in molds that they'd brought to form the concrete blocks. After just a few minutes, they'd remove a block and leave it to stand, dry, and harden in the sun. Typically, concrete needs a month to reach full strength – but these blocks were used after just a day or two of curing.

"My jobs as an able-bodied nineteen-year-old varied. Mostly I carried things – bags of cement, buckets of water, and finished concrete blocks to the work site, where other locals were mortaring them into place. The original church had been nothing more than a structure of sticks marking the area and providing a bit of shade. They hadn't even used any homemade daub to make it more permanent. The new church was being constructed around it.

"We settled into a routine – making blocks, laying course after course as the walls rose, constructing roof joists for when they'd be needed, and then relaxing in the evenings. Dr. Roberts would see patients at night – mostly children, some with terrible injuries that he couldn't treat, such as open wounds covered with gnats, or one lad who'd burned his knee in a fire. The skin had healed too tight, and he couldn't bend his leg without it splitting open each time. There were many children who showed signs of malnutrition, but their mothers sought medical attention with the faithful hope that the English doctor could do something just by putting his hands upon them.

"I became friends with all the men – Old Able Welsh and my teacher Mr. Birch and Doctor Roberts. The Bills: Bill Brewford – the youngest of them in his early forties – and Bill Brown. Harrison Tipton, an engineer who worked out the best way to build the roof joints, and David Mayer, the father of one of my old school friends who took me under his wing. Perhaps the only one that I didn't get close to was the leader of our little band, Reverend Garrison Anderson, the assistant minister at our church who led these mission trips."

(At the mention of Reverend Anderson, I saw that Holmes showed a flicker of extra interest, perhaps only obvious to me, but he didn't interrupt Enderby's narrative.)

"They were all good men," continued our visitor, "giving of their time and energy to help this little village in the middle of nowhere that no one had ever heard of. You'll never find it in any reference book, and it will never be important for anything, but for a time, it was our entire world.

"The days rolled on as the church grew, and anything that broke the monotony was of great interest. Water was always of great concern. As many of the trees had long-since been cut on La Gonave, it never seemed to rain. Apparently Petite Source was named for a small spring, but I never saw exactly where it was. We had been in our routine for so long that when clouds began to build one afternoon, it seemed to shock us into a new wakeful feeling that we hadn't felt in weeks.

"The wind continued to rise, and the clouds became blacker and blacker. Dr. Roberts was running everywhere, urging everyone to gather whatever containers we could find to catch the coming cloudburst, but actually the locals were already doing so. I worked with Daniel and Marulla to fix a bent gutter that led into the cistern, while others were tying down our supplies from the now gale-like wind. But soon we were forced inside, as the storm began to throw sizzling lightning bolts all around us, one after another, more than we could count. The cracking and deafening thunder from each crash ran together into one long explosive rumble that seemed to last more than an hour. The entire hillside around us seemed to be struck over and over, and we nine huddled in our main building, aware of the sheet metal roof above us that seemed likely to loosen and blow away at any second.

"Eventually the storm passed, and – to our great disappointment – there had been little or no rain at all. Just the terrible electric force from the skies – more destructive than we initially realized.

157

"An hour or so after the storm finished, the last bit of daylight returned, along with great cries and lamentations from someone down the path leading to the village, getting closer with each minute. Daniel stepped that way to converse with some of the locals who were congregated there, whispering, as the wailing voice along the trail came closer. Then he returned to tell us what was happening. During the vicious lightning storm, a boy of eight or so had been killed. Amazingly, he was one of five brothers, and three others had also been killed by lightning in recent months. The boy who had just died had been treated by Dr. Roberts for an infected wound only the night before, and now the last surviving brother, a man of twenty or so, was on his way to confront us, believing that somehow we were cursed, and responsible by our presence for the death of his last brother.

"I noticed that as we heard this story, standing there in the dirt clearing before the main building in the last of the day's light, each of the men in our group seemed to pull in a bit, crossing their arms defensively, and moving a little closer to one another. Before we had a chance to ask further questions, a party of locals came into view along the trail to the south. In front was a tall young man, raising his voice and raving at the heavens. When he saw us, he leaned forward and began to walk faster in our direction. I saw a liquor bottle of some sort in his hand, and he raised it to take a drink as he approached.

"When he was just fifteen or twenty feet from us, lurching our way with mayhem or vengeance on his mind, he was suddenly stopped by the appearance of the matriarch, along with her daughter, Marulla, who both stepped directly into his path. He bobbled to a halt and said something, a sob in his voice that became a snarl while pointing our way with his free hand. I have no idea what he said, but the matriarch raised a heavy arm and slapped him, twisting his head violently sideways. Then she swung her arm again, knocking the bottle from his hand, where it landed to one side and shattered on a stone. She grabbed his collar and shook him, and then slapped him quickly twice more before he cried out and collapsed in a heap at her feet, wailing and shaking his fists at the sky. Some of the men in the group who had been following him stepped forward and dragged him upright, and then pulled him back the way that they had come. But several of them looked back over their shoulders in our direction, and their expressionless and judgmental faces were more terrifying than if they too had been glaring at us with rage.

"'She said that he was embarrassing the village,' explained Daniel. 'She told him that we did not cause the death of his brother, and that to threaten the nine of you – or to curse God as he was also doing – was a sin that she would not tolerate.' He didn't provide any further explanation.

"Reverend Anderson tapped Daniel on the arm to join him, and then they walked over to the matriarch and Marulla. As they conversed in low tones, the rest of us, by unspoken agreement, adjourned back to the main building. Surprisingly, there was no conversation, as everyone seemed to be turned inward. I would have expected much more discussion in a frantic manner, such as what would have occurred at school if something like this happened, but these men reacted in a different way. Later, Reverend Anderson joined us and pulled a couple of the older men aside, whispering, but the rest of us weren't included in their counsel, and we drifted to our sleeping spots.

"The next day was subdued, but the work continued as normal. By now the roof joists were in place, and as work continued on the walls and placement of sheet meal on the roof, a number of us gathered rocks which we tossed into the church's interior to serve as a floor. After hundreds – likely thousands – of rocks had been brought in, we set about leveling them, bending and fitting the rocks in such a way that they compacted and didn't roll when walked upon. Perhaps it was because I was so involved in this that I didn't speak to any of the others that day, and didn't know what was going on or being discussed.

"The day progressed as usual, and that night we were preparing our evening meal when the sun began to drop behind the mountain to the rear of our building.

"It was then that we heard the drum.

"We had become so accustomed to the sounds of the village – the wind, the hammering and construction sounds during the day, the conversations and voices of both the locals and the men from England – that anything like this would be unmistakable. It started as a simple steady beat – *Boom Boom Boom* – every few seconds. Everyone within sight, locals and visitors, came to a halt in their tracks and looked upward toward the mountain. Somewhere up there in the blackening shadows, the drummer was maintaining a vigil of sorts, his efforts magnified acoustically by the downward slope that carried the sound directly toward us. At first it was simply unusual – almost too strange to understand, but vastly primitive in a way that sent chills along my spine. I didn't realize what it was – I just knew that it was different. Then Daniel softly explained, '*Vodou*.'" There was fear in his voice. "The drum plays for the dead boy – and as a curse.'

"Marulla scolded him, saying something in Creole in a scathing tone that made Daniel wince. Her meaning was clear, but he didn't retract his statement, instead looking at each of us meaningfully, as if willing us to understand him, even if he couldn't explain further.

159

"The drum had started with a steady beat, continuing in this way for an hour or more, as the sun finished its descent and the village darkened. A number of locals, more than usual, gathered at either end of the clearing where the trail vanished in two different directions, but they only talked amongst themselves and came no closer. We went about our usual nightly tasks, and then at some point, the rhythm changed – subtly, but no longer the steady beat that had almost matched a resting heart rate. Now it quickly modified and became more complex – what I demonstrated for you. It took on extra, irregular pulses, seemingly random, but then repeating after a moment, as if there was a longer pattern than we are used to comprehending in Western music. It got under one's skin and could not be ignored.

"Reverend Anderson was in and out. He spent quite a while talking with the matriarch and Marulla, along with Daniel and a couple of the older men in our group. Finally, when the sun was fully set, he returned and gathered us close.

"'There is danger here,' he said. 'We've decided to leave at first light. The native workers can finish what's left of the church without us. There will be a wagon in the morning. Pack only what you need – we'll leave the tools and crates. We'd planned to do so anyway,' he added when Bill Brown started to protest. 'The journey back will go much more quickly, as it's downhill to Anse-à-Galets. With any luck, we'll be back across the bay and in Port-au-Prince by nightfall.'

"The night was long and cold, and the drum never wavered. The complexity of rhythm it had maintained became our only reality. We would have known if it changed – as if someone counted from one to six over and over for many hours, and then suddenly skipped the number four. It seemed that every repetition conjured some evil and terrifying image in my mind – which was certainly the drummer's intent. This was only intensified by the cold wind blowing up the long draw from the sea.

"We agreed that having faith in God to protect us, while of great value, wasn't enough, as God helps those who help themselves. With that in mind, we armed ourselves as best we could with our more dangerous tools and set shifts as guards – but the fact was that none of us slept. All night the drum continued, and that pattern became unforgettable. To this day, as you saw, I can reproduce it.

"Our escape was something of an anti-climax. The matriarch had a wagon waiting for us in the morning. Some of the villagers were there to see us off, and they didn't have the cold antagonistic expressions of those who had been watching us from a distance the night before. They reached out to touch us, whispering prayers and blessings in Creole, their words a mystery as always but their expressions caring. Daniel climbed up to join

160

us, but of Marulla there was no sign. The last I saw of any of the villagers, or the church we'd labored to build, was when our wagon turned on the northern trail, and the matriarch was waving goodbye.

"We crossed from Anse-à-Galets to the main island within a few hours on the same decrepit boat, although I have little memory of it, and then sent word to Jack Helford, who came to escort us back to the capital. We spent several days there sightseeing while our early passage back to England was arranged, and then we said goodbye and sailed for home. The members of the church – and my family – were surprised at our early return, but we reported that the work had gone quickly and we'd finished ahead of schedule. We'd agreed that it would be better not to relate the danger from the drums, as it would worry our families and the church, and future trips might not occur. Instead, we said that since the church was finished, there was no need to stay and keep being a burden on the village in terms of them being displaced or finding us water.

"And so life went on. In a year or so, there was something of a schism in our home church, wherein Reverend Anderson – respected by a great many of the congregation – left to start his own church. I returned to university and my church attendance dwindled and then stopped. Many who had thought I was being called to be a missionary seemed to be disappointed when that didn't turn out to be the case. Over the years, I believe that most of the other eight men who made the trip have died, and I haven't had any contact with them in longer than I can remember."

Chapter III – The Resolution

"Your journal," asked Holmes. "You recorded all of this?"

"I did. I'm able to recall it so vividly now after so many years because I recently re-read it as part of the research for my new novel."

"You say that most of the other men have died," asked Peake. "How do you know?"

Enderby shrugged. "Various ways. I heard long ago by way of my late parents that some of the older men had passed. Over the years, I've seen obituaries in the newspapers."

"So their passings were widely spaced, as far as you know," clarified the consulting spiritualist. "None were recent, or could have been connected with any sort of curse."

"That is my belief. But again, I really know nothing substantial about any of them since our last real contact in the mid-1860's."

"And Reverend Garrison Anderson?" I asked, glancing toward Holmes, who had showed interest when the name was mentioned. He gave a small nod in my direction.

Enderby frowned. "I haven't heard that he's died – but if he's still alive, he must be nearly eighty by now."

"He is," confirmed Holmes, standing and walking to his shelf of scrapbooks, on the wall to the rear of where I was seated. After thumbing through them for a moment, he related, "You are correct. Born in 1825. Associated with various churches from his twenties onward. Widowed in his mid-forties – never remarried. Currently the minister of The Baptist Temple at 14 Shouldham Street since 1876. I've noted that he is something of a king in his own little kingdom."

He closed the book and returned it to its place, and then reached for another. He brought it back with him to his chair and sat, opening the book upon his knees.

"*Vodou*," he said, flipping through the pages and loose sheets tucked between them. "Watson and I have had our share of past encounters with this curious religion. The dockland murders – remember those? The affair at the lodge in Eccles, where we found evidence of a *vodou* sacrifice." He tapped a finger on the book. "I pasted in my notes from Eckermann's invaluable volume. There was the matter of Lady Chatterley's *vodou* dolls, and the matter between Professors Tarrington and Collingwood. There was that confounded affair of that *vodou* woman and the Betrayer Moon – Don't smile, Peake! – and Watson and I won't soon forget Dominic Langley, the sugar merchant's son. There have been several others as well – " He shut the book with a snap. " – but nothing along the lines of what we've heard today." He looked toward Peake. "I'm sure that you have more specialized knowledge on the subject."

The spiritualist investigator nodded. "There have been some instances where *vodou* – or imperfect attempts to copy it – have been noted here in the capital, but for the most part, it hasn't taken much hold in England. It's uniquely Haitian, there's no real Haitian community here. It's a curious mixture of Roman Catholicism and traditional African religions, wherein the African divinities are equated and substituted with Roman Catholic saints.

"Those who practice *vodou* see no contradiction between their religion and the Christian aspects that are infused into it. There are good features to it, in that it can be used to promote healing and cleansing of the spirit. But there is a dark side as well that has gained the most attention. There are those who use it for divination which, as we know from their counterparts here in England, can be used to manipulate and cheat believers. There are the sacrifices of animals to obtain desired outcomes, or to appease the *vodou* saints. There are the curses – such as the *vodou* dolls and fetishes, and also through the use of the drums. And then there are the terrible bogey-man stories of the *vodou zombies* – the reanimated walking dead, similar in some ways to the vampire stories found 'round the world, and particularly in the Eastern European mountains."

"And your personal thoughts about it?" I asked, knowing that Alton Peake was quite willing to expose charlatans, but he also kept an open mind.

"There are more things in Heaven and Earth, Watson," he quoted, "than are dreamt of in our friend's philosophy." He jerked a thumb in Holmes's direction with a smile. "I have *seen* things that defy the dictum that 'No ghosts need apply.'"

"Ha!" said Holmes, rising to his feet. "A discussion for another time." He walked to the shelf and returned the commonplace book to its spot. "Right now we're considering Mr. Enderby's situation. More research is needed, but I have the beginnings of a plan in mind."

"You already seem to have some idea about all this, Mr. Holmes," Enderby replied. "I can't imagine what you've heard in my story that might provide you with an understanding about what's going on."

"I believe you overestimate my grasp of the affair," countered Holmes, "but I do have an intimation where answers can be found, and certain aspects can be examined more closely. In truth, however, the only way to move forward is to catch this *vodou* drummer in the act." He looked at me, and then Peake. "The man will certainly be back tonight. Can you join me in setting a trap?"

Peake said, "Of course," and I added, "I've made arrangements to be free for the rest of the day."

Holmes nodded. "Then we should each pursue our different lines. Peake, can you delve more deeply into this *vodou* business? Clearly in this case it's only a contrived intimidation to obtain the journal, but the method presents certain curious aspects. And Watson – can you accompany Mr. Enderby back to his home in Hampstead and retrieve the journal, and read through it to see why it might be of interest?"

"Certainly."

"Excellent!" He turned to Enderby. "When you sent your wife away, was it obvious to anyone watching the house, or did you do it discreetly?"

"The latter. As nearly as I could arrange it, I've left the house with the impression that she's still there during the day. I have an excellent set of locks on the doors and bars on the windows – the house is rather lonely, after all, and I wanted my wife to feel secure – so anyone trying to get in would find it difficult, and he or she certainly believes in any case that my wife is still in residence."

"And there have been no signs of attempted entry?"

"Not as of this morning."

163

"Good. When you both retrieve the journal, get in and out as quickly and quietly as you can. Our drummer is unlikely to be watching during the day. Leave the impression that your wife is still at home. Then adjourn to The Spaniards Inn and wait until Peake and I join you – around sunset, I think. That should give us time to complete our research and get the pieces in place." He looked at the three of us. "Any questions?"

"Mr. Enderby," I said, shifting forward in my chair, "you indicated that you haven't mentioned plans to use your youthful Haitian experiences in your new novel, but I do recall from your most recent book, *The Regent's Solicitations*, published just a few weeks ago, that there is a minor character, Davison, who references in passing a similar trip to Haiti while in his teens. Knowing that you reuse background characters in following novels as the main protagonists, is this fellow to be the main character in your new book?"

"He is, and bless me, Doctor, and that's very perceptive of you. I'm thrilled to learn that you must have already read the new novel."

I nodded. "I enjoy your books a great deal, and I picked up the new volume at Hatchard's in Piccadilly on publication day."

"Thank you for mentioning that, Watson," interjected Holmes. "That small fact has some bearing on my thinking."

"That this recent interest in the journal only arose when someone saw a mention of Haiti in the new book?" asked Peake.

"Exactly. Are you sure, Mr. Enderby, that no one knows of your plans for the next book and its Haitian theme?"

Enderby sat back and thought for a moment, slowly shaking his head until he suddenly seemed to remember something. "I was at a small gathering at a bookstore in Bloomsbury, answering questions about the new novel, and I told the store owner that I was researching my next book. I explained that in addition to my own journal from when I traveled there in my teens, I might be interested in seeing what they had that was available in terms of a Haitian history volume to supplement my own journal and already-gathered materials. Perhaps someone who was there overheard me mention the journal . . . ."

Holmes nodded. "Quite possibly. Now, if there's nothing else, let us separate to our various tasks. Peake and I will arrive shortly after sunset. Then we'll let this drummer walk into our trap."

We all put on our coats and hats and trooped downstairs together. Outside, Holmes and Peake set off walking toward Marylebone, bent together in conversation, while Enderby and I found a hansom for the long climb to Hampstead.

Having traveled across much of the world in my youth, and a few times to that part of the world, I was full of questions, and Enderby was

164

happy to provide more information about his past journey to the little-known Caribbean island.

"My first full day in Haiti was quite a surprise. Remember, I was just a lad who had barely traveled around the southern parts of England. When we arrived at our destination the night before, it was dark. Only when I awakened could I see just how foreign this land was to my experiences.

"We were up early that first full day for the final push to our destination. As I mentioned, we were to sail fifteen or twenty miles to La Gonave, an island situated in the middle of the bay, which is rather shaped like a fish surrounded by crab claws on that end of the main island of Hispaniola, where Columbus first landed in 1492. Haiti occupies the western side of the island, and the Dominican Republic takes the eastern – and much more prosperous – half. But prosperity isn't safety, as the Dominican Republic was involved in a war just then. Fortunately, it didn't spill over into Haiti, which had its own problems.

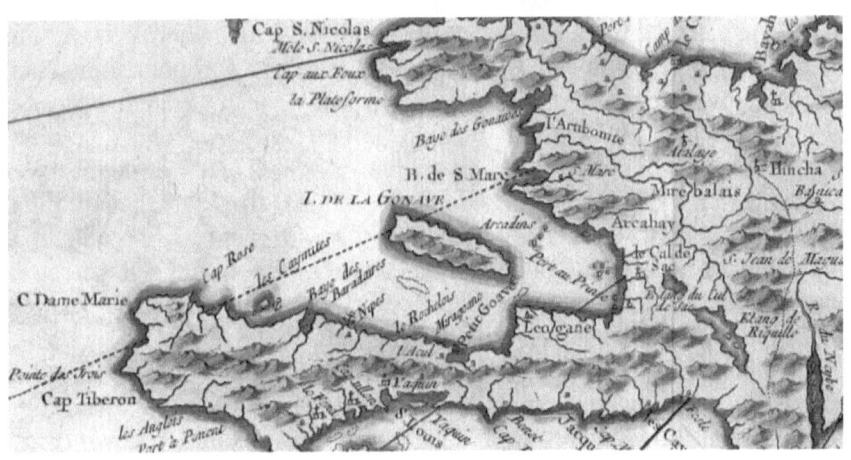

Haiti and La Gonave

"Much of the island, and particularly La Gonave, was already irrevocably damaged then by all of the logging that had been done for decades to build ships. I'm sure that it's only worse now. The climate had changed, leaving it quite barren and brown – not what one would expect to find in a Caribbean island, and quite different from the Dominican Republic not that far to the east. The Haitian people live in incredible poverty, and La Gonave is worse than the rest of the county – not even acknowledged by the official government, and receiving little or no assistance. This was where the missionary, Jack, had asked us to go and serve.

165

"A part of me had wondered about these mission trips that had been supported by our church, and what I'd find when we arrived. There had been some joking during the months of preparation about how we were secretly going to Monte Carlo or some other pleasant spot, but in fact we were visiting a most unpleasant and possibly dangerous place. The eight men, all of whom had businesses or comfortable positions that allowed them to leave the country for several months at a time, were truly dedicated to the work, as I quickly saw, and their willingness to return on multiple occasions spoke well of their character."

He went on to describe the monotony of the days as work continued to build the little church, and also what they did to have a bit of fun.

"One day, David Mayer and I took the afternoon off to climb the mountain behind us, giving us a wonderful overall view of how our village lay in relation to the surrounding countryside. The view down to Anse-à-Galets was much clearer up there as well. On another day, we were running short on water – always a concern, especially as so much was being used to make concrete for the blocks, and also simply for the visiting water-fat Englishmen. We obtained various buckets, pitchers, and gourds, and set off to the north to another village to buy water – much to the displeasure of the matriarch, who felt that such work was beneath us and should be left to the women. (That was according to Daniel, our translator.) We walked through several other villages of equivalent sizes, and then through a market town of twenty or more buildings, all of which were selling vegetables, before finding a house with a cistern that would sell us water. Carrying it back was much worse than you can imagine, especially, as we had wandered so far to find it.

"Occasionally the village was visited by agents of the dictator's secret police. The mood was always subdued during that time, and I was dimly aware that there was a feeling of danger in the air, but nothing ever came of it, and eventually the policemen would wander on, either on foot, or riding on donkeys.

"And still our routine continued. I became strong and brown and slept wonderfully each night. I made friends with many of the laborers, and we tried to communicate – although I suspect that the Creole phrases that they taught me were off-color, for their own amusement. The more I got to know the men from our church, the more I knew them as people. They often surprised me – also occasionally telling humorous stories, or simply sharing aspects of their normal lives that they found frustrating. As a nineteen-year-old, it was a very surprising and important introduction into what it meant to be an adult.

"Things that had bothered me at first – gigantic insects and massive tarantulas hiding under every surface and in each nook and cranny –

become nothing more than things to be ignored or brushed aside. I thought of home, realizing that wars could have begun and family members lost and we wouldn't know the difference. The days ran together, and by the time of the storm, and the drumming, I'd lost track of how long we'd been there, and how much longer our journey was intended to continue. Each day was so much like the previous one, and it was a simple life with clear tasks from sunup to sunset, and then deep dreamless sleep."

He then asked me about some of my own experiences, as he'd read my published works and picked up on the hints and allusions to past adventures of my own. The conversation then turned to writing methods, and how he strictly plotted each of his books, with strands stretching forward and backward into his other works, while I recorded actual events, but necessarily changed names and dates on occasion to protect the innocent from needless scrutiny and exposure of their secrets. And so we whiled away the slow journey northwest into the higher elevations above the Thames valley.

We reached Whitestone Pond, and I glanced to my right, along East Heath Road, as I always did when passing this way. I couldn't see Charles Augustus Milverton's old house, but I would never forget that night, and how Holmes and I had kept to the shadows before returning to this intersection, to then make our way more sedately back toward Hampstead village. Then our hansom turned on Spaniards Road alongside the Heath, and our conversation resumed.

We passed the inn and continued around to the northeast. Soon Bishop's Wood stretched away to the north, and not long after, our weary horse turned down the lane indicated by Enderby, bringing us to a most tidy little house tucked in the trees and set well back from the main road.

Asking the cabbie to wait, we walked to the front door, while I looked around, hoping to see if we were being watched. There was no sign of it, as the forest was deep and dark on nearly every side, and I could only trust Holmes's idea that no one would be observing us at this time of day, several hours before the drumming typically began.

We stepped inside, and from the entryway I could see that it was a well-kept abode. Mrs. Enderby had a good sense of what made a nice home, and I knew that my own wife would enjoy my descriptions of it. Alas, I was unable to see very much of it, as Enderby excused himself and went upstairs to retrieve the journal, leaving me alone by the front door. He returned in just a moment, and then we stepped back outside. He locked the door, tested it, and we returned to the cab. Our travel back along Hampstead Lane and then to the Spaniards Inn went quickly and, after Enderby paid the cabbie a sizeable amount and tip, we went inside, finding a quiet corner and ordering both cider and a late but hearty lunch. And there we spent the afternoon and early evening, Enderby making notes on a manuscript that he had also retrieved from his home, while I read the Haitian journal.

I could see very quickly that Enderby's description of his earlier self as "naïve" was accurate – and I wondered if it was still true. Certain things that he had recorded when he was nineteen seemed to leap off the page, and yet he hadn't mentioned them, implying that he hadn't read between the lines in his own journal. Borrowing a sheet of blank paper from the noted author, I made a number of notes to share with Holmes when he and Peake arrived later that evening.

The time passed quickly enough and, after completing my examination of the journal, I shared a long conversation with the innkeeper, an old friend who I had first known in the late eighties when Holmes and I, stopping at the Spaniards for a restorative whisky, had been drawn into the unexpected rescue of the man's daughter, taken as leverage to force him into providing an alibi for a planned jewel theft. He had been grateful ever since, and it was always a pleasure to renew our acquaintance.

Just before sunset, Holmes and Peake arrived, and with them was Inspector Youghal, whom I hadn't seen in several months. Holmes introduced him to Enderby, and while our client repeated his story for the policeman, Holmes, Peake, and I spoke quietly at the bar.

"Only two of the original nine church members to make the trip are still alive," Peak related. "Welsh, Birch, Roberts, and Tipton were all around seventy or older in 1864, and have passed away from natural causes. Brown and Mayer were in their fifties, and died in 1889 and 1893, respectively. Bill Brewford, the youngest of the adults on the trip, was only forty at the time. He died in 1877, having rescued three children from a burning building. While there wasn't time to fully investigate whether there were darker aspects to the deaths, it seems that there was nothing unnatural about any of them – and there were no signs that any type of *vodou* curse was involved."

"And Reverend Anderson," I asked. "The other survivor? Holmes, you had him documented in your scrapbooks for a reason."

"Quite true. He has come to my attention before, although there has never been a way to bring charges against him. The man has had a history of molesting women from the churches where he's been a pastor – although the laws and the circumstances have conspired to allow him to get away with it. I've been keeping track of him for several years, after first becoming aware of him in the mid-nineties by way of a story told to me by a despondent maid who needed my help. I knew that Anderson's day would come, and when I heard his involvement with this affair, I

168

thought that now might be the time. Hearing that he's the only other living member of the expedition besides our client is highly indicative."

"And what you've stated fits with what I read in Enderby's journal," I said softly, going on to explain that Enderby himself didn't seem to realize what he'd innocently observed and recorded so many years earlier. I flipped open the sturdy book and, referring to my notes, showed Holmes page after page of where Enderby had noted that Reverend Anderson appeared to be paying a great deal of unwanted attention to the young lady, Marulla, who had returned to her village to help with the care of the visitors. "All this, plus the many occasions where he documents Anderson's many off-color stories and jokes, paint a vivid picture of the man that is much more rounded in a dark way than the simple mentions of his presence when Enderby told us of the trip."

Holmes nodded. "Excellent, Watson. This explains why the journal has assumed such importance, and augments what facts I was able to discover with my own research."

I nodded toward the inspector across the room. "So Youghal's presence means more than the simple arrest of the harassing drummer."

"Indeed. The case may have international implications. In 1866, a Haitian man in his twenties named Daniel Toussaint arrived in Paris, attempting to find out about a group of Englishmen who had been on La Gonave two years earlier. Soon after they had left Haiti, the body of a young woman, identified as Marulla Laurent, had been found buried under a pile of stones near her village – in what passed for the local cemetery. Due to the remote nature of the area, and the Haitian government's indifference to La Gonave, attempts to obtain some sort of justice went nowhere. Daniel – who was certainly the translator described by Enderby – saved his funds and journeyed to Paris."

"But why didn't he go straight to England?" I asked.

"I would speculate that it was due to Haiti's long-standing relationship with France, from whom they gained their independence nearly one-hundred years ago. Perhaps he felt that France was the place to begin his search, and if he could get the French to take an interest, he'd have more clout when he shifted his efforts to England."

"But how do you know this?" asked Peake. "That's quite a bit of specific information to obtain in one afternoon."

"Watson and I are quite fortunate to know a most notable and gifted French policeman, François le Villard of the *Sûreté*. Over the years, he has become masterfully organized, and my shot in the dark in his direction paid off beyond measure. I had cabled him to ask if he had any records related to possible crimes in Haiti in 1864, and specifically taking place on La Gonave. I was simply hoping for any indication about some incident

169

that might have occurred then to explain what was happening now. I only asked to make sure that I'd looked under every stone, having no hope that anything useful would be uncovered. Luckily le Villard has an encyclopedic knowledge of the Sûreté's unsolved and still-open cases, and he recalled seeing a report from nearly forty years before about Daniel Toussaint's visit and how, when he wasn't satisfied with the indifferent French response to his queries, he'd indicated that he was next sailing for England. Nothing more was ever heard from him, and as relations between England and France were tense then – you will recall that Britain had refused to join the French plan to aid the Confederacy, afraid of assisting the Confederate traitors and angering the legitimate American government, and also England rebuffed Napoleon III's attempt to gain British support when he invaded Mexico to forcibly place his lackey, Maximilian I, on the throne. Thus, there was no follow-up to determine what happened to Daniel Toussaint."

I tapped the journal. "I fear that he came to a bad end."

"Very likely. And perhaps, after all these years, we'll learn what happened to him, and see justice for Marulla Laurent as well."

Holmes spent several minutes intensely reading through various parts of the journal, nodding occasionally and muttering to himself, while Peake related to me some of the additional details regarding the prosaic and uncursed deaths of the Haitian construction party. Then, when Holmes had concluded his research, we rejoined Enderby and Youghal, and Holmes noted that it was now dark enough for Enderby to start for home, as if returning from work on a normal day, and the rest of us to make the short journey to Bishop's Wood, where plans were already in place to capture the mysterious *vodou* drummer.

"Enter the house as normal," advised Holmes, "and then simply go about your business. You will almost certainly hear the drums begin anew. Don't leave the house as you have on previous nights. Instead, when we have the drummer in hand, we'll bring him to you."

"You know who it is, don't you?" asked the author.

"We believe so, and tonight should provide us with the evidence we need to see the end of this business."

Saying goodbye to the innkeeper, Enderby climbed into a nearby hansom cab while the rest of us hailed a growler. After letting Enderby gain a head start, we set out along the same route, and in less than ten minutes, we'd been set afoot a few hundred yards from Enderby's lane. Then, with Holmes leading the way, we entered the woods, stepping carefully through the ancient trees in the last of the dying daylight.

When we'd gone a distance from the road, Holmes drew us aside by a great oak and whispered. "I scouted the woods earlier today and found

170

where the drummer has been conducting his singular performances, and also the route by which he arrives and departs. It was then easy to set various Irregulars in place to catch him. When he begins, we'll interrupt the concert and drive him into our trap. Now, this way." And he turned and led us deeper through the silent forest.

Fortunately for that time of year, sunset was early, and it was a mild night. Holmes placed us behind several trees and indicated a general area toward the south where we should direct our attention. "Be careful when we go forward to capture him," he added. "Don't blunder into the Irregulars' trap."

I raised an eyebrow, which he saw but chose to ignore, my question being just what sort of trap to expect. I knew that he wouldn't say, too interested in providing a surprising performance, in the same way that a magician doesn't reveal quite what to expect until the trick actually occurs. I tried to imagine the Irregulars – that band of urchins who were so at home in the London streets, carrying out tasks as Holmes's agents – out here in the woods, seemingly far out of their element. Yet I knew that they were quite adaptive and clever, and whatever Holmes had asked of them would not be beyond their capabilities.

I have waited in many worse places, and the time passed quickly. It almost surprised me that we hadn't waited longer when the drum began.

At first, from somewhere ahead of us, it was a single beat, repeated as one monotonous tone at the pace of a resting heart. I tried to recognize if there were any added points of emphasis, breaking it into the rhythms recognized in the western world of the 4:4 march or the 3:4 waltz, but there was none of that. I had tried to count – "One – two – three – four" – but soon it became meaningless. The terrible insistence and pondering regularity began to cause an involuntary response – intimations of something older than man and his pitifully arrogant civilizations, built on darker foundations, with no true permanence. And then, when the beat had gone on long enough to cause my own heart to be synchronous with it, a complexity was introduced.

The steady pulse continued, but other flourishes were added – an extra doubling here, and preemptive strike there, sometimes doubled or tripled, but never quite in a way that could be predicted, or perhaps part of a bigger pattern than could be retained and recalled consciously before it began anew. It was the same as had been demonstrated in the sitting room by Enderby and then copied by Holmes – but now, in the dark and suddenly dangerous-feeling woods, it was real, and in my ignorance, somehow I understood.

I could only imagine Holmes and Peake's sharp interest as the complexity of the pattern increased, and I wondered what poor Youghal must be thinking. But I knew that the man was a steady as a rock, and with a rock's imagination as well, so I was certain that he was simply waiting for Holmes's call to action – and when it came, we were ready.

Ahead of us, as the drum continued its assault on our nerves and sensibilities, there was suddenly a high-pitched scream, and then another, followed by a dozen more. Enderby had mentioned nothing like this – surely it was the Irregulars, part of Holmes's plan.

It must have worked, because the drumming stopped. Even as Holmes yelled for us to follow him forward, I heard the sound of scrambling through the brush, and then a cry – from an adult, a man. The screams turned to boys' yells jeering and hollering with joy at the apparent success of their efforts. We entered a clearing just as a number of dark lanterns were opened to reveal a most curious site.

In a great arc on the far side of the clearing was a network of stretched ropes, tied from tree to tree, stretching from the ground to waist-height. Anyone running in that direction in the dark wouldn't have seen them, and would have been blocked from escape, bouncing back before understanding what had happened. On the ground nearby was a man, trapped under a great net, working frantically but uselessly to extricate himself, and hurling ever-stronger curses toward the dozen or so gleeful boys dancing around him. Nearby was a long drum, and as we arrived, one of the lads, taller than the others, leaned forward and stood it upright, giving three taps on the stretched skin top with his thumb. It was clearly the same instrument that had worked so effectively just minutes before – but now it was nothing but a curious artifact, diminished to insignificance.

Holmes and Youghal stepped forward, reaching across the net to lay hands on the trapped man's collar and yank him upright, while Peake congratulated the boys on their fine work. They calmed down to watch as Holmes worked the net from the captured drummer, revealing a heavy-set old man, his white hair wild upon his head, and a snarl of rage twisting his reddish features. He began to curse in a most un-Godly way, and Holmes gave him a shake.

"Not in front of the children."

The boys laughed, and then Holmes handed over the prisoner to the inspector and walked to the tallest lad. He provided words of praise, and then fished a substantial amount of coinage from his pocket, which was transferred to the Irregulars' current leader – an older boy named Creighton Cross. Then, their work done, they began chattering amongst themselves as they drifted away into the trees, back toward the road. In seconds, it was as if they had never been there.

Meanwhile, Youghal, who had cuffed the old man's hands behind him, stated, "You're fair caught, Anderson. Now let's go somewhere and talk about it."

With Holmes leading the way, we soon reached the back of Enderby's house, where we found a note on the back step – a duplicate of the six that had proceeded it. Holmes looked at it and then passed it to Peake and me without comment as we climbed the stairs and knocked on the door.

Inside, it took Enderby several moments to comprehend that we had a prisoner, and he had no initial recognition of the elderly and disheveled disgraced minister. Only when we told him who it was did he begin to see some points of familiarity.

"But why?" he asked the minister, who refused to look at him, instead muttering under his breath and invoking meaningless curses upon all of us.

Holmes then began to explain what he had learned earlier in the day, to Enderby's shocked amazement. When I pulled out the journal, Anderson became quiet, his eyes focused on it like some sort of lizard who is suddenly deathly still before striking. Youghal took a firmer grip on him.

As Holmes spoke, he shifted his attention from Enderby to Anderson. "The journal clearly shows your interest in the girl, as well as her distaste for your unpleasant regard. It's all recorded there, even if Mr. Enderby, at the age of nineteen, naively didn't realize what he was seeing, or if he gave you the benefit of the doubt because of his respect for your position." Holmes glanced at Enderby. "In your colorful recollections, you note that the hillside behind the village was dotted with various graves, randomly located instead of localized in a cemetery. You describe these as cairns, with the bodies covered by local stones, such as the ones you used to line the floor of the new church."

He shifted his attention back to Anderson. "Daniel Toussaint, your interpreter, came to Paris in 1866, two years after your visit. He reported that days after your group departed, the girl was discovered in one of these graves. Wild dogs had dug her up. She was horribly violated, and then whoever killed her had opened an old grave, placed her there, and then restacked the stones. Based on your history, Anderson, can there be any doubt of your responsibility – especially since you were instrumental in getting your group out of the country as soon as possible?"

"Girl?" replied the old man. "She was a tease – flirting with all of us. If there was a murder, it was one of the others – Brown or Tipton or Birch. Or this one!" he snarled, jerking his head toward Enderby. "He talked with her quite a bit, as I recall."

Holmes shook his head. "No. After you left your home this afternoon, you were followed on your various errands before winding up in the woods

173

with your drum." He glanced toward the policeman and then continued. "After you departed, I happened to find myself within your quarters, where I noticed that you also kept a set of extensive and well-hidden journals – going back well past 1864." Youghal pointedly ignored this bit of burglary, and Holmes pulled several little shabby and much-fondled leather books from his coat pocket.

"Men such as yourself," he continued, "need to relive their crimes. You're really quite proud of them – or so one would think, reading your rather prosy descriptions of what you did. You are especially boastful of how you killed the girl on that last night and then – cleverly, in your own opinion – thought of where to hide the body. I'm not sure how you contained yourself on the journey home, so thrilled you seemed to be at getting away with it and then successfully escaping. It almost makes the description of how you killed Daniel Toussaint in 1866, when he came to England to find you, seem dull and rote by comparison."

Anderson began to lunge this way and that, seemingly trying to pull his arms from their sockets as he jerked one and then the other, trying to retrieve the journals from Holmes's firm grasp. Youghal was compelled to restrain him more effectively, leaving the old killer gasping on the floor.

"I'll need to take your journal with me as evidence," explained the inspector to Enderby.

"Of course," eyeing it in my hands with great distaste. "I shan't be needing it back. It's of no use to me now."

I understood that whatever his next book would be, there would be no reference to Haiti.

Garrison Anderson's arrest set off a small hurricane of interest. There were international implications, as France was interested in his capture, and hoped to use the event to gain some goodwill between itself and Haiti, with help from England. Meanwhile, more and more women came forward to indicate that they, too, had been molested by the minister under the guise of "marriage counseling". In several cases, he had then blackmailed them, based on the situations in which they found themselves.

More information was uncovered related to Anderson's activities at the time of the "schism" described by Enderby at his boyhood church, a few years after the trip to Haiti. The principal minister at the time, Reverend Regal Black, had come forward to describe a number of rumors that had divided the church at the time, with many unflinchingly and ignorantly supporting Anderson in the face of certain revelatory accusations. All too often, ignorant fools follow blindly after immoral and evil men.

It was unclear what the immediate future held for the disgraced killer between his arrest and the hangman – Would he be held in England, or transported for trial in Haiti as part of some convoluted diplomatic arrangement?

In the end, he cheated all of the different outcomes. One of the women with whom he'd had a relationship, refusing to believe his guilt in the face of overwhelming evidence, managed to visit him in prison, bringing a double-dose of lethal cyanide. The two of them were found not long after her arrival, their limbs twisted in what must have been agony upon the floor, and their lips covered with foam. The woman's husband of thirty-two years was shocked, and he grieved for her terribly. No one was concerned about Anderson's fitting and long-overdue passage into Hell.

Holmes had confirmed that Anderson was visiting the Bloomsbury bookshop on the day Enderby that answered readers' questions, and it was generally felt that this was when he must have heard of Enderby's plan to use the journal for a future book – causing him to fear exposure, and to set in motion the bizarre plan to intimidate the author into giving him the journal. It was also agreed that if much more time had passed without result, Anderson would have killed again.

Before his death, Anderson never provided any information about his crimes, and Daniel Toussaint's body was never recovered.

Peake found a new interest in the practices of *vodou*, which stood him in good stead when he had call to investigate certain matters in the coming years. I maintained a friendship with Enderby, and was later surprised to find a disguised version of myself acting as a character in one of his novels.

And I accidentally learned some years later, without his knowledge that I knew, that Sherlock Holmes had made a sizeable contribution to a Haitian missionary organization in Port-au-Prince to see about making long necessary improvements and restorations at the small church in the village of Petite Source, on the much neglected island of La Gonave.

NOTE

By interesting coincidence, I was also able to make a trip to the small village of Petite Source on La Gonave, in Haiti, when I was nineteen years old in the summer of 1984. Even more coincidental was the fact that I accompanied eight older men from my church who had made the same trip several times before. In fact, my journey mirrored Enderby's pretty-much exactly – without any murders – except that I traveled from eastern Tennessee instead of England.

On our second day in Haiti, we departed the main island from a dock near Port-au-Prince on a small overloaded sailboat with a tree limb for a mast (See Photo 1 – that's me in shorts and T-shirt at the left edge of the stacked boxes). Once on La Gonave, we traveled to a small three-building settlement where we helped to build a church, replacing the existing stick structure (Photo 2, with the home-made days-old cinder blocks going up around the existing stick building). The village really did have a matriarch and her aged-before-his-time husband (with whom I'm posing in Photo 3 in front of the finished church).

The daily work and living conditions in 1984 were just as described in this story. And most interesting of all (and tragic), the lightning strike that killed the young boy – whose three other brothers had also recently been killed by lightning – really occurred, as did the unsettling *vodou* (voodoo) drums which began playing somewhere above us on the mountainside the next night.

There were no murders, however, and none of the eight men on the trip resemble those described in Watson's narrative – and none of our party were criminals. We didn't pack up and leave the day after the drums played. Instead, we remained until the church was completed, although we did depart a bit earlier than planned because our continued presence was placing a huge water-burden upon the small village.

– DM

The Tragic Affair
at the Millennium Manor

The drapes were suddenly pulled back, letting in the weak morning light. I groaned and shut my eyes tighter, but it was too late, and it was no surprise when Sherlock Holmes said, "Five minutes, Watson! Downstairs. The lady seems insistent on sharing her story."

With my eyes shut, I heard as he walked from the window to my bedroom door, shutting it behind him without another word. His statement held no meaning, and I had no idea as to the identity of the lady in question.

We were in Keswick at the urgent request of one of Holmes's old school chums, Sir Kelvin Demery, in regard to a missing painting with deep historical significance to the area. Locating the item itself had been easy enough, but doing so had revealed a wider and more subtle conspiracy, seemingly against the aged knight, his much younger wife, and his infant son. A final reckoning had occurred late the previous night during an aborted sacrifice of the child at the Castlerigg Stone Circle, revealing that the threat against the family came from within – specifically Demery's ne'er-do-well elder son from a previous marriage. Circumstances were such that afterwards we couldn't remain at the Demery estate in Watendlath, some five miles to the south of the Druidic ring of stones and, it being far too late to return to London, we had instead settled into a nearby inn of rather dubious quality and a surly landlord (irate for being awakened at such a late hour) for the remainder of the night until we could make our way to the Keswick Station, and so on back to the capital.

Wondering if this was related in some way to the Demery affair, I made my ablutions and then descended the narrow staircase to the small inn's dining room where Holmes was sitting in the shadows near the fireplace, his back to the wall, and facing a young woman. I couldn't see her face yet, but her dark clothing seemed to be of good quality, and heavy enough to protect her from the sharp autumn chill that permeated the room.

I glanced to the bar where our host stood, holding a mug of coffee. He nodded, seeming not quite so irascible this morning as when we'd knocked him up after midnight – just a few hours earlier, I sadly noted, stifling a yawn. He raised the mug with a questioning look on his face, and I nodded gratefully before moving to join my friend and the unknown lady.

She heard my footsteps and stood, turning to reveal that she was just in her early twenties. Her complexion was dark, as was her hair, and even in those limited conditions I could see that she was a rare beauty indeed. As I had thought, her clothing was moderately expensive – not gaudy, but well-made and serviceable. She presented confidence and poise, and yet her fingers were twisted anxiously around a misshapen handkerchief.

Holmes stood. "Miss Thirkell, this is Dr. Watson, my associate."

We greeted one another and seated ourselves, and at that moment, the landlord placed the much-appreciated hot coffee before me. Holmes and Miss Thirkell already had their own mugs as well. Holmes had made a good start on his, while the young lady's was untouched.

"Mr. Holmes," she said, "I learned that you were here from our cook, Mrs. Weaver – she's friends with the cook at the Demery house – and I knew that I had to ask for your help before you departed – or I think that I shall go mad!"

Her voice rose in tone, and I leaned forward to urge that she calm herself and take a sip from her cup. She nodded and did so, visibly relaxing while Holmes spoke.

"Before the Doctor joined us, you stated that you are being watched – 'terrorized' – was the word you used. Has this been since your return to England, or did it begin in India?"

She looked up sharply, surprised at his simple deduction. However, even I could see that her naturally dark features were even more so because of long-time exposure to hot and dry weather, far different than our British autumn, and that her simple jewelry was clearly from northern India, where I myself had been not so many years before. I noted these facts for her, and she nodded.

"I only returned a short while ago, after leaving India in late summer, summoned home following the death of my Uncle Raymond. It is an uncomfortable situation – he had named me as his sole heir, in spite of the fact that he had two sons, one of whom is especially deserving. I . . . I'm not sure that I wish to claim this inheritance, but my presence was necessary to disentangle certain legal questions. Now – now I wish that I had never returned!"

"And someone is watching?" I repeated.

"I'm – I fear that my fiancé, Philip – he is the younger of the two sons – is watching me."

Holmes raised an eyebrow. "That statement is rather unusual, and vague – not indicative of your level of distress. You fear your fiancé? Further explanation is required."

She nodded. "I'm telling it out of order. You see, I've only been back in England for less than a week, and I expected Philip to meet me when my ship docked. Instead, I learned that he'd angrily departed from our

179

family home more than a month ago, following an argument with his older brother, Sterling, and there has been no sign of him since.

"Soon after I arrived here, I felt the need to move out of the large house where I'd been staying and into a small cottage on the property, not far from here. Since then, I've had the impression that I was being watched. At first I didn't know who it could be, although I suspected that it was Sterling, as he'd hinted since my return that he also has an interest in me romantically." She lowered her voice. "He was the reason I left the main house for the cottage."

Holmes raised a hand. "Your story indicates that you were initially staying at your fiancé's family home with the two brothers, but you also called it 'our family home', and these brothers are your uncle's sons. Are we to make the connection, then, that these two brothers are your first cousins, and it is their father who left the fortune to you, rather than to either of this two sons?"

She nodded. "Yes, I'm sorry that I wasn't more clear about that."

"And you don't trust your older cousin, Sterling – it is due to him you moved to the cottage – but it's your missing fiancé, Philip, that you fear."

She nodded. "The cottage where I've been staying, on the grounds of the estate, is surrounded by a number of large trees. Sometimes, when looking from my window, I've seen movement amongst the nearby trunks by the drive leading to the road as someone seems to slip into hiding when observed. Last night around dusk I went out at dusk to see if there were any signs of who it could be.

"I was no more than fifty feet from the cottage, but I felt as if something were wrong – my senses had a vague sense of alarm, and I felt a chill that had nothing to do with the cold, as if I could perceive some threat. Then, alongside one of the trunks, I found this."

She reached into her bag and pulled out a bracelet. It was silver, with large links and a wide flat plate. She handed it to me first, as I was closer, and I saw that it was engraved with the initials *PT ST*. I read them aloud before handing it across to Holmes.

"*Philip Thirkell*, no doubt," Holmes clarified as he examined. "And the letters '*ST*'?"

"My first name is Sheila. It was a gift from me to Philip before I left England. It expressed my feelings for him before we openly acknowledged them, and our plans for marriage."

"And it was simply lying on the ground?"

She nodded. "Near the trunk of one of the larger trees, quite obvious. As I picked it up, I felt a shiver – had Philip dropped it inadvertently while watching me from this hiding place? Was he still nearby? Had it been him watching me all along, instead of his brother Sterling, as I'd first thought – and feared? If it is he, why has he not made any effort to communicate?"

As she spoke, Holmes continued to turn the bracelet this way and that, holding it to the light, examining the links with great attention, and even holding it to his nose and sniffing it. He slightly raised an eyebrow – one who didn't know him probably wouldn't have even noticed – and then handed it back to Miss Thirkell.

"I called out but there was no answer," she continued, putting the bracelet back in her bag. "Just the sound of the birds in the trees. I hurried back inside and locked the door. Later last night, when Mrs. Weaver came down to check on me as she has often done since I moved from the main house, I broke down and told her what I'd found, and how it had unnerved me. She sympathized, but could offer no explanation. She was certain that Philip had departed in anger more than a month ago, following an argument with Sterling – she'd seen him herself walking away from the house toward the station, carrying his bag. She said that if he is back, he would have notified me as soon as possible. She thought that perhaps Sterling had been watching me, although she couldn't explain the presence of Philip's bracelet, and she stated that this situation needed to be resolved – that it's unfair of me to be left in such a position of ignorance. That's when she remembered hearing from her friend that you were here, and that you might be able to offer some guidance, based on your experience.

"After she left, I pondered her words, and later, as I read my Bible and prayed on the matter, I realized that she was right – I'd be best served by asking for your help."

She looked to Holmes with a hopeful countenance – an expression I'd seen on many a face in the years that I'd known and worked with him. By that point in our friendship, I had learned that Holmes was able to accomplish what ordinary men could not.

Holmes took a sip of coffee, leaned back, and said, "I am intrigued, Miss Thirkell, but I think that a clearer picture of the situation would help before we move forward. Please go further back. How did you end up in India to begin with?"

She composed herself for a moment. "My family has lived around here – Watendlath – for ages. Centuries in fact, and Thirkell Hall has been our ancestral home for several hundred years. Through the generations, the family fortunes sometimes waxed, but mostly waned. My grandfather, Eustace Thirkell, went to sea in his youth and came back with a fortune that revitalized the family. He then made a number of improvements to the original house while cannily keeping track of his investments, increasing his wealth many times over. He never revealed its source of his fortune, but I gathered that it wasn't earned honorably, which may have had something to do with his behavior in later life, as he tried to atone for past sins in his own way. He was filled with regrets in his later years, turning his attentions toward religion in a most unique and fervent manor, even as he stepped away from the running of his carefully built businesses.

"He had only two children: Uncle Raymond, and my father, Desmond, the younger brother. Upon reaching adulthood, Raymond followed his father's path into business, further increasing and consolidating the family wealth, while my father joined the church – although not following the same strict path that his father, Eustace, would later settle himself upon.

"My father married a young woman from his congregation and I was born in 1866 – twenty-one years ago next month. My mother died when I was small, and as I grew, Father and I moved around from parish to parish. We would, however, regularly return here to see my Uncle Raymond and his two sons – my cousins Sterling and Philip. Grandfather and grandmother had both died by then, passing before I have any memories of them.

"Sterling is the older of Uncle Raymond's two children – around thirty now – and when Philip was born, their mother passed at his birth. Philip is nearly my age and, being motherless like me and much younger than his brother, we were always particularly close, although we only saw one another every year or so when Father and I would journey back here to visit Thirkell Hall. However, Philip and I have always corresponded, even when Father decided that we were going out to India.

"As he grew older, Father's faith sustained him less and less, but rather than give in and abandon it, he only delved deeper into its pursuit. When he heard of the opportunity to carry out mission work overseas, five years ago, it seemed to awaken a new spirit within him, and I was willing to go along. And it was the saving of him. Once there, he had the energy of a man twenty years his junior, and he was instrumental in setting up a hospital for the poor villages. Then, early this year, he was suddenly down with a fever, and dead within a week."

She paused, not to swallow any grief, which had apparently been managed long ago, but instead to have a sip of coffee.

"I remained there," she continued, "in India, to carry on with Father's work. I wouldn't have stayed my whole life, but it was a plan for the meantime, and I knew that what I did was important. Throughout, I maintained my correspondence with Philip, and over time – perhaps due to the safety provided us by distance and carefully-crafted letters – we came to have an understanding that when I decided to return home, he and I would wed.

"In the late summer, I received a wire from England – most unusual, as the correspondence that typically arrived was by letter – explaining that Uncle Raymond had passed away unexpectedly from an apoplectic seizure, and that I must return home as soon as it could be arranged, related to him naming me as his heir. Other wires arrived, and my responses followed. I was surprised at Uncle Raymond's decision, but perhaps I shouldn't have been, as Uncle Raymond had become more unpredictable as he aged. As Philip had intimated in his letters, my uncle had become more cantankerous in his middle years, particularly when expressing his disappointment in his two sons, leading to a widening estrangement – more on his part than theirs. In one of the wires from the lawyers, I learned that, after an argument with Sterling in which he felt that Philip didn't take his side enough, Uncle Raymond had the family lawyer remake his will in my favor – an unusual move, and probably something he would have changed back soon if death hadn't taken him so quickly afterwards. Neither the property nor the fortune is entailed to the elder son, and so legally I find myself the sole possessor of more than I'd ever imagined – and a burden of which I never wanted any part.

"I settled my affairs in India and turned over the running of the hospital to several locals who I hope will continue its success. I'd eventually planned to leave there anyway, so this simply advanced my timetable. After a long and tedious journey to the coast, and an equally monotonous return home by sea, I set foot on the dock in Portsmouth a little over a week ago in a cold autumn rain, just as the season was turning cold. It was a great shock, having been away for five years, to find such a different climate and way of life. I had sent a wire when I departed, telling of my planned arrival, and another when we temporarily docked in Bilbao, so I was expecting to be met by someone – particularly Philip. However, there was no sign of him – or anyone – when the ship made port, and rather than leave for Watendlath on my own and miss him, I sent a message. The return wire from Sterling shocked me. That was when I first learned that a month earlier – around the time of my departure from India – he and Philip had fallen into a bitter quarrel, after which Philip was seen leaving the house the next morning and hadn't been heard from since.

"In haste, I returned to Thirkell Hall on my own, finding it much diminished since I'd last seen it. Philip had given some indication that his father had become rather stingy as he aged, but I could see that in just a few years, he'd barely done anything toward the upkeep. Sterling greeted me when I arrived, and even though I wished to discuss where Philip might be, he instead began an immediate and ongoing litany that has been equally divided between the unfairness of the new will and what needs to be done

183

toward the physical improvement the estate, now that his father is out of the way.

"As those early days passed, I also noticed an uncomfortable fact: Sterling seemed to be paying attention to me in a rather bold way – more than he ought – as if he has conceived a romantic interest in my direction that was never before demonstrated. He began to particularly press his attentions on me during my very first evening back, after he'd had a bit too much to drink and when dinner had concluded, I had to ask pointedly if he was aware of the understanding between his brother and me. He admitted that he was, but he stressed that clearly Philip had changed his mind, fleeing from the house before my arrival would force him to honor his promise.

"He then shared the details of their argument, which had begun with a discussion of the inheritance, and had progressed to the point where Philip revealed that he'd regretted our arrangement almost from the beginning, and that the added weight of my inheritance made the match most unsuitable, as he wished to continue his preparation for the ministry, and such wealth on my part would be intolerable. Sterling had argued to him that I was on my way home, and that he would change his mind when we were together once more, but that had only made Philip more adamant and upset, and he had angrily vowed to find a new life before he would ever allow himself to be trapped in one with me.

"'After he left,' Sterling explained, 'I sent wires to his old school, and his friends, but he hasn't returned to his classes, and no one has heard from him. I also informed the constable, who put some questions about at Keswick Station to see if his direction could be determined, but nothing was learned. It seems that he simply didn't have the backbone or the stomach to wed you after all, my dear.' And then he stood, with something of a leering smile on his red face, as if he intended to relocate and join me where I occupied the settee – perhaps to provide me with something that he likened to comfort. As I found that idea quite distasteful, I arose and quickly excused myself.

"What he told me made no sense. Philip and I have always had the same sensibilities, and I'm quite in agreement with his attitude that the inheritance is an added weight that neither of us needs. Surely if he and I could talk, I could make him understand. And yet, I cannot comprehend the rest of the argument, in which Philip had changed his mind about our engagement. His expressions of love and affection, which grew over time, were always most sincere and proper, as he is a quiet and thoughtful man. The idea that he could argue with his brother, and reach the level of anger as described to me, feels as if he were under some other strain of which we know nothing.

184

"Over the next day or so, I found Sterling watching me more and more, or looking for further excuses to attempt conversations *tête-à-tête*, ostensibly about the estate, but with the underlying obviousness of his new and unwanted attentions. Finally I had the idea of moving to the cottage beside the Millennium Manor, and to Sterling's surprise, I relocated there the next afternoon."

"The 'Millennium Manor'?" I asked.

She paused here and took another sip of the now-cold coffee. "It is an old stone building on the property, built by Grandfather Eustace in his later years, related to his religious beliefs. There is a tidy little cottage – the Woods Cottage, as it's called, beside it, which is where I moved to escape Sterling's attentions. It's always been well maintained, in contrast to the stone Manor, although rarely used.

"It's much more suited to my needs than the large house, and I can do for myself there – a fact that has discombobulated the servants to no end, as they don't quite know what to do with the fact that after I had the place stocked with provisions and my possessions moved over, I've proven quite self-sufficient. I let the attorneys know where to find me, and of more importance, I indicated to Sterling that he should keep to himself as well – without quite stating explicitly yet that his attentions are offensive.

"I've been there ever since, reading and enjoying my solitude, and worrying about Philip, and considering what the attorneys have told me during their nearly daily visits. The wealth of the estate is much greater than I'd imagined, as Grandfather Eustace had originally left things in the hands of good managers, and Uncle Raymond and then Sterling were quite capable in their own right. At times, I believe that I could happily walk away from it all, although I've decided (while considering the situation during my long journey home) that I will remain involved after Philip and I are married – at least initially, until I understood the entire situation. And yet, with Philips concern and disappearance, I'm completely at odds and ends as to what to do now.

"As the days have passed, I've become more and more anxious, and except for the attorneys, my only visitor has been Mrs. Weaver, who comes down from the big house to check on me. I had always gravitated to her company when I was small during our visits to the house – perhaps she has been like the mother I never had – and I still find her a comfort now. She can offer no explanation as to where Philip might have gone, or why. The staff was aware that he was angry that night – they could hear his voice through the closed doors during his argument with Sterling, and it seemed most unlike him. Although the engagement between Philip and myself wasn't common knowledge, Mrs. Weaver was one who did know something of it, and she believes that he was happy with the arrangement. Now she's as worried as I am.

"Two days ago I visited the constable, and he had nothing to tell me, having had no success in tracing Philip following Sterling's original request. And so I wait, with the feeling that there is something wrong. It has only grown worse in the last few days – and with the feeling that I'm being watched, and finding Philip's bracelet . . . ." She leaned forward. "Can you help me, Mr. Holmes?"

I expected that he might ask more questions, but instead he stood, surprising both the young lady and myself. "Do you have a carriage waiting outside?"

"I do. When I decided to come here, I walked up to the main house to tell Mrs. Weaver, and she roused the driver."

"There are aspects of this that make me uneasy," Holmes responded. "Watson, join me upstairs to retrieve our coats and hats."

A moment later, I stepped into the close upstairs hall, having donned my coat. Holmes met me in his Inverness, and with his fore-and-aft cap in hand.

"I heard the same story as you," I said, "but there was nothing too terribly urgent."

"Ah," he replied, "but you didn't thoroughly examine the bracelet."

"I saw nothing unusual."

"Likely not. But you didn't take the opportunity to *smell* it."

With that, he led me back downstairs, where we joined Miss Thirkell outside and settled in the carriage for the drive, which she assured us was only a few miles.

There was a frost on the ground, and as the sun rose, its light muted by the overcast sky, I could see that we were passing along a narrow roadway, with hills sloping up steeply on either side. Everywhere I could see were rocks, broken by the eons and scattered in ancient times, some probably still lying in the same spots they had occupied for thousands of years, untouched by man throughout that entire time. It was a bleak landscape, and I could only imagine what it was to return to it after a sojourn of five years in the hot and colorful climes of India.

"I'm intrigued," said Holmes, breaking the silence. "You mentioned an old stone structure near the cottage where you're stating – the Millennium Manor, I believe you called it. What is the story behind such a place?"

"The tale is as strange as the name implies," replied Miss. Thirkell. "I've told you of how my Uncle Raymond and my father became estranged from their own father, Eustace. This was due to his ever-increasing interest in religion – not in the way that my own father was interested, in terms of ministering, or Philip's interest in being a pastor. Rather, it was an Apocalyptic belief in the end of the world, as described in *The Book of Revelations*. This had been developing within him for many years before I was born, and was very much the cause of the separation between him and his sons, who were both such a great disappointment to their father.

"As his mind increasingly turned toward the end of the world, Grandfather Eustace began to believe that he was one of *The Chosen*, the 144,000 righteous souls as described in the seventh chapter of *Revelations* – although he was not a member of the Tribes of Israel, as specified therein."

"'*Do not harm the land or the sea or the trees until we put a seal on the foreheads of the servants of our God*'," quoted Holmes. "'*Then I heard the number of those who were sealed: 144,000 from all the tribes of Israel*'."

The young lady nodded. "That's right. Assuming himself to be one of these elect, Grandfather planned to live on earth with Jesus for one-thousand years after the Lord's return, which he had calculated to be imminent. He and his wife, Enid, without benefit of the aid of servants or other laborers, began to construct a home in which to live out the Millennium following Jesus' return.

"Over the course of eight years, the both of them, then in their sixties, labored to create an Apocalypse-proof, thousand-year-strong fortress. I'm told that Grandfather often explained it by stating, 'I believe in preparing to live instead of preparing to die.'

"They rejected any building material that would rot or rust or burn, such as wood or metal, instead gathering the stones which lie in abundance here in Watendlath. They burrowed into a wooded hillside not too far from the main house and built an all-rock, fourteen-room, two-story monstrosity. It's estimated that just the two of them together hauled and placed hundreds of tons of stone, and then mortared it all together with over two-hundred tons of cement. One can only imagine the curiosity they generated amongst the locals. Working alone, they built wooden forms for the walls and ceilings, and then stacked rocks over these forms using Roman arch-and-key methods. Theoretically, we were told once by a visiting medieval expert that the structure alone was self-supporting, but by pouring the cement over the top of it as they'd done, it was over-built by two- or three-hundred percent, and could in fact stand for one-thousand years.

"Sadly, Enid died soon after the building was completed, and Eustace lamented that, 'Her faith just wasn't strong enough.' He, however, remained firmly committed to his belief that he would live on earth with Jesus for the next thousand years – and by his own interpretations, he was

187

certain that such would begin any day. He died, however, just a few years after his wife. They're both buried near the manor in unmarked graves, as he wished. I must confess it adds to my agitation when I think that I might have inadvertently strolled across their final resting places.

"After their deaths, the stone house – which came to be called 'Millennium Manor' – was abandoned. After all, it is nearly indestructible, unless someone intentionally attacks it with carefully placed explosives or picks and hammers. But while the place was being constructed, Eustace and Enid hired someone to build an attractive little wooden cottage beside the stone house, where they could live so that they could be closer to their tasks, and because the ostentatious vastness of Thirkell Hall had become distasteful to them. Millennium Manor was left to itself after their deaths, and as far as I know, the only visitors to that stone pile since then have been when the servants sometimes look around while caring for the Woods Cottage, or when Philip and I would play there as children."

As she finished speaking, we turned off the road, and after a hundred yards or so we stopped before a pair of most dissimilar buildings, set near a grove of trees. We stepped down beside the closer of the two, a charming wooden cottage, well maintained, and constructed to resemble some sort of fairy-tale dwelling. It showed strong, exposed timbers, mullioned windows with complex metal-work, and a good-looking thatch roof that might last a century. But as interesting as I found it, my attention was inevitably drawn to what stood looming behind it – the Millennium Manor.

As described, it was completely made of stone. Two stories tall, it was rough looking, and the stonework showed no obvious skill or eye toward beauty. No stone was regularly shaped, and each was stacked in place solely with the thought as to where it would fit with its irregular neighbor. There was what seemed to be a main doorway centered, in the ground floor, as well as several other doors and openings for a number of windows, but they were all open to the elements now, and if wooden doors or window-frames had ever been there, they were long-since gone. The upper floor had several curved arches, as if in the shape of a three-humped camel. Clearly the builders, the old man and woman of deep religious convictions, had made use of ancient Roman methods, for one could see that massive weight of the house was placed so that it held itself together. I couldn't imagine what force would be required to take it apart.

It was a grim and brooding place, and one could almost imagine the ghosts of the builders watching from within it. I shivered, and it was only somewhat related to the coldness of the morning. The flinty and dour atmosphere was made complete by a number of ravens which were scattered about, some on top of the building, and others on the ground at either side, their raucous speech being the only sound except for the sigh of wind in the dead leaves of the nearby trees.

The house seemed to hold a dark and immediate fascination, and I made a move to step that way, wishing to see the place closer, but Holmes held up a hand. "In a moment, Watson," he said. "Miss Thirkell, can you point me toward the tree where you found the bracelet?"

She nodded and indicated a tall tree along the front of the nearby grove. Though clearly a type of oak, the tree looked somewhat unusual to my layman's eyes, and it oddly retained its dead and darkened leaves, even this late in the season.

"Thank you. If you will wait inside with Doctor Watson, I'll make a quick examination."

With that, he turned away, heading not directly to the tree, but rather into the old stone house, passing through the ground-floor doorway and into darkness. I went inside the cottage with Miss Thirkell, who offered to make tea, but I declined, as Holmes might need us to join him at any moment. Instead, we sat in the cold, the cottage's fire having long gone out, and discussed common memories of India. At times, I could see Holmes moving back and forth across the narrow field of vision provided by the window. He went to the oak and the other trees around it, looking here and there at the ground, sometimes getting down upon hands and knees. He spent some time peering up into the tree, and then walked over to the carriage driver, with whom he carried on momentary conversation. I saw the fellow nod, climb down, and walk toward the cottage. However, he didn't come to the front door, but instead went around one side, returning a moment later with a ladder that must have been kept there for when it was needed during routine maintenance. Meanwhile, Holmes approached the cottage and then knocked on the door. I rose and opened it, and he gestured for me to join him outside.

"Watson," he directed softly as I pulled the door shut behind me, "I need for you to take Miss Thirkell to the main house, and leave her in the care of the cook. Then, find out from her which servants can be trusted, and have them make sure that Sterling Thirkell makes no effort to depart. Have the cook summon the constable to join us here. Then return with Coggins, the driver, as soon as you can."

"What is this, Holmes?"

"Deviltry." He turned away, back toward the tree. "Oh," he said over his shoulder. "When you return, bring a long rope."

I returned to the cottage, summoned Miss Thirkell, and explained that we needed to go on to the main house. She complied, and soon we were back on the main road, traveling at a brisk pace north. She questioned me, but I could offer no explanations, and refrained from describing Holmes's instructions. She then turned to the driver, asking, "Coggins, what did Mr. Holmes do?" The driver, however, simply shook his head – which rather surprised me, as she was one of his masters. He had seemingly received instructions as well.

We arrived at the house and were driving to the rear. As we stepped down to enter what turned out to be the kitchen door, I turned back and asked Coggins to find a long rope. He nodded as if he'd already been told that too, and then I followed the young lady inside. I then requested that she let me speak with Mrs. Weaver. I could tell that Miss Thirkell was becoming quite impatient at being kept in the dark, but I didn't know the reason, having no knowledge to share, and simply followed Holmes's directions. When the cook arrived, she being a woman of trustworthy mien in her late-sixties, I quietly and to one side explained who I was and what Holmes had asked. She seemed to understand that something grim was in the offing and led Miss Thirkell deeper into the house. I returned outside to find Coggins, along with three other steady-looking fellows. The driver showed me a long rope that he'd found. Then, together we returned to the cottage.

I shall never forget that grim and terrible task. Holmes explained what he'd found during his search of the grounds, and we were soon spread around the large oak where the bracelet had been discovered. The ladder was set beside the trunk, and Holmes called me over to point at a fresh-looking gash. "Note, Watson, that this was already here, at nearly the same level where I placed the ladder. Someone has been here before. Additionally, before I placed the ladder, I found deep marks still in the soil beside the tree where it had already been stood. The leaves still on the tree protected them from being eradicated by the weather."

With that, he climbed the ladder to a point within easy reach of the lowest limb. From there he stepped into the tree, working himself higher, confidently climbing steadily upward. I looked up to see his goal, now somewhat visible in the increasing morning light. I nearly could not believe it.

While we stood there, the constable arrived, and Coggins whispered to him while pointing up into the tree.

Holmes had carried the rope with him, and by then he'd secured it to the object hanging high above us before cutting the other rope that fastened it to the high limb. Then, with the assistance of the men from the house, the dead body of Philip Thirkell was solemnly and carefully lowered to the ground.

Coggins identified what was left of him and turned away. The poor fellow was greatly decomposed, and the ravens that lived in and around the stone house had been at him.

Holmes explained. "He's clearly been here a while – likely since just after the argument between the two brothers, and just before his supposed 'departure' for parts unknown. The condition of the corpse shows that. Does the older brother, Sterling, have a limp?"

"He does," confirmed the constable.

"His footprints are all over the place," responded Holmes. "In the dust on the floors of the stone house, and in the soil under these trees. This is *Quercus palustris* – the Pin, or Swamp Oak, native to North America, but transplanted to England in the early part of this century. They hold their leaves through the winter, shedding them gradually through the season instead of all at once. After Philip Thirkell died – and we don't yet know the reason – his brother Sterling chose to hide him, rather than make the death known. He brought him here, thinking this to be the most out-of-the way place for quick disposal. He couldn't dig a grave – the ground around here is too rocky, and he might be seen, or the excavation might be noticed. Here, he could hang the body where it would remain undiscovered for quite a while. The leaves would conceal it, even after the season changed, giving him time to think of a better place. He likely believed that no one would come here – not realizing that his actions of harassment against his cousin would drive her to move to the cottage almost immediately."

"But how did you know to look here?" I asked.

"I mentioned to you that the bracelet, found on the ground here by this tree, had an odor. I know it well – that of a rotting corpse. If you had smelled the bracelet, you would have recognized it yourself. When the body was hung, the weather was warm – it has only just now turned cold – and decomposition proceeded rapidly. Over the last month, the wasting of the hand and wrist progressed to the point where the bracelet slipped off and fell – probably just in the last day or so. Thus, I already suspected that the body was hidden in the tree. When we arrived here, and I saw the limping footprints, I was further certain. As I said, the ground under this tree is protected from the rain and elements by the remaining leaves, and the footprints were quite obvious, both from when Sterling Thirkell hung the body, using this same ladder which is kept beside the cottage, and also more recently, during the past week, when he has lurked about, in both the stone house and underneath the trees, spying on his comely cousin."

Our return to the house was a terrible affair. Miss Thirkell became overwrought upon hearing of the death of her fiancé, and she broke away before she could be stopped, running to the wagon which held the body, throwing back the tarpaulin and seeing the terrible wreckage of her long-time companion and love.

Sterling Thirkell was still asleep upstairs, hung over from his drinking the night before. He was a lanky man, old before his time and clearly dissipated. When he understood that the truth was known, he collapsed, repeating over and over again that it had been an accident. He and his brother had argued over Miss Thirkell's return. Sterling had wanted to bully her into relinquishing the inheritance, or if not that, then he'd insisted that he be the one to marry her, as he was the elder brother, and the one with the most right to becoming the owner of their late father's estate through her. Words had come to blows, Philip had fallen, and his head had split on a fireplace andiron. In a panic, Sterling had wrapped him up, hidden him behind a sofa, and then transported him to the trees by Millennium Manor in the dead of night. His motives were as Holmes described. After hanging him out of sight, he'd returned to the main house. Early the next morning, he walked away in his brother's hat and coat, carrying his brother's bag, making painfully sure to move without his customary limp and to be seen by Mrs. Weaver and the others in the kitchen. He had spread the story of the argument and Philip's angry departure. No one had believed that the man they'd seen leave could be the older brother, as he never rose that early.

Sterling Thirkell was arrested, but his story of an accidental death was believed, and in spite of his actions in hiding the corpse, the case never even came to trial, showing the pervasive influence of the wealthy, particularly in rural areas. Against all advice, his cousin relinquished her inheritance and returned to India.

I happened to be in Watendlath again several years later, this time without Holmes and on my own business, and I happened to stay at the same inn. Finding the host much more genial when not bothered after midnight, I spent some time talking with him. It was he who told me that Sterling Thirkell still lived in the big house, and that his business was still vastly successful, no thanks to its proprietor. The man was slowly drinking himself to death.

I didn't mention to my new friend that I'd stopped by the Millennium Manor the previous evening, intending to explore it further, having missed the chance some years earlier. The small cottage beside it was empty and dark, and the wind was up, sighing through the same trees around where the unfortunate Philip Thirkell's body had been found. As I approached the building, the ravens' cries became louder, and some hopped or landed nearby as if they meant to defend it. The place may have been built to await the Savior, but there was something sinister about it, and after many long minutes considering whether to press forward and enter that darkness, I turned away.

I learned one further fact of interest from the innkeeper: Miss Thirkell had insisted that her fiancé, though dead, had still found a way to warn her of the dangers posed by his older brother by dropping his bracelet where she would find it, beneath his body in the tree in which he was hanging. Throughout her remaining time in the village of Watendlath, he told me, she had grasped the bracelet as if it were a talisman, twisting it around her white fingers as if she'd never let it go.

I only knew her for a couple of hours, and have no idea where she ended up in the world, but I will never forget that look of wrenching despair when she realized that her love was gone. I feel as if there was some sort of lesson in her anguished features, but all these years later, I have yet to find words adequate to express what I should have learned at the Millennium Manor

The Canterbury Manifesto

Part I

As a man with an experience of women which extends over many nations and three separate continents, and as a husband with experience of three separate wives, I can attest that there is special emphasis put on certain events – particularly firsts. Such was certainly the case throughout December 1902 as my new wife planned for our first Christmas together in our Queen Anne Street residence. Thus, when she insisted on changing those plans at the last minute, I was quite surprised – but probably no more than she was. Instead of supervising the preparation of the Christmas Day feast as intended, she was spending Christmas Eve in a first class compartment (*not* a smoker!) on a train bound for Canterbury, engaged in polite conversation with Sherlock Holmes.

They were pleasant enough to one another, but I expected the worst at any moment. My wife's plans had been spoiled after I had been summoned to the Diogenes Club on the previous evening, and Holmes had certainly never envisioned that she would accompany us to famed cathedral city.

Late the night before, on the evening of the twenty-third, I had voluntarily sequestered myself in my study, doing what any sensible man would in such a situation, the house being in a controlled uproar while the holiday celebration was being assembled. My wife, Priscilla, [1] had taken delivery of various items – chiefly comestibles – throughout the day, and on those rare occasions when I ventured forth to scavenge supplies and gather intelligence in order to get some sense of what was being organized, I couldn't believe the amount of food that was being assembled

By common agreement, we both ate a light dinner that evening, and I had only just returned to my study when the doorbell rang. In a moment, my wife appeared at the door, an envelope in her hand bearing a distinctive crest.

"I am afraid that you shall have to go," she said, handing it to me. I recognized its origin, as did she.

"Hmm?"

"To Pall Mall. To the Diogenes Club."

She said it in a flat tone, and I knew that she feared that I might be gone for longer than that evening, possibly even for several days. It was a fear that I shared.

194

Of course my wife knew Mycroft Holmes – in fact, his existence was much more common knowledge than either Holmes brother would have liked, due to my thoughtless indiscretion back in 1893. At that time, still grieving over what I believed was Holmes's death at the hands of Professor Moriarty atop the Reichenbach Falls, I was writing and publishing a series of narratives describing Holmes's past cases, so that his memory would remain green and his true gifts would be known and remembered.

I had written up quite a few of these accounts, and my literary agent, Conan Doyle, had been helping select which ones to place in *The Strand*. He liked the tale of the Greek prisoner and the interpreter who had been taken to communicate with him, and how I was introduced to Mycroft Holmes by way of the case. By that time, I was well aware of Mycroft Holmes's unique and valuable role within the government, but in the late summer of 1893, I was still grieving the death of my wife Mary, and my sensibilities were numb and blunted. Thus, I let Doyle talk me into publishing the story, not realizing the problems that it would cause for Mycroft when his existence was announced through the pages of a popular periodical. Fortunately I left the description of his duties rather vague, or it might have been much worse.

But I had withheld no such details from Priscilla, and she knew that a summons from Mycroft meant that the matter was serious – although she rather sarcastically asked if my opinion was needed to help in the selection of his brother Sherlock's Christmas gift. All I could do was laugh politely and get into my coat, hoping that whatever the problem was could be resolved quickly.

It hadn't taken long after I first met Mycroft to understand just how important he was in the functions of the British Government, and particularly in the secret intelligence services. In fact, it was soon clear that the Diogenes Club, while truly fulfilling its purpose as a place for unclubable men to spend their time, was also the location of much that occurred within the government to organize and manage those agents of Britain's secret intelligence services. And as such, I was almost certain that it was this connection that was behind my summons to the club that night.

I had received the message to attend the meeting at a little after nine p.m., and it wasn't much past the half-hour when the hansom deposited me at No. 78 Pall Mall, the modest building housing the Diogenes Club. I've written enough elsewhere about this unique establishment that a great deal doesn't need to be addressed here. Suffice it to say, the club was originally founded by Mycroft and several others as a retreat where they could go and avoid conversation for a time. No speaking was allowed within the club, save in the Stranger's Room on the first floor, overlooking the street. Over the years, I have been in that room, one way or another, more times than I can remember – with Holmes in order to confer with or receive information from Mycroft Holmes, or summoned there with the request that I assist in an investigation. At times, I've even been there on my own, to seek advice or guidance or help in various confidential matters that have sprung up on occasion.

Sherlock Holmes was already in the Stranger's Room when I arrived. He and I had recently been involved in some business that finished up at the London Hospital, and just the night before we'd been in a rough altercation, but he now looked rested and refreshed. He nodded as I entered. Mycroft waved in my direction, spoke a greeting, and indicated that I ought to pour something for myself from the sideboard. I did, taking a nice portion of the club's very memorable brandy.

While doing so, I noted with amusement the contrast to my own home. There, no open surface remained that didn't have some sort of holiday-themed greenery. Our door had a sizeable wreath upon it, and there were candles burning in every window. There was no such frippery here, and I wondered if any concession would be made, even on Christmas Day, by making the slightest changes to the otherwise rigid menu. I knew from encountering many of them that the Diogenes members maintained gruff exteriors – men who, like Mycroft, ran on fixed rails between work, the club, and home, with no time for what they considered foolishness. Yet was there some place deep within them that wished for a bit of holiday festivity, and a return, if just for a moment, to that sense of childlike wonder which unexpectedly makes itself known during the holiday season – even a solitary candle in the Diogenes window? Or were all sparks of sentimentality extinguished in their stony hearts? I knew that no answer could easily be found.

Before I drifted into a full reverie on the topic, I turned back toward my intended chair. When I was seated, Mycroft spoke.

"Have you seen the news?"

I frowned. I hadn't taken the time to read the late editions, and I recalled nothing of importance earlier in the day. I shook my head.

"The Archbishop of Canterbury died several hours ago."

"Frederick Temple?" I asked. "That's unfortunate," I added, but not certain yet what his death implied.

Sherlock Holmes spoke. "There is no indication of foul play – for now. The man had been ill for several weeks, after collapsing during a speech earlier this month."

"He was, after all, in his eighties, I believe," I said.

"Eighty-one," confirmed Mycroft.

"Then if there is nothing suspicious connected with his death, what is the interest of the . . . umm, Diogenes Club in the matter?"

The question held implied meaning. When I had first met Mycroft Holmes in September 1888, I'd believed that he held some small position within the government. It wasn't long after that, however, that I began to be aware of his much greater influence. In fact, he held a most unique position as something of a clearing house of information, able to see connections and hidden paths and links that others could not. Due to the value of his oversight, he often functioned *as* the government, his word deciding policy and guiding the country through some very rough waters that the average man might never perceive.

"One of the Archbishop's papers has been taken," explained Mycroft.

I raised an eyebrow, wondering what sort of paper belonging to a church leader could fall under Mycroft's purview. "I wouldn't have thought that would be a cause for concern – unless there was something in his past that might discredit him."

"Nothing of the sort. He was a man of the highest moral character. I assure you of that with all the authority of my position."

"Then did this paper hold information that might be used to embarrass someone else? Or to tarnish the Archbishop's reputation and legacy in some other way?"

"The latter," said Mycroft, "but his reputation is not our concern. The damage, should this paper be published, will be far worse to the nation as a whole – at a time when such things cannot be tolerated. What was taken was a previously unknown essay – a *manifesto* – that Temple was preparing which could rock the Established Church, and the rest of the nation along with it – apparently a fundamental shift in doctrine which he has apparently come to espouse in recent months, and which he had taken upon himself to aggressively announce, without reaching any sort of agreement to do so with others in the Church who should also have a say."

"Apparently," said Holmes with a smile and shake of his head, "the Crown is concerned as well.

"They are 'dismayed'," corrected Mycroft. "The King expressed distress that the man who so recently carried out his duties in the Coronation could take it upon himself to 'hijack the ship', as he put it.

"Temple was always something of a progressive type," Mycroft continued. "In some ways, I suppose it's a wonder that such a fellow espousing those views, good as he was, managed to be elevated to the position of Archbishop. Over forty years ago, he was promoting the values of science alongside faith, and seeing nothing within certain scientific theories of the time that were contrary to the teachings of religion. And more recently, he has preached at least one sermon espousing greater educational opportunities for women."

"Nothing so terrible in that," I said.

"Ah, but apparently he has been much more specific as part of this new overall proposal that he was working out on his own – a full-blown dash toward science as the new God, along with suggestions of radical Socialism. We should have seen it coming, I suppose. Even in the early 1860's, Temple welcomed the insights of Darwin's evolution theory, by way of a series of lectures. In recent months, from what we've been told by his secretary, one Stephen Smythe, Temple knew that his health was starting to fail, and he was hurrying to complete a document so shocking that it would leapfrog debate about various current issues and disagreements that he felt are hindering the Church so that the country will be ready, or so he believed, for whatever faces Britain in the new century."

"I'm puzzled," I said. "Are you referring to Germany and the Kaiser?"

"I am," confirmed Mycroft. "The Archbishop has been part of a committee assembled to examine the threat of rising German nationalism. Representatives from all areas of government and important industries have been meeting for several years in order to prepare for the eventual, inevitable German war which is bound to occur. Temple represented the Church."

I was well aware of the growing sense within a certain segment of the country's leadership that war with Germany would absolutely occur at some uncertain point in the future. The King's nephew, the Kaiser, had been ever-envious of Britain, and the aggressive expansions of Germany's military were ongoing and increasing. Mycroft had long been an advocate for being prepared, and he'd been pressing more and more for his younger brother to devote his energies in that direction, instead of wasting his time on those lesser cases that he viewed with disdain, once describing them as "the usual petty puzzles of the police-court". A sizeable number of Holmes's recent investigations had related to circumventing the Germans' activities, as I well knew from my own involvement.

"This missing paper," I asked. "Is there any sense that it was been obtained by foreign agents in order to cause disruption or embarrassment?"

"Not so far," answered Mycroft. "All we know for certain is that it is missing. We were caught unaware of Temple's intentions until earlier this afternoon when Smythe informed us that Temple planned to publish them on Christmas Day, against Smythe's advice. Apparently this young man was the only one included in Temple's secret plans, and only he knew the explosive nature of the Archbishop's proposed thesis. He was encouraging a delay, and to seek other opinions or approval before pulling the trigger, so to speak, but Temple must have sensed that his time was short, for according to Smythe, he'd spent much of the past week or so racing to finish the document. And Smythe confirms that as of just a few days ago, Temple *did* finish it."

"Can you be more specific?" asked Holmes. "Is it something really so dangerous?"

"Oh yes, very much so. It is a specific statement aligning the Church with a number of scientific theories – all correct, of course, or they are according to our current understanding, but still controversial to those of less-educated backgrounds. Smythe says that he has gone all in with the current thinking on evolution, for instance, and also investigations into atomic theory and universal astronomy – both of which have far more connections between them that one might think, despite the vast differences in scale between the two.

"And then there is his abrupt and unexpected push for reconciliation with the Catholic Church – which he felt was absolutely necessary to be in place as a unified guiding force when the great conflict breaks out. It seems that Temple has written that all of the various treaties between nations – secret and otherwise – which are looped 'round and 'round the necks of the various European countries, along with the ever-increasing need for raw materials from around the globe, and the competing and fractious colonization that goes with it, will eventually pull every great nation into a terrible world-spanning conflict, such has never been seen before."

"But you've predicted as much yourself," said Holmes. "Why is Temple's document any different? Why should it be so feared?"

"Because my opinions have been private – behind the scenes – with an eye toward preparation for something which cannot be avoided. To openly discuss it now – to incite the public to discussing it – might precipitate an acceleration toward the war. And Smythe says that the essay is written in just such a way, pushing British interests first so that it cannot help to offend others, and more likely throw us into war within a week – even with our allies. If such a thing were made public under the name of such a highly placed figure, it would only and immediately increase the nationalistic tensions and advance the pace of the coming war by decades – and England is nowhere near ready for that.

"For such a document to simply appear, with the Archbishop of Canterbury coming down on the side of legitimizing evolution and also suddenly proposing reunification with the Catholics in the same sweeping manifesto, and while doing so in such a highly offensive manner, will be perceived as the height of arrogance. Opinions will immediately inflame in all quarters, spinning into a nationalistic furor. The nation celebrates Christmas in two days. By New Year's day, the peace we enjoy would be finished."

"And this Smythe fellow was the one who sounded the alarm," I commented.

Mycroft nodded. "As soon as Temple passed, Smythe realized that something should be done to secure the man's papers. The absence of this new doctrine was immediately obvious. He had rushed to secure it and found that it was gone. He then notified me."

"Is he one of your agents then?" I asked. "You had a man watching the Archbishop of Canterbury?" I wasn't entirely comfortable with the idea."

"I have many agents – for without accurate and complete data, how else can I make good decisions? But in this case, the answer is no, Smythe is not working for me. However, the Archbishop and I have had some dealings with on another – there is more to his position, you understand, than just overseeing the Church and presenting the occasional important sermon – so it was no surprise that Smythe had heard of me as well, and when he perceived that the document was missing, he correctly sought me out."

I wasn't truly surprised, and to belabor the question would serve no purpose. "Who could have taken it?" I asked instead.

"That," answered Sherlock Holmes, "is what we have been tasked to discover."

I thought of my wife, and all the efforts that she'd made toward constructing our first Christmas as husband and wife. It was already late on the evening of the twenty-third – how many hours were left until Christmas Day? I glanced at the clock on the mantel. Almost ten p.m. So twenty-six hours until the 25th. Or something around thirty-four hours until that morning, when the day would actually begin for us when we awoke. It wasn't much time.

I suppose it was my look toward the clock that informed them both of my train of thought. "At least we don't have far to go," I said. "The Archbishop's residence is just across the river – a mile as the crow flies." I stood. Time was passing. "Should we make our way in that direction?"

Mycroft shook his head, and Holmes gave me a rueful smile.

"You're correct, Doctor," said Mycroft, "to think that starting at Lambeth Palace would be the proper place. Temple did pass away there. But for some reason he had gone out to Canterbury a few days ago, in spite of his failing healthy and that was where he completed work on the essay. He left it there when he returned to London, and that's where Smythe went

200

in such a hurry – to secure it, only to find when he arrived that it was gone."

"So we must go to Canterbury," said Sherlock Holmes, looking my way and surely realizing what that meant to me and the chances of having a first successful Christmas in my new home and with my new wife.

If Holmes and I left immediately, I thought, we could be in Canterbury in the early hours of Christmas Eve – provided that we found a train running so late. Could we engage a special, much as Professor Moriarty had done over a decade earlier when we observed him from a hidden spot as he pursued us toward Canterbury after we'd decided to go a different way? Unlikely. And what could we accomplish in the middle of the night when we arrived? And even if we left immediately and didn't sleep when we got there, waking people up and working through until morning, could the matter be resolved in time to have me back in Queen Anne Street when my wife's Christmas plans were to be set into motion?

I looked back at Holmes, realizing that a bit of panic might be showing in my face. Of course he had read my thoughts as if I'd said them aloud. I never should have glanced at the mantel clock.

"We can but try," he said, with no indication that my staying behind was ever an option. "To be back as soon as possible. We can but try. I wouldn't want to add another grievance to that list with my name upon it that the good Mrs. Watson already maintains."

I started to protest that there was no such list, but in fact, she did have a few objections to my long-time friend – my being shot earlier in the year while assisting him being one of them. But before I could defend her, Mycroft interrupted.

"Nothing can be done tonight. Travel down first thing in the morning. I'll send word to the Archbishop's wife to be ready for your arrival. I trust that this will be resolved quickly."

"His wife?" I asked. "She's in Canterbury? Surely her place is here, with the body of her husband."

Mycroft shook his head. "Mrs. Temple is particularly strong-willed. When she learned of this essay and its explosive nature, and that it was now missing, she insisted on traveling to Canterbury, leaving the arrangements for her husband with others here that she trusts. She says that she knew Temple better than anyone – certainly true, I'm sure – and that she should be there in case her help is needed in any way."

Mycroft turned to his brother. "The woman is strong and capable. But her husband has died. Be . . . diplomatic, Sherlock." Then he forced himself to his feet from the heavy red leather chair that had likely been specially constructed for him long ago and placed there in the Stranger's

201

Room. "And apparently, as it's Christmas, this makes his death even worse. Emotions will be on edge. Go carefully."

Then, with a nod our way, we were dismissed. Holmes and I walked out, passing through the silent building where no conversation was allowed. At that time of night, in rooms unseen to both sides of us, the place could have been mostly empty, or filled to capacity, and we wouldn't have known, as the members always took great pains to remain silent. Such a place definitely had its attractions.

Outside, in the brisk December air, I began. "Holmes, I – "

He raised a hand. "I understand, Watson. I was unaware until I arrived that Mycroft had involved you. If he'd asked beforehand, I would have convinced him to let you stay home for the holiday, but he rightly pointed out that your participation can only make the chances for success that much better."

I nodded at the compliment and didn't bother to correct him, for I had instead been about to try and convince him that my wife didn't have any great antipathy toward him, as he apparently believed. Yet now was not the time for that discussion, and we would have several hours the next day to hash it out on the train.

Holmes indicated that he had some research to do before our departure in the morning, and asked my opinion as to whether Lomax might still be found in the nearby London Library. I expected that he was, and offered to go along, but Holmes encouraged me to return home instead, and I didn't argue. We wished each other a good night, and then I had to walk to Waterloo Place before encountering a hansom. It wasn't a long journey from there, but the going was slow along Regent Street due to the upcoming Christmas holiday, even at that hour, and I had time to ponder my wife's general antipathy toward my best friend.

Just months before, in mid-1902, I had wed for the third time, at a period in my life when I had no expectations of entering such a state ever again. My first marriage in 1886 had lasted little more than a year before my wife, Constance, was taken far too early due to general poor health, greatly stressed at the end by an unexpected illness. My second bride, Mary, was also taken from me in 1893 after four years of marriage by a combination of maladies. When she passed, I assumed that I would remain a widower for the remainder of my life. However, that changed when I met Priscilla, and after a reasonable period of acquaintance, we both agreed that it was inevitable that we should join our destinies.

At that time, I had been living in again Baker Street for eight years, having moved back in the spring of 1894 following Holmes's return to London following the extended period when he was believed to be dead.

After Mary's death, I had maintained my practice, but with very little enthusiasm. Upon Holmes's invitation to return to my old digs, I sold out and resumed assisting him in a great many of his investigations. It was through the course of one of these that I met my future third bride, although neither of us initially knew then how our stories would join.

Priscilla was quite a different lady from Constance or Mary. I had met the former during a time in the mid-1880's when I traveled to San Francisco. Upon our marriage, we settled in London, but the intolerable fogs, so different from those of the northern California coast, had terribly afflicted Constance to the point that she was often forced to travel away with her mother, seeking restoration of her health while I remained in London, attempting to build my practice and our future – while still having time to assist Holmes as needed.

I had met Mary when she presented herself one morning in September 1888 as Holmes's client, and it was through that investigation that we quickly fell in love, being married the following spring. Due to this initial connection with Holmes, and having seen him in action, Mary had no objections when I joined him on his cases.

But Priscilla had a different perspective.

At the time of our marriage, I was about to turn fifty, and my bride-to-be was in her middle years as well. By then, each with several decades of accumulated adult experience, we approached our upcoming union with a certain practicality, and sensible plans were made in terms of purchasing the lease on the house at No. 9 Queen Anne Street, not very far from Harley Street, which would contain both my new practice and our residence. Arrangements were proceeding at a stately and comforting pace a few weeks before our wedding was scheduled when I was shot.

It occurred, as one might expect, in connection with one of Holmes's investigations. Perhaps I had become too complacent over the years, but I should have been more careful when dealing with a cornered criminal known by the sobriquet of "Killer" Evans. The bullet did no more than graze my thigh, although in such a way as to cause a burning sensation for quite some time afterwards while healing. I had received far worse wounds during my military service, and quite a few more after my return to England when associating myself with Holmes's investigations. (These included taking an unexpected Jezail bullet to the leg – and who expects to receive two of those in one lifetime, with the second wound occurring in England? – and also being stabbed in the upper chest with a red-hot poker. Both of these had occurred at different times in '88, and over the years there had also been numerous other cuts, breaks, punctures, gunshot wounds, and occasional poisonings.)

After being wounded by Evans, what I had thought would be an interesting story to tell Priscilla had turned into another of our firsts: Our first argument. The gist of her position was that as responsible husband, I should henceforth forego any activities which might put my life in danger, and instead settle meekly and for the rest of my days into my new role as a West End physician.

I disagreed.

The matter was gradually tabled without an absolute agreement acknowledged either way (although I held firm to my position), and we married as planned. Holmes, as he had been both times before, served as my best man, and he and Priscilla settled into a stiffly polite acquaintance with one another, while I walked the fine line between the two worlds of Baker Street and Queen Anne Street.

It had seemed to work rather well so far, as my practice was immediately successful (although I was fairly certain that a great number of patients initially crossed my threshold because of my association with the famed detective), and I also still found time to join Holmes on many of his cases. Most were rather benign, and in the instances where I encountered danger, I wasn't shot, so the question of being a responsible husband and avoiding such circumstances hadn't been reopened – but it was never entirely forgotten either.

And then came the Christmas season, and my wife's complex expectations for our first Yule holiday together, which I knew was at cross-purposes with the summons I'd received from Mycroft Holmes.

I'd had plenty of time to consider how to share my upcoming plans with her, as the journey from Pall Mall was quite slow. The second Boer War had ended half-a-year earlier, and while nothing about it gave the country any sense of pride or joy, there seemed to be some unspoken agreement that this season's celebrations should be especially festive. The shops and stores were highly decorated, and many had stayed open late with window displays that fought to outdo those of their neighbors – each successful enough to attract the great crowds who chose to stop and tarry for a while at each one instead of moving along. Those who did need to get from one place to another more quickly were often diverted out into the street in order to circle around the paused throngs, and that rippled into a general constriction of traffic.

I saw it all – the decorations and the crowds (with so many individuals awkwardly balancing their brightly colored purchases) and the unusual holiday smells, savory and sweet, that wafted above the typical horsy odors of the thoroughfare. For those of a mind to appreciate it with wide eyes, the journey would have been a treat. But I was headed home, with the premonition of my wife's reaction to my news.

And yet she surprised me. We turned from Regent Street into Mortimer Street, passing along Cavendish Square before traversing the short distance up Harley Street and so into Queen Anne Street. I had the cabbie release me several doors early and walked the remaining distance, pausing for a moment to look at the cozy building, with windows lit on all four stories by single candles, more powerful in their simplicity than the vast and ostentatious decorations that were to be found at other finer houses throughout the city. It was so different from the Christmases of my youth, growing up in Scotland where the holiday was nothing more than another religious day to be noted on the calendar – no gifts, no feasts, and certainly no Father Christmas.

My wife met me at the door. "Where are you off to, then?" she asked, trying to make her voice bright and interested, but the expression in her eyes revealing her true thoughts.

"Canterbury," I said as she stepped aside to allow my passage. "The Archbishop has died, and one of his most important papers has gone missing."

She stopped abruptly, turning around to fully face me. "The Archbishop? Oh, poor Beatrice!"

"I'm sorry?" I asked, nonplussed.

"Beatrice. His wife. I know her." She paused, not more than a pair of seconds, and then said, "I'm coming with you."

Over the remainder of the evening, I half-heartedly tried to talk her out of it – but I also remembered how useful Mary had been on a number of investigations. (Sadly, Constance's poor health had prevented her from providing any meaningful assistance.) Priscilla was practical and intelligent, and there was the added advantage that she knew the Archbishop's wife, a long-standing friendship that had begun long before Reverend Temple had been enthroned as the Bishop of London in 1885. They had maintained contact with one another ever since, although this was the first I'd known of it.

Priscilla set about pausing some of the Christmas preparations – but not those that would affect the staff, who would not be deprived of their holiday. And I wrote a short note to be delivered to Baker Street, explaining that Holmes and I would be accompanied to Canterbury in the morning. I expected no reply – frankly I hoped for none – and by the time we went to bed, there had been no response from that quarter.

Part II

Priscilla and I joined Holmes in the morning at Victoria, and there was no discussion as to Priscilla's presence. Holmes accepted the inevitable nature of the situation, and he seemed to flash a glance of approval at the very light amount of luggage brought by my wife – barely more than I carried myself.

I was relieved to find that Holmes and Priscilla got along well as we traveled, and he had no qualms at fully taking her into his confidence – or at least as much as he had me. He explained the circumstances to her, repeating much of what I'd related the previous evening after returning from the Diogenes Club, but also providing a bit more information that neither of us knew, concerning the names of a few rather concerned government officials who were monitoring the situation quite closely.

"Your friend Lomax was invaluable," Holmes explained. "It isn't just the forgotten dusty tomes that he can lay a hand on in an instant. He knows right where the information concerning current events might also be located. Within fifteen minutes, I had three other names – important men – and as I visited each in turn, they were able to tell more than even Mycroft had supplied." While the identities of those men isn't important, they did tend to confirm the concern that was felt by the Archbishop's sudden streak of independent thought when he sensed his time was short.

Holmes questioned Priscilla some about her friendship with the newly widowed Beatrice Temple, and I could see that her presence fit somehow with his plans, as he asked her to be especially certain to comfort the bereaved woman. Knowing him so well, I knew what he was really asking was for her to distract the new widow at those times when his investigations needed to be carried out without the woman's knowledge.

When asked to describe Beatrice Temple, Priscilla replied, "She is a strong woman – as much responsible for her husband's success and advancement as he was. She's originally from Kensington – she's several years older than I am, and she was originally a friend of my elder sister. We were thrown together much as I grew up, and eventually we became rather close.

"Her father died when she was young, and the entire family was forced to become stronger because of it. She and Frederick married more than a quarter-century ago, and they have been very happy together. I rather lost touch with her when her husband was enthroned as the Bishop of London in the mid-1880's, but she took time to reach out to me five years ago when he became the Archbishop. I've been down to the Archbishop's Palace quite a few times since then, but I see her much more often at their London residence in Lambeth Palace."

206

Holmes questioned her about Temple's sudden shift in belief, which had led to him writing the inflammatory document. Priscilla shook her head, puzzled. "He was always interested in everything, you see – science, nature. People and politics. Not what you'd think of as the titular leader of the Church at all. I suppose when I was younger, if asked, I would have imagined the Archbishop of Canterbury as a monastic type, given to gloom and grim pronouncements, dressed all in black and emanating final judgments wherever he turned. But Frederick was a laughing man – happy, intelligent, and a good leader. I can only think that his final illness had either given him some sense of urgency to accomplish a long-held secret agenda, or that his mind had been affected in ways no one realized, causing him to become so reckless at the very end."

As we each fell silent and into our own thoughts, I held my wife's hand while looking past her and out onto the winter-locked Kent countryside. The trip from London to Canterbury was only seventy miles or so, and accomplished in less than two hours, but in some ways it might have been a journey back in time. The little farms dotted here and there, decorated with their fascinating oast houses, probably looked the same as they had four-hundred years before. Living in the city, with every day being a headlong rush further into the Twentieth Century, sometimes made one careless in one's thinking, believing that everyone had the advantage of modern advances in electricity, transportation, and sanitation. Seeing this space between our departure and our destination made it clear that more of the country than not was still living within the constraints of the old ways, and would likely be doing so for quite some time to come.

I looked for some signs of Christmas along our journey, but it was rarely seen. A wreath here and there on a barely seen station, perhaps, but nothing on the distant lonely farms and houses. I could only hope that there would be seasonal happiness in all of them, and I silently wished them well.

We were quiet and pensive until our arrival at the newer eastern Canterbury Station – newer in the sense that it was constructed fourteen years after the western station, which was built over half-a-century before. Holmes and I followed Priscilla, who knew the way, out of the modest brick building to the cab rank, where she motioned for a growler. Holmes glanced toward me with a small grin, and I recalled his maxim, which he himself only honored on certain occasions, to take neither the first nor the second cab which might present itself. This was much more difficult when obtaining a cabbie's services in the ordered lines outside a station, and in any case, it seemed unlikely that any attempt would be made to abduct us here – although it wasn't entirely unknown in our combined experiences.

Once aboard, Priscilla surprised us both by giving instructions to set out for the Old Palace, as she called it. I had believed that we were bound for the Cathedral and the Archbishop's chambers there, and I could tell that Holmes had believed the same. Priscilla explained. "The Old Palace is within the limits of the Cathedral. When Frederick was installed as Archbishop, he set about restoring an Eleventh Century building on the grounds. He is – *was* – the first Archbishop to have lived there since the Seventeenth Century."

She barely had time to explain this as we reached our destination. If not for Priscilla's presence, I believe that Holmes and I could have walked, even carrying our light luggage, as it probably wasn't more than half-a-mile from the station.

I had been to the Cathedral before while joining Holmes in several different investigations, including the events which uncovered the true facts about the suicide of Thomas à Becket – a story for which the world is truly not prepared. I had never visited at Christmastime, and was surprised to see that very little had been done to decorate for the season. But upon reflection, I recalled that the typical festive decorations that we know so well, many having been adopted from various ancient pagan religions, probably had no place here.

The portion of the city through which we passed had embellished for Christmas, but the mood was notably muted, no doubt following the death of the Archbishop. Groups of men and women huddled in conversation, and as we approached the Cathedral, more and more of them seemed to be looking that way, as if speculating as to what might be occurring inside.

There was a large Christmas tree set up on a wide cleared spot, and nearby was a Nativity scene with nearly life-sized mannequins in familiar poses. But we only had a chance to see them for an instant before arriving at our destination.

The Old Palace was a lovely stone building, ranging intermittently between two and three stories. We turned into the circular drive off Palace Street and passed by a decorative fountain, stopping before a front door that opened from a small angled covered projection extending from the main building. There was a jarring mixture of traditional Christmas decorations (including colorful ribbons and secular holly and ivy) and black mourning drapery being installed across the front of the house by church workmen, as if both types of adornment were competing, and the winning theme had not yet been decided.

A stout woman in black had emerged as we drew to a halt, her hands clasped before her and holding a handkerchief. Beside her was a tall and painfully thin fellow in his early thirties, also dressed in mourning, his hands behind his back while he stooped forward, rather stork-like – apparently his natural posture.

Priscilla stepped down from our conveyance and went immediately to the woman. They embraced. Then, while still in that pose, the woman looked over my wife's shoulder toward Holmes. "We received your wire," she said, her voice steady and strong. "Thank you for coming. My husband's study is ready for your examination."

Clearly, in spite of her loss, she was a strong woman who had a clear idea of what needed to be done.

"Although it isn't necessary after all," said the man behind her. "The document has been recovered."

The woman – clearly Mrs. Temple – released Priscilla and stepped back. She glanced toward the tall man with a fleeting frown. "This is true. I suppose that Frederick thought he was being clever, but he hid his essay underneath a false bottom in a desk drawer. Stephen had forgotten about it, and I only thought to look there this morning, when we were straightening the mess in the office for your investigation, Mr. Holmes."

I didn't look at my friend, but I could imagine the reaction that he was struggling to suppress upon hearing that statement. If a Scotland Yard inspector had been so foolish as to utter such a thing about cleaning up and in the process destroying clues, Holmes would have had no hesitation at releasing a blistering rebuke. But this was the new widow of the Archbishop of Canterbury. Such a thing was not done – even by Sherlock Holmes, who typically had little regard for social mores.

"That is a relief," Holmes replied, his voice level. "Still, might Watson and I visit the study, and speak with Mr. Smythe, while you and Mrs. Watson reacquaint yourselves?"

Mrs. Temple nodded. She glanced again at Stephen Smythe. "Of course. I would like to gain some understanding why my husband have taken this course." She appeared to be on the verge of speaking further, but stopped herself, took Priscilla's hand, and turned to walk away toward the door, leaving us on the drive with the secretary.

"This way, gentlemen," he said after a few seconds, holding out a hand toward the door where the two women had just vanished, as if to prod us into motion.

"One moment," countered Holmes, seemingly oblivious to the cold December morning, or the fact that the tall thin man facing us had no winter coat. "As I understand it, you hurried down yesterday after the Archbishop's death to secure his papers."

The man nodded, folding his arms pointedly and tightly around himself in an obvious attempt to stay warm.

"You knew of this document. Was that specifically what you wanted to secure?"

"It was."

"If it was so important, why was it left here? Why didn't the Archbishop carry it back with him to London?"

"That I cannot say. I had been responsible for packing up most of the Archbishop's papers before our return to Lambeth Palace last week, but he himself took care of those he considered most important or confidential. It was only yesterday, before his passing, that he happened to mention that he'd left it here, in Canterbury. I assumed that he had a reason, but it didn't seem appropriate for me to question why. Not long after that, he died, and soon it occurred to me that this document needed to be secured. Explaining in generalities, but not specifically referencing the document in question, I excused myself to Mrs. Temple, came here as soon as I could, and found it to be missing."

"But then it was found this morning. Mrs. Temple recalled that it was hidden in the desk drawer."

He formed a small smile. "Actually, it was me who thought of the hidden cavity in the desk drawer, but Mrs. Temple was closer, and she opened it first. She now seems to remember that she thought of it." He shook his head, as if it were a charming memory.

"We found the original, but – " Here the smile slid from his face and he lowered his voice, although there was no one around to hear us. "I didn't inform Mrs. Temple, as I didn't want to disturb her fragile peace of mind, but there were *two* copies of the document – the original, and one made when it was typed, using carbonic copying paper. That copy, gentlemen, *is* still missing."

Holmes, who had seemed to be losing interest by the minute, straightened a bit, like a hound who hears a distant horn. "Then by all means," he said, "there is still work for us to do here. Please lead us to the study."

I could almost hear Smythe's thoughts expressed aloud: He had been attempting to show us in that direction when Holmes had paused, and he could have just as easily told us of the missing copy inside, where he would have been warm. The skeletal man didn't have much meat on him for such a cold day.

The transition from the chilly outside air to the front hall was abrupt, and I was glad to shed my overcoat. A servant took it and my hat, and collected Holmes's Inverness and fore-and-aft cap as well. I sniffed. The house was filled with a most enticing spicy smells suggesting the holidays – quite at odds with the recent death of the head of the house.

Smythe noticed my reaction. "Preparations for the Christmas celebration were already well under way when word came of the Archbishop's death. It was decided that the cooks should go ahead and carry on. If no celebrations occur here in the Palace, then the food can always be distributed to the poor rather than go to waste. Mrs. Temple is very forward thinking, you know, and quite practical. She has been a tower of strength so far, but I'm concerned that she will break at some point. They were married for over twenty-five years, you know. I'm glad that your wife accompanied you, Doctor. Mrs. Temple thinks the world of her."

He had shared this while leading us through the fine house, passing along corridors and through various parlors and sitting rooms before reaching a stairway up to the first floor. More turns brought us to a small room along the rear of the house. "This was the Archbishop's working study," he explained. "He has – *had* – more formal rooms elsewhere in the house for meeting with dignitaries and other important officials."

Smythe started to lead us inside, but Holmes held up a hand, preventing him. "It's too late to see the room entirely undisturbed," he said, "but I still may glean some obscure fact." Then he went ahead on his own, stepping carefully as he examined the space from different vantages before moving from the general to the specific.

"I apologize for Mrs. Temple clearing things up," explained the secretary, watching him curiously. "After the document was found, I didn't want to upset her by revealing that a copy was still missing. She seemed so relieved. Thinking that all was now well, she began to put things back in order that had been shuffled during the search. I'm aware that you might have learned a great deal from the scene if it had been left alone – who else might have been in here, and who might have taken the copy." He turned to me with a smile – quite ghastly on his cadaverous face. "I'm rather a student of Mr. Holmes's methods, Doctor, and an admirer of your published works. Your narrative of that Dartmoor devil dog earlier this year was rather fascinating, you know, and I was quite surprised at the conclusion. It never seems to be who you think, does it?"

I shook my head, paying more attention to Holmes than the words of the thin young man beside me. By now, Holmes was seated at the desk, looking half-heartedly through the stacks of documents on top before pulling out the drawers.

"Do you suspect," he asked Smythe, "that someone might have taken the copy?"

"I don't know. There have been no signs of break-ins, and the staff is completely trust-worthy. And there have been no visitors for the Archbishop in this office for months – long before he wrote his . . . his *manifesto.*"

"We've been informed of the general nature of the thing, as you related to my brother," said Holmes. "Have you exaggerated?"

Smythe shook his head. "Not at all. In some ways, it might be worse than what I was able to convey. I know what it *said*, but there are those who will be able to pull it apart and twist it and imply things that are much worse." He looked from one to the other of us for a moment, to see if we understood. "There is much there for those who wish for an excuse to become angry. Very angry."

Holmes thought for a moment and then pulled some stacks of random files and pinned pages toward him across the desktop, turning them this way and that as he examined them. He then pivoted to look through the few sheets that were contained in the Archbishop's wastepaper basket beside the desk before shifting back to the desk, pulling at his ear for a moment before leaning forward and opening the deeper lower drawer on the bottom right. He looked inside and then leaned back to examine the outer dimensions. Then – apparently deciding that the inside was much indeed more shallow than the outside – he reached in, made a motion with his hand, and lifted the false bottom of which we'd been informed. I stepped forward and peered down. It was empty, which was no surprise at all. Still, I'd wanted to see it for myself.

"Was there anything else here besides the original document?" Holmes asked, leaning back in the dead man's chair.

"Nothing."

"And where is the original document that you recovered?"

"Here," said Smythe, pulling some folded sheets from inside his coat and handing them across the desk. "See for yourself – these are dangerous thoughts."

"Where is the typewriting machine?" I asked.

"Why, it's that one," said Smythe, gesturing behind me. There, along a wall near a window, was a much smaller *L*-shaped desk. The shorter leg of the *L* jutted into the room, holding an old Standard machine, manufactured in America by Remington. "We had it cleaned and refurbished earlier this year," the secretary continued. "It was becoming intolerable."

As I stepped over and leaned down to look at it, attempting to see the striking surfaces in the weak sunlight from the window, Holmes asked, "Did you type this, or the Archbishop?"

"Oh, he did," replied Smythe. "He copied it from his handwritten notes. I only knew of its existence when he was finished and asked me to read through it."

"When was that?"

"Less than a week ago. Let's see . . . It was on Saturday afternoon. The 20th."

Holmes took a moment more to read through the document, then looking at the edges and back of the pages before handing them to me.

"Strong stuff," he said. He gestured at the Archbishop's desk. "Where are the handwritten notes? I've only made a cursory search, but there isn't much here. I suppose he kept the bulk of his papers in London, and I see nothing related to this – no drafts, no supporting documents that might have been used for his research."

Smythe shook his head. "Last Saturday, when he let me read it, he said that he'd destroyed all the notes, as they might be too dangerous, and that there were now only two copies – 'Tossed them in the fire,' he explained about his notes, adding that no one had any business reading the unpolished version. I had the impression that it was more abrasive and offensive than what he eventually typed."

As he spoke, I myself looked through the four sheets and saw that this was indeed much more explosive than anything we had previously been led to believe. Not only did it contain the thoughts, ideas, and suggestions that Mycroft had described, but it was written in a highly nationalistic and insulting manner. For instance, it didn't simply suggest reunification between the Church of England and the Catholic Church – it advocated the complete absorption and subjugation of the latter by the former, with the removal of the Pope entirely, along with the recommendation that he be punished publicly for heresy.

It quoted scripture in twisted ways to affirm England's chosen status, while greatly diminishing – in extremely belittling terms – our Continental neighbors in a most jingoistic manner. And the xenophobic comments about immigrants were some of the most unchristian statements that I had ever seen, outside of disgusting letters to certain disreputable newspapers.

I was aware of how small turns of phrase and the most subtle of nuances could alter the meaning and outcome of diplomatic documents. There was no subtlety here. Should this be made public, as signed by the Archbishop of Canterbury, there would be fighting in our own streets within the week – and that wasn't even taking into account what footing England would find itself upon against other offended nations who only sought the slightest excuse to escalate toward violence.

"We will need to inform Mrs. Temple about the copy," said Holmes. "Can you go and fetch her?"

Smythe nodded and left the room. We heard him walk down the hallway, his footsteps fading until that side of the building was deadly quiet. Then Holmes jumped from the seat, where he had appeared to be slumped in some sort of middle-aged and defeated weariness. "Watch the door!" he hissed before seating himself at the secretary's desk.

I looked both ways down the hall, but we were alone. "The document – " I began, but Holmes interrupted me.

"No carbon," he said in a low voice. "There is no indication that a carbonic copy of the document was actually made – no smearing of the carbon ink at paper's edge, or where a finger might have touched the ink and then the original. And sometimes when a typewriter strikes a period or comma, it perforates the paper. When a carbon sheet is underneath, this carbon will show up on the back of the original sheet – on the perforated indentation. None of that exists. See for yourself."

I did and confirmed that the back of the sheets in hand were unmarked in the way he described. As I did so, Holmes was quickly opening and closing the drawers, pulling out various typewritten documents that were filed there. Then with a low whistle, he located a box of carbonic paper. He opened it and held some of the top sheets to the light. "New – not previously used." Then he replaced the box and began to go through the sizeable amount of litter in the wastepaper basket beside the secretary's desk.

"Some of these documents are more than three weeks old – clearly it hasn't been emptied in a while. Neither had the Archbishop's basket. There are no used carbon sheets in either place, so it's almost certain that none were thrown away. That's enough proof, I think. No carbon sheets were used, and the fact that the document you hold shows no signs of being copied in such a way is also enough."

"Enough for what?" I asked. "What does this mean?"

"You don't think that I came down here without doing my research?" he asked. "The only person who knew of the existence of this document was the secretary. It was he who took the trouble to notify Mycroft that it had been written and was missing. He has thrown us all – not just you and me and your good wife, but the entire grim machinery of the government – into a frantic scramble of attempted recovery and frantic preparation with his description of how destructive it might be.

"Now, having read it, we see that it's much worse. And how were we able to read the original? Because it was conveniently found for us. Smythe even let us know that it was he who thought of where it was hidden, although he noted that it was Mrs. Temple who recovered it. Now we don't have to take his word for how bad it is – we can read what it says for ourselves! But then he went on to inform us that there is a copy – and it's missing! A copy exists, and we only have only Smythe's word for that too, and as to how this extra document was produced in the first place – a story that's demonstrably false."

"Who is this Smythe?" I whispered. "It seems as if the has much to explain."

"Indeed. And yet, we can't show our hand too soon, before we understand his game. Clearly – "

But it was too late for him to explain further, as I gave a soft "Hist!" when I heard returning footsteps. Holmes slipped out of Smythe's chair, quietly replaced it under the desk, checked to make sure that the secretary's work area and wastebasket looked as they had before, and then settled back in the Archbishop's seat, slumping to the pose he'd held just moments before. He was that way when Smythe, Mrs. Temple, and Priscilla came in, but he pulled himself wearily to his feet and faced them.

"Mrs. Temple," he said, glancing at Smythe, who looked concerned, "it appears that things are not as resolved as we thought but few moments ago. We've just learned that there was a copy of the document, and it is still missing."

The widow held herself steady, only allowing her concern to be expressed by the appearance of a deep V between her brows. "I have read the sheets, Mr. Holmes," she said. "I understand what this could mean." Then Mrs. Temple's voice broke and Priscilla, her arm already holding her, squeezed tighter. "I . . . I don't know what could have happened. What could Frederick have been thinking? Do you think, Doctor," she asked, shifting her gaze from Holmes to me, "that he might have had some illness – a tumor perhaps – that would have made him take such an unexpected and dangerous path? This is so unlike . . . so unlike . . . the man who I was . . . ." With that, she began to weep – possibly for the first time since her husband's death – and pivoted to lay her head on my wife's shoulder.

I nodded toward Priscilla, and she led Mrs. Temple from the room.

"What now, Mr. Holmes?" asked Smythe. "What should we do? Where should we look next?"

"A very good question," responded Holmes. "Time is short, and the copy may already be in the enemy's hands."

I glanced from him to the secretary, my mind racing to catch up. Holmes had determined to his satisfaction that there was no copy, and yet he was going forward as if it actually existed, and allowing Smythe to agree with him. Further, he had proven that the secretary's story of the copied version was false, as well as pointing out that no one actually knew of the existence of this copy except for the secretary who reported it missing in the first place. What was Smythe's game?

The secretary nodded. "I attended the Archbishop's meetings, including those with members of Government. I understand what's going on in the wider world. By 'enemy', you mean Germany."

Holmes nodded. "Our relations with the Kaiser have never been easy, and have only deteriorated since the Queen's death." He paused, looking back and forth across the room as if to see if anywhere else needed examination. "It would make the most sense," he continued, "that, after hiding the original here, the Archbishop carried the copy with him upon his return to London. Are you sure that it isn't there? Did you search his office in Lambeth Palace before traveling here?"

"I did, but not as carefully as I might have. When I recalled that the document was here, I assumed that both copies would be together and hurried down to retrieve them. Then, when I found only the original, I kept the knowledge to myself, not wishing to upset Mrs. Temple further, and also because I knew that you were on your way."

Holmes nodded. "Then there's a good chance that it's still in London. Can you return there as soon as possible to examine the Archbishop's papers? In the meantime, if it truly is missing, I'll alert the Government to take the next steps toward mobilization."

"What do you mean?" asked Smythe.

"Simply this: If the copy of that document has fallen into our enemy's hands, war is imminent. Watson and I have been told that by my brother, Mycroft, whom you know and notified yesterday. If so, we will need every minute – nay, every *second* – to do what we can to prepare, ineffective though it might be."

Smythe swallowed and nodded. "The Germans – they are ready to fight now. That's what the Archbishop thought – that we should fear the Germans."

Holmes nodded. "I'm glad that you understand. Now hurry back to London – on the next train. Search anywhere in the Palace that the Archbishop might have left the copy and let my brother know what you find. In the meantime, I'll see what we can do here."

The secretary nodded and left the room. I followed quietly to the door and made sure that he was gone before turning back to face Holmes.

"Can you explain?" I whispered with some urgency.

"Not entirely," was his tense reply. "The idea of the copied document is an unexpected twist, and the fact that Smythe so clearly lied about it makes his other statements highly questionable as well."

"I see. For instance, we only have his word that Temple typed it."

"Exactly. I've established that Smythe typed it, not the Archbishop. This document – " And he tapped his finger on the four sheets that had been left lying on the desk. " – was executed by a skilled typist. Similar examples can be found in Smythe's desk drawer – samples that he clearly produced. But Temple was a very unskilled typist of the two-finger variety with a very uneven style. This can be verified from documents in his own desk that he clearly wrote himself. So that too is another one of Smythe's lies. The question is *Why*? What does he hope to accomplish, other than to throw the entire Government into a frenzied preparation of war?"

"So you believe, then, that just because there is no carbonic copy then there is no other actual copy at all? If he's such a good typist, he could have simply prepared another original."

"That is true, but he had access to the carbonic paper, and his story is that there was a copy, so why not go ahead and make a copy? For that matter, why 'find' the original and claim there was a copy, when he could just as easily give the original to whomever he wished and stir up as much trouble that way.

"No, he's playing a deeper game. Perhaps all he wishes is to have the country seen to be preparing for sudden war. Our enemies – and allies – can't help but notice it and become concerned, and they may then suddenly begin to escalate for war too. It might take longer for conflict to arise that way than if the letter were to simply be delivered to an embassy or published in the press, but the end result would be the same."

"But how does it benefit Germany to go to war with us now? From all that I've heard from Mycroft over the years, it's inevitable, but they aren't ready yet either."

"Not Germany, Watson. During my research last night, I asked questions regarding several of the players in this drama – some of whom you haven't met, and likely now won't need to. The staff at both the London residence and here, for example. A short *précis* of their various biographies contained a great deal of information, almost all of it quite useless. But I did see that Smythe is a Cambridge man, and that has certain implications."

"What?" I asked. "I don't understand."

"I'll explain later, when I've seen how things progress. In the meantime, I want you to stay here for a few minutes and help your wife comfort Mrs. Temple."

"A while?"

"Yes. Return to London on the next train – it leaves half-an-hour after the one that Smythe will catch – and I'll leave word for you at Victoria when you arrive. Your wife can remain here. In fact, it might be best."

"And where will you be?"

"I intend to be on the same train as Smythe – without his knowledge."

Holmes then instructed me to return downstairs, where he would join me in a few minutes. "Tell them I'm examining the house for signs of intruders."

I found the two women in a small parlor, and was relieved to see that once more Mrs. Temple was in control of her emotions. I explained the

217

secretary's mission, leading them to believe that there was a possibility that the copy was still at Lambeth Palace, carried there a few days earlier when Temple had returned to London. Although I disliked withholding information from Priscilla, I didn't mention that in fact it was almost certain that such a copy as described did not exist, and that the secretary had apparently told us two demonstrable lies, thus undermining anything that he might profess.

Holmes had just rejoined us when Smythe presented himself to us before departing for the station, informing us that if he left then, he'd be in time to catch the next London train. As soon as he was out the front door, Holmes retrieved his case from one side of the room, where it had been left along with our bags since our arrival, and excused himself. Both Priscilla and Mrs. Temple looked at me in confusion, and I rather ineffectively explained that Holmes intended to travel back to London as well, after he made a few preparations.

"What preparations?" asked Priscilla with something that looked like amusement. I realized with a start that she might be enjoying this.

"I don't wish to be identified," replied Holmes, reentering the room almost as soon as he'd stepped out, and setting the case down where he'd removed it a few moments earlier. When stepping into the hall, he'd taken the opportunity to change his appearance into a familiar figure – at least to me – of the venerable old priest who had shared my train compartment as we fled the capital in April '91, just ahead of Professor Moriarty. Back then he'd used his skills to look older, but now, in his late forties, he had grown into the part. I recalled well the wide-brimmed hat and the black cassock. Clearly he'd expected to make use of them, having packed them ahead of time. But then, Sherlock Holmes wasn't anything if not prepared.

"Might I use your telephone?" he asked, and he was directed to a room at the rear of the house. "Any of the staff can show you," added Mrs. Temple.

After he had stepped out once again, I saw that both women had reached the end of their patience and wanted to know what was going on, but I was still evasive. Priscilla seemed to accept that, but the older woman was less tolerant.

"If there is something that you know – something else that is relevant – then I want to know it too." Her square face had a commanding expression, and any hint of the weeping woman from just a few minutes before was gone. Clearly she was able to set aside her grief when necessary.

I was uncertain how much Holmes wanted shared, and simply repeated what they had been told. "Holmes feels that as the original was left here, it only makes sense that the copy might be found London. Mr.

Smythe didn't look for it there before he came to Canterbury yesterday, and he's going back now to check."

Mrs. Temple shook her head. "Clearly Mr. Holmes intends to follow Stephen. I want to know why."

"I'm sorry, Mrs. Temple." I felt uncomfortable being evasive with the two women, one of them my own wife, and the other the widow of the Archbishop of Canterbury. "At times during an affair like this, it's best for knowledge to be held close to one's vest. Holmes likes to hold all the cards – "

"Nonsense! If there's some reason to suspect Stephen, then my opinion needs to be considered!"

"And that is?" asked Holmes, returning into our presence. His telephone call must have been quite brief.

"That I don't trust him. I haven't from the time that Frederick hired him a year ago."

"And why is that?" Holmes glanced at the mantel clock.

"Because he insinuated himself too earnestly, and too quickly. And Frederick was too – it was a weakness he had, especially over the last few years. He wasn't a proud man. He considered it a sin – and rightly too. But he did like it when someone listened to him, nodding and wide-eyed and encouraging him to express his thoughts wherever they might lead. Stephen did that, and I watched with amusement at first, and then with a bit of contempt, I supposed. Finally I quit paying attention to it at all, but I never lost the sense that Stephen cannot be trusted. He never seemed quite sincere, but he was always ambitious."

"I believe that you are correct to think so," said Holmes. He then looked to me. "As I've told Watson on many occasions, I have the greatest confidence in a woman's intuition. What I have strived to learn with such long effort and practice in the way of observation and inference often comes without thought to a woman who sees a dozen different little clues and behaviors and then senses – sometimes without even being consciously aware or able to put into words – that a certain person is exhibiting dishonest behaviors, or any of the objectionable aspects that mankind so often manifests."

I kept silent, remembering when he'd said the exact same thing a year or so after Mary and I had wed, when her opinion had been of especial value during an investigation into the activities of a highly respected minister who in truth was carrying out the most vile and dishonorable acts. Holmes had gathered the evidence, but it was Mary's intuition that had initially pointed the way for him to look.

"I believe that you are correct about Mr. Smythe," continued Holmes. "We'll know in a few hours – and we'll also have determined if the nation is truly at risk because of this dangerous document, or if this is all some sort of conjurer's misdirection. I wish that I had time to discuss it with you further, but now I must fly, for I have just enough time to walk to the station."

"Let me summon the carriage," said Mrs. Temple, rising to her feet and clearly pleased that her opinion had been respected, but Holmes held up a hand. "No need. I can be there shortly. I'm aware of several short-cuts." He turned to me. "Remember – the next train. I'll send word." And then he was gone.

Part III

The next ten minutes or so were rather awkward. The ladies had seen just a hint of Holmes in action, and both knew enough about him to understand that something exciting and important was happening. They also knew that I had knowledge that I wasn't sharing, and they continued to try – at least initially – to get me to tell more than I was willing. It was Priscilla who gave up first, physically throwing her hands in the air with a good-natured smile and telling Mrs. Temple that they would know soon enough. "They like their secrets," she said. "I've already learned that." Then she shook a playful finger in my direction. "But as soon as you can, John, we want the entire story."

I agreed, but saw that Mrs. Temple clearly wasn't prepared to stop querying me that easily. And yet, she too knew that I had told all that I could, and seemed to respect it. Eventually that time had passed and I rose, intending to walk to the station as well, explaining that I was looking forward to it before I too could be offered the use of a carriage.

And in truth I was. It wasn't far, and in spite of the Christmas Eve cold, I wanted to see the famed town decked out in its holiday best, even if I had to hurry through it. Kissing Priscilla and telling them both goodbye, I went to the front hall and retrieved my coat and hat. Then, letting myself out, I set off to the station.

The brisk walk was pleasant enough, but I soon forgot to pay attention as my mind wandered to the curious question of the Archbishop's secretary, and what he was up to. Clearly a document containing such dangerous rhetoric was of great concern, but how it might be used opened up too many pathways of speculation. Arriving at the station, I realized that it was useless to ponder "What If's" without further data. In hopes of mental diversion, I bought a newspaper which contained a great deal about the life of the deceased Archbishop, as well as additional articles about other men who had held the same office, and managed to stay distracted by it during the return trip to London –

– Or at least the portion of the trip wherein I remained awake. I'd discovered that as I aged, I tended to become more sleepy when I allowed myself to relax – and the rocking of a train on Christmas Eve easily contributed to my slumber. I awoke as we arrived at Victoria, and had barely stepped upon the platform while still gathering my senses when a ragged lad approached.

It was Derrick Britton, one of Holmes's current crop of Irregulars. He was a quiet and unsmiling lad, and I wondered if there wasn't some tragedy in his background. However, that was true to some degree with a great many of the Irregulars who had worked with Holmes over the previous decades, and I knew that in spite of their pasts, each was fortunate to be an Irregular, as my friend took them under his wing, making sure that they were fed and clothed and educated, and when they aged past their usefulness as his agents, he found them jobs or other opportunities.

Without a word, Derrick motioned for me to follow. I stepped lively to keep up with him as he nimbly danced through the crowd vacating the train, and soon we were in the street outside and at a cab driven by Abel Whitaker, a long-time acquaintance who frequently made himself available to Holmes when needed.

He nodded. "Step lively, Doctor. We must get you to Clerkenwell."

I turned to offer Derrick a few coins, but he had already vanished into the crowd. Looking back, I saw that Whitaker was favoring me with an impatient expression, so I quickly climbed into his hansom and had barely seated myself when we lurched into motion.

"Where in Clerkenwell?" I called up.

"37a Clerkenwell Green," was the reply. "Mr. Holmes said you'll remember it."

I sighed, recognizing the address. It wasn't more than a couple of miles from Victoria on a straight line, but the separation between the two couldn't have been greater.

Traveling by the shortest route, we would cross the Thames and be almost within sight of the Palace before riding along some of the city's more prosperous and vital streets. But then north of Holborn, conditions would markedly and rapidly decline. I'd heard the story about how one of Charles Booth's assistants, when making his famous London poverty maps, had asked a constable to describe Clerkenwall. "It's a melting pot," was the reply – not in the sense that Americans use with pride when describing their own country and the strength which comes from the diversity of its many and varied immigrants. Rather, what he meant to tell Booth's man was that the area was "where all the stolen silver or jewels come to be melted or disassembled."

Holmes and I had been there just a few months earlier, when retrieving the specially made anointing oil, made from a secret and ancient recipe that was used on those rare occasions a Royal Coronation took place. It had been stolen in a poor attempt to delay or prevent the event from occurring. [2]

At the time the oil was stolen, we had followed a trail from the Palace to the chemist who prepared the oil, and so on to its recovery. Our way had taken us by 37a Clerkenwell Green and the shabby offices of *Iskra*, one of the many Russian revolutionary newspapers that one found all over London. Knowing that was our destination, I began to shift my perspective as to whether the responsibility for the current situation could be laid at Germany's feet after all.

We turned north along Red Lion Square and into Theobalds Road, winding through an ever-narrowing confluence of streets and dark-bricked buildings. However, instead of driving straight to No. 37a, I found that we were a couple of blocks away. No sooner had we pulled to a stop than Holmes appeared, stepping from a dark alley in our direction.

"I'll settle up later," he called up to Abel Whitaker.

"Right you are, Mr. Holmes," said the cabbie, touching a finger to his cap and turning the horse down a side-street. Rather than watch him depart, I followed as Holmes took my arm and led me into the alley from whence he had appeared.

"Things progress quickly," he said softly as we walked. I pulled out my service revolver. "While still at the residence in Canterbury, I was able to quickly question a few of the staff members. They have no liking for Smythe – 'A snake, that one! A cold snake!' said the cook – and they confirmed that he was often on the telephone when staying in Canterbury."

"But surely that would be part of his job," I said, striving to stay caught up as Holmes turned this way and that in the narrow lanes.

"Ah, but he had two behaviors when making telephone calls – those related to his honest profession were open and above-board. But there were others, late at night when it was thought he was alone, which seemed quiet and secretive. 'Sneaking!' affirmed the cook."

"Perhaps a romantic entanglement . . . ?" I asked.

"Perhaps. But while also still at the Canterbury palace, and before my departure, I telephoned Mycroft to set his Myrmidons in motion. As he'd already begun investigating Smythe last night, discovering whom the secretary was calling was no great difficulty. All of the calls were placed to our friend at 37a Clerkenwell Green."

"So it is the Russians who are behind this."

"So it seems."

"And that is where Smythe has gone now?"

"Where he was directed to go. By me."

"What? How did you accomplish that?

"I contrived it on the journey back to London. The next train from Canterbury had several stops, and I was able to send a telegram to Mycroft during one of them with my plan. He set it into motion as Smythe and I completed the remainder of the journey. Your train was an express, so you've actually arrived at the perfect moment, being able to travel straight through, despite your later departure.

"When our train arrived at Victoria, Mycroft had Bert Deacon in place, ready to meet Smythe and offer him cryptic instructions that he should get to the *Iskra* office immediately – while of course taking all precautions. Thus, Bert was able to take an exceedingly tedious and round-about way to Clerkenwall while the rest of the plan was put into place."

Bert Deacon was an old acquaintance of ours, a former rampsman-turned-cabbie who owed his life to Holmes after being falsely charged with a capital crime. He made himself available whenever necessary.

"In the meantime," Holmes continued, "Mycroft sent a note to our acquaintance Jacob Richter at *Iskra*, seemingly from Smythe, announcing that he was on his way, and that Sherlock Holmes and Dr. Watson were involved – nothing more than that. Bert should be dropping Smythe off in about five minutes – just enough time for us to get into position."

By that point we had navigated a thoroughly confusing series of alleys, passages, and near-tunnels, some of which we could barely squeeze through while turned sideways. At times the smell was atrocious, and occasionally we were watched by taciturn residents, standing and smoking with apparently nothing better to do. I had felt that we might go on like this for a while longer when Holmes stopped short and nodded toward a plain wooden door in a blackened brick wall. We had only been there for a moment when we heard a low whistle from around a nearby corner. Apparently it was a signal that Holmes recognized, for he nodded and crept forward. He had a lock-pick in hand, but there was no need. The door was on the latch, and he began to open it very slowly – enough so that any noise that it might have made was avoided. We might not have been heard even if the door had squeaked, for there were angry voices at the front of the ground floor.

"Why are you here?" snarled a man with a high-pitched Russian accent – clearly Richter, whom we had encountered the previous August when tracking the holy anointing oil. "I have nothing for you here! And this message – " There was a pause, and I could imagine him holding a paper out to Stephen Smythe. "'*Sherlock Holmes and Dr. Watson are involved.*' Can you imagine what this means? Involved in what? The

Archbishop's statement? What have you done, Smythe? You were told to lie low when the man died."

"It isn't the time to lie low!" was Smythe's hissed reply. "What better time to reveal this, when the Archbishop cannot deny that he wrote it?"

"You have set things into motion which you don't understand, you fool," countered Richter. "Yes, England and Germany will be pushed into war, but our own forces are not yet strong enough to take down the Tsar. We weren't ready for this yet."

"You are a coward, Richter," snarled Smythe. "You have been here since last April, and all you do is meet and plot, scurrying in the shadows like a rat, and you accomplish nothing! I have forced your hand. I've forced all of your hands!"

"You go too fast! The Committee does not agree with how you wrote this." We heard the rattle of paper. "We have been debating it, and choosing who will do the revisions. It wasn't time yet for the document to be released."

"Revisions! Who among you is worthy to revise it? You? Nadya? Georgy Martov?"

"If you're so proud of it," asked Richter, "and so confident that you've done the right thing, then why did you write that Holmes and Watson are involved? Why did you come here seeking my advice?"

"Write to you?" replied Smythe. "I didn't write to you. Who wrote that message?"

"You did. See here?"

There was a pause, and then Smythe answered, his voice suddenly more soft, as if he sensed danger. "I didn't write that. I'm here because of this message from *you*!" And there was another pause, as I imagined Smythe pulling a similar note from his own pocket and handing it to Richter.

The Russian groaned. "Ah, we are undone, you fool! You have walked us into a trap!"

I was surprised then by the sudden loud burst of a police whistle at my side. Without seeing Holmes repeat the action, and knowing what was coming next, I walked forward into the front part of the building, my friend at my side.

Iskra, or *The Spark* as it was known in English, was a shabby operation – nominally a newspaper, but nothing more than an outlet for revolutionary spew. The main office consisted of a number of tables piled with stacks of flyers and pamphlets, written in a number of languages besides English and Russian, and all espousing the same Socialistic clap-trap demanding the overthrow of ordered society. Numerous places like this had sprung up all over London in recent years, some with much more influence that the one in which we now stood, facing the two men that had been speaking.

Even as Holmes and I stepped in front of them, their eyes drawn to my service revolver, the front door opened, allowing a number of burly constables and one smaller inspector to boil through.

"Nice to see you, gentlemen," said Inspector Lestrade. I assumed that he meant Holmes and me, and not the two figures standing between us.

Smythe had a wild look in his eyes, as if he might bolt or do something else equally foolish. Whatever might have happened was prevented as he was seized by two Bobbies before he could move. Richter, however, simply looked disgusted, and obviously there was no fight in him.

As when we'd met him in the summer, there was a strong stench about him, as if he'd never washed in his life. He was a very curious fellow to observe, with a high rounded forehead, and a prominent receding hairline that was so noticeable that it seemed to be made of wax. His eyes had a stretched and Mongol-like appearance, and his head was bulbous at the top, and narrowing toward a pointed chin, tipped with an asymmetrical and untidy goatee. As I had previously noted, his complexion was terribly marked by angry red patches of *Erysipelas*.

"You have no right to be here," Richter snarled. "Whatever this man has done has led to nothing. He typed a letter. Has it been published? No, it has not. There is nothing more terrible there than if you, Mr. Holmes, wrote an angry letter to the editor of *The Times* – a really vitriolic thing that would get you sued for all you were worth should it appear – but then you did nothing but file it away. Whatever this man has written has caused no damage at all."

"Wrong!" I cried. "He has impugned the reputation of a dead leader of high noble character whose only mistake was to trust a dishonest man." I flung the words at Smythe, but instead of shame, he simply smiled.

"Richter is correct," he said. "Nothing has been published yet. And in any case, I will swear that the Archbishop wrote that document. One way or another the truth will be told."

Holmes stepped forward, taking care to stay out of the path of my gun, and plucked a series of sheets from Richter's fingers. Looking at them, he nodded.

"He did make a copy after all – but it wasn't a carbonic copy. Rather, it's another original." He looked some more, and then pulled the sheets found in Canterbury from his pocket. Comparing them, he added, "There are some differences, but not enough to mention."

"There are other copies," said Smythe, trying to gain the upper hand, but there was something desperate about him. He would have made a poor card player, as his bluff was desperately obvious.

"I think not," said Holmes. "And even if there are, the government understands the nature of this threat now, and can act most expeditiously to counter it."

Smythe was crumbling, but Richter seemed to become more bold. "Where is your warrant, Inspector?" he asked, turning to Lestrade. "You have invaded my premises, and I see no evidence of a crime. I believe that my attorney will advise that I have grounds for a lawsuit."

"I think not," answered Holmes before the inspector could respond. "You see, Richter – or should I say Vladimir Ilyich Ulyanov, or Nikolai Lenin, or whatever name you're using this week – it's known that your return to London after last summer's ill-advised visit is illegal. The best you can hope for is to be deported back to Russia – although the Tsar's Government will be notified of your return, which might spoil your homecoming considerably. One can only hope. In any case, I would advise that you say away in the future."

He turned to Smythe. "And as for you? Once you tried to set this in motion – no doubt motivated by the death of the Archbishop – your background was immediately given the most thorough scrutiny. It wasn't difficult to see that you had been radicalized while at university." Holmes turned to me. "There is a certain group of Cambridge scholars who have an unhealthy admiration for revolutionary extremists like Mr. Richter here. We would be well advised to keep an eye on them in the future."

Looking back at Smythe, he asked, "The business about a copy – that was to panic the government into preparation for war, setting into motion mirrored activities amongst our friends and enemies, leaving the revolutionaries to carry out their own agenda amongst the chaos. But why not actually make additional copies? Why falsely claim to have done so?"

"I was adjusting my strategy as I went," was Smythe's reply. "When the Archbishop died, I decided to set things in motion, despite this coward's attempts to stop me." He sent a glare toward Richter. "I notified Mycroft Holmes, understanding that he could make the most occur quickly. But then he involved you, and you were coming to Canterbury, and I had no time to make more extensive plans."

"And you didn't notify Richter what you had done, preferring to let things grow on their own so that you could present him with a *fait accompli* before he could object."

"It doesn't matter!" snarled Smythe. "I'll tell the press what was in the document. I'll swear it. Some will believe it! And Richter here – he'll have no choice. He'll have to agree, because it serves his interests as well. He'll – "

"He'll do nothing," interjected Lestrade. "You'll be in an unmarked grave after an early morning firing squad at the Tower if you open your mouth, and Richter is too much of a weasel to say anything, knowing that he's being watched by the British Secret Service. And when he gets sent back to Russia . . . ."

I must have shown my surprise, because Lestrade said to me, "The Yard has been briefed on threats from people like these, Doctor. There's a war coming, all right, and we won't have our hands tied." He glanced back at Richter. "You can tell that to all of your vermin friends."

With that, the inspector jerked his head toward the door and the two revolutionaries were shuffled outside. Richter was deported, but he was back just a couple of years later after the events of Bloody Sunday in Russia in January 1905. He stayed for a while at 16 Percy Circus, this time under the name of Lenin, and with much more notoriety. As for Stephen Smythe: I never heard of him again, and have no idea as to his eventual fate. When I asked Holmes about it a few years later, he vaguely replied that it was a topic best left unexplored.

Within moments, the police had departed, leaving Holmes and me standing in the street in front of No. 37a. I realized that the door was left unlocked, but I made no move to do anything about it, or to ask if Holmes might use his lock-pick if no key was evident. We would do no favors for Richter.

There were a number of idlers watching us from different directions. All had faces ranging from expressionless to hostile, and the idea that this was Christmas Eve was clearly meaningless here. Surely there was no loyalty to a filthy specimen like Richter, so their attitude could only be something deeper. I realized that I still held my service revolver in my fist. Consciously and conspicuously, I slipped it back into my coat pocket.

Holmes, meanwhile, raised his fingers to his lips and blew a shrill whistle. In seconds, the sound of a cab lumbering into motion was heard, and then Bert Deacon drove around a nearby corner, sitting atop a hansom cab.

"Baker Street?" he asked.

"No," said Holmes. "Lambeth Palace."

The journey across London was mostly accomplished in silence, except for a few comments on my part as I thought of them.

"You thought it would be resolved more quickly to bring Smythe and Richter together."

Holmes nodded. "It was a unique opportunity, and by delaying Smythe's arrival, we were able to get the pieces in place to hear their

227

conversation. Each thought the other had arranged the meeting, and fortunately, their previous disagreements gave them enough to discuss that they didn't immediately realize they'd been tricked. In any case, it was really unnecessary – Smythe's plan was already essentially understood at that point. It was just helpful to confirm with whom he was working, and just how many copies of the document we were dealing with."

Holmes pulled out both sets from his coat pocket, flipped through them once more as if to confirm that he had all the sheets, and then replaced them.

"I suppose those will disappear into Mycroft's files," I said.

"They will. He has a number of contingency plans squirreled away that aren't so different from these, but tailored to disrupt an enemy as this would have disrupted us. Perhaps there is some nuance here which will be of use to him – although I doubt it. Mycroft is already a master at these games." He frowned in distaste. "And he keeps trying to pull me in."

I started to reply, but he continued. "And the sad part is, I see no other option but to do so. War is coming Watson – if not with Germany, than with the revolutionaries, or combinations of the two, or even other possibilities that we haven't even imagined yet. It will be an ill wind, and those of us who can stand against it will have to do so, at whatever the cost . . . ."

His voice faded, and his gaze seemed to be focused far beyond the bit of passing street that we could see from the cab.

We arrived at Lambeth Palace some time later, and the door opened as we walked toward it. I was most surprised to see Priscilla coming toward me, her arms outstretched, as if I was a soldier returning home after a long war. She then held me closely for a moment without speaking, and I realized that to her, my participation in Holmes's cases would always seem to involve a certain amount of danger. That, and the death of her friend's husband, had made her especially sensitive on that day.

Inside, Holmes explained to me that he had sent a message to Canterbury at the same time he'd wired Mycroft, during his return to London, telling the ladies that they could return on the next train. They had done so, and had arrived at the Palace just before we showed up. He then spent the next quarter-hour describing our own adventures, thankfully downplaying any danger that we might have faced. (And in truth, when compared to so many other encounters that occurred during our investigations, this was not dangerous at all.)

Priscilla offered to stay with Mrs. Temple, but the older lady stoutly refused. "Be with our own husband on your first Christmas together," was her reply. "I shall be fine. Knowing that Frederick did not write that vile document, and that his faculties had not deserted him at the end, has comforted me more than you can know. Go, and make the best of your holidays."

And so we departed. Outside, Bert Deacon waited atop his hansom, and Holmes waved us toward it. "I'll walk," he advised. "I must brief Mycroft, and in turn learn if anything else is required to clean this mess up." He patted his coat. "And I have a couple of documents to deliver."

"I do hope that you'll join us tomorrow for Christmas Dinner," said Priscilla – not the first time she'd invited him.

He responded as usual. "Thank you, but no. I intend to conduct some chemical experiments – a rather quiet day – and then I'll wander over to see Mycroft at the Diogenes Club."

Having expected that response, Priscilla and I nodded and climbed into the hansom. But as we drove away and saw him following in the same direction on foot, I knew that there were other plans afoot to lure him to our house and our first Christmas together.

But that is another story entirely . . . .

Rev. Frederick Temple, The Archbishop of Canterbury,
and his wife, Mrs. Beatrice Temple

NOTES

1. There is a great deal of controversy over Watson's third wife, whom he married in 1902. Canonically, we know very little about her. As related in "The Illustrious Client", by September 1902 Watson had moved to Queen Anne Street, not so very far from Baker Street. This new residence was in the medical district surrounding Harley Street, and was certainly combined with his new medical practice. In *Hot on the Scent: A Visitor's Guide to the London of Sherlock Holmes* (Calabash Press, 1999, p.73), Arthur M. Alexander has identified Watson's residence and practice as No. 9 Queen Anne Street.

    In January 1903, we learn from Sherlock Holmes in "The Blanched Soldier" that *"The good Watson had at that time deserted me for a wife, the only selfish action which I can recall in our association."* This discreetly implies that Holmes didn't get along as well as he might have with the third Mrs. Watson – but as the many post-Canonical stories in which she appears show, their friendship and respect became a very real and tangible thing.

    In "Watson's Wives and A Question of Chronology", found on my irregular blog, *A Seventeen Step Program* (see link below), I provide some information about Watson's first two wives, and explain why this 1902 wife was Watson's third. I also list a number of stories involving her as pulled from Watson's Tin Dispatch Box by the likes of Michael Mallory, Michael Hardwick, Val Andrews (sometimes writing under his own name, and at others as John North), Stuart Palmer, Bert Coules, M.J. Elliott, Lorraine Daly, Daniel D. Victor, Stephen Kendrick, Donald W. Holmes, Philip Jose Farmer, and Nicholas Meyer, among others. They provide her with a variety of names: Amelia, Tilly, Coral, Emelia, Jean, Anna, Violet, Mary, and Julie – to name just a few.

    The name "Priscilla" as Watson's third wife is first introduced by my friend and excellent author, Tom Turley, in his story, "The Adventure of the Disgraced Captain", to be found in *The MX Book of New Sherlock Holmes Stories – Part XXVII: 2021 Annual (1898-1928)*. I'm very glad that that this current entry, "The Canterbury Manifesto", confirms what Tom introduced to us in that earlier volume.

    https://17stepprogram.blogspot.com/2019/11/watsons-wives-and-question-of-chronology.html

2. These events are described in "The Problem of the Holy Oil" in *The MX Book of New Sherlock Holmes Stories – Part VI: 2017 Annual*, as presented by David Marcum from Watson's original manuscript.

The Noel Street Oracle

Our visitor collapsed back into his chair, his eyes wide. "Mr. Holmes – I am astonished! Could it be that you are the very man that our Society has sought? For surely only a mind reader could have known what I would ask, and have such an in-depth report ready for my arrival."

I glanced across to where Sherlock Holmes sat in his usual chair, his back to his chemistry table alongside one of the tall windows looking out upon Baker Street. I was uncertain as to how he would accept this statement, for his visitor might not have been simply expressing amazement at Holmes's recent pronouncement. As an investigator of the occult, Henry Sidgwick could very well, and with great sincerity, be declaring Holmes a clairvoyant, and the uneasy truce between the two that had only held for only a few moments might just as quickly be sundered.

Sidgwick's initial arrival had started on civil-enough terms.

"I believe," said the older man to Holmes as he adjusted himself to our basket chair, "that we might have some relatives in common," As an opening gambit, my interest was piqued. I had known Holmes for well over a year by then – in truth nearly two – and during that time I'd learned precious little concerning his past. He was as good at protecting his own privacy as he was in ferreting out other's secrets. The idea that this somewhat gaunt and bearded man of middle age might cause Holmes to confirm or reveal a rare personal fact made me sit a bit straighter.

"Really," said Holmes, his response level and even. My increased attention hadn't gone unnoticed. I observed perhaps the faintest smile bending his lips, but I could also tell that his interest in the prospective client was thus far unengaged. He held himself with – perhaps – even the slightest edge of overly polite hostility, and from the manner that he'd accepted the visiting card presented to him just moments before, all signs were that the interview would be a short one if things didn't change soon.

"From your manner of speech," Holmes added, "I place you originally from somewhere in the Craven district, west of York. I'm unaware of any of my people residing in that side of the county."

"Nevertheless," said Henry Sidgwick, crossing his legs and settling back, making himself comfortable for a longer stay. One could see that with his thin frame, he appreciated our warm fire on that cold November morning. "I can tell that you're a Yorkshireman like me, although you have worked to mostly eliminate the tell-tale signs from your way of speaking. So we have that in common, at least. One of my father's cousins always held a willful streak, and it's my recollection that when she bolted over thirty years ago from Skipton, where we were from, it was toward the North Riding, and the Dales beyond Thirsk. The story goes that it was a man named Holmes in those parts who offered her more in his poverty than anything that she might have found if she'd stayed near her family." He'd been reflectively stroking his long gray beard as one might absent-mindedly coddle a cat. He suddenly sat up and leaned forward to peer closer at my friend, grasping and squeezing his beard into a tight rope, a speculative look upon his face.

"What are you?" he asked Holmes, an intent look in his eyes. "Surely you aren't yet thirty."

"I'll be twenty-nine in early January."

Sidgwick nodded, settling back again. "I was born in '38, and my cousin was older than me – old enough to be your mother, in fact. What was your mother's name – Edith, perhaps?"

"It was not." Holmes glanced my way, as if weighing how much information to provide. Then, he shifted and carefully laid the man's visiting card on the octagonal table kept beside his chair. "Her name is Violet, and she was not from Skipton. But that is neither here nor there. You requested an appointment for something else. Your note mentioned a matter of blackmail."

"It did."

"But you provided no specifics. Understandable, I suppose." Holmes tapped the card. "And is it in relation to this . . . *Society* of which you are the leader?" He said it with a curious flatness, but I could tell with ease by that stage in our friendship that he was masking a certain contempt for the organization that Sidgwick led, as named on his card.

"It is," replied our caller, his tone now also shifted as he sensed Holmes's implied judgement and prepared to defend himself. I wondered how often he, a man described in Holmes's commonplace books as both a noted economist and philosopher, had found himself of late making the same excuses for being the leader of a recently formed group that investigated the occult.

"The Society of Psychical Research was conceived to investigate phenomena," added Sidgwick, with just the barest defensive hint in his tone, "not to actively and blindly promote it like some circus barker."

"I see," said Holmes, his lips tight. "And of the investigations that you've completed since the group was organized nine months ago, how many occurrences have you happily certified as genuine?"

"None."

That answer was unexpected, and surprised both Holmes and me. When Sidgwick's message requesting an appointment had arrived earlier that morning, Holmes had recalled the man's connection with the newly organized group, and his initial reaction was to refuse to see him completely. I believe that if the rent hadn't been due in a few weeks – and in those days, Holmes's share was always less certain than my own, as mine came from a steady wound pension – Sidgwick wouldn't have gained entry at all.

"I believe," said the older man, his tone becoming just the least bit more sharp, "that you have accepted the inaccurate press reports of the Society's formation at face value, without taking the time to obtain additional facts. I expected better of you, Mr. Holmes." Then he smiled, as if making a point to a favored student. "One really mustn't jump to conclusions." I almost expected him to end the sentence with a benevolent, tolerant, and condescending, "young man", but that, at least, was withheld, which was probably why Holmes seemed to listen and take in the offered lesson in the spirit that it was apparently intended.

"I agree," he responded, nodding, "and you are correct. When I first read of your organization at the time of its formation, and subsequent reporting about its subjects of investigation, I did make assumptions that were unwarranted. I apologize."

But then he sat straighter still. "But what is your agenda, sir? You haven't yet found a legitimate psychical occurrence, but do you still hope to? I'll grant you the benefit of the doubt that your tests will be fair, but is it your desire to find that one overwhelmingly convincing occult circumstance that will serve as incontrovertible proof that such things do exist? Because if that is the case, then I am not the detective you seek."

Sidgwick shook his head. "Dear me, Mr. Holmes, you're still making assumptions! I'm not an advocate for occult phenomena. Nor am I the enemy of it. I don't promote or deny. I want to *investigate* – To seek the truth! – just as I'm sure that you strive to remain impartial when investigating a case of slander or theft or . . . or blackmail – without any preconceptions."

Holmes nodded. "Then I apologize again, and instead of seeking to lead you around to some sort of debate, perhaps you should simply tell us why you're here, and I can determine if I might assist you."

Sidgwick nodded as if to say, *"Finally!"* but he held his tongue, showing that at forty-four – his age as based on his statement that he was born in 1838 – he had learned discretion and tact. It was something that I didn't always see in my highly intelligent but often impulsive friend. And yet, instead of immediately relating the nature of the blackmail, Sidgwick seemed to become hesitant, veering off to give us a *précis* of his institution, and I feared that Holmes's forbearance would now be terminated for sure.

"As you know," explained Sidgwick, "the Society for Psychical Research was formed in February of this year to investigate occurrences of psychic phenomena. Telepathy, ghosts, spirit writing – it takes many forms. My associates and I have actually been involved in something along these same lines for several years – investigating such things – and as I was the one who was initially curious and motivated enough to ask the questions, our gathering was sometimes called by certain wags the 'Sidgwick Group'. When we made it more formal, I was named founder and chosen as the first president.

"My training is in the fields of ethics and economics – seemingly two very different paths of study, each of which might be explored for years without reaching bottom. And yet, if one thinks for just a moment, is there any field that needs ethics more than economics? But conversely, can ethics truly survive untainted when economics are a necessary consideration? It's a fascinating question – at least for me it is.

"These interests, combined with my own personal struggles related to religious belief, led eventually to interest in the legitimacy of the various practitioners of the occult that seem to be spreading like mildew across the Kingdom. If these men and women are charlatans, then it is for their own economic benefit, and when they play on people's deepest hopes and fears, without conscience or concern, it becomes an ethical question. As I pondered the questions that one topic raises in connection to the others in a cold academic way, I must admit that my interest began to bloom in a more vulgar manner – as if I were a boy at the carnival, wishing to be fooled by a trick, and yet at the same time wanting to know that it *was* a trick, and how it was accomplished, and what mechanisms were employed."

He was becoming more enthusiastic, sitting forward in his chair, his hands punctuating his words while looking from Holmes to me, judging how he was being received. Rather than allow this explanation go become a sermon, once again giving Holmes the feeling that he was being recruited to a debate, I interrupted. "But the blackmail, Mr. Sidgwick – Tell us of that."

He stopped short, no doubt ready to pivot to his next point, deeper and deeper into an explanation of both the obvious and hidden connections between economics, ethics, and supernatural showmanship.

"Ah yes," he said, caught up short. "The blackmail. Yes." He looked back toward Holmes. "In the last month or so, a new thought-reader has set up shop in Soho – in a little house in Noel Street, near Wardour Street.

"Indeed. Señor Esteban Carvalos."

Sidgwick nodded and started to speak, but Holmes continued. "This self-styled oracle was originally named Sidney Stephen Blevins – also known as Steven Carvel, sometimes Benjamin Brooks Stanton or Alfred Endicott, and at one point, Dr. Basil Heath. I believe there were other names as well. He is an American – although most wouldn't know it now – originally from a district near Manhattan known as 'the Bronx', and he only fled to these shores in 1877 after New York became too hot for him, first setting up shop in Liverpool and then Manchester, before shifting his operations to the capital."

Sidgwick collapsed back into the basket chair, his eyes wide. "Mr. Holmes – I am astonished! Could it be that you are the very man that our Society has sought? For surely only a mind reader could have known about what I would ask, and have such an in-depth report ready for my arrival."

Holmes shook his head. "The information I just provided is the result of my continuous professional effort to stay even with the activities of those less-than-salubrious residents of this city and whatever schemes they are enacting from week to week." He was speaking rather pompously I thought, as if putting the older man in his place. "I have a number of informants who bring me regular reports of such men as Blevins – as we will call him, as that's his real name. Keeping track of him and ascertaining details of his past with a few telegrams to my American contacts, along with one sally into enemy country earlier this year to get a look at him in person, was enough to confirm what I needed to know.

"I have no ethereal gifts," he continued, "other than painstaking attention to detail. If anything, you might look to yourself for mind-reading powers, Mr. Sidgwick – for you seem to have chosen the one man in London who can likely help you. I take it that your Society became aware of Blevins and attempted to test him, and in doing so, some among you allowed him to discover information that is now being used in an attempt to increase his own personal wealth at your expense."

"That's it exactly!" cried Sidgwick, slapping the arm of the chair.

"When setting up the appointment, he asked who would be attending."

"He did."

"And how long between setting the appointment and its actual occurrence?"

"A little over a week."

Holmes turned over a hand. "He is nothing if not thorough. With those names in hand, and with the resources he's already put in place, there was more than enough time to turn his full attention to those men. Apparently your fellow members, sir, have secrets."

"Who doesn't? But I'm not ashamed of mine, so when this man asked for a meeting after our initial examination to explain what he was up about, and to accept my 'donation' for him to keep my secrets, I laughed in his face. But afterwards, I recalled that two of the three men who had accompanied me were both acting differently when we recently, and I began to wonder if they too had also been approached. I spoke to both of them in private, and such is the level of our friendship that they confided in me – not *why* they're being blackmailed, you understand, but that it is occurring, and by whom."

"And you say Blevins requested to meet with you?"

"The reptile sent a message, asking if he and I could have a private discussion over what he claimed to have read in my mind during our first meeting. He went on to mention a couple of names that hold great significance to me – but are no one else's business! – and offered his services to make sure that the Press didn't learn of them."

"For how much?"

"Five-thousand pounds."

Holmes raised his eyebrows and whistled. "These names must be important."

"They are – and for their sakes the connection needs to remain hidden. But I don't have that kind of money. The very idea is ridiculous. If Blevins delved deeply enough into my background to find those names, then surely he knows that too. He seriously misjudged his scheme. When I told him so, he shook his head with a sad little smile and said he'd give me time to reconsider before the information appears in the newspapers. Still, I cannot imagine that it will matter much even if he does offer the names to them, as my doings and those who know me wouldn't be of interest to anyone."

"And the other men? You say that two of them had similar experiences?"

"Exactly."

"What about the third?"

"He resides outside of London, and I haven't had a chance to confer with him."

"What was the position of the two you've questioned?"

"They also seem inclined to let Blevins do what he wants and reveal what he's discovered rather than pay. But I feel responsible. I led these men into this situation, and now something must be done."

"Tell me more of your initial visit to Blevins' chambers."

"It was just over a week ago, on the eighth – a Wednesday. Seven o'clock. Blevins does all of his readings in the evening. We four were just on time, and the door was answered by a manservant – a tall fellow in a turban."

"That would be Lyle Statton," interrupted Holmes. "Originally from Berkshire."

"Really. Well, he was addressed as 'Hakim' when I saw him. I would have sworn that he was from somewhere in the Far East. I should have caught that he wasn't truly foreign – we all should have. In any case, on

237

the night of our meeting, we were taken to a front room, very tastefully furnished.

"After five minutes or so, the turbaned fellow returned and announced that Blevins was ready. We were then taken back to the hall and deeper into the house to a book-lined study, dimly lit by the fireplace and a desk lamp. Chairs had been arranged before a solid old desk, covered in books and papers, but pushed aside so that Blevins could rest his arms on it before him, fingers laced.

"He didn't stand or offer to shake hands, and we didn't offer in return. Instead, we sat, and he welcomed us. The chap with the turban provided us with drinks."

"Did everyone have the same thing, or was there a variety?"

"A small variety. I had water – I am teetotaler. Blevins and . . . and two of the other men had whisky. One of them noted that it was a fine Scottish blend. The fifth chose brandy."

"Did you have any sense that your water had been tampered with? Any feelings of light-headedness or confusion? Suggestibility?"

"No, nothing like that. I suppose that it wasn't necessary. He was going to read our minds, not try to fool us with ectoplasm or table-knocking. If he already knew certain aspects of our past, as you suggest, then having us alert and nervous instead of relaxed would have served his purpose much better.

"He immediately seemed to know who was who without introduction. Of course he'd had our names ahead of time, and must have researched us, so identifying us like that wasn't impressive."

"These other men?" asked Holmes. "I note that you are withholding their names. Are they well known?"

"One is. The other two are not, but I suspect that they have it in them to become great one day." He seemed to expect further questions about them, but Holmes shifted away for the moment.

"I expect that I know what happened next," he explained to Sidgwick. "Blevins explained that he became aware of his 'gift' at a young age. It was initially a burden before he learned to be selective – otherwise constantly hearing the thoughts of everyone around him would have driven him mad. He made no claims about being advised by a friendly spirit or a dead Egyptian or other similar rot – this is a skill that is all his own. He then proceeded to settle into something of a trance, making cryptic comments to each of you in turn that held no meaning to the others, but were suggestive enough to indicate that he knew of your secrets. Then he roused himself, asked if that gave you a sufficient indication of his skills, and suggested that additional visits would be useful, without mentioning a monetary aspect."

"That's it!" said Sidgwick, thumping his knee with a fist. "As if you'd been there yourself."

"And not long after, he made private appointments with hints of more specific information, telling you and the others that he'd actually read much more from your minds then he'd initially let on, and that your financial support in the matter was essential to keep what he knew from being revealed."

"Yes."

"And why don't you believe him? Why don't you think that this is the very evidence you've been seeking of the existence of a true thought-reading oracle?"

"Because I'm not a gullible imbecile!" was the suddenly testy response. "He did nothing in our initial meeting to inspire great confidence that he had true abilities. All of us talked afterward and, without explaining specifics concerning our individual readings, we were in agreement. None of us were impressed."

Holmes nodded. "Then at this point, I need to know the names of the other three men."

"That isn't possible." Sidgwick shook his head. "And I don't really see why. Their experiences were the same as mine. What would that accomplish?"

"I don't know that yet, but I'm not accustomed to having information withheld from me by my clients. One never knows what factors might become relevant. My time should be effectively reserved toward solving your problem, not initially excavating what you haven't told me so that I can only then begin the real job."

Sidgwick was quiet for a moment before replying. "Give me a chance to ask their permission. I'll let you know later today."

"Given that they will agree," Holmes replied, "then what is it that you need from me? It sounds as if you all intend to ignore Blevins' threats, so the threat of blackmail is negated. Clearly you can all weather the storm that the revelation of these secrets might cause. To prosecute him would bring undue attention to you and your friends at a point where you're trying to gain credibility for your Society. So what do you want? To chase him from London and let him prey on the residents of a different city? For that is surely what he'll do."

"I . . . I suppose so, although that doesn't seem exactly right either – to set him loose on other innocents. I just knew that I wanted to consult with someone – to do something." He gave a thin smile. "Perhaps something will suggest itself as you progress."

Holmes uncrossed his legs and stood, signaling that the interview was complete. "Provide me with the names of the other men, and then I'll examine the situation and see what options we have."

Sidgwick considered this and then nodded, rising as well. "I will be in touch, and do what I can. Thank you both for your time." Then he offered his hand to each of us, turned, and departed.

Holmes stood silent until we heard the front door close. Then he stepped to the door and retrieved his Inverness.

"I'll return before lunch," he explained. "It's time to become reacquainted with the latest particulars concerning Mr. Sidney Blevins, known of late as Esteban Carvalos. Although," he added, taking his fore-and-aft cap in hand, "without the names of the other men being blackmailed, I have no intention of wasting any more of my time." With a wave he opened the door and was off.

I considered whether I too wished to venture out into the cold November air and found that I did not. Ringing downstairs for more coffee, I settled into my chair with the morning newspapers, maneuvering until I found a position that helped to ease my aching shoulder. By then, over two years since I'd been wounded at Maiwand, I had more days than not when I felt essentially healed, but the cold always seemed to aggravate the problem.

I read with interest events from the previous day of which I had been sadly unaware. Apparently astronomers at the Greenwich Observatory had reported a red "*coronae borealis*" on the horizon the previous night, consisting of a "*pale-green light fringing the upper edge of the London smoke cloud*". This was related to what was described as a strong electrical storm due to solar activity, first observed in the form of dark spots on the sun a month or so before, which had resulted in numerous disruptions of the electrical and telegraphic systems, causing wires to ignite and instruments to melt. This left me wondering how the human body itself might react to such stresses, and whether fields of electricity passing through us without our knowledge could work for good or ill. Perhaps my own aches and pains that day were less due to my old wounds or the cold, and instead were connected to the invisible energy storm around us. But neither Holmes nor Sidgwick had showed no signs of being affected.

That led me to consider how such acts of nature might be perceived by the ignorant among us, and how men like Blevins are able to prey upon the foolish and the gullible. Conjurers and magicians have certainly been around for as long as civilization itself, and it was truly a wonder that simple-minded credulity hadn't been bred out of the human species by natural selection long ago. Those who could not outrun the predators did not survive to reproduce, or so Mr. Darwin's thinking went, but nothing

240

seemed to prevent the naïve victims of men such as Blevins from reproducing and passing on those foolish characteristics to their descendants.

At midday, Mrs. Hudson brought up my lunch, and I confirmed that Holmes had promised to return. She nodded and left the tray on the table, and beside Holmes's place she put a small note in a sealed envelope. "This was delivered just a few minutes ago," she explained before returning downstairs.

I was just tucking in when the downstairs door opened and closed and energetic footsteps dashed up the stairs. It was Holmes, of course, and he quickly divested himself of hat and coat before joining me at the table. He rubbed his hands when he saw the envelope.

"I hope that these are the names," he said. "I should hate to let go of this matter on principle because my client is keeping secrets." He took the clean butter knife and slit open the envelope. Then, dropping the knife on the table with a clatter, he pulled out a folded sheet. "Ah," he said after reading it. "All three of Sidgwick's comrades are willing to be interviewed."

He tossed the sheet my way and turned his attention to the ham sandwich on his plate.

"I've met one of these men," I said. "He's a doctor – graduated about a year ago from the University in Edinburgh. We were introduced when he was down here earlier this year with Dr. Bell for a seminar. We've run across each other a few times since then, but I'd heard he moved to Portsmouth back in the spring or summer."

"Well, apparently he was in London a week ago as part of Sidgwick's expedition to Noel Street. What of the other two?"

I shook my head. "No idea about one of them, but I expect that Sir Clive is the fellow that Sidgwick felt is well-known." I laid the envelope and note aside. "I don't know him. Is he well-known to you?"

"I have heard of him, but only because his name came up last year peripherally connected to an embezzlement scheme at one of the banks in the City. I'm sure that he was guilty, but there was no proof. Perhaps it's something related to those events that the supposed mind-reader uncovered. In any case, Mr. Sidgwick needs to be more careful in terms of whom he allows into his little club if Sir Clive is representative. After all, they're trying to make themselves respectable."

He said it with something of a jibe and a sneer, and I felt that I had to question him further. "In the time that we've known one another," I've said, "you've turned down any number of cases involving supposed supernatural connections. With your obvious disdain for that type of thing, I would think that you would leap at the chance to discredit the many humbugs, mountebanks, and quacks who victimize the too-trusting sheep among us."

He finished chewing a bite of sandwich, swallowed, and then took a sip of water. "It's a steep and slippery path to walk," he explained, "and such work might quickly consume me, taking my mind from better and more productive things, as there's a never-ending supply of it. I have a friend that I met several years ago while living in Montague Street – Alton Peake is his name – who does just that sort of thing. He's set himself up as something of a 'Consulting Occultist' – a fine fellow, and not at all fooled by the hoaxers. And yet he keeps his mind dangerously open to possibilities – rather like Sidgwick described. Perhaps a little too open, to my way of thinking. One of these days, in his enthusiasm to encounter a real ghost, Peake is going to miss a clue, and when the truth is known, all of his credibility will be lost."

"You say that he keeps his mind 'dangerously open', but along those same lines, mightn't yours be 'dangerously closed' to the possibility that there is more to the world around us than what we can understand? I can tell you of some truly strange and amazing things that I saw in India and Afghanistan – "

"I have a maxim for such situations as this," Holmes interrupted. "You have no doubt heard it before. 'No ghosts need apply.' If I were to credit the existence of spirits and phantoms as active agents amongst us, then why bother trying to seek a rational explanation for any crime? Any miscreant could blame a ghost and who could naysay him? How could anyone prove a negative? Young Smith didn't pour the cyanide into Auntie's tea – it was her dead husband that did it – either because he'd always hated her, or conversely because he missed her and wished to rush her along because he's lonely. Any occurrence might be blamed equally upon man or spirit, and by opening up the possibility that something was done by ghosts or demons or mischievous sprites, my suspect list becomes infinite."

He reached forward a finger to tap Sidgwick's note. "Here is a list of three men. I can find out things about them: Are they telling the truth? Are they in league with the blackmailer? We can add Sidgwick to that list, because I never take a client's story as stated. What if he was somehow behind the blackmail, working through Blevins, and trying to be clever now by bringing the story to me? It wouldn't be the first time. And then add in our false mind-reader and his turban-wearing toady. Now our subjects of interest number six. Who knows how many more might be involved before we're done? What if Blevins is himself but a pawn in the blackmailing scheme, controlled by someone else on the other end of his strings – and not Sidgwick? Now there is another living person to consider.

242

The list of those involved – and those who must be investigated and either eliminated or, at the very least, understood – grows, sometimes exponentially. Now tell me," he said, pushing back his plate, "what I'm supposed to do if, in addition to these men, and any others we have yet to discover, I have to take into account the infinite dead as well?"

In the course of this fascinating declaration, we hadn't heard the door open behind us. "Dead?" said a familiar voice. "Well, there's one more dead man in the world, and I've been told, Mr. Holmes, that you can provide additional information about him."

We both turned to find Inspector Lestrade standing in our doorway, a wicked grin on his face. "I understand you've cast your eye on Mr. Sidney Blevins. Well, he won't be bothering anyone anymore."

As I shepherded our friend over to the table to join us for lunch, Holmes rose with a gleam in his eye. "I suspect that Mr. Blevins didn't shuffle off his coil peacefully."

Lestrade, who had gratefully accepted a cup of coffee from the pot, nodded. "Not a bit of it. He was found seated behind his desk just a couple of hours ago – shot between the eyes with a small-caliber gun. No powder burns on his face, so it was certainly from whomever was across the desk from him. His manservant discovered him this morning. He rushed into the street, crying for a constable."

"Why wasn't he found any earlier?" I asked.

"His servant, another wrong 'un named Lyle Statton, had been given the previous evening off. There aren't any other servants in the house. Statton was only required to be back by ten o'clock today."

"Did he actually leave?"

"The cat's meat lady who works that corner saw him go around the time that he said, and there's no reason as of now to think that he came back. He's given us an alibi – a lady friend all the way out in Whetstone. It's being checked." Lestrade took another sip. "One might argue that if Statton did the killing, he wouldn't have made such an obvious stir of finding of the body. He could have just as well stayed out of town – or never come back at all. He was living there in disguise, as a Middle Eastern fellow, and he might have figured that no one would know who he really was if he were to up and vanish."

"Aren't there any other servants?"

"Not a one," replied Lestrade. "It seems that the late Mr. Blevins had a mistrust of his fellow man. I suspect the only reason Statton was able to stay around was that he had something to hold over Blevins."

"How did you find out about us?" asked Holmes.

Lestrade had folded half a sandwich, and he finished swallowing a bite before replying. "Before he left last night, Statton let in a visitor –

243

there by appointment. This man was also seen by the cat's meat woman. Statton gave us the name, and it was also confirmed in Blevins' appointment book: Henry Sidgwick. It was him who told us of his visit here this morning."

Holmes glanced my way. "He indicated that he'd spoken with Blevins, but he neglected to mention that it was less than twenty-four hours ago. I suppose we need to discuss that with him further. Do you have him at the Yard, or is he under request to stay at his home?"

"Better. He's in a growler downstairs. We were waiting for him when he arrived home – from his visit here, he says, followed by a few other errands – and when he heard what had happened, he insisted that we bring him right back and discuss the matter in your presence. Shall I have him brought up?"

"Better yet, let's go to Blevins' home and see what we can find there."

It was so agreed, and within a moment we were downstairs and on our way. When we were situated within the carriage, Sidgwick began to speak, but Holmes immediately held up a hand.

"I understand from Inspector Lestrade that you met with your blackmailer last night. Why didn't you give us that information?"

"But I did! I told you that he had arranged an appointment where he revealed what he intended, and where he explained his terms to hold back my secrets."

Holmes nodded and looked my way. "Note this, Watson. I failed to ask the proper questions – or at least enough of them. I felt that I had enough to be going on with, while I was instead building my assumptions on sand. I should have more thoroughly established when events occurred." He looked back at Sidgwick. "You mentioned that when you saw Statton, he was called 'Hakim'. I had taken that to have occurred on just the one occasion – when all four of you visited the dead man together. Did you also hear him called that last night?"

"I did. That's what Blevins called him both times that I was there. Last night, the turbaned man let me in, but then he departed as I arrived. He was gone for the rest of my visit."

"And did the rest of your encounter with Blevins occur as previously related."

Sidgwick nodded. "I'm sorry if I caused any confusion. I suppose that I thought the intent of my story was what counted, whether my meeting with him occurred last night or a week ago."

"Probably you would have been right," countered Holmes, "if the man hadn't been murdered. Do you have anything to add concerning last night's meeting?"

"Not at all."

At that moment, Holmes knocked on the roof of the four-wheeler with his stick, asking that we stop in front of a nearby post office. Then he asked that Lestrade briefly join him inside to send a telegram. Noticing the inspector's initial reluctance and glance toward Sidgwick, Holmes said with a smile, "You can leave your prisoner in Watson's safekeeping."

Lestrade frowned and Sidgwick sputtered, but he then climbed out and joined Holmes as they crossed the street.

Sidgwick and I were left sitting in an awkward silence. To fill the time, I considered relating an incident that had been on my mind since his earlier visit, concerning a supernatural occurrence that I had seen some weeks before Maiwand. But I realized that I would have barely begun before Holmes and Lestrade returned, so I held my tongue.

I was surprised that Sidgwick didn't ask me questions, but then again, he may have seen me as a nothing more than an extra on the stage of this drama, or perhaps he resented that I had been designated as his guard. In any case, he was quiet until our companions rejoined us.

"We have wired to Portsmouth," said Holmes. "Lestrade has used his authority to have the fourth man of your initial group investigated as to his whereabouts last night. We've also requested that the other two to be brought to Noel Street."

"It may take a while for the message to get to the Portsmouth police," said Lestrade. "After yesterday's electrical storm, some of the wires are still down. But once word gets through, they'll make a good job of it. I sent the message to Inspector Breeden – he's very thorough."

The expression on Holmes's face gave his opinion as to any policeman's thoroughness, but he held his tongue and instead resumed his questioning of Sidgwick. "You indicated that you remembered two of your friends acting differently after the initial meeting on the first, and that you spoke to them, whereupon they confessed that they too were being blackmailed. If you didn't meet with Blevins and learn of his blackmail plan until last night, then questioning your two friends – excluding the fellow in Portsmouth – must have occurred last night as well."

"It did. I went to both of them and each told me what Carvalos – Blevins, I mean – was up to. I was returning home afterwards when I thought of you, Mr. Holmes, and so sent the note asking to see you this morning."

"These two men – how did they take it that you had determined that they were also subject to blackmail?"

"Both were upset, I suppose, but they weren't too surprised that I'd also been tapped by Blevins, and knowing that I had my own secrets, I suppose that they felt that they could trust me."

"Did they tell you what he held over them?"

"Of course not."

"After you saw both of them, where did you go?"

"Straight home – where I remained until this morning when I came here to Baker Street. Anyone there can vouch for me."

I could see that Lestrade was unimpressed. A man's family and servants were not good alibis, and even if they were, they couldn't absolutely swear that the man of the house hadn't slipped out in the night without their knowledge to commit murder. And what did later alibis matter if Sidgwick had killed Blevins before he even departed from the man's house earlier in the evening?

As if reading my thoughts, Holmes asked Lestrade, "Has the coroner determined a time of death."

"Inconclusive. Twelve hours from when he was found this morning, and within an hour or to either side of that."

"So Mr. Sidgwick could have killed him at the time of their initial meeting, or he could have returned to do it later."

"Why, I – " blustered Sidgwick, but Lestrade interrupted.

"True. Or it could have been someone else."

By then we were slowing to a stop before a house in Noel Street. Number 1 was a narrow four-story brick building in a narrow little street. Normally the lane would have been a passage that one simply walked through quickly to get from one place to another, but now it had become a place of interest. There were a number of constables standing in the street, while even more loungers stood around them in an arc, ten or fifteen feet back, speculating about what had been found inside.

As we stepped inside the house and shut the door on the noise behind us, Holmes asked, "Has the autopsy been scheduled yet?"

His voice was low, to match the sudden quiet within.

"Too soon," Lestrade shook his head. "There were several bodies to deal with last night. It seems that these electrical storms cause people to go a bit mad in the same way that they're affected by the full moon. But as I said, he was shot between the eyes – death was instantaneous."

Holmes nodded and gestured with his hand, indicating that we should be taken to the dead man's study. Yet when we arrived, finding a constable standing at the door, he asked that we remain outside while he investigated the room by himself. By that point in our association, I understood that he would be gritting his teeth that the room had already been invaded by a number of policemen, but I was confident that he would still see more in that disturbed state than the rest of us would have found when the room was still pristine.

Lestrade, having seen Holmes's methods of investigation before, pulled the constable aside and spoke in whispered tones. Sidgwick watched from the doorway, fascinated as Holmes stood for long moments simply looking at the room's arrangement before shifting slightly and then doing the same from a different perspective. Then, without warning, he would drop to his knees, crawling here and there across the carpet, and making a series of low murmurs, whistles, and clicks of his tongue. He stood, examining the desk from both sides, and then the chairs on either side: One that had been Blevins', and the other across from it, where his visitor – and killer – had apparently sat. On either side of the desk were two glasses, and the desk itself was covered with several stacks of papers, all collapsed to some degree and spread out in a jumble.

As Sidgwick and I continued to observe Holmes's methods, I heard the front door open, and soon we were joined by four men – two constables, and two others dressed in suits. When they saw Sidgwick, they rushed forward and began to talk over one another.

"Sidgwick, what is the meaning of this?" said one, a man in his fifties with a bushy mustache.

"I have no involvement with this!" growled the other, about the same age, clean-shaven and wearing an expensive looking suit.

"I had you brought here," interrupted Lestrade, who then introduced himself. "Mr. Blevins has been murdered, and Mr. Sidgwick was here last night, to discuss business that I understand involves both of you as well. Which one is Sir Clive Underwood?"

I had already decided that the expensively dressed man was Sir Clive, and I was right. His eyes narrowed. "I'm sure that a lot of people had business with this . . . fraud who got himself killed. I'll be having a word with the Commissioner about this!"

Lestrade's expression indicated that this bothered him as much as it had on all the other occasions he'd heard it. "You must be Abel Hitchcock," he said to the other man, who simply nodded, having seen how effective Sir Clive's threat had been.

Lestrade turned to the constable. "Bring him from the kitchen." As the policeman departed, Lestrade added to me, "We kept Statton here after he found the body."

It only took a moment for the sole servant to be led into our group. A tall dark-skinned fellow with a prominent Adam's apple, I could see how, with a turban, he might fool some people into thinking that his given name was "Hakim". But without his head covered, he was just a bald-headed scarecrow of a man who could have been taken as a worn-out laborer in a rail yard.

The three members of The Society for Psychical Research began to yammer at him, while reserving further comments for the inspector.

247

However, mere seconds later their quorum was interrupted by Holmes, who announced that he was ready for them to come into the room.

The study itself was dark, with drapes closed to our left as we entered. There were crowded bookshelves containing various tomes with dark unreadable bindings. Aside from the two chairs on either side of the desk, there were several others pushed back along the walls. They remained there, as none of us were given any invitation to sit.

"Mr. Statton," said Holmes to the tall thin man, "you may not remember, but our paths crossed a few years ago, when you barely avoided arrest in that Hinde Street business. My name is Sherlock Holmes."

Statton reacted with a start, and his mouth dropped silently open. Holmes continued.

"How are the chairs normally arranged in this room?"

"Depends on the visitors," Statton said after swallowing, his Adam's apple dancing up and down and back again. "When no one was coming, Blevins kept them all pushed back. He would pull them up to the desk as needed." He looked around. "When these gents were here a few days ago, along with another, he pulled up four. He liked to do it himself – didn't want anyone in here very much if possible. Last night, when this one was coming over – " He jerked a thumb toward Sidgwick. " – he pulled up just the one."

"And after you saw Mr. Sidgwick at the front door, you left?

"I did."

"Why?"

"Blevins gave me the night off. He did that a lot when he didn't want me to hear his other business."

"'Other business'?"

"Not the mind-reading. The other – where he took money to keep quiet about their secrets." He took a step, leaning forward a bit. "That was between him and the men – I had nothing to do with that!"

"And you didn't return until this morning."

"God's truth. And Betsy Willis will tell you so too." He looked at Lestrade. "You find her. She'll tell you."

Lestrade made no reply.

Holmes looked at the two recent arrivals. "Sir Clive. Mr. Hitchcock. I am Sherlock Holmes, and Mr. Sidgwick visited me and Dr. Watson this morning concerning this business with Sidney Blevins – whom you knew as 'Carvalos'. He has informed us of your initial investigation, and how each of you was notified not long after with the information that Mr. Blevins was willing to protect your secrets for a price."

Both men started to yap angrily at Sidgwick, but Holmes talked over them until they became quiet once more.

"Mr. Blevins had a long history – known to the police and me – for this sort of thing. But I believe that we can arrive at a satisfactory solution by an examination of the room." He pulled a notebook and pencil from his coat pocket. "Mr. Hitchcock, could you take notes? I would ask Dr. Watson, but he's recovering from a recent injury."

That statement was pure twaddle, but I knew that Holmes had some goal in mind with this game, and I didn't disagree. Lestrade also held his tongue, watching Hitchcock with a new interest.

"And Sir Clive – would you stand by the window. When I tell you, please open the drapes to flood the room with light. Keep ready, sir – when I say so, the need will be immediate."

Sir Clive looked equally peeved and puzzled, but he went to stand at one side of the window and raised a hand, grasping the drapes firmly for when the order came.

"Inspector," Holmes said, "was there any sign of a struggle in relation to the body?"

"None at all. He was sitting in his chair, with a surprised look on his face."

"Where was the chair positioned?"

"He was facing forward, and the chair was pushed up to the desk."

"The wound was centered, you said?"

"Between the eyes."

"And as you told us, the bullet is likely small caliber, and there were no powder burns upon his forehead. He had a visitor last night – one who sat in the chair on the other side of the desk. Mr. Sidgwick? Or someone else? This person rose – perhaps to leave, perhaps in anger – and pulled forth a small-caliber gun. As they aren't very accurate beyond a few feet, he would have had to lean forward. Before Blevins could react, he died. Then the killer made a cursory search of the desk, as seen by these scattered papers. But then, perhaps not realizing that there weren't any other servants in the house and fearing imminent discovery, he fled."

"Sidgwick!" snapped Sir Clive. "You were here last night! What have you done?"

"Mr. Sidgwick wasn't the killer," said Holmes. "His left foot has a slight left twist, similar to the inspector's, and Mr. Sidgwick's is rather narrow as well. His footprints are here, in front of this chair on the visitor's side of the desk, but there are others on top of them – a later visitor." He glanced toward Lestrade. "Of course, no one has sat in this chair after the police arrived."

"No one," said Lestrade flatly. Holmes nodded.

"There are two glasses on the desk, on each side – one for Blevins, and one for his visitor. Both are empty, but they each have dregs of fluid in them, and – *Now, Sir Clive!*" cried Holmes. "*Throw open the drapes!*"

I expect that all of us jumped. I know that I did. Sir Clive was shocked, and nearly dropped his hand before remembering his instructions and jerking the drapes back. Light flooded the room, revealing countless illuminated dust motes. Some of us were set to coughing. In the meantime, Holmes stepped to Sir Clive, pulling a pistol from his pocket. "Take this," he said urgently. "Stay alert – there is danger in this room."

The older man nodded and accepted the gun. He then pointed it forward, moving it back and forth toward anyone who might pose a threat.

"Here now, Mr. Holmes – " began Lestrade, but Holmes held up a hand to silence him.

"Just a moment, Inspector, and all will be clear." Then he walked back to the desk and gestured toward the two glasses. "There is a small table beside the visitor's chair, but luckily the empty glass was placed on the desk. Watson – if you were sitting in the chair and facing the desk and Mr. Blevins, which side would the glass be on?"

"Why, my left," I said, starting to understand.

"Correct. Mr. Sidgwick," he said, jumping his attention to our client. "When you and the others were here the other night, you said that you had water."

"That's right. I don't imbibe."

"And you said that the others had whisky."

"Yes. Someone said it was a good blend."

"But didn't you also say that one man had brandy instead?"

"I did! I remember! It was – " His glance turned sharply from Holmes to another.

"Blevins' glass held whisky. The visitor's glass has remnants of brandy. Last night," Holmes continued, his voice more harsh, "after you left, Mr Sidgwick, another visitor arrived, after you had visited him to discuss the blackmail, and before you decided to consult me in the morning. His distinctive footprints overtop yours in front of the visitor's chair. Blevins offered the man a drink. The visitor asked for brandy instead of the fine whisky. They talked. The second visitor lied to you last night, Mr. Sidgwick – his secrets *are* dangerous, and he had no intention of rolling over or paying blackmail regarding the facts from his past that Blevins had uncovered during his research to perform his thought-reading act. The visitor finished his brandy, set the empty glass on the desk instead of the small side-table, stood while pulling out his gun, and then leaned forward, shooting his host.

"Mr. Hitchcock – have you been recording this?"

"Umm – I've rather lost track . . . ."

"No matter. I see that you're holding the notebook in your left hand, and the pencil in your right."

"Yes."

"The killer was left-handed. He set the glass on the desk to the left of the chair as he stood. He – "

"That's enough, Holmes," said Sir Clive, still standing by the window, Holmes's gun clutched in his left hand. "I may be finished, but I might as well have some satisfaction before I swing!" And he lifted his arm full-length, aiming it directly at Holmes.

With a cry, both Lestrade and I sprang into motion, but it was too late. Sir Clive's finger pulled the trigger again and again. But even as he went down under the combined weight of myself and the inspector, I realized that there had been no shot, only clicks on empty chambers.

"A man with any good working knowledge of firearms," said Holmes as we picked ourselves up, "would check first thing to see if the gun that was handed to him was loaded. I simply needed a quick way to verify that you were the left-handed man we sought. If either Mr. Hitchcock or Mr. Sidgwick had also favored their sinister hands, I would have had to resort to something else."

He smiled at Lestrade. "You're learning, Inspector. If the room had been disturbed any further – if the glasses had been gathered and taken away to the Yard, for instance – I doubt that the case would have been solved. I hope that I'm beginning to impress upon you and your colleagues the value of preserving evidence until it can be properly examined, evaluated, and recorded. If you will recall in the matter of the Biggleswade Autonomy, when I – "

"Take him away," Lestrade snapped to the constables now grasping each of Sir Clive's struggling arms.

Outside, the crowd had enjoyed the spectacle of the angry and well-dressed killer being loaded into a Black Maria. In the meantime, Holmes spoke to Lestrade, Sidgwick, and me while still standing just inside the front door.

"There were any number of reasons that I might not have been able to get at the truth so quickly. The evidence could have been removed. There might have been no additional discernible footprints, meaning that you couldn't be eliminated so quickly, Mr. Sidgwick. As a matter of fact, when I arrived, I had no idea that we would accomplish anything more useful than questioning the suspects and gathering some facts. I had seven separate ideas of how to proceed – but then I saw that the solution was already waiting here, laid out before me and ready for interpretation, so I rather forced the issue."

"You kept Sir Clive off balance," said Lestrade, "and that's a fact."

"He was already nervous. I doubt that he's killed before – but who knows? Perhaps he has murdered after all – that might be what Blevins found out about him, although it's more likely something related to the scandal in the City in which he was involved last year. Whatever it is, it will now be rooted out completely. In any case, he was certainly on edge already, and then to be brought back to where he killed a man less than a day later . . . . Manipulating him was child's play.

"I wanted to see if Sir Clive and Hitchcock were right- or left-handed. Hitchcock immediately took my pencil in his right hand, so it was less likely that he placed the glass to the left side of the visitor's chair. Sir Clive grabbed the drapes with his left hand, but then I realized that this was an inconclusive test – he might have used either hand in order to stand where he could see what was going on. So I then handed him my emptied gun, as he would definitely grip it in his dominant hand.

"Of course, the killer might have simply been shifting his glass back and forth from hand to hand prior to rising and shooting Blevins, and the fact that it was in his left hand when he did so could have meant nothing. Fortunately, the evidence of the footprints helped to further establish Sir Clive's presence, and his attempt to kill me made his guilt certain."

"It was clever," said Sidgwick, "but there were other considerations: Just because the one of the men drank brandy on the first night didn't mean that he would choose it last night. One of the whisky drinkers on the first visit could have simply asked for brandy instead. And you haven't yet verified that my friend in Portsmouth was at home last night, or whether he was right- or left-handed."

"These statements are true," said Holmes. "I don't know anything about this other man – What was his name, Watson? Conan Doyle? – Although I don't know if he is right- or left-handed, and it wasn't established that he was one of the whisky drinkers, in the end it didn't matter, as the situation today allowed for a quick solution based on the evidence we found, without the necessity of completely verifying all of those extra facts. There are cases when it's not so simple."

"I saw it in Sir Clive's eyes when he realized where you were headed," said Sidgwick. "When you made me recall that he was the one who drank the brandy a week ago, while the other two had whisky. He knew that the game was up. He certainly made it easy for you."

Sidgwick put out his hand. "I cannot thank you enough, Mr. Holmes. I can't imagine what might have happened had I not thought to ask for your help."

He dropped Holmes's hand and leaned forward. "Having you in The Society would be invaluable! With your gifts, we would never have a

252

doubt if what we investigated was true or not. And when your reputation is associated with us – "

Holmes shook his head once, decisively. "Thank you, Mr. Sidgwick, but no. The idea is – " He pursed his lips. I suspect that he would likely have finished the sentence with the word "repugnant" or something worse, but instead he concluded by saying, "No, let it suffice to say that I'm not interested."

Sidgwick started to argue further, but he was intelligent enough to cease. I glanced at Lestrade. His face was expressionless, but his eyes were merry as he, like I, imagined such a group with Sherlock Holmes as a member.

We parted then, and not long after Holmes and I were back in Baker Street, arriving at 221 just as another cab was departing. A middle-sized fellow of our similar age was left standing on the pavement, watching with a smile as we disembarked.

"Watson, may I introduce Alton Peake, stalker of the night, and exposer of frauds and con-men?"

"More of an evaluator," laughed Peake as he stuck out his hand. "A pleasure to finally meet you, Doctor. I hope that you're a bit more open-minded than our mutual friend here."

His pleasant countenance and nature elicited a similar laugh on my part. "Well," I stated, "I have seen a few things over the years that have kept me from entirely closing the door on such ideas."

"Excellent! You must tell me all about them!"

Holmes waved a hand to the doorway. "Shall we, then? I think you'll be interested in our most recent activity, Peake. We just came from the scene of Sidney Blevins' murder."

"Carvalos is dead? The Noel Street Oracle? Well, that is news!"

"After we tell you about that," Holmes added, "you and Watson can regale each other with ghost stories. I have some chemical matters to investigate."

And with that we went inside, closing the foolishness of the world outside for a little while as we sought some small answers to the greater mysteries.

Henry Sidgwick
(1838-1900)
Founder of The Society of Psychical Research

The Well-lit Séance

"You are considering a holiday?" asked Sherlock Holmes as he attempted to light the somewhat-dried dottles left over from his previous day's pipes. "Is Mary in on the planning, or will it be a surprise?"

"At this point, it's only the vaguest thought of my own," I said with a smile. "Of course, you watched as my gaze wandered from my old desk which has become rather buried under your own books and papers, and thence to the bookcase, specifically the gazetteers there on the second shelf, and finally to the cabinet used to store your impressive collection of Ordinance Maps. No doubt my expression became unfocused at that point as I pictured various pleasant locations, and I recall that I touched my wedding ring."

"That, and the fact that yesterday you mentioned that Mary's health has been somewhat off of late, and that you had prescribed a change." He tossed his match into the fire and sat down across from me with a smile. "Sometimes it isn't so much sharp observations and deductions as simply interest in a friend's plans. Do you have anywhere in mind?"

I related my ideas for a few possible sites, but I was a bit limited in my choices due to the fact that it was October – not always the best month for making a journey. However, winter would soon follow, and if we didn't go now, we might be forced to wait until spring.

I had dropped into Baker Street that Sunday morning in order to meet with Holmes and Inspector Peter Jones regarding any remaining details that needed to be discussed concerning our activities the night before in the vaults of the Coburg branch of the City and Suburban Bank. It had been a most remarkable affair resulting in the arrest of John Clay, a man that Holmes considered was the fourth smartest in London. His plan to tunnel into the bank had been bold, and the distraction he'd devised leading up to it, tricking the poor man who owned the shop at the other end of the tunnel into leaving every day to copy the encyclopedia while the tunnel was being dug, was audacious – but one would never think of Clay as smart based upon the way he acted after his arrest. He devolved into a ranting foul-mouthed jackanapes who had to be restrained by four constables before he could be locked into the police van.

"The Professor will be upset," Holmes had murmured as the criminal was driven away.

But that was yesterday, and for now the escalating game that Holmes was playing with London's criminal element was paused for a moment. Over coffee, Holmes and I debated the strengths and weaknesses of various holiday locations until the doorbell rang. In moments Inspector Jones had joined us and, over a pleasant breakfast prepared by Mrs. Hudson, we elaborated on the facts that led to the previous night's events.

"It's an airtight case, thank the Lord," said Jones, wiping his mouth. "Clay's argument that he was just a bystander is absurd, considering that he was the one who first pushed up the vault floor before the eyewitnesses – each of us waiting in the vault – and even his mates behind him in the tunnel have turned on him. And yet, with Royal blood in him, and considering the fools who regularly sit on juries, it's very possible he still might get off. I want to sew this one up good and proper."

Jones made no mention of Professor Moriarty, Clay's shadowy master, and neither did Holmes nor I – Jones because he may or may not have known of the Professor at that point in time, and Holmes and I because we still didn't completely know whom we could trust, even on the official force.

We talked for a few more minutes, about attempted bank robbery and other cases, and a bit of gossip regarding the other Scotland Yard inspectors. Our visitor could only shake his head when the conversation turned to the Yard's *other* Inspector Jones, Athelney. "Bless him," said Peter Jones, "his heart's in the right place, and there's no one braver – you know most of all, Mr. Holmes, with what he was willing to do to his own reputation and career during the Ripper mess to save The Crown – but if the rest of us didn't keep him on the rails . . . . And if I see the two of us confused in the newspapers one more time – !" He tipped up his cup and finished his coffee. "It's enough to drive a man to drink!" He stood up with a grin. "I know you wrote about Athelney in that book earlier this year, Doctor – the one about the Sholto murder. Should you ever record me in one of your tales, please promise to be a bit more kind!"

I nodded. "I simply record the facts, Inspector. You have nothing to fear."

Then, with a nod and thanking us for our help, and for bringing the matter to him – he'd long coveted the capture John Clay – he departed. We heard him pass Mrs. Hudson on the landing, thanking her for breakfast, and then the good lady entered, bringing Holmes a note before gathering the breakfast dishes.

"It was hand delivered by a nice-looking fellow," she explained while Holmes examined the envelope. "Tall, well-dressed. About thirty, I'd say. He had a watch fob with the initials '*R.B.*', and his fingernails were clean."

"Thank you, Mrs. Hudson," said Holmes, who had by this point read the letter and passed it to me.

256

As Mrs. Hudson departed and pulled the door shut behind her, I said with a smile, "She is becoming more observant. Your methods are rubbing off on all of us."

By that time we had moved back to our chairs beside the fireplace, and Holmes was relighting his pipe. He gestured with the stem toward me, saying, "Then tell me what *you* observe."

I examined the letter, noting that it was expensive paper with a matching envelope. "The address in Mayfair indicates wealth. The writing, both on the envelope and on the single sheet, were made by a right-handed man using a pen with a nib in good condition and expensive ink. There was no sign of hesitation or emotional distress – the lines were firm and clear, running evenly from left to right. It is signed *Richard Birlsthorpe*. An interesting name," I added. "And his father, Giles Birlsthorpe – Surely that must be the same fellow responsible for Birlsthorpe's Gargling Oil, and all those other patent medicines produced by that company."

"And the letter?" prodded Holmes. "Can you make anything from the limited contents?"

I read it again:

Mr. Holmes,

> *Please forgive my intrusion on a Sunday. I have a family problem related to my father, Giles Birlsthorpe, which is mounting by the day, and after the events of last night, my mind is made up that I must do something about it. When I get a notion, I can't rest until it's settled.*
>
> *If possible, may I visit you on Monday to explain my situation? A reply to the provided address will serve to fix the appointment time.*

Very best,
Richard Birlsthorpe

I replaced the folded sheet into the envelope and again pondered the address – Hill Street, just west of Berkeley Square. "Nothing but the obvious – that it concerns something related to his father, an ongoing situation that escalated last night."

As I spoke, Holmes rose and walked around his chair to the shelf of ponderous commonplace books to the left of the fireplace. Pulling out a volume near the middle, he carried it over to the dining table. I rose and followed.

I could see that he had chosen the volume for "*P*", which I could only assume stood for "*Patent Medicine*" rather than "*Birlsthorpe*". His filing system was definitely something of his own devising, but I had come to have a limited understanding of it during the years I'd known him, and at times I could even make use of the books on my own.

"Books" is too generous a term, I suppose. They were great scrapbooks, filled with newspaper clippings that Holmes found of interest related to people, places, and things which might be of use to him. Often he saw connections and patterns, sometimes running back and forth across years, and his documentation of these had been useful on more occasions than I could count. In addition to the various clippings, there were countless loose items tucked into the pages – theatre tickets and pamphlets, more than one type of feather, and occasionally envelopes filled with soil samples. Once I'd opened one of the volumes to find a small vial of blood tucked inside, which started to fall when freed. I barely caught it, and my admonition about putting something so fragile in such a place seemed to have found root, because as far as I knew, Holmes never again stored objects of that sort in such an unlikely location.

"Hmm," he said, reading the biography of Giles Birlsthorpe. "Born September 1818 – he turned seventy-two last month. Married late, had one son, Richard, born 1859. Mrs. Hudson was nearly right about his age. The wife died five years ago. The father is famous, as you recognized, for the invention and marketing of a number of patent medicines, starting with his Gargling Oil in the 1860's. Before that, he'd had a tedious job working for a London chemist in Shoe Lane. He started selling his Oil on his own time, and within a year, he'd earned enough to turn around and buy his employer's shop. After that, success followed success as he came up with more and more of his medicines: Birlsthorpe's Bitters for Seasickness, Birlsthorpe's Black Draught, a purgative full of saline, and – most curious – Birlsthorpe's Eclectric Tonic, to regulate the body's inner electricity. *Eclectric . . . ?*"

"And the son?" I asked. "Do you have any notes related to him?"

Holmes shut the book with a disappointed look. "Nothing beyond his date of birth as part of his father's narrative." He shelved the volume and turned to look at me. "Would you be interested in hearing his story? If so, what time should I have him arrive?"

"I would, and four o'clock, if that's acceptable. Monday's are always busier – catching up after the weekend."

Holmes nodded and indicated that he would make the appointment by return note. After a few more minutes, I left. Walking home to Paddington, I considered what I knew of Birlsthorpe's *faux* medicines, and realized that it wasn't much, except that I would never prescribe them, and whenever a patient told me about using them, I quickly recommended something else. From what I'd heard, they were harmless – unlike some others like Fowler's Solution, full of arsenic, that were sold as a treat-all for many illnesses which they could never cure, including some forms of cancer. Then there was Godfrey's Cordial, full of laudanum and often called "Mother's Friend" because it was prescribed to quiet cranky children. But too often it was overused, and children died.

I had never heard anything bad about Birlsthorpe's potions – except that those who used them wasted their money, bottle after bottle – funds that could have been better-spent elsewhere.

I reached my own doorstep with quite a bit of curiosity as to what Richard Birlsthorpe might have to tell us on the morrow. Possibly his father had become involved in some unsavory or dishonest business deal.

It turned out that I couldn't have been more wrong, and it was nothing that I could have imagined. But that was usually the case.

"What do you know of the human aura?" asked the man sitting in the basket chair. I could see that Holmes was, for once, in the dark. He glanced at me, and I nodded that I'd heard of it.

"There is a belief," I explained, " – *not* shared by the majority of the medical field – that all living things produce an energy field." I wondered how this related to the sales of bogus medications. "Based on the field's strengths, its ebbs-and-flows, and even its coloring if one can see it, the state of the organism's health and well-being can be determined. If this field shows signs of darkness, for instance, the patient is in a condition of spiritual and electric illness, and should be treated accordingly."

"From your tone," said our visitor, "I gather you don't put much stock in it."

"It's claptrap," I replied with certainty. "Ineffable twaddle."

"Quite right," Richard Birlsthorpe nodded vigorously. "I agree entirely, Doctor, and thank you for your honesty." Then he looked toward Holmes. "My father, however, is a convert to this . . . this *'ineffable twaddle'*. He believes in it, and is well on his way to becoming a missionary for it. He's even managed to get a few legitimate medical men interested. It's bad enough he made his fortune selling quack remedies and nostrums to the gullible. Now he's trying to read other people's 'atmospheres'. He thinks he has the 'gift', and it's because he's under the influence of someone – a fraud – that I want you to investigate."

Truly, this was not what I expected, and I could tell that Holmes was caught afoot as well. As I'd discussed the affair with Mary the night before, I'd convinced myself that the Birlsthorpe son was seeking a consultation about some prosaic matter – never anticipating that it concerned human auras. And yet, I thought that once the peculiar trappings of this nonsense were stripped away, the idea was really no different than other forms of patent medicine.

Once again, I couldn't have been more wrong.

When I'd arrived at 221 Baker Street on Monday afternoon, Richard Birlsthorpe was stepping down from a cab. He was handsome and carried himself with confidence. He paid the cabbie, and then took a moment to look up and engage the man in conversation, asking if the fellow was married or had children. When the cabbie affirmed both, Birlsthorpe gave him something extra, causing the cabbie's eyes to widen. He expressed enthusiastic thanks before moving on.

I had introduced myself and said that I'd be joining him and Holmes, if that was all right. He'd heard of me, and indicated that he had no objections at all. Then I rang the bell, rather than using the key that I still retained. Mrs. Hudson nodded to me with a smile and said that Holmes was upstairs, and that she'd be right up with tea. I led Birlsthorpe up to 221b and introduced him to Holmes, and thus there was no chance for a comparing of notes before refreshments were served and the man began his narrative.

"This fraudulent person," said Holmes. "What can you tell us about him?"

"He is my father's secretary. Clayton Kenneth Pounds. He's about fifty – from up north somewhere. My father . . . he is a difficult man. He always has been, but particularly so for the last five years. It has become more and more difficult for him to retain a secretary. Father is seventy-two, but he refuses to retire, or to hand over the reins to his managers, each of whom are more-than-competent to continue running the business.

"After his last secretary quit, having put up with far more abuse than should be expected, Pounds interviewed and obtained the job. He's unmarried, and I don't know much about him. He's close-mouthed, and has never responded to my efforts to find out more about his private life. I've considered hiring a detective before, just to discover out more of his past, but I never followed through. However, recently the man's influence on my father has become more and more fixed, and it's he that's encouraging my father to pursue his interest in these 'atmospheres' and 'auras' that supposedly linger around the human body like a colored cloud."

"Is he encouraging your father toward questionable business dealings?" I asked, thinking that my theory might still be verified.

"Probably. But what finally drove me to take action is the séances."

I had been perched forward on my chair, but this caused me to settle back. I glanced toward Holmes, and there was a glint of interest in his eyes.

"Tell us more," he said.

Birlsthorpe nodded. "Last March, when the previous secretary quit, interviews were held to replace him. Pounds was hired, and from what I've seen of his resume, there was nothing about him that was any more or less qualified than the other applicants. As my father runs through secretaries like others wear out socks, the interview process has become rather standardized.

"As I said, Pounds is a taciturn man, and my efforts to get to know him have been for naught. I like people, and take an interest in them, but Pounds seems to have a wall around him. Not just with me – I understand that some people are private, and others just don't get along, but Pounds makes no effort to create any connections with any of the rest of my father's staff. In fact, the only person that seems to have that connection is my father himself.

"While I no longer live in the Mayfair house, I'm a regular visitor, and I have certain duties within the company that require that I visit my father daily. Through these visits, I've seen Pounds begin to have greater and greater influence, setting himself up as something of a gatekeeper around my father. This is only made easier as my father gets older and becomes more feeble and dependent – although he would never admit it, as he believes he's just as strong and capable as he was twenty years ago.

"My father's successes have been documented, but he found his calling, such as it is, before I was born, so I don't know what he was like then. However, by the time I was in my teens, I could see that he truly believed that his brews, elixirs, and philters were fully efficacious in dealing with people's ills. He becomes quite contrary if someone gives any indications that they are merely colored water and flavored tonics with no actual benefit, other than that which the patient convinces themselves to believe – the *placebo* effect, I believe it's called, Doctor."

I nodded.

"At least our products don't injure or kill people. Father has never been one of those who believe that a small dose of poison has benefits – since there are too many people who think that if a little is good, more must be better, and they take greater and greater doses of some of our competitor's products, with the result being a permanent injury or death." He glanced at me. "You know the ones of which I speak."

"I do," I said. "Fowler's, of course. And then there are Dr. Rush's Bilious Pills and Godbold's Vegetable Balsam, both containing mercury. Someday they will be illegal."

"And don't forget Soliman's Water and Swaim's Panacea – also dispensing medicinal mercury by way of the shelves of every chemist in the nation." He shook his head. "It's enough to disgust you with human nature."

"All very interesting," interrupted Holmes. "But what of the séances?"

"Right. About six weeks ago, Pounds showed my father something new – lenses that apparently allow the wearer to see the 'atmospheres' surrounding a person. My father was quite enthusiastic about it, and couldn't wait to show me on my next visit. I must admit that it was a curious sensation. Pounds had found a set of leather goggles – he was quite vague as to where – which had dark-tinted lenses, rather like what one sees on eyeglasses worn by the blind. The goggles fit tightly around one's head, and then . . . and then, when looking at a person, one can see an outline around them, as if they are lit from behind by a bright light – rather like how the moon looks during a solar eclipse. I've only tried it twice, and to be honest, the experience is quite unpleasant, although Father insists it becomes easier with practice. It made my eyes burn and water."

"And did you see the different colors?" I asked with interest, thinking that this in fact might be a diagnostic tool, different from the useless "medicines" bottled by the elder Birlsthorpe.

"I'm not sure," replied the son. "I . . . I may have, but as I said, looking through the looking through the lenses hurt my eyes, and I wouldn't trust what I saw."

He looked at Holmes. "I can see that you're getting impatient to hear about the séances. They aren't that, precisely – not the same mumbo-jumbo that the spiritualists usually display. My father doesn't summon ghosts or attempt to transmit messages back and forth from the dead. There are no knockings on the table or floating phantasms. Rather, he gathers a small group and, using the goggles, he makes readings about them, and their conditions. He started by simply commenting on their atmospheres, and whether someone looked healthy or unwell. But lately, with Pounds' encouragement, he's been delving deeper, claiming that he can see details of their everyday lives – their relationships, and their jobs, and their financial situations. He claims that as he uses the goggles more and more, he becomes attuned their waves and vibrations – and that everything he's said has been confirmed to be correct. He first talked of making them into a product that we might sell along with the medicines, but now – enjoying the attention he's receiving, I suppose – he wants to keep having his 'counseling sessions', as he calls them, and he selfishly wants to be the only one who has such a power."

"And Pounds is encouraging this."

"He absolutely is!" said Birlsthorpe, suddenly pounding his fist on the arm of the basket chair. "I have no idea why, except that it makes him even more trusted by my father. He's saying what my father wants to hear, while any reasonable word to the contrary that I provide is only driving a wedge between us."

"Which do you want?" asked Holmes. "For Pounds to be investigated, and exposed if he's some sort of confidence man? Or do you want the truth about the goggles and the séances?"

Birlsthorpe looked to each of us. "Both, I suppose. Whichever one is necessary to free my father from this man's influence, and also to prevent whatever is going to happen in relation to the goggles. Public embarrassment? A lawsuit? I have no idea where this is headed."

"Tell me the truth, Mr. Birlsthorpe," said Holmes, sitting up straighter and setting aside his pipe. "Are you concerned that the increasing divide between you and your father might lead to you losing your inheritance?"

Birlsthorpe looked a bit nonplussed, but he showed no signs of anger. Holmes continued.

"After receiving your message yesterday, I did a bit of research. I found that, as expected, you are your father's only heir, and that you expect to receive a sizable inheritance upon his death. His financial dealings are of interest in various quarters, as it's hoped that the business will remain stable after his passing. You are not the only one concerned about the influence of this man, Pounds, but you *are* the one who stands to lose considerably should the secretary obtain full control over your father."

Birlsthorpe nodded, showing no anger or irritation as I might have expected at Holmes's statement. "I do want to make sure that I receive what's coming to me. But it isn't greed, Mr. Holmes. It's responsibility.

"My father married late, and I was born when he was already in middle age. He was already the man who built up his business from nothing. But my mother was a good soul who saw the good that was still in him, and she was a wonderful influence on him while she lived. He realized it and appreciated it. But then she died, and in his loneliness, he has slipped back into the rather ruthless fellow that apparently he once was.

"I am ashamed of how my father has taken advantage of those who needed better help than they received, and how that part of him seems to be on the ascent once again. I love him, for all his vexations, and I will miss him, but when he's gone – when I'm in control – I intend to use the money for good."

"That may cause as much consternation in various boardrooms as if Pounds were to gain control," said Holmes. "I take it you don't plan to continue producing and marketing your company's ineffectual products?"

263

"I do not. I plan to pivot to items of proven and beneficial value." He leaned forward. "You say that there is concern about the direction of the company – and how my father is being manipulated?"

"There is – but I heard no mention of these atmospheric readings as part of the vague distress. That . . . intrigues me." Then Holmes nodded. "I will take your case. When is the next . . . *séance*, as you called it?"

"Tomorrow night. Pounds is now running several of them a week. The one on Saturday night was the most outrageous yet – at least that I've seen. I don't go to every one of them, and I certainly have the sense when I'm there that I'm not a welcome visitor, but I haven't been obnoxious when I attend, so my father allows me to stay. I simply sit and watch . . . and wonder what's going on. In this last case, there were eight people present besides my father, Pounds, and myself, and father gave very specific advice to six of them – quit your job, for instance, or your wife has deceived you. He told another that the child he thinks of as his own son belongs to another. Regardless of whether these 'atmospheres' exist around a person, there's no way he could *see* that kind of information – and no reason that he should be sharing it, true or not. Pounds has convinced him of his own skill and authority, and it's only going to get worse. It must be stopped."

"Can you arrange to have Dr. Watson invited to the event tomorrow night?"

I didn't react at this inclusion in his plans without Holmes first verifying that I might have other commitments, but I too was intrigued, and if I had been otherwise obligated, I would have attempted to free myself in order to attend the meeting. Birlsthorpe drummed his fingers on the chair arm for a moment and then said, "I can. It will be a bit difficult, but father won't deny it – especially if it seems as if I'm coming around to his side." He looked at me. "Number 4, Hill Street, in Mayfair. Eight o'clock. I'll meet you outside five minutes or so beforehand."

I nodded. "Perhaps I should attend under an alias?"

"Do you have something in mind?"

"Perhaps . . . Dr. Jabez Roylott?"

Birlsthorpe frowned, and Holmes interjected. "Possibly something that doesn't sound like a circus ringmaster, Watson."

"Campbell, then," I replied. "James Campbell."

"Excellent," replied the client. Then he looked at Holmes. "Do you need anything else from me?"

"I think not. There is plenty of time between now and then for me to set further inquiries into motion."

We rose and shook hands, and then Birlsthorpe departed. After we heard the downstairs door shut, I turned back to Holmes. "Circus ringmaster?"

He laughed in that peculiar silent way of his. "You must admit that 'Jabez Roylott' is a bit over the top."

I nodded, laughing as well. "Is there any assistance that I can provide before tomorrow night?"

"I think not. Discovering Pounds' background should be routine, and I have some thoughts about the séance. I believe that while you're in attendance at the main performance, I'll see what I can determine backstage."

"I'm not sure what you hope to find," I said. "It sounds as if the usual bogus séance tricks aren't used – no tooting horns or ectoplasm. Birlsthorpe's father doesn't even pretend to be possessed by a five-thousand-year-old Pharaoh."

Holmes nodded. "In addition to researching Pounds, I'll see what I can found out about the household. When researching the Birlsthorpes *père et fils*, I learned that the old man has very few servants. In fact, since Pounds has come to work for him, the number has dropped to a maid, a cook, and an old man-of-work who carries out odd jobs."

"Funny that the son didn't mention that – another example of Pounds isolating the father."

"He told us the gist of the story. Perhaps he simply neglected to think of it. In any case, it means that the house will be that much easier to visit tomorrow night during the performance."

"What do you expect to find?"

"I have no idea – but I'm confident that I'll find something!"

The next morning, I completed my rounds near Covent Garden and, having some time before I needed to return for office hours, I decided to do some further research of my own. I hailed a cab, instructing the driver to cross the river and carry me to St. Thomas' Hospital, directly across from the Palace of Westminster. Big Ben was just striking eleven at the top of the great clock tower when I went inside, asking to speak with Dr. Walter John Kilner, who I had found mentioned in several journals the previous night while researching the curious question of atmospheres and auras.

I had met him a few times before, but we were not close friends. On the first occasion, I was eating lunch with my friend Doyle, always rather too impressionable and credulous when faced with pseudo-science, when he spotted Kilner at a nearby table. He introduced us, stating that Kilner was the medical electrician at St. Thomas, and was in charge of electrotherapy, delivering measured charges of current to the body to treat various ills. Barts, where I had been associated, had been involved in medico-electrical research since the mid-eighteenth century, but it was never an area that I had bothered to examine – or to which I had given much credence.

Kilner was an average looking fellow, thick dark hair parted in the middle over a wide forehead. He had straight brows across expressionless watchful eyes, and a mouth that seemed wider than it actually was as his face narrowed toward his chin. He never seemed to smile, and in spite of Doyle's typical jovial efforts on the day that I was introduced, the man didn't make any interested response.

I probably wouldn't have bothered with talking to him at all, except in my limited researches the night before, his was a name that I recognized, and he was in London.

I was led to a basement laboratory where Kilner's office was located. I couldn't put my finger on it, but there was a feeling there that I didn't like – the same as one finds when touring the torture rooms of old castles. There is something about the old buildings that have absorbed terrible human suffering, wherein they have their own atmospheres and auras. Holmes has scoffed at this when I've mentioned it to him, but at times when we've visited such places, and he hasn't realized that I was watching, I can see that he is aware of such things too.

Kilner was welcoming enough when I knocked on his office door, and willing to take a few minutes to answer my questions. I explained that I was involved in an investigation as to whether humans could produce atmospheres that couldn't be seen by the human eye, and also a new lens device that I'd heard of that was used to observe them.

"No," he said, "I'm unaware of any such thing, or atmospheres such as you describe, but that doesn't mean that they don't exist. I take it that you have the layman's knowledge of electricity," he added.

"I believe that I do. I understand current, and how voltaic batteries and generators work. The principles of circuitry – "

"Yes, yes," he interrupted impatiently. "Well, the body generates electricity too. A very small amount, certainly, but it's there none-the-less. The heart, for instance, has an electrical current, and so does the brain. One can see the effects that electricity in different levels has on tissue. Large amounts, such as a lightning strike, can burn the flesh, or superheat the water inside the body so suddenly that it explodes. But smaller controlled amounts of electricity can do amazing things. We're only in the early stages of understanding it, you realize – regulating heart-beats, stopping seizures, using shocks to treat insanity or discourage deviant behavior. But we progress daily. Who is to say that we will find next? Ritter discovered ultraviolet light nearly a hundred years ago. He only did so by seeing how some unknown factor was discoloring silver chloride. Perhaps the body does emit its own fields. It would explain a great deal, wouldn't it? Those who scoff at human beings' *spiritual sides* – that there is such a thing as a *soul* – might acknowledge such a thing as an electric aura, generated by the body during life, and then – after death . . . ?"

He rattled on for quite a bit longer, talking about conservation of energy and showing more enthusiasm than I'd seen from him on any previous meeting. His professional focus was something that provided him great joy. Yet, I quickly began to realize that Kilner had very little to offer that would be useful to me, so I gradually disengaged myself with thanks. He rose from behind his desk, offering his hand. "Please tell me what you learn. What you have suggested is fascinating. It opens up all sorts of possibilities for treatment . . . ."

Outside, I was glad that I hadn't specifically mentioned Birlsthorpe, as Kilner would likely be calling on him by day's end. In hindsight, I wondered at the wisdom of my visit. Now that Kilner was aware of the concept, it might lead him to further investigate it, wasting his time on a dead-end path. On the other hand, possibly there was something to it after all. Kilner's explanations about the electrical nature of the body were enough to realize that we really know very little indeed.

I found a cab and returned to Paddington in time for office hours, but too late for a proper lunch.

At five-minutes-to-eight that night, I stepped from my cab at the corner of Hill Street and Berkeley Square, and then walked the short distance west to Number 4. Waiting on the street was our client, dressed in a conservative dark suit. He offered his hand. "Dr. *Campbell* – so good of you to join me." He emphasized the name, as if to make sure that I'd noticed he remembered. "They're expecting us."

I looked both ways but no one was nearby. "Was there any difficulty in making the arrangements?"

He shook his head. "My father didn't care. He's so convinced by his own powers that the idea of another stranger stopping by is of no concern. Pounds was quite tight-lipped about it, but what could he do?"

"Have you heard from Holmes?" I whispered. "Did he give any indication of his plans – how he intends to enter the house?"

"I spoke with him this afternoon and let him know the best way to obtain access, and how to stay out of the way of the remaining servants. He seems very capable, doesn't he?" He nodded toward the door. "Come inside. They'll start soon."

It was a handsome house, but I was rather surprised that it wasn't larger. Surely the elder Birlsthorpe could have afforded something much grander in scale. It was a corner property, four stories plus a basement that could be accessed by an areaway, and an attic, as indicated by dormer windows. Curiously, the entire right side of the building and the ground floor of the left were painted white, but the upper three stories on the left were of red brick. It gave the place a most conflicted appearance, as if one type of house had sprouted out of another.

Birlsthorpe appeared to read my thoughts and stopped on the stop step. "My father originally lived in a much finer house, closer to Hyde Park, but when he married my mother, she insisted that something more modest was proper, and he agreed. She was a very beneficial influence on him, and it's truly a tragedy that she passed." Then he knocked, and almost immediately the door opened. A tall shadowed man saw us and then stepped aside for us to pass.

"Master Richard," he said, as if he were addressing a school-boy instead of a man in his early thirties, "you're nearly late." Then the man looked at me, measuring up and down to see what I presented. Apparently he wasn't impressed.

"This is Pounds," said Richard Birlsthorpe. "My father's secretary." He shed his coat and handed it, along with his hat, to the man as if he were just another servant – an intentional diminution to put him in his place, I was sure. I handed him my outer garments as well – Why should I undo our client's efforts?

"We'll go in now," said Birlsthorpe, giving the man no further attention. I followed down a darkened hallway, and then left into a well-lit parlor.

It was tastefully furnished with a few small tables here and there, supporting vases or bowls. I suspected that this was the lingering influence of the dead wife and mother. I noticed them only for instant, however, as my gaze was drawn to the center of the room, where a large round table rested underneath a bright electric chandelier of the type that one occasionally saw in finer homes. The table was surrounded by chairs – seven of them. Four were already filled, and one was soon taken by Pounds, who quickly sat down next to an elderly man who projected an air of authority.

"Richard," the man grumbled, "you were almost late. I would have had Pounds lock the door. The readings cannot be disturbed. You know that! This is your friend?"

"That's right," said Birlsthorpe as he directed me to one of the two remaining empty chairs, directly across from his father. I sat at

Birlsthorpe's right and took a moment to look at the other members of our party.

Across the table was Giles Birlsthorpe, with what could only be the atmosphere-reading goggles lying before him. To his right was Pounds, and then – between the secretary and Richard Birlsthorpe – was an elderly bird-like woman who was watching the father and son with great interest, her gaze darting back and forth as if she expected some sort of lightning storm to spring up between them.

"You're Doctor Campbell," declared the old man. "Where do you practice?"

"Barts," I replied. "I consult on trauma cases."

"Hmm," he replied. "I'll bet you have a story or two. I can't wait to see *your* atmosphere." Then he gestured to the woman.

"This is Mrs. Emmaline Calvert. A widow. She's been here before." She nodded at me, and I could see as the light shifted that she was in her sixties. Her small frame had initially given the impression that she was younger.

"And these two," continued the elder Birlsthorpe, nodding his head to his left, "are John Reynolds and Vaughn Taylor." He referred to the two men that sat between him and me, both in their thirties, and lounging back with the same shared attitudes that they were tolerating a foolish elder in the hopes of picking up some useful scrap along the way – even if it was just an amusing anecdote for later use at their club.

Giles Birlsthorpe lifted a blue-veined hand gnarled and knobbed by arthritis and laid it on the goggles. "Let's begin." He grasped the strap awkwardly and lifted the device toward his head. Pounds rose and stepped behind him, helping to place the strap in the correct place and seat the lenses before the old man's eyes. I risked a glance at Richard Birlsthorpe, and could see the pain in his expression at his father's feeble condition, and also a hint of anger at the involvement of the secretary, Clayton Kenneth Pounds.

As I watched, I wished that I knew what Holmes was up to. I'd meant to go by Baker Street during the late afternoon and see what he'd learned, but an emergency call had prevented that. In fact, I'd been lucky to get free in time to attend this gathering. Was Holmes already in the building? And what did he hope to accomplish after he arrived? If there were no typical séance tricks, there was no one to catch upstairs or in the cellar, manipulating objects that might be mistaken for ghostly manifestations. Apparently Giles Birlsthorpe simply wore his goggles and made comments about his guests – all very trite, except for the bizarre nature in which the comments were generated.

There was no effort made to dim the light, as I had seen so often before at spiritual séances. It was often explained that the bright lights scared away the ghosts – when in fact it made it too easy for the participants to see wires or assistants dressed all in black moving behind the chairs, reaching in to shift objects or touch things. No, these proceedings were well-illuminated.

With the goggles in place, Pounds returned to his seat, looking expectantly at the old man. He in turn looked around the table, one after another, silent for several minutes. Then:

"You all have atmospheres. That's good. I'd hate to meet someone who didn't!" He laughed – the first such emotion I'd heard from him – and it was actually engaging, as if this might be a pleasant fellow after all. He looked foolish, however. The goggles were a great leather piece that completely covered his face from forehead to lower cheeks. A raised section of darker leather was spliced in to arch over his nose, and his white hair stuck out over the top, tousled and uncombed, giving him a look of madness. The lenses themselves were great greasy-looking black circles, held in place by additional circles of leather trimmed in the same shape, and apparently riveted to affix them on either side of the nose piece. It was a solid construction, and it wouldn't be falling apart anytime soon.

I wasn't surprised when I was Giles Birlsthorpe's first subject.

"Campbell," he said. "Good atmosphere – Red. That's energetic and well-grounded. You have hints of green – that means you're social – and some yellow as well. The means you're creative. The edges are straight – no jagged places that would indicate emotional turmoil, or dark intruding spots trailing from out cancer or other illnesses." He nodded. "I'm glad my son brought you. He does well to have such friends. Come back again. As I'm able to make subsequent readings about a person, I can tell more about them. It will be useful for you – you'll be glad you did."

Then his attention turned to the others at the table. Next was Mrs. Calvert. He asked her if what he'd told her about her son's financial secret had turned out to be true.

"It was!" she exclaimed, bursting into motion like a beater-flushed pheasant. Her hands and arms flapped as she enthusiastically sat up and chirped for several minutes about all that Birlsthorpe had told her, and how every bit of it had been correct. Meanwhile, the man in the goggles just watched her and nodded sagely, unsurprised at everything she listed.

Then Birlsthorpe turned to the two men beside him. "Reynolds, you've been gambling again. I see that you lost several hundred – no, just over a *thousand* pounds at the tables last night."

Reynolds suddenly looked sheepish and dropped his gaze. "That's true," he mumbled. "It's all right though. I'll make it back tonight." He looked back up. "What do you see? Am I showing any orange? Will this be a good night?"

Birlsthorpe nodded, the light glinting off the round black lenses. "Absolutely. In fact, if you can beg or borrow some more funds, take them with you. You're set to win tonight – and big!"

Reynolds nodded and sat back, satisfied. Then Vaughn Taylor perked up, knowing that his turn was next.

Birlsthorpe watched him for several silent minutes, and the mood around the table, which had been rather charged following the announcement of Reynolds' impending good luck, began to feel rather grim.

"You didn't follow my advice," was the elder Birlsthorpe's declaration, and Taylor grimaced.

"I . . . I couldn't. She wouldn't have listened."

"She's your *mother*, man!" Birlsthorpe's expression was neutral, the goggles revealing nothing, his voice was angry. "Her atmosphere is still intruding upon yours. I can see it there, edging in toward your own heart – and unless you do something, she will die within a fortnight! Do you understand what I'm telling you? Do you?"

"I . . . I do. I'll do my best. But if she won't listen – "

"She must! I have been given this gift – to help. To *heal*! But how can I do so when you refuse to listen?" Then he reached up and pulled the goggles from his head, tossing them aside in disgust. "It's too much," he muttered. Then, louder, "We're done for tonight. I can't see such suffering and know that nothing will be done to prevent it. Don't you know that I can see when you're lying, Taylor? It might as well be tattooed on your forehead! You have no spine to stand up to your mother, and without treatment she will die."

He turned in his seat. "Help me to bed, Pounds. I'm done here."

And without another word, he stood and shambled from the room. He seemed to stumble for a moment before finding which direction he wished to go. The secretary stood as well, looked around at each of us for a few seconds, his expression turning speculative as it passed over me, and with the hint of a frown at Robert Birlsthorpe. For the others he had no expression at all. Then he followed his employer into the hall, and in a moment I heard them both ascending the stairs.

The rest of us stood, encompassed by an awkward silence. Then, without any additional conversation, we all went outside, pulling the front door shut behind us.

I was surprised that our client hadn't remained behind to check on his father, but perhaps he felt that it was better to stay with me. We stood outside the door as the two men walked off together to the west and into

271

the October darkness, while the little woman continued down Hill Street back to Berkeley Square, no doubt to find a cab. When they were gone, Birlsthorpe whispered, "Mr. Holmes said that he'd meet us here."

And in fact, it was just seconds later that he did so, appearing from around the corner to the mews. It was too dark to see his face, but his silhouette – his notable Inverness and fore-and-aft cap – made his identity quite obvious. He gestured to us. "Hurry – if we don't lose her, we may have this affair settled within the hour."

I was used to Holmes's unexplained commands, and thankfully, Birlsthorpe didn't question him, but instead joined us as we moved along Hill Street toward the better-lit Square a few hundred feet away. As we approached it, Holmes held up his hand and we paused. Then he darted ahead and looked to the south. Then, with a gesture, he hurried us forward.

"She has found a hansom. Hurry – summon that growler before we lose her!"

The driver was quick to act, understanding Holmes's instructions to follow the hansom without letting us be seen. Then, when we were in motion, he settled back with an explanation.

"Her name is Annie Henderson – Annie Sweet, they call her, because her of supposed kindly disposition."

"You know her then?"

"I know of her – and what I know convinces me that her involvement is all we need to know about this charade. Now we just need specific details."

"Did you find anything when you searched the house?" I asked.

Holmes nodded his head. "To be honest, I didn't really expect too, but the opportunity couldn't be ignored. Thank you for your information, Mr. Birlsthorpe. I was able to enter and move about exactly as you predicted, without encountering anyone or being seen. Of course, there was nothing to find in relation to a typical supernatural séance, so I didn't bother. Instead, I looked through your father's papers – and more specifically, the secretary's papers, as well as his bedroom. What I found was most instructive."

Birlsthorpe gestured with a hand, rather impatiently, for Holmes to continue.

"It seems," said Holmes, "that Mr. Pounds is accumulating a little trove of documents, all signed by your father, which are steadily giving him more and more power within your father's business, and in some cases, more and more bits of ownership as well. There are powers of attorney, deed and property transfers, and outright financial payments – quite substantial in size. Additionally, there are instances where your father has even signed over the rights to patents for his different medications."

Birlsthorpe was speechless. Then – "I knew that Pounds was up to something, but I had no idea what, or to the extreme that he's carried it. He's managed to completely worm his way into my father's confidence and do all of this in the little time that he's been employed?"

"Much less time than that, in fact. The dates on the various documents are no older than five weeks."

"Just after he began wearing the goggles," I said. "But what's the connection?"

"I suspect, from the research that I was able to carry out today, that he's being systematically blinded, and as Pounds accelerates his schemes, he's having your father sign papers that he cannot see, based on the misplaced trust he has in his secretary."

"Blinded?" cried his son. "How?"

"When he stood tonight," I said, "to leave the room, your father appeared to stumble, and to correct his course before heading straight to the door. Diminishing sight might explain that."

"It's the goggles," said Holmes. "I managed to reach Doyle on the telephone. He is an optic surgeon of our acquaintance," he added for Birlsthorpe's benefit. "When I described the goggles, he said that they might be coated with various dyes that would give the illusion of an aura or atmosphere when light passes through them. The best dyes for this purpose would be coal-tar derivatives, which – when placed that close to the eyes, and for longer and longer extended periods – would produce a quite-deleterious and cumulative effect."

Birlsthorpe's mouth became a tight line. "If we weren't going to find out more about what's been occurring, I'd stop the cab right now and go back to the house, and beat that man within an inch of his life."

As we'd talked, our route had taken us south and east, and we were then crossing the Lambeth Bridge. The night had cooled, and the river was flat and dark. The reflections from the gaslights were still – there was no chop or ripple upon the water. Then we were on the other side, moving slower down Old Paradise Street. A couple of turns to the south, and the hansom before us in the distance turned into Hamish Street. We reached the corner as it stopped halfway down, and the small lady disembarked, tossing up a coin to the cabbie.

Holmes knocked on the ceiling of our cab and we stopped as well. He told the driver to wait, and then we three set off down the street toward Annie Henderson – introduced to me not so long before as Emmaline Calvert, a widow.

273

She heard our footsteps and turned, suddenly tense. I couldn't blame her, and I felt ashamed – three men hurrying toward a single woman on a dark street. It wasn't so long since the Rippers had roamed the lanes of the capital. "Mrs. Calvert," I called, attempting to calm her.

She leaned forward, peering toward us. Her expression lightened. "Why, it's Mr. Birlsthorpe and his friend, the doctor." She straightened and a warmth came into her voice. Then she saw the third member of our party, and his distinctive garb. Her voice faltered and hardened. She no longer sounded very sweet. "And – I know you, Mr. Sherlock Holmes." Her tone was now flat and toneless.

"I expect so, Annie," said the detective. "Now what's to be? Will you answer our questions here, or at the Station?"

She sagged as if a string had been cut. "Here, I suppose. I've done nothing wrong." She looked over her shoulder. "Do you want to come inside?"

"No need. This will take five minutes, I think."

"That's right, it will," she agreed. "I was just doing a favor, you see, and earning a little bit besides."

"Who hired you?" asked Holmes.

"Mr. Pounds – the secretary. All I had to do was show up and agree with whatever the old man said, and remember it so that when he asked me about it the next time, I could agree again, as if whatever he claimed was correct."

"To make him think he had magical powers?" prodded Holmes. "That he could see auras, or give accurate advice and predict the future?"

"That's right. Whatever he said, I was supposed to act like he was right."

"I don't understand," said Richard Birlsthorpe.

"It's something of a reverse confidence game," I said, comprehending what was going on. "Pounds convinced your father to try the goggles – coated in something that causes an 'aura' in bright light. He wants your father to wear them more and more so that the coating will blind him."

"Blind him?" asked Annie Henderson. "I didn't know that anyone was supposed to be hurt! I thought that it was just to fool some of the other people who came to the little parties."

"I suspect that the others there were all also playing the same game," I said, and Holmes interjected, nodding.

"The goggles were making him go blind. Pounds hired people like you, Annie, and no doubt the other two men at the table tonight, along with others, to do what you were doing. They simply had to show up and let their atmospheres be read. Your father, Mr. Birlsthorpe, would then make announcements about what he thought he saw, and everyone would always happily agree. As his confidence grew in his abilities, he would make more statements and predictions, ever bolder, and whatever it was – a financial matter, a wager, a sick relative – the attendees simply agreed, further giving Birlsthorpe the belief that he has powers – and making him more and addicted to the wearing of the injurious goggles – and also becoming more and more dependent on his secretary, who had first directed him toward this miraculous 'gift'."

"You were listening from the hallway tonight," I said. "After you finished your search."

Holmes nodded, adding, "That's how I recognized Annie here, and knew that we had the opportunity to follow her and find out what her involvement was in all of this." He looked at her. "The other two men – John Reynolds and Vaughn Taylor. Of course they were hired by Pounds as well."

She nodded. "I don't know Reynolds, but Taylor is really Seth Peters. He'll do whatever you ask, if the money's right."

"I believe we'll find that every one of those who have sought readings will have been paid by the secretary to agree with whatever comments are thrown their way. Watson's invitation must have left Pounds nonplussed – here was a man who wasn't in on the game." He looked at the son. "Fortunately for Pounds, your father was cautious in his initial readings about a stranger. Have there been any other outsiders at these parties?"

"None that I know of for sure. I haven't been to every séance, but Dr. Watson is certainly the only outsider that I've brought."

"I believe that's right," added Annie Henderson. "I've known some of the others that have attended, and had the feeling that the ones I hadn't met before were also in on what was happening. And this man that you call Pounds? His true name is Willard Gables of Stepney. I've known him forever. I realized that when he was hired as a rich man's secretary, he must be up to something. A man like him couldn't simply accept his good fortune and make an honest go of it. His type has to turn it nasty." She turned to look at the younger Birlsthorpe. "I'm sorry, sir. I had no idea that your father was being injured. He seems a good sort." Then, back to Holmes. "I suppose that I have to make a statement to the police."

Holmes nodded, and within moments we were back in the four-wheeler, crossing the bridge and traveling alongside the river to the new building where Scotland Yard had recently relocated.

Our friend Inspector MacDonald was on duty, and he quickly understood what had occurred. Birlsthorpe swore out a complaint, and then we, along with several constables, were headed back to Mayfair.

Birlsthorpe unlocked the front door and allowed the policemen to enter quietly. He then led them upstairs, but after indicating where Pounds could be found, he went a different direction, to his father's room in order to explain what was happening, even as the secretary was being dragged from his bed and so downstairs.

Holmes and I stood in the hall, about midway between the two bedrooms. From Pounds' room we heard muffled noises, and then angry bellows. Then the secretary was being pulled from the room and into the hall, fighting the two burly officers gripping him on either side and looking ridiculous in his nightshirt and uncombed hair. When they reached the bottom of the steps and he saw Annie Henderson standing there, all the fight went out of him. He understood then that his scheme was undone.

Holmes stepped into the parlor and then returned, carrying the curious goggles. He glanced at the man in custody, getting his first good look at him before handing the device to MacDonald. "For the Black Museum, Mr. Mac," he stated. "Not quite as sinister as Jack's letter from Hell, but rather memorable nonetheless."

It was then that Richard Birlsthorpe assisted his father downstairs. The old man pulled his arm loose and stepped in front of Pounds, looking up at him while his mouth worked, as if he were chewing his rage into something manageable.

"I trusted you," was finally all the he could mutter. He raised a feeble arm as if to strike the secretary, but his son stepped forward, gently taking and lowering his wrist, and putting his other arm around his father's shoulders before turning him away.

"That's it, then," said MacDonald. "Belk, go upstairs and get this man some clothes. He can change at the Yard." Then he looked at us. "Will you join us – to go over the finer points?"

"Certainly," replied Holmes. "But there's no need for Watson to stay out any later. He has calls to make in the morning."

MacDonald nodded. "Still, I may stop around tomorrow, Doctor, if that's satisfactory, in order to confirm a few points."

I nodded. Then, with a general shuffling, everyone moved toward the door. I saw that Annie Henderson was also glumly now in the custody of a constable. I glanced over my shoulder to where Richard Birlsthorpe was explaining things again to the wizened man before him.

Mary was waiting up when I arrived home, and made for a most fascinated and attentive audience as I related the events of the supposed séance and subsequent journey across the city to obtain the true facts from Annie Henderson. Two days later she remained with curious interest as we entertained Dr. Kilner, who had stopped by at my invitation to hear more about the curious goggles. I understand that he was initially skeptical, but as the years passed, he ended up devoting a great deal of time and energy into his explorations of the mysterious auras and atmospheres that supposedly surround the human body.

Clayton Kenneth Pounds, more properly known as Willard Gables of Stepney, lost all interest in the topic on the night of his arrest. After a stretch in prison, I understand that he relocated to Australia, where I'm sure that a man with his dark and stunted character quickly found new ways to cause trouble.

Richard Birlsthorpe, on the other hand, was able to generate a great deal of good from the affair of the blinding goggles, convincing his father, who had thankfully suffered no permanent damage to his eyes, to evince a much more generous and charitable spirit before his passing a few years later. The secretary's plan, in a round-about way, had accomplished some good after all.

The Templarian Tattoo

Sherlock Holmes was speaking, but I still wasn't quite used to hearing him do so.

"I came over at once to London," he was saying – or so I thought, as there was a ringing in my ears – "called in my own person at Baker Street, threw Mrs. Hudson into violent hysterics, and found that Mycroft had preserved my rooms and my papers exactly as they had always been."

I took a sip of brandy, and then reached for the flask to pour some more. I felt that I deserved it, as just moments before, I must have fainted for the first and the last time in my life. There was no other explanation.

My study had been invaded by a wizened old book collector who had apparently followed me home from Park Lane, on the other side of Hyde Park. He was prattling about how he owned a little bookshop in Church Street, just around the corner from my Vicarage Gate home in Kensington, and that he had just what I needed to fill a five-volume gap on one of my shelves. I'd turned to look, and even as I was formulating a polite response that I wasn't in need of the titles he was selling – *British Birds*? *The Holy War*? – I saw that the man who had entered my study had vanished – replaced by Sherlock Holmes, who had died years before.

In a wide experience of surprising, mysterious, and sometimes unexplainable events which extends over many nations and three separate continents, I had never before looked upon something that shocked me so significantly. But then, the very last thing I would have expected was for Sherlock Holmes to suddenly return from his watery grave.

I was only half-listening as he continued speaking.

"So it was, my dear Watson," said he, "that at two o'clock today I found myself in my old armchair in my own old room, and only wishing that I could have seen my old friend Watson in the other chair which he has so often adorned."

I shook my head and glanced at the wall, where a small but significant framed document was hanging. My thoughts spun back to nearly three years earlier, when Holmes and I had been involved in seemingly random pilgrimage across the Continent, leaving London for a time while Professor Moriarty's organization was broken and the scurrying pieces were gathered up for prosecution. As that had occurred, I had simply followed where Holmes wished, only realizing later that he was drawing the Professor along in our wake to trap him, as he understood that Moriarty was too wily to be caught in the nets being cast about London.

The Professor had made a few feeble and anonymous attempts on our lives as we traveled east. Once, as we passed over the Gemmi along the border of the Daubensee, a massive boulder was dislodged from high above us, passing nearby and then into the nearby lake. One might have thought it a natural occurrence, but something about the event alerted Holmes that his plan was working – the Professor was dogging us.

I, however, was still unaware of it, and on the fourth of May, 1891, I was regretfully lured away from Holmes's side by a clever ruse. Holmes understood what was happening, of course, but he allowed me to go, ensuring my own safety while he willingly walked into the trap. Moriarty then forced an encounter between the two of them atop the awe-filling and awful Reichenbach Falls, nearly a thousand feet high and at the peak of their deadly flow from the upstream spring thaw.

Realizing that I'd been tricked, I'd rushed back up the mountain to find that Holmes had vanished. It was only by way of the short note that he'd left for me, three pages torn from his notebook and tucked under his silver cigarette case on a rock above the chasm, that I understood what had happened: He and Moriarty had fought there, and presumably both had died. These three small pages were now framed upon the wall in my study, and I glanced at them again while Holmes spoke.

After his "death", I had returned to London, nearly broken at the loss of my friend. Over the next year, I had sold my Paddington practice and residence and repurchased my older one in Kensington. To distract me, the inspectors at Scotland Yard had taken to involving me a great deal in their investigations, and I'd become something of an unofficial police surgeon. Additionally, I'd had some success fulfilling a long-standing desire to be a writer, as I'd published two-dozen short sketches of Holmes's methods in a newly-formed periodical. These, along with the two longer accounts that appeared a few years before, had served to fulfill my old agenda wherein I would make Holmes's gifts and accomplishments known to the wider public.

But throughout that period, my successes were marred by the steady decline of my poor wife's health, resulting in her passing from a combination of various illnesses in April 1893.

After that, much of the next year was a blur. My friends at Scotland Yard were most attentive and kept me busy, and my Kensington practice remained successful enough, but in the dark lonely evenings, I could only look down the road of my life and see a bleak sameness, day after day and year after year.

I was not well during those months.

However, in spite of my broken spirits, I somehow continued to function, and even though I didn't realize it, I did hang on to a faint spark of curiosity and interest in life. It was such that had led me earlier that evening, around six o'clock, across Hyde Park to Park Lane, the eastern boundary of the park – usually a pleasant walk for those so inclined to appreciate it. I'd made the journey to see the location of a recent mysterious murder – that of young Ronald Adair, whose head had been destroyed by a soft-nosed revolver bullet in a locked upstairs room.

After working with Holmes and the police for so long, the idle speculations of the crowd standing around on the pavement before the house seemed amateurish and irritating, and I'd turned to go, only to accidentally stumble into a hunched and crotchety old man – apparently a bookseller, for he carried a bundle of bound volumes in the way that such merchants sometimes do. I apologized, but he snarled and turned away. Then, having satisfied my own interest in the Adair matter, I'd turned and walked back across the Park to my lonely home.

I hadn't been back for more than five minutes when the bell rang. Thinking it rather late for a patient, I assumed that someone from the Yard had sent for my assistance. I was astonished when the maid brought in the old bookseller.

I had risen, wondering how I could shoo him out, as he appeared to be one of those rather aggressive sorts, perhaps a touch mad, who had unexpectedly fixated upon me. He must have followed me straight across the park. Then, in the time it took for me to turn my head toward my shelves and back, the hunched figure with shaggy white hair had vanished, replaced with a taller man. Even as his features came into a sharply recognized shape, my vision clouded, and I fainted.

I was surely unconscious only for a moment or two, awakening to find Sherlock Holmes, back from the dead, with a brandy flask in hand and deep concern across his features. "My dear Watson," he said with a tentative smile, "I owe you a thousand apologies. I had no idea that you would be so affected."

I struggled to my feet, finding that I was in my desk chair – either I had collapsed there, or Holmes has helped me into it without my knowledge. I crossed the room and grabbed his arm, confirming that he was in fact corporeal. My mind raced with countless questions: How was he alive, when all indications had apparently confirmed the contrary? Where had he been? Why had he now returned?

Over the next five minutes or so, he gave me a brief *précis* of his experiences during the last three years – how he had survived the struggle on the ledge over the Reichenbach, and his subsequent escape. He told of how he had chosen to remain "dead" in order to continue the work in destroying the remnants of Professor Moriarty's organization, and then just a bit of his journeys around the globe, carrying out work for his brother, Mycroft, and the British Government.

It was a truly remarkable and incredible narrative, and again and again I internally tested myself to confirm that I wasn't hallucinating. After telling me of his own adventures, Holmes gave me to understand that he was not unaware of my own situation, as he'd kept up with me through Mycroft, who had been in on his secret. He knew of my own sad bereavement and, as was his way, unchanged after all that time, his sympathy was shown in his manner rather than in his words. "Work is the best antidote to sorrow, my dear Watson, and I have a piece of work for us both tonight which, if we can bring it to a successful conclusion, will in itself justify a man's life on this planet."

I asked for him to explain, but he was reticent as usual, preferring to keep all of his cards close. That hadn't changed either. "You will hear and see enough before morning. We have three years of the past to discuss." He glanced at the clock – it was just then seven o'clock. "Let that suffice until half-past nine, when we start upon the notable adventure of the empty house."

Another question was forming upon my lips when the front doorbell rang.

Holmes frowned. So many years away hadn't changed that expression. The idea of a visitor was upsetting to his plans.

He moved over to a space behind the door to the hall where he would not be seen. "Whoever it is" he instructed softly, "get rid of them!

I maneuvered from behind my desk and toward the door. The maid was due to leave at seven, so it was possible that she'd already gone, but she might also still be around to answer the door. The rest of the staff, such as there was, had departed long before. I employed a combination housekeeper and cook during the day, and she usually made an evening meal that I warmed and ate alone in the evenings. There was an office assistant who left at five, and a page who brought patients in and out of the consulting room, but he typically left at six. Otherwise the house was empty.

I knew that Holmes must have gone to a great deal of trouble to arrive at my door unidentified, although I didn't yet understand why. He'd described how he returned to Baker Street at two o'clock that afternoon, arriving as if he'd simply been away for an overnight holiday to Margate. Whereas I had fainted, Mrs. Hudson had become agitated and distressed, and it had taken Holmes a bit of time to calm her, and to explain where he'd been and why he'd chosen to disappear for so long.

Then, after firmly and publicly establishing himself in residence, he'd risen and gone to the trouble of disguising himself and slipping away again, in preparation for some plan that we would be carrying out in a few hours. And now, someone unexpected had arrived at my door, and Holmes, who had shed his disguise, needed to avoid being seen, lest somehow the fact that he wasn't currently in Baker Street might be discovered.

I had just reached the study door when a series of heavy footsteps approached on the other side – and not the maid's. I had the impulse to rush forward and lean against the door, like a child trying to keep someone out of his bedroom, but before I could do anything except glance apologetically toward Holmes, the door opened to reveal a most unexpected figure: Inspector Athelney Jones.

"Doctor!" he bellowed, his great red face shining. "Is he here?"

Holmes was still hidden from Jones's view, behind the opened door. Without answering, I raised a finger and stepped past him to the hallway – passing on Jones's side away from the door, so that as he turned to look my way, he would be facing away from Holmes. I didn't know how that could help my friend should he wish to remain undiscovered, for there was no second door in my study through which he could escape unseen and, after removing his disguise, he was in a dark suit – nothing would camouflage him if he tried to go unnoticed on the sofa or a chair.

In the hall, the maid was standing by the front door, ready to leave for her own home.

"I'm sorry, sir," she said softly. "He just came through – said he was with the police and needed to speak to you."

"What did he say, exactly?" I quietly asked.

"'I'm a policeman, girl,'" she replied in what she thought was an imitation of Jones's officious growl, "'and I need to talk to Dr. Watson right away.'"

Good, I thought, nodding to myself. Jones hadn't mentioned Holmes. The girl could leave without any knowledge of my friend's resurrection, so the fact that he was secretly here wouldn't be revealed – at least not by her.

Thanking her, and telling her that it was all right, I let her out and locked the door. The practice was definitely closed for the day.

Back in my study, I found that Holmes had chosen to reveal himself – as he really had no choice. He was standing before Jones, who was shaking his hand frantically without any signs of stopping.

"I heard you were back!" he was saying in a rush, his Welsh accent adding a pleasing difference to the otherwise normal words. "I overheard Lestrade and Gregson whispering about it. I went right over to Baker Street to seek your advice, but your landlady said you were asleep and couldn't be disturbed. For anyone else, such an excuse wouldn't have prevented me from carrying out police business, but I owe you, Mr. Holmes, I most certainly do. Then, as I stood on the pavement, it occurred to me that the doctor would be the next best thing – that he could put in a good word for me once you were rested. I never thought to find you already here. Why, this is a most useful turn of events!"

Holmes's expression was polite, but I could see that he was irritated. I didn't yet know what had prompted his return to London after nearly three years roaming the globe, nor had I yet learned why he'd taken the trouble to arrive at my Kensington home in disguise, going to the trouble to give the impression that he was still back in his Baker Street rooms. But I did sense that Jones's unexpected appearance threatened to upset his plans, and that his mind was racing to see a solution. Finally, he appeared to accept the path of least resistance, at least for the present, and welcome Jones's presence. Freeing his hand and offering the brandy flask to the policeman, Holmes said, "Here, Jones, have a start at that, and I'll be right back to hear what you need to tell me." Then he led me into the hall and shut the door.

"Holmes," I said, "that cognac is *grande champagne*! It was given to me last year by the Duke of W------ when I cured him of a -------- -------! Jones will guzzle it like water!"

Holmes ignored my distress. "As you've gathered, Jones's arrival is most inopportune. I don't mind that word of my return has spread – that's what I wanted. But it's imperative that I'm believed to be in the Baker Street sitting room for the rest of the night." He looked around. "The maid – is she already gone?"

"She was done for the day and on her way out when Jones arrived. He brushed past her. Don't worry – I questioned her, and he didn't mention that he was here to see you – just that he was a policeman and needed to see me. As far as she knows, I was still in there with the old bookseller."

He nodded. "We must somehow contrive to keep Jones from revealing my presence here before we depart at nine-thirty. I suppose hearing his story is as good a way as any to pass the time."

We returned to the study and I was dismayed to note that the level in the bottle was already down a good inch. Even as I realized it, Jones reached over from the chair he'd occupied near my desk and poured another glassful. He took a long swallow, licked his lips and closed his eyes tightly, and then smiled. Then, setting the bottle down – but close by – he reached into his coat pocket and pulled out a wadded handkerchief, tossing it onto my desk.

It was bloody, and as it fell, it draped open to reveal what appeared to be a piece of meat.

Holmes, who had been in the process of pulling a chair over near Jones, stepped closer, leaning down and carefully opening the cloth for a better view. "Your glass, Watson."

I had seated myself behind my desk and quickly pulled my magnifying glass from a right-hand drawer. Holmes took it and began a thorough examination of the object, while Jones continued to sip my brandy and smile benignly, nodding to himself and watching Holmes knowingly.

Holmes lifted a pencil from my desktop and pushed the object around. I stood and leaned closer, suddenly realizing what it was.

When it had first been revealed, it appeared to be a lump of flesh, oval-shaped, about three inches long and two wide. Then Holmes flipped it, and I nearly gasped.

The other side was hairy and pale – unmistakably human skin. In the harsh light of my desk lamp, I could see that it was covered with fine wrinkles and whitish hairs, implying that the former owner had been middle-aged or older. But what was most shocking, perhaps, was that centered in the excised piece of flesh was a tattoo.

I had never seen anything like it. The design consisted of a cross. But unlike the Christian symbol, with the lower length longer to represent the device used for crucifixion, the four arms were of equal length. They were narrow in the middle where they joined, but widened at the outer edges, almost forming the edges of a box. The inner segments were red – a bright crimson really – but the outer arms were four different colors – white, red (of a different, darker and more blood-like shade), black, and gray – as labeled in this sketch:

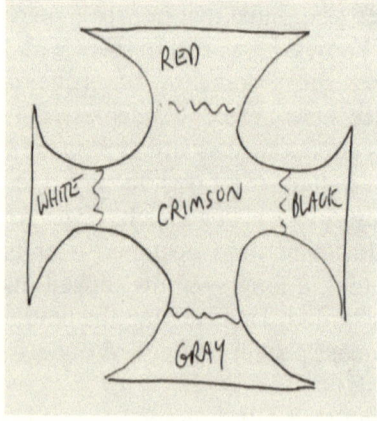

"Do you recognize it, Watson?" Holmes murmured. "It's the symbol worn by the leader of the Templarians."

Softly, I replied that I'd never heard of them while he continued to poke the chunk of skin with the tip of the pencil. "Almost certainly removed from him against his will – and not that long ago. It would have been taken as proof that the leader is gone – dead – and for his replacement to use as a talisman."

He stood, dropping the pencil upon the desk and retrieving the flask from Jones, who was about to pour another serving for himself. "I take it, Inspector," he said, setting the flask further back on the desk, "that this means Lord Retford was murdered."

Jones, already a bit bleary-eyed, looked with regret at the brandy, now placed quite the distance from his chair, and took a much smaller sip from his glass, as if to conserve what he had left.

"He was, Mr. Holmes," replied the policeman, "though how you can tell it is a wonder."

"It is indeed a wonder, Jones, when one considers that I've been away for three years. Succession to the apex of the Templarian leadership is a violent game, and Retford might have been killed before today without my knowledge. However, based on the freshness of the . . . *sample* that you brought, along with the unique design of the tattoo and the apparent age of the victim – the fine wrinkles, the aging of the skin, and the occasional white hairs are most obvious – and knowing that the two other candidates to replace him as leader of the Templarians are quite a bit younger, identifying Retford as the victim was a safe assumption."

"*Temp . . . Temp . . . .*" Jones's tongue tripped on the name. He might have had difficulties without a few glasses of brandy. "Who are these people?"

Holmes sat down and crossed his legs. Meanwhile, I stepped across and found another glass, pouring a reasonable amount of the brandy and setting it before my recently and unexpectedly returned friend. Jones hopefully waggled his glass toward me, and I added another inch or so before also refilling my own.

"The Templarians split off from the Freemasons nearly thirty years ago, having decided that the Masons' beliefs of morality, charity, and obedience to the law of the land were too restrictive. They want to form a different society, wherein the masses are led – *controlled* is a better word – by a forceful strongman who can suppress opposition and criticism by being in charge of wealth, and resources like food, and even the press, in order to spread their own message and no others. They see the poor as beasts to be controlled for the benefit of the wealthy, and the wealthy to then be controlled by the few of them at the top. I believe that they were first set in motion by some sort of reactionary fear related to ideas espoused in Marx's *Das Kapital.*

"In spite of their rather radical beliefs, they've always been relatively harmless – except to each other – and very few know about them. I gave them some special attention in '88 while investigating the various Rippers, and while they appeared to have fallen in line for a time with those Masons holding high positions in government – some responsible for the crimes, and others satisfied with what was occurring – they didn't have any direct involvement in the actual butchery. In truth, the Templarians seem to exist only to entertain one another with their fiery rhetoric and decadent gatherings."

"*Templarians*," said Jones, speaking the word carefully and correctly. "What does it mean?"

"They see themselves as the true guardians of the legacy of the Knights Templar – although in truth there is very little about the Templarians philosophy that's recognizable in comparison to that of their namesakes. Their symbol is the Templar's Cross – the design of the tattoo – but the original is completely red, while this one – " He nodded toward the object on my desktop. " – has four different colors at the ends of the cross, representing the Four Horsemen of the Apocalypse, as described in the Book of Revelations, Chapter 6, Verses One through Eight: White for conquest, red for war, black for pestilence, and pale – or gray in this case – for death."

"It sounds," I said, "as if, along with knowing who the dead man is, you have some idea of who might have killed him."

"I do – although being away for three years means that my knowledge is a bit dated."

"Nevertheless, Mr. Holmes," countered Jones, "I'm glad that I found you, as I need advice on how to solve the man's murder."

"Indeed," said Holmes. He took a sip of brandy and added, "Tell us what happened."

Jones nodded, took a larger sip of his own, and began. "We received notice around four o'clock that a man had been stabbed to death in Farm Street, just behind Berkeley Square. Number 12. Everyone else seemed particularly busy today at the Yard – not sure why, but something's up tonight for sure. I was free, so I took it. I arrived to find that it was Lord Clive Retford's home. I was met at the door by a constable, and another was inside, watching the staff. He had the servants waiting in the dining room – just a pair of them, as it seems the dead man kept very much to himself and didn't go in for a large household. Indicating that I would interview them momentarily, I had the constable from the front door take me through to the body.

"Retford was a big man, about sixty, with bushy gray hair and along unkempt beard. In truth, for a man of his station, he was rather shabby, wearing mismatched but comfortable-looking clothing and worn bedroom slippers. He had no coat, but was instead wrapped in an old threadbare dressing gown. There were dried food stains upon his waistcoat, and a rather musty odor about him.

"The room was crowded with bookshelves and tables, all crammed and stacked and piled with old volumes and loose documents in very untidy heaps and jumbles. The dead man was lying on his back in the center of the room, with a large ornate dagger plunged thoroughly into the center of his chest. He had bled a great deal, and the old rug underneath him was soaked with blood. I learned from the constable that the servants had summoned the police just after the murder, and that I had been called not long after, so he'd been dead no more than an hour when I examined him.

"As curious as all of this was, what I found most intriguing was that the right-hand sleeves of the dead man's dressing gown and shirt had been pushed up, and he had a terrible wound on his right forearm. A sizable piece of flesh had been carved out: That one right there on your desk, Doctor. That wound hadn't bled – and I'm sure that you gentlemen will both realize that's an indication that the mutilation occurred after death, when the heart had stopped beating."

He looked at both of us with satisfaction as he explained his deduction, and then he took another sip of my expensive brandy. As his consumption of it had slowed, his relative soberness had returned.

"Having seen all that there was to see in the study, I repaired across the hallway to the dining room, where the servants, a husband-and-wife named Handel, were waiting nervously, clenching each other's hands across the table. I noticed that they both look well-fed, and I suspect that they've had no hesitation at making free with the master's victuals. If servants can't be trusted with the small things, then it's no great leap that they might consider murder.

"Their stories were simple: They had worked for the dead man for nigh onto twenty years. Retford had always kept to himself – turned funny, he was – and he had no other servants. He'd never married, and rarely had visitors or went out. He spent much of his time in his study, writing and doing research on some project which took most of his time. He occasionally had three other visitors, never on a regular basis. All that the Handels knew was that each of the other men were younger than Lord Retford, and they never visited at the same time. Twice a year, Retford dressed up and went out at night in a carriage that came for him – once in the fall, and again in the spring – always returning after midnight. Most recently he went on – " Here Jones fished in his coat for his notebook, the first time he'd needed to refer to it. " – on March 21st."

"The Spring Equinox," murmured Holmes. "It's a date that they find important in their rituals. Go on, Jones. What about the tattoo? How did you acquire it?"

"Right. I didn't have to work hard to get it. It was lying on the dining table when I interviewed the Handels. Their story is that this afternoon, unknown to them, Lord Retford must have had an unexpected visitor. Normally whenever someone stops by, the front bell rings and one or the other of them answers it, then showing whichever visitor it is into Retford's study. Today they heard no bell – or so they say. They both heard a cry from their master and came into the hall – both from the kitchen at the rear – and so to the study door, but they found that it was locked. They could hear noises on the other side and further cries from Retford, who sounded as if he were in distress. While they debated how to proceed, they heard one final outcry from their master, and then a thud as something hit floor. Then, before they could think any further about it, the door suddenly unlocked and flew open. A man dashed past them to the front door, which he then flung open, and so on outside.

"Mr. Handel gave chase, even as he heard his wife starting to scream behind him when she saw the dead man. Outside, Handel saw a running figure to the left and he went after him. He was unable to stop him, but he did lay a hand on him – or so he says – and in doing so, a white bundle – that handkerchief – fell from the killer's grip and onto the street. At that point the man got away, and Handel picked up the item, sickened to see what it held.

"He claims that he's never seen Retford's forearm where the tattoo was cut off, so he can't confirm it. The same for Mrs. Retford. Still, I matched it to the wound – it's Retford's, all right. It's also the Handels' story that they can't identify the man who committed the murder. He was in a dark heavy overcoat – black-dyed wool, she thinks – and he was wearing a hat and his face was covered by a muffler."

"I assume that you're arrested the servants," said Holmes with a knowing smile.

"Certainly. That story is very shaky, as I'm sure you'll agree, and I saw nothing to indicate that there had actually been a visitor as they describe."

"And their reasons for cutting off the dead man's tattoo? Or for immediately notifying the police before coming up with a better story that was less likely to arouse your suspicions?"

"Clearly it was in their interest to notify the police as soon as the man was killed. They likely understood that we can roughly determine the time when a man was killed, and to wait too long before reporting it would raise more suspicions. And we both know, gentlemen, that people of their class can't come up with clever stories. But what does have me puzzled is the removal of the tattoo. Did they do it just to confuse things, or to make it seem more believable that some mysterious visitor committed the murder?

"I went back to the Yard to ask Lestrade or Gregson or MacDonald about it, but they were all busy with whatever else is planned for tonight and had no time for anything else. Then I overheard that you were back in London, Mr. Holmes, and I decided to get the jump on them and see what you thought about it. And here we are."

Holmes glanced at the clock, which now said half-after-seven. He tapped his fingers on the desk, frowning. I could see that he was thinking furiously, and finally he rose. "I believe, Jones, that I can offer some assistance – specifically the names of three men, one of whom is almost certainly the murderer, but I'll need to review my scrapbooks. Wait here, and I'll be back as soon as I can." Then, without awaiting a response, he opened the door and into the hall.

I jumped up as well, nodding to a confused Jones (who was already reaching for the flask), and followed Holmes, pulling the door shut behind me.

"Holmes!" I said urgently, and he stopped, turning to face me. "I don't know yet what purpose brought you here tonight, but I sense that it's of the gravest importance – that this is why you decided to return to London and life. Surely Jones's problem can wait until tomorrow."

"I fear not, Watson," he replied. "The last time the Templarians had an abrupt change of leadership – and this is certainly what is occurring now – there were a number of peripheral innocents killed in the process. It's a wonder that the Handels weren't murdered along with their master. Even as we speak, whatever has started is spreading.

"When Retford became the leader, in the late seventies, nineteen people died before it was all over. No case could be made against him, and there is every likelihood that the facts were concealed by those in authority who were able to do so. I interested myself in the affair, and in those days, few even knew about the Templarians, let alone who made up their membership. I've been quietly learning about them ever since, and only I can provide names to the authorities so that they can all be questioned and a light shined on what they're doing before things get much worse."

"You say you need information from your scrapbooks," I countered. "Then tell me what it is and I'll go. I can be there and back in half-an-hour. After all," I added, "if you're trying to give the impression that you're still in Baker Street, that notion will only be reinforced when I go to visit you there."

"No, Watson. The risk is too great. Your house is also being watched."

That surprised me, and a thought occurred to me. "If so, then they saw the old bookseller arrive – and they still believe him to be here. I can wear that disguise and travel to Baker Street."

Holmes thought for a moment. "No. That would only serve to draw a connection between the bookseller and Baker Street, possibly hinting that I'm out and about in a disguise. I have a better idea."

And so it was, five minutes later, that I departed the house – not as myself or the bookseller, but rather wearing Athelney Jones overcoat and hat, attempting to walk and carry myself as the inspector would. It was an unexpected challenge.

Before I left, Holmes and I had returned to my study to find Jones nursing along with the brandy – possibly the best he'd ever had. Holmes immediately topped off his glass, and I suddenly understood that he now wished for the inspector to become drunk – and then to fall sleep. It was one way to keep him quiet and prevent him from leaving and sharing that Holmes was in Kensington instead of Baker Street, and I suspected that it was also likely that Holmes, seeing the need to spend a half-hour with the policemen, preferred it to pass with Jones unconscious.

While the policeman was distracted by his quest for inebriation, Holmes helped me into his overcoat. "Your house is being watched," he repeated, "but I was careful to time my arrival to just before they changed their shift, so the fact that I'm still here has hopefully gone unremarked. However, a visit from a known Scotland Yard Inspector would have gathered much more notice, and seeing him leave here and then travel to Baker Street will help affirm that I'm still in the sitting room there, where I've spent the entire day."

I walked from my door, west along the street, doing my best to imitate Jones's curious shuffle. Finding a cab in the High Street at that hour was no great difficulty, and within moments – having promised the cabbie a substantial fee for a quick trip – we were in the Bayswater Road, moving at a brisk clip back to the east.

For the first time since Holmes had unexpectedly returned – Could so much have changed in less than two hours? – I had a moment to myself to consider what had occurred. My life had suddenly changed in ways that I couldn't yet even understand. For the past year, since the death of my wife, I had lived a dull and downtrodden existence, my daily routine only broken by the occasional summons from a Yarder to ask my opinion regarding dome curious incident or another. Each time, I warned them that I was no Holmes, but they sought me out anyway. Sometimes I was able to help, but even when I wasn't, they were perhaps a bit too effusive in their thanks and praise. I knew that they worried for me, and that they were doing what they could, in their own ways, to keep me connected with and interested in life. And yet, throughout all of that terrible period, all I could see was a dull gray straight road before me, leading over a distant hill to a dark horizon.

Now, Sherlock Holmes was back. I could not imagine what would happen next. I only knew that suddenly the world seemed alive with possibility once again. I suddenly had that same interest and energy as in the old days, when the ringing of the bell would cause both Holmes and me to sit up a little in our chairs, awaiting the sound of someone climbing to the sitting room, foretelling that something of interest was about to begin.

Later I would learn more about what Holmes had done during his travels, and I would examine the fact that he had trusted his brother with the knowledge that he lived, and yet had kept it from me, but for now I set that aside. All that mattered was that once again I was on an urgent errand for my friend, and I resolved to simply enjoy and exist in this moment.

Not long after we'd turned north, and almost before I knew it (and yet not soon enough) we were arriving at 221 Baker Street.

During the past three years, I had been there occasionally, sometimes by necessity, sometimes to visit Mrs. Hudson, but never without a terrible sense of loss. Now it was different. My heart was pounding with excitement. I didn't know what was happening, which wasn't unusual, but I was in the thick of it, and the game was once again afoot.

Loudly, and doing my best Jones, I told the cabbie to wait, and then made an effort to look as if it was he lumbering to the front door. I rang the bell, and within just a moment, dear Mrs. Hudson answered.

Her first response told me that I was initially successful in my impersonation. "Inspector," she said loudly, "I told you that Mr. Holmes isn't seeing visitors – " Should couldn't have spoken more effectively if she'd had a script.

Then she recognized me, and her lips were starting to speak – likely to exclaim "Dr. Watson!" and ask what I was up to – when I surreptitiously raised a finger to my lips. "Pretend that I'm Inspector Jones," I whispered, sure that I was soft enough that no one, even a passerby just a few feet away from us, could hear, but still aware that somewhere in the gathering gloom, a watcher was certainly lurking.

"I must speak to Mr. Holmes!" I said, possibly overacting a bit, but I wanted my performance to be a success.

"Oh," she said. "Oh, Inspector. Yes, please come in." Then she stepped back to let me slide by.

She had barely shut the door when she gripped my arm with both hands. "Doctor! He's *back*!"

I nodded, taking off Jones's hat. "I know. It's amazing."

"But . . . but I don't understand! When I asked him where he'd been, he said that there will be plenty of time for all of that tomorrow. He's lost weight, Doctor. And he's worried about something – you know how he looks when something is happening. Like that time when Dr. Dexter was hiding down in the basement, and he knew it but couldn't tell us – "

"We have to trust him, Mrs. Hudson," I said, patting her hands and then freeing my arm. She looked at me for a long minute, and then nodded and released her grip.

"He's at my house right now," I explained. "He arrived just an hour or so ago, with need for my help tonight. He apparently has a plan of some sort that will be carried out – but a complication has arisen. The inspector showed up, looking or him and needing his help."

She looked at Jones's hat and coat with disdain. She had never cared much for Athelney Jones. "He was here earlier – but I guess you know that. Somehow he'd learned that Mr. Holmes was back. I put him off – Mr. Holmes made it clear that people should believe that he's here right now. When he left in disguise, he went out the back, as he used to do when he didn't want to be seen." Then she took a step back. "But you must be in a hurry. You wouldn't be here if it was urgent." She gestured toward the stairs. "I'll let you be about your business."

I thanked her, adding, "I'll only be a moment. I just have to retrieve a scrapbook."

Then I dashed up the steps, faster than I'd done in many a year. Since Holmes's supposed death, every time I'd climbed to the sitting room – always curiously preserved for no apparent reason, although I now understood that Mycroft Holmes had kept the rooms *in situ* for his brother's eventual return – had been a labor, and I'd always felt that I was conveying a twenty-stone burden upon my back. Now I covered the distance to the landing, and then from there to the sitting room door, like a young man of twenty who had never been wounded in battle, nor one who carried the weight of over four decades upon his bones.

Opening the door and then looking neither left nor right, I went straight ahead until I reached the wall to the left of the fireplace, where a row of shelves was mounted. Here was where Holmes kept his scrapbooks – sometimes referred to as his "commonplace books". They contained an incredible amount of material – clippings, notes, and small physical objects – that were of incredible assistance to his work. I pulled the relevant volume from the shelf and stopped a moment, opening it to check that it did indeed have the information that I sought. I confirmed the entry

292

for *Templarians*, along with a short list of names, addresses, and notes quite incriminatory toward a number of noted members of the ruling and political classes. Then, closing it and holding it close under my coat, I spun around and went back downstairs.

Mrs. Hudson had waited by the front door, and she laid a hand upon my shoulder. "Good luck, Doctor," she whispered, and then stepped to the door. Opening it, she said – rather loudly – "Mr. Holmes is in for the night, Inspector. He has been away for quite a while and is quite weary. Please keep that in mind and don't come back until tomorrow!"

I made a Jones-like grunt and, being careful to stay in character, re-entered the cab, giving instructions in my best loud Welsh accent that we should make all haste to Scotland Yard. I had no idea whether anyone was watching, or was close enough to hear any of this gimcrack dialogue, but if so, I hoped that it had been effective.

I turned around several times as we sped along and, as near as I could tell, there was no sign of anyone following us. At our approach to Oxford Street, I knocked on the roof and called for the cabbie to turn west instead, and to set me afoot at Palace Gardens Terrace. Along the way, I'd removed Jones's coat and knocked his hat into a different shape before replacing it on my head, so when I disembarked and surreptitiously made my way through the back streets and alleys to the rear entrance of my home, my silhouette and manner looked nothing like either the policeman or myself.

I found Holmes in the study, pacing, while Jones, eyes closed, reclined supine in the chair where I'd last seen him. I was tempted to check his breathing, noting that the brandy flask was now quite low.

"Good God, Holmes, have you killed him?"

My friend smiled, even as Jones gave a great snort upon hearing my voice, rousing himself for just a moment before then shifting sideways and falling back to sleep.

"No, and it's been much more quiet here with him asleep. You have it, I see."

"Yes, and I confirmed that the information is there."

"Excellent. Oh, I truly lament trying to catch these volumes up after a three-year absence!" But his sorrow at the thought was not his main focus, as he quickly found what he sought.

"There," he said, laying a finger underneath one of the names. "Sir Stephen Bennett, without a doubt. Politician, financier, the next leader of the Templarians upon the death of his predecessor. Thankfully I've recorded enough here for Mycroft to take him in."

He moved around my desk and sat in my chair. After a second or two, he said, in a rather accusatory tone, "No telephone, Watson?"

I shook my head. "I haven't needed it – and in truth, for quite a while, I haven't wished to be bothered after hours."

He nodded, seeming to understand what that implied. "It's just as well," he said. "There are ways of listening to telephone calls, you know – attaching wires that run to separate speakers, sometimes quite a distance away. It wouldn't be worth taking the chance." He frowned. "I suppose you could slip over to a neighbor who is on the telephone? Do the Parkers still live nearby?" Then he shook his head. "No, the safest way, while slower, will have to do." He looked at me. "Where are your telegram forms?"

He then took a moment to arrange this thoughts before carefully composing the wire. "This is to Mycroft," he explained, laying down the pencil – the same one he'd used to examine the piece of the dead man's arm, now wrapped in the handkerchief in which it had been recovered, along with another, presumably Holmes's, to hide the blood stains. "He will understand, and can set things in motion to round up the various other members of the Templarians. They've been on a long leash for quite a while, seeing which one would get tangled first and bring about the destruction of the rest of them. Whoever let his ambitions run away from his good sense and killed Retford today has set in motion a series of events that will leave this nation in better shape than it was yesterday."

"What about Jones?" I asked, setting the man's coat and somewhat repaired hat on a nearby chair. Holmes nodded.

"He at least deserves a bit of acknowledgement for having the sense to consult me." He added another line to the telegram. "This will assure that he receives the credit – as Mycroft certainly wouldn't take it."

"Nor apparently you as well," I added.

He waved a hand in the air. "Unnecessary." He folded the telegram form and pushed it back on the desk. "I regret that we can't send that immediately, but we should limit our appearances, and sending it an hour or so from now will do just as well." Then he rubbed his hands together. "I don't suppose that you can offer something nutritious to a weary guest, now back home from many a far land."

"I can indeed. I believe that the cook left her noteworthy chicken pie, which seems to suit this occasion down to the ground."

"Indeed. Lead on!"

We reconvened in the kitchen, where we wiled away the time with him telling me much more about where he'd been and the things he'd seen. If it had been anyone else sharing those tales, I would have suspected that the fellow was an irredeemable braggart, or hopelessly mad, but knowing Holmes, I was also sure that I was only hearing a fraction of what he'd accomplished.

As the appointed hour for our departure approached, we returned to the study, where Jones was still asleep. As he looked most uncomfortable, I got him to his feet and onto the sofa. He did his best to help a bit, although he was clearly unaware of what was going on outside of his thoroughly inebriated skull. Meanwhile, Holmes bent to the bag which had held the books used to complement his disguise, unbuckling and unpacking for a moment until he pulled out his Inverness and deerstalker. As he pulled them on, I felt a chill: The best and wisest man that I'd ever known had truly returned. This was not a dream, and we were really about set forth into the dark night. I knew not where, not yet, but understanding would come soon enough. For now, I was simply content to once again have my best friend, my brother in bond if not in blood, back once more.

Holmes picked up the wire, intending to send it to Mycroft at the first available opportunity, which wasn't long in coming. Seeing that the clock finally said nine-thirty, we left a slumbering and snoring Jones, carefully departed the house by the rear entrance, and made our way to Kensington High Street where we could obtain a cab . . . .

It was indeed like old times when, at that hour, I found myself seated beside him in a hansom, my revolver in my pocket, and the thrill of adventure in my heart. Holmes was cold and stern and silent. As the gleam of the street-lamps flashed upon his austere features, I saw that his brows were drawn down in thought and his thin lips compressed. I knew not what wild beast we were about to hunt down in the dark jungle of criminal London, but I was well assured, from the bearing of this master huntsman, that the adventure was a most grave one – while the sardonic smile which occasionally broke through his ascetic gloom boded little good for the object of our quest.

– Dr. John H. Watson,
April 5th, 1894
"The Empty House"

The Betrayer Moon

"Ashes to ashes, and dust to dust," droned the minister.

From our spot, standing underneath a tree and watching the small group at the open grave, but still within earshot of the service, Holmes whispered, "I've never found those to be words of comfort."

I didn't bother to comment, but instead kept my eyes on the young widow, who hadn't appeared to need any comfort at all. With her newly inherited fortune, she would already have all of the comfort she could buy. I couldn't see her face for the black veil that covered her eyes, but I knew that they were fixed on Holmes.

"The actual verse," he continued, "from *Genesis* 3:19, goes, '*In the sweat of thy face shalt thou eat bread, till thou return unto the ground; for out of it wast thou taken: for dust thou art, and unto dust shalt thou return.*' More of a warning than a consolation."

He raised himself a little straighter. "This has gone on long enough," he said, and then raised a police whistle to his lips.

The shrill tone ripped through the silence. The dead man's two friends, our client Colonel Clipperton, and his old physician Dr. Forsythe, had both been warned what to expect. The minister had not, and he looked both ways as if someone had yelled for him to jump and he didn't know which way. I hoped that he wouldn't leap into the grave, and again disagreed with Holmes's decision not to tell him, worrying that his "performance" wouldn't appear genuine. The three others in attendance were surprised too in greater or lesser degrees, but this soon gave way to further shocks as the police swarmed around the widow, taking her into custody.

When the scrambling around the open grave had subsided, Inspector Lestrade led a blonde woman from behind one of the nearby tombs. She held him tightly, as the drugs which had been meant to kill her were still having an effect. Seeing her for the first time alongside the ersatz widow, her veil now lifted, gave me to understand how the imposter had hoped to get away with her scheme. They might have been twins. In fact, they were cousins, but whereas the old man's actual widow was – according to everything we'd learned – a good and decent woman, the other, who had attempted to kill her and take her place, was a schemer of most viperous nature.

It was the quick thinking of the observant Colonel Clipperton who had brought Holmes into the matter, and his evaluation of various aspects of the imposter widow – a phrase that I quite liked, but which could never be used as the title of a story, as it gave away the ending – quickly revealed her plan. We had waited and watched, and Holmes had arranged for this moment of revelation, here amongst the curious and atmospheric ground of ancient church cemetery. Now, with the fraudulent spouse and heir exposed, her true nature confirmed by the foul and vulgar epithets spewing from her snarling face, we found that Lestrade was less than amused.

"Why all this?" he said, waving his hand to either side. "We'd rescued the actual Mrs. Simms. We knew what her cousin Claudia had planned, and could have laid our hands on her at any time. Instead – all this?"

Holmes smiled. "Major Simms still needs to be buried, so the funeral was going to occur regardless. And . . . ." Here words actually seemed to fail him for a moment before he smiled. "And why not? Tell me, Lestrade, would you have rather knocked on Claudia Holt's door and simply arrested her, interrogating her for a confession, or done it this way? You'll never forget it, will you?"

Lestrade wanted to stay angry, but a small smile twisted the edge of his lips, and there was a twinkle in his eye – I thought I'd seen it when Holmes first explained the plan, but the policeman had suppressed it. Lestrade turned to me and said with a shake of his head, "Art in the blood." It was a phrase that the inspector had heard Holmes mention numerous times, and in spite of the necessity of Lestrade's official necessary stance that he make use of the simplest and most direct and effective methods possible, we all knew that he'd be telling this story for days back at the offices of Scotland Yard. Glancing at the constables, I knew that it would be the same in their parts of the building, with word spreading from one to another along the beats as well.

The minister continued to stand beside the grave, looking alternately confused and angry. Once he appeared to forget himself and nearly sat upon the nearby coffin before a lady shrieked and he remembered himself, snapping upright. In the distance, a couple of gravediggers sniggered. In the meantime, the snarling woman, along with her new coterie of attentive officers, had departed for the local station, and Holmes was explaining to the true Mrs. Simms, the Colonel to whom she clung, and Dr. Forsythe how he had determined the truth, verified the identity of the false widow, and rescued the true one, along with obtaining evidence of the true method behind Major Simms' death, when I became aware that one of the men who had been hanging about on the periphery of the mourners had approached and was standing slightly to my rear. I turned to face him.

He was a young fellow, barely in his early twenties. He was thin and rather wan, as if he spent most of his time indoors studying. The look of young scholar was written all over him, from his clothing to his manner, and to the slight stoop of his shoulders from studying old books instead of standing straight and facing an outdoor horizon.

As a medical man, I could see that he was suffering from some sort of anxiety. His manner was quite nervous – darting glances, slightly shaking hands, fingernails gnawed to the quick, and the meat of his cuticles ragged and in some cases scabbed with blood, both old and fresh.

"Were you a friend of Major Simms?" I asked, thinking that while some of his highly strung aspects might be related to grief, many of the indicators had clearly afflicted him for far longer than that.

"No, no. Of course, I knew who he was – we all did here in Fobbing. I'm only here to see Mr. Holmes."

I glanced that way, seeing that Holmes appeared to be nearing the end of his explanations. "And you are – "

"Abel Meisner, of Iron Cross House." He tossed a hand vaguely to the south and the river. "About a mile that way – a bit to one side alongside the Corringham Marsh. Mrs. Whitton, my cook – well, she's also something of the housekeeper as well –was one of the people that Mr. Holmes sought out yesterday when he came to town. He asked about her dealings with the Simms household. It was she that informed me that he was here – and you too of course, Doctor. I wrestled with myself all night, and finally decided that I couldn't pass up the opportunity to meet him – and you – and to lay my problem before you both." He widened his eyes, as if he'd somehow already told me what that problem was, and now wondered if I would agree to commit myself, and Holmes too, to helping him. But Holmes's moods were mercurial. He might be willing to assist, or at least listen, or instead he could have already set his mind upon a quick return to the capital.

I became aware that Holmes had disengaged himself from Mrs. Simms and her protectors and was walking our way. As he reached us, I started to introduce Meisner, but before I could do so, the young man tried to speak for himself, but suddenly he gave a small cry and began to sway, as if he might pass out.

I reached out to steady him, and Holmes, having just given him the quickest glance, said, "Hold up, man – You're nearly ready to collapse! Been using yourself up a little too much lately, I see." He glanced at me. "An acquaintance?"

I shook my head. "Abel Meisner from a nearby house. He learned that you're hear and wants to discuss a problem with you."

Holmes checked his watch. "The London train doesn't depart for nearly an hour. Let's get this fellow something to eat and drink and hear what he has to say."

Meisner, looking alternately grateful and sheepish at his sudden weakness, smiled at us both. I held to his arm as we walked from the cemetery and along the short village street to a nearby pub, just opened for the morning.

Inside, the landlord spoke in a friendly manner but kept a curious eye on us as his wife brought an early lunch of bread and cheese, pickles, and a most excellent beer. Meisner tried to speak several times, but both Holmes and I refused to listen until the young man had some food in him. It was five minutes that we wouldn't get back before the London train departed, but it was necessary. After a swallow of cheese, washed down but a long pull at his beer, Meisner explained why he needed Holmes's help.

"I'm afraid that the family ghost will kill me tonight."

I glanced at Holmes to judge his reaction. It had long been a maxim of his that "No ghosts need apply." On more than one occasion in the early days of our friendship, he had explained in various ways something along the lines of: "If I were to give credence the existence of spirits and phantoms, either evil or playful, as active agents amongst us, then why should I even waste my time trying to seek a rational explanation for any crime? Anyone who was caught and accused could turn around and blame the family ghost for carrying out the clever killing behind a locked door, and with the possibility of ghosts acceptably tossed into the mix, who could disagree? How could anyone prove the opposite? Mr. Smith didn't stab his father in the neck – the deed was done by his jealous dead brother. Acts of evil might be blamed equally upon man or spirit, and by allowing the possibility that something was done by a spiritual remnant still walking among us instead of going to the beyond as it should have done, my list of suspects becomes infinitely unmanageable."

I had noticed that while Holmes avoided involvement in questions of whether or not some supernatural thing could be proven, he would devote his time to cases where the idea of a supernatural aspect might pose a danger to a helpless victim. Seeing that Meisner appeared to fear for his life, I suspected that this might meet Holmes's requirements. Still, it wouldn't be certain until the story was told. I indicated that Meisner should do so.

"I'm not sure how to begin – "

"You mention the family ghost," said Holmes, a touch of skepticism in his voice. "Perhaps that is good place to start."

Meisner nodded. "I suppose I should explain first that I've only lived here about six months, having moved down when I completed my studies at Cambridge – mathematics, you know. Study of celestial orbits and all that."

Holmes's expression narrowed, but only enough for an old friend to notice. He'd long held a distrust of mathematicians – especially one who had delved into matters of asteroids and their dynamics before shifting to a more criminal intent.

"My family was from Cambridge – I grew up there – and I stayed after my parents died two years ago in a carriage accident. Their cab overturned on the ice." He blinked and continued. "My uncle – Silas Meisner – was my father's older brother, the owner of Iron Cross House. He died on New Year's Eve of '95 – he had inexplicably wandered onto the marsh and was found the next morning, drowned. Inheritance of the estate is a complicated thing, and as he had no children and I was the only child of the next oldest brother – my father – it came to me, along with a sizeable amount of money.

"As I said, I remained in Cambridge, coming down here upon rare occasions and letting my uncle's managers continue to run things in a very successful way. But having completed my studies last spring, and feeling the need for a change, I came here. And only recently have I learned of the ghost, and the dark history of Iron Cross House."

Holmes said nothing, but I could almost hear him sigh, "Ah!" as we reached the key part of Meisner's story.

"My direct ancestor – he was a grandfather, but I'm not even sure how many 'greats' should be appended to his title – was Abner Meisner, a sea captain who made his fortune in journeys between England and the West Indies. Shamefully, the greater portion of his money came from the slave trade, and he owned a number of them himself."

I was aware of Britain's terrible involvement in slavery, and how the fortunes of thousands of British families had been made in the 1600's and 1700's before it was outlawed in the early nineteenth century. Holmes and I had encountered such terrible legacies before.

"In 1786, as the tale is written, Abner retired from the sea and purchased a sizeable amount of land around Corringham Marsh, where he built a rather large and brooding stone house – the same one that I've inherited. His wife had died years before while he was at sea, and by the time he settled in, the son whom he barely knew was grown and wanted very little to do with him, as he was pursuing his own business interests in London.

"Growing ever more lonely and embittered, Captain Abner shut himself up in the house as the weeks and months passed, becoming more bitter and paranoid with each day. It was at that point he became convinced that one of his slaves was stealing from him.

"The slave's name isn't recorded in the document that I was shown, but his fate is – he was chained to a tree in front of his little cabin on the estate and whipped, the captain becoming angrier with every lash as the slave refused to confess to something that he likely hadn't done. It was then that events took an even more tragic turn.

"The slave's wife – who is identified by the name Alourdes – rushed to defend her husband, carrying her young child in one arm. She grabbed at the Captain who, in his rage, pulled his gun and turned, shooting at her. The bullet passed through her child, killing it instantly, and gravely wounding the poor mother. Then, turning back to the chained slave, my grandfather many-times-removed fired again, killing the poor man where he was trapped.

"According to the story, the killing urge left the Captain then, but it did not matter – his fate was sealed. Alourdes survived, and it was then that Abner learned her true nature. For she was a witch, a Haitian *vodou* woman, captured and brought to England, removed from her land but not diminished in her powers. She was sworn to *sevis lwa*, or 'service to the spirits' – and she decreed that these spirits would make the Captain and his descendants pay for what he had done. On the two nights preceding the Betrayer Moon, she would appear as a reminder. Then, on the night that the moon rose, she would appear a third time, and then the captain would die, as would his male descendants. She declared this before all who were there – with many witnesses both free and slave – while still holding her dead child and sunken to the ground alongside her murdered husband.

"In a rage, the Captain gave a cry and raised his gun, firing one last time, killing Alourdes as well. And then he returned to the house, and things returned to normal – as terrible as 'normal' was for that cursed man.

"The story doesn't say how long it was before the next Betrayer Moon was due, but two days before it, at sunset, the Captain was looking from his study window – the same room where the study is still located – and saw Alourdes standing in the distance, watching the house. With a cry, the captain ran outside, firing his gun in that direction, although the woman was far beyond the range of any possibility of hitting her. Then, she vanished.

"He ordered the slave cabins searched, thinking that one of the women there was pretending to be the murdered *vodou* woman, but nothing could be found to establish this. And then Alourdes was seen the next night – this time by both the Captain and the household staff.

"The following night – the night of the Betrayer Moon – the Captain shut himself in his study, getting drunk on rum and crying and bellowing at odd and random intervals. Nothing is recorded about what else happened that night, although no one reported seeing a figure on the marsh, as had been observed on the two previous nights, but come morning, a servant tentatively knocked on the study door. When there was no answer, he opened it to find the room empty. A search quickly found the Captain, face down dead in the Marsh near where Alourdes had been seen. There was no sign of violence, and he may have drowned or died from shock. There was never any reason found as to why he would have left the safety of his study.

"His son came down from London, sold all the slaves, and tried to clean the stain of his father's ownership. No specifics are provided – the story simply says that after a number of years, on the next Betrayer Moon, the son also fell victim to Alourdes' vengeance, and that she will never tire of it, and her hunger for the deaths of the Captain's heirs will never be sated."

"And you have seen her as well," said Holmes softly.

The young man nodded. "The first time was two nights ago – looking from the study window at twilight. I knew the story by then – I knew who she was."

"Did you tell anyone? Ask for confirmation from another member of the household?"

"I did not. I have no other family members here, and I don't . . . I could not speak of such a thing to the servants."

"And you saw her again last night?"

"I did. And no, I didn't seek any confirmation then either. But having learned of your presence here from my cook, I decided that I'd be a fool if I didn't seek your help."

At this point, I had to ask, "What is the Betrayer Moon? It's a term that I haven't encountered before."

Holmes started to answer, but Meisner spoke first, the first touch of enthusiasm that I'd heard in his voice since meeting him – no doubt related to his celestial studies. "The Betrayer Moon is when there is a second full moon within a month. There was one on August 2nd, and tonight – the 31st – will have another. It may have been called that simply because one naturally understands there to be only one full moon in a month, or twelve in a year instead of thirteen, and it betrays what we expect, but I believe that it might relate to smuggling, when the darkness of the new moon is always preferred, and the brightness of an extra full moon is despised."

Meisner looked at Holmes, the small enthused light in his eyes from sharing an interesting fact dying as he asked, "Can you help me, Mr. Holmes? I am alone here. I will certainly avoid the marsh, but I fear that even if I joined you and Dr. Watson on the train to London, somehow Alourdes and my fate would find me there."

Holmes didn't answer, instead asking his own question. "This story of the Captain and the curse – how did you learn of it?"

"Why, through this. It was given to me by my cousin, Windham Meisner, when he recently visited."

He reached into his coat and pulled out a document, folded and brown and speckled with age. Holmes examined it for quite a while before unfolding it to see the closely-written text on one side.

From my side of the table, I could see that it was about eighteen-inches square, and written on what appeared to be vellum. The handwriting was small and cramped, and the ink was faded, but still clearly visible. After five minutes or so – during which time Meisner nibbled more on his fingers than his food and I checked my watch, wondering if we were staying or ought to be finishing up and heading for the station – Holmes handed the document to me.

I skimmed through it and saw that it matched the story told to us, although it was related in a laborious and old-fashioned manner, with many curious and archaic misspellings. The heading declared that it was a "*True Account*" as laid down by B. Meisner, 1826.

"There isn't much time," said Holmes while I skimmed my way through it. "And I confess that I know less than I should about *vodou* and its practices. I need to run back to London and consult an expert."

"Peake?" I asked, folding up the document. I started to hand it back to Meisner, but Holmes asked if he might keep it for a while, and the young man agreed.

Then Holmes nodded and answered my question. "I'll see if he's available."

Alton Peake was a friend of Holmes's – and now mine as well – who was something of a practicing "Consulting Occultist". Holmes had met him years before when he was living in Montague Street. At the time, both of them, young men of the same age trying to make a successful start in their chosen professions, had encountered one another doing research in the British Museum. Holmes was trying to gain a thorough understanding of those various topics which might be useful to a detective, while Peake spent his efforts pursuing stories of curses, hauntings, and otherworldly encounters.

I had first met Peake following the affair of the Noel Street Oracle, and I'd found him to be a very likeable and ordinary fellow. My mind has always been a bit more open than Holmes's after some of the things I've seen, particularly in Afghanistan and India, and thus I've enjoyed conversing with Peake, even though I too don't quite give the credence to various tales that he asserts. Still, to his credit, he is not gullible, and he has debunked just as many charlatans as those whom he claims are legitimate.

Whatever Holmes thinks of the occult and the idea that it need not be a consideration in his work, he does acknowledge that Peake is an expert, and it was no surprise that he would go to seek his advice. Also of no surprise was Holmes's next instruction:

"Watson, please accompany Mr. Meisner back to the grimly named 'Iron Cross House', where I'll join you before tonight, after I've run up to London. I need to ask a few questions about your inheritance, Mr. Meisner, and also consult with a friend of mine, Mr. Alton Peake. He's an expert in certain areas outside my typical purview."

Outside the pub, Holmes pulled me aside for a moment. "The manuscript is only partially legitimate. A more intensive examination is necessary, but I could tell right away that while the bulk of the narrative was written in the early 1800's – telling the story of the Captain's murder of the slave family – the final portion, relating the curse by the *vodou* woman and subsequent deaths occurring during the Betrayer Moon, has been added recently. Oh, the forgery is first-rate, but to a trained eye, it's still obvious."

"You suspect this cousin, Windham, of giving him the document to stir up Abel's fears – a first step toward murdering him."

"I do. I think that I'll quickly find that Windham is the next in line if our new friend passes suddenly, and with no heirs of his own." He looked toward Abel Meisner, who waited patiently for me to join him with a bland dog-like expression. Now that help had been obtained, his nervousness had markedly decreased.

"This quality of forgery," Holmes continued, "could only be accomplished by three men, and one of them is speaking with you now. I need to locate the other two and confirm Cousin Windham's involvement, and get an idea why he's chosen this particularly method of murder. It's overly elaborate when a bullet fired from a distance would accomplish the same quite easily, provided that Windham has established an alibi."

"You believe that Windham has crafted some scheme rather like that directed at Sir Henry a decade ago."

"I think so. Try to find out all you can about him – but discretely. Meanwhile, further investigation is required elsewhere – and a bit of luck for me to accomplish what I need to in London and get back by tonight. I'll send some wires from the station before I depart to set things into motion."

"And Alton Peake? If this is but a fabrication, is his opinion even necessary?"

"It cannot hurt – I'm delinquent in my studies of *vodou* – and I think that seeing one of these *faux* ghost stories play out this way will be an added argument in our favor for the next time that he's telling us about another vampire hunt through a Hampstead churchyard."

It wasn't the first time that Holmes had mentioned that particular incident, the hearing of which had somehow rubbed him the wrong way, as Peake had insisted on relating it on a day when he really didn't have time to listen.

At that point we parted, with Holmes setting off for the station, and Meisner and I striding in the opposite direction. "I try to walk whenever I can," explained my young companion. "I'm not the most healthy chap, you know. I have a weak heart, a weak constitution really, and I'm afraid of everything. Sadly, my parents raised me to be that way – I see it now – and I wonder if it was because they knew of the family curse and its unavoidability."

"How did your father die?" I asked. "Did he also succumb to a violent death?"

"No, not at all – at least not that I knew at the time. He passed in his bed, during the night. But perhaps I don't know the full story. Suppose he saw the ghost of the dead woman and kept the knowledge to himself?"

"Did he die on the night of a Betrayer Moon?"

Meisner frowned. "You know, I'm not sure. It never occurred to me to check. But I did verify that there was a second full moon in December 1895 – on the night my uncle died, nearly three years ago."

"But you never heard of anything suspicious about his death?"

"No. I wonder why my parents never warned me."

"Perhaps they never knew of this curse either," I replied, withholding my knowledge by way of Holmes's interpretation that the added details of the curse were fraudulent. "If it was only recorded in the manuscript, then perhaps your parents never learned about it."

"That's quite possible, I suppose."

"Tell me more of your cousin."

He shook his head with a fond smile. "Oh, we couldn't be more different. Where I'm rather fragile, he's quite hearty. He is my only cousin – like me, he has no brothers and sisters. My father was one of three brothers – the middle one. The elder – Uncle Silas – had no children, and the youngest, Theodore, was Windham's father. They always lived in Winchester, and we only saw them on rare occasions. When Windham was grown, he went out to sea, and I've seen him even less since then, although we've written over the years. He showed up a few weeks ago without any warning – down for a visit while he was in port and wanting to see the old family digs."

"And that's when he gave you the manuscript."

305

"Right. He said it had gotten side-tracked to his side of the family ages ago, and that it ought to be back with the house. We both agreed that our distant ancestor the Captain was a terrible man, and that there is much despair soaked into the grounds, but he laughed at the notion of the curse, and said that if anyone can cheer up the place and give it fresh life, it's me." He looked down. "I suspect that I'm in over my head, Doctor, but we shall see. Thank heavens for good managers to act as stewards for those who don't know how to do it themselves."

As the conversation progressed, we'd ambled away from the village and along a narrow road, choked at times by wild growth, undeterred by the August heat, and at others with a view of the flat lands stretching away to the horizon. One might think that they were simply fields, but I knew from experiences with similar locations that setting off across them might turn treacherous, as what appeared to be solid ground could turn instantly into a plant-covered mire, wherein one might plunge deep by way of a single wrong step and never be found.

Iron Cross House was much as I'd imagined it – a wide dull-colored building constructed of massive fitted stones. There were windows and a central door facing us, but nothing of personality which might do anything to break the bleak presentation with character or cheer. It could have been the administration building of a prison for all of its warmth. I could see how the notion of a curse could be generated in such a place, whether or not it was really true.

It was on something of a rise that jutted out into the surrounding marshland. The day was sunny, but there were hints on the horizon of evening storms. The late August heat was muggy, and the sound of a million insects all around us would have rivalled the noise of a busy city street.

As we moved to the front door, I glanced around, and except for a few low out-buildings, there were no visible structures in any direction. I knew that other villages were over the horizon in every direction, but one might have thought that we were on an island without any other inhabitants. Quite the lonely spot for the retreat of an already lonely young man, particularly after his days in a university town. I knew not how this business of the inheritance would play out, but if possible, I decided to try and advise Meisner to find a different path than residing in such a desolate place.

After the humidity of the approaching mid-day, entering the building was a pleasant shock. The inside was rather dark, and at least twenty degrees cooler. I supposed that the stone walls were so thick that the warming effect of the sun really had no effect at all.

The furnishings, what there were of them, were solid and substantial, but uncomfortable looking. We entered the front door into a wide hall that led straight through the house – I could see a window in a room at the far side of the building. There were a few doors on either side of the hall, and a substantial staircase rising along the right wall. Meisner gestured vaguely to each side as he led me toward the back – sitting room, library, dining room, parlour. Then we were in the back room, which he called the study. It was set up as a rather more comfortable place with inviting chairs, a very cozy fireplace, shelves of books, and wide windows looking out upon the nearby marsh, just twenty feet or so from the house. Without giving time to poke around, Meisner walked on through a door to the right, and after passing through a dark hallway, we found ourselves in the kitchen.

Sitting at the table was a middle-aged couple, one in cook's attire, and the other clearly some sort of laborer. I was introduced without explanation, and their names were provided as Mr. and Mrs. Whitton – the cook and housekeeper, and the caretaker to maintain everything outside the house.

"They've been here for ages," explained Meisner. "I don't know what I would have done if they hadn't been waiting when I arrived."

Both seemed reserved but pleasant enough, although they kept a wary eye in my direction. In spite of what we'd recently eaten at the pub, Meisner asked if we might have a bit of lunch – in the manner of a child who was uncertain of what reply he might receive. Mrs. Whitton pulled herself wearily to her feet, while her husband excused himself and departed, and within a few minutes, the cook had set out the remains of a cold ham and a portion of a loaf. A crock of beer – not nearly so good as what we'd had in the village – completed her efforts, and she nodded without asking if anything else were required and left.

"Do they know that you intended to seek help?" I asked. "Do they even know of this curse?"

"I did ask questions about Mr. Holmes when I hear Mrs. Whitton telling her husband about him, but I didn't explain why, or what I planned," was Meisner's reply through a full mouth. "It didn't seem appropriate somehow to share my troubles."

"So you haven't asked them anything about the curse?"

He shook his head.

"How long have they worked here?"

"Twenty years at least. More, probably."

"And they were the caretakers during the years between the last owner's death – your Uncle Silas – and your move down here."

"They were. The attorneys who look after the estate and the business worked closely with them. I think," he said, lowering his voice, "they're worried that I might make some improvements around here, and won't need them anymore. It's absurd, of course, but how to bring it up without it being awkward? But I'll think of something." This his tone darkened and he set down the remains of his sandwich. "That is, if I get through tonight. It's the Betrayer Moon."

That recollection seemed to dampen his spirts considerably, and it was a mood from which he never really roused himself during the rest of the day. After our second lunch, he and I settled into the comfortable study, and all my attempts at further conversation or to find out more about his family – Cousin Windham and any others – was fruitless. I pulled a novel from one of the bookcases, and after twenty minutes or so, Meisner excused himself and went upstairs for a nap.

I considered questioning the Whittons, specifically to see if they were aware of the curse, and about the circumstances of Silas Meisner's death on New Year's Eve 1895, but I didn't know if doing so might upset Holmes's plans. While I was often responsible for seeking out information in situations such as this, I also knew that in this case, with things coming to a head so quickly, I shouldn't do anything to cause additional ripples. My presence there had already set enough of those in motion.

After reading until I was also nearly ready to fall asleep, I set the book aside, stood up, and went back to the kitchen, where the Whittons were again sitting around the table. They were both lost in their own thoughts, and there was no conversation to disturb. Instead of being too specific, I tried asking some general questions about the age of the house, its history, and what the nearby area was like, but they simply provided monosyllabic answers with steady regularity until I gave up and went outside to pace the grounds.

A hot wind had risen, and there was a curious sea-like smell to it, and a freshness as well. There was a storm coming, and I wondered if it would pass and be finished before the night's business began, or if – as had happened too many times in the past – I would be out in it, without adequate rain apparel, squatting in the blackness and waiting for something to happen, or chasing someone (or some *thing*) nearly unseen as it fled in front of me into the darkness. Looking at our surroundings, I vowed that if such a person (or thing) ran into the marshes, particularly during a violent storm, I would happily let it go, and insist that Holmes do the same.

Eventually I had walked and explored as far in each direction as I cared to go, and had learned nothing. I made my way back to the house, settled in with the same novel (and re-read a substantial portion of what I'd already seen, as I had no memory of it) and let the afternoon slide by without purpose or accomplishment. I felt that Holmes would return and expect me to have something valuable to contribute, but I would have defied him to learn anything more than I had. But even as I thought that, I realized that he could have done so. I took a sip of the brandy which I'd poured form the decanter on a nearby sideboard and congratulated myself that it was an important skill to understand one's own limits and be satisfied with them.

Sunset at that time of year would normally be quite late, but with the steady arrival of storm clouds all afternoon, it was dark by six o'clock. Abel Meisner had come down from his long nap not long before, but he didn't look any more healthy or refreshed than when he'd left me after lunch. He asked how I'd fared, but didn't seem too interested when I showed him the book I'd found. I could see that he was distracted and rightfully concerned by the expected visit later that night of Alourdes, the *vodou* witch who had supposedly cursed his family and died a hundred years ago. I was tempted to tell him that it was all a trick – the lines on the manuscript detailing the curse were forged, and that responsibility likely fell at his cousin's feet – but Holmes had made a point of privately sharing his conclusions, so it wasn't my decision as to what was revealed. And I also knew that there were other possibilities and explanations that required my silence. Perhaps Abel Meisner was much more clever and dangerous than he appeared. It did not seem so, but I had been fooled before, and there were many times when Holmes had been consulted in order to give some wily plot a sheen of credibility. Better to keep my own counsel.

At Meisner's invitation, I joined him back in the kitchen. The Whittons were gone – I was told that they went to bed quite early and would already be in one of the small out-buildings I'd passed during my explorations – but that an evening meal was prepared each night. It was indeed – if one considers the remnants of the same ham and bread loaf to be a prepared meal. As we had hours earlier, we both made plain dry sandwiches, although this iteration was even less pleasant than before. I had the sense that the ham was starting to turn and limited my portion accordingly.

The wind was rising, and nothing could be seen by then in the blackness outside the windows. We ate slowly without conversation, but eventually we were done and – putting the last of the ham and bread in a nearby cupboard until morning (where I feared it would be our breakfast if this lasted that long), we adjourned back to the larger room along the rear of the house. I worked up a small coal fire and we settled into chairs, pulled around to face the windows. All was in darkness except for the small cheery glow flickering in the fireplace, and the flickers of lightning in the distance above the black marsh. The lightning and thunder were initially far in the distance, and I counted the seconds between flashes and rumbles to gauge the distance and speed of the approaching storm. Ten miles at least, and then five, and then it was upon us.

The sound of it was more muted than I would have thought, but this I attributed to the thickness of the building's walls. The lightning was vicious and frequent, and the cracking thunder sometimes rattled the room around us. I knew that the house was of heavy sturdy stone, but I wondered about the roof, with its ancient dried timbers. If it was struck, would the slate shingles be any protection, or would the incredible heat or a stray spark catch on the flammable beams and set the place to burning? It hadn't happened before, I supposed, and therefore it was unlikely that night as well.

I glanced toward Meisner to see that he was huddled within himself. I imagined that he was pale, although there was no true way to know in that jumble of firelight and sizzling hot brightness flashing from the sky. He had a sick look on his face, and he was staring through the great windows before us, into the featureless darkness that enveloped the marsh surrounding the house.

And then he gave a cry.

I turned my head in time to see, standing right at the window and illuminated by the burst of another lightning bolt, the angry yet smiling face of a black woman, cradling a baby in one arm, her hand raised and pointing toward the marsh behind her.

I gasped. I may have given a cry as well. Almost as soon as the hot white light flared and faded, I could see nothing while my retinas recovered - nothing but the hazy shape of the woman imprinted upon them. Then the thunder crashed again, shaking what felt like the entire house around us. I felt no logic then, no intellect. I was simply a defenseless creature, wishing to do nothing but curl in upon myself and hide, hoping that the danger passed by – that the roving predator went on without noticing me, or the flying hunter chose to skim over me while seeking an easier meal. Nothing in that second of time could have made me recall who I was or why I was there.

Except for the sound of Sherlock Holmes's voice.

"Watson! He's in the house!"

I blinked and stood up. I don't know why. I had no idea what to do after I'd done so, or where to go, but it was an instinctive reaction. There was no need to hide or flee. I would react. I would fight back.

Turning as my vision cleared, I saw in the light from the fireplace a man – a burly grimacing figure – a foot or two behind Abel Meisner's chair. The young heir was still facing forward, frozen with his mouth hanging open in that way that some small animals are when instead they should jump and move and run. Even as I stood and turned, the heavy-set man looked my way, his expression one of shock. He hadn't expected me to be here – that much was clear. I took a step toward him, seeing as I did so that a rope of some sort was stretched between his hands. It couldn't have been more than a second or two since Holmes had called to me. This man – certainly Windham Meisner – must have been as surprised at hearing Holmes as he was to see me stand up beside him. I took a step forward, ready to knock him down. To detain him. To punish him as a target for my recent surge of fear. The lightning and thunder had charged me with strength and emotion, and it cried for release. But before I could reach Windham Meisner, he was surmounted from behind by consulting detective.

The struggle was brief. Holmes pulled Windham Meisner over backwards, locking him in a wrestling hold until I could step forward and place my pistol at the man's temple. The fight went out of the sailor immediately, and after calling to our client several times, we were finally able to get him to rise and light a lantern. He seemed to slowly comprehend who it was that was being held at gunpoint.

Abel swallowed, and then, after doing so again, turned and stumbled to the sideboard, where he poured himself a splash of whisky. Drinking it down and the coughing seemed to bring him back to himself, and he stepped again before his cousin with a puzzled and hurt expression.

"I don't understand . . . ."

"Your cousin planned to kill you," Holmes said, disengaging himself and rising to his feet. "For the inheritance. The terms were quite easy to establish. The house – and more importantly all of the business interests and funds – they all go to the oldest male heir. With your death, your cousin Windham is next in line. He had the original manuscript that you showed us. That part of his story was true, and it did end up with his branch of the family, but he had the ending with the curse and the Betrayer Moon and all of that fairy tale added by an accomplished forger."

Holmes glanced at Cousin Windham, lying before us on the floor. "I've spoken to Pinchbeck in Distaff Lane. He confirms your intent. He's been half-expecting you to come back and try to tie off that loose end. If you'd done so sooner, he and his pistol would have been ready for you, and we would have never had this opportunity to meet here tonight."

Windham Meisner snarled and made as if to roll to his feet, but I raised my service revolver another inch and caught his attention, reminding him why he was on the floor to begin with.

"Who was the woman?" I asked. "The black woman pretending to be the *vodou* witch?"

"She is Windham's wife, whom he brought back with him from the West Indies. She was with him when the arrangement was made with

311

Pinchbeck. By the time I'd assembled all the pieces, I had Alton Peake with me, and he and I came down from London together. Sadly for him, he's still out in the storm. It's his job to keep an eye out for the woman, and to follow her. I knew from the nature of the false curse, as described in the forged part of the manuscript, that she would be the one putting in an appearance as the dead conjuring woman. Peake and I hid outside, and we saw both her and this man, her husband, arrive a good half-hour ago. She went one way, and Peake followed her. He has a talent for that sort of work. It's too bad that he chooses to chase after myths instead of real criminals, as he did tonight.

"After we separated, I kept an eye on Windham here, and at the height of the storm, he entered the house by way of a window on the far side, opening into an unused ground-floor room. After he was in and had moved deeper into the house, as I observed from outside, I climbed in and followed him. He was in the doorway of this room, unaware that I was behind him, when his wife appeared at the window. I must admit that it was quite effective – I nearly gasped myself and gave the game away. But I withheld, and when Windham moved in, unaware of your presence, Watson, and carrying a rope by which he meant to strangle his cousin, I called for help and moved to stop him."

"But how did he hope to make such a thing work?" I asked. "I assume that he has an alibi in place, well away from here, but how did he think it would work? A curse, for heaven's sake!"

"I expect that he thought his cousin Abel would make his concerns widely known, so that when he died – his body likely to be tossed into and later recovered from the Marsh – there would be inevitable talk of the curse."

"But that wouldn't have worked," I said. "I have the sense that Abel told no one but us. Is that correct, Mr. Meisner? Abel?"

The young scholar roused himself when I said his name, and then agreed. "That's right. There's no one to tell but the Whittons, and I didn't share the story with them."

"It isn't too late!" snarled Windham Meisner unexpectedly. "The curse is real! The story has been told in our family from generation to generation." He cast and evil glance upon his cousin. "Just because your parents withheld the truth from you doesn't make it any less true. Yes, I had Pinchbeck add it to the old account, but I didn't make it up – the story has been told on our side of the family for over a century." He stood then and took a step toward Abel Meisner, despite the presence of my revolver. "I know everything – including the truth about your side of the family. You haven't a clue. The estate is *mine*! It always has been – and you won't keep it!"

He looked back at Holmes. "You may charge me with harassment, although I'll claim this is simply a joke – a bit of fun played on my poor cousin who took it the wrong way. But there is no other crime! The crime is your friend here, holding me at gunpoint. And I'll be bringing charges at first light – see if I won't! But in the meantime – " And he looked back at Abel Meisner, who seemed to be curling in upon himself. " – the curse will take you, my fine foolish cousin. Before morning – count on it! This is the night of the Betrayer Moon, and Alourdes wants her payment!"

And suddenly he turned, pivoting on his foot with the quickness and grace of the sailor that he was, toward the great window. The storm was still raging outside, and as the lightning flashed I could see the black woman from before, now ten or fifteen feet back from the building instead of pressed to the window. With a leap, Windham Meisner leapt and crashed into the glass with one shoulder, hurling forward into the night. He rolled when he hit the ground and carried through until he leaped to his feet. Then, he and the black woman together vanished into the night.

Holmes cursed under his breath, but quickly recalled young Meisner and set about getting him seated back from the broken window while I poured another inch of whisky into his glass.

Holmes was explaining that while Cousin Windham had been correct in his assertion that criminal charges against him might not hold up, the idea of the curse was false – something concocted as a distraction when Abel was murdered.

"But the curse isn't false," said a familiar voice behind us. "It's a well-known story amongst those who keep track of these things."

I turned to see Alton Peake's smiling face, somewhat drenched, but displaying his typical good cheer. It didn't falter when Holmes said, in a rather peeved tone, "I thought you were going to keep track of Windham's wife."

"I did. After they separated, she turned tail and made straight for the village. I stuck with her right to the point where she climbed on a train for London, and I saw her out of site. I sent a wire to your friend Gregson at the Yard to meet her when it arrived and to hold her, should we need to ask some questions."

Holmes was silent for a moment, as if what he wanted to say was no longer relevant and must be re-calibrated. Finally I expressed what he must have been thinking.

"If Windham's wife is on her way to London . . . then who did we see at the window? Who was standing outside just now when Windham escaped? Whomever it was, she ran off with him toward the Marsh."

Holmes had no answer, and Abel Meisner simply stared into his whisky glass, occasionally taking the tiniest of sips. Alton Peake, however, simply turned his head and cocked a knowing eyebrow when our eyes met. In the dim light from lantern and fire, augmented by the flashes of lightning through the broken window from the receding storm, I thought I could see an expression of amusement on his face, as if he had known the answer to a question all along that we were unwilling to acknowledge, but could not deny.

We stayed in the house through the night, and then looked outside in the bright sunlight the next morning to see if Windham Meisner's path as he'd fled could be determined. It wasn't difficult, and he hadn't gone far. He was dead a hundred or so feet from the house. He'd been running along the edge of the Marsh when he'd apparently slipped, falling forward and across a newly fallen limb. One of the jagged branches had landed upright and had gone through his throat.

Alton Peake's expression was innocent as he pointed out Windham Meisner's footprints, still clear in spite of the storm, indicating that he was running when he'd lurched forward to his death. "Just *his* footprints, you'll note," Peake clarified. "No others. Almost as if the woman who left with him didn't leave any footprints of her own at all . . . ."

The Whittons were not the unsympathetic couple that I'd first perceived. Seeing their master's distress, they rose to the occasion and cared for him. I had a glimmer that perhaps they were seeing him in a more sympathetic light when they heard the story of how he'd been mistreated. In any case, we left Abel Meisner in their care, convinced that the curse was false and that he had nothing more to fear. I vowed to check back on him soon and see if he was all right.

At the station, Holmes found several telegrams waiting. He passed one to us without comment. It was from Gregson. Windham Meisner's wife had been detained for questioning when she'd stepped off the train, and she'd explained that she was through with his schemes. To have arrived in London at the time she was met, she would have been on the train when we saw Windham Meisner join the other black woman and run into the night.

Holmes remained convinced that the sea-faring cousin had made use of another black woman of his acquaintance, and that it was she whom we had seen from the window in the lashing of the rain and wind, but no word as to who she was or her whereabouts could ever be discovered. I knew that the question of the woman's identity continued to pester Holmes long after the matter had otherwise been replaced in our thoughts by subsequent affairs.

I, on the other hand, would always regret that I had been unable to actually observe the Betrayer Moon on that terrible night, as it rose and set unseen behind the great canopy of the terrible storm.

In the train back to London the next day, Holmes was quiet, and Alton Peake watched him intently. He had known Holmes longer than I had, and we could both see that our friend was working something out in his own mind. Finally he spoke.

"You have never been the type to gloat," he said to the occultist, "so I can tell you this one final fact because you will appreciate it, and with the knowledge that, as friends, you won't throw it up to me in the midst of some future argument."

Peake nodded and said, "I suspect that I know what you're going to say."

"Indeed?"

"Yes. You're going to say that during your researches yesterday, you found that Abel Meisner is not the true heir."

Holmes isn't often surprised, but he was this time, and didn't try to hide it. "And you knew this how – ?"

"It isn't unexpected. After all, the true *vodou* woman did kill a Meisner, and I doubt that she would make a mistake. Windham Meisner followed her into the storm, and died just minutes later. On paper, Abel Meisner was the heir – so if she didn't kill him, she had a reason. Thus, Abel isn't the true heir. Windham was."

Holmes nodded. "I had wired ahead yesterday as I left for London. Thus, relevant documents were waiting for my inspection when I arrived at Somerset House. Although apparently forgotten now, Abel's father was adopted. He was an orphan whose parents worked for the Meisners – not a true Meisner at all. His father was apparently a fair man who shared his estate equally between his two real sons and Abel's father, and after years it was forgotten – except by Windham. You'll recall that he implied that he was the true heir, but without explanation. When it came time to pass on the estate, Windham was likely at sea on the other side of the world, and lazy attorneys took the simple path to Abel without doing deeper research. When Windham returned, he contrived using the curse to take the estate. He would have been better off simply relying on legal documents to establish the true inheritance."

Peake shook his head. "He was the true heir. Last night was the Betrayer Moon. He was doomed to die. But at least the curse has ended. Windham had no children, and Abel is of a different bloodline. There are no true Meisners left. There's no reason for Alourdes the *vodou* woman to stay. Her work is done. She can finally rest in peace."

"There is that, at least," I said, and Holmes scowled.

"So, Watson," he grumbled, but without true ire, "now you've also gone over entirely to the supernaturalists."

We debated the question the entire way back to London.

The Distasteful Affair
of the Minatory Messages

CAVEAT: A bit of familiarity with the events of The Hound of the Baskervilles *would not go amiss when reading this narrative. Watson, having recorded these events in his journals several months after* The Hound *occurred in September and October 1888, likely had no idea then that he'd later be publishing the Baskerville narrative, or that he might be spoiling some details of that initial investigation's solution . . . .*

It had been less than a year since I stood before Baskerville Hall, and while I'd always supposed that I'd return someday, being there that afternoon was a complete surprise. When I'd arisen that morning, in an inn a hundred miles north, I'd had no expectation of traveling later that day to that ancient pile of weathered black stones, mullioned windows, and centuries of dark history. But it had seemed like the best course of treatment to prevent Sherlock Holmes from dropping into one of his black moods.

Throughout my life, with travels and experiences across three continents, Holmes has been the best and wisest man whom I have known, but he has his limits. Early in our association, when I had nothing better to do than heal from certain devastating war wounds and try to learn more about my new flatmate, I had constructed a list, attempting to catalog what I knew of him, but it mostly consisted of tallying what technical and learned subjects he did or did not know. I had thrown it into the fire in frustration before moving on to those questions of his character and personality.

Even in those early days, I had found that he was contradictorily quite proud of his abilities – he'd once cried, "What is the use of having brains – I know well that I have it in me to make my name famous!" – while curiously willing to let the police take credit for his successes.

Holmes has little patience for willing and intentional ignorance, but if someone is curious and interested in learning or bettering themselves, no one will make more of an effort to help than he. His sense of justice is second to none, and those who have been victimized by the strong earn his special attention. And yet, for every instance where I am aware of him making an effort to aid and assist someone, there are certainly a dozen others which I never know about. He tends toward secrecy, for a number of reasons. He is discreet when dealing with the affairs of others, and withholds information when necessary, even from me. Additionally, he likes to keep back some of his cards until such a moment when he can make a dramatic revelation. But mostly he tends to keep a tight grip on all the threads that he's gathered, refusing to make any final declarations until he is certain he has all the facts in his possession, as well as a complete understanding of their importance and relation to one another.

Another more unfortunate aspect of his personality is his occasional tendency to fall into extended brown studies – although that has lessened markedly as the years have passed. I well remember how he'd warned me of it within minutes of our introduction to each other in one of the old laboratories in Barts on that long-ago New Year's afternoon. "I get in the dumps at times," he'd explained, causing me to smile at his forthright explanation – which was hard to credit seeing how enthusiastic he was at that moment – "and don't open my mouth for days on end. You must not think I am sulky when I do that. Just let me alone, and I'll soon be right."

We had shared rooms for a number of months before I ever saw the first signs of this aspect. Even before I knew of his profession, I was aware that he was always moving about – seeing his mysterious clients in the mornings in our shared sitting room (after I'd excused myself and retreated upstairs to my own bedroom), and then departing on various errands – sometimes returning quickly, or occasionally vanishing for several days in a row. It was only in the late spring of that first year that I first saw a sign of these "dumps" as he'd called them.

I knew he'd been burning himself rather freely. For the most part in those early days I didn't join him, as my own health was still fragile – although even then I realized that assisting Holmes on his investigations, which required me to rouse myself from the tempting womb of our comfortable sitting room, was the best rehabilitation that I could have. I came down that morning to find him very unexpectedly on the settee, wrapped in a blanket, still in his sleeping clothes. It took him quite a bit to convince me that he wasn't ill, and I finally recalled his initial warning that these moods occasionally came over him, and that eventually all would be well. And it was – within a day, a new case had captured his attention, and we were departing for Morcott, in the East Midlands.

Over the years, I had seen the same symptoms occasionally present themselves, only to depart again quickly enough, and I'd learned that some sort of distraction was usually the best way to get things back on track quickly. On the morning of which I intend to write, the ninth of June, 1889, we were in a small sitting room in a nondescript hotel, where we had just spoken with a most remarkable visitor, now departed. I glanced from the just-closed door and back to Holmes, where I could see the incipient signs of one of his dark moods stirring.

We'd just heard the confession of an elderly man in relation to a recent killing. His future son-in-law was being held for the crime of murdering his own father, and now we knew truth. But what to do with it? Both Holmes and I felt that the affair was unpremeditated and long justified. The old man had told us of the years wherein he'd been blackmailed by the dead man, and how the situation had finally become intolerable.

We were in a delicate position: We had knowledge of a killer's identity, but we were choosing not to reveal it for what we'd determined was the greater good. Did we have that right? I knew that Holmes's sense of justice confirmed the decision in his own mind, and I agreed, but that gave us no legal standing whatsoever. We'd had the killer – I hesitate to elevate the designation to "murderer" – sign a statement confessing his guilt before he walked from our door as a free man. And now we were withholding evidence.

"Well, it is not for me to judge you," Holmes had told the old man just before he left. "I pray that we may never be exposed to such a temptation." Then, when the man had gone, Holmes had murmured after a long silence, "God help us! Why does fate play such tricks with poor, helpless worms? I never hear of such a case as this that I do not think of Baxter's words, and say, 'There, but for the grace of God, goes Sherlock Holmes.'" And his voice faded away, his gaze locked on something far from that sitting room in a small hotel located near the Boscombe Valley.

When Holmes had first sent me a wire the previous morning, asking if I'd like to join him for a couple of days in the west of England, I had initially expressed reluctance, as my practice's list was rather full at that time, but my wife Mary had said, "Oh, Anstruther would do your work for you. You have been looking a little pale lately. I think that the change would do you good, and you are always so interested in Mr. Sherlock Holmes's cases."

As I went upstairs to grab my case – as I'm always a prompt and ready traveler – she had joined me, stating that she'd been worried about my state overwork in recent weeks, and that the trip would do me the world of good. She'd gone on to say that after the investigation was complete, I should extend it for a couple more days, making it a proper holiday. It was with that in mind that I suggested something of the sort to Holmes, hoping to deflect his grim ponderings from our recent visitor before they had chance to take root.

His gaze returned from wherever he'd been focused, almost looking surprised to find himself back in that small sitting room. He seemed to understand the reason for my effort, as he didn't ignore my idea completely, or reply with a sigh and some snide comment that he wasn't interested. "Where do you suggest?" he asked instead. He waved a hand dismissively. "Here? Somehow I think we've already exhausted the charms of Rye."

I was at a loss, as I had considered this to be an excellent base of operations from which to explore the countryside, particularly the beauties of the nearby Wye Valley, of which I'd heard much throughout the years. Seeing that I was losing his interest, I had another thought.

"I had a letter," I said, surprised that I'd forgotten to mention it already. "Just the other day – an invitation, really. Sir Henry has returned to the Hall, and asked if we might visit him. At the time I ignored it – for how often do we find ourselves in this direction with nothing to do? But now it seems rather like a perfect idea."

In fact, I wasn't so sure. The previous fall, Holmes and I had spent an extensive amount of time in Dartmoor, over a hundred miles to the south, assisting a young Canadian who was the victim of a long-standing plot to cheat him of his inheritance. Holmes's solution, to which I admit some regret because of the danger in which our client was placed, had involved allowing the young baronet to walk unknowing across the foggy moor as bait, luring his scheming enemy into making an attack. Holmes had felt that there was no other way to conclusively catch the villain except to force him to act. Sadly, before we could reach the young man, Sir Henry Baskerville, the attack had begun, and he was somewhat physically injured in the process. Worse, however, was the mental breakdown that followed as the terror of the incident, following weeks of stress while accustoming himself to a completely new life.

It was recommended that Sir Henry get away – and he had done so, travelling extensively throughout the past winter. He'd been joined on his journey by a fellow Dartmoor resident and recent friend, Dr. James Mortimer, who left both his patients and his patient wife for the duration of the journey. I knew that however friendly Mortimer's motives had been, he was also being practical: Sir Henry's continued well-being, and his willingness to reside on the bleak moor in the ancient family home, would mean the world to the local community. Should Sir Henry move away – into London, or even back to Canada – the financial resources and support that he would provide by his presence and stewardship of Baskerville Hall would vanish, as would whatever other advantages might have benefited the nearby residents.

Now Sir Henry was home and wished to see us, and this seemed to be a perfect opportunity. Rather than give Holmes the chance to raise objections or change his mind, I set about efficiently arranging our departure. Within the hour, we were packed and on the train, first to Gloucester, where we passed the impressive cathedral on our right within a few hundred feet of the station, and then on to St. David's Station in Exeter, bypassing Bristol entirely on the way, and pausing for only a moment in Taunton. In Exeter, we weren't far from their cathedral, where Holmes and I had previously had some grim business a few years earlier, but as it wasn't directly on our way, I was unable to see it on that day.

The further we removed ourselves from the morning's earlier conversation, the better Holmes's mood seemed to be, and I was glad of it. I could see that I'd made the correct decision, and felt fortunate that the option of returning to Dartmoor had been available. Holmes had bought a stack of newspapers when we left Gloucester, and he spent most of the longer leg of the trip reading them, occasionally making comments as we headed south. He told me a bit of his brother's involvement in the passage of the recent Naval Defence Act, which led to questions whose answers revealed a bit more than I'd known about Mycroft Holmes's unique position within the government. Then, as we left Exeter for the shorter trip to Coombe Tracey, Holmes mentioned that one of the newspapers had noted that the previous day was the Feast Day of Ephrem the Syrian, and he just had time before we reached the station to relate the story of a short investigation he'd carried out for the Orthodox Church in relation to the Saint a decade earlier, in those years before I knew him when his practice was in Montague Street, alongside the Museum.

Before we'd departed Ross, I'd sent a wire to Baskerville Hall, and there was a reply from Sir Henry waiting for me at the station in Exeter, announcing that we were more than welcome and would be expected. I'd also sent one to Dr. Mortimer, but there had been no response. However, we found him waiting for us when we left the small wayside station at Coombe Tracey, with a wagonette parked outside the low white fence. He greeted us with great warmth and ushered us aboard his vehicle. Then, gigging the pair of cobs hitched to it, we lurched into motion for the final piece of our journey, leaving me impressed, yet again, with how easily it was in that modern age to journey between various regions of the country as compared to the difficulties one had faced when I was a lad.

We spent the first part of our reunion reacquainting ourselves, and Mortimer told us some details of their international journey – initially back to Sir Henry's original home in Canada, where his health had improved, even if his spirits had not. "It was the betrayal, you see, that broke his heart," the doctor explained. "He had truly loved that woman, Beryl, and he believes that she loves him – he still believes it – and he has struggled to understand how she could have allowed him to remain in danger."

"And your opinion, Doctor?" asked Holmes "How do you assess the lady?"

321

Mortimer was silent for a while. Then, "I think that she did – does – love Sir Henry as well. Any secrets she kept from him were due to fear of her husband and what he would do if she betrayed him." He shrugged. "You saw her condition when we found her – what had been done to her when she did try to warn Sir Henry."

"Where did she go after her husband died?" I asked, recalling those grim events from the previous October, and the terrible damage that he been left upon the unfortunate woman.

"Go? Why, she never left. She remained at Merripit House. I don't know the state of her funds, but I can't imagine she has much left. My wife and a few of the local women have done for her what they could, but the lady is proud, and will only accept so much charity – although she has been wise enough to at least accept some, or she would have been much worse off than she is, and much sooner too. I believe," he added as we lurched around a corner and the grade steepened, "that she has been waiting. For Sir Henry to return."

"And have they reunited?" asked Holmes.

"Not to my knowledge – and I think that I'd hear. My wife seems to know everything that happens on the moor."

As we'd progressed, the sun was lowering into the sky, although full dark would still take several hours to arrive, so close as we were to the summer solstice. We climbed gradually higher, and our gaze was constantly drawn this way and that by the jagged rocks pushing from deep inside the earth, some no more than scattered discolorations, while other great tors towered so high that they could be seen long before we reached them.

The early evening was clear, with none of the rolling fogs or sudden rains which so often swept across the area. We constantly trundled past free-roaming sheep and the moorland ponies, most ignoring us completely, while a few raised their heads to note our passing with otherwise no reaction. We went by patches of darker green contrasting with ploughed earth alongside lonely stone moorland cottages, and overhead the evening birds flew here and there, catching insects and dipping and diving to impress one another with their energy, and simply full of the joy of living in that beautiful spring setting. For it *was* beautiful, despite the grim history and mysteries of the place, and the sometimes-terrible lonely feeling that would occasionally sweep across when one is there long enough.

We had fallen into silence after Dr. Mortimer finished speaking, each with our own thoughts, and I idly watched as we reached and then passed the great tor where Holmes had stood on that night, just three-quarters-of-a-year ago, silhouetted briefly against the moon while Sir Henry and I foolishly wandered about below, searching for an escaped convict as the terrible cries of a hound echoed across the dark and ancient moor. The night had been so dark, and neither of us had been able to see much beyond our own hands, for even in the stark light of the October moon, the shadows had been absolutely black. But in spite of our limited physical vision, that search had been one of the most vivid experiences of my life, with my senses sharpened in a way that has rarely ever occurred. I doubted that I should ever forget it.

I saw that Holmes was glancing toward the tor as well, and I felt like pulling his typical trick of seeming to read my thoughts based on where he'd looked. But the mood wasn't right just then for such a glib conversational gambit, and in any case, Dr. Mortimer chose that moment to speak once more.

"He still isn't well, you know," he said. "Sir Henry. After Canada, and then traipsing around the Continent, he said that he was ready to come back here. 'Back home,' he said. I had my doubts, but I was also selfish. I missed my wife and my practice, and my studies. It's longest I've ever been away, and in spite of seeing parts of the world where I would have never been able to travel otherwise, I wanted to come home, too. So I let him talk me into it – in spite of hearing from my wife that conditions here might not be best for Sir Henry's recovery."

"Conditions?" I asked, as Holmes turned his gaze from the distance toward the doctor. "Do you mean Beryl Stapleton?" I feared some new *faux*-supernatural threat.

Mortimer nodded. "As I said, the lady of his affections is still here. Perhaps she had nowhere else to go, but my wife seems to think she's waiting for Sir Henry." His lips pursed. "As if she hasn't caused him enough pain."

I withheld comment. I understood Dr. Mortimer's protective stance, and I knew full well the lady's complicity in the previous year's crimes, but I also had been with her on several occasions, and had seen she and Sir Henry together. True, she'd been a married woman when they met, though in secret, but she couldn't have truly loved such a brute as her husband, scoundrel that he was, and if she wanted to await the baronet's return, I would not judge her.

Our day's journey was drawing to a close. The land before us dropped into a small cuplike valley, ringed 'round with bent timeworn trees that had stood for ages before the sometimes-terrible Dartmoor storms and ever-steady winds. They served to both protect the manor which we approached and to mark the boundaries of its immediate grounds. A pair of high towers rose into view, and the rest of the building became visible as we rounded a turn to find ourselves before the aged and weathered lodge gates. Each was surmounted by a large carved boar's head, curiously representing the Baskerville family. I'd always wondered why these were chosen, as the story of the legendary hound was so much more associated with them. However, I also instinctively understood that such a reminder and connection would not be something that they would wish to be reminded of, or to promote to their visitors. I wondered how many hundreds of years it had been since the last boar had traversed these lands. The fact that such was chosen as their symbol was another indication of how deep were the Baskerville's roots in this primitive and curious place.

We clattered down the avenue toward the front door. When last I'd passed this way, it had been fall and the passage was like a dark tunnel, muffled by countless fallen leaves along our path. Now the evening was still bright enough that the building itself looked interesting rather than grim, with its lichen-blotched stonework and countless mullioned windows arranged haphazardly at different levels across the face of the structure. To our right was a newer, half-constructed building which had been started by Sir Henry's predecessor, his uncle Charles Baskerville, before the man's death just over a year before, in May of '88. I could see that no work had progressed since Sir Henry had departed – not a surprise. Neither was the fact that there was no sign of the Swan and Edison electric lamps that Sir Henry had declared would be up within six months of his initial arrival.

As we waited at the door to be admitted, Dr. Mortimer whispered that the Barrymores, the servants we'd met on our first trip, had left the region for Penzance, where they used their savings and a legacy from Sir Charles to purchase a small pub. Currently the Hall's needs were being seen to by Mrs. Hayes, a local widow, who lived there with her young son. It was the former who answered the door. She was a gruff woman of middle years, her countenance dour and weathered, but she was welcoming enough as we entered the old building, and she seemed to hold no resentment about extra visitors showing up nearly unannounced. We set our bags down in the entryway, telling her that we would take them up ourselves when the time came, both being familiar with the place after our visit the previous year. That little bit of consideration seemed to thaw her just a bit.

We were led into the great room where Sir Henry was rising from a deep chair to meet us. He was the same man that I'd known before, but changed nonetheless. He moved as if he was recovering from an illness – a slowness to his movements as if he were conditioned to expect pain from every motion. And there was a gauntness to him now, with an expression that looked as if he were constantly expecting to flinch from a blow. Dr. Mortimer saw it as well, and while I wasn't surprised, based on what I'd heard, apparently it was worse than our friend had expected.

"What has happened, Sir Henry?" Mortimer asked, taking a step forward before we could even exchange greetings. Clearly some sort of set-back had occurred.

"Nothing, nothing," the man replied nervously. Then his glance cut toward a nearby table, with an opened letter upon it. One didn't need to be Sherlock Holmes to observe such an obvious reaction.

"It's those notes!" explained Mrs. Hayes, still standing behind us in the doorway. "Fourth one since he's been home. And now those scratchings on the moor wall . . . ."

Sir Henry frowned. "That's enough!" he snapped, his voice shrill. Then, in a slightly more controlled tone, he added, "It's nothing. It's my problem. It's time I stood on my own two feet again."

"May I?" asked Holmes, stepping forward without acknowledgement or permission and retrieving the sheet.

"I've found them propped by the front door, every time," said Mrs. Hayes. "Maybe I shouldn't have delivered the others after I saw how the first one upset him. And I never would have told him about the scratchings – but Davey opened his mouth."

Sir Henry seemed as if he were trapped in some sort of electric current, jittering as if he wished to storm from the room in anger, while also paralyzed into place. Finally he dropped into his chair and sagged back, covered his eyes with a shaking hand. Dr. Mortimer knelt beside him, offering him soft words of comfort. I stepped over to Holmes's side and read the letter over his shoulder.

It was a typed note, simply stating: *You will pay. Vengeance is mine.*

Holmes looked up toward the housekeeper. "The other notes?"

She shook her head as Sir Henry replied, "I destroyed them."

Holmes handed the sheet to me for closer examination. It was on plain cheap paper, with matching envelope. I noted that the typing was uneven and, having been around Holmes enough to pick up a bit of information, I could see that it seemed to have been composed by an amateur typist who was using two fingers instead a more learned and practiced method wherein all the fingers labor equally. The envelope was similarly typed, and addressed simply as "*Sir Henry*".

"Were the other notes of a similar nature?" my friend asked.

Sir Henry lowered his hand and looked up. Somehow having Holmes taking charge seemed to give him strength. "Not exactly. One – the first – had a Bible verse – I cannot remember which. The second something about a ghost who walks. The third . . . the third said that blood – *my blood* – will be spilled to pay the debt."

Holmes pursed his lips. "And you didn't keep the others."

The baronet shook his head, his eyes locked on Holmes's features. "I burned them."

"Why didn't you tell me?" asked Dr. Mortimer, rising to his feet. "I could have helped!"

"How?" cried Sir Henry, his control cracking as he sat upright. "What could you do? Is this place cursed to me even now – after what I went through? Is there no safe haven to be found here? And besides," he said, his voice lowering, "how could I ask even more of you, my friend, after you traveled with me, and worked so hard toward my recovery over these last months? I have no claim upon even more of your time."

"You have every claim!" snapped the doctor. "For the very reason that you *are* my friend!" Then he clapped his mouth shut, as if afraid to say more.

"These 'scratchings'," said Holmes, turning back toward Mrs. Hayes. "You said they're on the moor wall. Can you show us?"

She nodded, and then seemed to wait, as if to determine whether Holmes meant right then. He did, and he started toward her. From the corner of my eye, I saw Sir Henry pull himself to his feet. Dr. Mortimer took a step forward and grasped his arm.

"Is this wise?"

Sir Henry nodded, his mouth a tight line. "When – when the first message arrived, I suppose that I thought of you, Mr. Holmes – of whether you could help me. But it was too much to ask. Even with the other messages, I couldn't presume . . . But finally I – I finally couldn't wait. I wrote to you, Doctor Watson, without specifically defining the problem. Doing so at least made me feel as if I'd made some effort to fight back, little enough though it was. I had no hope that it would actually result in your visiting here. To receive your wire this morning – that you were in the area and wished to stop by – It seemed like a miracle. I was suddenly hopeful again. But then Mrs. Hayes found the latest letter, just an hour ago, and Davey told me right after what was marked on the wall, and it felt as if I'd had my feet kicked out from underneath me all over again. Now, however – having you both here – I feel as if there might be an explanation for this after all – that you will find it."

I nodded, not wishing to mention that it was only by the merest chance that we'd ended our day in Dartmoor. If not for Holmes's dark mood, and the need for a change and a distraction, with the realization that we couldn't find it in the area of Rye, we might never have even thought to journey in this direction. And then what further suffering and persecution would Sir Henry have faced?

The five of us walked through the house and out the back, toward the Yew Alley and the gate that opened onto the Moor. As we passed I looked for indications of the housekeeper's son, Davey, but saw no signs.

We reached the gate, which was at the end of the long row of ancient yews. As had been the case every time before that I'd passed this way, I glanced at the ground, fruitlessly trying to locate in just which spot Dr. Mortimer had seen the footprints of a giant hound when Sir Charles Baskerville's body had been discovered there. I glanced toward Sir Henry and saw him doing something similar. Perhaps he would never be able to walk that path without considering what had occurred there, and the evil intent that had caused it.

The old gate wasn't very high, and it squealed with disuse when we opened it and passed through. Instead of heading onto the moor, which rose before is in a distant dreamlike vision, Mrs. Hayes turned sharply to the right and led us back along the yews until they ended at a six-foot stone wall that continued on around the back of the grounds. She then pointed toward one of the wider wall stones, about five feet above the ground, which had several curious markings upon it. "Found that this morning," she explained.

Holmes thanked her and then indicated we should all stay back. Before looking at the wall itself, he bent to examine the ground before it. I could see the indications of where someone had stood, but I didn't know if they were the prints of the housekeeper or the person who had defaced the stone. Holmes glanced toward Mrs. Hayes, whose shoes were visible beneath the hem of her plain skirt.

Satisfied with what he'd seen, Holmes then took a step closer to the wall. Even from where I stood, I could see what the markings represented. They were scratched into the lichens adhering to the face of the rock – a wide triangular shape at the bottom, forming a base for four smaller elongated ovals arranged across the top of it. They could only be meant to imply the footprints of a hound – a giant one, based on the unusually large size.

The markings were clearly fresh. The newly exposed stone was white, almost gleaming in the fading light. Around the marks, the lichens had been uprooted, peeled away and hanging limp, further highlighting the stylized footprint.

Holmes had pulled out his glass and was leaning in to examine the stone further when a curious thing happened. A chip of stone suddenly exploded from one of the stones just a foot or so higher than his head. It was so unexpected that none of us save Holmes had any reaction for a second or two. He however immediately jumped back and turned, dragging Sir Henry to the ground. His action set me into motion, and I pulled the housekeeper down as well, even as we heard the echoing sound of a distant rifle shot. Dr. Mortimer remained upright, looking like a confused long-legged bird, until I hissed for him to drop like the rest of us.

I myself wanted to rise and look around – it was instinctive curiosity – but I knew that the service revolver in my coat pocket would be a useless defense from someone shooting our way with a rifle. The revolver was only accurate at a very limited range, and based on the time between the shot hitting the stone and the following sound of the gun's discharge, the unknown sniper was quite some distance from us. The good news was that whomever it was that had fired the shot was probably far enough away that he couldn't approach very quickly now that we were pinned down – assuming that this person was working alone and didn't have a nearby confederate. The bad news was that we had to find a way to get back inside the house without being exposed to further shots.

Sir Henry was surprisingly calm. I had expected more of an emotional reaction after this attempt on his life, but he seemed to have snapped out of what was plaguing him. Perhaps the idea of an actual physical enemy with a very prosaic firearm versus anonymous threats with the weight of supernatural associations gave him something to focus upon. In any case, he was calmer than Dr. Mortimer, who was muttering to himself and becoming more agitated as the seconds passed.

Holmes had crawled over to the bushes that shielded us, and he returned to report that he could see nothing on the distant moor. "I suppose that it could be a coincidence – a stray hunter's bullet hitting just where we'd paused along the wall – but I'm inclined to think that this was intentional." He turned his head to Mrs. Hayes. "As I recall, we can continue along this wall to the turn at that corner, and there's another back entrance on around."

She nodded, and I was impressed that she appeared to be more irritated than frightened. Without being asked to lead, she took that job on her own, rose to a half-crouch, grabbed her skirts, and then started along in a curious scurrying that might have been comical in another setting. We followed in a hurry, and I had the terrible sense the entire time that I was in someone's cross-hairs, but we made the corner and then the turn without further incident.

Inside, Holmes set us to making sure that the doors and windows were closed and locked, and then we gathered in one of the central ground-floor rooms. In the meantime, Mrs. Hayes had wasted no time in gathering her son, Davey, and he stood watching us silently, a boy of about eight with dark curious eyes and sandy hair.

"We cannot just hide here!" snapped Dr. Mortimer. "This attacker can't simply lay siege to the Hall until we step out to be shot."

"I suspect that all of us but one are safe," said Holmes, "unless we were to be accidentally shot if the real target is missed."

Sir Henry sighed at that. "I don't understand. I'd never planned on coming here to this place, to Dartmoor – not in my entire life – but then the inheritance was thrust upon me. Since then, it's seemed as if I'm suddenly in a boat, and the river is rushing faster and faster toward a dark destination that I can't see, and I have no way to stop or steer to the shore – I can only go forward. Since I've arrived here, it's been nothing but danger and fear and . . . and heartbreak." He closed his eyes.

"We will put an end to this, Sir Henry," said Holmes firmly, taking a step forward and gripping the young baronet's shoulder. "And I suspect before nightfall."

"But what can you do?" asked Dr. Mortimer, his skepticism threatening to undo whatever confidence that Holmes had hoped to impart. "The moor is vast. The shooter might have already vanished – or he could be creeping closer even as we speak to invade the house!"

"Calm yourself, Doctor," said Holmes. "I believe that, with a few verifications and conversations, this affair will be soon be at an end."

I already had a sense what he suspected, although he probably had a dozen reasons more than my one vague notion. He turned to me. "I'll need to slip out and move around a bit. Can you maintain calm here?"

I nodded. He didn't need to ask if I could keep things safe as well until his return. I would do my best, in spite of wishing to join him. I knew that he could move quicker alone, and that he would find the answers he needed with the quick precision of a skilled surgeon. In any case, the occupants of the Hall didn't need to be left unprotected.

"I'll be back when I can – or I'll send word. Watson, I'll have my messenger knock in the same pattern as Fleming did in the Elford affair. Do you recall it?"

I did, although it had been five years at least. I wasn't likely to forget such a grotesque and tragic murder.

Without further comment, he turned to go, but I followed him into the hallway.

"The typed messages?" I asked softly.

He nodded. "I suspect so. It fits with what we already know. As you recall, I continued to ask a few questions when the matter last fall was concluded – to satisfy my own curiosity." He gripped my shoulder as he had Sir Henry's. "Stay alert. And see what weapons you can find. Who knows what this deranged villain may try next."

Then he slipped open the front door and was gone. I saw him vanish around the corner of the unfinished building, and could only imagine what he would be forced to do in order to get away unseen from the estate.

I closed and locked the door and returned to the inner room – something of an unfurnished windowless passage between the rear of the building and those large front rooms where the Baskervilles had spent their idle hours over the centuries. I queried Sir Henry about our defenses, should it be necessary, and he led me deeper into the house to a mostly disused gun room. There were a few rifles, apparently stocked by Sir Charles before his death, that were in reasonable condition. We brought all of them back to where the others waited, along with several boxes of ammunition, and spent a quarter-hour getting them cleaned and loaded. Mrs. Hayes took a rifle, and clearly she knew what to do with it. Then we brought in some chairs from the dining room – carefully, as there were tall undraped windows there – and settled in to wait for word from Holmes. It would prove to be a long evening.

Occasionally soft conversation would begin, but it would fade away just as quickly, as if people preferred their own thoughts – or perhaps they didn't want to miss the sound of stealthy approaching steps. A few times early on, Dr. Mortimer alternately expressed outrage that we were in such a position, and then he would ask who could be responsible, but no one offered any answers. He had set his rifle aside early on, but he would reach out and touch it regularly, finding comfort in the cold steel.

Sir Henry was a curious study, and I watched him closely. He had also set his rifle down on the floor, and then folded his arms tightly, as if he were very cold. He didn't move from that position, or loosen his grip upon himself, throughout the long vigil. It appeared as if he were trying to hold himself together, and if he relaxed, even once, he would separate into pieces and slide to the floor.

I had been listening as closely as I could to the sounds which made their way into the inner room. Such a place, even one as old as that which had been settling for centuries, still had creaks and ticks as the sun set and the air cooled. It was difficult to know which sounds were natural, but I heard nothing that indicated someone was trying to enter the building – and certainly nothing as dramatic as a broken window or forced door.

It was in one of the long periods of silence in which we'd settled that Mrs. Hayes abruptly stood. "I'm getting food and drink," she whispered. "Davey, stay here," she added in a tone that didn't allow debate. Then, before I could respond, she had slipped into the darkened hallway that ran from that room to the back of the great house, leaving her rifle behind.

I stood up, rocking with uncertainty for a few seconds. Sir Henry still held himself, and Dr. Mortimer looked to me as if seeking some kind of explanation. I finally muttered, "Stay alert," and followed the housekeeper.

330

She was in the kitchen, efficiently setting meat and bread and a couple of jugs of something on a tray that already held a small stack of plates. She glanced up when I came in, but said nothing as she then reached for five glasses. I looked past her, toward the windows that were lit with the last of the dying June sunlight. Without approaching the windows, I tried to be aware of any threats that might be lurking there, half-expecting something to suddenly appear before me, suddenly silhouetted. Should such a one appear, would I have time to react? Forcing myself to breathe deeply, I resisted the urge to raise my service revolver and hold it ready to fire. At the same time, I cursed to myself regarding Mrs. Hayes's thoughtless impulse to seek food. "Please hurry," I whispered, my voice tight.

She spared me a glance of the sort that is recognized by men instantly, wherein the woman makes it clearly known that she will do what she wants, and in her own good time. Fortunately, she was nearly finished, with only utensils and napkins left to complete her efficiently loaded tray. Then, without comment and ignoring my offer to assist, she lifted the whole thing, pivoted, and headed back to our refuge.

After she stepped away, I moved forward once more to look carefully from the window. The view was limited across the back of the house, a distance of fifty feet or so before a series of closely planted trees separated the grounds from the moor. The kitchen being darker than the outside, there was still enough light to illuminate the portion of the grounds that I could see, and all looked well. But I knew that this was just a fraction of the entire perimeter, and our enemy – should there actually be one, and this not just the result of an errant hunter's bullet – could be approaching from an entirely different direction, even as I tarried at these unapproached windows. I hurried back to join the others.

They were already sharing out the food, humble though it was, and Dr. Mortimer's mood in particular was markedly improved, to the point that he started softly relating some tale or another of a Cavalier who had hidden on the moor in days of old in a cave otherwise reputed to have sheltered a witch. Barely had he begun, however, than I reminded him of the need for silence. He stopped speaking abruptly, and there was something of a wounded surliness in his manner after that, until I caught his attention and directed him toward Sir Henry, who was eating nothing. After that, he resumed his normal solicitous manner.

Although it was already dim in the room, we'd had some residual light by way of the adjacent rooms with their tall windows. We were near the longest day of the year, and the sun set late, but even so, it was getting darker with every minute. I dreaded when the night fully arrived, and we had nothing to do but sit in the black room, listening for every noise and adjudicating whether it indicated a threat. It was while I was pondering such thoughts that a loud knock came from the front door.

Mrs. Hayes gasped, and Sir Henry sat up straight for the first time since we'd retreated there. Dr. Mortimer half-rose with a jerk, and Davey, who had made no sound since I'd met him, gave a small whimper and leaned toward his mother.

I listened – three knocks, followed by a long silence. Then five more, with the second and fourth considerably softer. Then four more in quick succession, much faster than the deliberate effort of the others. It was the same pattern used by Clifford Fleming when he'd arrived with a surgeon during the affair of Lionel Elford's abominable inheritance.

Holmes had returned – or someone representing him who had been taught the secret signal.

Motioning for Dr. Mortimer to say where he was, I slipped through the shadowy house to the front door. Unfastening the great lock, I stood to one side, gun in hand, and pulled it open to find Holmes before me, along with a constable that I vaguely recognized from our previous visit.

"Doctor," the man nodded.

"Officer Claiborne," I responded, remembering his name just in time. Meanwhile, Holmes walked past me, into the house. The constable and I followed.

Back in the darkened room, I could just make out the faces of the others as they circled Holmes, questioning looks upon their faces.

"There is nothing to fear here," said my friend without preamble. "All is known, and there's nothing left but to confront your persecutor, Sir Henry. If you'll join us, we'll have the matter settled before another hour has passed."

The young baronet looked confused, as if he didn't understand the language. Meanwhile, Dr. Mortimer said, "I shall join you."

"There was never a doubt," said Holmes. "We have a carriage outside large enough to carry all of us." He glanced toward Mrs. Hayes. "We shall return in a few hours – might you have something hot waiting for us?"

The woman, in spite of her grim features, seemed to have a look of relief about her, and she brushed a hand across her son's head. "I will." She waited and watched without moving, however, as we all left the room, heading toward the front door.

In spite of Holmes's assurances that all was now safe, I still kept my hand resting on my service revolver, and glanced here and there around the courtyard as we all found seats within the carriage. Then, with two sizeable horses pulling us, we set out through the gate and away, back on the same track we'd driven only a few hours before.

"After the events of last fall," Holmes began without further preamble, "I continued to investigate, as there were a few unanswered questions. At the time, I felt sure that, based on what I'd learned, the matter was at an end. But your return, Sir Henry, shows that there was still a grievance against you that someone wanted settled."

"It's Stapleton," muttered Sir Henry. "You were wrong – he didn't die on the moor as you said. As you *promised*!" His voice cracked a bit then, and Constable Claiborne gave him an appraising stare, as if thinking *Is this the rich man who is supposed to do so much?* I could see that he was not too impressed by our young Canadian.

"No," said Holmes, raising his hand. "All indications are that Stapleton did indeed perish while trying to cross the mire. His carelessness – and his hubris – destroyed him. No, this was someone else who also has a grievance."

"Who, then? Who is this person?"

"All in good time. Soon, all will be known."

I looked at Holmes with a bit of irritation. As was typical, he wished to reveal the truth in his own way – as if he couldn't help doing so in a dramatic fashion. In this case, if I were him, I would have shown Sir Henry a bit more mercy and simply revealed the name then and there. I thought that I knew it myself, and was tempted to go and say it – but then I realized that I wasn't entirely certain, and this carriage was no place to debate the matter.

It was no surprise – to me at least – when I perceived that our route was terminating at a centrally located and well-appointed set of rooms in Coombe Tracey. I had been right, and the typewritten notes had been the clue. I had been working with Holmes long enough by then to recognize certain aspects of the message – the manufacturer of the typewriter, as based on the type, and various indicators by way of the two-fingered typing style. While I was unclear of motivations, I had expected that this person was involved in some way. I glanced at Holmes and saw that he recognized that I wasn't surprised, and he smiled.

When I had first visited Mrs. Laura Lyons the previous fall, I had initially been struck by her extreme beauty. The rich hazel color of both her eyes and hair were uniquely attractive, and her freckled cheeks had been flushed with rose over a complexion that one typically found on a brunette. Altogether, it was most striking, but my second impression had almost immediately been that there was something subtly wrong with her face, a coarseness and looseness which otherwise spoiled her near-perfect features.

When she'd first greeted me the previous year, it had been with a pleasant smile of welcome. Now there was no such expression upon her face. With a snarl upon seeing us, she tried to slam the door, and then leaned into it, but it was useless. The solid figure of Constable Claiborne was immovable, and with a quiet tone, he informed her that we were inviting ourselves inside "for a little talk".

I looked at Sir Henry, who appeared to be baffled. I realized that he likely had never even met the lady, although he might have heard about her. She was the estranged daughter of one of his neighbors, old Frankland of Lafter Hall, an amateur litigator who would rather fight with his neighbors than get along. In typical fashion of one of his type, he had disowned his daughter when she'd married against his wishes, and then provided no help when her scoundrel husband had abandoned her. It had been up to many in the local community to provide what aid they could, and Sir Charles Baskerville had been helped to set her up in a small typewriting business to make ends meet.

Stapleton, the man who had made Sir Henry's life such a living hell the previous year, had wooed Laura Lyons, making use of her help in his own plot. She hadn't known that he was already married, and whatever hopes she'd had for improving her own future had been dashed with Stapleton's death. I could understand that she might seek some sort of retribution.

We settled ourselves in her small parlor and I glanced over to the nearby desk, where her Remington typewriter sat, the same as it had the previous fall.

"It's late," said Holmes, "and there's no need to beat around the bush, Mrs. Lyons. Of course you know of the letters that Sir Henry has recently received – you wrote them on that typewriter. Both Watson and I recognized the typeface of machine that wrote the messages – a Remington. From our visit here last fall, I had observed that you owned a Remington and, while there may be one or two others in the surrounding area, it's unlikely that any of the other owners have a connection to Sir Henry's affairs.

"Additionally, it was obvious that today's message was typed with two fingers, but the uneven strength used for the different letters was indicative in that an effort had been made to give the impression that the message was prepared by an unskilled typist – when exactly the opposite was apparent. You would have been better off to write the messages by hand.

"Regarding the scratching of a hound's footprint on the stone wall – that was simply a lure to get Sir Henry outside so that you could take a shot at him, after having unnerved him for several days with the anonymous letters. You clearly placed scratchings there early this morning. Alongside those of the housekeeper and her son who discovered the markings, there were footprints still on the ground that match the unusual shoes you're wearing now – and were wearing last fall too. I noted them at the time Watson and I visited you on the morning of Stapleton's death, and after examining the typed notes which implied your involvement in the matter, I wasn't surprised to see the same footmarks along the wall by the stone wall. Those same footprints were also in the mud near the tor where you'd climbed this evening with your rifle, lying in wait for Sir Henry to come out and look at the markings. No doubt you learned to shoot from your father, old Frankland, when you were young.

"I suspect that you've had vengeance in your heart for months after the death of your lover, Stapleton, and when Sir Henry returned, you set out to carry it through. It's only fortunate that Watson and I happened to be on hand."

Through Holmes's recitation of the facts, as one link in the chain followed by another, the woman had expressed a gamut of expressions, from feigned shock to indifference to anger. But as Holmes finished his last statement, her expression turned to amused contempt. Then she laughed – a jarring sound in the small room.

"Mr. Sherlock Holmes – the high-and-mighty detective who understands everything. You understand *nothing!* I wasn't trying to kill Sir Henry. I was trying to kill *you!*"

It isn't often that I see Sherlock Holmes taken aback, but this was one of those occasions. He sat back, his eyes wide, as if this was a solution that he had never predicted. I imagine that the same expression was on my face as well.

"You thought you were so *smart!*" Laura Lyons snarled, rising to her feet. "You both came here that day to ask me about Jack, and then you let me know that he was married, as if it would turn me against him. You fool! Of course I knew that he was married! I was helping him with his plan! When he couldn't care for that beast out on the moors, I offered my assistance. I grew up here – I knew the moor better than he did. When he was able to kill this one – " She tossed her head toward Sir Henry. " – his wife would have been next. He and I would then be together, free to leave this cursed place and go wherever we wanted. And you ruined *everything!*"

Her voice rose, and I considered what she had revealed. I had wondered at the time about the wisdom of telling the woman that Stapleton was married. I had feared that her wrath would be overwhelming, and that she would in turn try to contact the man immediately before our trap was ready and somehow warn him. But I had underestimated Holmes, who had made additional arrangements of his own.

"You were unable to warn Stapleton that day, weren't you?" he asked. "After we revealed that we were on to him."

She nodded but didn't speak.

"Do you recall why?"

She frowned, and then her eyes widened. "Because before I could get word to Merripit House, I received a wire to meet him in Exeter, as fast as I could get there. But I went . . . ." Her voice faded, and then she swallowed and continued. "But I went there immediately, and he was nowhere to be found. There was just another wire, where he told me to stay there, in the restaurant of the Great Western Hotel until he called for me. I waited and waited, but he never arrived. I finally sent a wire back to him – "

"A wire that I intercepted," interrupted Holmes. "It was I who arranged for you to be falsely summoned to Exeter to prevent you from letting him know that he was discovered, and I also arranged to have a watch kept on you while you tarried in Exeter. When you sent the wire back to Stapleton, its delivery was prevented. I suspected that you would try and warn him – it was a perfectly reasonable response from someone who thought that she loved him and had learned she was cruelly wronged, but we couldn't allow you to disrupt our plans. Unfortunately, your message of warning was vague enough that you gave me no indication that night of your own involvement or guilt – it simply informed him that he was under suspicion. If you'd been more specific, and described your complicity in the affair, we would have arrested you then and there, and avoided today's little skirmish."

Even as the woman considered that Holmes had outmaneuvered her from the beginning, he continued.

"As I mentioned, the typewritten messages immediately alerted us to your possible involvement. After slipping out of the Hall following the rifle shot, I worked my way around to see if I could locate the shooter on the moor. You were gone by then, but indications of your unique footwear were easily located. From there, it was only a matter of making my way into Grimpen and getting a message to Constable Claiborne, and then trying to locate you while making sure this house was watched. You made it easy for use by simply returning home. Once you were trapped and corked in this bottle, we fetched Sir Henry and the two doctors, and here we are.

"I only have one question," he added. "If I was your target, why make your attempt in such a convoluted manner? You could have simply come up to London and shot me through my front window from the house across the way while I looked down upon the street."

At that, tears rimmed her eyes. "I would have done so, were I able to afford the trip. I barely get by – the purchase of a train ticket to London is far beyond my means. My father won't – He still won't help me, now more than before. I . . . I could only hope that you might return here someday – to walk into my trap. Then, I learned that Sir Henry was returning, and it seemed likely that you might visit him. From there, it was no great leap to decide that possibly I could manipulate events so that he would have to summon you, sooner rather than later. I started sending him the warnings. I have my own agent – a lad who is in my pay. He runs errands for the telegraph office. He saw your wire this morning that you were coming down later today, so I put the rest of my plan into motion. I hurried out to the manor and left another message, along with scratching the dog's paw on the wall.

"I knew that Sir Henry was bound to mention it to you. I got into position and I had you in my sites. And then . . . then you leaned over, and the rest of you dropped to the ground after my shot missed, and I realized that I'd lost my chance. There was nothing to do but make my roundabout way back here." She looked around the room, looking at the bleak four walls that must have already seemed to her like the cell she'd soon occupy, and repeated, "Here – " but that time with a grinding combination of sadness and contempt, as if her meagre existence had finally overwhelmed her. It wasn't worth pointing out that her problem was technically solved – she would soon be leaving this place and wouldn't be coming back anytime soon.

There wasn't anything left to discuss. The woman's guilt was confirmed, and her motivations explained. The constable stood, took her arm, led her to the door, and it seemed as if she had no fight left in her. Then she yanked free and spun to face my friend.

"You killed him! *You* did it! After you shot the dog, you couldn't let it drop – No, you had to pursue him into the mire! It would have been over then, and he and I could have still been together, but you had the follow him – "

Constable Claiborne had retaken her arm or I think she would have jumped forward to claw at Holmes's eyes. By then he'd risen too, watching her as if he were an alienist clinically observing the symptoms of madness.

"It would never have been over for Stapleton," he replied gravely. "Such a one as he is a cancer, and as such, his removal was the best possible treatment. It's unfortunate that your life had to be bound up with his."

"I won't forget," she countered. "He wouldn't want me to forget. They won't hang me for this. I'll survive – and I'll remember, Mr. Holmes. I'll remember that excellent suggestion of yours – to watch you from the street. When you someday look out from your window . . . ."

337

They departed, leaving the four of us in the woman's sitting room, and it suddenly felt very close and oppressive.

Sir Henry took in a deep breath and then let it out with a long shudder. He looked up from one to the other of us, as if waking from a long illness.

"I am ashamed," he said softly. "I had thought my recovery was more settled. It certainly didn't take much to knock me off the tracks."

Dr. Mortimer opened his mouth as if to reply, by Holmes spoke first.

"Nonsense. You have no reason to be feel that way. You were the victim of a terrible plot – one that was already long in motion when you were drawn into it. There is no way that a man can prepare himself for such a thing. If anyone should be ashamed, it is I. After your injuries last fall, I never had the chance to properly apologize to you – for placing you in such danger. I had a plan in place, but I never took any account of the fog. I – "

Sir Henry raised a hand. "You owe me no apology, Mr. Holmes. Without your intervention, I would have likely been murdered not long after I came to the moor. I understood that even as I recovered from my injuries. And it sounds as if you even suspected the possible danger posed by this woman here today, for you took steps to keep her from warning Stapleton on the day I was attacked."

"Apparently I suspected less than I should have," was Holmes's reply, "for I certainly never thought that I would be her target."

"Then possibly this has been useful for both of us," countered Sir Henry. "I hope that this roots out the last of my enemies, and you will have learned to be more careful yourself, as she has vowed further vengeance."

"Perhaps. In any case, you can now return home in peace."

"Home," Sir Henry murmured. 'Home. Is it, though?"

"You have the chance to find out," I offered. "No more threats await you, and you have several months of beautiful summertime to explore the moor properly – possibly, dare I add, with a certain lady who still resides here?"

Sir Henry's gaze sharpened, but he suddenly saw nothing there in the room. He wasn't looking at any of us. Rather, I knew that he pictured the woman he had loved half-a-year before, and who had loved him as well – I was sure of that. Beryl Garcia – that had been her name had been before her husband, also a Baskerville, had taken the false names of Vandeleur and then Stapleton. Originally from Costa Rica, she was now left alone in this strange land. Seeing Sir Henry's features soften as he thought of her, I was confident that she would not be alone forever.

And I was right. Holmes and I would return that fall for their wedding.

But for now, Sir Henry still needed some settling. We returned to Baskerville Hall and informed Mrs. Hayes and Davey of the details of what had happened in Coombe Tracey. The latter's eyes were wide, while the housekeeper, who knew of Laura Lyons, declared that she was not surprised at all.

Holmes's mood improved markedly from when he'd apologized to Sir Henry, and when I considered how I'd feared the approach of one of his brown studies just that morning, I was quite grateful for this unexpected trip – for more reasons than one. As I sat and sipped whisky and listened to the others talk, I pondered if there was an overall plan that had led to today's events, a higher view – something greater than all of us. In London I would scoff at such thoughts, but here, with the moor just on the other side of the walls and yew hedges and gates, where an ancientness brooded beyond our understanding, the idea didn't seem so ludicrous.

I took another sip and settled deeper into my comfortable chair.

The First Spivey Encounter

I settled back in the chair with a sigh, newspaper in hand, and a cup of tea on the small table beside me. After the morning I'd just faced – delivery of rather stubborn twins – a visit to my former rooms in Baker Street had seemed just the ticket before returning to my Paddington practice.

When I'd arrived, Holmes was out, and I started to continue on my way. However, Mrs. Hudson, perhaps sensing my weariness, had urged me to stay for a just a while longer, as she expected Holmes to return at any moment. I was easily convinced, and I went upstairs as she returned to her kitchen at the rear of the house, promising that she'd have tea ready in an instant.

The sitting room was arranged as always, seemingly cluttered at first glance, but more organized than might be expected if one knew exactly how to examine it. There were stacks of books and documents filling most of the flat surfaces – including half of the dining table and all of what had been my desk when I'd lived here. More books were stacked on the floor in front of the shelves, and various curios filled in many of the other empty spaces – the left side of a skull, for instance, smoothly sawn from top to bottom to reveal the brain and various sinus cavities, was set beside the gasogene, turned so that the openings faced the room. This wasn't a teaching object from a hospital, as might be supposed. Rather, it was the telling evidence in the Bass murder, and if one looked closely, flecks of dried brain matter were still adhering to the inside of the cranium.

There were half-a-dozen bottles of various colored liquids on one end of the mantel – poisons one and all – and what looked like a two-inch lead pipe was lying on the dining table where I used to eat my meals. It wasn't something that would be used by a plumber. It was the barrel of a prototype air-gun, which Holmes had obtained at great cost (and a bit of illegality) the previous month from a former associate of Von Herder, the blind German mechanic. What he needed with it I didn't know, but he had been quite pleased to acquire it.

But for all the chaos, there were places of order as well, Holmes's scrapbooks being the most obvious. Placed on a shelf to the left of the fireplace, they were always kept in the best of condition, as was his chemical corner, on the opposite side of the mantel by one of the front windows. Elsewhere in the room, mounds of papers had an organization to them, wherein Holmes claimed that he could find documents in his various stacks based on the thickness of the dust on top of them – to Mrs.

Hudson's great frustration. This might or might not have been true, but no such dust could be found where he conducted his chemical researches.

As Mrs. Hudson brought in the tea, I took that morning's Times from a stack of metropolitan newspapers resting on the settee and dropped into my old chair. I was engrossed in an article on the front page when I heard Holmes arrive, and within moments he had joined me, divesting himself of his Inverness and constant fore-and-aft cap. He brought a feeling of the January cold in with him, and he approached the fire with a nod. As he stood rubbing his hands briskly, he noticed the newspaper in my hand.

"Anything of interest?"

I nodded. "I didn't have a chance to read this earlier today," I said. "Sir Thomas Spivey * died yesterday."

With a raised eyebrow, Holmes replied, "Indeed. So he's finally escaped his informal house arrest and gone to meet his final judgment."

I nodded, recalling far too easily the events of late 1888, just a little over one year earlier. On occasion, I still felt the pain from when I'd been wounded during the final days of the hunt for the various Rippers, that diverse band of killers who had joined the Wild Hunt when certain powerful men declared open season in order to end a secret. In fact, I was still in hospital the morning after my worst injury when Holmes confronted the Prime Minister, the Home Secretary and Sir Charles Warren regarding their deep complicity – and Sir Thomas Spivey as well, for his direct role in committing some of the murders.

Much has been written elsewhere regarding that terrible Autumn of Terror, and there is no need to revisit it here. It suffices to mention that Sir Thomas's health had already been destroyed by the second half of 1888 from a series of crippling strokes that began in 1887. Possibly it was these that had so damaged his sense of morality and decency, wherein he participated in both the planning and execution of the diabolical scheme to silence all those who knew of an unwanted Royal marriage and the subsequent birth of a child perceived to be dangerous to the monarchy. Sir Thomas, conspiring with a certain high-ranking and like-minded individuals in positions of power, had set in motion their barbaric plan – little realizing that such a juggernaut would attract other killers who used the murders to further their own agendas. Sir Thomas had himself committed some of the killings of the poor unfortunate East End street women, although exactly which ones he had specifically slaughtered might never be known, as his mind was severely damaged by the time his involvement was revealed. Terribly crippled, he would have been unable to carry out the horrific crimes if not for the help of a Royal coachman, himself dead since November 1888. But Sir Thomas had survived, protected by his peers and allowed to live out his remaining days in his

341

own Brook Street home rather than at an asylum or prison – or more fittingly finishing abruptly at the end of the hangman's rope.

I knew that it galled Holmes that Sir Thomas Spivey had been allowed to continue his cursed existence less than a mile from where we sat that morning – just a brisk walk south along Baker Street to where it becomes Orchard Street, and then turning east at Grosvenor Square for only a few hundred more feet down Brook Street. I couldn't count the number of times we had passed Sir Thomas's residence, either together or apart, since late 1888, but I know from my own experience that on each occasion my eyes were drawn to that inconspicuous building, pondering the wreckage of the man slowly dying inside. He had lived there during the Ripper murders. It would have been from there that he was loaded aboard the black coach that carried him to his East End hunting grounds, where he lured those poor women to their deaths simply because they knew of a marriage and subsequent birth of a child. I could not say that I had any sadness at all that the evil man had finally gone to his just and eternal punishment.

Mrs. Hudson had brought fresh tea, and Holmes had gratefully accepted a cup and settled into his own chair. It was a cold morning, and the fire was only somewhat effective against the creeping chill.

"I knew him before," said my friend after a couple of sips. "Sir Thomas, that is. Back when I first came up to London."

I shifted in my seat. It was only on rare occasions that Holmes shared details of his past – and when the mood might strike him was not to be missed. He had told me a number of his early cases just two years earlier, at a time when I'd moved back to Baker Street following a personal tragedy. I believe he did so as a distraction, and it was much appreciated. I'd heard of the Musgrave family's curious ritual and about the old Russian woman. He shared the true details of Lord Culver's unintended plague, and one of his early investigations into the theft of the Heka idol from the British Museum – the telling of which then almost spiraled beyond our control and so nearly cost our lives.

I tried to recall what he'd told me about those early days. "Was that in '74 – after that matter concerning the Norfolk squire and the coded message about hen-pheasants?"

"More correctly, it was in the middle of it." He took another sip of tea, and I stretched out my legs, glad that I'd stopped by . . . .

If you recall, [*Holmes continued*] I had gone down to Donnithorpe for a month of the long vacation, at the invitation of my friend, Victor Trevor. While there, I had impressed his father with my ability to make deductions, and he had recommended that I ought to become a detective – 'That's your

342

line of life, sir,' he told me, 'and you may take the word of a man who has seen something of the world.'

"It was the first time I'd truly considered such a thing, although you know, from other examples that I've shared, that I'd been involved in a number of investigations before then – but always as an amateur with an interest in such things, and usually because I happened to fall into the affairs instead of having them find me. It was an intriguing notion, becoming a detective, but not one that I was yet ready to embrace. My father had set me on the path to becoming a civil engineer, and there was no arguing about it – or so I believed then.

"Still, I began to secretly nourish the impossible thought of becoming a detective, even as things became increasingly tense around the Trevor household when Victor's father turned more and more to drink. I ended up leaving early and coming up to London, rather than traveling back to Oxford.

"At that time, Mycroft resided in the rooms at No. 24 Montague Street that I would later occupy, as his own position within the government was still rather new, and as a low-level clerk, he had yet to come to the attention of those above him who would learn to make use of his unique and valuable skills. He had originally obtained the rooms at No. 24 because the building was owned by an aunt of ours by marriage – a bitter widow who took him in, but never failed to express her resentment towards the Holmes family who she felt hadn't supported her well enough when her husband, my uncle, had died. She gave Mycroft rooms on the very top floor, just under the attic, and it's lucky that he was somewhat thinner in those days, as reaching that last upper level was more like a climbing a ladder than a set of steps.

"The events in Donnithorpe had all occurred during the first month of the long vacation, and after I went up to the Montague Street rooms, I spent the next seven weeks working out a few experiments in organic chemistry – with a small laboratory set up in the corner of the room near the front window, much like the one behind me here, but in this case overlooking Montague Street and the British Museum. Needless to say, our vexatious landlady, Mrs. Holmes, would have been quite unhappy with the arrangement, should she have ever discovered it. But I didn't just confine myself to chemistry. I have always been curious about everything – I've had to be careful about what I load into my brain attic, you understand – and it was during this time that I began to make use of the laboratories at Barts, courtesy of a family friend for whom I'd done a favor. Sadly, it's a story that I can't even share now, sixteen years later. In any case, through his good word, I was allowed to come and go as needed at Barts, carrying out what research suited my fancy. I'm sure that many in those days, just like you at our initial encounter, thought of me as another student, but I wasn't bound by the limits of the official curriculum.

It was in late July, just a week or so before I'd be summoned back to Donnithorpe for the sad conclusion of that affair. I was in the smaller morgue at Barts, making an examination of some of the bodies in order to see what form different deaths took. My experience with death then, while already quite a bit wider than that of most twenty-year-olds, was still unsystematic and ill-informed. There were several students there as well, all going about their own business, when I heard the sound of approaching footsteps, from more than one person. They were striding briskly and, as there were no other rooms at the end of that long stone corridor, I knew that they were bound for that grim chamber.

Three men entered. First was Dr. Niels, who was head of the hospital's Forensics Department – such as it was in those days. He knew me and of my special permissions to access the facilities, and he glanced my way with a nod as they approached. Another man was behind the other two, and he seemed rather insignificant, as if he were a small dog following after two of much greater strength and importance. It was the third man who seemed to draw the most attention. As you will have surmised, this was Sir Thomas Spivey. I knew who he was – even then, he had a certain status after he'd successfully treated the Prince of Wales for typhoid just a few years earlier. It was unusual to see him at Barts, as he was mostly associated with Guy's Hospital in Southwark, where he'd made several notable advances in various treatments.

On that day in the summer of '74, he was in his late fifties, a man of medium build, but obviously of great strength and vigor. He had great oblong head with bright sharp eyes and a quick way of speaking that seemed to expect the same from those around him. He was certainly a far cry from the mad shell of a man we encountered in late '88 who, by then, had become a wrecked simulacrum of what he once was back in his prime.

Of course, he paid no attention to me or the other students in the morgue as he was led to a covered body, resting a few feet away from where I stood. I watched curiously from nearby, where I had just finished my examination of a broken sailor who had passed terribly after being crushed underneath a dropped pallet. Dr. Niels leaned forward, lifting the sheet from the corpse on the table while the Sir Thomas stepped closer, even as the insignificant lackey behind them eased away, a hand covering his mouth and a sick look in his eyes.

I had already examined the figure under their scrutiny just a few minutes earlier – a girl in her twenties who showed no obvious signs of death. Various callosities upon her hands and feet, as well as certain signs of slight malnutrition, indicated that she was in service, but had not lived a life of total hardship. Her clothing, which was in a basket nearby, had confirmed this. She had been a maid.

Sir Thomas nodded. "It's her, all right." His deep voice rumbled in the low-ceilinged chamber. "Sarah Dunstan. She's been in my service for a little over a year." He frowned and nodded to Dr. Niels. "Thank you for notifying me. To be found dead in the street – Ah, I'd hate for the poor girl to have gone to a pauper's grave because no one knew who she was, or how she came to be here." He stepped back. "I'll have Styles make the arrangements to remove her to the undertaker's."

The young man behind them lifted his eyes, glancing from Sir Thomas to the girl and back again. This, I realized, must be Styles. The famed physician then turned to go, followed by Styles and Dr. Niels. I cleared my throat and stepped forward.

"Excuse me, but the cause of death isn't obvious to me."

The men stopped, with Dr. Niels turning first to look my way with a frown. Styles, the closest to me, stepped sideways so that when Sir Thomas pivoted my way, he wouldn't be between us.

"And you are?" asked Sir Thomas, turning the full intensity of his gaze upon me.

"This is Mr. Holmes," answered Dr. Niels quickly, with perhaps a bit of exasperation in his tone. We slightly knew one another after my presence at the hospital had been arranged, but I suspected that there was a bit of resentment about the arrangement on the doctor's side.

"Sherlock Holmes," I added.

"One of your students, no doubt."

"No," replied Niels. "He has special permission by way of an institutional benefactor to carry out extra-curricular research here."

"I examined the body not long before you arrived," I said. "There is no sign of trauma, and no obvious indication as to why she died. For a girl in her early twenties to simply pass away – "

"Sometimes people just *die*, Mr. – *Sherlock Holmes*, is it?" Sir Thomas tightened his mouth into something like a polite smile, but his eyes did not change, except to perhaps focus more sharply upon me. "Curious name."

I nodded, noting that Styles looked quickly back and forth from me to his employer.

"Sarah had been unwell for some time," Sir Thomas continued. "She had a weak heart. This fact was not known to the staff – " He glanced at Styles, and then back my way. " – but she had shared it with me. In confidence. This . . . this sad ending was not entirely unexpected." And he turned again to leave. As they approached the door, Dr. Niels looked back and our eyes met, but there was nothing to be read there, beyond a tightness to his lips. I suppose he was apprehensive that I would speak again. The younger man also looked my way, and then with a nod he followed the others into the dark hallway.

As their steps receded, I considered why I hadn't spoken further – to ask why no autopsy seemed to be planned or required, or why no questions were being asked as to the circumstances of the girl's discovery – about which I knew nothing, except that it seemed the idea of Sarah Dunstan dropping dead in the street somewhere was to be treated as expected and normal, with the young woman's demise to be ignored as easily as she was probably ignored in life. Someone should find out what happened, I thought. And yet, I was young then, and uncertain, and without any official standing in the matter, so I simply let them walk away.

But I didn't let the matter drop. Instead, I made a renewed examination of the body.

As part of my arrangement, I had access to the occupants of the morgue in the same way that a medical student is allowed to make examinations to further his practical experience. Of course, the bodies there are not to be treated the same as those in the dissection room, for those in the morgue are not released for full medical research. While many are brought there as initially unidentified corpses, there is always the chance that they will be claimed. Sarah Dunstan was one of those, and soon the undertaker would arrive to carry her away. But until then, I had an opportunity to carry out further research.

With the assistance of one of the other students – Jack Berkham, whom I believe you knew before his untimely death on Bloody Sunday – I made a further study of the body. I realized that there was only a limited amount of information that I could determine, as I had no right to carry out a full autopsy. Yet, I hoped that something would be obvious with a closer examination.

As you'll recall, Berkham was always chattering – he apparently felt that silence was uncomfortable – so I had to put up with his constant narration as we made our inspection. We could find no sign of a wound on the girl's head underneath her thick dark hair. Likewise, there were no contusions along the body, and no indications of infection or illness. I even looked, without success, to see if she had recently been pierced by a hypodermic needle. However, there were some small broken veins along her eyelids, and the whites of her eyes were rather reddish, suggesting that she had been ill prior to death. Yet without any sort of internal evaluation, I feared that there wasn't much more to tell.

Berkham had looked in her mouth but reported nothing of interest. I wasn't satisfied to simply accept his judgment, and thus I looked as well, turning her head this way and that to catch the lamplight. There was no sign of anything abnormal – no burns, for instance, indicating that she might have ingested something caustic. There was, however, a slight odor – beyond that associated with death – that indicated she'd possibly vomited at some point before her death. If such an action had been violent, this might be an explanation for the reddish eyes and small broken capillaries on the delicate skin of her eyelids.

I was about to lower her head back to a resting position when something caught my eye. Asking Berkham for a set of fine-tipped dissecting forceps, I repositioned her open mouth and probed between the second and third molars on her lower right side. Her teeth were in good condition, and generally clean, but something was stuck there – reddish against the teeth and contrasting with the pale pink flesh beside her tongue. Slowly I worked the object loose and then laid it upon a cotton pad provided by Berkham. Then we both looked at it with curiosity before Berkham laughed softly. "Now we can say what she had for her last meal – Nothing but a bean hull."

And in truth, that's what it appeared to be – but unlike any bean that I'd seen before. It was about the size of a typical bean or pea, but instead of the usual brown or green shade that one would expect from one of those, it was a bright red over most of its surface, with one end a sharply defined black, surrounding a small light-colored circle where it would have been attached to the plant which produced it. In truth, it looked like the wings of some sort of unusual ladybug.

Ignoring Berkham's chuckles and mutterings, I wrapped up the cotton pad and tucked my find into a pocket. Then, re-covering the poor girl with the dingy morgue sheet, I thanked our mutual acquaintance for his assistance and left, making my way upstairs until I reached the courtyard. I strode briskly across to that familiar door with its encouraging motto, "*Whatsoever thy hand findeth to do, do it with thy might.*" Then I entered and stepped the short distance to the doorway leading into the medical library.

I'm not sure how much time you spent there, since you were pursuing your studies at the University of London, which had its own facilities. That was the first time that I visited there, but it would end up being a valuable resource over the next few years as I worked to develop my skills, dividing my time between those rare cases which presented themselves and the various self-directed trails of study that I set myself upon in the Museum and the British Library. Both of the latter have always impressed me, but I won't forget that first time I entered Barts' Medical Library, with its well-lit alcoves, the balustraded balcony running around all sides of the main floor and filled with ranges upon ranges of fascinating volumes, and the decorative busts at the end of those upper-floor shelves, each of some famed medical figure peering down upon the students below. For a moment I was stopped in my place as I breathed in the rarefied atmosphere of *knowledge*.

I was still there when Mr. Lux, the head librarian, approached and introduced himself. I believe that he retired or died before your time, Watson, but he was a true scholar. Tall and thin, he gave the impression that he maintained his stature due to regularly forgetting to take nourishment in favor of enthusiastically pursuing his enquiries. Ah, I see you smile as you attribute that same reasoning to my own spare frame. Perhaps it's true. Certainly Mr. Lux turned out to be a kindred spirit, if not the best at keeping a confidence, and when I showed him the unusual hull, along with rather carelessly explaining where I'd found it, he was quite interested, and he immediately pointed me in the correct direction. He didn't find the answer for me – that wasn't his way – but he showed me how to find it for myself, which was infinitely more helpful in the long run.

And it didn't take very long. A perusal of one of the later editions of Orfila's *Traité des Poisons* quickly identified the hull as *Abrus precatorius*, also commonly known as the jequirity bean or rosary pea. Ah, I see you know it. The seeds aren't native to England, instead usually being found in the more warm and temperate regions. Curiously, because of their bright colors, they're often strung together as beads for jewelry. Although various components are watered down and used in ritualistic ceremonies in some remote parts of the world, they aren't meant for human ingestion. Even the smallest amount of the poison within the beans, *abrin*, can be toxic. Symptoms of abrin poisoning include nausea, vomiting, convulsions, liver failure, and death – usually after several days.

I began to suspect that Sarah Dunham had died from ingesting abrin by chewing the beans – leaving one of the hulls stuck in her teeth, and causing the vomiting which had left indications around her eyes. But why would she have done such a thing? And if death took several days, where had she been during that time? I didn't know anything about her last days – whether she had disappeared from Sir Thomas's home, or why she had been discovered dead in a London street and brought to the morgue. Then it occurred to me that I might be able to learn something from the police.

Obviously, I didn't have any sort of relationship with the police in those days, but I was young enough to arrogantly think that I could walk in off the street as a concerned citizen and request information. I set off for Scotland Yard – walking, of course, as I didn't have coins to spare in those days for a cab. Fortunately the weather was pleasant, not yet too hot, and I made good time down through Blackfriars and then along the Strand to the Yard. But there it seemed as if I ran into a wall.

The constable at the desk seemed to willfully misunderstand what I needed to ask. Instead of simply giving me information about whether a young lady had been listed as missing, or the details of how the same girl's body had been subsequently discovered, he instead repeatedly insisted on finding out who it was that I myself wanted to report. When I couldn't make him understand, he became rather gruff, as if I was doing something suspicious by even presenting myself at his desk. It was then that he summoned an inspector.

I thought that I was now getting somewhere, but actually this only complicated matters, for the man that came from somewhere in the back of that great hive was Inspector Dodge, by then a long-time fixture of many decades, and well beyond any possible hope of providing assistance. He was already sick then from the illness that would carry him off within a year, and it was quite plain when he took me aside to hear my request for information that he had no interest in what I was asking. It was only when I mentioned that Sir Thomas Spivey had been the girl's employer that his rheumy eyes widened a bit and he gave me a better look.

"Oh, that girl," he wheezed. "What's your interest again?"

I explained – once more – that I had been in the morgue that morning when Sir Thomas identified the girl. "I'm tasked with following up on how she came to be there," I said, leaving it vague that I was the one doing the tasking. "Where was she discovered?"

"In the gutter along Adelina Grove, near the pickle works."

"When?"

"Why, just this morning." He squinted at me. "Why don't you know that already?"

"Because," I countered, "Dr. Niels didn't relate that information to me." It was the truth. "Had she been reported missing?"

"No, she hadn't." That didn't seem to be unusual to him.

"Who found her?"

"Some late workers coming along from the pub in Greenwood Street noticed her. They notified the constable."

"And how did anyone know to summon Sir Thomas to Barts?"

"His address was written on a letter," replied Dr. Niels, "twisted up and pushed down deep into one of the pockets in her dress. From someone she'd known growing up."

"Do you know who is in charge of the investigation?"

"What investigation? I hear that Sir Thomas has identified her and will take care of the burial arrangements himself. A fine man."

"No investigation? But what about determining the cause of death?" I was hesitant at that point to mention my own conclusions – at least to

349

this indifferent wreckage. I had planned to explain what I'd found to the inspector handling the case – but then I learned that there was no case.

"No investigation," Dodge confirmed. "Sometimes people just die, Mr – What did you say your name was again?"

"Holmes," I responded absently, thinking to myself as I did so. "Sherlock Holmes."

He fished in his pocket and pulled out a dirty scrap of paper and the stub of a pencil. Licking the tip, he carefully wrote my name and then obtained my address. I watched with a fair amount of unexpected uneasiness – just what was I letting myself in for? If the police should become interested in the girl's death after all, they suddenly had the name of a stranger who had come around asking questions for no apparent reason. I was certain that this seemingly inept relic would be a firm believer in the old adage that the guilty always return to the scene of the crime. Here I was, a mere student, asking whether the police intended to carry out an investigation into an unexplained death. They hadn't planned to – but now they might, and they would be wondering why one Sherlock Holmes was interested. Should they come knocking at my door, it might do me more harm than good to then pull out the carefully preserved hull and explain that possibly the girl had died from eating poisoned seeds. I would have Berkham's testimony that he had been with me when the hull was found and retrieved, but if the police already had a narrative in place with my name as a main character, a little thing like Berkham's support would have no value whatsoever.

You must bear in mind, Watson, that at this point, in spite of a number of interesting adventures that were already in my *vitae*, I was just a twenty-year-old engineering student. Old man Trevor had put the idea in my head that my future ought to be as a detective, but right then, I had given such a notion no serious consideration. Uncertain as to how to proceed further, I let the matter drop and returned to my chemical studies.

A week passed, and although I scanned several newspapers, there was no report of the girl's death or subsequent funeral. On those occasions when I visited Barts – and I arranged to visit there perhaps more often than usual – a few casual mentions of the dead girl elicited no response. It was as if she had never been.

And then I received a curious invitation.

One evening as I returned home, turning out of Bloomsbury Square into Great Russell Street, a man leaning against a nearby post straightened and walked my way, clearly intent on speaking with me. In fading light, I was surprised to see that it was Styles, the young man who had been with Sir Thomas in the morgue. Now able to devote more attention to him, I could see that he was about my own age, or perhaps just a few years older.

He was of average size and coloring, and wearing average clothes – altogether forgettable in nearly every way. In an average voice, he said, "Mr. Holmes? Perhaps you recall me? Lloyd Styles. I work for Sir Thomas Spivey."

I nodded. "Yes, I remember. How are you this evening?"

"I'm well, thank you. I trust you are the same." After I nodded again in agreement, he continued. "I come tendering an invitation. Sir Thomas has learned of your interest in poor Sarah's death. He'd like to have a confidential conversation with you about it."

I raised my eyebrows in surprise. "How did he – ? I'm afraid there's been some mistake," I lied. "I have no interest in her, other than as a passing curiosity. What makes him think – ?"

"Your name was apparently provided to him by Inspector Dodge of the police," Styles answered. "He visited Sir Thomas about the matter. It seems that your questions raised a small bit of interest from the police – although isn't any reason to think that there was anything suspicious about Sarah's death – " he hastened to add.

There wouldn't have been, I thought grimly – for I had removed the evidence from her mouth that might indicate something sinister had happened. It was a valuable lesson, Watson, in the need to maintain a trustworthy chain of custody. Now, a week later, any credibility that I might have had with my discovery, research, and conclusions was irretrievably tainted.

"Does Sir Thomas wish to meet now?" I asked.

Styles shook his head. "Tomorrow evening, at nine o'clock. Do you know his address?"

I did not, and Styles recited a number and street in Mayfair – this was before Sir Thomas moved to Brook Street.

"I'll be there," I said, and Styles thanked me without further explanation or comment, spun around, and walked back to the west. I watched as he passed the Museum and then out of sight where Great Russell Street veers to the north.

The rest of that evening and the following day, I found that my thoughts kept turning to my upcoming meeting with the famed medico. I had no idea what to expect from him, but I was prepared to make my case concerning the detritus of the poisonous rosary pea that I'd retrieved from the dead girl's mouth.

The next night, I set out with plenty of time to walk the distance required and still reach Sir Thomas's home by nine. By Mayfair standards, I recall that it was rather modest – narrow and tall, but quite well appointed nonetheless. At exactly the correct time, I stepped to the door and rang the bell. After I moment, I was surprised when Sir Thomas himself answered the door.

I was nonplussed as he greeted me by name, and then stepped aside to allow me to pass. He then leaned out and looked each way along the street. "You told no one of this meeting?"

"I did not. Your associate said the matter is confidential."

He nodded and shut the door behind us. Then, taking my hat and placing it nearby, he indicated that I should follow him deeper into the building. The hall was poorly lit, and we passed several closed doors and a stairway ascending to a darkened upper floor before we stopped at what appeared to be a study, containing a desk with filled bookshelves on either side. Behind it was a window, but the blinds were tightly drawn. Those walls not covered by shelves were decorated with a dark green paper – as near as I could tell, since the only light came from a decorative lamp sitting on a round table to one side of the desk. A tray sat beside it, with a teapot and two cups.

Sir Thomas indicated that I should take one of the two chairs beside the table, and as I sat, he poured tea into the cups, placing one of them in front of me.

I hadn't known what to expect when summoned here, but I found that I was quite tense, and rather defensively pulled in upon myself, my arms crossed and legs tight. I consciously willed myself to relax and decided rather firmly that I would not be sharing any of my conclusions after all – at least until I was quite sure of my ground.

Sir Thomas raised his cup and took a sip of tea. "So, Mr. Holmes, I hear from Dr. Niels that you are not a traditional student, as I'd assumed."

"That's correct," I replied. I started to go further – to add a bit how I was an engineering student with interests in chemistry and many other topics, but I restrained myself. I would provide nothing beyond what was required. There was a tension here in this dark house I didn't understand.

"Is your family away?" I asked, gesturing vaguely toward the rest of the building. "Your servants?"

He nodded. "They've traveled down to my Reigate house for the weekend. But before I join them, I wanted to discuss poor Sarah with you. I'd heard from Inspector Dodge that you had questions."

"Not particularly," I lied. "I happened to be at Scotland Yard on another matter later the same day after you identified the body, and thought that I'd see if the police knew of any additional information."

"Another matter?" he asked with a smile. "What business could a lad of your age have with Scotland Yard?"

I smiled in return. "I'm afraid that it's a confidential affair, and I'm unable to share any of the details."

352

His face still retained its pleasant countenance, but something changed in his eyes. Apparently he didn't like it when any sort of resistance to his will was demonstrated.

"It's been over a week," I said, suddenly interested in seeing if I could drive the conversation from this point. "Have any other details regarding the girl's death revealed themselves?"

"I'm afraid so," he said, his expression suddenly saddened. "And in a rather dramatic fashion." He took another sip from his cup, and then nodded toward the table before me. "Drink up before it gets cold."

But I didn't. Instead, I asked, "Has something been discovered about how she died?"

"Not 'how', necessarily, but the 'why' has been answered." He shook his head. "It's all quite tragic."

He took a deep breath, and then let it out in a great weary sigh.

"I'm sure you understand how things are in a house such as this," he said. "Your bearing and behavior indicate that you were raised as a gentleman. You understand how a family and their servants can . . . *interact* with one another.

"Sarah had been employed here for about a year. She was from Colchester, but had moved to London for better opportunities, and she came with good references. She arrived at about the same time as young Lloyd Styles, who served as my trusted aid."

"Served?" I asked. "Is he no longer employed?"

"Not as of this afternoon – not after what I learned. You see . . . ." He rubbed a hand across his face, his expression now gray and empty, as if looking upon something dire. "You see, under our noses, Lloyd and Sarah were . . . they were carrying on with one another. Their . . . intimacy had apparently been going on for quite some time. Lloyd was using his authority, such as it was, to intimidate her into cooperating – although to hear him tell it this afternoon, she wasn't entirely unwilling."

"This afternoon? Has new information come to light just this day?"

He nodded. "Apparently after Lloyd . . . after what he did, he had a guilty conscience. It's been eating him up this past week. When Inspector Dodge stopped by the other day to ask if I knew you, or what your interest might be in the matter, Lloyd felt that what he'd done . . . that he would shortly be exposed. So this afternoon, he came to me with his admission."

He took another sip of tea.

"And what did he do?" I asked after a long moment while the famed man sat, simply pondering what he knew. Then, he finally continued.

"It seems that poor Sarah found herself in a family way. She was pregnant, you see."

I recalled the examination of the girl's body, and the slightly distended stomach that I'd taken for an indication of malnutrition. It was another lesson to make sure of my conclusions.

"After learning of Sarah's condition," Sir Thomas continued, "Lloyd became fearful for his position – for abusing the trust that I and the household had placed in him. He didn't know what to do. He convinced her to come away with him – to a rented room somewhere in the East End. He wanted to have her vanish from the house, so that no questions would be asked. We would assume she'd decided to run away, and we'd simply replace her. And to entice her away, he told her that they would wed. Possibly he even meant it, although it seems to be a very poor plan, and not well thought out at all – very typical of Lloyd, I might add. I don't know why she believed him, but she did leave. Then . . . then the next evening he went to check on her, and found her dead.

"He didn't know what to do. He could have left her there, but he believed that the landlord would identify him when the body was found. If there was some way to trace her back to this house, he would be tied to what happened."

"Yet she was traced back to this house," I interjected. "Inspector Dodge told me that she was found with a letter bearing this address, from a friend she'd known growing up."

"True. When Lloyd told me what happened, he said that he'd carelessly overlooked searching her pockets when he . . . when he disposed of the body."

"In the street," I added.

Sir Thomas nodded. "As I said, he was fearful that the landlord might somehow identify him – particularly if he left the girl in the lodging house to be discovered. So late that night, he managed to move her outside, leaving her in a nearby street."

"Terribly disrespectful," I said, to have something to say. I raised my hand toward the teacup, and was most interested to note the sudden gleam of interest which lit Sir Thomas's eyes – and then the narrowing frown when I removed my hand, leaving the cup untouched.

"What was the reaction of the police when these additional facts were revealed?"

"Oh, they will dismiss it as an unfortunate accident."

"And Mr. Styles? I take it he's quite relieved."

"Well, I suppose he will be, when he learns of it. After confessing to me just this afternoon – sitting right where you sit now – he was dismissed from my service, and I have no idea where he's gone. Of course, I notified Inspector Dodge what had happened."

He leaned forward, looking at me more intently than before.

"And what about you, Mr. Holmes – Did you learn anything else about the matter before Inspector Dodge satisfied your inquiries? I understand from our mutual friend, Mr. Lux in the medical library, that you were doing some additional research on the day that we met."

My surprise at this revelation was quite genuine. It did not go unnoticed.

"Word spreads quickly at a place like Barts," he explained. "When it became common knowledge that my maid had been found dead in the street and brought 'round to the closest morgue, Lux recalled that you'd been in there earlier that day – and that you brought a rather unique research question to him in relation to something you'd discovered when illegally examining the poor girl's body." His tone became more harsh and his breathing quickened.

"What did you think you'd found, Mr. Holmes?" he asked. I noticed that he wasn't blinking. The whites of his eyes were quite visible all around his pupils.

"Nothing," I answered, sounding like a child caught stealing food and ridiculously lying about it.

"Not long afterwards, you showed up at Scotland Yard," he continued. "On your 'confidential affair' – the details of which you refuse to share."

I simply nodded. The house around us was completely silent. No one else was there, and we were deep in the dark building, far from the street.

"I often confer with representatives of the Yard," I said, hoping that my obfuscation would unnerve him a bit. "It's part of my trade, you see."

"Your 'trade'?" he said, almost with a sneer. "And what would that be? I understood from Dr. Niels that you are some sort of engineering student who traded a few vague favors for permission to use the hospital laboratories – although I have no idea what an engineering student could hope to accomplish there."

"*Former* engineering student," I corrected, feeling my way forward as if I were hopelessly lost somewhere in his unfamiliar house, trying to find my way out to the street. "Earlier this summer, I was advised that I ought to change my career plans – that I should become a detective. The weeks since that time have been spent preparing for that."

"A *detective*?" There was a new wariness in his eyes now. The aggressive tone he'd adopted only moments before became suddenly cautious as he considered further just how much I might know . . . or surmise.

I considered my position. Of most immediate concern was that he was between me and the door. Once I was past him, it was a straight path to the street. But he was a big man, tensed and still in his prime, and I sensed with certainty that he didn't intend for me to leave.

Or perhaps I was misreading everything. I was young, and still quite inexperienced. Was I simply imagining too much – a danger that wasn't there?

I reached again for the tea and saw again his sudden interest. That decided me. Before my hand could touch the cup, I pulled my feet back underneath me, rose abruptly with a rushed, "Thank you for your hospitality, Doctor," and was by him before he could react. Was I mistaken, or did his hand reach out for me as I passed? I could not say for certain, as I was already in the darkened hall, streaking toward the front of the house. I raised a hand as I passed toward my hat, successfully snagging it while the other touched the doorknob. Thankfully the door opened easily, as I'd forgotten to take into account that it might have a complicated lock, and if I'd had to negotiate finding and turning a key in that darkened entryway, I could have been irretrievably delayed.

I thought that I heard a roar behind me, but I didn't turn to confirm it. I threw the door wide and pounded onto the pavement, surprising a couple walking sedately in front of the house nearly as much as they surprised me. Then, finding my footing, I pushed my way left and hurtled east toward Berkeley Square. There, in the shadows of a side street, I paused to catch my breath and consider. I couldn't confirm that I knew anything for certain, whatever my suspicions. The story that Sir Thomas had told me could be completely true, despite his curious attitude in the dark house, and his rising accusatory tone as he revealed what he'd learned of my actions the day that Sarah Dunham's body was brought to the hospital morgue.

At a loss regarding what else to do, I resolved to return to No. 24 Montague Street and confer with my brother.

In those early days, Mycroft worked some very long hours, but he was in our small shared rooms by the time I made my appearance, after carefully crossing the city. I told him everything – from Sir Thomas's arrival at the hospital and my examination of the body, of the curious hull, and then my visit to both the medical library and Scotland Yard. I related how my invitation to visit Sir Thomas had been tendered the night before by Lloyd Styles, who showed no signs of stress when doing so, and then what had happened at Sir Thomas's empty and unnerving house.

Mycroft agreed that there was something questionable about what I'd told him, but he was also unwilling to fully admit that my suspicions were concrete – for obviously I suspected that Sir Thomas had himself had a hand in the girl's death, which had occurred with some connection to the ingestion of poison berries. However, a conversation with Lloyd Styles would clear the matter up quickly. Or so I thought.

I stayed in all the next day, in those cramped rooms at the top of the building. That night, Mycroft returned with an interesting story.

"Lloyd Styles is dead," he informed me. "By his own hand, in a cheap rented room in Aldershot. He drank cyanide and left a long confession in which he described impregnating the maid, Sarah Dunham. He wrote that he convinced her to come away from the house and stay under an assumed name until they could marry. But he wrote that he had no intention of doing so. Instead, he fed her some poison berries, and when she became sick, he convinced her that he was caring for her, when in truth he was letting her die. He then moved her body to the street, where he thought she'd be found and buried, unidentified. Instead, she was linked to Sir Thomas's household – her employer and his – and he knew that it was just a matter of time until he was implicated. Or so he believed. He confessed a series of half-truths about the matter to Sir Thomas – without admitting that he murdered the girl, and instead implying that she died of natural causes – and then he fled. When the guilt overwhelmed him – "

"The confession," I asked. "How do the police know that he actually wrote it?"

Mycroft gave a bitter laugh. "Sir Thomas confirmed the handwriting."

I started to protest, urging that there was surely another story – the *true* story – to discover, and that we needed to speak to the police immediately. Perhaps we could find the room where the girl was taken to die. If we could prove that Sir Thomas rented it instead of Lloyd Stiles –

Mycroft raised a hand to silence me.

"It would do no good," he said. "I've done some quiet research into Sir Thomas. He has powerful friends – very powerful. He's rich, and a member of a most influential and ancient secret brotherhood that stretches to the very top of society. Before any charges could be brought – before any truth could be discovered – they would band together to crush those who oppose them."

"But . . . but . . . ." My younger self was speechless. Finally I formed a coherent thought. "Surely . . . What if Sir Thomas was actually the father of the girl's baby? Did *he* kill her, and then arrange this complex charade to shift the blame onto the poor secretary? He must have! We can't let him get away with it!"

"I'm afraid that we must – at least for now. Neither of us is in a position to do what would be required to find the truth, and insure that justice is done."

"But what can we do?" I cried.

"We wait. We wait and watch, and someday we'll be in a position to expose him. I only hope that he doesn't do further damage before we arrive at that point . . . ."

Holmes and I sat silent for several minutes, each contemplating various aspects of what I'd been told. Then, a thought occurred to me.

"The tea," I said. "He was trying to kill you."

Holmes nodded. "I'll never know for sure, but I'm satisfied that he was. When a doctor goes wrong, as you know, he is the very worst of criminals. Later examination showed that Lloyd Styles was already dead by the time I visited Sir Thomas's house. He'd given no indication during the short time that I conversed with him the day before that he was in any sort of distress, or had any plans to end his own life.

"Sir Thomas was alone at his house, and he seemed to be more-than-interested that I consume the tea that he'd prepared. He drank from his own cup several times, so he must have placed something in my empty cup before he poured the tea from the common pot."

"And yet," I said, "there is really no evidence, is there? Lloyd Styles' note could have been legitimate."

"I suppose," Holmes replied. "I certainly didn't have the resources to conduct an in-depth investigation at that time, and as Mycroft pointed out, I would never have been able to interest anyone with more authority to assist me. In fact, doing so – and drawing attention to myself – would have been dangerous."

I smiled. "Danger never seems to deter you very much."

"And it didn't then either, but I knew that I'd be more effective if I lived long enough to properly investigate the matter."

"And did you investigate?"

He nodded. "I did, with Mycroft's help. We discovered a number of indicative facts, although nothing absolute. In the meantime, we both kept an eye on Sir Thomas – but he never gave any further obvious indications of similar behavior. When he had his first stroke in 1887, we thought that whatever threat he'd been was neutered. Little did we know of what horrors he was truly capable . . . ."

After a moment's silence, I asked, "What were some of the indicative facts?"

"Oh, several things. His family's trip to Reigate that day had been sudden and disruptive. The doctor suddenly announced that everyone – staff included – would make the trip.

"We were able to confirm with staff that worked there at the time that Sir Thomas had likely behaved inappropriately with the maid – it wasn't the first time – but Sarah Dunham was made of rather stern stuff. Based

on surreptitious interviews with those who had known her, it seems likely that if she was carrying a man's child, she'd expect something for it. If Sir Thomas was the father, what would she want? And would he be driven to murder to avoid giving it to her?

"And then there was Lloyd Styles – an orphan with no family or ties, and no one to cry out for justice at his passing. He had no special knowledge of poisons, so why would he have chosen such an unusual method to rid himself of the girl, if the events described in his suicide letter were true?"

"He could have picked up such knowledge from his association with the doctor," I replied.

"True – but why complicate things? Sir Thomas already knew such things, and would have had easier access to poisons, even obscure ones, that his secretary would not."

"But why would Sir Thomas complicate things? Why not just give her some of his poisoned tea?"

"Who knows? Perhaps as a physician he thought it would be easier to convince her that the poisoned rosary peas had some sort of therapeutic value in relation to her pregnancy. As you know now from experience, when a man sets out to murder, the plan is often far more complex than necessary, as killers tend to arrogantly overthink their actions. Look at how Sir Thomas orchestrated the Ripper murders – instead of simple killings, the arcane and symbolic rituals he added made them then center of a national panic.

"In any case, Mycroft and I continued to wait and watch, as all we had were our suspicions. But I've learned to trust my instincts, and I believe the man was guilty."

"It's good that you had those instincts," I said, "for they were what likely prevented you from drinking that tea."

Holmes nodded. "And they did something else, too."

"What's that?"

"They gave me to understand that old Trevor was correct – that I should turn my attentions to becoming a detective. It was almost a sign when, a few weeks later, I was called back to Donnithorpe to solve the curious puzzle that the old man had left just before his fatal attack. That confirmed in my own mind that I needed to alter my path. You can imagine how such an announcement was met by my father."

I raised an eyebrow. "I imagine that he was upset."

"You don't know the half of it. I thought I'd better tell him in person, so I journeyed home. Luckily, before he had a chance to completely lose his temper, there was a murder."

"I'm not sure that it was so lucky for the victim," I replied, "but as distractions go, I suppose you couldn't have done better."

"Indeed – especially as my father was accused of the crime." He shifted in his seat. "Do you need to get home right away, or do you have time for one more story? I can ask Mrs. Hudson to bring more tea."

Mrs. Hudson brought more tea.

NOTE

*   It's clear, based on various provided biographical details, that "Sir Thomas Spivey" is meant to disguise – barely – the identify of Sir William Gull (1816-1890). From humble beginnings, Sir William rose in fame and influence throughout his life, with his career receiving a noted boost when, in 1871, he successfully treated the Prince of Wales for typhoid. For this he was made a Baronet, and appointed to be one of the Queen's physicians. He made a number of significant medical contributions and died a wealthy man.

Over the years, his name has been repeatedly associated with the murders carried out by "Jack the Ripper" – either helping to conceive or cover up the crime, or possibly himself being the murderer. This theory had been explored extensively over the years in many books and films. In two of Watson's many narratives on the subject, (later published as *Murder by Decree* and *The Reign of Terror*,) Sir William's name was changed – as it was in this document – to "Sir Thomas Spivey".

More about Holmes and Watson's involvement in the events of 1888's "Autumn of Terror", their massive efforts during the truly monumental investigation, and the activities of the various Rippers who carried out the crimes, can be found in "November, 1888" (in *The Complete Papers of Sherlock Holmes, Volume III* by David Marcum, MX Publishing, 2021.)

Jonathan Sparler, Resurrectionist

It was not unusual for my friend, Sherlock Holmes, to stop at my lodgings in Queen Anne Street upon those occasions when he visited London, or even sometimes stay in my spare room. Since the death of my wife, his visits had occurred more often, and even though it was never mentioned by either of us, I was certain that he made the extra effort to journey up from his Sussex "villa" (as he liked to call it) to check on me.

By then I had long-since retired from my practice and, after the exertions of the War just a few years before, I was quite glad to take it easy more often than not. It was less than a year until my seventieth birthday, and I must admit that I was feeling my years more than I wished. In spite of friends, my club, and the general distractions of London, the loneliness of my home only exacerbated this.

When Holmes sent a wire that he would be arriving later that morning, I thought it no more than another of his friendly sojourns to cheer up an old friend. I expected that the day would proceed as many of these visits often did: Sitting in my study, sipping something while our discussions ranged from the news of the day to examining philosophical questions, or talking of the doings of Holmes's coastal neighbors – people that I'd also come to know over the years – and of course, reminiscences of past adventures. This would often be followed by a nice dinner at Simpsons, or some similar location if we had a taste for something different. It was just such a day that I was expecting when Holmes arrived, but I could see by the look in his eyes that something better was afoot.

"Ah," he said by way of greeting, "as you know me as well as I know you – and dear me, it's over forty years now! I can see from your expression that you've sensed that we have a matter to investigate."

"That much is obvious," I replied, taking his Inverness and fore-and-aft cap and hanging them on the rack beside the front door. My housekeeper knew that I preferred to greet callers – something to pass the time, and one less chore that she was glad to hand over.

I shut the door, rather regretfully, as the October sky outside was of a wonderful blue, and the air was invigoratingly crisp after the recent warm days. I had intended to take a stroll later in the morning, but my plans had changed when I received word of Holmes's arrival. Now there was a chance that I would still be going out, although not for a simple and meandering walk.

Holmes strode past me, down the hallway and into the study. Instead of making for his usual chair, however, he began to go through the stack of recent newspapers stacked upon a side table. Pulling out an issue from several days past, he stood straight and began to turn the pages. Then with a grunt of satisfaction, he found what he sought. Folding the pages like some Oriental paper puzzle, he reduced the overall area to a manageable rectangle, which he then passed to me. As I scanned the square foot or so of assorted advertisements, he leaned closer and put a finger on one centered upon the folded page.

Jonathan Sparler, Resurrectionist

Grieving? Unfinished Business?
End the Uncertainty – Speak with Your Dead!

By Appointment – Time is of the Essence!

No. 5, Princes Street, Mayfair, London

For centuries, mankind has wondered at the MYSTERIES of DEATH. Now, through the power of SCIENCE, death is NO LONGER A BARRIER between those who have moved to the next level, and those who remain!

Through a unique and confidential SCIENTIFIC process, Mr. Jonathan Sparler has OPENED THE DOOR that was ONCE FOREVER SEALED. The IMPENETRABLE BARRICADE between the living and the dead HAS BEEN BREACHED!

Do you need to speak final words to your loved one? Do you have questions that needed to be asked while a relative or business partner was still alive, but the chance was lost? Through Mr. Sparler's new scientific process, THE DOOR IS NOW OPEN!

But time is limited! The dead pass from this physical plane quickly. This process only works for the RECENTLY DECEASED. If you need answers from someone who has recently passed DO NOT HESITATE.

Please notify the Office of Jonathan Sparler, Resurrectionist IMMEDIATELY to make arrangements.

I read it again to see if I'd missed anything, and then looked up at Holmes. "Have you heard of this fellow?" he asked.

I shook my head. "You've taught me too well, I suppose, to give any credence to these carnival hucksters." I raised the paper a few inches. "This isn't uncommon, as you know. And perhaps it's worse now than it was years ago." I frowned. "It doesn't help that Doyle is running here and there trying to prove the legitimacy of this type of clap-trap." A sudden cold thought occurred to me. "He isn't involved in this, is he?"

Holmes's eyes narrowed. "I doubt it. He's been too busy lately looking under rocks for fairies."

I knew that Sir Arthur – or Doyle as I will always call him – had been obsessed of late with a series of photographs that had surfaced in Cottingley showing several children supposedly interacting with garden sprites. Rather disgusted that the public inescapably associated him with Doyle, and thus indirectly with such nonsense, Holmes had made his own study of the photographs, quickly determining that they were faked using cardboard cut-outs. He'd discussed the matter with Doyle, rather urgently with proof in hand, there in my study not so many months before, but our old friend had smiled and smiled and refused to listen.

Doyle always had a soft spot for the occult, all the way back to when I first met him in the early eighties, and the death of several family members in the War, plus the influence of his second wife (who believed herself to be the possessor of various supernatural gifts), meant that he had long gone over to the side of the supernaturalists. Fortunately he'd never tried to truly convince Holmes or me to join him – although he did regularly press me to play up supposed supernatural aspects to Holmes's adventures, such as the examination of the facts related to the Dartmoor Hound. When we'd discussed the fairies in August, Doyle had good-naturedly listened to us, and I could tell that he'd already expected this to be the topic of our meeting. Holmes presented his case, and kept his temper when Doyle blatantly refused to acknowledge the obvious truth, preferring instead to dive deeper into his childlike faith in spiritualism. It was no wonder that, seeing Sparler's advertisement, I might wonder if Doyle was somehow involved.

Holmes glanced at my mantel clock. It was already later in the morning than I'd thought. "I took the liberty of inviting two other visitors," said Holmes, "who shall arrive in ten minutes. We may learn more then whether or not Friend Doyle is mired in this bog."

I nodded and went to inform the housekeeper, and to request tea and refreshments.

When I returned, Holmes had settled into his usual chair and was lighting his pipe. I dropped into my seat across from him. In many ways, our seating arrangement before my fireplace mirrored the layout all those years before in Baker Street, not all that far away.

"Sparler," I asked. "What can you tell me about him?"

"Not much. I received a note yesterday from Mr. Wayne Wisham, who owns a manufacturing facility in the East End – he is a mirror maker. He apologized for bothering me – a nice start to his message – and went on to write that he'd been referred to me regarding his mother, who was apparently bilked by this man Sparler a few weeks ago, following the death of Wisham's step-father. He offered to come down to Sussex, but I was intrigued and realized that the investigation, should there be one, would take place here. With that, and an excuse to visit my good friend, I left this morning."

I was glancing at the clock when the doorbell rang. I pulled myself upright and shambled to the door, cursing my aging frame which so limited the still-young man – or so I felt – who was trapped inside.

After passing through the darkened hallway, I blinked when once again confronted by the bright blue morning. The sun was shining on the houses opposite along the north side of the street, and Mansfield Street, running away to the north, was well lit by that time of day, even though the sun was starting to rise lower in the sky behind my house with the approach of winter.

The man facing me was in his forties, a little over six feet, clean-shaven, and with laugh-lines at the sides of his eyes and a marked lack of frown lines between them. Even though the purpose of his visit concerned something unpleasant, he had an incipient smile, and when he spoke, I understood why.

"Dr. Watson?" he asked, glancing at the Number *9* upon my front door. "This is the address that was given to me. I . . . I can't tell you what an honor it is to meet you." Then he glanced past me. "Is . . . is Mr. Holmes here?"

I was amused, but took care not to show it. When I first met Sherlock Holmes, he was quite willing to let others take credit for his work, even as he said to me things like, "I know well that I have it in me to make my name famous. No man lives or has ever lived who has brought the same amount of study and of natural talent to the detection of crime which I have done." After I'd seen him work – what he was able to accomplish, only to have the newspaper accolades given to others – I swore that I would someday do my part to let people know of his gifts – although it took me several years to make that promise come true.

In the meantime, in spite of letting the police take credit for his brilliant successes, word spread of the consulting detective in Baker Street, and when I published a couple of narratives concerning a miniscule representation of his work in the late 1880's, and then two-dozen more in the early 1890's in a recently formed periodical during that three-year period when he was presumed dead, his fame only grew. After his return to London, this trend continued in an ever-escalating manner, and by those years following the war, boys who had read of him in those early days had grown, and now had children and even grandchildren of their own who were also interested in Sherlock Holmes's various adventures – a fact for which I was thankful, as the continued sale of those writing efforts were a blessed comfort toward funding my retirement. Clearly Mr. Wisham was one of those who had known of Holmes his entire life – and now he had the chance to meet him face-to-face. I could only hope that he settled down to business, as Holmes had very little patience toward those who became lost in celebrity worship.

I needn't have worried. Other than a bit of initial awe-struck hand-shaking, Wisham settled quickly into his seat. Unfortunately, I missed their initial conversation, as the doorbell rang once again.

I was somewhat taken aback. When Holmes indicated that two visitors were coming, I'd assumed that one was Mr. Wisham, and the other his mother, or some other interested party. When Wisham had arrived alone, my thoughts had turned to another of our long-time associates, Alton Peake. Holmes and Peake had known each other since the late 1870's, when both had more time on their hands than clients, and spent their free days in the British Museum, attempting to learn various esoteric branches of knowledge that would be useful in their chosen fields – Holmes as a consulting detective, and Peake working along similar lines, but instead focused on a scholarly examination of the occult.

For all of Holmes's disdain for beliefs of this sort – "No ghosts need apply!" was his credo on the subject – he did respect Peake, who approached his field with a certain amount of skepticism and a great deal of knowledge. (Unlike poor Doyle, who was ready to believe any wild claim just because it was uttered aloud.) Over the years, we had worked with Peake on any number of affairs, and while many had proven to be out-an-out frauds and scams, some solutions were more ambiguous, although Holmes never admitted a true supernatural explanation. I, however, was willing to be more open minded, having seen a number of things that seemed to extend beyond human understanding and experience. Because of this, Peake and I got along rather well, and it was he that I expected to see when opening my door that morning.

Instead, I was surprised to see the grinning face of Thomas Carnacki.

Seeing my expression, he said, "Admit it, Doctor: You were expecting to see Alton."

I could only nod as I let him in. As I took his overcoat, I tried to remember when I'd last seen him – surely it had been three years, in the autumn of 1918 when our paths had unexpectedly crossed when Holmes and I were called to Hurlstone in western Sussex, converted for the duration into a recovery hospital. A wounded soldier had been shrieking of ghosts, and Holmes's old school chum, Reginald Musgrave, had requested our presence. Unbeknownst to us, one of the doctors, acquainted with Carnacki, had sent for him as well. The matter fell firmly within Holmes's purview when it was determined that the young soldier was actually a wounded German who had taken the identity of one of our own dead infantrymen in order to infiltrate our side with damaging information, but before he could begin his mission, a reaction to his medications had caused him to have psychotic visions.

Carnacki had stayed busy over the years, although his fame had peaked in the years before the War when several of his investigations were written up and published by one of his friends in a popular periodical. I knew from an offhand comment that he'd made at the time that he was rather irritated in his own way at the attention he'd received, and he had managed to quash subsequent efforts to relate more of his affairs to the public. Holmes had once commented, with a significant glance my way, that Carnacki had successfully accomplished what he himself had been unable to do.

I was aware that some tragedy during the war had changed Carnacki, and not for the better. He was still pleasant, with a twinkle in his eyes, but some of the joy with which he approached his work was gone. It was unfortunate, but altogether too common in those years following the conflict.

"Alton is in Scotland," Carnacki explained as I took his coat, "attending to survivors of the sinking of the *Rowan*. Some of the deceased aren't passing over as easily as their tortured families might hope." He then asked after my health, and expressed his condolences over my loss before we turned and entered the study.

In my absence, my housekeeper had delivered the refreshments. Carnacki was introduced, with the simple explanation that his unique skills might be of great assistance. Then, once we were settled, and the tea poured and the biscuits passed, Mr. Wayne Wisham began his narrative.

He glanced at the newspaper, still folded open on the side table to Sparler's advertisement.

"That's him, then. You'll have seen his specious claims, but perhaps you don't know his game. I found out the hard way a week or so ago, and while it may be too late to help my mother, I can't let this go on any longer." He dropped his eyes. "I must admit, Mr. Holmes, that I first spoke

367

with someone else about the matter. When I approached the police, I was told by an inspector – Jamison, I believe – that this was beyond their purview without further evidence – my mother had willingly gone along with Sparler, and as she's still in her right mind, it's up to her to take action if she wants. But he went on to sympathize with me, and recommended that I speak to Mr. Pons in Praed Street. However, when I communicated with him, he had just been engaged upon another matter – something related to an aluminium crutch – and not knowing how long it might take, he suggested that you might be willing to hear my story."

Holmes nodded. "Pons called me on the telephone last night, not long before your message arrived. We often work together, or refer cases to one another. Please – continue explaining your difficulties with Mr. Sparler."

Wisham took a long sip of tea and set his cup aside. "Eight days ago, my step-father died. It wasn't unexpected – he'd been in poor health for quite a while, and was being cared for in a nursing facility. Shamefully, I hadn't visited him in quite a while, and really even then just to check on his care rather than spend any time with him. He was there a little over six months, after his condition became too much for my mother to handle, as she is a very small woman who, although in good health, had problems with the day-to-day tasks required for such a case.

"My own father died when I was very young, and my mother married Mr. Grayling when I was just ten. Although we were never close, we got along well enough, and there was no underlying animosity between us. He owned a jewelry business off the Strand which he'd sold for quite a tidy profit upon his retirement – more for the store's reputation and location of the building's lease than his stock, I believe. In any case, he was a good investor, and had saved well throughout his life, and so he left my mother a tidy-enough nest egg. In spite of this, I paid for his health care at the end, in order to preserve her funds – which is why I would sometimes check on him, as in his final months, he was completely unaware of his surroundings, or his visitors.

"My mother lived near where he was kept, and she visited him most days, and did what she could to help feed him in the evenings. As I said, his passing wasn't a surprise, and when I was notified that he was gone, I set in motion the arrangements that I'd previously made – the mortician, the funeral and the burial, and so on.

"But the day after he died, I received a telephone call from the mortician, asking me how long I expected the delay in burial to take? I had no idea what he meant, and he informed me that my mother had sent a man for the body, which he said would be returned within a week or less, after the 'procedure' was carried out. I had the sense that he knew more about it then he let on, but was leaving me to discuss the matter with my mother.

"Needless to say, I rushed to her home, where she explained that she'd arranged to have this Jonathan Sparler take the body in order to have one of his 'communication sessions' between her and my step-father."

He gestured again toward the folded newspaper. "I don't know if you've heard of this charlatan before – ?" I shook my head. Carnacki nodded, and Holmes gave no indication. Wisham continued. "I had never heard of him – had never paid any attention to these advertisements – although subsequent investigation shows that they've been appearing for a good six months. This is what he does, then: He advertises, and also makes his services known by word of mouth. What he claims to do will only work within just a few days of a person's death.

"If Sparler is hired by a grieving family, he arranges to take immediate possession of the body. He apparently insists that it has to be very soon after death, and before any kind of embalming or other intrusions to the body can take place. The, he takes the corpse to his building in Mayfair, where he makes his 'preparations', whatever those may be. When he's ready, the client is summoned to his place of business, where communication with the dead person can supposedly be achieved. It can only be done once, and has to be done quickly. Then the body is returned for burial.

"As I said, after I spoke to the mortician, I rushed to my mother's house, and she explained that she'd hired Sparler so that should could talk with her husband one more time. She'd had it in mind for quite a while – what she wanted to say to him – but his illness had taken him from her months before his actual death. I had no idea of the nature of this unspoken issue between them, and I urged her to let me have the body returned to the mortuary immediately – but she adamantly refused.

"That was the first time I checked with the police, and also an attorney. I learned that as the dead man's wife, my mother had final say in what was done with his body. As the burial was still planned for later in the week, this wasn't illegal – but everyone agreed that it was wrong, and that I should be on my guard.

"Two days later, at my mother's request – I'm her only child – we attended Sparler's 'demonstration'. It was late in the evening, and the street where his building is located, although just half-a-block off Regent's Street, is very quiet, dark, and deserted. I helped my poor mother to the door. She was weeping quietly, and my initial thought that she might be feeling guilty at committing her husband's remains to this disgraceful path was proven wrong when the door opened. A fat man stood in the doorway, his features shadowed in the dim light from the hallway behind him. Instead of regretting what she'd done, my mother shook me off and stepped forward, grabbing his hand and weeping more strongly now.

Obviously she knew him, and they must have met when she made the arrangements without my knowledge. Through her tears, she was asking if her dear Carl was ready to speak with her. The man nodded, put his arm around her, and guided her inside. Without acknowledging me, he left the door open for me to follow.

"Once inside, I had a better look at him. He was even larger than I'd thought – well over six feet with a leonine head surround by a great mane of dark hair, sitting upon very broad and rounded shoulders. His suit was expensive-looking – or so it seemed in the poorly lit hallway. His chest was massive, and suspended from it was a great pendulous belly, covered by a shirt and waistcoat that rolled away to unusually narrow hips and almost spindly legs. In form, he looked something like a walking hot air balloon, but not nearly so jolly.

"'Mr. Sparler – ' I began, ready to protest this whole affair, when he dropped my mother's hand to lift his own, as if to silence me. His other great arm still held her close, as if he were her relative and not me, protecting her from some menace.

"'You would be the son,' he said, his tone sibilant, and with some vague foreign aspect. 'I am Dr. Leviticus Hayes, Mr. Sparler's technician. I assist in applying his process to the unfortunates who arrive here, allowing them to speak one last time before going on.' Then, before I could respond, he turned away, leaning down toward my mother. 'Are you ready, Mrs. Grayling?' She nodded and allowed him to propel her forward into a parlour whose doorway was just across from us.

"The building was a former house, with a layout as one might expect, and not so different from this one, Doctor. The parlour wasn't exceptionally large, but it was rather empty, giving it the impression of wider space. There were three plain wooden chairs set along one side, near the front windows. The heavy drapes were pulled shut behind them. Across the room, against the far wall, was another set of drapes, fastened to the ceiling by a series of hooks. The only other thing there was a small table near the doorway, which held a variety of bottles, as well as pots of both coffee and tea.

"Dr. Hayes turned my mother that way as soon as we entered, offering her whatever she wished – 'to calm your nerves,' he said. At first she declined, but he went ahead to pour a 'medicinal brandy', as he put it, and she accepted it. Then he turned to me with a raised eyebrow. I didn't want any spirits, but I did decide take a cup of the black coffee, wishing to be as alert as possible. It was still quite hot, and must have been placed on the table just before our arrival.

"My mother and I stood beside the doctor for a moment, both of us somewhat dwarfed, and he peered from one to the other while we sipped

370

our drinks. I had the sense that we wouldn't proceed until we had finished up. I suppose that was wise – for there was no need for us to be holding our empty glassware during the . . . the *encounter* with the dead man." He closed his eyes at the memory.

"I thought it curious that Dr. Hayes made no effort to make small talk – but then again, what was there to say? In any case, we were soon finished, and the doctor took our cup and glass and placed them on the table. Then he led us the few steps across to the chairs, which faced the closed curtain, and indicated that we should sit, my mother in the middle, with Dr. Hayes on the side nearer the hallway door. Only then did he begin to speak, but my attention was immediately distracted by the entry of two other men, both rather burly and quite silent, but moving with efficiency.

"'Mr. Jonathan Sparler spent his younger years on the Continent,' Dr. Hayes was saying, his tone almost a whisper, 'working in a variety of electrical generating plants with the likes of Nikolai Tesla. It was there that a friend of his was killed in a terrible accident, leading him to understand more clearly that electricity can have terrible effects upon the human body – but also, that the body itself is a generator of electricity. With this in mind, Mr. Sparler began to spend much of his free time experimenting and studying, attempting to understand the connection between electric current and the secret processes within our bodies. Did you know, Mr. Wisham, that the human brain actually functions as an electrical device?'

"As he spoke, the two men went about their activities. One of them picked up the refreshment table smoothly and effortlessly and removed it from the room, carrying it into the hallway and then toward the back of the house, while the other set about dimming the old-fashioned gaslights until the room was quite dim.

"'After many years,' Dr. Hayes continued, 'Mr. Sparler was successful – his research revealed the type of electricity which courses through the human body – that which serves to vivify it. At first, his new knowledge was used to improve the health of the living. He opened a series of Continental spas featuring electrical treatment. That's when he and I met, and it became obvious to him that my own training along similar lines would be of much use to him. Then, when he was ready, this same knowledge was used toward the next most-obvious goal: To reanimate the dead.'

It was during this last declaration that the first man returned to the parlour, now with a tall candelabra in his possession, containing five white candles. While he was placing it near the curtain on the opposite wall and lighting the candles, another man, tall, elderly, and disturbingly

371

cadaverous-looking, entered the room, pushing the door to the hallway shut behind him.

"Dr. Hayes, hearing the click of the door-latch, turned around toward the newcomer. 'Ah! And here is our founder, Mr. Sparler himself.'

"I started to rise, but Dr. Hayes held up a hand. 'Please, please – Mr. Sparler shuns physical contact – especially before a procedure is set to begin.'

"I sank back before I'd fully gained my feet, glad enough not to cross the room and meet the man. If he'd spent a good amount of his time working out the practicality of using electricity to encourage human health, it looked very much as if he'd never applied any of what he learned upon himself. He was painfully thin, with his cheeks so sunken that he might have lost all his teeth. His eyes were so deep-set that his upper eyelids seemed to vanish into cavities curving back into the sockets – the thought crossed my mind that he could keep spare shillings in the empty spaces along the tops of his eyes. In the few seconds that he crossed the room, he never smiled or even cracked open his mouth, so I couldn't say for sure about his teeth. He was wearing a light-colored suit, and with his pale skin and whitish hair brushed upwards, as if he were already charged with electricity himself, he looked like a ghost.

"I watched him move from the door to the curtains, and then turned to crane my neck up to Dr. Hayes had risen to his feet beside us, blocking most of the little light, I suddenly felt a wave of dread, realizing what I must have known all along: Exactly what was on the other side of the curtain, where the two nameless men now stood, one on either side. I began to feel hot and rather dizzy, and the curiously foreign odors coming from the burning candles, rather like some of the sour incense that's burned in the shops of the East End, almost made my head swim. Only then did I recall my mother, and I looked to see how she fared, but she was simply staring straight ahead, anxious for whatever would come next.

"We didn't have to wait any longer – there was no mumbo-jumbo or chanting or invocation of spirits, as I've heard they do to fool the gullible at séances – no offense, Mr. Carnacki. Dr. Hayes dropped heavily back into his chair. Meanwhile, the two nameless men each took a different side of the hanging drapes and pulled them aside slightly, while Jonathan Sparler shambled into a lanky awkward motion from where he'd paused, passing between the drapes into the dark area behind them. Then, there was a hum, almost immediately followed by a sizzling sound, and something of a flash from behind the drapes that left my vision temporarily affected. When it cleared, I could see that the drapes were now pulled all the way back, revealing Sparler standing to the right of a massive throne-like chair, his attention occupied by a small stand set up nearby. It had some sort of panel on top, covered with various dials that he was energetically turning this way and that. A tangle of wires ran down from it, across the few feet of floor, and then onto connections attached to the throne. There were some other devices behind the chair, flashing and sparking and throwing off what looked like miniature lightning bolts.

"But all of that was inconsequential to the figure who sat upon the throne.

"It was my step-father, Carl Grayling – dressed in the suit we had provided to the mortuary for his burial. He was slumped to one side upon an arm of the chair, which dwarfed his old and withered frame. The placement of the candelabra now made more sense, as my step-father's face was illuminated – his waxy pallor reflecting the light so that his countenance was visible against the small storm raging behind him.

"Beside me, my mother half-rose with a sob, as if she intended to cross the room to her dead husband, but Dr. Hayes, from his seat beside her, leaned closer and laid a heavy hand upon her shoulder. She didn't fight him – rather, she sank back into her seat with a disappointed sigh. I reached for her hand while I glanced back and forth from her to the dead man, but soon I couldn't tear my eyes away from the other side of the room, and I nearly gave a cry myself. For Sparler's fiddling with the dials upon his panel had caused the various electrical surges sparking here and there along the devices to increase. There was a curious burning smell now in the air. And even as I watched, aware of a humming noise that was rising and rising, my step-father's eyes opened, and he stared at us."

Wisham looked at us then, each in turn, as if willing us to understand what he'd seen. "There was no doubt, gentlemen, that it was Carl Grayling – or what was left of him. The same face and hair, and the same withered body, left that way after months of wasting illness. His features were white and bloodless, and I doubt that his heart was beating at all – and yet, he found the strength to speak to us.

"His voice was dry and raspy – what one would expect from someone who had died just days earlier. At first he moved his mouth as one does after awaking from a long sleep – as if he were attempting to moisten his lips and tongue. But apparently there was no moisture was to be found, and in the end, he spoke as best he could.

"'*All . . . is well . . .*' he rasped. Only his mouth and eyes moved. His body remained slumped toward one of the throne's arms, his legs splayed before him as if the rest of his body were still dead. Perhaps the electricity from Sparler's invention was only powerful enough, or the process only refined enough, to enliven my step-father's head, while the rest of the body upon which it rested continued toward its inevitable decomposition.

"I can't say how long we would have simply sat and watched, while the dead man in turn cut his eyes from my mother to me, making no further effort to speak, but seeming to question if we had something to tell him. Then, I jumped in my seat when Dr. Hayes leaned in and said softly to my mother, "I believe you had something that you wanted to say?"

"Never taking her eyes off her husband, she nodded. Then – nothing. For the longest time, she continued to sit and watch. I remembered only then that I was still gripping her hand, and I leaned forward. 'Mother?' I prompted, and she nodded again.

"'Carl,' she whispered, her voice sounding almost as dry and awkward as his had been. 'I . . . I never had time . . . to tell you . . . I knew. I knew, Carl, about . . . about the other woman – Ableson's wife. I . . . I hated . . . .' She closed her eyes, and a tear ran down her cheek. 'I forgive you, Carl. You were weak. You were always . . . .' Then her chin quivered, and she managed to utter with a small cry, 'You were always weak!' before turning toward me, leaning in, and burying her face in my chest, wracked with sobs.

"Needless to say, I was completely dumbfounded, having had no suspicion of anything like this in my stepfather's past. I turned my gaze back toward his dead body, whereupon his eyes met mine, with something like the same surprise I must still be showing. Then he closed them, gave a perceptible slump, and vanished when the two nameless men dropped the drapes shut, hiding both the dead man and Jonathan Sparler, who had never spoken, and who never stopped turning the dials this way and that.

"The electrical currents must have been shut off immediately, for the room seemed to grow immediately black. Only after a few moments did my eyes readjust to the five candles and the low gaslight.

"After my mother's weeping subsided – only a few moments later – Dr. Hayes, who was by then standing before us, leaned forward, offering his hand to my mother who, by this point, was looking across at the closed drapes, possibly wishing that she could have had more time or, like me, wondering just what abomination she'd just witnessed.

"'I hope that was satisfactory," murmured Dr. Hayes. "The process is still in its infancy, and the electricity does a great deal of irreparable damage to the body during the reanimation." My mother closed her eyes at the thought and gave him her hand, and he helped her to stand. "Your husband will be returned immediately to the mortuary."

"She nodded, and I stood as well, feeling somewhat dizzy and disoriented at what we'd seen. I have little memory of the rest. Dr. Hayes walked us through the door to the hall, and then outside to the pavement. A cab was already waiting there for us, and the doctor called out my mother's address. We were bundled into it, and it was only as we were

374

driving away that the cold brisk air seemed to bring some kind of sharpness back to my senses."

He fell silent then, as if the most difficult part of his story had been told. It was Holmes who next spoke. "And what would you wish from us?" he asked.

Wisham nodded, almost as if to himself. "To expose this man. To prevent him – You see, if it was just providing my mother some comfort – the chance to unburden herself of this knowledge she had of my step-father's secret affair – then I suppose that I could live with it. But . . . after that night, the funeral proceeded as usual. Then, a few days later, I had a note to stop around at my mother's bank, where I'm known and also have a responsible access to her accounts. There I learned that she had paid out a bill to this Jonathan Sparler for nearly her entire savings! This single arranged encounter with her dead husband had taken nearly all that she had!"

"And even that is beyond the power of the police?" I asked, but Carnacki answered.

"Without better proof, they often can't – or won't – make the effort. At least Inspector Jamison had the sense to refer the matter on to a private consultant."

Holmes had been tapping his lip with his forefinger, his brows frowning. Then he looked to me, and over at Carnacki. "Shall we?" he asked simply.

I nodded, and the spiritual investigator smiled. "We should. I've been meaning to turn my attention to this Jonathan Sparler for a while now, but other matters prevented me."

"You'll check into the mechanics of it?" asked Holmes.

Carnacki nodded. "And you the participants?" Holmes agreed.

"And me?" I asked, seeing that the train appeared to be leaving without me.

"Ah, Watson," said my old friend with a sad shake of his head, "you may not have heard that the scandalous brother of our old friend, Dr. Hill Barton of 369 Half Moon Street, has just passed away. I understand that Dr. Barton has an urgent need to ask said brother for forgiveness about an old matter of long-standing dispute between them – something about a young lady's affections, I'm thinking."

With that he stood while I laughed aloud, grateful that this time I wouldn't have to devote hours of painful and useless study upon the subject of Chinese pottery, and could instead simply show up when and where I was told.

Soon after, my guests departed, leaving me alone in my study to ponder the curious history of the elusive Dr. Hill Barton. Nearly two decades earlier, Holmes had been asked by an illustrious client to intercede as necessary, doing what he could to save a young woman's honor from a most despicable murderer, the Austrian nobleman Baron Adelbert Gruner. Try as we and others might, every word spoken to the stubborn young woman concerning the Baron's terrible past only served to driver her further into his clutches.

Finally, Holmes, who was already recovering from a beating received at the hands of the Baron's agents, had conceived the idea that I would approach from the front, in the guise of Dr. Hill Barton, wishing to meet with the Baron about his passion, Chinese pottery, while Holmes entered the man's house from the rear, in the hopes of obtaining the physical evidence of the fiend's crimes and future intentions that we knew he maintained. In order to pass muster, I'd spent several days in preparation, intensely cramming as much useless knowledge and trivia on the subject into my weary head as I could stand.

After the investigation ran its course, Dr. Hill Barton was allowed to fade away. Now, Holmes had found a reason to resurrect him, so to speak. At that time, the matter of the Baron and Dr. Barton had yet to be published in *The Strand*, so it was nearly impossible that the Resurrectionist and his mountebank myrmidons would have heard of him. I could only imagine with anticipation how the matter would play out.

That afternoon, I saw in the late newspapers a discretely placed obituary for Wauford Barton, a suicide victim, Next of kin was the aforementioned Dr. Hill Barton. If the notice were to be believed – and it was not – Wauford Barton had been in his mid-sixties, a wine merchant and land-speculator who had thrown himself into the Thames following substantial financial losses.

"A bit informative for an obituary," I commented that night as Holmes and I sat on either side of my fireplace. "Typically, you know, they simply list relevant dates, next-of-kin, and burial arrangements."

"It was Carnacki's idea," Holmes replied. "The sort of thing that an angry brother – you, my dear Watson –might have published without thinking it through."

"And have matters progressed?"

"They have. I arranged with the Home Office to take possession of a suitable body – the true dead man's manner of death actually suggested the nature of his obituary. Then, I sent a message – in your name, Dr. Barton – to Jonathan Sparler's establishment, requesting that your sad brother be revived so that the final discussion of those questions which still lay between you might be resolved. The response to Barton's address at 369 Half Moon Street – which is still a residence where I maintain some slight connection – was nearly immediate, and it wasn't long before two silent men – likely the same ones that Mr. Wisham mentioned as stage-managers for his own drama the other night – arrived at the cooperating mortuary to take possession of the corpse."

"And then?" I pressed. "There were many hours in the day. I'm sure that you accomplished much more than that."

Holmes nodded. "I determined, by way of several nosy neighbors on Princes Street who were willing to share what they knew with me, an out-of-work gas-fitter seeking odd jobs, that the Sparler building – claiming a Mayfair address, although this is true by only a few feet! – has quite a few more inhabitants than the four that were described. They all mentioned the two silent men, the tall overweight doctor, and the Resurrectionist himself, but they indicated that besides the irregular night-time visitors who arrive in various stages of grief and shock, there are a number of others who come and go during the daytime: Several women of different ages and shapes, and an equally diverse crew of men. Tall, short, fat, and thin."

"And what does that suggest?"

"I have some early ideas, and have set a few queries into motion – Pons is going to be sorry to have missed this one! – but Carnacki's report tomorrow morning should tell us more. Tonight he intends to burglarize the house."

I felt a pang that I seemed to be spending the investigation sitting in my study, but I knew that the occult investigator, quite a few years younger, was much more suited to that kind of work than I was by that time in my life. Holmes sense my mood. "Fear not, Watson. Carnacki will know specifically what he's looking for, and you will have your own part to play – for Jonathan Sparler has sent a message agreeing to re-animate Brother Wauford."

And with that I had to be satisfied.

The following day passed much as a normal one typically does. Holmes was out and gone when I arose, and no word came from Carnacki about what he had found. My housekeeper told me that Holmes had refused breakfast before leaving – which was no surprise. With no other calls upon my time, I settled into my typical daily routine, alternating between reading and taking my meals. In the afternoon, with no still word from about Mr. Wisham's investigation, I ambled into the mews behind my house as I often did, out and across Chandos Street, and along a short stretch of Portland Place to the entrance of the Langham. I had lived in Queen Anne Street since the autumn of 1902, and it hadn't taken very long at all to discover that route, thus cementing the constant temptation to step over to the Langham when the notion struck.

I sat and had my usual afternoon fortification, watching those around me with an interest that has never faded. Long ago, when I was just a boy, impatient to move on instead of simply sitting and waiting, my father had explained that, "People-watching is the greatest entertainment." At the time, just ten or so years old, I had given this statement no credence at all, but as I grew, I realized that he had spoken a great truth to me, and once I learned to appreciate it, I was never bored in that situation again.

When I returned home, Holmes was in my study, crouching by some low shelves and looking through a reference book of medical practitioners. "Dr. Leviticus Hayes is genuine," he said, closing the book, replacing it, and rising to his feet. "It's always good to confirm facts, and thank you for the use of your library. Elsewhere, I've learned that he was born in early 1883 in a village west of Farnham, on the Surrey border. He was raised by his maternal grandparents. Rumor has it, he was illegitimate, the son of a doctor who lived in that area and died in the spring of that same year. I wonder . . . ."

"You don't mean that he could be the son of Dr. Roylott?" I asked with some surprise.

Holmes shrugged. "Would it matter? If so, it would help to explain his wrong-turning, but he could have been a wrong 'un all on his own, possible parentage aside. In any case, you can decide for yourself, Dr. Barton – you're supposed to meet him in an hour in a tea-shop in George Street, to settle the financial aspect of this devil's bargain."

This was unexpected to say the least, and I left soon after. I entered the shop after an uneventful cab ride without much in the way of instruction, other than to state that my son would be joining me on the following night during Sparler's reanimation of my dead brother. By this point, Holmes and I had worked together for so long that he trusted me to pivot and adapt as necessary in such a situation.

The day was cold, and I kept my coat on as I entered and approached the table where a large man, presumably Dr. Leviticus Hayes, had risen, waving me in his direction. We were mostly alone, with only a couple of separately seated tight-mouth spinsters watching us. Although my frame had diminished with age, I found that I had to be careful on the spindly chair, and I could only imagine the monumental efforts made by my host not to splinter his.

"Dr. Barton," he said, his voice low and rumbling. He didn't offer his hand, and neither did I. While I adjusted myself, he waved over a lurking woman, requesting a pot of tea. "And do you wish for something to eat as well?" he asked, but I shook my head, aware that this meeting didn't need further extension, and also of my recent visit to the Langham.

He began by expressing his condolences, and it was obvious as the tea was delivered that he was already fishing for information about Dr. Barton's relationship with his dead brother. I was vague, intimating that I didn't normally go in for this sort of thing, but I had to know Wauford's intentions regarding an upcoming land sale, as it would affect my own financial position. "My son is the one who suggested you," I said. "Not normally my type of thing at all, you know. But he's read of you in the newspaper, you see, and I'm willing to try anything . . . ."

"Yes, yes," agreed Hayes, and I recalled Holmes's mention of the man's antecedents. Perhaps there was a hint of Grimesby Roylott around his eyes – and his frame certainly had much in common with the infamous doctor – but I could neither confirm nor deny for sure. After all, I had seen Roylott only twice – when he forced his way into our sitting rooms nearly forty years earlier to warn Holmes away from an investigation, and then less than a day later, when we found his corpse staring with horror into eternity following a particularly terrible death. I idly wondered what he would have to say, should he be resurrected.

Hayes was now going on about "unfortunate financial requirements" – how Sparler's process was so expensive, and the cost of moving their operation to London from the Continent, *etcetera.*

"How much?" I interrupted, rather sourly.

His spiel was disrupted, but Hayes took a folded sheet from his pocket and slid it across the table. I raised my eyebrows – five-thousand pounds.

"I don't suppose you'll bargain?" I asked.

He smiled unctuously and shook his head. "I'm afraid that wouldn't be possible, Dr. Barton."

I sat silently, letting my mind wander long enough to look as if I were debating the question in my mind. Then: "I stand to lose much more if I don't get this question answered, and in any case, my son insists."

"Good." Then he pulled out another sheet. "I'm afraid that, even for a necessary service such as this, there are agreements to be made."

It was a legal document, obligating payment of £5,000 from Dr. Hill Barton of 369 Half Moon Street, payable within one week of "consultation services" as provided by Jonathan Sparler. I grunted, pulled out my fountain pen, and scrawled something that could be argued to resemble *"Hill Barton"*, but could have just as easily said *"Hob Knolly"*.

I pushed back my chair and rose – clearly a man with other obligations. "Your message said tomorrow night." I tightened my mouth, as if this were unpleasant and distasteful. "What time?"

"Nine o'clock," he responded. "No. 5 Princes Street – just off Regent's Street. And you say it will be you and your son?"

"That's right." Noticing that we were still being observed by our fellow annoyed-looking patrons, I nodded. "See you then," I concluded, turning to walk out without looking back.

As I had learned long ago, I took steps to make sure that I wasn't followed before finally returning to Queen Anne Street. There, I found Holmes waiting, and I related what had occurred. He nodded.

"Well done. Babbling to him and over-acting would have simply given someone like him more ammunition. Better to leave things simple and clean."

"But surely," I countered, "he's already doing all sorts of research about Dr. Hill Barton and this ne'er-do-well brother, Wauford. It's what these bogus spiritualists do – find out all they can ahead of time to bolster their credibility."

"Ah, he won't be wanting for fact," Holmes responded. "Dr. Barton wasn't solely created and destroyed just for Baron Gruner all those years ago, you see. Mycroft and I saw the usefulness for such a man, and in the years since, quite a legitimate biography has been established and maintained for him – including the actual retention of the house in Half Moon Street by Mycroft's department. Even Brother Wauford has had his uses over the years. It was sad to kill him off just now, after coming to know his tempestuous life so well, but we did need someone close enough to Dr. Barton to require the services of a resurrectionist."

Talk then drifted along to some of the other affairs in which Dr. Hill Barton – later played by actors other than myself – had been involved, although none are repeatable, and revelation of a few of them here might mean the filing of criminal charges against me.

The afternoon drifted into evening, and still no report from Carnacki, although Holmes didn't seem concerned. I had long ago learned to take facts as they appeared, and to be patient during those times when information was wanting.

The following day began as had the day before – Holmes already gone, and my morning routine feeling like any other. With no news and no word to the contrary, I ambled to the Langham early that afternoon, and then, feeling energetic, set off to the south with the intention of visiting Hatchards in Piccadilly. It was quite the temptation, just south of Oxford Street, to look down Princes Street toward No. 5, our destination that night, but I kept my eyes facing forward, just another elderly man locomoting from here to there.

Sadly finding nothing of interest at the bookstore, I waved down a cab and returned home. It was nearly five o'clock and, still alone, I asked my housekeeper for something to eat and then cleaned my service revolver. At 8:45, I was standing out front when a cab pulled to a stop in front of my door.

I saw that the driver was Roger Deacon, the son of Bert Deacon, a former hansom driver in days long past who had owned his very life to

Holmes. It was through my friend's influence that Roger had received a decent education, with a future in the medical field. After the War, however, he had lost his stomach for such work, and became a cabbie as his father had been before him. He nodded to me, jumped out, and held the door while I climbed in beside Thomas Carnacki, my "son" for the evening.

"Is everything ready?"

Carnacki nodded. "It should go like clockwork." He smiled as something crossed his mind.

I understood. "Holmes told you not to tell me," I said, and he nodded.

"Something about your reactions appearing natural so that Sparler and the others won't catch on."

"Typical. Well, I'll sit back and enjoy the show. Should I be aware of anything special?"

"No. Wait – I almost forgot." He reached to one side, retrieving some sort of vulcanized rubber object. "Slip this into your pocket – it should fit unseen. It's waterproof, and lined with an absorbent cloth. When we're offered drinks, in the same manner as the Wisham and his mother, request something small, like whisky. Then, when I've distracted Dr. Hayes, pour it unseen into your pocket. Don't drink it."

"You suspect something hallucinogenic in the refreshments?"

"Well, possibly not that strong, but certainly enough to make Sparler's clients a bit more willing to believe whatever is suggested to them. Recall that Wisham indicated that he felt hot and dizzy – he blamed it on the scented candles, and he felt better when they left and he was in the cold night air." He settled back in his seat. "And if you could also distract Hayes for just a bit – we'll stand to either side so he can only see one of us at a time – I'll dump my drink as well."

I pulled aside my overcoat and fit the device in to my left coat pocket – that side would be a bit more awkward, but the right was already filled with the comfortable weight of my service revolver.

By then we'd made the short trip and arrived at No. 5 Princes Street. It was a typical London house, similar in many ways to my Queen Anne Street lodgings, and 221 Baker Street as well – a ground-floor door, and three stories above it, each floor with two windows looking down on the street. It was somewhat shorter than buildings on either side, and there was nothing to make it stand out as unusual in any way. It was neither well-kept nor dilapidated, but rather just one more building that, unless one had reason to pay attention, would look no different than any other.

We dismissed the cab, as there was no reason for Roger Deacon to stay, and Wisham's story was that a cab had been waiting for him and his mother when they departed. We had no wish to deviate from established practice. We mounted the single step and rang the bell, which was opened immediately by the imposing figure of Dr. Leviticus Hayes.

By then, the light had long left the sky, and his easily identifiable silhouette was a dark shadow limned by the faint light from the hall behind him. He let us in, murmuring words of greetings as he took our coats. I introduced my "son", but the doctor's interest was directed to me. He didn't go so far as to lay an arm across my shoulders – he certainly saved such attentions for smaller grieving women, I'm sure – the sense of hovering concern was still there nonetheless.

The house was warm, and there was a curious scent of incense – possibly from the candles that we would likely soon see – mixed with the somewhat dank odor of a house that has stood empty for too long. Sparler and the rest had been here for several months, but I suspected the house had been untenanted before that and, judging from the lack of furniture in the entryway, they were apparently doing nothing to make it more livable during their own stay.

Hayes shepherded us through an open door and into a parlour – the same as described by Wisham. The three chairs were there on the left, along the draped front windows, and across from them was the curtained area on the opposite wall. They were heavy drapes, and dense-looking, as if taken from some defunct theater and cut down to size. I knew that the corpse was resting behind them, and based on the layout of the house, I also suspected that there was a doorway leading deeper in the house, so that the "stage" behind the curtain could be accessed by the various actors before the show began.

Just inside the door was a small table containing half-a-dozen spirit bottles, as well as pots for coffee and tea. Turning us that way, Hayes asked what we wanted. Rather than fight the notion before giving in, I gruffly said, "Whisky," and the same was requested by Carnacki at my side.

After receiving our glasses, we stepped apart, and Carnacki asked a question – something about how long Mr. Sparler had been back in England. While Hayes answered, "Since the spring," I found it too easy to slip the small glass into my pocket and tip it into the lined receptacle. Then, stepping back and drawing the doctor's gaze, I said, "Why not provide this service on the Continent?"

Hayes turned to me and Carnacki wasted no time in emptying his own glass. "They are too . . . *superstitious* there, Doctor," was the reply. "Fear of the dead is bred into them. Unlike the enlightened British, they do not understand the *science*. Before long, they would be burning us out and driving stakes through our hearts!"

Even as Carnacki was removing his glass from his pocket, the two silent men of whom we'd been told entered the room, one taking a station

382

beside the drapes, and the other by the drinks table. Seeing that our glasses were empty, Hayes took them, placed them on the table, and then laid a hand upon each of our shoulders to nudge us toward the seats.

When I was settled, I looked back to see that the second man and the table were gone. Yet just seconds later, he returned with the promised candelabra. And then, right after him, came the fellow that I'd especially wanted to see . . . *Jonathan Sparler, Resurrectionist.*

He was an even more of a curious contrivance than Wisham's description: Tall, gaunt, pale, and sickly, he moved with a fascinating jerking motion, as if the muscles on his stringy limbs had atrophied to the point where movement was just about unattainable. I'm surprised that some case wasn't occasionally made that Sparler himself had died and been reanimated by his own machine – some would have paid more to consult with such a man. He did have terribly protruding cheek-bones with great hollows underneath, and Wisham's description of a total lack of teeth seemed quite accurate. The man neither looked left nor right from his deeply socketed eyes, but instead moved straight to the gap in the drapes, opened for him by the two men. He stepped inside where the dead body of my supposed brother waited for viewing. Knowing what was coming, I shut my eyes.

The flashing when the electrical devices were started could be seen through my closed lids. When it seemed as if they had settled somewhat, and my eyes had already adjusted to some degree, although closed, I cracked my lids to see that the curtain was now pulled entirely back, revealing the slumped figure of an elderly man, collapsed against one side of a large but plain throne-like high-backed chair.

To the side, as expected, was Jonathan Sparler, standing before some sort of table whose top was covered with various dials and switches. It was at an angle, so that I could see both what he was doing, and also enough of his face to observe the peculiar intensity of his expression as he focused intently on his task. Faster and faster did his hands move, and I was surprised to see the slightest bit of drool at the corner of his mouth, shining in the sparking light from the various devices flashing behind him.

I glanced away from him. Without looking right at him, it was still obvious that Leviticus Hayes was watching me instead of the resurrection. I looked back toward the "stage", able to perceive that I had been correct: There was a closed door behind the throne. I looked back at the body in the chair.

The skin was very white, and there was nothing about this man who seemed to be alive. The effects of the electricity were doing nothing – not a twitch or shift was evident.

But then, as the electrical activity from the various devices located nearby increased, this dead stranger opened his eyes, looking straight at me and trying to speak.

It was fascinating, and there was something of a visceral terror associated with it as well. Holmes had indicated that my reactions ought to be sincere – and I'm sure that they were. I had never seen anything like this before, and it was impossible to look away. I forgot what was expected of me. I could only watch, even as the thing in the chair watched me in return.

"Doctor," whispered Hayes in my ear, his foul warm breath washing over me. I'd had no sense that he was leaning closer. I realized too that his hand was gripping my arm. "He will not be reanimated for long. The process – it is too damaging to be sustained. What are your questions?"

"I . . . umm, I . . . ." I cleared my throat. "Wauford, is that really you?"

The body worked its lips and blinked several times. Finally, "*Yessss* . . . ." The word extended in some terrible sibilance, and I realized that if I did have a legitimate question, it would only be answered in the briefest of responses – which no doubt helped Sparler and Hayes and the others avoid saying something that would unmask them.

"Wauford," I continued, finding it hard to speak myself. "The girl – " I said, having no idea what to say next. "What is her name? The child – I need to know whose it is. Your will – We cannot complete the agreement without settling that question, and finding your heir."

Having said that, made up spontaneously, I realized that Hayes and the others might learn of some serious secrets through this process. I wondered if, after they had received payments for the various resurrections, their clients found themselves some months later being blackmailed for what was discussed here in this room on nights like these.

The dead man ground his lips tighter, blinking his eyes as if trying to force out a response. I knew that I had stumped them, for there had been no hint of this in the conversation I'd had earlier with Hayes. Then, I'd implied that I simply needed a response about whether to complete a land deal. Now I'd added a complication.

The dead pale white face reflected the light from the candelabras, its mouth working while most of his body remained in shadow. I had to concentrate to see him clearly as the electrical currents and arcs behind him continued their motions. I looked back to Jonathan Sparler. His hands continued to flash from here to there, turning knobs, flicking switches back and forth, and occasionally turning some sort of handled wheel.

"*I . . . I . . .*" groaned the figure of Wauford Barton. "*I –* " And then he shrieked – in a much different tone than what we'd heard before.

Beside me I felt Hayes stiffen – apparently with surprise. But my attention stayed on the figure before me, because he was now no longer sagging upon the throne. No, he had risen abruptly, and taken a step forward, wringing his hands, still crying out, but this time cursing in the same manner that my brother had once done upon blundering into a hornet's nest.

As he stepped closer, I could see that the dead waxy face now seemed rather puckered around the eyes and mouth, and a line was visibly obvious around the man's ear. He was clearly wearing a mask.

Abruptly, the electrical display died, and the sudden silence was replaced by a number police whistles. I could hear the front door bang open, and seconds later, half-a-dozen constables boiled into the room, truncheons pulled in case they faced resistance. Among them was the burly figure of Inspector Seymour Jamison.

Meanwhile, to the right of the throne, Jonathan Sparler continued to turn his dials and toggle his switches, accomplishing nothing.

With a roar, Dr. Leviticus Hayes rose beside me, taking a step forward as if he could tear the policemen to pieces with his hands. It took no extra effort reach out with my own foot and give a solid push against the back of his knee. His leg bent and crumpled and he fell to the floor, only to be surrounded before he could cause any harm.

Into this confusion strode Sherlock Holmes with a smile. Apparently his plan had gone off without a single deviation.

The mask was removed from the *faux* Wauford Barton to reveal a small-framed middle-aged man, looking as if he wished to take his chances and run. Holmes stepped in front of him.

"Clayton Fulford," he said. "Quite a step down from St. Martin's Theater. I take it that things have been lean since the War?"

The man shook his head. "Just a job, Mr. Holmes. We're hired as needed – whatever type of body they need. Fat, thin, tall short. Then we just sit in the chair for a few minutes."

"Not quite so simple as that, I'm thinking. We'll let the police sort out just how complicit you and the others are. But you will tell us the names of the other actors, of course, it will go a long way toward showing your good faith in the interest of leniency."

"You can be certain of that, Mr. Holmes," said the man before he was led away. Hayes, in the grip of two burly constables beside me, growled as if he wanted to threaten the other man into silence before he lost his chance, but he restrained himself. Holmes and Carnacki stepped up, ranging themselves in front of Hayes. I glanced over at the curtained area. The two burly men had already been taken outside, and a constable was disengaging Sparler from his activities, his hands still making motions even as he was pulled back from the panel. I realized that he had no notion as to what was going on. He had been used, another actor in this bizarre drama.

"You should be ashamed," I said to Hayes, realizing that he never would be.

His eyes raged, but he shrugged. "Others could have worked the dials, but Wenzel's curious physiognomy was useful – and he does so enjoy playing with dials and buttons."

"Wenzel?"

"His real name – I don't know if it's his first or last. I found him pushing a broom in a café in Blois. He's been useful in any number of ways since then." He smiled, an ugly thing. "I bequeath his care and feeding to you, Doctor."

I started to respond, but Holmes interrupted me.

"They obtained the corpses from their clients, by way of the advertisements and word of mouth," Holmes explained for my benefit, while watching Hayes – if that was his real name. "They wanted them fresh, both as part of the scheme that they needed to be that way for their electrical process, and also to give a sense of urgency to the matter that would make clients comply in desperation without thinking too much. Then, when the body was in their possession, a rubber mask of its face was constructed, and whichever one of their stable of down-at-heel actors best fitted the corpse was hired for the evening. A little research, a few facts provided to the actor as to what might be asked – if it could be determined – and then, after putting on the mask and getting suitably ready, the players took their places and the very brief show performed. Afterwards, the body was released back to the family for burial, the fee, as legally contracted, was collected, and at times, the information learned here was put to further use down the road."

"I wondered about that," I said. "A perfect way to support a blackmail scheme."

Holmes nodded. "Carnacki found the mask-making apparatus last night when he – " Holmes glanced at Jamison, who pointedly looked away. " – when he 'researched' the house here. It was then that he made a few modifications of his own."

"I electrified the chair," he said. "It was obvious what they had done – run a current to these little toys behind the throne, like the Tesla Coil and the Jacob's Ladder – in order to impress their gullible clients. The actual hook-up for that device was in the cellar. The panel where Sparler stood wasn't connected to anything at all. I managed to run some extra wiring through the hole in the floor and onto the chair, where the occupant, his feet grounded in front of him, would get a shock." He grinned. "It worked better than I expected."

I started to make a comment about possibly killing the man – the Americans had been using the electric chair as a method of criminal execution for decades – but I decided that such talk right now would be a distraction, and I doubted that Carnacki would ever have the temptation to try this similar method of exposing a fraudulent spiritualist again.

"So what now?" I asked. "I suppose that we should see about returning the stolen funds back to the bilked clients."

Hayes growled. "It was paid voluntarily!" he grumbled. "I shall fight!"

"An interesting defense," said Holmes. "I wonder if you can find an attorney to support your argument – knowing that if you lose, you won't have any money to pay his fees. I shall be watching with interest to see how that turns out."

Carnacki, who had observed the exchange with amusement, raised his hands toward Hayes. Waving them, he motioned. "Out you go!"

Outside, the cool night air was refreshing after the stuffy atmosphere of the small room.

"I'm glad we didn't drink any of the whisky," I said.

Holmes nodded. "Carnacki obtained some samples last night, and I had it tested. Everything was mildly tainted with a mild drug that would make the visitors more open to what they were seeing."

A number of police wagons were still on the street, and I nodded my head across the way to Jamison and Inspector Japp, who were standing beside another vehicle – a hearse – where the body of "Wauford Barton", whomever he really was, was being loaded for return to whence he'd been borrowed.

Holmes glanced at his watch. "Not yet ten," he said. "Is it too late, Watson, for a little celebration?"

I considered. If I stayed up late tonight, and slept in the following day, would that be such a bad thing? No, I decided. A bit of shake-up to my routine was definitely the recommended treatment.

"We are just a short walk from Claridge's," I said, and Holmes nodded, while Carnacki said something about that suiting him down to the ground. Thus, we set off along Princes Street and then along the edge of Hanover Square into Brook Street. Claridge's turned out to be a fine choice, and the night ran long as Holmes confirmed what we'd thought about Leviticus Hayes's parentage, along with sharing other facts he'd since discovered about the man. We told one another of tales and adventures, with Carnacki sharing some that were most unusual indeed, and the next morning, I didn't regret the decision to celebrate the successful resolution of the case in that way at all.

The Sethian Messiah

Chapter I

Within hours of being introduced to Sherlock Holmes in 1881, he and I – two total strangers – were sharing rooms. We met on New Year's Day for just a very few moments, long enough to agree to look at apartments that he'd identified in Baker Street. On the second morning of January, we met there and found them to be quite satisfactory. In fact, they were desirable in every way, and so moderate were the arrangements when divided between us that we entered into possession at once. I was glad to have the opportunity, since my meager wound pension would never have allowed me to afford them on my own.

I moved in with my few slight and battered possessions that very night, and Holmes began doing the same on the third – although he brought quite a bit more than I did. Soon after we'd settled in, I turned my attention back to recovering from the grievous wounds I'd received at Maiwand the previous July, and Holmes went on with his life – although at that stage, I couldn't have explained exactly what that meant.

He was often away, and I assumed that he was carrying out his further curious researches at Barts, where we'd first met. I suppose that I had some vague idea that he must be a medical student, in spite of the fact that he was getting rather old for it – he'd just turned twenty-seven that January, although I didn't yet know his actual birth date. When he began to have visitors from all strata of society, I initially believed that he might be providing them with some sort of medical treatment, using our sitting room to consult with his "patients".

Holmes was always most solicitous about my health, and he would graciously ask if I minded allowing him the use of the sitting room during those mornings when a plethora of his "clients" climbed the stairs to meet with him. I would defer and remove myself up one flight to my bedroom, or when the weather was tolerable enough I'd take a walk through the nearby streets or in Regent's Park. I learned that Holmes was generally finished with these "consultations" by about eleven a.m., and it was then safe to return to my fireside chair for the rest of the day.

But this was not what I agreed upon when we first discussed sharing a flat, and as much as I objected to rows because of my shaken nerves, I felt that I was being steadily positioned into saying something if his regular use of our joint sitting room was going to be a permanent arrangement. While I never thought that I would be there for more than a few months –

I planned to return to the Army later in the year when my recovery was complete (or so I thought then) – I was paying my half-share, and that included full and free access to the sitting room, which was already more filled with Holmes's possessions than mine.

As my journal records, it was on Monday, the 28th of February, 1881, that I resolved to speak to my fellow lodger about my rising sense of injustice. I expected that it would be a civil exchange, for we had never been anything but polite with one another, and I was fully confident that my point of view would be expressed, heard, and honored.

I made a point of rising a bit early, for I had a leaning toward getting up at all sorts of ungodly hours, and knowing when Holmes's visitors started arriving, I made sure to be downstairs and fed a good fifteen minutes beforehand. I recall that I was nervous, which makes no sense at all, because just half-a-year earlier I had faced the butchering Ghazis on the worst day of my life. I suppose that even then I very much appreciated having a refuge at 221b and feared that taking my stand might muff it.

Holmes and I had finished our meals, each mostly silent, and I was preparing to speak my peace when the doorbell began clanging loudly, followed in moments by a cry from Mrs. Hudson and then scrambling thumps as someone awkwardly climbed the stairs. The door to the landing slammed open to reveal a wizened fellow of elder appearance, although later I was to learn that he'd aged prematurely due to his demanding lifestyle. With a rather wild-eyed look, he muttered, "Mr. Holmes . . . ." and then collapsed to the floor.

Although I didn't yet know it, this was Bartholomew "Bertie" Tolliver, one of Holmes's many associates in that low and gray-shadowed area of society that so many preferred to ignore. Bertie, like his forefathers before him, was a *tosher* – a "profession" whose existence I'd never even considered before beginning my medical training in London some years earlier.

For those who don't know, a word of warning: Toshers have chosen a career of sorts that places them in the filthiest of conditions and most unhealthy locations. Specifically, they venture into the city's sanitary sewers in search of lost or discarded valuables.

I first became acquainted with such men when they sought the free treatment provided by medical students when I was at the University of London, and after that when they would seek aid at Barts. As one might expect, they inevitably carried a certain . . . *aroma* about them different from that of the men who regularly worked with animals, or those who carried out the awful tasks required in the tanneries and abattoirs scattered throughout the capital. Once such a scent had been identified for us by one of my aloof professors, it was never forgotten.

Now I smelled it again as I rose from my breakfast chair and crossed the few feet to the doorway. Dropping to my knees with more than a twinge of pain, I leaned over my unexpected patient. He wasn't unconscious yet, but appearances indicated that such a condition wasn't far off.

He grasped my hand and whispered, "Food . . . ." He grasped my wrist and urgently tried to speak clearly. "I need something to stave off the shakes before it gets worse . . . ."

I understood, and further hurried examination confirmed my tentative diagnosis. This was more than simple hunger. He was one of those poor unfortunates who suffered from *diabetes mellitus*, wherein the afflicted were required to maintain very strict and careful diets, along with constant vigilance, in order to prevent a cascade of worsening symptoms, possibly resulting in death. But for now, I knew nothing of the man except that I should quickly provide him with certain items from our breakfast table.

The improvement was dramatic, and within fifteen minutes he was up and sitting in a dining chair – Holmes's, I was glad to see – as if he'd walked straight there from the door when he arrived, instead of detouring by way of a prone position upon our floor. Throughout the man's recovery, Holmes had stood to one side, watching with a gimlet eye in the same way that some of my past professors had once done when adjudicating my choice of treatment.

I questioned the man, who then provided me with his name, information about his further symptoms, and that he was already quite aware of what he needed to do to care for himself. "But I've been using myself up too freely for the last few days," he explained, "and I rather lost track of things. Won't happen again, I assure you." He was a small fellow with an unaccountable twinkle in his eye, and he spoke in a sing-song manner that would have sounded rather like a leprechaun if his accent had been Irish instead of East London. I advised that he continue to obtain medical treatment and be careful, and he agreed that he would – although I'd heard too many others promise the same thing over the years to accept such a statement on total faith.

When Bertie and I had nothing left to discuss, Holmes then spoke up, referring to me formally as "Doctor" and thanking me for jumping in so ably, and then asking – once more – if he might borrow the sitting room to speak with his visitor for a few minutes. As I wondered again if Holmes was some type of medical student, and whether he was already treating Bertie for this or some other condition, I also recalled my intent to assert my rights regarding the shared usage of our space, but decided that to do so now would appear rather petty, as my time for doing so was lost. With a nod, I swallowed the last of my now-cold coffee and retreated upstairs.

I said nothing further about the matter over the next week or so, again working to pick up my nerve, and then the matter became moot on the fourth of March, when I learned that Sherlock Holmes was a *consulting detective*, and that these visitors of his were clients in need who were seeking his unique services. I became involved that very day in the matter of the Lauriston Gardens murder, and then another case after that. More and more often in the coming months, I helped with his investigations when I could, and in ways in which I was able. Over the next few years, I saw Bertie Tolliver again on numerous occasions when he would visit us, understanding afterwards how he served as Holmes's trusted agent in that specific portion of London.

He was of particular use to us during the unreported siege of Wakeling Street, and also in the midst of the unfortunate affair of Madame Belasco's defenestration. The longer I knew him, the more he impressed me. In spite of the way he earned his bread and cheese, he was well-spoken, and more than once his comments had given me to understand that he was knowledgeable about current events, along with other learned topics. He once casually mentioned that he read a lot, and I could believe it. One curious fact about him was apparent as the years passed – I felt each and every one of those years, but Bertie seemed remain the same wizened and unchanging little fellow that I'd first met in early '81. It seemed as if the fumes of his workplace were preserving (or pickling) him somehow, and he didn't appear to noticeably age.

Bertie was perhaps of the greatest service to us just a few years before his death. It was early on the morning of Wednesday, 26 November, 1884, and Holmes and I had just returned from Knightsbridge, where a particularly grim murder had threatened to defame the carefully maintained image of Harrods store. The business had burned to the ground nearly a year before, and as the remodeling was nearly complete, a body had been discovered lodged in the forgotten framing under a stairwell. In spite of its condition, the corpse was quickly identified as Eustace Beynard, who had gone missing a decade earlier. Holmes's brilliant examination of the stitching wounds on the body identified Crane Wickham, Beynard's jealous former assistant, as the killer. The fervent thanks from the store's management were ringing in our ears as we departed the premises in the early hours

It was with these thoughts in mind that I stirred up the fire and settled into my chair, considering whether to stay where I was or make my way upstairs for a few hours of sleep. Holmes was jotting something in one of his scrapbooks, and I had just decided to wish him good-night – at six in the morning – when the doorbell rang. The perceptive reader, having seen him so thoroughly described earlier in this narrative, will rightly assume that our pre-dawn visitor was Bertie Tolliver.

I knew that Mrs. Hudson was up – her day began long before six a.m. – but I rose and went downstairs to answer the door, finding Bertie on our front step, a rather uncharacteristic grim tightness to his mouth. "Mr. Holmes in?" he asked, and I nodded and let him pass me. Then, seeing Mrs. Hudson approaching from the rear of the house, I let her know that we would apparently be staying up and would appreciate a pot of coffee. "Strong," I added.

Back upstairs, I found Holmes and Bertie standing in the center of the room, facing one another about four feet apart, with the smaller man looking up at Holmes with an alert expression. Holmes, however, was staring at something in his upturned hand, tipping it this way and that. He fiddled with it for a moment, and then began unfolding a tiny slip of paper which had apparently been attached to it. He flattened the small sheet on his palm, looked at it closely, and then offered what he'd seen to me.

I reached out with a sigh, correctly suspecting where a fellow of Bertie Tolliver's occupation would have found the object – whatever it was. And in fact it turned out to be a ring, thankfully clean – or as far as I could perceive at any rate. More curious was the tiny and stained piece of paper which had been wrapped tightly around the band.

The ring had been made for a man, apparently gold, and heavy. The object itself was plain enough, and narrow at the back side where it would rest beside one's palm. It widened on each side toward a squared front, where a stylized cloisonné black-and-white griffin was fixed in white enamel, decorated sparsely with a tiny red tongue and bloodied claws. That was curious enough in itself, but there was more. The square decoration pivoted on the connecting ring-posts, rotating to reveal a second image on the back – another white enamel space enclosing a secret emblem that would normally be kept hidden against the wearer's finger until intentionally exposed. And I had seen this wicked little sigil before.

It was the suggestion of a human figure, but drawn more like a stick figure than a man. A circle made up the head with a couple of irregular dots for eyes, and a downward slash placed a cruel and bitter-looking mouth. A few lines below sketched the shape of a body and legs. There was only one arm, holding a straight line seemingly representing a spear. Instead of the other arm, another smaller circle touched the line of the body in the semblance of a shield.

Holmes had made himself aware of countless secret societies throughout the nation, ranging from the harmless and silly to those with angry and dangerous agendas, and some with the means to create great mayhem. Through my association with his investigations, it was inevitable that I would learn more of these shadowy organizations, and the ring in my hand represented one that we had brushed against before: *The True Knights of Seth.*

The folded piece of paper was no more than two inches square, cut sharply and neatly on two adjacent corners and ragged on the other sides – clearly it had been torn from the corner of a larger sheet, perhaps the flyleaf of a book. It had been folded many times into a tight thread, so that it would have been no wider than a sliver of wood before being wrapped around the ring's narrow band. Written in dark pencil was this curious message:

Gladstone – Thursday 10 – Return for details

As I looked at the tiny paper, Holmes was questioning Bertie Tolliver.

"Where?" he asked tersely. There was no need to query whether Bertie knew what he'd found. He'd been with us the previous February when we'd prevented a group of The True Knights from assassinating the Lord Mayor – for they were aggressive in advancing their agenda.

"Just below the Bow Street Police Station – over from the Tottenham Court trunk line."

Holmes stepped to one of his bookcases and returned with a large-scale map of that segment of the city. Pushing aside a stack of books, he unfolded it on the table and leaned down to study the arrangement of the streets.

"Once again, I'm reminded that I need to obtain a map of the capital's sewers," he said while running a finger along one of the wider thoroughfares. "The routes aren't widely known for a variety of reasons, but in my work – "

"If you don't mind, Mr. Holmes," said Bertie, pushing in beside him, "I can show you easier than you trying to puzzle it out." He put a finger down on the map. I leaned in and saw he was pointing at Bow Street, as mentioned. "The sewer here runs roughly northwest to southeast, from up here along Gower Street, and parallel to the Tottenham Court trunk which runs the same direction – but that one's set off to the west, you see. The both cross the larger Piccadilly trunk here – " He moved his finger back and forth a couple of times from west to east to west on a line north of the police station. " – and then both veer inward a bit to nearly touch one another here. Then they separate again, and the line below the Bow Street Station carries on toward the Savoy, emptying into the Victoria Embankment low-level interceptor line just west of Waterloo Bridge."

He stepped back. "As you know, we all have our areas in the sewer that we 'farm', and Bow Street is one of mine – me and a few others. I was making my rounds there this morning when I found the ring – and when I saw that symbol, I knew that you needed to see it as soon as I could get here."

Holmes nodded. "You did well, Bertie." Then he seemed to focus inward as he considered what to do next. At that moment, Mrs. Hudson arrived with the coffee, and Bertie and I quickly poured cups for each of us, and for Holmes as well, should he want it. I knew that I should drink mine as quickly as possible, as we might be leaving abruptly at any moment, and if so, Holmes would gulp his down before dashing out the door. Better that his should have a chance to cool before then.

Holmes paced slowly as he considered, staring at nothing and pinching his earlobe. I took the opportunity to retrieve the appropriate commonplace book from the shelves near his bedroom door and review what little we knew of The True Knights of Seth.

Holmes had first made note of them in mid-1881, as their actions became more public. These criminals were not to be confused with the similarly named *Knights of Seth*, an ancient religious group. As Holmes explained it to me, the original Sethians were a Gnostic sect that flourished in the Mediterranean in the early years of Christianity. They named themselves after Adam's third son, Seth, whom they believed was some sort of Messiah with secret knowledge and a special understanding of the nature of reality. It was their idea that what we perceived as the physical world was in fact an illusion, while man's spiritual side was the true reality. Their symbol was a lion's head on a serpent's body. The original Sethians had an elaborate creation myth involving events that occurred before the making of Adam and Eve, in which various spiritual powers were infused into the first humans' bodies. These beliefs then merged into what is more widely known in the book of *Genesis* concerning the Creation.

The neo-Sethian Knights of the mid-1800's were made up of wealthy young English and Germans who were more interested in an excuse for a gentleman's club of sorts than forming an actual religious movement. They simply draped the tenets of the millennia-old Sethians onto their own foolish order, which they liked to call the *Ordo Equester Sethiani*. But as is too often the case, there were a few within this group of wayward young men who felt the call to something darker.

These few believed that there is a true God and a false one, the latter being known as the *demiurge*. It was he, named by them as *Yaldabaoth*, whom they credited with actually creating the world, and in doing so replacing the true and benevolent God. They also believed that Adam's son, Seth, was the original Messiah who could enact Yaldabaoth's will in this shadowy construct we think of as the actual physical world, and that other messiahs had followed in Seth's footsteps in the ages that followed.

Holmes had first perceived that such a group was in motion after the murder of Somerset House clerk. The killer had been easily identified and caught, but he refused to provide information as to who had instigated the crime, or the reason behind it. However, a search of his possessions had turned up a ring exactly like the one now resting in my pocket. Two other murders had followed which gave every indication of being related to The True Knights of Seth, and four others had been prevented. And Holmes still had no complete idea of who the new "Seth" was, or how to identify him.

The previous February, Holmes had deciphered a coded reference to Yaldabaoth in the Agony Column, leading him to spring into action while the latest outrage was actually in progress. We had been involved in another case at the time in which Bertie Tolliver had an interest, and he was swept along with us in the mad chase across the City to save the Lord Mayor. As our growler had raced east from Baker Street, I had given Bertie a short sketch of the organization we were facing, explaining the history and the rings, and his eyes had widened at such primitive idiocy and evil going on in our modern times. It was with this awareness that he had identified the significance of the ring brought to us that morning.

And now, it was possible that we had an unexpected indication as to the True Knights' next plan – and to the identity of one of the members as well. Perhaps even the self-proclaimed modern Messiah himself . . . .

"Bow Street provides good pickings, I suppose," said Holmes suddenly, back from his reverie and with his gaze focused on Bertie.

The small man nodded. "Many are arrested with things that they don't want found on them. As soon as they can, they get them off their person and down into the sewers. Often it's money, or jewelry. The pipes downstream from the police stations are all prime, as you might suspect, and are well defended by those of us who claimed them long ago."

"Where was the ring found?" asked Holmes. "Somewhere along the pipe, or specifically at the Bow Street Police Station sewer connection?"

"At the station," was Bertie's prompt reply. "We have a basket fixed there beneath the pipe. Makes it easier to rake, and to be sure that nothing is lost. That the ring and the note came from straight above our spot – no doubt. It was lying right on top of the . . . on top of what was in the basket. It couldn't have been there for more than half-an-hour. You get a sense of how long something has been in the sewers, you understand. And when I saw it – saw what it was – I knew that you out to have it."

"Your . . . profession," pondered Holmes, "isn't well known. Whomever dropped this ring wasn't just ridding himself of it to keep it from being found on him when he was thoroughly searched at the station. The note shows that. By adding a message, it indicates that he – whomever it was that got rid of the ring – knew that it would be found in the sewers by someone who would be looking for it – someone who would know where and what it was, and what to do with it. The note instructs the finder to return for more information, so presumably another message will be sent down the pipes." He took a step forward, shortening the distance to the smaller man. "How well do you trust your fellows – the other toshers with whom you work – who regularly examine that particular area?"

Bertie frowned. "I see what you mean. They would be the ones to know where to be watching for such a message. Well, I trust some more than others. Those that I do are like family. But then, there is one . . . Willoughby. We accept him, but he isn't trusted, you see. Not yet – he's too new among us. Do you think he might be working for The True Knights – the one who was supposed to find the message?"

"Possibly. Their reach seems to be both broad and deep. If so, he hasn't received the message from the prisoner upstairs yet, because we have it – and he'll be looking for it. Was anyone with you when you recovered the ring?"

Bertie shook his head. "I made my rounds early this morning. When I found the ring, I got out as fast as I could and washed it off at the trough near Cleopatra's Needle. Then I hurried here."

"Then we have a chance to take control of the situation. Watson," he looked at me, and I thought I spied pity in his face, "put on your very oldest clothes – nothing that you need to keep." Then he stepped over to my desk, pulled a blank sheet from a pad lying there, and picked up a pencil. Leaning over, he scribbled something on a corner and then tore it off, approximating the look of the message found on the ring. Rolling it tightly, he then turned to me, his hand out. I placed the ring in his palm and he set about attaching the small slip of paper.

"I've left Gladstone's name as before, but changed the day to Sunday – four days away, instead of tomorrow – to give us time to maneuver and possibly wreck their plans. I also left instructions to deliver the ring after it's found to a house in Crutched Friars. The message barely fits." He looked at Bertie. "We need to get the ring back to the sewer as soon as possible. Is there a way in without alerting your . . . associates?"

"The easiest way is up from the Victoria Embankment by the bridge, but that's like a regular tosher highway. Instead, we can come down Goodge Street alongside the Museum. But there are only so many routes, and whoever is looking for this ring might use any of them, depending on which way he decides to approach. We'll just have to be careful – and lucky."

I turned then to go upstairs and find my oldest set of clothes. This was not my first trip into the London sewers, nor even my tenth. In fact, during the years of my association with Sherlock Holmes, such journeys had been required far too often for my happiness. I had long-since learned to retain old worn-out clothing at hand for when sojourns such as this, and sometimes even worse, became unavoidable.

Downstairs, I found that Holmes had also changed into a quite disreputable outfit – his in much worse condition than mine. While Bertie warmed himself by the fire, he was drinking his coffee in one steady draw. Then he set down the cup, picked up three dark lanterns that he'd retrieved from one of the storage cabinets while I was upstairs, and led us down to the street. We walked south for just a moment before encountering an early-morning growler. "Endell Street at Short's Garden," Bertie instructed the cabbie, and we lurched into motion.

Chapter II

As we traveled, each holding to our own thoughts, I considered what I knew about the London sewer system – which wasn't very much in 1884, except for my prior visits there. I only learned about its history and construction in greater detail years later, when Holmes told me of the time in 1877 when he'd been consulted by Sir Joseph Bazalgette, the famed civil engineer. *

It was Sir Joseph who had, beginning in the 1850's, been the designer and driving force behind the construction of London's massive sewer system. By '77, he'd already completed most of his great engineering works, and was only dabbling in the occasional consultation, which was how he'd discovered an elaborate underground dene hole, far east of London. That was during those early years when my friend was residing in Montague Street and first establishing himself as a consulting detective. It was after that meeting that Holmes had bothered to learn more about the man and the sewers, and I knew that he'd remained friends with the famed civil engineer until the man's death in early 1891.

But it was back in the 1850's when Sir Joseph earned his fame, as necessitated by the terribly unhealthy conditions facing Londoners every day.

Those had been the days of The Great Stink, when the sewage for the entire massive city had emptied directly into the tidal Thames. The Pool of London had been a gigantic heaving cess-pit, toxic and festering, and the health crisis that it caused was both deadly and unceasing. Sir Joseph was appointed as Chief Engineer to the Metropolitan Board of Works and given the monumental task of fixing it.

Up to that time, the city sewers, if they existed at all, were randomly located and undersized pipes, emptying into streets or streams, which in turn filled the Thames along the length of the city. More often, raw sewage ran in the streets and ditches and was emptied from windows, making walking anywhere a hazard both above and below. As the city grew, the situation became worse, and diseases, particularly cholera, ran rampant as the local water supplies, chiefly wells whose ground water was polluted by sewage, were affected.

Growth of the city also meant that many streams and rivers were literally enclosed and covered, some lost forever as they were artificially forced underground and forgotten. Sewage choked these as well.

The famed engineer had showed amazing foresight in terms of his estimate for the future growth in the capital. After he'd completed his calculations for the size required to handle the amount of sewage being produced in the 1850's, he'd then looked at his numbers and doubled everything, stating that, "We only have the chance to do this once, and there's always the unforeseen." For me personally, that planned oversizing of the sewers meant that many of the brick passages beneath the streets of London were constructed high enough to walk through – which was the only pleasant aspect of where we were headed.

London was a stranger to me in those bygone days when I was just a boy, so I can only imagine the filth and pestilence of the place. Sir Joseph's plan was to create great underground sewers of vast diameter, oversized brick tunnels as large as the underground rivers. To these would be connected hundreds of other smaller constructed brick pipes and passages running under streets and back into the various neighborhoods and absorbed villages, all carrying the accumulated sewage downstream into larger and larger pipes like branches joining limbs, and then becoming part of a great tree trunk. Then, at the lowest elevations in the city – along the banks of the Thames – the largest of these trunk pipes, constructed underneath the Albert Embankment, the Victoria Embankment, and the Chelsea Embankment, would turn and follow the river east, out of the city and far away, keeping the sewage from directly entering the river. Many miles downstream, the sewage would then be treated, stored in reservoirs until the pollutants had been consumed and eradicated by various natural water-dwelling creatures of microscopic size. Only then, when this bacteriological treatment had occurred and the sewage water was of a more natural state similar to river water, would it then be released into the Thames to complete its journey to the sea.

The streets were still empty and dark, as our conversation with Bertie in Baker Street had lasted no longer than fifteen minutes. The cab released us in short order at the poorly lit corner on Endell Street, and our guide into the Underworld led us into Short's Garden, with Christ's Church and the workhouse on our left, and the Lying-in Hospital on our right. Our footsteps echoed off the cold black bricks rising on either side of us. Halfway down the narrow passage in the direction of Drury Lane, Bertie directed us to the left, toward a circular metal lid darkening one side of the street. Reaching into his coat and retrieving a short pry-bar (a tool of his trade), it was but a second before he had the lid raised and then lowered quietly beside the now-opened void. I smelled the unmistakable odor of our destination.

Holmes had been lighting the lanterns, handing one to each of us as he finished. Keeping the third for himself, he gestured for Bertie to lead onward. I pulled on a pair of old and thick gloves and followed the little man down into the literal bowels of London.

We had kept the lanterns darkened in the street, but after Holmes had pulled the round metal lid closed over the top of us, we each widened the apertures, illuminating our surroundings. We were in an arched brick passage, about seven feet tall, and five or six feet wide. I could only imagine the incredible effort in terms of time, manpower, and materials that had gone into the building of these vast underground passages, less than a generation earlier. At the time, the streets along the routes would have been completely removed, dug down by removing dozens of feet in depth and thousands of cubic yards of ancient soil. It was uncertain how many archeological ruins, Roman and older, had been uncovered and destroyed in passing by the workmen, as there had been little time to properly excavate and study what was revealed, as the project could not stop and would not be slowed.

Millions of bricks and tons of Portland cement had been brought into the excavations as the underground branches of the sewer line were slowly extended and connected. While this had occurred long before I arrived in London, I had seen something similar in my own adult lifetime as the Underground was being installed in much the same way – entire streets burrowed to great depths, and brick-walled tunnels formed in place before being covered over once again. I could only imagine the incredible engineering involved in designing both systems, and the problems that would have occurred when the sanitary sewer and the Underground found themselves in conflict with one another – each with a required route, slope, and depth that might be blocked by the other.

The tunnel was warmer than the street, in the way that a cave maintains a constant temperature, but that isn't to say that it was pleasant. There was a fogginess to the air that held the lantern-light close to us, keeping it from extending too far in either direction. It was enough to see the nearby walls, where the cement between the bricks was somewhat swollen and crumbled, and rotten-looking. There was a dark running line on either wall about eye-high – clearly a high-water mark for those times when the rains flowed into the sewers and filled the pipes beyond their daily design capacity, accumulating more and more as they approached the river downstream, causing overflows at manholes and storm drains that even Sir Joseph's amazing plans couldn't overcome. I was relieved to recall that no rains were expected for several days, so that morning we only had to contend with the steady flow of filth beneath us, in a foot-wide channel molded into the sewer's floor. It was surprisingly clear and steady. Bertie saw me noticing it.

"It's early in the day, Doctor. Not much sewage in there yet. That's ground-water seeping into the pipes."

He saw my eyes dart to the right, where I'd sensed a movement. But it was only a rat.

"That's a good sign," explained our guide. "When they can live down here, so can we. No sour damp, you see."

I knew that he referred to the rotten-egg smell of Hydrogen Sulfide, which permeated sanitary sewers. It was detectable by the human olfactory system in the smallest amounts, mere parts per million, and deadly when present at just a bit more. As if reading my thoughts, Bertie tapped his nose. "This will keep us out of trouble. And we don't have far to go."

"Then lead on," said Holmes, surprisingly patient when considering that we weren't already in motion. "And carefully. We don't want to alert the person who will be seeking this ring, should he already be down here too."

"Willoughby," muttered Bertie.

"Possibly. You would know best."

Without responding further, Bertie set off.

It wasn't far, but I wouldn't want to repeat it, and I suppose it could have been worse. Conversation was at a minimum, but Bertie did softly call out the intersections we passed. We went back underneath Short's Gardens in the direction we'd arrived, and then turned south into a wider passage running down Endell Street. There was a slight but perceptible slope downward in the direction we were headed, enough to keep the sewage flowing steadily without pooling or ponding. The channel running along the center of the floor widened and deepened, and the fluid within became murkier, but the wide floor on either side remained relatively passable, apparently washed clean by the last rain event. Both in front and to our rear, we could occasionally hear the squeaks of the rats, but they gave us wide berth, and we progressed steadily. I was always trying to sense if there was any change in the toxicity of the atmosphere, but mostly it was just a cold dampness that gave the back of one's throat a rawish feeling.

When we passed underneath manholes with their lids vented by small holes, the temperature would lower slightly, and the air seemed a bit more fresh, although that may have been my imagination. Bertie noted when we crossed the intersections of Betteron and Castle Streets, and then he laughed when the air became noticeably more unpleasant soon after. It wasn't an increase in the deadly Hydrogen Sulfide. Rather, it was a thick yeasty smell that made me want to scrape my tongue against my teeth.

"It's from the brewery just west on Long Street, at The Elms." He nodded at the flow in a floor trough joining the main channel from that direction, its contents more of a thick sludge. "Always a bit chewy. Fancy a pint, Doctor?"

He gave one of his elven laughs, but then, when he saw Holmes's pursed lips, he fell silent.

Within just a hundred yards or so, we reached a wide spot in the tunnel. It seemed as if some of the bricks were newer than what we had previously seen. "They did some work here to accommodate the Opera House," said Bertie, nodding to one side. Then he stepped to the opposite of the tunnel. "But this is what we've come for."

Holmes frowned. "I had hoped to stop and reconnoiter before we arrived," he said softly, "to make sure we aren't being watched, or to see if there were any footmarks nearby."

"I'll see," said Bertie, skipping ahead down the tunnel. He was back in a short moment. "No one down there, and no place to hide. The floor is clean – as much as it can be, at any rate. No fresh footmarks. We can do our business and be away." He stuck out a hand. "The ring, please – unless you want to place it yourself."

Holmes reached into his pocket. "You are welcome to it."

Bertie took a couple of steps to one side of the tunnel where a six-inch pipe, possibly of iron but quite tuberculated and rough-looking, jutted out of the brick-work. It had been mortared in at some point, but now there were gaps around it, and there was a small amount of clear liquid running out of the wall below the pipe and down to the floor below – more of the groundwater, I assumed, although I couldn't be certain.

A wire basket of about one cubic foot was affixed to the pipe by a thick corroded wire, so that the flow would empty there. It was a most inefficient and disgusting arrangement, but clearly one that worked, as the toshers relied it on as a labor-saving device, allowing them to retrieve all sorts of treasures that otherwise might be lost, carried away along the floor channel.

The basket was half-full, and I wrinkled my nose in disgust. Bertie placed the ring on it, message-side up, and stepped back. "Just as I found it – on top and winking in my light."

"Which means, as you said, that it was sent down the pipe not long before," added Holmes, "with the near certainty that whomever did so is still, even now, under arrest and located in one of the cells above us." He looked farther down the tunnel, as if concerned that someone might be approaching at any moment. "Time to go, Bertie. Watson and I must speak with someone upstairs."

Bertie led us thirty or forty feet onward in the downhill direction in which we'd already been heading, and then took a sharp right turn into a smaller shaft, now only about six feet in height. Leaning down to avoid brushing the ceiling, I congratulated myself upon having stayed essentially clean throughout this trip, while recalling the time in autumn 1888 when pursuit of one of the Rippers had necessitated a race beneath the streets in tunnels so small that I could barely fit by turning sideways, scraping along tighter and tighter until I feared I'd be lost and forgotten down there forever.

We exited into a wider brick chamber with the choking odor of rotting vegetation, much of which was mounded along the sides of the floor at the walls. "Covent Garden Market?" asked Holmes, and Bertie acknowledged it. He led us to a rusty ladder which he mounted carefully, climbing eight or ten feet to another of the round lids that sealed away these Stygian passages. We followed, finding ourselves in the first light of dawn and under the curious but otherwise indifferent gazes of the various vendors setting up around us. Bertie replaced the metal lid and walked us back out to Bow Street. As we stood next to the corner of the Floral Hall, Holmes gave low instructions to our short companion, confirming that there were locations within the sewer where Bertie could observe the basket beneath the police station pipe discreetly.

"Once someone finds the ring," Holmes added, "surface and let them know in the police station across the way immediately. I'll arrange to be notified."

"But what if it's one of my mates finds it who is innocent – and not Willoughby?" asked Bertie. Seeing Holmes start to answer, he added, "There are three others besides me who 'own' that spot that might check at any time, finding the ring without being guilty at all. One of them might pick it up like they would any other trinket, not knowing about messages and criminal societies.

"I know that I'm maybe suspecting Willoughby too much," he continued hurriedly, "but I have a certain feeling about him. If one of us was supposed to retrieve the ring for this Sethian fellow, it will be him, you can be certain. He hasn't been around nearly as long, and has never made himself overly trustworthy.

"Who are to ones that you do trust?" queried Holmes.

Bertie frowned. "Jacob, Harry, and Silas. Willoughby is the wrong 'un for sure.

"I honor your instincts," said Holmes. "If Willoughby is the one to retrieve the ring, let him go and follow him, but if one of the others finds it, speak to them and have them put it back. In any case, time is short. Go back to your hiding place and watch. Meanwhile, Watson and I will confer with the police."

Walking the short uphill distance a dozen or so feet above the route we'd just taken, we crossed the street and entered the station, where we were initially met with the suspicious look from the officer on duty that our shabby appearance demanded. Although we'd both been careful not to intersect with any objectionable detritus within the sewer tunnels, we'd doubtless absorbed a certain amount of the unforgettable scent within our clothing, carrying it with us like an invisible but unmistakable fog. I could see the officer's nose wrinkling as he started to speak, and then he recognized us. A bit of merry twinkle flashed in his eyes for just an instant.

"I can only imagine, sirs, where you both spent last night – " He tapped his nose knowingly. " – but I have definite ideas." He sat up a bit straighter. "Inspector Bradstreet is on duty this morning."

"Excellent, Coggins," replied Holmes, "and I'm sure you'll rejoice with us that we aren't in worse shape. Shall you announce us?"

The officer waved a hand generally toward his right. "You know the way. And may I say that I hope your day leads you along better paths than wherever you've already been."

"Amen to that," I agreed, while Holmes simply nodded and then turned toward a doorway on the left.

We made our way down a stone-flagged passage and were nearing an office when a man in a peaked cap and frogged jacket strode out, carrying an empty mug. He looked at us in surprise, and then grinned when he recognized us. "Good to see you, gentlemen. I'm must about to have some tea." He wrinkled his nose. "I expect that you could use some too."

I knew that Holmes wanted to set things in motion immediately, but I spoke quickly and accepted Bradstreet's kind offer.

"Just step into my room here," he said, "and I'll be right back."

It was no different than the many times we'd visited there before: A small, office-like space, with a huge ledger upon the table, and a telephone projecting from the wall. In a moment the big inspector had returned, carrying three mugs in his sizable hands. Placing one before each of us, he sat down at his desk with the third.

"What can I do for you, gentlemen?"

"May I see your list of prisoners currently on hand?"

Bradstreet knew of old that Holmes wouldn't be wasting his time, so he silently turned 'round the ledger in front of my friend. "The bottom six names," added the inspector.

Holmes only took a few seconds to glance along the list, and then he nodded, tapping a finger underneath one name for my attention. I leaned forward. *Brendon Hanover*. I nodded. While the other five names, all unknown to me, might be our man, their various petty crimes, along with notations of their shabby criminal history, indicated that they were not the influential man that we sought. Hanover, however, was well-known to anyone well-up on London society, and he fit with what I would have required if picking a member – perhaps even a leader – of The True Knights of Seth.

In his mid-thirties, he was the second son of a North-country textiles magnate and his American dowry wife. There was none of the idea on the part of Brendon Hanover's old father that only first sons gained the benefit of the family wealth – he would have happily made use of Brendon's innate cleverness and brutal tenaciousness had the young man gone along with the plan. But the son wanted no part of his father's operations, instead moving to London more than ten years before and then making himself over into someone completely different. He worked hard and created a successful law practice, involving himself in a number of controversial suits that steadily increased his fame. He was initially willing to take either side of a question, alternately being praised and then burned in effigy, but gradually his emphasis shifted toward an antipathy toward the establishment of his forebears. In the meantime, his hard work during the day was matched by how aggressively he pursued a social life at night – albeit with an almost palpable anger toward those with whom he associated. He went amongst the others of his age and position at dinner parties and the usual clubs, but his attitude was always truculent, as is challenging those with whom he associated, slyly reminding them that their existence was without purpose.

"And how did Mr. Hanover end up in your cells?" queried Holmes.

"The usual story – he was someplace where he didn't need to be. Specifically, a vicious brawl that erupted at the Tankerville Club after a cheating accusation. He wouldn't have been involved, but he made the mistake of being intoxicated and attacking an officer when he otherwise would have been ignored. The officer's injuries aren't life-threatening, but bad enough that Hanover won't be released anytime soon, in spite of his influence. He only became more belligerent after he arrived here – we didn't know who he was at first – and he ranted that he had somewhere he had to be this morning. Such an attitude made us decide that he needed to learn a lesson."

"It's fortunate that you did so," said Holmes. "You may have saved the Prime Minister's life."

Bradstreet removed his cap, ran a hand through his hair, and widened his eyes. "Tell me a story, Mr. Holmes."

Holmes did so. Bradstreet already knew some about The True Knights, so it didn't take much to get him caught up on that aspect. "We know that it's their ring," continued Holmes, "and that they've committed murders and tried assassination in the past. Seeing Gladstone's name written with a specific date and time – tomorrow – where he'll be on public display seems to be an indicator of planned mayhem."

"But it's no secret where the Prime Minister will be for those who want to know," countered Bradstreet. "Why take the time to leave the note on the ring, and then go to such trouble to get the message out in such a way?"

"Perhaps The True Knights have a list of several targets," I answered. Holmes nodded and I continued. "Possibly Hanover feared that he would be sequestered here for so long that he couldn't get the word out before their window closed on choosing Gladstone. And if he's seen by his lawyer, perhaps he doesn't trust the man to relay the message in the proper manner."

"But if he could make it understood to someone that he'd drop a ring into the sewer," asked Bradstreet doggedly, "couldn't he have just mouthed the word 'Gladstone' to whoever was watching him?"

"One would think," agreed Holmes, "but no doubt there were other circumstances of which we aren't yet aware. In any case, the ring *was* dropped into the sewer for someone to specifically find, and we have a chance that we wouldn't have had otherwise."

The story of the ring in the sewer a few dozen feet beneath us was of greater interest to the inspector.

"Well, I never . . ." he muttered. "I feel foolish – of course we know they get rid of things that we haven't found – our searches can never be completely thorough. Evidence – money, jewelry, what have you – it goes down the drain. But I suppose we assumed at that point it was irretrievable. Of course we know of the toshers, but if they do find anything, it's useless to us as evidence – for how can we connect it up with a specific prisoner here in the cells? To think that those fellows are straining what leaves the building right below us . . . ." He shook his head. "I'd dearly love – No, I started to say that I'd like to go down and see it for myself, but I'm not sure that I really would after all. It would be too frustrating to see the evidence appear from the pipe, and yet know we couldn't link it to the criminal who disposed of it. The lawyers would have a field day if we tried."

He shifted in his chair. "You bought us some time by shifting the day from tomorrow to Sunday – that might confuse them. But if they already have plans for a specific event tomorrow, they might not be convinced – they might not change anything. They'll likely ignore whatever confusion your new message generates and still make the effort to kill Gladstone tomorrow morning."

"Which is why I added the instruction take the ring to the house in 44 Crutched Friars – so that we can insert ourselves into whatever is happening. You may not be aware, but I know that property is currently vacant, following the recent decampment of the Wyatt brothers."

"That was not known to me, but arrangements can be made immediately to keep it under additional observation." He rose and stepped to the telephone. Soon he was speaking to officers located near Fenchurch Street Station, giving precise instructions as to how the building should be discreetly watched.

"I must also get there as soon as I can," Holmes said, rising. "I'll stop by one of my hidey-holes along the way and further alter my appearance to meet whomever shows up with the retrieved ring – Willoughby, if Bertie is right. Then I can contrive to work my way further along the chain."

He turned to me. "Find Wiggins and some of the other Irregulars. Get them into place around Crutched Friars as soon as possible to supplement the police, and then wait nearby." He glanced at Bradstreet. "You should let the boys take the lead in following whomever arrives or leaves. They will be more subtle."

Bradstreet nodded with a rueful smile. "I learned that long ago."

With that we separated. Outside, Holmes and I walked quickly south until we reached the cabs starting to congregate near the Strand. There we each went our own way without comment, he heading east and me back to Baker Street. Later, I learned that not long after we departed from the police station, Bertie Tolliver emerged once again from the Covent Garden sewers and related to Bradstreet the intelligence that Willoughby, as anticipated, had just retrieved the ring. As Bertie watched unobserved from the nearby darkness, Willoughby unfolded the revised message as soon as he picked it up, read it, and then made his way topside before hurrying east on foot. It would be close, but Holmes would be at the meeting place, in disguise, in time to intercept him.

Meanwhile, I rounded up a dozen lads from around Baker Street and gave them all instructions before we climbed into a pair of four-wheelers. Like good soldiers, they understood what was required.

The streets were waking up, but our journey went quickly. Crutched Friars was a narrow bow-shaped lane located in The City, several hundred feet north of the Tower. I had the notion, based on something read long ago, that the original Crutched Friars had been a Catholic religious order, suppressed in the mid-1500's during Henry VIII's dissolution of the monasteries, when he and his cronies carried out their massive theft of properties belonging to the King's religious enemies. I had some sense that the friars had once held a connection with St. Olave's Church, still standing at the corner of Hart Street and Crutched Friars, and it was at that corner where I waited after sending the Irregulars scattering in different directions, in order to follow Willoughby in whichever direction he chose. They needed no further instructions from me as to how they should best carry out their business.

I was still in those same old clothes that I'd worn into the sewers, so I felt rather inconspicuous. Still, I didn't want to draw any more attention than necessary until I heard from Holmes. I found a place near the church door, which was still locked tight at that early hour, and leaned against the rather grimy stone work, as if I were someone in need of aid with nowhere else to go. I occasionally glanced to the west toward where No. 44 was located, pondering if it was the building located before or after a one-story enclosed brick passage stretching over the street, connecting first floors of the two structures on either side. It formed something of a low tunnel across the road, and I wondered how long ago it had been constructed. I watched idly as a dray cart barely passed underneath, the driver's body laid over to one side, and considered how often something was knocked against the lower side of the building by carelessness. I was still looking that way when I heard a shuffle coming up behind me. Turning, I found a shabby fellow, hunched in on himself as if he was hungry or sick. It was very convincing, but I recognized Holmes none-the-less.

"Has Willoughby been here yet?" I asked softly.

He nodded. "Been and just gone. I've set the Irregulars on him. He arrived five minutes ago. We talked for several minutes in the doorway of No. 44. I looked past him and saw you standing here at the church. By that point, I had another name from him – someone named Nichols. That's who he expected to find when he got here."

"Did he accept you as legitimate?"

"I believe so. There was some initial suspicion, but I was able to speak with enough knowledge of The True Knights that I think he was convinced."

"And did he confirm an assassination attempt on Gladstone?"

Holmes nodded. "He did. I sent him on his way with new and erroneous instructions – to tell The True Knights to postpone tomorrow's attempt in lieu of a better opportunity on Sunday – with more information coming soon."

"All of which likely seemed credible since it went along with the reference to Sunday that he independently found in the message on the ring which brought him here."

"Which he believes came from Hanover – who may be their 'Messiah'."

"Did he tell you where is he's headed to deliver the new instructions?"

"One of the streets behind St. Paul's – where he would have gone in the first place had I not inserted this detour into his plans." He pulled his coat a bit tighter, looking every inch like one of the countless unfortunates who have nothing and fill every corner of the capital. "We'd best hurry or Willoughby and the Irregulars will leave us behind."

He walked past me and around the corner into Hart Street. We hadn't gone far before a lad of eight or nine leaned out of a dark side street, beckoning us to follow and pointing west. Soon we were trailing some distance behind Willoughby while the lads surrounded him on all sides, hurrying down side streets to get ahead of him and anticipate any changes in direction, and shifting with his path like a murmuration of starlings. I could only hope and assume that Bradstreet's forces were also somewhere behind us.

"This is more of a practice exercise than anything," said Holmes softly, "as Willoughby provided me with the address. Still, we're prepared in case he decides to bolt in a different direction."

"Or if he lied," I added. Holmes nodded with a smile.

"Any sign of the police?" I asked after a moment, looking back over my shoulder.

"No, but Bradstreet is smart enough to fall back and let the Irregulars do the work."

We walked in silence for a few moments, and then Holmes told me what else Willoughby had said.

"He was a bit puzzled when he found me there – and also suspicious. 'I don't know you,' he said. 'I expected to find Nichols.' I replied something about there being more of us than he knew, and he nodded, as if that fit his expectations. Then I asked him if he had the note from Hanover, and that settled whatever doubts he still had. He nodded and handed it to me.

"'And his ring?' I asked. 'Give it to me.' He provided it, but with a bit of reluctance." Holmes patted his waistcoat pocket. "Then I asked which of the locations he'd thought was his destination before being diverted to Crutched Friars, and he volunteered 'the Watling Street house'.

I told him that there were other aspects of the affair which he didn't know about, and that the plans were changing. He accepted that too. 'I read the note,' he said. 'It looks like Sunday is now the day.'

"I nodded. 'You're the tosher, aren't you? We've had good reports of your service.'

"That pleased him, and I said, 'We saw the arrest at the club but lost track of what happened next. How did you know to retrieve the ring – and the message?'

"'Just luck. I happened to be near the Bow Street Station,' he answered, 'when the Maria stopped and they took Mr. Hanover out. He must have recognized me. He yelled out about being mistreated – I suppose to get my attention in case I hadn't already noticed him. "I'll take this to the Prime Minister if I have to!" he cried. Then, when he saw me looking, he managed to point to his ring, and then down to the ground. It took me a minute to work out what he was telling me. Not long after that, I went down into the sewer to wait for the ring to appear. I checked back several times through the night, and finally this morning I found where it and the message had finally come down the pipes.'"

"We were lucky," I said, "that Willoughby didn't carry out an all-night vigil by the pipe. Otherwise, Bertie never would have found the ring first, and we wouldn't have had this opportunity to derail their plans."

"Or even know about them," Holmes added. "It's almost enough to convince me that Fate occasionally takes a hand in nudging events toward a better outcome. After Willoughby told me his story, I pretended to think for a moment, and then said, 'You'd best get this message on to Watling Street,' and I gave him back the paper. 'In the meantime, I'll pass along the change of plan to some of the others.' He nodded as if that was what he'd expected to hear, and then we parted company."

"Do you have any notion as to who this 'Nichols' might be?"

"Perhaps. One of Hanover's regular confederates is Vincent Nichols. He's already been under some scrutiny for his rather heavy-handed methods at enforcing various illegalities. He comes from a good background, rather like Hanover, but he has fallen far from where he began. If it's he that's associated with The True Knights, I wouldn't be surprised in the least."

Throughout this conversation, we'd passed through Candlewick Ward, along Cannon Street, and then turned into Budge Row. We occasionally received reports from this or that Irregular who dropped back and informed us that Willoughby has proceeded without deviation toward St. Paul's, apparently completely unaware that he was being followed. It was near where Budge Row became Watling Street that little William

Styers joined us, relating that our quarry had turned into a dingy brick house up ahead on the right, between Bread Street and Friday Street.

"Very good," said Holmes. "Find Inspector Bradstreet – he and his officers should be coming along behind us – and lead him and his men to surround the house." He checked his watch. "Tell him that Doctor Watson and I will enter at five after nine." As the lad ran away, Holmes added, "That gives them fifteen minutes to find their places, which should be more than sufficient." Then he took the lead, walking closer to our destination. I had no worries that we might look suspicious, as there were quite a few others on the streets by that time of morning, and our disguises were good. Still, we didn't know whom we might encounter who was also headed for the same house.

Within moments the inspector had surreptitiously joined us. As we stood just past the public house, east of Bread Street, he listened with interest to Holmes's report, and then said, "I suppose we raid the place?"

"Possibly," said Holmes. "But first, Watson and I will go in and see what we can determine, and if enough of them are present to arrest now, or whether we should give them more rope and see how they scatter, to widen the net."

Bradstreet asked the question that also occurred to me. "Is that wise, Mr. Holmes? Even if you two aren't recognized, they'll be suspicious of sudden strangers in their midst – and if we let these go, we might lose track of some of them."

Holmes brushed off his concern. "Willoughby was quick enough to accept my involvement. I believe that this group is so widespread that there are multiple cells, each with limited knowledge of the others, so that they won't know who else is involved. Speaking with confidence about the little we know should be enough to dampen their suspicions.

"But," he added, "If you hear a window break, hurry into the building with all due speed through every entrance."

Then, without any further discussion, he nodded in my direction and we continued along Watling Street.

Chapter III

One of the Irregulars was crouching near a doorway, apparently engrossed in some game of his own devising involving gravels he'd gathered from the adjacent street. He ignored us completely, but his presence at that door alerted us as to which building was our destination. As we passed, he held up two fingers, signifying which floor. I glanced up but didn't see any lit windows. Perhaps the room in question was at the back.

Inside the narrow entryway, we were assailed by the strong odor of cooked cabbage, with something worse and old and foul underlying it – though not as foul as the sewers. I involuntarily cleared my throat and stayed with Holmes as he moved to a narrow stairway leading upward. He stepped carefully and silently, and I followed in his footsteps as well as I could, mostly managing to stay quiet. Within a moment, we were outside a closed door with a bar of light showing underneath. Through the door, I could hear the rumble of low conversation – several voices, sometimes talking over one another, but not loud enough to determine what was being said. Holmes glanced at me and I patted my coat pocket, where my service revolver rested. He nodded, and then he knocked twice, sharply, and opened the unlocked door. He boldly stepped inside, and I followed closely.

I immediately saw that we had entered very deep water.

It was a small apartment with four featureless walls. Opposite the door in which we stood was another, possibly leading to a bedroom, or perhaps simply a closet. The space was empty of any pleasantries whatsoever. There were a dozen rickety chairs of various ages and styles, and one bare table in the center. All of the chairs were circled around it, facing two men who stood there, one of them possibly Willoughby and the other Nichols. Each of the chairs facing them was occupied, and there were just as many men who were standing behind them, pressed against one another and the surrounding walls.

The man on the right had obviously been speaking when we entered. He was in his mid-thirties, tall and thin, with stylish dark hair. He was well dressed – quite incongruous for the setting in which we found him. His voice held a sneer, and he spoke in a tone that betrayed more education and advantages than most of the other men in the room had ever known. He glared at us, and his hostility seemed to be matched by the looks from the other two-dozen figures ranged around him. There was danger here, and I wondered if Holmes would have any chance to spin his tale for them before violence erupted.

Remembering Holmes's instruction to Bradstreet about how the police would be summoned when needed, I muttered with despair, "There isn't a window."

"Indeed," was Holmes's barely audible reply. Then he boldly stepped forward. "Has Willoughby told you about this morning's set-back?"

"Who are you?" growled one of the standing men, while the man who had been speaking looked Holmes up and down.

"That's him," interjected the man beside him – presumably Willoughby. "The man in Crutched Friars. He said he was going to tell the others – not that he was coming here."

"Do you refer to Hanover's arrest?" asked the other man, ignoring Willoughby. "That shouldn't have changed anything," he said. "Do you have further information as to why he's delayed the event until Sunday?"

"I do," said Holmes. "He managed to speak to me when we were both in the police van after being arrested."

The man looked at Willoughby. "Was he with Hanover when you were outside the Bow Street Station?"

Willoughby shrugged. "Might have been. I was looking at Hanover after he raised his voice to see what he wanted."

"They turned me loose early," Holmes explained, diverting the subject away from Willoughby's identification. "Hanover might have been free by now, too, if he'd kept his temper. He'll be lucky to be out by next week. But he told me to get along to Crutch's Friar and wait for Willoughby."

"Now that doesn't make any sense," said the man, the sneer now shadowing his dark features. "Willoughby was just telling us about his unexpected detour, and I can't see that it made any difference to go all the way there, just to come back here. Why would Hanover send him there to meet you, for no apparent reason except to go there, when you already knew all about it? And why would he go to the trouble of putting a message on his ring if you were with him at the station? He could have simply told you about the change of schedule. Willoughby, did you tell this man anything when you got there?"

"Not a thing. He was expecting me, and seemed like he already knew what's what."

"And then he shows up here. He likely followed you." The man moved around the table and took a step closer to us. "I'm not like the rest of these men," he said. Was there just a shade of contempt in the way he said *men*? "I've made the effort to study those who might oppose us. I expected a better disguise from someone of your reputation – *Mr. Holmes.*"

There was a shuffling amongst the two-dozen True Knights who filled the room. Some might have been familiar with Holmes's name, while others simply knew that the man challenging us was becoming more hostile, and they took their cue from him.

"And you would be Nichols, I suppose," said Holmes. The man raised an eyebrow but didn't provide any confirmation. "Hanover informed us how to find you when he made his full confession last night."

The man looked at Willoughby. "Did you tell him my name?"

Willoughby chewed his lip. "I suppose I did."

Nichols looked back at us. "Not very clever, Mr. Holmes. Our Messiah would never confess anything."

413

Holmes took a step forward. There was now a low grumble from the assembled Sethians.

"Is this the lot of you, then?" He gestured toward the men. Those who had been seated were now standing. They seemed to take up more space than a moment before. Apparently The True Knights of Seth recruited from the laboring classes, as these were big men – those who labored. They could do a great deal of damage before they were stopped.

"Not entirely. These are our loyal soldiers." The sneering man looked at the crowd. Their anger was palpable. They likely didn't understand what was happening, but they knew enough to recognize enemies in their midst. "There are more than enough of them, I'm thinking – even if Dr. Watson pulls out that gun he's fondling in his coat pocket."

"And there are no more or you hiding in the other room?" asked Holmes, suddenly taking a few steps forward, into and through the midst of the crowded enemies like Daniel marching into the lions' den.

I tensed, ready to shoot the first one who made a threatening move toward my friend, but they seemed too surprised by his action to respond. Several even stepped aside, the Red Sea parting around Holmes as he passed through the taller and bulkier men. He reached the door on the opposite wall without hindrance and threw it open, revealing a darkened room beyond – but not so dark that there wasn't a window. He disappeared within and no one seemed inclined to follow, as perhaps they knew that he had nowhere beyond to go.

Immediately there was the sound of breaking glass, followed by the door to the far room slamming shut with Holmes still inside and the lock turning with an audible snick.

Taking that as my cue, I backed up through the still open door behind me, stepping into the hall and pulling the door shut. I had no way to lock it from my side, and as soon as I saw the knob start to turn, I shot into the wall beside it, only somewhat concerned whether the thick old plaster would stop the bullet, or if it would instead pass through and into one of the conspirators.

Another rattling of the doorknob brought another shot, this time aiming downward through the door. For certain that bullet passed through, and I heard a scream and knew that whomever had been at the door now had a wound in his foot or leg. I wondered how much further I would be able to discourage them, or if they had their own guns which they would begin to fire back in my direction. I only worried for seconds at most, however, before the sound of many rushing footsteps were ascending the stairs in my direction. Bradstreet was leading several dozen officers, and they swarmed past me, kicking in the door and flooding the room, their truncheons rising and falling faster than the eye could see, and the sound

414

of strong seasoned wood hitting criminal skulls pleasantly reminding me of the break of balls on a billiard table.

Over it all, I saw the door across the room open. Holmes stepped out, eyeing with satisfaction as the Sethians fell, one by one, in very quick succession. Nichols was edging through it, his escape route before him, when Holmes grabbed him, spun him around, and dropped him with a smart right cross. Then Bradstreet was blowing his whistle, and still more constables arrived, dragging their opponents upright and then downstairs, where they would be transported back to the Bow Street cells. Holmes took Bradstreet aside and had a quick word, and then the inspector hurried out to speak with the officers in charge of the police vehicles. It was over in minutes, and in the street below, those who lived in the neighborhood watched in amazement as so many criminals were hauled away in haste. In moments, they were gone as if they it had all been a dream. Only a single growler was left for us, waiting in front of the building.

Meanwhile, Holmes also dismissed the Irregulars, who had gathered on the pavement to watch with amusement as the damaged Sethians were loaded unceremoniously into the Marias. Holmes instructed Wiggins, the head of the Irregulars, to stop by Baker Street that evening for payment. Then he and I, along with Bradstreet, were left standing on the pavement as the prisoners departed and the curious neighbors dispersed, whispering amongst themselves.

"Nichols let slip that they consider Hanover to be their 'Messiah'," Holmes explained.

"So this should mostly take care of them," commented Bradstreet.

"Possibly . . . ." said Holmes.

"But you aren't certain," added the inspector. "That's why you had me make sure that when the arrested men get to the station, no one lets Hanover know what's happened."

"That, and Nichols implied the men you just arrested were but foot soldiers. I hope that Hanover might share what else has been planned."

"He won't talk," Bradstreet pointed out.

"He will if he thinks he's been turned loose."

That statement was met with silence for a moment. Then I said, "That may be, but he might recognize you, Holmes. Nichols did, in spite of your disguise. They seem to have been warned that you would one day be on their trail."

"Exactly," replied Holmes. "Therefore, when Hanover is released, I'll follow behind him to make sure he doesn't escape the net. It will be up to you, Watson, to gain his trust and find out if they have any other plans – things that only their 'Messiah' would know."

Bradstreet looked at me to see my reaction. I could only recall all the times that Holmes had commented that my forthright nature prevented me from convincingly prevaricating, or how he had withheld information from me so that I might not inadvertently reveal something before it suited his plans. Now, it seemed as if he were putting a lot of unexpected faith in my acting abilities.

"Just be yourself," he said, sensing my doubts. "The True Knights are obviously made up of men from all walks of life. The worst that can happen is that he knows each and every member, and he's never heard of you. However, I suspect that as the 'Messiah', he regularly delegates many of his affairs, including interactions with the riff-raff. And you'll have this to convince him of your legitimacy . . . ." He held up the Sethian ring.

"That's Hanover's own ring," I said. "What if he recognizes it?"

"Improvise. If he doesn't recognize it, all is well. If he does, tell him you retrieved it from your friend Willoughby. In any case, offer to take him to an emergency conference with Nichols. Head for Baker Street. When we decide to re-arrest him, it will be on home ground, and Bradstreet will have men waiting for us there."

"And what am I supposed to find out from this 'Messiah'?"

"Whatever you can. Their plans. Other members. Who else is in their sights. Timetables." He shrugged. "Or nothing at all. Do your best."

I nodded. "Why not?"

Bradstreet laughed. "Why not, indeed?"

Chapter IV

I was back at the corner of the Floral Hall, where we'd stood only hours before. Holmes had looked at my old clothing and decided that I would do. Now I simply waited for Brendon Hanover to be released. He would be accompanied to the street by Constable Giles Bates, an old acquaintance. After that it would be up to me.

Holmes was somewhere nearby, but – of course – he would only be seen when he wished to be.

I'd waited no more than five minutes, keeping back toward the building and out of the way of the hurrying pedestrians, when I saw Bates and another man exit the station. With no more than a word or two, the constable turned and went back inside. Hanover hunched his coat higher around his shoulders, looked up and down the street, and set off toward the Strand.

I crossed the street, intersecting with his path near a fire hydrant. As I approached, I made a low "*Hsstt!*" sound through my teeth, catching his attention. He stopped and tightened defensively – understandable at any time when a fast-striding stranger approaches, but more so when one has just been released from the Bow Street cells.

I maintained eye contact but raised a hand peacefully. Then, when I was within a couple of feet, I turned it so that he could see my palm, with the ring tightly on my finger, and rotated to that the sigil of The True Knights was visible to him. A curious frown settled on his face. He didn't yet relax, but I was allowed to approach.

"Nichols sent me," I said softly, allowing my voice to settle into the Scottish burr of my youth. "There are complications."

"Complications?" he asked. His voice, even in a near-whisper, was a rich baritone, and I could see that he would be a compelling and influential speaker. He wasn't as tall as I'd expected, being rather compact and athletic. His features were strong, with intelligent light-colored eyes under dark heavy brows and a high forehead, and his mouth was tight and tense. However, I could see a number of laugh lines, showing that when he was in the mood, he would appear to be charming and unthreatening.

I nodded. "Gladstone's schedule has changed. The next time we'll have a chance is Sunday."

My response was unplanned, as Holmes and I hadn't discussed what I would say. I only sensed that it must not be too outrageous – and in any case, it didn't matter what I conveyed, as Hanover would be re-arrested in the near future. I only needed to convince him to speak about any plans that might be in the offing, and with any luck reveal more about these modern Sethians.

"Your message was found in the sewer as you intended," I added. "The tosher took it to Watling Street. I'm supposed to convey you to Nichols the minute you're released."

"Where at? Watling Street, or the Lambeth house?"

"Neither. There's a fellow with more information – a clerk who works in Gladstone's office. We're supposed to speak with him at a coffee shop in Portman Mansions."

He nodded. I was thinking that perhaps this didn't seem too unexpected to him after all. Then he said, "Tell me which one."

I shook my head. "I'm supposed to bring you," I responded, my mind racing to think of a reason why that would be.

"Who are you?" he said, a new suspicious tone in his voice.

"Roylott," I said, with the first name that popped into my head. "Grimesby Roylott." I thought about elaborating – saying that I'd recently moved to London from Stoke Moran on the western border of Surrey, or that I'd formerly been a doctor in India. But remembering Holmes's idea that liars often spoil their game by simply attempting to fill awkward silences, I held my tongue. Fortunately that worked. Hanover nodded. "Nichols told me that he'd been recruiting. Find us a cab."

A hansom had been moving slowly down the street, and I raised a hand to attract the driver's attention. I directed him to the coffee shop in Portman Mansions, and within minutes we were in motion, passing through several small streets and lanes until we were moving steadily north along Charing Cross Road.

"This new information," said Hanover. "Is it certain?"

"As much as can be at this point," I answered. "When Nichols got word, he called off tomorrow's sortie – the information in your message was no longer valid."

"It isn't up to Nichols to make those decisions," he said, clearly irritated.

"That's not the way I heard it," I said, suddenly seeing a way to rattle him a bit. "From what I was given to understand when it was arranged for my organization to work with you people, he's the brains, and you're the figurehead – convincing these ignorant toadies of yours that you're some kind of new Jesus."

His color darkened, and I continued. "I was at Watling Street today for the meeting. Nichols made it clear that he's doing the planning – which is probably a good thing, since otherwise we would have been trying to kill Gladstone tomorrow and he would have been two-hundred miles away."

"Nichols doesn't *plan* anything," he said tightly, his voice low and dangerous. "He doesn't *decide* anything. *I* do. It's my right – *I'm* the one with the divine gift. Who did you say you were?" he suddenly asked, his eyes refocusing sharply in my direction, new suspicion on his face.

"Grimesby Roylott. So if you're still the leader," I pressed, "then whose fault was it that the Lord Mayor is still alive? Nichols put that failure down to you. He was pretty clear about how it happened, and he promised that it won't happen again. For my people to be involved, it had better not."

By now we were well along Oxford Street, and moving surprisingly fast. It wouldn't be long before we turned north into Orchard Street.

"The Lord Mayor only escaped because of a chance accident. My plan would have worked. It *should* have worked!"

I shook my head. "I spent time in Afghanistan," I said, goading him further. "I was at Maiwand. I saw what happens when a plan is too simple – when the person making the plan is too inexperienced to account for contingencies and happenstance and the unexpected. It nearly got me killed. Then Nichols said that you only think two-dimensionally – that you can't plan a campaign with the bigger picture in mind. He promised that when he's running things, it will be different." I looked him up and down, as if judging him and not liking what I saw. "That's what we signed on for."

Hanover was becoming more and more angry as I prodded him, and I was grateful that he wouldn't have been released by the police with any weapons in his possession. Still, his fists were clenched and his knuckles had turned white, and I saw the flickers of madness in his eyes. This was more than him embracing revolutionary ideas and taking on the mantle of omnipotence simply as a display to control his gullible followers – I was beginning to understand that he truly believed that he was a Messiah.

"Nichols went over your plan to kill the Prime Minister," I said. "Today in Watling Street, for all of us. And then he showed his own in comparison. Even those brutes you've recruited realized that his is far better. But I wouldn't worry any – he'll keep you around to raise funds. Can't have enough of those."

"Nichols knows *nothing*!" he hissed. "He has no *vision*!"

"I'd say that he sees exactly what needs to be done," I responded. "He told us what he has planned after the Prime Minister – one of them after another, without end. His plan – "

"*His plan?*" he shrieked, and I sensed that he was suddenly at a breaking point. "He knew nothing until I allowed him to enter into my councils – "

"Speaking of that," I interrupted. "It seems as if your organization is a bit thinner than I was led to believe. You and Nichols? Who else, besides those brutes in Watling Street?"

"Raymond Wright," he snarled. "And John Devereaux of the Foreign Office, and Colin Fraser as well. They have supported me from the beginning."

Excellent, I thought. And concerning as well. Hanover had just named a prominent banker, a Foreign Office Under-Secretary, and a cabinet secretary.

"But Nichols' plan – " I prodded.

"What does someone like him know of a *plan*? *I* was the one bold enough to suggest killing Gladstone. *I* was the one who understood how the Royal Family must be removed, and it was *me* who comprehended the way to send them to Hell where they belong! Nichols is *nothing* – Without me, he would already be dead. Without *me* – !" And then he turned, raising his hands and lunging in my direction, grabbing my coat and trying to shake me, his rage now out of control.

With a lurch the cab turned out of the traffic and stopped abruptly. The driver jumped down and then reached up, pulling apart the low front doors holding us inside. He grabbed Hanover's collar and, with a great heave, pulled the man off me, propelling him out and backwards onto the pavement, where he landed heavily and with a cry.

"I trust that you're uninjured," said Sherlock Holmes, who had been our driver.

"I didn't recognize you," I grunted, climbing out and straightening my clothes. "This was a better plan than you following along behind us."

As I spoke, several other hansoms and growlers pulled to a stop around us, and several policemen, including Inspector Bradstreet, disembarked, solely for the purpose of taking Hanover back into custody.

"Could you hear?" I asked Holmes as Bradstreet joined us.

"For the most part. Your testimony will be more effective than mine."

I shook my head. "I doubt that he will stand trial. I believe the man is teetering on the edge of insanity."

"Well, you can testify at Nichols' trial then. That was rather brilliant, by the way – nudging him with increasing evidence that his grip on The True Knights was evaporating, along with betrayal by his trusted lieutenant."

I started to sarcastically suggest that perhaps acting was in my future, but Bradstreet spoke first.

"This was all a bit too coincidental for my liking," he said. "If Hanover hadn't gotten himself arrested last night, and if your tosher hadn't found that ring, their plans might have been successful."

Holmes started to speak, but I interrupted. "Holmes spoke earlier of Fate taking a hand and nudging things in the right direction. Perhaps that's sometimes the best we can hope for."

"I would prefer something a bit more definite," commented the policeman.

Holmes nodded. "As would I. But at least we can be prepared to take advantage of opportunities when they present themselves – and find ways to be more vigilant as well. We can but try."

He looked up the street toward Mrs. Brett's coffee shop, long a favorite location. "Watson, I believe that before your improvisation with Mr. Hanover began – " He glanced toward the man, now handcuffed and raving as he was placed into one of the police vehicles. " – you directed me to the coffee shop in Portman Mansions. Shall we continue that way and have some breakfast?" He turned to Bradstreet. "Inspector, if one of your men could return the cab to its owner – he'll be waiting in Bow Street – it would be our pleasure if you would join us."

Bradstreet smiled. "That would suit me down to the ground."

It suited me as well, and soon the hot coffee was insulating us from the cold late-November morning. Yet even as we sat there, I could still smell the slightest hints of the Bow Street sewers hanging in my old garments, and I looked forward to returning home in nearby Baker Street and finding a chance of clothes.

NOTE

*   For more about Holmes's first meeting with Sir Joseph Bazalgette, see "The Civil Engineer's Discovery" in *The Collected Papers of Sherlock Holmes – Volume III* (MX Publishing 2021) or *Sherlock Holmes: Stranger Than Truth* (Belanger Books 2021)

The Outpost Incident

For Sherlock Holmes, the years between 1903 and 1914 will always be something of a mystery, even to me. While I saw him during that time a great deal more often than I've implied, many of his investigations – if they can even be called something as simple or straight-forward as that – were carried out in solitude, and often at great personal peril.

"As well as can be expected," Holmes would say when he and I would cross paths and I would ask how he was – sometimes with great regularity, but also following long gaps where he had been alone on some dangerous task or perilous journey.

"You know better than most," he would explain on other occasions when I would ask why he was working so hard, "that time is running out. We shall do what we can, and we can but try."

In October 1903, for reasons both personal and professional, Holmes had announced his departure from London for Sussex, and the supposed retired life of a reclusive apiarist. This was not entirely unplanned, for just a year or so before Holmes had acquired a small farm – or "villa" as he liked to call it – set immediately north of and below the slope which leads up to the mighty cliff of Beachy Head. This small site, only a few acres enclosed by a wall of local stone, and with a fine house and nearby outbuilding of nearly the same size, suited him perfectly.

He had long before discovered a fascination with bees that appealed to the side of him that enjoyed scientific study. It was a natural progression from those long hours when he found relaxation hunched in a corner of our old Baker Street rooms, working out chemical reactions, sometimes repeating an experiment that had already been well documented just for the systematic comfort of the process, while allowing his great mind to find distraction in orderliness and expected repetition.

But Holmes had never truly planned to fully become the character of the hermit bee-keeper that he played. With my help, and that of some of his most trusted London associates, the word was spread that Mr. Sherlock Holmes had retired. This, in truth, was not the case.

"We wish for you to resume publication of your stories in *The Strand*," Mycroft Holmes had told me one morning, not long before Holmes left for Sussex.

"'We'?" I had asked. "Who is the 'We' to whom you refer?"

"Mycroft is referring to himself," answered Holmes with a smile, "although his use of 'We' is less in the royal sense, and more to simply give the impression that blame for this idea can be spread to additional people."

"It's true that I conceived the notion," Mycroft interjected, "but others with whom I've discussed it have been in accord."

Before I could ask, Holmes posed the question forefront in my mind. "And what purpose would this serve?"

"An extra decoration on top of the cake," answered Mycroft. "It will be another way for us to spread the word that you are retiring." He went on to explain that a line dropped here or there into my narratives would be quite effective for those in the various embassies who would be combing through the stories to read between the lines. "For example, Doctor, you might casually mention that my brother's restriction on publishing the stories has been lifted, intriguing those who are reading it. 'Why has it been lifted?' will be asked. Later, you might mention that Sherlock is no longer in actual professional practice – that he has definitely retired from London and betaken himself to study and bee-farming on the Sussex Downs. You can give the impression that he's become a hermit, and that notoriety has become hateful to him, and he has peremptorily requested that his wishes in the matter of his privacy and seclusion should be strictly observed. It can only help further the impression that he's ensconced in Sussex, rusticating permanently on his little plot until such time as he shuffles off."

Some time later, Holmes had offered his own request that I enact Mycroft's plan.

"You must help me once again, old friend," he'd said. "Resume publishing your stories in *The Strand* – and note that you now have permission to do so. Make them understand that I have *retired*."

This had all become necessary, for Holmes and his brother Mycroft, along with what assistance I could provide, had long labored to prevent, or at least delay, the upcoming European War which was becoming ever more certain. A tangled knot of treaties, both known and unknown, was slowly tightening and strangling the diplomatic obligations of the various countries – the major players, and those less-significant remora whose interests were served by alignments with them. Additionally, rising conflicts between monarchies and other forms of government, as well as outlying and unworkable movements based on repressive beliefs – Socialism, Nihilism, and so on – poured fuel on the as-yet unlit bonfire. A constant need for raw materials to feed the starving industrial might of the different nations led to escalating colonial conflicts and horrors on far-away patches of ground. And finally, family entanglements extending like twisted roots from the source of our late Queen, and particularly in the form of her jealous and aggressive grandson the Kaiser, meant that a war was inevitable.

And yet, the Holmes brothers – and myself as well – did all that we could to stop it. In dozens of instances that I know of, both before and after Holmes's supposed retirement, and many more that will never be shared with me, Sherlock and Mycroft Holmes derailed this or that plan that sought to advance and even accelerate the plunge into conflict. Some of these plots were promoted by Continental governments, and others by private individuals – rich men who cared nothing for humanity, but simply saw opportunity in conflict. Holmes's long-ago foe Professor Moriarty had an anarchistic bend and a hatred for his homeland that defined him as a criminal, and he was more than happy to sell his talents to those who would foment conflict. Other newer players with the same tendencies were always revealing themselves – Ennesfred Kroll, for instance, whose dangerous scheme in Yorkshire in 1896 might have gone undiscovered and unchecked without Holmes's perception of the greater pattern.

Throughout that period from 1903 to 1914, Holmes did indeed spend time at his home near Birling Gap – where he lives to this day, I might add. (Rumors of his death constantly surface, but he will outlive us all.) However, he was able to slip away as needed, presenting himself here and there to accomplish some otherwise impossible task. This included one of his greatest deceptions, when he played the part of Altamont, the disaffected Irish radical, from 1912 until the very beginning days of the War. Even then, he managed to get home often enough so that *Sherlock Holmes* was seen in Sussex, and certainly having no connection with *Altamont*, last seen in Chicago or Dublin or New York, all the while convincing his enemies that he was no longer a relevant factor that should trouble them.

The case of which I write now occurred in those shadowy years leading up to the Great War, between Holmes's retirement and when he became Altamont. The terrible conflict was still far on the horizon, as one perceives distant thunder on a still-sunny day. And yet, Sherlock and Mycroft Holmes saw threads in these particular events which could be traced directly to the tapestry being weaved by Ares himself . . . .

In a year that must be masked – even in these notes that are to be locked away for at least a century – Holmes and I found ourselves quite far from home. In the months leading up to our journey, Holmes had been tasked with carrying out a greater number of his brother's errands, much in the same way he had done during that period from 1891 to 1894 when the world – and even I myself – had believed him to be dead. During those three years, he had hurried from one side of the globe and back again on ever-more complex missions. This current trip, planned for the United States, and this time with my participation at Holmes's invitation, had initially seemed simple enough, and certainly much more linear in nature. However, after we had successfully shored up British interests in certain American quarters, we then received word that there was further work to do in Canada. We moved north, and then from east to west. At that point, it only made sense to accept Mycroft's next assignment, and so we crossed the ocean to Japan. I was truly beginning to wonder if I would ever get back home.

As we traveled, the nature of our missions became more grim – sliding from mere diplomatic representation and behind-the-scenes maneuvering to tasks of greater weight with life-and-death consequences.

Holmes observed my growing concern. "You have often asked me about those years from '91 to '94," he said, "when I was acting as Mycroft's agent. The world has changed since then in many ways, but much is still the same. My skills are as useful in this realm as they were as a consulting detective, but the personal tolls upon one's ethics can be much more . . . challenging. But you were a soldier once, Watson, as well as being a doctor, so you understand the conflicting pull of both responsibilities. Right now we are soldiers, although working in secrecy, and as such we must be prepared to act accordingly."

I understood his words, but I wasn't sure that I was comfortable with them.

While in Japan, Holmes was able to clear up certain questions related to a long-ago investigation which had been solved from his armchair in Baker Street. But then, since we were somewhat in the neighborhood – if a thousand miles could be considered "in the neighborhood" – we received instructions from Mycroft to proceed across the Sea of Othotsk, and specifically to a curious and rather spontaneous conference being held regarding future peace in the region, where we would be the sole representatives of British interests.

"Kamchatka?" I said while sipping *saki* in our Morioka hotel room. "I don't believe that I've ever heard of the place. What do you know of it?"

"Very little," said Holmes "I heard vague mentions of it in the early nineties when I was traveling in the East. An isolated peninsula north of Japan, almost completely uninhabited." He tapped a finger on Mycroft's latest wire. "Very rugged and remote. The Government is curious as to why a conference is being held at all, let alone in that Godforsaken spot. As Japan's ally, Mycroft feels that Britain should be represented, and he's managed to use up some owed goodwill to arrange for our invitations and transport."

Holmes's instructions were in code, and his follow-up questions to London extensive, running to a fortune in back-and-forth cables between the brothers. Soon after their telegraphic exchange commenced, Holmes explained what he'd learned so far. "There will be a Balkan leader touring the area who has increasing ties with the Russians. He has notions of mining in Kamchatka, and wants to consider a consortium that will involve both the Russians and the Japanese – a venture of 'good will' for them both to work in tandem following the brokering of their peace treaty by the Americans. He foresees markets in Asia, as transport back across Russia to Europe would be problematic. The fear is that the vast amount of raw materials suddenly coming out of Kamchatka might cause new tensions and unaccounted threats in a world already approaching a dangerous juncture."

When Holmes finally finished decoding the last of the cables, his mouth was a tight line. "I don't like it, Watson," he said, before giving me a wider outline of the matter, and the true reason for our attendance. After learning what we should expect, I had to agree with him that we had no business being there – but at that point, we were committed, and someone had to represent British interests. In any case, by then we were no longer the detective and the doctor of days gone by. Rather, we were agents of our government, a transition that that had happened in my case so gradually that I couldn't look back and pinpoint exactly when the demarcation had occurred.

Holmes showed me the final coded cable, and particularly the last line, which he translated for me: "*Imperative that this be successfully accomplished*," it said, before the single identifying letter that served as a signature, "*M*".

And so, after a bracing journey north, first by train to Hachinohe and then by ship, we found ourselves at a small insignificant compound located on the most-southern tip of the Kamchatka Peninsula. The stark beauty was unlike anything that I had ever seen. We were there in high summer, but even so there was a coldness to the air, so close to the Arctic Circle, and I could only imagine what the barren place must look like in winter. I was glad that we would be gone long before true cold weather hit – or so I hoped. So far, nothing else about that long globe-circling trip had gone exactly according to plan – from the numerous extensions to our original brief to the supposed straightforward tasks which we'd been expecting. I ruefully recalled when I had initially believed that Holmes and I would be spending just a few weeks in the United States – "*The best laid plans*" and all that rot.

426

"Where did they find the lumber to build it?" I asked as we finally arrived at our destination. It was morning, and Holmes and I were on deck as we approached the bleak shoreline. Over the past couple of days, our world had been the small ship that carried us from the northern tip of Japan and across the frigid sea for something near a thousand miles. We had dined with the captain and his officers, but they, knowing very little English, had been polite and on task – namely eating the plain but adequate food quickly before returning to their duties. Now, as we approached land, we could see the new-looking stone dock facility, constructed literally at the bottom edge of nowhere, and the single-story wooden structure located about one-hundred feet inland. It was a low and sturdy building, and in winter, I knew that it would likely be buried under drifts of snow before soon collapsing. It shined with newness, and had clearly been placed here for a sole purpose.

"More importantly," asked Holmes, "*why* did they build it? What purpose could it serve here, so far from anywhere?"

For those who will be looking for some explanation, I will disclose now that we never learned the true purpose of the place, or why it was situated so remotely. There was some talk that it was to be the first of many buildings, but it hadn't been properly constructed for true winter conditions. Others mentioned that the conference was held there as a good-faith effort, so that all involved would set foot on the ground being discussed, but that never made much sense. I understand that those who are regularly involved in these messy affairs become acclimated to regularly unresolved questions. In the end, the building was simply where this affair occurred, and its location was not the mystery or the problem. The Russians and their reasons are ever inscrutable, and it has been ever thus. To my knowledge, after the events of this narrative ended, nothing more was ever learned of the rugged and remote facility, and I wouldn't doubt that it has long-since vanished.

Our ship, the sturdy Japanese *Nisshin Maru*, maneuvered into place with much backing and filling and laboring of the steam engine, and we were soon brought ashore by a launch. Standing by the dock was a head-high sign consisting of a thick wooden post held upright by rocks and a nailed-on crosspiece – a board with the word аванпост burned into it. ("'*Outpost*'," Holmes translated for me softly.) A couple of sailors placed the limited luggage we'd brought on the ground beside us, as we would be leaving the rest of our things on board the ship. We'd packed just enough for the two days and nights that we'd be attending the remote conference.

In the distance, the *Nisshin Maru*'s engine rumbled again, and once the launch returned, the ship backed away to wait a mile or so off-shore until time to reclaim us and return to Japan. In the meantime, three men were walking toward us, down the slope from the lonely building. As they came closer, I could see that all were wearing Russian military uniforms – heavy winter clothing, in spite of temperatures that morning that felt to be in the fifties.

The largest Russian of the three introduced himself quite briefly and with a thick accent – "*I am Golubev.*" With a flick of his hand, he directed that the two other silent brutes, nearly as big as he, should take our bags. Then he gestured that we should follow him toward the building. Without waiting for acknowledgement or offering any comments, he turned and fell into step with his two lumbering Sherpas. Holmes glanced at me, his eyes amused, and conveying without words that once again the game was afoot. My expression, or so I hoped, was more along the lines of "Out of the frying pan, into the fire."

As we approached the building, the rough and very new construction became more apparent, with the smell of freshly cut lumber quite obvious. Nothing was done halfway, and yet, while the building would certainly be effective and weatherproof in the current conditions, I doubted that it would be of any use when winter arrived. It was too flat, and any significant snow would cave in the roof, which had insufficient pitch for it to slide off. However, this snug-to-the-ground construction would be good protection against winds, which I already felt were starting to pick up. Holmes had noted this as well, and he nodded. This building was most likely constructed *just* for this conference. It was most mysterious.

The direct route from dock to doorway was already a churned line of muck, rather slippery as the thawing ground released trapped water from seasons past. If any longer-term activities were planned here, a better arrangement would need to be constructed. Golubev, who had passed the two porters and made his way to the front of our line, reached the door, where some gravel had been thrown down. He stomped his feet, knocking mud from his boots, and stepped inside. We followed suit, and it was suddenly warm and comfortable enough, although the heat was not overwhelming. We would definitely need to remain in our heavier clothing.

After passing through a short dark entryway, we found ourselves in a large rectangular room, the longer dimension running from front to back. The floor was bare wood, with no rugs or carpets. For the most part, the lumber fit together well enough, but there were gaps, and one could see that the bare earth was only a few inches beneath the wood. As we spent time in the room, we would find that the smell of the damp soil just underneath the floor, made worse by rains which arrived later that day, gave the space the sense of being in a grim wooden cave.

428

The joists upon which the floorboards rested were spaced too far apart, so there was sagging and bouncing as one crossed the floor. We were lit by a number of kerosene lamps hanging from nails hammered in the low-hanging rafters. As we would soon learn, Golubev and his two soldiers refilled the lamps several times during our stay. They, and a couple of kitchen staff, appeared to be the only people there besides the conference attendees. There was no attic over the great room. Rather, it was just a dark open space underneath the low-pitched roof. As I considered it, yet again I doubted that the building would survive a single winter.

At one end was a great stone fireplace, and the mortar keeping it upright was new and white. Nearby were standing a great many coal buckets, and the fire was immediately the most pleasant part of the wide space. There were a number of mismatched chairs located around the fire, constructed purely for sitting and not lounging in comfort. There would be no relaxing in one of those with a book and a pleasant beverage to pass a cold evening.

A long table was near another wall, with a dozen or so chairs around it – all very functional. A door that we soon learned led to a kitchen was nearby, and another went into a hallway that extended through the farther half of the building, with bedrooms on either side.

Of more interest was a makeshift bar to the right side of the fireplace. While the two brutes carried our luggage down the hallway that led to the bedrooms, Golubev walked to the bar, the two of us behind him, where we were introduced to the two men standing there. The taller was another Russian who simply gave his name as Petrov. He was silent and surly, although he shook our hands firmly enough. The other was Ando, the Japanese representative. Like Petrov, he had a drink in his hand. There was no bartender, and Holmes and I busied ourselves in pouring whisky.

After making general conversation with the Japanese man for a moment about the cool weather and the remoteness of the location, Ando asked, "You arrived on the *Nisshin Maru*?" As we both nodded, he continued. "She is a good ship. My son served aboard her . . . ." His face darkened, and he suddenly glanced at the Russian. He took a sip of his drink, and fell silent. I didn't need to be Sherlock Holmes to perceive that something had happened to this son during the Russian-Japanese War of 1904 and '05. Petrov, who had said nothing to that point, said nothing still, not even looking up from whatever ruminations that were holding his attention focused upon his glass.

Golubev, who had been waiting nearby, rumbled, "We are waiting for the last representative to arrive. The other is asleep in his room. We will gather this evening. In the meantime, your time is your own. Lunch

429

will be in two hours. Please don't wander far. There are dangerous areas just inland behind the building – unexpected holes in the ground, and mires from which there is no escape." He gestured to Holmes and me. "Now you will see your rooms."

I knew little of Kamchatka then, that untouched wilderness of both beauty and danger, and just a bit more now. In truth, I really saw none of it. The coastline where we stayed was barren, and we would have had to journey some ways north along the twelve-hundred mile peninsula to view the notable volcanoes and mineral springs. We might have encountered some of the extensive flora and fauna had we ventured any distance from the building, but we did not. We had landed at the very bottom of the peninsula in a region called Cape Lapatka, and the sunshine that greeted us that morning was a rarity. By early afternoon, the regular rain and fog returned, and any explorations that Holmes and I might have planned, despite Golubev's warnings, were canceled in favor of spending time in the large room. And an unpleasant time it was. I was re-reading *Our Mutual Friend* by Dickens near the fire in one of the uncomfortable chairs, while Holmes sat close, his back to the fire and facing the wider room, smoking and pondering. Petrov and Golubev huddled in a pair of chairs along a far wall for most of the afternoon, their conversation rising and falling and completely unknowable, as I didn't speak Russian. Holmes understood some, but I couldn't tell if he was able to listen, or was instead ignoring them. Meanwhile Ando kept to his room – as did the other mysterious participant, who must have been weary indeed to sleep away the entire day. When I asked Golubev who he was, his guttural response was simply, "The Balkan."

Lunch was a poorly cooked roast beef and a few overdone vegetables. At least I was able to sample it early when it was freshly prepared and somewhat more edible, because we had it again for dinner, and by then it wasn't nearly as presentable. Four of us – Holmes, Petrov, Golubev, and myself, sat at the table without conversing. Afterwards, we returned to our previous spots, and I realized that it would be far too easy to sip whisky all day to alleviate the boredom. From that point, I limited my consumption.

Around four o'clock, Golubev abruptly stood and went outside. Petrov watched him go, and then settled back in his chair and dozed off. After passing some further time in silence, there was a scraping noise from the direction of the dock. Apparently another launch was docking and the final guest was arriving. Petrov awoke. A few minutes slid by, and then we heard approaching footsteps. The door opened to admit Golubev, followed by an Asian and one of the luggage-toting Russians.

430

Golubev paused to introduce the newcomer as Pakk. Our host, if that's what Golubev could be considered, further explained that the newcomer represented one of the mainland regions that was loosely aligned with the Russians. Pakk nodded at Golubev's introduction to each of us, and then he walked toward the hallway with the bedrooms as if he already knew the way.

Not long after, we were told that we would gather for dinner in an hour, if we wished to prepare. There was no conversation as we separated. Holmes and I had already held any necessary discussions, so there was nothing to do but stay alert.

That evening, we were still in the large room. The tedious day had transitioned somewhat into what was supposed to be a small reception. Ando had returned, now standing near Petrov beside the fire, each facing outward instead of toward one another. Nearby was Pakk, surveying both intently, as if he were attending a play and not wanting to miss out should anything occur.

Holmes and I also stood apart, each watching everything, but both certainly getting something different out of what we saw. After many years assisting in Holmes's investigations, I was no longer as helpless or useless as I had once been when we first met, but of course he would always observe more than I ever would see.

I was most interested in finally meeting the last member of the group to show himself, the man who had been resting unseen for the entire afternoon, for I had learned much about him in recent days by way of Mycroft Holmes's cables. He had apparently arrived before us, very early that morning with Petrov, Golubev, and the staff. Ando's ship had put him ashore soon after that, but it seems that by then the mysterious Balkan visitor who had arranged the meeting had already taken to his bed – too much drink on the crossing, according to Golubev.

Earlier, standing in the hallway leading to the bedrooms – ten of them, five on each side – I had tried to hear some sign of where the man was sleeping – if he was snoring, or murmuring in his dreams. But there was nothing. Now I was glancing at my watch, though time seemed to have no meaning in that remote location, when I heard heavy footsteps approaching from the hall.

And then he was among us.

My gaze revealed a large man, his gross appetites obvious upon first glance. Finally he was facing us in the person, the true reason for our visit to this lonely location: Adolph Trommel, the leader of a minor Balkan kingdom, and a man who had inherited a massive amount of wealth from his father. Despite his inept management of both his funds and his country, he was somehow still both rich and ruling. His own country had the tempting combination of natural resources and geography that were coveted by his Russian neighbors, and despite his own people's resistance to it, he had been aligning himself with the Great Bear over the last few years. During the war with Japan, he had arranged some sort of deal wherein these ties had grown ever stronger, and he had become and even wealthier man following the signing of their peace treaty.

As Trommel entered the room, what little conversation had been taking place fell to silence. If the big man noticed it at all, it didn't seem to bother him. As he loudly demanded a drink, setting Golubev into motion, I had a chance to study his costume – for that is the only way that it could be described.

For the reception, he had chosen a long red coat. The barrel-resembling torso was covered in gold braids that looped in repeated rows from top to bottom, across the chest side-to-side, and then under the arms. It had the curious illusion of amplifying Trommel's fattish build, making him look like a many-layered and unappetizing desert. There were fringed epaulettes at his much-padded shoulders, running to a high stiff collar that pushed up his bullfrog throat, causing it to nearly absorb and obscure the bump that was his weak chin. His graying yellow hair sharply contrasted his puffy red face, covered with broken veins. He wore his hair combed back and long in the Continental fashion, somewhat tucked behind his ears, but many strands were loose, some dropping greasily to his collar, or the thinner ones waving about his head like fumes as he moved. They only contributed to and enhanced his long-earned dissipated appearance.

From the little I knew, his background had no nobility in it, no bloodlines of notable honor or worth. His grandfather had been a coward who had fled Germany years before to avoid military service, and had then made the beginnings of his fortune running a brothel. Trommel's father Friedrich had increased it tremendously to the point where he was able to become the financial backbone of a small Balkan nation, his cancerous roots running in any direction that offered the least resistance, increasing his influence by blackmailing those that he couldn't buy outright until removing him was nearly impossible. His son, Adolph Trommel, had used his late father's money to stage a violent coup, overthrowing the legitimate government and installing himself as a dictator. He also controlled the press in his small part of the world, allowing his machinations to manipulate a gullible and ignorant public. After he'd put down his opposition, he'd then sought closer ties with the Russians, who in turn had gulled him into using his own money to their benefit – including whatever this odd project in Kamchatka turned out to be.

432

For most of the previous year, Trommel had been traveling, leaving his little kingdom in the hands of his two corrupt sons and conniving daughter while he was shuffled around by the Russians like their version of a celebrity. In our recent discussions as we prepared to meet the man, Holmes had wondered if Trommel would have a kingdom to return to after his children were finished with it. There was certainly no loyalty on their part, and a coup – bloody or otherwise – would not surprise anyone.

The ways of these people disgusted me, even as I tried to understand how such things could happen – how they could rise to positions of power. It almost made one long for a simpler world, wherein modern communications and illusory economic theories couldn't be used so easily by bad men to become rich from the terrible human suffering that they would never personally see.

There was no need to gauge Holmes's reaction at seeing Trommel in person. We had learned a great deal about this man in Mycroft's wire, and nothing that we saw in person was unexpected.

After taking the glass, Trommel grabbed at Golubev's arm as he started to move away. Then, while holding him in place, the fat man tipped up the liquid in his glass and swallowed it in one swinish gulp before holding it out to be refilled. Golubev reached for the bottle and did so, adding more than before for this round. This was repeated an astonishing four times before Trommel took a final replenishment, this time to sip, and finally freeing Golubev. Only then did Trommel look around, blinking through his puffy eyes. He stepped toward the cluster of guests.

The fat man faced Petrov squarely, offering his hand, which the Russian ignored. As I wondered why, Holmes whispered, "That will cut him." I hadn't been aware he'd stepped closer. "Trommel values nothing more than Russian esteem."

"What sort of Hell is this place?" bellowed Trommel in accented English, the only common language of the attendees. He was unpleasant to hear, as if his vocal chords had been scorched by a lifetime of consuming excessive alcohol. "Give me six months, and I'll have a hotel here that will rival the great spas. This will be the destination of choice!"

I would have expected Petrov to fawn over the rich dictator, but surprisingly he showed no reaction, instead turning away to the bar to refill his own glass. In fact, he had a look on his face that judged Trommel to be a diseased and filthy beast that had crawled up, shivering at his feet, and needed to be kicked away or put down.

Finally finding enough awareness to see that he had apparently been rebuffed, Trommel pivoted toward the Japanese official, Ando, who reluctantly offered his hand. They exchanged words of introduction, and then, Trommel turned and did the same with Pakk, who shook hands as well, although with more enthusiasm than his Japanese counterpart had evinced. Trommel then shuffled around to Holmes and me, looking us both up and down as if we were zoo exhibits.

"Heard of you," he said to Holmes after swallowing more whisky. After one glance, I was ignored. "Not sure why you're here – nobody has stolen the Minister's mistress, or whatever dirty business it is that soils you."

"Britain has interests," Holmes replied. "And questions. We happened to be in the area, and – "

"And you decided to push your beaky nose into someone else's affairs. A nasty way to go through life – bottom-feeding off matters that don't concern you."

I was tempted to make a rebuttal, but it would serve no purpose, for we were here to observe, whatever happened, and becoming too involved was not part of the plan.

Trommel leaned forward, as if to see Holmes more clearly for the first time, his puffed eyes blinking while he did his best to focus. Then he glanced up. "Where's your silly hat? The one normal people from your country wear for hunting."

"The Scots wear them for that. I am English. The hat is called a 'deerstalker', and it's in my room – although this room is so cold, retrieving it becomes more and more tempting as the day progresses."

Trommel nodded, finding something that he and Holmes could agree upon. He nodded, looking toward Golubev. "More coal!" he cried, gesturing toward the fireplace. "Warm this place!"

Golubev nodded at one of this men, who walked over, retrieved a small shovel leaning against the fireplace stones, and shifted a meagre pile of coal onto the flames. There was a marginal reaction, and I suspected that the coal was of the local bituminous sort which burned poorly, but was rumored to found in vast quantities in Kamchatka – one of the many raw materials there that were being considered for future pillage.

Seeing very little result from the niggardly amount of fuel added to the fire, Trommel gave an impatient bellow and lumbered into motion. As he reached the fireplace, he cast aside his glass without thought, shattering it against a nearby wall. Then, with an angry bellow, he bent down and retrieved one of the coal buckets, causing Golubev's man to step quickly aside. With a grunt, Trommel stepped forward and emptied the bucket into the fireplace. Most of the coals rolled to one side or the other, but some settled onto the flames, nearly snuffing them. However, there was enough coal dust in the bucket to reignite the fire, and even as Trommel let the scuttle clatter to his feet, the flames grew back, brighter than before.

"Must a man do everything himself?" Trommel growled before turning back to the bar, where he found an unopened bottle of whisky. Opening it, he ignored the need for a glass and began drinking straight from the container.

Apparently no one expected any better from the fat Balkan, and he was generally ignored from that point on, apparently to his satisfaction, rarely speaking or being spoken to.

What followed for the next two hours does not bear reliving, except in barest summary. As mentioned, the meal consisted of what was left from lunch, supplemented by more over-cooked and tasteless vegetables. There was no bread. I again had to wonder why such a gathering was planned so far from anywhere, requiring a new building to be thrown up with great difficulty, and yet, when the meeting actually occurred, if only for a couple of days, no one had brought better food.

Trommel, as fat as he was, seemed indifferent, gathering his sustenance from alcohol. As the evening progressed, he became increasingly intoxicated. Becoming more abrasive and offensive – his normal condition, as we had read. He would wander the room, wobbling, correcting his course, and then seemingly steering toward some new impending disaster. When he did sit before his dinner, such as it was, he collapsed in his chair, somewhat separated from the rest of the party both by an actual distance that had been arranged by the Russians – to which Trommel was too drunk to either notice or object. Before the meal was halfway finished, he rose abruptly and loudly announced that he didn't feel well and was going to bed.

The mood markedly improved upon his departure, and Petrov frankly and unexpectedly apologized to the rest of us about the man's inclusion in the affair.

"He has interests here, you see," he explained. Ando nodded, as if past diplomatic experience gave him an understanding of such unpleasant requirements. Pakk simply scowled.

As the evening progressed, and the tension that had been caused by Trommel's presence gradually eased, conversation became more open. In spite of a war between them just a few years earlier, and whatever had happened to the Japanese representative's son, Petrov and Ando found some commonality. Pakk, while not joining in, nodded several times in appreciation. Holmes – and also me by way of association – was questioned about some of his past investigations, and he recounted a couple of them. (It must be noted, however, that his dry and rather scientific presentation of the facts, as if he were lecturing at a university seminar upon the topic of criminal and forensic detection, left his audience rather ready to change topics.)

Eventually the long evening ended and, with perfunctory and largely insincere wishes for a good night, and meaningless comments about whether the pure cold air of Kamchatka would aid in sound sleep, we separated and found our own rooms. I considered simply staying up, but it had been a long day, and any rest, even that which I knew would be interrupted, was better than none.

I had been asleep for several hours when there was a knock at my door. Holmes leaned in. "On deck, Watson."

"Trommel?"

"Just as expected. In his room."

I looked at my watch to find that it was nearly six in the morning, much later than I'd expected. I was glad that I'd chosen to sleep, and surprised at how much time had passed. I hurriedly dressed and grabbed my medical bag, wondering that I had already missed. I exited my room to find Petrov, Pakk, Ando, Golubev, and Holmes outside a door further down the hall.

"What's the problem?" I asked, because as a doctor I would be expected to do so.

"*Herr* Trommel," said Petrov with distaste. "He's dead."

"Some sort of attack?"

"That is uncertain at this point," said Holmes. "He was clearly a man in poor health."

I hefted my bag. "This is unnecessary then, if he's beyond help. But I shall examine him, nonetheless, and make the official medical declaration."

"That is what we hoped, Dr. Watson," said Ando.

"Holmes," I said, "will you assist me? He is a big fellow to try and wrestle around."

"Certainly." And we stepped inside, shutting the door on the others, who showed no indications that they were offended about missing anything.

"I expected that he'd be found sooner," I whispered.

"Just be thankful that he wasn't discovered until late morning," was Holmes's reply. "It was always possible that Trommel would be left alone, assuming that he was sleeping late, and we'd have been sitting around waiting for someone to knock on his door and find him. At least we'll be able to leave depart tomorrow – later today, I mean – instead of sitting through the further pretense of a conference."

"My report will be that he died of apoplexy, or perhaps a coronary," I said, eyeing the dead fat man sprawled across his bed. He was still in his ridiculous costume from dinner, as he must have collapsed and died almost immediately after retiring here, before he'd even turned down the bed. "I'll indicate that it was brought on by his atrocious lifestyle. Is there any need to carry out an actual examination?"

"The information as to what substance killed him might be useful, if it can easily determined, and if it's nothing too obscure. Get a sample, and hopefully it won't break down before we can get it to a laboratory and analyze its make-up. Mycroft's agents may face something similar someday, and it would be useful to know what tools the enemy keeps upon his workbench.

As I approached the body, I asked, "Who did discover him?"

"Golubev decided to check on him."

"That's a bit odd," I said. "Trommel wasn't his responsibility, and it's quite early to awaken someone like that. Trommel was the type that would sleep late."

"I agree, but the real reason probably doesn't matter. Possibly the Russians also didn't want to sit around all day before finding him – since it's very likely that they were as aware as we were about what was planned. In any case, when there was no answer to his knock, Golubev opened the door and found him. He roused Petrov, and since I had been listening for such an occurrence, I quickly joined them in the hallway – as did Ando and Pakk."

"Both of whom," I added, "were likely listening as well. I was apparently the only one who slept through it."

My cursory examination didn't take long at all – especially as Holmes told me where to look: The back of the Trommel's right hand had a small but irritated wound, no larger than an insect bite. "Exactly where you said it would be."

"I saw it when it was done."

Thinking back, I nodded. "I believe that I did too, although I kept looking for something to be put into his food – or more likely his drink. But Golubev and Petrov kept his glass filled, so it didn't come from that quarter."

"I didn't waste my time in that direction. After all, we already knew who was going to kill him. I kept my eyes upon the murderer."

I shook my head. "I'm still not sure how I feel about this. It's almost as if we goaded the killer into committing the murder by merely being here."

"It would have happened whether we were here or not, Watson, but perhaps our presence did hurry it along by a day or two. And besides – "
He nodded toward the bloated body on the bed. " – our government has deemed this man a threat and a danger. We were told to observe, and to let him die. We are soldiers carrying out orders."

"But we aren't at war. At least, not yet."

"I'm not so sure. An actual war is coming, but does it have to be declared by a resolution or an official piece of paper, beginning at exactly one fixed minute on one defined day? If one country's actions are an attack upon another, even secretly, isn't there an obligation to defend oneself? Trommel's activities, as he attempted to consolidate and advance his own agenda, have been bringing all of Europe dangerously closer to conflagration, much more immediate instead of that which is unavoidable, but still much farther in the future. In spite of his blundering and crude ways, this man was single-handedly, with his deal-making and greedy corrupt chicanery, lighting a fuse which could not be put out. His absence will give us more of a chance to prepare."

I glanced at the body. "Good riddance, then. And if it's all the same to you, I'd prefer to avoid examining him further. I've obtained a sample from the wound – " I held up some fluid in a closed test-tube, which I then returned to my bag. " – but I doubt that I can do any more to identify some obscure Oriental poison with the limited assets on hand, and I feel like we've already done enough for King and Country. Now, we only have to officially declare his death and our work here will be done."

Leaving the dead man stiffening in his bed, we stepped back outside, locking the door behind us and reporting to the waiting men, all of whom had abandoned the hallway for the main room, where they were drinking strong coffee. Although still quite early, the sun was rising, and the light from the small eastern-facing window revealed lined faces and red puffy eyes. I looked from one to another – the murderer, and the others who either knew the truth or suspected it. Surely they didn't think that I was gullible enough to accept what I'd seen as a natural death. I somehow hoped that they saw in me another who was smart enough and trusted enough to share their common secret. But I had a part to play, and they expected to see me do it. I explained that the man had died from heart failure – technically true, as far as I could determine – although I didn't add that this failure had certainly occurred due to some slow-acting poison, administered early the previous evening when Trommel had first joined us, yet only killing him after he had retired back to his room.

Gradually, Petrov, Golubev, Pakk, and Ando drifted away, down the hall to their temporary chambers, leaving Holmes and me sitting to one side of the main room, sipping our cooling coffee. When nearly an hour had passed, Holmes stood and nodded. I followed him as we silently made our way down the long hallway, stopping before one of the plain and unobtrusive doors. Holmes knocked, and a low voice bade us to enter.

Inside, the room's occupant was sitting in a chair, his back to the small window, smoking a cigarette. The smoke was lazily drifting up for five or six feet, before suddenly being pushed toward the center of the

438

room by some unseen air current forced in through a miniscule opening in the wall.

The room was cold, and no fire had been lit in the little fireplace. This would surely been as the occupant had instructed, for he could have requested a fire, and I wondered why he wished it that way.

Our host nodded toward two chairs which faced him, as if he'd already placed them there for just such an interview. We sat, and Holmes asked if he might smoke his pipe. When he received a nod, my friend went through the process of packing it with shag and then getting it lit. Two or three minutes passed before he spoke.

"It seems as if you expected us, Mr. Pakk."

"Yes," the man grunted. "I was afraid that I might have left some clue that a man of your reputation would see."

"We didn't really need to search for a clue," Holmes replied. "We saw you kill him."

"Really?" The stone-like expression finally broke to reveal an actual emotion, something like surprise, and perhaps a bit of amusement. "How so?"

"Because we were watching for it. Petrov wouldn't shake Trommel's hand. Ando did reluctantly. But you showed no hesitation. In fact, you even used your left hand to grasp Trommel's from both sides. The wound is visible on the back of his right hand where you pricked him with the poison."

Pakk nodded. He held up his hand. In the light from the window, I could see that he held something between forefinger and thumb – a small cap with a needle protruding from it.

"This is a little trick from my country – a *gom*. It is worn over the end of the finger, and the tip is coated with a slow-acting but inevitably deadly poison. Just a tiny scratch – ! I didn't know when I would get my chance, but sooner or later I would have my revenge. I should have known that you would detect me." But then he paused, frowning. "But you said that you were watching for it?"

"Yes. That's why we're here. It was anticipated that you would use this opportunity to remove Trommel. We were sent to deliver a message – after you had done so."

"Anticipated? Hmm. Certainly by that legendary brother of yours, then."

"That's right. He has long known of your personal antipathy toward Trommel. More recently, he became aware that it was probably through your own ingenious machinations that this meaningless and difficult-to-reach conference was scheduled. Your manipulations to get everyone here, so far from anywhere, was masterful."

Pakk waved a hand. With some, it might have seemed to be self-deprecation, but he made it look as if he were discouraging mosquitoes. "Time was running out. He had to pay."

"The information that we received by way of my brother's cables was limited, by necessity. I sense that your solution goes beyond Trommel's various business practices, many of which might lead to your country suffering excessively when the next war occurs."

"*When*, you say, and not *if*. Very perceptive. More prognostication by the infamous Mr. Mycroft Holmes?"

"Yes, and others as well. Mycroft was initially a lone voice crying in the storm. Now others have come to understand what initially only he perceived."

"In my country," countered Pakk, "we have our own version of Mycroft Holmes. He is greatly valued as an asset. I wonder how he and your brother would fare in a game of chess. Do you play chess, Mr. Holmes?"

"Passably. I find it tedious. There is some argument to be made that the training it provides in strategy and scheming and teaching oneself to plan multiple alternatives many moves ahead is of value, but the harmless structure of it all provides no personal incentive. I learned much about the game when, as a young man, I played with my former mathematics tutor. It was only later, when he and I later battled in the real world – move and counter-move – that it became truly interesting.

"Mycroft, on the other hand, has a mind that is much more attuned to that rarefied intellectual plane. It has served him well, particularly in being able to accurately perceive what will inevitably take place."

"Well, he – and you – are correct. A war is coming, one which will ensnare the world. But I didn't care about any of that. Trommel had to die for other reasons."

Holmes simply raised his eyebrows questioningly, and Pakk continued. "Several years ago, during one of his round-the-world junkets, Trommel . . . violated one of the daughters of my country. Irretrievably."

"More specifically," interrupted Holmes with sudden understanding, "he violated *your* daughter."

Pakk's eyes narrowed. "Yes. It seems you can perceive everything. My own daughter. I wanted to kill him then, but his resources and connections were deemed too valuable to my country's leaders. It was forbidden. So I had to bide my time. But gradually, I became aware of his other activities, and his malignant importance as a point of nexus in events that might cost millions of lives rather than thousands – or even one. He could no longer be allowed to live."

"You said 'Time was running out.' His . . . or *yours*?"

"Mine. I was told several months ago that I have less than a year to live. That is only an estimate, but based on how I feel, it was a generous one, as if to give me a vague hope. Of all the affairs that I must get in order, this was the most important. Now I can die fulfilled." He shifted in his seat. "You mentioned a message, Mr. Holmes?"

"Yes. Doctor Watson and I were sent to inform you that your plan to murder Trommel – "

"To *execute* him."

"Very well. Your plan to *execute* him was known, and that for our nation's silence upon the matter, to avoid an incident which would be detrimental to your country, an accommodation with British interests will be required in the future."

"So you weren't sent here to prevent the murder?"

"Not at all. In fact, my brother believed that our unexpected presence here might actually instigate it sooner than later. He gambled, you see, that your personality would see it as something of a challenge. This would cause you to go ahead and act with certainty, where otherwise you might have hesitated at the end. He expected that you might commit yourself to action, if for no other reason than to see if you could get away with it under my nose, adding yet another level of satisfaction for you."

"And you, Mr. Holmes? You are here, so you went where you were sent – a good soldier – but did you and the Good Doctor *agree* with orders?"

"We did not. It was difficult to stand by knowing a man was being killed, even such a one as Trommel, and also to obfuscate the true solution. But from what we understood, you planned to kill him regardless, and there was really no good reason to preserve his life. Fortunately, you got it out of the way before Watson and I had to spend even more wasted time here."

"If you understand me so well, then you know that this message – the ultimatum – from your brother means nothing to me. I am dying, and my life is fulfilled. I'll carry no message back to my country, whining to make special allowances for British interests."

"I do understand that. For all of his amazing abilities, sometimes Mycroft doesn't understand the subtle shadings of individual personalities. However, Watson and I have fulfilled our obligations, and you may return to your country with the knowledge, for whatever it's worth, that what has happened here is known – even if only at those shadowy levels of diplomacy where so many secrets are treasured."

"Ah, Mr. Holmes. Perhaps you don't know any more than your brother about 'subtle shadings'." He raised his hands from where they had been folded in his lap. On his right forefinger rested the *gom*. Then he raised his left forefinger, which was marred by a single dot of blood.

"This time, I applied a stronger dose of the poison than what I used for Herr Trommel. It will act quickly."

Holmes looked at me, but I shook my head. Even if we knew what it was – and there were too many unknown possibilities – I had nothing with my medical supplies that would be an effective treatment.

"I really had no choice," continued Pakk. "I am ethically against the act of murder. I find it abhorrent. It is an offense to the miracle of life, and contrary to all that I believe. Only in the case of someone so evil as Trommel would I violate my beliefs. But now, having done so, I must pay." He coughed, a rattling sound in his lungs. I suspected that Trommel had coughed in a similar manner, but his extreme inebriation had probably prevented him from giving it much importance.

"The murder of myself – it is the taking of a life which has been much more valuable than Trommel's. It is ironic that to make payment for his, I must sacrifice my own. Yet I must confess: I'm afraid that in making this payment for my sin, I will committing other murders as well, although indirectly." He shuddered and seemed to collapse a bit into himself. A sudden sweat had broken across his brow, incongruous in that cold room. Then, in an act that gave me a chill of premonition, he smiled.

"'Other murders'," Holmes repeated. "Who else will die?"

Pakk coughed again, and then his eyes seemed to focus more sharply. He smiled. In the brightening morning light through the small window, his gums looked black against his teeth. "*You* will, Mr. Holmes – and Dr. Watson as well – although not as quickly as me. I admit I feel more guilt about that than I had expected, but you are also agents of my country's enemy, and the chance to take you with me overcame my ethical objections. If there is an afterlife, perhaps we can discuss it there.

"You were right, you see. When I learned that you would both also be here, I *was* goaded into action, but it was because I thought that you were being sent here to *prevent* me – and what I did had to happen. I assure you that there was no effort on my part to outwit you in some intellectual challenge whilst I hid my crime and you detected it. I simply wanted the time necessary to complete my work. But I did think that you were here to stop me. Now, knowing that you tacitly assisted me, if only by doing nothing, I somewhat regret what I've done – although not completely.

"I mentioned my country's version of Mycroft Holmes. It was he who helped plan my vengeance, assisting as I made plans to kill Trommel – one doesn't easily obtain a *gom* and appropriate poison – and when he learned that you and the doctor would be joining us, he sent last-minute word to me and wove that thread into his tapestry." He coughed one last time, and

442

his voice was much weaker when he resumed, as if some essential thread inside him had severed. "Two birds with one stone, I believe is the saying. I have removed Trommel – and also struck a blow against Britain, a nation that is our enemy, if only because you were allied in the recent war with our *true* enemy, Japan.

"Not long ago, while you were waiting in the large room, I went into each of your bedrooms. There I left evidence that you and the doctor were responsible for killing Trommel. It will be found. It's likely being found by our Russian friends right now – along with proof that you have killed me as well. I don't know if they'll believe it, but nevertheless it will be a good excuse for them to remove you from the chessboard. If they don't kill you here – if you aren't taken outside and shot – " He raised his left hand and removed the *gom* from his right, before tossing across to land at Holmes's feet. "Your country took Japan's side in the war – supporting their desire to overrun my homeland. To own it. To desecrate it. I . . . I feel no . . . ."

And with that, he died.

At that time in my life, I had been associated with Sherlock Holmes for something over a quarter-century, to varying degrees. In the early days, my war injuries prevented me from joining him on every investigation, and also I was not always invited. I had also initially felt less-invested in the proceedings, as I then believed I'd soon be rejoining the army, or that I'd at least be well enough to find regular work in a hospital. Later, during periods when I was married and working to establish medical practices, my time was often directed elsewhere. But I accompanied and assisted Holmes as often as I could, and throughout that time, I became more accustomed to the unknown and unexpected, and to sudden threats and danger. Even when Holmes was supposedly dead for three years in the early 1890's, I regularly assisted the police, sometimes in dangerous situations.

Those many experiences, combined with prior time spent in the army on the battlefields of Afghanistan, had given me a certain well-earned calmness in the face of jeopardy. But that seemed, for one moment, to have vanished – to be worth nothing as a strange, primal, and atavistic fear consumed my thoughts following the threats of the now-dead man.

Holmes and I were alone in this far-flung hellish place, save for strangers upon all sides, none of whom had any reason to consider us as friends. There would be no interest from these men in determining truth or separating it from lies. If Holmes and I were accused of two murders, by way of the unchallengeable evidence contrived and placed by one of the dead men, it would an elegant solution to the problem that would satisfy everyone there – except the two framed Englishmen so far from home.

I wanted to rush from the room and see what false evidence had been left. Simultaneously, I wanted to flee from the building entirely and get as far away as possible, although such an action would be taken as an admission of guilt. And I wanted to lock the door to the room where we were waiting quietly to prevent the discovery of the latest death, so that Holmes would have time to decide what to do – for in my sudden uncertainty, I still had faith that he would lead us from this new and unexpected danger.

I looked his way and was relieved to see that none of the panic I had suddenly experienced seemed to have affected him. His brows were knit in fierce concentration, and he tapped a finger rhythmically upon his tightly compressed lips will staring at Pakk, as if waiting for Trommel's killer to reawaken just long enough to reveal one further fact that might be of some use. Finally, when Pakk offered him nothing, he spoke, even as he leaned down to retrieve the *gom*, wrapping it in his handkerchief and slipping it into his pocket.

"This isn't entirely unexpected," he said, looking more confident than I felt he should have. "In any case, I believe there's a good chance that we can talk our way out of this. After all, the consequences, should something happen to us, would be far reaching. I believe that Mr. Pakk overestimated the Russian's desire to have an excuse to eliminate us."

I glanced toward the dead man. Ever since I was a child, taken to wakes and funerals by my parents, I've been intrigued by the curious optical illusion that the dead seem to still be breathing. I recall sitting for several hours across from the body of an uncle, lying face up in his coffin, certain that my careful observations were seeing his chest slowly rise and fall. Now, looking at Pakk, it seemed that I saw the same effect. Then, with a start, I realized that I hadn't actually confirmed his passing. As a doctor, I should have stepped forward to see if there was something to be done, but I had not. And I resisted the urge to do so now.

Holmes was looking around the room. I knew him very well, and could see that he was deciding whether it was worth the extra time to search the dead man's effects for any important documents before we departed, on the slim chance we could get away. Then he shook his head, speaking aloud as if he'd heard my thoughts.

"If he brought anything useful, he would have destroyed it, and anything of less importance would only serve to incriminate us if found on our persons during a search. No, it's best to slip out on the slim chance that the planted evidence hasn't been discovered yet and see what we can do to mitigate the situation."

He stepped to the door and then slowly opened it. I looked back one last time at the dead man, wondering if he had found some joy at the end in the completion of his vengeance, or if he'd had one last burst of guilt as he crossed into eternity.

Perhaps, I thought, if there's an afterlife, he and I could discuss it.

Holmes had the door open a foot or so and stuck his head out, listening carefully. Apparently seeing no threat, he widened the opening and stepped through. I followed, seeing that we were alone in the hallway, and hearing no sound whatsoever.

"Quickly," Holmes whispered. "Search your room for any evidence. Fortunately we brought few possessions with us, so anything foreign will stand out. Look in any obvious hiding places. It won't be too well hidden – Pakk wouldn't have wanted to make it difficult for anyone to locate. I'll join you in a moment."

Then he slipped into his own room, and I turned the other way to go to mine.

As he said, it hadn't been difficult to locate, but I searched everywhere else just to make sure that there weren't more surprises. It was a set of documents, poorly made, authorizing me to kill Trommel in the name of the British Government. This license would appear official enough as proof to someone who was already looking for an excuse to shoot me as a murderer and a spy. Handwritten in ink at the bottom was an additional instruction: "*Kill Pakk – M.H.*" Written, I supposed, by Pakk himself at some later time, as he'd mentioned, to also frame us for his death – along with the added benefit, from his perspective, of seemingly laying the authorization at the feet of Mycroft Holmes.

I didn't need to confer with Holmes about what to do next. I immediately lit the paper on fire and let it burn to ash. This was no souvenir that I wanted to carry away with me, should we be allowed to leave, with the intent of storing it in my old dispatch box. No, this was as deadly to me as if I'd found a ticking anarchist's clockwork bomb tucked underneath my pillow.

I was making yet another pass around the room to check for further falsified evidence, wondering that Pakk's effort hadn't been more sophisticated, when Holmes slipped in. He sniffed, smelling the evidence of the recently burned paper. "Just the one sheet?" he asked, and I nodded.

"And you?"

"The same. I believe that you can stop searching. We've found whatever was hidden here. Now we have to go out and face the music with whatever he might have left for the Russians to discover. Put on your most confident face, Watson. We may have to bluff our way from here back to the ship."

With a nod and a deep breath, I nodded, and we walked out into the hall with forthright strides, striding down the hallway as if we had no cares in the world except possibly seeking something for breakfast. Without looking back, Holmes opened the door to the large room and entered – and then stopped abruptly. I stepped around him and stopped too.

Everyone that we had met since our arrival yesterday was in the room: Petrov and Golubev were slumped in chairs near the fireplace, their eyes closed. Nearby on another chair sat Ando, in the shadows, his feet stretched out before him. Lying stretched on the floor by the Russians were the two porters who had met us at the dock, carried our luggage, and functioned throughout as servants. Alongside them, in the same state, were the two men who had worked in the kitchen.

I stared from one to another, trying to comprehend that we were the only ones left inside this hellish structure. I blinked my eyes in the dim light, seeing once again, just as I had with Pakk, the illusion that all of them were still slowly breathing.

From where we stood, there were no apparent wounds, and I wondered if they had all also been poisoned, and if so, how? Pakk had intimated that these men would be waiting for us, ready to accuse of his and Trommel's murder, and to exact justice of some type. And yet they too were now dead as well. Was there some other concurrent plot besides the one we just barely comprehended? Was there a stranger here whom we hadn't yet encountered who, having hidden outside in the rain since the day before, had slipped inside and somehow murdered everyone else but us? Were we, even now, being watched? Would we, at any moment, join these others, laid out like so many irrelevant carcasses?

"Holmes," I breathed softly, "who has done this thing?"

"I rather think we owe a debt to Mr. Ando," he replied, his voice jarringly loud in the grim room.

I glanced into the shadows where Ando was seated, propped in a chair like the two senior Russians. I couldn't see him very well. It was his slight shape more than his features that identified him. But then I saw that his arms were crossed over his chest in a pose that would be difficult for a dead man to maintain, and that at the end of his stretched crossed legs, one foot was slightly bobbing. Then, as I was still getting used to the notion that he was not dead, he suddenly pulled back his feet underneath him and arose.

"What have you done?" I asked the Japanese representative as he strode toward us. Closer, and in the light, I could see that he was, in fact, very much alive. There was an amused expression upon his face at my shock and anger.

"They aren't dead," he said, nodding toward the six men who still appeared to me to be lifeless corpses. "I drugged them. I found some of the evidence that Pakk had planted, implicating you, and understood immediately what his intent was. After that, I was watching to see when the Russians would find their copies as well. But then I grew tired of waiting, so I put something into their drinks and sent them to sleep. They'll awaken in a few hours, long after we've departed."

I looked at the Russians, trying to ascertain if he told the truth, and whether there were truly any signs of life.

"And Pakk's 'evidence' against us?" asked Holmes. "I assume that since you're assisting us to escape this attempt to frame us, you've taken care of that as well."

"Burned in the fire." He nodded toward the fireplace past Petrov and Golubev. "While you were in the back of the building with Mr. Pakk – and I hope that you'll share with me what he said to you both – I made a quick search and located the documents – all hidden poorly so that they were meant to be easily found. All were duplicate handwritten notes, individually addressed to each of us and signed by Pakk, indicating that he saw you both slipping poison into Trommel's drink last night, but that he was afraid to implicate you – especially because you both knew by then that he was a witness, and that he feared you would kill him next."

"But you chose not to believe him," I said.

"His attempt to blame you was idiotic," Ando replied. "And in any case, I knew ahead of time – as I suspect you did too – that Pakk was here to execute Trommel. This was just his little last-minute diversion." He glanced toward the hallway. "Is he still alive?"

Holmes shook his head. "While explaining his plans, he committed suicide, applying the same method that he'd used on Trommel, and living just long enough to explain about his faked evidence to implicate us – his feeble little cock-a-doodle of victory."

Ando nodded, in a way that made me think he didn't quite believe that we hadn't killed the Korean after all, but also that he didn't particularly care one way or the other.

"What is your purpose in this?" I asked. "Why did you step in to save us?"

"Because we are allies, Doctor," the smaller man replied. "Britain stood with us during the war with the Russians." He glanced toward the unconscious men, a look of hate fleetingly crossing his otherwise expressionless face. "Trommel was working to set up some plan with the Russians for the rape of this land, with the idea to sell the materials that the Russians didn't keep for themselves to Asian countries, including Japan, their new partners – as if we could forget the atrocities that they committed during the war, just a few years ago. As if *I* could forget . . . ." He became lost in thought for a moment. Then, "We are allies," he repeated. "We may not be so in another generation, but for now, for here in this spot, that is enough."

He pulled a watch from his pocket. "We must hurry. After I put them to sleep, I walked to the shore and fired off a flare to summon the ships. Gather your things and meet me at the dock."

I saw then that his bags were already standing by the front door. Without another word, he turned, retrieved them, and then slipped outside. I could hear the steady hiss of the rain before he pulled the door shut, and I realized that it had become such a part of the place that I'd forgotten to be aware of it.

Holmes and I looked at one another, but there was really nothing to say. We each went down the hallway and quickly retrieved our meagre luggage. Holmes, now having the chance, made a quick pass through Pakk's belongings, as well as the Russians, retrieving the bottle of poison and a number of documents which he folded and put into his coat pocket. "In for a penny . . ." he responded as I waited by the door to the large room.

The Russians were still asleep – I stopped to verify that each was in good health, and that they were in truth alive and likely remain that way. Then, pulling our coats tighter and our hats low on our heads, we left that place, slipping and sliding down the muddy path to the dock.

A lighter was already docked, and Ando stood nearby, waiting for us. I was glad that he was honoring his statement that we were allies, for I had half-feared that we'd reach the shore to find that he'd left without us after all. He took my bags, handed them to one of the crewman on the boat, and then helped me aboard. Holmes followed just behind me.

The rain was too heavy to see any great distance, but I could identify two nearly identical ships waiting not far away, both with their steam up and smoke rising from their stacks: The *Nisshun Maru*, which had dropped us off less than twenty-four hours before, and the unknown Japanese vessel which had brought Ando to Kamchatka not long before that.

After Holmes quickly briefed Ando on Pakk's last statement, I turned to him and started to speak, but he raised a hand.

"No need for thank you's, Doctor," he said. "As I said, we are allies. I was at the ceremony after Tsushima when the British representative presented a lock of Admiral Nelson's hair to our nation, in honor of our victory over the Russians."

"It was only fitting," I responded. "It was possibly the greatest sea battle since Nelson's victory at Trafalgar."

"Nevertheless, it was an incredible gesture of honor from your country. My son died in that battle . . . ." He swallowed and began again. "My son died in that battle. His ship exploded and he was thrown into the water. This was told to me by one of his friends, who survived. I don't

448

know what might have happened, but his chances were ended when Russians turned machine guns on the swimming survivors. They . . . ."

This time he stopped and didn't continue. Even when we reached the side of the *Nisshun Maru*, he could only shake our hands, without any additional comments.

On board, I found something hot to drink and eat, and insisted that Holmes partake as well. Then, for the better part of the journey back to Japan, he holed up in his cabin, studying the documents he'd retrieved from Pakk and the Russians. Upon docking on the northern Japanese shore, he disappeared, seeking a secure location to send cables to London.

Four hours later he returned to our shared sitting room at a small hotel near the docks. He had a sheepish look on his face – not something seen very often displayed by Sherlock Holmes.

"The information?" I asked. "Is it useful?"

"It's like dynamite," he replied. "Petrov was most indiscreet to bring it with him. Mycroft was quite pleased . . . ."

Something in his tone made me suspicious. "And?"

Holmes shrugged. "Since we've come this far . . . ."

I gave him a speculative but knowing look. "Back to the United States," asked wryly, "or shall go forward and make a true circumnavigation of the globe?"

"Not so much forward," he replied with a smile, "but *sideways*. What's it been – nearly thirty years since you visited India? And after all, from there it's just a hop and skip toward home."

"I doubt if it will be that simple," I answered. "But we've come this far . . . ."

"Excellent!" he said, clapping me on the shoulder. "What do you know of Malcha Mahal?"

I vaguely recalled stories of the place. "A hunting lodge," I think. Built in the fourteenth century, and taken over by the British in '56. Supposedly the original inhabitants somehow hid themselves there and have remained to the present day, taking potshots at the current inhabitants, and making the locals think that they're ghosts. Why? Why does Mycroft need to send us there? Surely not to investigate such a ridiculous legend."

"Malcha Mahal is located halfway between Agra and the Punjab, and it's also just a hundred miles from the Nepalese border. That's where our real business lies." He once again patted me on the shoulder. "Get some sleep, Watson. We still have far to go."

449

Kindred Spirits

Editor's Note: *As mentioned in the Foreword of* Sherlock Holmes and The Eye of Heka (2021), *I was fortunate to stumble across a vast cache of Watsonian Manuscripts while in London during my second Holmes Pilgrimage, having boldly knocked on the door of Watson's former Queen Anne Street lodgings and finding a distant descendant living within. This person, assured of my sincerity by my deerstalker hat and knowledge of Watson's life, has since given me access to these various accounts – of which I've only scratched the surface. Among those papers was the following letter, written by a most unexpected author . . . .*

– DM

You ask how I knew Jonathan Small? Well, there's a tale, and no mistake. Some people creep into your life like the first light of the false dawn – you look around and they're there, but it really makes no difference at first. Then they're there some more, and then the light is shining all around you, until you can't remember a time when that person wasn't the most important thing in the world to you. That's how it was with my beloved. The first time I ever saw her, she was just another girl – a curiosity – being helped down from a carriage by her father. I happened to notice her when I looked up from some task as she walked past me and inside one of the officer's buildings – it was ten seconds at best. And from right then my life was never the same.

Others slip into your life just as silent as the shadows that come at night with a long sunset, but they bring the darkness instead of light. And then there are the others – like Jonathan Small – who burst upon you like whirlwind – but full of shadows and darkness just the same.

I hadn't been back in England from my long years abroad for very long. As I told you when we first met last September, when one gets old, one has a longing for home. For all the years of my sojourn in India, I'd been dreaming of the bright green fields and the hedges of England. At last I determined to see them before I died. I saved enough to bring me across, and then I went where the soldiers are, for I knew their ways and how to amuse them and so earn enough to keep me fed. I'd learned a few conjuring tricks from the natives, and showing them off to the soldiers always earned me enough to keep body and soul together. It was all I ever really expected by then.

While I had a hunger to revisit all of England, no place seemed quite right to me. There was one spot in Hampshire that I was avoiding then, because I knew that my beloved was living there, so wherever I slept except there was as good as any other. And thus it was that I was plying my meagre trade in the pubs scattered around the Fulworth Barracks when I angered an ill-tempered brute who didn't like to be fooled, or made to look the fool in front of his mates.

I had performed the same tricks as always, and I finished up to their laughter and enough coins for a pint and my supper too. But this one fellow who'd had too many cried out that he'd been cheated. You know me – you know that I can't fight after the way I was broken and bent in India – so I chose to depart rather than let things get any worse. I slipped outside, hoping that was the end of it.

But he followed me, that great brute, and his anger seemed to feed something in his friends as well. They weren't all violent – not yet – but they followed along behind him to see what he might do. This only emboldened him, and he reached for me as I tried to move away as best I could, pulling me backwards and into the dirt by the side of the building.

The others gave a roar, as if this were very fine entertainment, and they roared again when my pursuer lobbed a kick of his great boot toward my head. I managed to throw up an arm to deflect it, but I knew that I couldn't get away, and that there was something ugly growing in this crowd that I couldn't defend against. My attacker pulled back his foot to kick me again, and that's when Jonathan Small sailed into the throng.

I wish that I could have seen it better – that I was one of those crowded around watching, instead of trying to scramble away in the dirt. I just knew then that a man had leapt in from one side swinging a club – or so I thought then – and laying out the big drunken soldier as if he were a side of beef. Thanks heavens Small didn't actually kill him, or the crowd might have turned even uglier, but something about the sight shocked them into standing still and coming to their senses.

As I pulled myself to my feet and looked up, I saw the strangest thing: My rescuer was hopping on one foot – his other leg was missing – and the club he was swinging overhead was his own wooden peg-leg! Even as I watched and tried to straighten my ragged clothing, Jonathan Small – for it was he – jumped from side to side, from one group of men to the other, screaming an unholy mixture of curses in English and other Indian dialects while his face turned brick red and the spittle flew from his mouth. There was rage and madness there, and none of those watching felt that defending their fallen comrade was worth any further association with this seeming lunatic. Finally they bent down, dragged the moaning attacker to his feet, and went back inside, leaving me and my rescuer alone.

His rage seemed to leave him immediately, like pinching a candle to kill the flame. He moved with ease and grace, hopping on one leg as easily as some walk on two. I used to walk that way once myself, smooth and

451

without giving a thought about it, and none of the pain that now comes with every step.

While he buckled the peg-leg back into place, I had a chance to study my rescuer closer. He was fifty or so, about my age, but he seemed older somehow. He had thick wrists and forearms, and his bare head was covered with thick black-and-gray curly hair. He had heavy brows and a prominent chin and – ah, but I forget that you've already met him, so you know what he looks like. You'll recall how sun-darkened he was, with his face cut up by a map of wrinkles and creases which told of his hard life. Since I'd been back in England, I couldn't recall seeing anyone who looked so roughened – and he was probably thinking the same about me, as my features, as you know, are much the same way.

I suppose it was only natural that we would fall in with one another. He looked me up and down and said with a laugh that, "Neither one of us is going to win a foot-race." Seeing that life had been cruel to both of us gave us an immediate connection, and by the time we'd made our way to another pub, we'd introduced ourselves to one another, and confirmed that we'd both been in India during the Mutiny, and not all that far apart. We'd both been in the Army, but he'd been invalided out of the service somewhat before my time when a crocodile bit off his leg. When the fighting started, he'd been working as an overseer on an indigo plan near Lucknow. I was in a group that was sieged not far away at Bhurtee, near Cawnpore, but in spite of each of us beginning our respective journeys during the Mutiny not fifty miles apart, our long and curious paths had never crossed until that spring night in 1888, more than thirty years later.

Well, as the days passed, we became more acquainted with one another, and it was nice to have something like a friend after so many lonely years. We met in taverns and pubs – not the one where I'd been attacked – and I found that he had been getting by much like I had, debasing himself for whatever charity the soldiers might toss his way. I had my conjuring tricks, and sometimes I would make up a little show with my small menagerie, but Jonathan Small – ah, his performance put mine to shame.

As you will recall, I have a tame mongoose that is quick on cobras, and I'd brought back one of them without the fangs. My mongoose would catch the cobra every night to please the folk in the canteens and pubs – it was always an interesting little demonstration. But Small – well, he had Tonga.

I know that he was a killer, but I can't help believe that he didn't understand what he did, and I hate that the poor little fellow came to such a bad end, and so far from his home. I became friendly with him – as much as one could – over the months that Small and I were pals. For the public,

Small played up Tonga's savagery – and make no mistake: He was as deadly as a cobra himself with his little poisoned darts, but mostly he would just sit and nap by the fire, like an old spaniel. He hated the cold English weather – and after so many decades in India, I was in agreement with him about that, as I fancy sitting by the fire as well. Tonga could barely savvy any English, but we could make each other understand what was needed – Hand me this, and pass me that – and Small could make him understand too, although his method was generally to shout and rant until Tonga somehow figured out what was what and got the deed done.

After a time we moved on from Fulworth, working our way south. We earned a living through the summer at fairs and other such places by working up something of a double bill, with me as the opening act – my tricks and my mongoose – and then Small would exhibit poor Tonga as "The Black Cannibal". He would eat raw meat and dance his war-dance, so that we always had a hatful of pennies after a day's work.

I learned more about Small as we traveled. Most of the time he was genial enough, but I never knew when he would lose his temper. It was never directed at me – he seemed to recognize that I was a kindred spirit, and in all of England, he was unlikely to find someone who'd had such a similar experience and could understand him – or tolerate him. Not that our stories were all that similar. While I'd been a soldier up until my captivity, he had left that behind following his injury, working as an overseer until the Mutiny. After that, I was vaguely aware that he'd also been held captive for a number of years before escaping – and that somehow along the way, he'd acquired poor little Tonga, but he was always quite close with the details of what had occurred over those years. That was all right – every man is allowed his secrets. I had mine, and he only got close to it once, when he suggested that we try our luck in Aldershot next. I was quite quick to put the kibosh on that notion, and he agreed without argument, sensing that I would go anywhere but there – because I knew that was where my sweetheart lived.

He was always interested in the rest of my story, though – what happened to me in India. Like him, I kept many details of my past to myself. The betrayal, for instance, where I was sold into captivity, was explained in the vaguest of terms, but I had a lifetime of other stories about what happened to me afterwards – when my captors fled into Nepal and took me with them, and then afterwards up past Darjeeling. The hill-folk up there murdered the rebels who had taken me, and I became their slave for a time until I escaped. I had to go north after that, until I found myself among the Afghans, where I wandered about for many a year, at last coming back to the Punjab, before finally deciding to return to England.

We settled into a comfortable routine, and I suppose I would have been happy to go on like that for a while. But as time went on, I began to learn still more about Jonathan Small, and I realized that I'd only seen the very edge of the man.

I've mentioned his temper, which could go off like a powder-keg at the least provocation. I was often exacerbated by his tendency to drink. Most times he was genial enough, with keen, twinkling eyes that more-often-than-not had a hint of humor in them. That's why his rages were so unexpected and disruptive. I recall once in the late summer of '88 when he ran across a newspaper story that set him off. He began to cry out, angrily d---ing all the gods in heaven and hell for the injustice of it all. He threw a bottle against the wall, where it shattered into a thousand pieces. Poor Tonga, who had been asleep in his little bed by the fireplace, leapt up and ran behind one side of a bureau in the sitting room of the cheap lodgings where we were staying, wisely getting out of the way in the same manner that a dog will run and hide when the master becomes angry.

Small's tantrums never affected me, other than causing a disruption that I didn't need or appreciate After all, I'd heard and seen much worse during the years of my captivity. After he tossed aside the newspaper, I retrieved it to see what had caused such a reaction, but at first I perceived nothing there of any relevance. Only after he calmed himself a bit – as quickly as he'd burst into his fit – did he direct my attention to a small article relating the apparent loss at sea of a ship bound for Africa, the *Fuwalda*, a barkentine of about one-hundred tons, and specifically a young man and his wife, John and Alice Clayton, who had been traveling aboard her. I failed to understand his reaction, and by that point of our association – I hesitate to call it friendship – in June or July of 1888, I wasn't hesitant to ask him about it.

"Clayton was helping me," Small replied. "Before he left. I've been working out a solution to a problem, and Clayton once did me a kindness after I returned to England. When he learned of my problem, he agreed that an injustice had been done to me. He was looking into a legal way to address it. But then he was sent to Africa – diplomatic service. Still, he assured me that he would keep an eye on the affair, even from down there, and see that the whole thing was fixed up legal an' proper. Now he's gone – lost at sea – and I have to start over again, and find another way to get what's mine – to get my fair share, and that of the others too."

That was all I heard about it then – just another one of his secrets. But a month or so later, he'd been drinking again, and that night he was in a talkative mood.

"I wonder which of us had it worse," he said to me, holding his glass and staring at the firelight through the whisky. "You were a mistreated and beaten slave, and I was a prisoner of the Crown – first sentenced to death, but then my sentence was commuted to penal servitude for life, like my three mates."

This was the first I'd heard of this particular secret. It was a quiet night, and he showed no signs of falling over the edge into one of his sudden rages, so I took a chance and, recalling his conversation after the sinking of the ship, asked, "Would those be the same ones who have shares – in that legal matter you were mentioning?"

He gave a snort. "'Legal matter.' That makes it sound like dear old Auntie died without leaving a will, and me and the cousins are squabbling about it. No, this is much more than that – a fortune, such that men would kill for it." He took a quick sip, and when he spoke again, his voice was quieter, as if he were speaking from somewhere far away. "I *did* kill for it – and look where it got me. Imprisoned in Agra, and then to Madras, and from there to Blair Island in the Andamans." He tossed his head toward the corner. "That's where I found Tonga."

The little fellow, mostly asleep, roused when he heard his name, but seeing that it was nothing more than a passing part of the conversation, he settled back down to his fireside slumber.

Seeing that Small was in a friendly-enough mood, a rare thing, I pressed for more details. "If you were imprisoned for life, how did you get back to England?"

"Escaped," he said shortly. "By then Tonga was devoted to me, for I had saved his life, and we stole a boat and got away from the prison island. After that, I had no choice but to come back to England." He raised a hand to stop my inevitable question. "You see, this was where the treasure is."

With this my years perked up, as anyone's would. I'd known Jonathan Small for several months by then, and seen him when he was up and down, friendly or mean, but I'd never observed any indications that he was mad. Yet it's a rare day when someone in England talks of a treasure as if it's a real thing. I'd certainly never encountered a person who knew of a treasure in my limited circle. I suppose my skepticism showed on my face, because he continued.

"The Great Agra Treasure," he explained, as if I should have heard of it. "I was part of a group – a volunteer corps of clerks and merchants – that was trapped in the old Agra Fort." Then he stopped, glancing my way as if judging whether I was trustworthy. But by then he'd known me for a bit, and he knew that I was as friendless as he, and my own crooked physical wreckage was much more debilitating than his, so the chances that I could steal his treasure were slim. He took another sip and continued.

"To make a short tale of it, I was on guard one night at one of the abandoned fort entrances alongside the river – me and the two Sikhs who had been put under my command. In a moment when my attention drifted, one raised his rifle while the other put a knife at my throat. 'Don't make a noise,' said Abdullah Khan, the one with the knife, and when I started to struggle anyway, he added, 'The fort is safe enough.'

"Then he went on to explain, 'You must either be with us now, or you must be silenced forever. The thing is too great a one for us to hesitate. Either you are heart and soul with us on your oath on the cross of the Christians, or your body this night shall be thrown into the ditch, and we shall pass over to our brothers in the rebel army. There is no middle way. Which is it to be – death or life?'

"Well, how was I to know what I was agreeing to? I said that I'd have no truck with anything that endangered the fort, but he shook his head. 'We only ask you to be rich.' Then he went on to explain that the servant of a rajah from the north country, traveling under the name of Achmet, was on his way at that moment, and likely nearly there, attempting to seek the safety of the fort by way of the gate which we guarded. He was being led there by another of their group, Abdullah Khan's foster-brother, Dost Akbar. He would be met at the water by the other Sikh in our group, Mahomet Singh, and then taken through the gate. All I had to do was let them through.

"Achmet was carrying a treasure – half of the rajah's fortune. 'The most precious stones and the choicest pearls,' explained Abdullah Khan. And if I let the man fall into the clutches of these Sikh killers, a share would be mine."

He fell silent for a moment before continuing. "In Worcestershire, the country of my birth, we're told that a man's life is a great and a sacred thing, but it's very different when there is fire and blood all round you, and you have been used to meeting death at every turn. I had killed before – seeing my rifle drop man-shaped targets in the distance was no difficulty, and I'd fought and killed hand-to-hand when we were over-run. Now I was tasked with condoning a murder – and when I considered the treasure, I found that whether Achmet the merchant lived or died was a thing as light as air to me. I agreed, and swore to be with them, all three, heart and soul. I never realized what such a Devil's bargain would cost.

"It progressed as planned. Dost Akbar, he largest Sikh that I'd ever seen, led a fat little man ashore and I allowed them to pass beyond me and into the tunnel. But the little goat must have sensed something, because I heard a cry and a scuffle, and then suddenly Achmet came running back my way. This wasn't the plan – I had done my part. But before the fat man could sound the alarm, I shoved my rifle between his running feet. He sprawled and then tumbled upon the ground, and I think his neck was already broken before one of the Sikhs was upon him, driving a knife twice into his heart.

"After that, we hid the body and took a look at the treasure, which Achmet had been carrying in an iron box. It was more vast than even my new friends had expected. There were over a hundred-and-forty diamonds of the first water, including a huge one that is said to be the second largest stone in existence. There were nearly a hundred emeralds, and almost two-hundred rubies, and that many sapphires. There were carbuncles and agates, beryls and onyxes and cats'-eyes and turquoises, and so many others. Then then there were pearls – nearly three-hundred of 'em, with the twelve biggest and finest set in a gold coronet."

As he spoke, his tone rose a bit, and his gaze was such that he was seeing them in front of him, as they had been on that night so long ago. I brought him back to the present.

"You said you were a prisoner," I said. "You were caught for the murder, then."

"We all were. They found the body and knew from the knife wounds that it was murder. We four were arrested and charged – three of us because we had were in charge of the gate that night, and the fourth, Dost Akbar, because he was known to have been in the company of the murdered man. We were tried and convicted – but none of us told a word about the treasure, and no one asked, for the rajah himself had been deposed or killed in the meantime.

"The night of the killing, we'd hidden the box of jewels deep within the old fort and made four documents for us to sign and swear to. Then, with that solemn ceremony in place, we swore again and burned the documents, so that they wouldn't be found upon us. It was enough that each of us had faith in the others' honor, and we all remembered where the treasure was hidden. And there it remained through our long captivity."

"But you said it's here in England now, and you've been trying to get it back."

He nodded. "I ended up in the Andaman Islands, thinking that would we where I sweated out the rest of my days. But I became aware of a couple of officers stationed there who seemed likely enough to get me off that rock. They were in a deep over cards, and I played them like fish, teasing them with my knowledge of where there was a hidden treasure that would buy them out of their debts. Mind you, I never intended to just save myself. It was all done for the four of us – Abdullah Khan, Mahomet Singh, Dost Akbar, and myself. We four had made the sign, you see, and we were sworn to protect the interests of one another. Through Hell itself, if necessary.

"The two officers stewed on it, and I told them just enough to convince them. We arranged a meeting – the four of us, and the officers, Sholto and Morstan. The plan was for Sholto to go to the fort to verify the treasure's existence, and then come back and arrange a boat for the four of us prisoners to use for our escape. We would then meet Morstan at Agra and retrieve the treasure. But it wasn't to be. Sholto went to the fort as planned, but he never came back. Morstan later showed me in a newspaper where Sholto had claimed to have received an inheritance from an uncle, so he was resigning his commission and returning to England. But there can be no doubt – he stole the treasure for himself, and then came back here to live like a king."

"Have you approached him about it? What did he say?"

"That was over ten years ago. Some time after that, Morstan went back to England to confront Sholto, but he never came back. Not a word has been heard of him ever since – and I think we know who's to blame for that! In the meantime, I escaped – Tonga and me. We got away from the islands and were picked up by a band of Malay pilgrims. Here and there we drifted about the world, but there was always something to keep us from London. But I never lost sight of my purpose. I dreamt of Sholto at night – a hundred times I've killed him in my sleep. Strangled him. Pushed him from a high place. Bashed his head in with my leg . . . . " This thought caused another short reverie. Then –

"Several years ago, I finally made it back to England. Finding Sholto's house in Upper Norwood was no great difficulty – it's a massive place, and that 'inheritance' of his has done him quite well. But he could have bought ten of those estates and only touched a fraction of the value of the treasure – and I still mean to get it back from him, for the four of us who swore an oath to one another."

"But you didn't answer my question," I pressed. "Did you approach him about it?"

"I went to his house but was turned away. He has several brutes working there as bodyguards. So I began to lurk about the place, and I paid a coin here and there as I could afford to get news about him when there was something to tell – which wasn't much, as his health was ruined since his return, and he never left the estate. But finally word came to me that he was dying. I slipped into the grounds, taking my chances and hoping to confront him before he was gone – to tell him that he hadn't escaped entirely, and to find out where the treasure was hidden. But as I reached the house and looked into the window where he was lying in his deathbed, I knew that I was too late. He stared toward the window and saw me, and his eyes became fixed in horror even as he died. His two sons were on

458

either side of him, and I don't think they ever spotted me. I slipped away as soon as I realized that I'd missed my chance.

"Tonga and I traveled some more, but I always returned to London to learn what I could. When next we came back, I found that the two sons had wrecked the grounds of the estate – digging for the treasure. That's how I figured that they didn't know where it was either. It was during that time that I made the acquaintance of young Clayton, who ended up owing me a favor. He'd been out to India once, and we talked. I shared a bit of my story and he became interested, and he started legal proceedings on my behalf. But now he's died before they can be completed, and without his aid, I can't do anything!" He shook a fist toward the heavens. "Another betrayal!"

I started to ask how Clayton's death due to shipwreck could be perceived as such, but I didn't want him to become angry at me too. Meanwhile, he fell silent, while I pondered the story he'd related. I glanced around his room, where we'd been sitting as he spoke. For all of his roughness, he was an intelligent man, and there were a number of books lying around that he read when he had the chance. I'd never been much for reading myself, but there were a few there that I'd enjoyed on my own, including one from five or six years earlier, *Treasure Island* by Stevenson. I glanced from it and then back to Small, whose eyes were fixed on some distant place far beyond the shabby walls of the rooming house where we were staying. It was then that I started to wonder if he was a bit mad – for this story of treasure and abandoned forts, murders and maps and sacred oaths, was just a bit too unbelievable. Was he having me on? Had he concocted the whole thing – his own version of Jim Hawkins and Long John Silver and Captain Flint's treasure? But I thought not. For all I'd seen of him, he didn't have that kind of imagination, and he certainly wasn't the type to spin such a yarn just to while away an evening.

We spoke no more about it for several weeks, until one afternoon when Small came in. He was in great spirits. We had gone on to London by then, for he was interested in seeing what was new with the Sholtos, and whether they were still searching for the treasure. Small seemed to think that I was now involved in his quest, as he'd shared the story with me. In truth I was interested, but I had no faith that he could ever retrieve such a treasure, should it truly exist, and I couldn't imagine that he would truly try to preserve the shares belonging to the three Sikhs if he actually managed to re-acquire it. I was also a bit nervous as he seemed to continue this obsession, which seemed a slippery slope toward the kind of attention that he couldn't afford to attract.

"There's a man," he said as he came in, "who I found. He might be able to help me with the Sholto affair."

I looked up from the small stool where I sat hunched before the fire. It was a hot day, but after my years of Indian captivity, I could never warm myself after returning to England. "Who might that be?"

"A retired colonel – he had service in India. He was in the Jowaki Campaign, and Afghanistan. Part of the 1st Bangalore Pioneers. This colonel works for a man who will be able to help us with the Sholtos."

It didn't escape my attention that he'd use the word "us" when describing the situation. "Is this colonel just doing this out of the goodness of his heart?" I asked, but Small didn't seem to hear the skepticism in my voice.

"No. If I can retrieve the treasure, the man that he works for will get a share."

"Wait – can you just give away a share like that? What about the oath you swore to the other three?"

An angry look crossed his face. "It's the best that I can do for the others. Right now it's all been stolen from us. We were going to give a share to Sholto and Morstan. This will be the same as that fifth-share. The others will understand."

I didn't mention what was uppermost in my mind: The three Sikhs were probably long since dead, and should they still live, how would he ever convey their shares to them?

And yet, he seemed to have firmly convinced himself that it was still possible to rescue the treasure, and to hold true to his vow to the other three as well.

For the most part, our days in London weren't much different than usual. We stayed on the outskirts of the city, down near the artillery barracks at Woolich. Small tended to go off on his own a bit more than when we were out in the country, and I knew without him saying so that he was journeying over to Upper Norwood to prowl around the Sholto manor. I was curious myself, but not enough to ask to go along, or to think of trying to find it on my own. This story would play out, or not, regardless of whether I took an active interest.

Then, one afternoon in early September, we had a visitor.

There was a knock, and when Small rose to answer the door, I could see from my fireside stool that it was a large and virile man of middle years. He had a high brow and a sinister face. But most noticeable were his cruel eyes with their drooping lids, and the fierce, aggressive nose perched above his bushy moustache.

He looked at me with a hateful gaze, but after my lifetime of experiences, such as him didn't frighten me. Without mentioning my name, Small introduced our visitor – this was the colonel whom he had mentioned, the man who was going to help retrieve the treasure, with a one-fifth share going to the colonel's boss. Seeing this man in person, I felt that Small would be lucky to escape with his life if the treasure was actually found – and I was glad that my name hadn't been mentioned. Or so I hoped. Looking at this dangerous colonel, it was then that I began to consider that I might need to separate myself from Jonathan Small and his obsessive goals.

"They've found it," said the colonel, his voice with something of a curious rasp, as if he had spent so much time out-of-doors that he lost the ability for indoor conversation. "The treasure. We don't know the details yet, but our agents in the neighborhood report that the Sholto brothers had discovered it – hidden somewhere in the house." He glanced my way again – the briefest look, as if to make certain that I wasn't faking my crooked stance in order to lull him before I attacked. I turned back to stare into the fire.

"Be ready in the morning – nine o'clock – and we'll plan how to get the treasure away from them. I'll send a carriage for you."

He didn't ask if that was agreeable. He just turned and left, pulling the door shut behind him. I expected Small to immediately address me – to start talking about how his long quest was nearly at an end, but he remained silent. It went on for so long that I turned on my seat to face him. He was staring straight ahead, deep in concentration. Finally he seemed to decide something and looked my way.

"I have to go out – to find out what has happened for myself. Can you join me tonight? Be at the Upper Norwood Station at nine o'clock." He walked to the door without waiting to see if I'd agreed. As he walked out, and just before he pulled the door shut, he added, "And bring Tonga with you."

I thought long and hard about it, but in the end I did as he said and, wrapping Tonga up well, as we had to do when taking him out and about, we set off for Upper Norwood.

Small met us at the station, carrying a long coiled rope. A fog was rolling in by then, which suited his plans perfectly. He told me that he'd scouted the house and spoken with his own agent that he'd had in place. That reminded me, and I pulled a telegram from my pocket that had arrived for him that afternoon after he'd departed. He nodded and read it, explaining that this was the notification from his agent that the treasure had been found. "The colonel," he added, "has better troops than I do to have found out even before I did."

I started to use that to warn him that this colonel seemed like a dangerous sort who would most likely try and take all of the treasure, and that he shouldn't get any more involved with him, but before I could speak,

461

Small said something that only made it worse, even if it confirmed what I was also thinking.

"That's why we have to get the treasure tonight."

"But he'll kill you!" I blurted out.

Small just shook his head. "We both know he'll try to kill me either way. At least this way, I have a chance to get the chest and the jewels into my own hands." We walked into the fog as he explained that the Sholto manor, known as Pondicherry Lodge, wasn't all that far – which was a good thing, as my own poor condition didn't lend itself to very much of such movement.

Small explained that he'd learned of the house's layout, and that the treasure had been found in a secret attic at the top of the house. He'd had no idea about how to spirit it away until he realized that there was a trap door in that same spot. "It seems to me that we can manage the thing easily through Tonga. He can climb like a cat."

We had no problem getting inside the walls. Small theorized that since the treasure had been found, the rough men that the Sholtos hired to keep watch had been pulled back to the house. The grounds looks like they had been shelled with artillery fire – holes dug here and there as they delved for the treasure which had been inside all along. In some places trees had been pushed over and abandoned, and in one instance the wall had collapsed underneath the weight of one fallen tree, which made a convenient place for the three of us to climb and enter – not much worse than a going up and down a set of steps.

Small led us to one wall, deep in shadows, and wound the long rope 'round Tonga's waist. Then, after muttering to him in some lingo that the native appeared to understand, the little fellow scampered up the wall as if he were walking on level ground. In a moment, the rope dropped beside us and Small grabbed it. After giving a couple of pulls, he muttered, "Keep watch," and then started climbing, his peg-leg causing no problems at all, as he simply lifted himself up with the strength of his thick arms.

I leaned into the shadows by the wall, hoping to soon be finished with this madness. I was already considering what to do afterwards. When the colonel returned in the morning, Small might or might not meet with him. Would he admit that he'd retrieved the treasure early and offer the colonel the promised fifth share, or would he try to keep it all, pretending innocence when it was discovered missing? In either case, I suspected that the colonel and whatever organization he represented would have no further need for Jonathan Small – or Tonga, or their crooked friend. It was looking more and more as if I would be moving on and fast when we returned to the city.

It was probably no more than ten or fifteen minutes when I heard a noise above me. A few scrapes and bumps later, and I could perceive a dark shape being steadily lowered down the side of the building. As it reach the level of my head, I reached up and took it, guiding it to the ground. It was a heavy iron box, and the ironwork was two-thirds of an inch thick all round. It was massive and well-made and solid, and it landed with a solid thump.

In a moment, Small came down the rope rather quicker than he went up, sliding in a couple of places when his feet couldn't find purchase. As he set about untying the chest, I could see that in a couple of places he'd stripped the skin from his palms. I started to ask about Tonga when the rope began to rise.

"He's going to close it up and leave the way he came – through the trap-door." Then he cursed and kicked the stone wall of the house."

"What?" I asked.

"That d---ed heathen! He killed Sholto with his blow-gun! When I pulled myself in through the window, he was strutting about the dead man as proud as a peacock!" He passed a hand across his eyes. "This treasure – will it never soak up enough blood?" Then, without another word, he leaned down, grabbed the chest by the handles on each end, gave a grunt, and stood with it. "Let's go," he hissed.

We had reached the wall by the time Tonga joined us. I noticed that he'd left the rope behind, but didn't ask where or why. Perhaps I should have mentioned it, but I just wanted to get away, and Small might have decided to send Tonga back for it. Who else might he encounter during a second intrusion into the house – and who else might die because of it?

I don't know how he did it. Perhaps Jonathan Small is the strongest man I've ever met, or possibly it was sheer will that gave him the strength to carry that heavy chest all the way back to the station. In any case, we arrived a quarter-hour later, in time for the up-train. We had a compartment to ourselves and, with my coat across the window so we couldn't be seen, Jonathan Small opened the chest.

I can't begin to describe what I saw. It was only a moment, but I shall never forget. Even in the dim carriage light as we rocked north through the night, the contents seemed to blaze like captures sunlight. There was no order to it – diamonds were poured beside rubies, emeralds swirled with pearls, and stones for which I had no name flowed like liquid fire through all of them.

Tonga thought it a curious thing, and reached a hand toward the box when a small growl from Small made him jerk it back. But it turned out it wasn't his ward's curiosity that vexed him. No, he sensed that something was missing.

He thrust in his hands, and at first I thought that he just wanted to feel the stones. But then he became more urgent – although never enough to cause a single jewel to spill out of the box. Finally he jerked his hands free and sat back in disgust.

"It's gone!" he uttered, his face red as if he might fly into a rage.

"What?" I asked, for I couldn't imagine any other treasure which might be missing from such a vast hoard.

"The chaplet! The pearls – twelve of them. The most beautiful matched set you might ever see. Possibly the most perfect set ever assembled in the history of the world!"

My first thought was to suggest – rather stupidly, I later realized – that he might go back and see if they were in the room where the chest had been recovered. Instead, I lamely offered, "I suppose that Sholto pulled them out to be kept elsewhere."

He nodded, as if considering a way to verify this without betting arrested. Then an idea lit his eyes.

"Or they already gave them to Morstan's daughter – to buy out her share."

"His daughter? You haven't mentioned a daughter."

He looked at me, and I could hear his unspoken thought: *Even you don't know all my secrets.*

"She lives in Camberwell – she's a governess." He nodded. "Once I get this chest squared away, I might just make a visit there, and see if she has my pearls." Then he glanced at the huddled figure on the bench beside me and smiled – an evil smile. There, in the light reflected on him from the myriad of jewels, I could see the truth: The sickness of the treasure was upon him. Whatever he might say from here on out about protecting the share of the other three who had helped steal it, they would never be offered their part, even if such an offer were possible. He would rationalize it in such a way that in the end, he would have it all – or no one would. I became more resolved than ever to be on my way as soon as we reached London.

But first, I had to make one effort.

"You can't bedevil Morstan's daughter," I said, trying to sound firm, but with an unwanted pleading tone in my voice. "Small – Jonathan . . . This is enough. That – " I gestured to the chest between his feet. " – is enough for a hundred men. A thousand. There has been enough suffering without you bringing more on a poor girl who doesn't deserve it."

I could see his eyes change, as if for a moment he had stepped back and seen the edge where he was standing. But then his expression went empty, and I knew that he was making an effort to hide whatever he was thinking by giving the impression of careful neutrality. He was lost.

464

"Perhaps you're right, Henry," he said to me, and then he presented a smile – the most ghastly one that I've ever seen on a man's face, living or dead.

We spoke no more, each with our own thoughts and plans. Small had quickly closed up the chest, and afterwards the carriage seemed unnaturally dark. At Victoria, he muttered something about me seeing Tonga home while he took care of an errand, and then he lifted the chest with a grunt and set off to look for a cab. It was clear that I wasn't invited. I never saw him again.

I shepherded Tonga back to our lodging house and got him settled for the night. Then I went down the hall to my own room, where I collected my scanty possessions – my few clothes and books, my mongoose Teddy and the old cobra – and slipped into the night. I wondered what Small would think. Would he be glad that I was gone, now that I knew too much? Or would he worry that my disappearance was some move in a new chess game, planned so that I could steal the jewels from him in a way that he didn't expect? Someone who had treasure sickness like that would lean toward the latter, so I knew that I had to get away very cleverly – both from Jonathan Small, and the colonel, whose anger was likely to be dangerous.

I considered where to go, and finally there seemed to be no better place than Aldershot – the one spot on earth that I'd avoided so long, because of she who lived there.

But before I left, I tried to find Morstan's daughter – to warn her. But I only knew that she was a governess in Camberwell, and in my own condition, talking to people and gathering information was hopeless. And then I feared that word about me might get back to the colonel. Finally I gave up and went down to Aldershot.

A few days later, I read in the newspaper of Small's capture and poor Tonga's death. You did the right thing to shoot him, Doctor, although I did know him well enough to see some of the good in him. I knew that I'd been correct about Small when I read that he dumped the jewels over the side of the boat while you pursued him: If he couldn't have them, no one ever would.

I thought about visiting him in prison, but I quickly quashed that notion. When I read that he was stabbed to death a week or so after his arrest, I could only think that the colonel's revenge had been certain and quick.

Meanwhile, I hid in Aldershot, making coins entertaining the soldiers as I always had, and finally believing each day that I was a little safer. It was when my guard was finally easing that I encountered Nancy, my beloved, after so many years – the very person who I had wished to avoid for so long.

She didn't seem dismayed at my crooked frame, and she finally understood how her husband, now Colonel Barclay of the Royal Mallows, had betrayed me to the enemy so long ago, resulting the decades of torture and captivity. But you know all of this. If not for Mr. Holmes, things might have worked out differently. And if not for you, Doctor, my life might have still been empty and meaningless. I still cannot express my gratitude, nor my disbelief at how my life has changed.

If you and Mr. Holmes had simply left after finding me and hearing my story, I might have departed the next day for parts unknown. But your intervention – telling the truth of my story to the other officers of the Royal Mallows so that they felt an obligation – helped restore me to something like the man that I once was. And when Nancy regained her health – Ah, Doctor, I can barely speak of it. It is a dream that I'm living, and do not want to awaken. The fact that she still loves me, even in this broken shell that I now inhabit, is beyond my comprehension. Our marriage just a few weeks ago –We did not wait. Convention and respect for her widowhood be d----ed! – has made me the happiest man on the earth. For all that you did to facilitate that, Doctor Watson, I will forever be grateful.

I hope that this account of my passing acquaintance with Jonathan Small will be of some help. I was interested to learn that you're preparing a narrative of the events of his capture for publication, and I look forward to reading it.

Please wish your own bride my best wishes. Take care, and deepest regards.

Henry Wood
Corporal (Retired)

466

Enquiry in Conduit Street

He had always hated the cold, and spring was late this year. The discomfort he felt upon stepping outside was exacerbated by the damp fog that immediately found its way under his collar, and he cursed under his breath – and then cursed again for allowing something so petty as physical discomfort to elicit an emotional response. He should be above that – a thinking machine, a logician, a *brain*. But it was his own fault. He had forgotten to take his muffler as he walked out the door. Yet, he would not go back for it. To do so would be an admission of a mistake.

Not that Alfred Bassick would care. The man was as loyal as a street dog who had been tamed by a few scraps and a little attention. If the Professor chose to make him wait on his cold seat atop the carriage while he stepped back inside for just a moment or the rest of the night, it wouldn't make a jot's worth of difference to the shabby little man. He was there to serve, and in his eyes, the Professor could do no wrong.

James Moriarty felt that way about himself as well, and he therefore refused to waste any more time on something that might contradict that opinion. The little bit of extra cold from the chill March evening would simply serve to remind him to be more careful going forward – and after the recent months, such a reminder would be of special value.

As he climbed into the carriage, careful to make no audible grunt from the effort, he considered his foe. Early in the year, Holmes had crossed his path. It wasn't the first time, of course. They had known each other for so long – many more years than what it took for the bright young man to figure out just what his former mathematics tutor was up to. Even when the indications could not be ignored, Moriarty had sensed that Holmes didn't quite believe it. But he had been too complacent, and could not say exactly when Holmes had crossed the line from uncertainty to aggressive action.

It had certainly been before that business in Sussex three years earlier. The Professor had been consulted upon a simple matter – to find an expatriate American that had changed his name and hidden himself away somewhere in the English countryside. He didn't care why, nor was he interested in the petty revenge scheme of those who sought him. It took no great effort to find the colorfully named "Birdy Edwards" – now calling himself "John Douglas" – burrowed into a manor house near Birlstone village on the northern border of the county. Moriarty had notified his American client, a bitter and surly criminal named Ted Baldwin, and there

467

the matter should have rested. How the two foreigners settled their dealings after that was their own affair.

But nevertheless he'd been curious – something had niggled at him about that bit of business, and he didn't know why, but he'd learned to honor his hunches. He'd sent Moran down to Sussex, following Baldwin without his knowledge. The killing had occurred as planned – but then Moran unexpectedly spotted Holmes and his lick-spittle dog, Watson, in the company of policemen – one of whom was the same Inspector who had visited him not long before, asking questions, almost certainly at Holmes's behest. He had no idea how they had become involved – perhaps John Douglas had previously hired Holmes because he too had some itching premonition that danger was nearby. Moran hung around the village long enough to determine that it was, in fact, Baldwin who had gotten himself carelessly killed, and Douglas, the prey, had survived.

After that it was a matter of honor – and business, of course, for the Professor couldn't allow the affair to remain unresolved. He was trying to expand his operations into the United States, and such a failure could seriously damage his reputation there. It was no great problem to send one of his lesser but still-effective assassins after Douglas, who had soon after departed on a sea voyage without knowing his killer had joined him.

In due course, Douglas's death was reported – supposedly he had fallen overboard in a storm, but for those who knew better, the truth was obvious. It was something of a loose end that Moriarty's assassin seemed to have also gone over the side in the struggle, but overall that bit of business was concluded satisfactorily in the end, and his reputation with the Americans was salvaged.

But it also alerted Moriarty to the serious concern that Sherlock Holmes was becoming a bit too interested in his business.

Since then, they had played cat-and-mouse with one another, and so far Moriarty had let the mouse dance away after each encounter – it was almost an intellectual treat to watch how Holmes met each challenge. Also, it was useful to him to see how Holmes played the game, and in their moves and counter-moves, Moriarty always gained information – Who else Holmes used as an agent, for instance, besides that dullard medico who tagged after him. There were those beggar children, of course – such an army would be invisible to most people, but Moriarty had his own sinister equivalent of such a group. Other children in his pay, of course, as well as a legion of beggars and petty criminals who knew the streets and byways every bit as well as Holmes's "Irregulars".

Moriarty already knew which policemen he could buy, and those that he couldn't, but seeing who Holmes recruited to his side helped provide additional affirmation of these facts. Still, whatever small amounts of information that Moriarty was gaining seemed to be decreasing, while his losses were mounting.

His and Holmes's paths had crossed on the fourth of January – score one for the detective. Just three weeks later, Holmes had incommoded him, and by the middle of February, he was becoming seriously inconvenienced.

Now he was finding that his plans were absolutely hampered – and just when he could least afford distractions, he had received word of a possible Judas within his ranks.

Thus, his nighttime journey across fogbound London to the traitor's rooms in Conduit Street, to find what he could and see what he might see.

Bassick let the carriage lurch as he made the turn south out of Russell Square and into Montague Street. To the Professor's right, the Museum was now dark, but the vast building was silhouetted along the roofline by the bright lights to the west, making the fog glow and twist. Moriarty could remember being fascinated by fog as a boy, sitting outside to watch it long after it was time to come inside. Even in those days, he had worked things so that his two younger brothers took care of his chores, leaving him time to ponder those questions which so fascinated him – matters of science, and the way the universe worked, from the macroscopic to the microscopic. Fog seemed to flow like a liquid, but Moriarty knew that if one looked closely enough, it was made up of individual particles – water and dust and smoke – each tiny piece like a planet, and moving with its own directions and behaviors.

As a murmuration of birds appeared to be one single sweeping creature, in truth it consisted of countless individuals, all moving together – for a while – with seemingly one mind, maintaining similar distances and directions. Bits of fog were similar – moving together in the greater swell and surge, but each little fragment holding its own position – almost as if the minute parts were able exert the forces of magnetism upon one another – attraction and repulsion. Or perhaps they too had their own infinitesimal gravity, allowing them to hold their places in eternal freefall, kept apart, but also drawn together to form bigger and bigger clumps.

Even at a young age, he had read of Brownian Motion, and Darwin's theories of gravity, and he sought a connection between them – but only in his own mind. Keeping track of such thoughts had never been a difficult. Perhaps, he sometimes wondered as a boy, such a connection could be applied to studies of heavenly bodies as well – planets and stars and asteroids. And once the dynamics of such were understood, similar knowledge of the atom would present no difficulties either, and his findings would make his fame.

By the time he was twenty-one, he was well on his way, having written a book of such rarefied and pure mathematics that no man in the scientific press capable of criticizing it. With that reputation, he had won a mathematical chair at one of the smaller northern universities, and with his eye fixed on the path to even greater and more accelerated advancement. He had no doubt that he was this generation's Darwin.

But then the rumors began to gather around him like a parliament of owls – tales told by lesser men who resented him, their jealousy making them bold. They did not realize that he wasn't simply a harmless academic, his head filled with mathematical equations and unhelpful theories. He had learned early that he had another gift – the manipulation of lesser beings. And he had also helpfully realized early on that all but he were lesser beings. His envious colleagues never had a chance.

But his academic undoing was a valuable lesson. He had honed his manipulative skill on his brothers and parents – almost too well – and by the time held his university position, he had become arrogant and careless, forgetting that subtlety was also necessary to have his way. Too late he learned how much he was resented by the other professors – they would never have been his peers – and he was finally forced to resign, moving to London and setting himself up as an army coach. But as tedious as that was, it allowed him to turn his attention in other directions – quietly executing plans to increase and consolidate his power and influence, and making a position for himself unlike any that had ever been seen before. There really was no defense against such a one as he.

Along the way, he began to carefully recruit those who would assist him, to serve as intermediaries between him and the drones and dreck that formed his dark army. Many of the lesser creatures didn't even know who he was. Oh, sometimes there was a rumor, but when he needed to, he squashed it – permanently if necessary. And for carrying out such tasks as these, he formed his own elite Praetorian Guard.

Early on, he'd considered recruiting his old pupil, Holmes, but he'd soon given up that idea. Holmes was possibly the fourth smartest man in London – with himself being the first, the young criminal nobleman John Clay next, and third being Mycroft Holmes, Sherlock Holmes's smarter brother – and unfortunately just as incorruptible. But Clay was a temperamental stripling, unseasoned and vain. There had always been the eventuality that he would bend when strength was needed. And then it happened . . . .

Just the previous October, Clay had planned and nearly executed what should have been a brilliant attempt on the vaults of the City and Suburban Bank, just 'round the corner from Saxe-Coburg Square – but he had been arrogant, believing that the success of his scheme would be absolute, and that he'd remained undetected. Neither was true. He'd unknowingly spoken with Sherlock Holmes just hours before his arrest, when he should have taken the trouble to identify the enemy and expect him, and he'd foolishly drawn attention to the clever distraction he'd constructed in order to have time to dig his tunnels by posting a notice – for no reason at all – that the distraction had closed its doors.

Moriarty's plans for the bank's French gold had been extensive, and John Clay's carelessness had cost the Professor dearly, requiring a quite unexpected re-routing of his funds for an important job – ironically in France. And now Clay was gone, and there was no one who could replace him in terms of intelligence – certainly not the object of this night's enquiry.

As Moriarty had constructed his organization, he'd found that he needed a Chief-of-Staff, someone who could be trusted – as much as that was possible – to keep order, carry out the unpleasant tasks, and think for himself when needed. Such a one as that didn't need to be brilliant – just some animal cunning and dogged persistence. Perhaps a former military fellow, but one of dubious-enough reputation that he wouldn't mind working outside the lines of the law.

Such a man was Colonel Sebastian Moran,

Now just over fifty years of age, Moran had been born in London, the son of a former Minister to Persia. He'd attended Eton and Oxford, and seemed to have a bright future – but at some point, for no apparent reason, a dark spot in his character warped him in a different direction. From what Moriarty had determined, after Moran joined the 1st Bangalore Pioneers and went overseas, he managed to run through any situation he countered like a wolf meeting a herd of penned sheep, always finding a way to turn things to his advantage.

He served in various campaigns, including Jowaki in '77, and he was at Maiwand in '80. It was there that he got into a bit more trouble than usual – Moriarty had to pay a sizeable amount to winkle out that story. Apparently Moran had been double-dealing, working for the Russians, and he was forced to hunt the man who held evidence against him. The trail took him right into the heart of the Battle of Maiwand as it erupted around him, and he was forced to shoot and kill several British soldiers, using his well-honed skills, before he brought down the correct target. After that, he escaped back to Peshawar, and not long after, sensing that he had worn out his welcome, he resigned his commission.

He remained in the East, hunting in the western Himalayas and through the lower jungles – the experiences of which generated a couple of books which Moriarty read with initial interest before soon judging them tedious. How useful for a man to thoughtfully record his thoughts so

471

that another could adjudicate him. He found Moran to be a vain man, but with an animal cunning and brutal stubbornness.

Their paths initially crossed in the early eighties, when the Professor was finding that the idea of a second-in-command would be useful, and an arrangement was made – which had proven satisfactory, right up to the present. But now word had come to him, by way of a document never meant for his eyes, that Moran might no longer trustworthy – and that idea must be investigated.

All of these thoughts had passed through the Professor's mind in mere seconds as he reviewed what he knew of the Colonel. He came back to himself as they passed No. 24 Montague Street on the left, its ground-floor windows dark. He remembered visiting there once, over a decade before. That was when Holmes had still lived there, before moving west to Baker Street. Moriarty had just come up to London and moved in right around the corner in Russell Square. He had knocked and been permitted entry by a sour-faced woman who told him that Sherlock Holmes lived in rooms on the top floor. With a sigh, the Professor started up the stairs, which quickly narrowed to the point that the last flight was more of a ladder.

Holmes had seemed glad enough to see his former tutor, but there were some reservations, and Moriarty recalled that their past interactions in Yorkshire at the Holmes family estate in the mid-seventies had not been pleasant. The willful young man had one of the finest minds that Moriarty had ever encountered – not clearly so fine as is own, of course, but with potential. That day in Holmes's Montague Street room, when Holmes was unknowingly being evaluated for a position within Moriarty's new organization, had convinced the Professor that the young man, who had set himself up in the ridiculous profession of "Consulting Detective", would not be suited to the duties that Moriarty would require. After a few minutes of rather pointless conversation, Moriarty said goodbye, and then climbed back down to the street without having even mentioned that he was now residing nearby.

By now Bassick was moving along Great Russell Street, in front of the Museum. The street was dark, the fog getting somewhat thicker. Occasionally the black shape of a man or wraith could be seen walking along the street, hunched against the insidious damp. Moriarty idly wondered which ones were in some form or fashion out this night upon his business.

A turn down the Tottenham Court Road brought them to the better-lit Oxford Street. Here, in spite of the unpleasant evening, there were more people about, and Moriarty sank back into the shadows of the carriage – he didn't even realize that he had done so. Despite his disguise, he didn't want to be seen. He spent very little time these days out and about amongst the riff-raff of the capital. Tonight, if he'd had another choice, he would have been indoors – in his study, with his books and calculations, relaxing his own peculiar way, and with the occasional glance at the lovely Greuze painting hanging nearby – one of his few indulgences toward the weakness of art and beauty.

Regent Street was more lit and populated than Oxford Street had been, but they only traversed it for a few moments before turning right into the darker path that was Conduit Street. The rather dull thoroughfare seemed an odd place for Colonel Moran to construct his den, but Moriarty knew that there was cunning in the old shikari, and that such a location, with its stodgy nature and lack of excitement, would make obvious any enemy intrusions.

No. 64 was just on the left, but Bassick knew better than to stop right in front of it. He continued a hundred feet down the street, slowing just long enough for Moriarty to climb down. Then he resumed his journey, with instructions to be back in one hour, precisely. That was all the time that Moriarty would need to determine Moran's guilt.

He ached as he dropped to the pavement, but he refused to let Bassick see any signs of it. Ever since the accident at the Tower, he'd been in steady pain. At times he'd even been tempted to try to ease it by way of a bit of morphine or cocaine, but he knew that was the first step upon a steadily steepening slope from which there would be no return. Furthermore, it would dull his intellect, which he could not afford. It was just one more debt that Holmes owed to him, and which he would have paid when all was said and done.

Moriarty's scheme had been brilliant: After Holmes had tried to have him convicted of the Lorray murder, only to have the whole matter dropped in court – a brilliant bit of chicanery which had fooled two-hundred members of the Royal Society into providing him with an alibi – Moriarty had realized that Holmes was off balance. The defeat had shaken him. With that in mind, the Professor came up with one of his most audacious schemes – namely, to steal the Crown Jewels.

He'd stirred up a devious little distraction for Holmes involving a mysterious drawing of a man and an albatross, a haunting song played on a South American flute, and a revenge murder. (Why did so many of those foreigners bring that sort of business to England's shores? he sometimes wondered.) Then, in the midst of this distraction, he'd planned to have a fake robbery of the Tower be prevented, after which he remained behind in the guise of a policeman.

It had gone according to clockwork – he had been locked in with the jewels, allowing him to start their workmanlike separation from the tattered and bulky crowns – but then Holmes had somehow divined what was going one and arrived before he was finished.

They had fought atop the battlements of the tower-tops, and it was only the fog-slick stone that had prevented Moriarty from being victorious. Instead of throwing Holmes to his death, he himself had slipped and dropped to the hard courtyard below. Fortunately Moran and Bassick had been waiting in the shadows, and they were able to slip away with him and seek treatment before he was arrested. After that, it was only Holmes and Watson's word that he had been there, and influence exerted on the police officials and politicians in his power had insured that Holmes's accusation was ridiculed. *Professor Moriarty tried to steal the Crown Jewels? Do you rave, man? Go back to your petty puzzles and stop impugning the reputation of one of our finest citizens! This bee in your bonnet, Holmes, will destroy you if you aren't careful.*

In spite of his escape from the law, the Professor still paid a price, both in the fact that any benevolence that he might have still held seemed to have finally vanished overnight, and also lingering physical pain. Only his knowledge of Eastern fighting techniques had allowed him to land as safely as he did. Otherwise, his skull would have split on the stones like a melon. And he'd felt it every day since then – including this night, moving through the shadows of Conduit Street.

Fortunately, the Professor had no need to create any kind of distraction, as Moran was out of the country – sent to France in order to carry a message to certain criminal overlords there who were in the process of being subsumed into Moriarty's organization – although they had yet to realize it. When all was ready, the trap would spring, and he would own them as he did so many others. There really never had been anyone like him before, and there was nothing they could do to fight back. No one, in truth, really had any clue as to his capabilities. Except for Holmes, of course, and he would be neutralized at the right time, when it would most benefit the Professor's goals.

Moran lived in the third floor of a wide building with several ground-floor shops. Moriarty went to the eastern end of the building, past the shop doors, and to a nondescript and shadowed doorway. Expertly picking the lock, he let himself in, shut and re-locked the door, and then listened for a moment, and then another. The building was silent, and the Professor slowly and steadily climbed the stairs, without making a single sound. His body ached, but he gave no outer indication. His breathing stayed level and even as he ascended.

Entering Moran's rooms, even with their expensive and complex lock, presented no more difficulty than he'd had at the street door. Inside, Moriarty shut the door and then breathed deeply and slowly while listening. Nothing. The room smelled like a gentleman's club – rich smoke had saturated the walls and furniture. Great leather couches and armchairs were scattered about, and well as various African and Indian curios brought back from Moran's travels.

Moriarty had been here before, and he wasn't surprised – or concerned – at the great size of the rooms. The expensive tastes on display here were not indications of treachery in and of themselves. Moran was well paid for his unique services, and there was nothing wrong about him fixing up his lodgings in the way that pleased him, and in the manner that he could afford. No, Moriarty sought deeper evidence than merely monetary expenditures.

He had received a letter – just a short note really – sent anonymously to the house in Russell Square. That in itself was concerning, as his residence there was not well known. The letter had been written by Moran to one of the men that he was now visiting in France, vaguely implying an otherwise unidentified arrangement between the two of which Moriarty had no knowledge. It raised a concern: If Moran was willing to conduct business like this on one occasion, then wasn't it likely there were others? And if that crack in the man's armor existed, then it could be widened . . .

.

The Professor was shaken. A lesser man might feel that ignorance of this sort about his most trusted agent was an error – something he should have foreseen or expected. But Moriarty did not make errors – of this he was certain. So some way of explaining this must be found, something that would confirm Moran's treachery while allowing Moriarty to continue to view himself as unbeatable.

In his continued self-admiration, the Professor did not see the danger of this self-made trap.

Methodically, as befitted a man of his intelligence, Moriarty searched the rooms efficiently, and effectively, and in a way that Moran would never spot when he returned. The Professor saw a few small traps and indicators that Moran had foolishly placed – single hairs across closed doors, for instance, or small pieces of paper or dust shut in the crack of a closed drawer, poised to fall unnoticed to the floor when they were opened. Moriarty felt as if he were some sort of God standing above a boxed maze – almost as if he could see Moran, the mouse, running from here to there setting these little hooks, so proud of himself at his own cleverness, and completely unaware of how pedestrian and insignificant his efforts had been.

It was Moran's journal, kept in an easily opened safe, that exonerated him. The details of this supposed side-deal were revealed: Moran was smuggling a sizeable amount of an American liquor to the Frenchman as a gift – to grease the wheels of their upcoming deal. There was no betrayal on Moran's part – he was simply being a good manager, and hadn't told Moriarty about it because it was a triviality that didn't need to be passed up the chain of command.

Moriarty continued to flip through the journal. He had time before Bassick's planned return.

It was interesting to see Moran's viewpoint on a number of their past business matters – and of concern that the Colonel would keep such detailed notes in a journal. That would have to be addressed upon Moran's return from the Continent. Perhaps Moriarty would bring the matter up in such a way as to reinforce his own omnipotence.

He continued to read.

As he looked deeper, beyond the obvious narrative of what had been accomplished by Moriarty's organization, he began to see a deeper pattern, one that made his lip curl involuntarily with disgust. |

Apparently, incredibly, Moran thought of him as a *friend* – and a close one.

Where, thought Moriarty, did the idiot get that idea? Moran was his employee – a blunt instrument, and nothing more. He was effective, certainly, and in some ways unique and indispensable, but that was the end of it. In fact, it was only Moran's usefulness and skills that made the crude former soldier tolerable at all. Moriarty looked up from the journal and glanced around at the room, which reeked of Moran's personality. The man was barely more civilized than the beasts that he hunted. He had animal cunning, but absolutely no other redeeming values. Moriarty had in fact always kept a special eye on Moran, expecting that someday he would become rabid and have to be put down. Perhaps, he considered, he would need to find a new Chief-of-Staff sooner than he'd thought – because any ideas that he and Moran were *"friends"* – and the idea gave him an unpleasant sick feeling – would not be tolerated.

With a snap he shut the journal and started to toss it back into the safe in disgust, only to force himself at the last minute to be more careful, replacing it as it had been found. Then he departed. There was no need to make any additional effort toward erasing his presence before he went – he had already done that methodically as he searched.

Bassick and the carriage were passing by exactly on time, and as soon as the Professor was aboard and seated, they were in motion again, this time to Limehouse. There was no need to direct Bassick, as he'd already been informed of their agenda earlier that night before their departure from Russell Square.

Moriarty had always been able to compartmentalize his thinking, and he did so now as the carriage wended its way east, through the prosperous parts of the city and on into those of a much different nature. He considered various jobs in progress – the Mona Lisa affair, which had required some of Moran's time in France, and also the Godolphin Street intrusion to retrieve the Ministry papers. These thoughts kept him distracted for a while, but he found that his mind kept creeping back to the notion that Moran considered him a friend. How on earth could that have happened? He had expected to read Moran's true thoughts in the journal, and that they would be the typical and expected criticisms of an employer by his employee – useful information for the Professor to have. But instead there was admiration – which was only right – but presented in a quite distasteful manner. He gave up trying to consider his other business and turned his thoughts completely to what he should do about Moran – but by the time they reached his Limehouse rooms, there was no solution.

Of the people that knew of his existence, most connected him with this location, rather than the Russell Square residence. He had seen the usefulness of having a stronghold here in the eastern side of the city, but getting established in this location had been something more of a chore than he'd first expected. They were very territorial in this district, and the Chinaman who was called "The Devil Doctor" had proven to be particularly resistant to Moriarty's presence. But an uneasy accord had been achieved when the Doctor understood that Moriarty's interests did not include taking over the elaborate criminal network that infested the Docklands. At least not yet . . . .

Still, Moriarty's Limehouse stronghold was quite close to the Chinese Quarter, hard down by the river. It was in the upper floors of an otherwise-abandoned warehouse, apparently in terrible shape: Broken windows, scarred brickwork, and abominable odors. But in spite of its neglected appearance, it was known to a certain number of disreputable people as the place where the Professor's organization carried out its business.

He kept another set of rooms just to the north, in Stepney, which could be reached from the Limehouse building by a series of closely-guarded tunnels, almost certainly originally dug by the Devil Doctor, but now reluctantly ceded to the Professor. Moriarty only used them on certain special occasions, and he rarely visited the Stepney location at all, except when the gas chamber there was needed. This night would require no such finesse. Instead of trapping and removing an enemy behind a locked door while the deadly gas hissed into the room, he would be in his own building when confronting the treacher.

Normally anyone entering the Professor's Limehouse headquarters would need to negotiate a series of locked entrances and narrow passages to penetrate deeper and higher into the building. But the leader of the organization was not required to put up with such foolishness, and he was quickly passed through into his inner sanctum. There he found several of his Inner Circle, all climbing quickly to their feet to indicate their respect. They spent a great deal of time here, keeping an eye on various aspects of his business. He had not shared with them his own enquiry in Conduit Street, or his intention to explore Moran's quarters, but they were aware that an accusation had been made against the Colonel, and that it would be investigated. They were also aware of the origin of the accusation – for there was no true trust within Moriarty's little "family", and when the anonymous note was delivered directing attention to Moran's supposed malfeasance, it took no more than a day to locate who had sent the message.

Moriarty had barely entered the room when one of the men standing to one side pushed himself away from the wall where he was leaning and approached him. It was his younger brother, Jamie, a sneer on his face.

"You're getting careless, Brother," he said with a drawl, his voice a bit too loud for the room – which was suddenly very quiet indeed as the breathing of the other men there seemed to stop. "You're allowing the troops to lose their fear of you."

Moriarty, in the act of removing his coat, gave the younger man the same look he might give a filthy beggar who had dared to crawl close and touch the hem of his garments. It was not lost on the younger man, who faltered and realized that he had overstepped his position.

"Jamie," Moriarty replied, his voice a low hiss, "I was unaware that you were invited here tonight. I'll let you know when something requiring your . . . *unique* talents occurs. In the meantime, don't you have one of your dollymops to visit?"

A flash of rage – just the barest glimpse – passed across Jamie's eyes, but then his intelligence superseded his inclination to respond hotly and, rather than say anything else, he turned on his heel and walked out, knocking one of Moriarty's lieutenants, Oldacre, to one side. Then the door shut – not quite a slam, but not quietly either – and he was gone.

The Professor knew that neither of his brothers could be trusted, but at least the middle one, Colonel James Moriarty, could be kept on his leash by manipulating his innate responses to authority. Jamie had no such aspect in his nature – he was the youngest, and the most spoiled, and with a sly intellect that was nearly on par with the Professor's – though without any of the true brilliant artistry that the elder brother often displayed. Jamie had started his career as a West Country station master, but the dark tendencies that were stirred into each of the brothers had soon tempted him into mistreating his position in such a careless manner that he'd been discovered and released – and quite lucky not to have been prosecuted.

He had drifted to London soon after and had obtained a position working with his older brother – and it was soon apparent to the Professor that the younger man hubristically believed that he deserved to be the leader. He certainly resented not being chosen as the Professor's Chief-of-Staff, and when the accusations had first arrived against Moran, he had been so vocal in supporting them without investigation that it seemed as if he might have fabricated them himself. However, no connection could be established between him and anonymous letter, so he was absolved – this time. But he would need to be carefully watched.

In fact, Moriarty was aware of at least one occasion when Jamie had intricately disguised himself as the Professor – and well enough to fool some of the Inner Circle. What he'd intended with that action was still uncertain, and the Professor was willing to give him some rope just to see how the situation progressed . . . but only for a little while, and it was becoming rather certain that Jamie would eventually have to be taken to the facility in Stepney for a final solution to this problem – possibly sooner rather than later.

But that was not on the agenda this night. Instead, the Professor intended to confront the man who had written the letter accusing Moran of high crimes, and to confirm the origin of the plot.

When he had finished removing the disguise he'd worn to Conduit Street, Moriarty and a couple of his men went through a side door and down a hall to a locked chamber at the far end. Although not specifically set up as a cell with iron bars, the walls, floors, ceiling, and door had been reinforced so that no escape was possible. Bassick unlocked the door and then went first – should the prisoner be feeling aggressive.

But Able Wenallt would offer no further trouble. He was curled upon his bunk, his hands clutching his belly, and regularly emitting a low whistling noise from his damaged face. Moriarty looked around at his men with a curious expression.

"He fought back during questioning," said Oldacre, flexing his big knuckles. "He took some damage."

"No matter," said Moriarty, taking a step closer. Then, in a louder tone, he said, "Wenallt!"

The man, in spite of his pain, forced a glance up at the thin shape looming between him and the doorway. He surely knew how this would end – he had been on the other side of such interrogations before. Escape was impossible, even if he'd been physically capable of it. And that wasn't the case anymore – Oldacre had broken something inside him. He could feel it grinding with every breath, and it was becoming more difficult to keep the spots away from his vision, or the darkness from crowding in on all sides. He was becoming cold.

"The letter," pressed Moriarty. "We know you sent it. Tell me – was Holmes behind it? Was he?"

A note of impatience crept into Moriarty's tone, and he forced himself to breathe deeper and control it. Weakness must never be shown.

"Holmes was behind it," continued the Professor. "I know he was – trying to sew distrust and dissention in our ranks. Somehow he found this letter, which might be misinterpreted, and hoped to plant a seed of doubt. He got to you, Wenallt. How? How did he compromise you?"

Able Wenallt coughed and tried to sit up, but then he collapsed suddenly with a small cry. He rolled onto his back, still gripping his middle, and Moriarty could see fresh blood at the corner of the man's mouth. He glanced with disgust at Oldacre.

"You've killed him, you imbecile."

Oldacre suddenly looked terrified – he had somehow offended the Professor, doing only what he thought was the right thing. He threw a pointed finger in Wenallt's direction. "He ain't dead. He's still breathing."

Moriarty shook his head. "Not for long, he isn't."

"Maybe a doctor – " chimed in Bassick, but Moriarty disagreed.

"For what? He's for the river soon enough anyway. All I want to know is how Holmes was able to turn him." He raised his voice. "Tell me, Wenallt – and maybe that sick brat of yours will survive the night, even though you won't."

This statement made the dying man gasp in shock, which in turn seemed to increase his pain. He groaned, crying, "Don't! Don't, Professor. Leave him be – !"

"Then tell us!" growled Moriarty, taking another step closer. He started to reach out and grab Wenallt's shoulder, but then he prevented himself from doing so. "How did Holmes turn you?"

"It was Molly. After the baby was born, and she was sick, we were going to leave – move away. But then she died. You told me she died. But she didn't! Mr. Holmes found me, and told me where she was – where you had taken her. So that I wouldn't be distracted, he said. You took her away from me so I would keep working for you.

"Mr. Holmes was going to take me to her. We would have taken back our baby and moved away, and you would have never found us. And Mr. Holmes told me how I could repay what you had done – I could slip in the letter from the Colonel – and make you doubt him. He said it would be a dis . . . a dis – "

"A distraction," finished Moriarty. He'd heard enough. It was generally as he'd thought – only the details had been required to satisfy his own curiosity. Then another idea crossed his mind – unlikely to be sure, but one that must be explored while there was still a chance.

480

"Wenallt," he said, his tone sharper. "Listen to me – Listen! Are you *Porlock*?"

Some of the men behind him cut their eyes to one another – a few knowingly, and others with puzzlement. Those in the know were aware of this curious name, but only in the smallest way. It had come to Moriarty's attention several years earlier that someone within his organization – and he'd yet to discover who – had been passing information anonymously to Sherlock Holmes concerning some of the Professor's various projects. A few times, Holmes had managed to get ahead in the game and spoil everything. It was only because of a few well-placed bribes within the police force that Moriarty had learned of this "Porlock" at all, and he'd never been able to dig any deeper. Whomever Porlock was, he was still uncaught – and unpunished.

Now, before Wenallt was gone, perhaps the Professor could cross off at least one possible suspect.

"Wenallt! Answer me – *Are you Porlock?*"

The damaged man could only shake his head. "No," he finally managed. "No. Never . . . never knew who . . . would have helped if I could . . . ." Then he coughed, and Moriarty wondered if he was simply starting to choke on his own fluids, or making a futile attempt to spit on the Professor's boots.

Moriarty was finished with the traitor. He nodded his head in the general direction of the nearby Thames. "Sink him."

As the Professor walked out of the cell, a part of him listened to hear if Wenallt might cry out in protest, but he didn't say a word, even as he was dragged from the filthy cot and onto the floor.

Bassick joined him as they returned to Moriarty's office. "Eliminate the child," said the Professor, loud enough for Wenallt to hear, should he still be alive. "Find the girl and do the same."

Walking behind him, Bassick didn't speak, and Moriarty found that he needed some sort of acknowledgement to his order. "Examples must be made. Do you *understand*?" He placed extra emphasis on the last word. There was more to understand here than the specific instructions about the fate of mother and child. Bassick's own safety was tied up with his efficiency in carrying out the order.

"Yes, sir," was the muffled reply.

At the door to Moriarty's office, he paused. "I have some additional work to do regarding the new French-British telephone lines. We have a client who is interested in hearing what is being said between certain Government officials on both sides of the Channel. While he's over there, Moran will be taking care of the French side of things. In the meantime,

I'll have instructions for you in the morning about whom to compromise here. You are up to the task, aren't you, Bassick?"

"Yes, sir," the shabby man repeated, his eyes downcast.

He feels bad about the woman and the sick child, Moriarty thought. A weakness – perhaps I'll need to rethink the hierarchy of the Praetorian Guard. I've become too complacent – too trusting of these weak inferiors. They have allowed Holmes to vex me too often of late.

It never occurred to the Professor that any of the blame for Holmes's recent successes might lie at his own feet. He was the sort who could never consider that possibility – for he knew with certainty that he was the smartest man in London, and mostly likely the world. It gave him a pleased feeling as he shut the door and sat down at his desk, pulling forward a blank sheet of paper where he began to list the points of his latest scheme, starting with *Number 1 . . . .*

Bassick was able to slip away later that night. He had been so careful for so long, but he never let down his guard. His position gave him a certain amount of invisibility. Moran was the Chief-of-Staff, and he always carried himself larger-than-life, which drew a lot of attention as he carried out some of the Professor's more ambitious plans. Bassick, however, was more subtle, his appearance making him seem harmless and worth very little respect, but in truth he was usually able to get things done without any fuss. When he left Limehouse in the early hours, it was assumed that he was faithfully on the Professor's business, as always, and no one gave him a thought.

He never traveled the same way twice when on one of these special errands, and he also found ways to pass along the messages in ways that were never repeated. He was just as careful this time, and when the short note had been sent, the Professor never knew. Bassick had no doubt that Mr. Holmes would decipher the coded message as he always had before – for no matter which new code that Bassick devised, the consulting detective in Baker Street never failed to figure it out. He did this time as well, and Bassick finally fell into his bed near dawn, relieved that once again he'd managed to accomplish something meaningful – a small victory in the greater war. It would never repay the debt that he owed, but he did what he could.

> *Wenallt discovered, killed. Attempt to discredit Moran failed.*
> *Make all efforts to save girl and child – will report that they*
> *have died as well, as ordered. Information provided soon*
> *regarding London-Paris telephone scheme.*
>
> *Porlock*

The Gillette Play's the Thing!

Chapter I

"**I** trust," said Sherlock Holmes over the last half of his pint, "that you've satisfied your commitment – that there will be no more of your little tales in *The Strand*." It was a statement, not a question.

His comment was unexpected at that moment, but not atypical in general.

I gave a quarter-turn of my own glass while I silently considered my reply.

Not long after the gales had assailed the eastern coast in early January 1905, when the pier at Scarborough washed away and Great Yarmouth flooded, I journeyed down to visit my friend at his Sussex cottage. Just weeks earlier, he'd been invited up to London to spend Christmas with us in Queen Anne Street, but my wife and I had known that it was very unlikely he'd make the trip, and we'd been correct. We both understood that he wasn't the type to feel lonely during the holidays, and he was quite able to entertain himself without any feelings of self-pity, but there is always a concern that arises, especially during that particular season, when thoughts turn to those we care about and we wish to have them close by.

I had set off that morning, driving south through the blue-gray twilight that had gripped the nation for a number of days. The countryside looked so different than in the warmer months when I usually made the journey, either by train or in my own automobile. When the sun was high over the vibrant summer fields and forests, it was more beautiful than could be expressed. Now the fields lay fallow and empty, with the ragged stalks of last year's crops silhouetted against the low sky, awaiting the return of spring. Often I would see distant cottages across the vacant pastures, with one or two lights showing in their windows and smoke rising from the chimneys. Sometimes a dark figure would be visible near a building, or perhaps a few animals might be silhouetted against the horizon, but mostly there was a sense of emptiness as everyone hid away from the dark day.

In spite of the bleak aspect, however, there was still an unmistakable charm and stark beauty to it too. Since Holmes's retirement a little over a year before, and move to the southern edge of the Downs, I had seen him quite a bit, both in Sussex and when he came up to London, but I realized how very little I'd made this journey during the colder parts of the year. I resolved to do better.

I arrived in early afternoon to find him researching a chemical question in the cozy little laboratory he'd set up in one corner of his study – specifically, he was analyzing which compounds were toxic to the ergot fungus, and which left it to survive. As if we were carrying on a conversation that had begun just an hour before, he explained that there were certain medico-legal aspects to his research, relating to the forced suicide of Lord Woodford the previous week. I had apparently arrived at a crisis, but within moments he had the result he'd sought and, after he'd recorded his results neatly in his laboratory notebook, he shut off his Bunsen burner, washed his hands, and settled me before the fire with a restorative whisky.

Our conversation, as it usually did, ranged from current events to past cases, and encompassed news about those whom we'd known over the years. Holmes would be turning fifty-one the following day, and I was a year or so older, so we'd arrived at that age when mortality was beginning to creep up on us. Still, it was always something of a surprise to hear that this or that person with whom we had been long acquainted had passed from natural causes – especially as we'd known so many who died over the years from violence.

After an hour we decided to adjourn to the nearby village for a pint or two. As the day was cold and the chance of rain still likely, I drove my automobile. (Typically we would walk the mile or so across the pastures behind Holmes's small farm.) We exited Holmes's property and joined the road running east-to-west along the base of Beachy Head, which was highlighted against the gray southern light and fast-scudding clouds. Within a few thousand feet we were passing below the Belle Tout Lighthouse, abandoned a couple of years before, and high above us on the left. Not much further and we reached Birling Gap and the Coast Guard houses. A right turn there, and then in less than a mile we had arrived in the small village of East Dean. Parking the vehicle, we walked into the grassy village square and so into The Tiger Inn. As we entered, familiar faces offered greetings, and soon we were in a warm corner, continuing our earlier discussions.

Holmes told me that he'd recently had a visit from Trevor and Edith Bennett, who happened to be staying in nearby Eastbourne. They brought the sad news that Edith's father, Professor Presbury, had finally succumbed to the madness that slowly overtook him following his personally detrimental experiments of a year or so before. "Apparently his undiagnosed dementia was seriously exacerbated by those injections," explained Holmes. "Bennett said that during the professor's final months – spent alone, as his engagement to his young lady had ended – he had to be restrained completely so as to avoid doing violence to himself or harming others."

We fell silent as I considered the fate of the professor, whom Holmes and I had always referred to as "the creeping man". I doubted that his injections of monkey gland derivative had actually caused any true deleterious effects on him. The instances when he crept about displaying simian behaviors – the reason that Holmes was initially consulted – were more likely related to his declining mental condition than anything he'd put into his body. As I continued to chase these thoughts, Holmes spoke again.

"I trust that you've satisfied your commitment, and that there will be no more of your little tales in *The Strand*."

I was abruptly returned to the present with the realization that I'd been thinking of publishing those very same singular facts connected with Professor Presbury, if only to dispel once for all the ugly rumours which still agitated certain learned societies of London and the university with which he'd been associated. Of course, perceiving my thoughts had been mere child's play of deduction for Holmes.

"I'm uncertain," I replied noncommittally. "With the publication of 'The Second Stain' last month, this series is complete – but Doyle wants to keep the door open."

Holmes shook his head. "He's certainly changed his tune. As I understand it, it was he who wished to cease your joint publishing venture a dozen years ago after you'd made public the events of my encounter with the Professor at Reichenbach."

"This is true. At the time, he felt that his own works were being eclipsed by the effort he was making to get your adventures published."

"You mean to publish *your* writing – *your* efforts," Holmes countered. "He has taken advantage of you, Watson. For years he's done it. From the beginning, and all the way down the line." His tone was peeved, and he had made this familiar argument before. "For heaven's sake! He offered to be your 'Literary Agent' – a job which you could have done yourself, especially in those early days – and then it's his byline over your story! You do the work – after you lived the actual events and faced the dangers! – and he reaps the credit and takes his substantial financial cut."

It was a conversation that we'd had in countless variations over the years, and would doubtless have again. The question of my 'Literary Agent' was one of those rare situations when I felt that I did not have Holmes's full respect. His opinion of my actual published works themselves waxed and waned, and I was never quite certain where he would land on the question at any given time. He was sometimes willing to admit that the stories had helped make him more well-known than he might have been otherwise, and while he didn't like having a reputation built on "that character in *The Strand*", as he sometimes disparagingly referred to it, he did agree on rare occasions that some interesting clients had found their way to his door who might not have otherwise have done so except for knowing about him by way of my stories.

The entire topic was something of a sore spot with me. When I'd first met Doyle – Sir Arthur to everyone else, but always Doyle to me – we'd both discovered that we each had ambitions to be writers. He drifted toward historical novels, hoping (I believe) to be the modern Sir Walter Scott. I had always simply been a writer – a keeper of journals recording my own experiences. In the mid-1880's, after making records of Holmes's cases for several years, I'd finally had the gumption to polish the narrative of the Lauriston Gardens mystery, as I'd promised Holmes to do not long after we met. I'd let Doyle read it, and he noted that it needed something more – a central section that he offered to write, detailing the long-ago and far-away historical events leading to the London murders. By then I was attempting to build a medical practice, and as such I had the notion that putting my name on such a sordid little tale might somehow damage my professional credibility. Doyle, who handled the arrangements of the sale of the story to a small holiday periodical, ended up placing his own name on the cover. He made an explanation about it at the time – something about liability and perceptions and a misunderstanding with the publisher – and I accepted it – which laid the groundwork for more of the same in years to come.

Just a few years later, I finished up a second story concerning another old vengeance brought to England's shores, and it was easy enough to rationalize along the same lines. I had a practice and a reputation to consider, and even though I had written the entire second book without assistance, Doyle again did the work of placing it for publication, attending a dinner with an American publisher when I was too busy to do so myself. Afterwards, we followed the same arrangement as before, and in hindsight, I was quite naïve in allowing him to again put his name on the cover instead of mine. (The second time seemed more deliberate.)

My wife was certainly unhappy about it, stating that it was as if Tommy Ryan had fought and won the fight, but his manager was given all the credit. And she was no happier when we repeated this method the next year after that, publishing shorter versions of Holmes's investigations in a new monthly periodical, *The Strand*. Sadly, she passed away some months before the last of them appeared, so when Doyle indicated that was ready to move on to something else and disassociate himself from any more of

Holmes's adventures, I agreed, no longer having any interest in publishing further – or in much of anything, for that matter.

But at the turn of the century, Doyle had visited the West Country, where he'd run across a few people who told him of one of Holmes's more *outrè* investigations there in the autumn of '88. He came back asking me for additional details, and before I knew it, he'd talked me into writing up the affair of the Baskervilles for publication. I'd checked with Holmes about this, of course, as he'd refused to allow any further publication of his cases following his return to London in 1894 after his supposed death. By the time *The Hound* began serialization in late summer 1901, Doyle had actually achieved his goal of becoming a famous author, and we agreed to continue the previous arrangement, as his name was so associated with the stories by that point, and he could also negotiate a much larger sale based upon his reputation.

In late 1903, Holmes had chosen to move to Sussex, part of his supposed retirement to give the impression that he was no longer in active practice, as in fact he'd transitioned into something of a specialized agent for his brother Mycroft's governmental department. It was in the best interest to spread the word that he was retired, and part of this was accomplished with the publication of thirteen more tales in *The Strand*, some with discreet references to Holmes having left London. But as of December 1904, the last of these had appeared, with no firm plans for additional efforts. Doyle, however, was suddenly pressing for more of them – I suspect the money was a factor – and hearing about the late Professor Presbury had reminded me of that. It was just the sort of thing that Doyle, with his growing and unhealthy interest in the occult, might appreciate – although I was sure that he'd want to emphasize the horror of it, to the diminishment of describing Holmes's methods.

When conversing with Sherlock Holmes, one never knew when this topic might rear its head, and I certainly hadn't expected to be defending my writing, yet again, in the warm and comfortable corner of The Tiger Inn. I tried to think of a new topic to discuss, but all that entered my mind was my other reason for visiting Sussex that day, in addition to celebrating Holmes's upcoming birthday on the morrow. I took a sip and, with a deep breath, tentatively broached the subject, aware that it was just as likely to elicit a similar response from my friend as that brought about when considering my recent publications.

"I have been asked," I explained, my tone neutral, "to attend the theatre tomorrow tonight. In Eastbourne – the Royal Hippodrome."

Holmes raised an eyebrow. "I do still read the newspapers, you know. It hasn't escaped my attention what is premiering there tomorrow night, and then playing for the next two weeks – a touring company's version of

Gillette's play." He said it with the same tone that a titled lady might use to describe an East End slattern marrying her precious son.

I nodded. "I was invited by the actor playing . . . well, playing *you*. Brian Singer. And he asked if you would join me. I believe that he has a problem and needs our help."

"Really, Watson," Holmes said as he leaned back. "You could have mentioned this earlier. When were you planning on bringing it up?"

"Soon. Later this afternoon. But then we ended up talking about publishing – "

" – And only then did your thoughts turn to this appointment, which has a loose connection with your other published works, by way of that drodded play." He turned up his glass for a sip. "What is Mr. Singer's complaint? Are you certain that he doesn't simply want to lure us to the theatre in order to have our presence bestow some sort of approval upon his performance?" His voice took on a rolling theatricality. "'Ladies and gentlemen, we are *honored* tonight to have with us Mr. *Holmes* – Do rise and take a *bow*, sir! And also here is Sir Arthur's scrivener friend – You too, sir! Don't be shy!'" He finished the remains of his ale and then said, his voice returned to normal, "Will a member of the press, perhaps a friend of Mr. Singer's, be lurking in the shadows to leap out and take our photograph, standing alongside the costumed actor? Will we continue to see it when least expected for years to come as it's used for his personal publicity, until both the photograph and we too have faded beyond visibility or interest?"

I thought he was being unnecessarily sarcastic, but I bit my tongue, hoping that he might be lured into accompanying me. But perhaps that was the wrong approach.

"Here is his letter," I said, pulling the missive from my pocket. "You can decide his veracity for yourself."

Holmes took is and, as expected, he first examined the envelope. I had long ago learned to do the same thing when receiving a letter, and while I generally don't see a fraction of what he does, I knew that what he observed was fairly straightforward. Apparently Holmes agreed, because he quickly pulled out the single sheet without comment, looked it over front and back, and then read it to himself.

"Singularly uninformative," he concluded, dropping it onto the table. "He identifies himself, apologizes for the intrusion on your time, indicates that he is in some unspecified danger, and then asks if we can meet with him tomorrow afternoon in his rented lodgings before the performance. Have you had no other communication with him?"

"I telephoned the theatre yesterday after receiving the letter. He was in rehearsal but broke away to speak with me. He didn't provide any more information than what he wrote, instead preferring to discuss it in person. He's being harassed, he said, by someone he knows. He believes that several attempts have been made on his life, but the incidents may have been accidental. When pressed, he wouldn't provide any further details. He simply hopes that we will meet with him tomorrow."

"If he's in danger, why not sooner?"

I turned over a hand. "I informed him that I planned to drive down here today, and asked about meeting with him this afternoon, but he seemed to feel that tomorrow would do just as well. The play doesn't open until tomorrow night, and apparently they're busy with rehearsals, and also becoming accustomed to the theatre."

Holmes shook his head. "A drowning man doesn't typically ask to wait and have the rope thrown to him tomorrow. I reiterate my fear that this is just some ploy to get us to the play."

"Possibly. He did say that after we met, he'd make sure we had tickets for the best seats in the house."

Holmes nodded and leaned back. "That's it, then – We'll meet and talk, and it will be some contrived excuse that amounts to nothing. We'll reassure him – all part of his plan – and then, when we're in our seats and least expecting it, a spotlight will find us and, before you know it, we'll be bullied into coming onto the stage."

I finished my ale and, after a moment of silence, said, "We will meet with him, of course."

Holmes's mouth tightened, but in good-humored resignation rather than irritation, and he nodded. "I suppose so."

"And I do wish to attend the performance," I added. "I haven't seen it in four or five years – since Gillette finished up at the Lyceum. I'm curious to see how it plays in the provinces."

"Why not? If we're singled out for special attention, it can only reinforce the notion that I'm permanently rusticating here, and no one will expect to find me anywhere else. Perhaps I'll dodder onto the stage and shock everyone with my feeble helplessness." And he then gave that silent laugh of his which so often boded ill for someone.

I nodded, took our glasses, and went to the bar for refills, considering what Holmes had just said.

In late 1903, a combination of circumstances – which I do not propose to recount here – had led Holmes, then only forty-nine years old, to announce his retirement. Some of what happened then was personal, but a great deal of Holmes's decision was also related to the perceived threat, understood particularly by his Holmes's brother Mycroft, that the European situation was becoming more and more tangled, and thus fraught with peril for England. Many politicians refused to comprehend this, while others in the government understood all too well what might possibly occur in the coming years.

For quite a while, Mycroft had been urging Holmes to turn his attentions from those "petty problems of the police courts", as he liked to call them, and focus his energies and talents on the plots and plans devised by the British Government to prepare for upcoming threats. It must be admitted that Holmes had a special skill in such areas, as demonstrated by his recovery of the Bruce-Partington submarine plans, or more recently, the capture of the deathbed visitor to the woman whom we'd spent a lifetime believing to be our Queen, and the subsequent retrieval of the two items removed from the woman's personal lock-box – one of which had the absolute power to immediately topple more than one European kingdom. (I'm believe that it was the latter case that finally turned Holmes around to Mycroft's way of thinking, and it's a narrative that I'm absolutely and forever forbidden to record.) When certain personal matters occurred in 1903, Holmes realized that he must assume new obligations. The die was cast, and he threw himself into his new life.

I believe that he was happy during his times in Sussex, and he certainly stayed busy – keeping his bees with a passion I wouldn't have expected, delving into various scientific researches, accepting Mycroft's urgent missions, and continuing to take on the occasional private investigations for the occasional someone in need – often with my help when I could manage to get away, or when he happened to be in London. Our invitation to the Royal Hippodrome on the morrow would be one such affair.

After another half-hour or so, we departed from The Tiger Inn and returned to Holmes's cottage, where a warm meal awaited us. We had further discussions regarding old cases and new, and a little ongoing matter that would require Holmes to visit London within the next few weeks. He indicated that while he was there, he planned stay for a time in the old rooms in Baker Street, which he had retained following his decampment to the coast for when he needed a temporary base from which to carry out his inquiries in the capital. We didn't make further mention of our meeting tomorrow with the actor playing the part of Holmes, because without data, what reason did we have to speculate further?

It was still early when I went up to my room. Holmes had turned his attention back to his chemical researches, with no indication that he planned to stop for the night – very much like old times.

Chapter II

The next day passed quietly enough, and I took advantage of my holiday to relax, sleeping late and then sitting and reading by the fire in Holmes's study. He was up early, as usual, taking care of various chores around the small farm, and then resuming his research.

He was already outside when I arose, so it was only later that morning when I was able to wish him Happy Birthday and present the small gift I'd brought from London – a package of his favorite tobacco, the strong shag from Bradley's that he so favored. He acknowledged it with simple but sincere thanks. He packed some to take with him just before we set out for Eastbourne and our meeting with Mr. Singer.

We departed about half-an-hour before our scheduled appointment, driving east along the coast road past The Gables, the well-known coaching establishment, and then circling Bullock Down to our left. Upon reaching Holywell I turned right, just before Warren Hill, and so entered the maze of Eastbourne streets, working my way steadily toward our destination. We stayed just inland, going straight when we could. Luckily, pedestrians in early January are quite scarce, and not long after we passed the pier, we reached the theatre. I gave it a glance as we went by, but almost immediately Holmes advised me to turn left into a winding warren of lanes and alleys, and within moments we found ourselves before a small but tidy house just a couple of streets away. This, then, was where Singer was staying for the time that the play would be rehearsed and performed.

The street was empty, with nary a vehicle or pedestrian in sight, so I pulled to one side and shut off the engine. We exited and stood for a moment, looking at the plain two-story brick building, adjoined to similar-looking structures up and down the narrow lane. Then Holmes pulled his coat tighter, glanced at me, sighed, and stepped the short distance to the door.

Seconds after he had rung the bell, we were greeted by a beaming lady no more than four feet in height, and nearly as round as she was tall. She looked to be in her sixties, and her white hair contrasted with her prominent cheeks, resembling red apples. She looked up at us with her round pink face wreathed in a welcoming smile and wheezed, "It *is* you!" Then she stepped back and invited us in. "Young Mr. Singer told me that Mr. *Holmes* and Dr. *Watson* were planning to call. I had no idea he knew such noted figures, but I supposed that since he's the star of the play . . . Such an honor, gentlemen! Such an *honor*!"

She bustled around us to shut the door while indicating where we could hang our coats and hats, all the while chattering about how the neighbors would be so jealous, and then pivoting effortlessly to inform us of the other visitors of note she'd entertained over the years, all apparently actors of one sort or another – Edward Righton and Wybert Reeve, Arthur Wontner and William Henry Pennington, to name a few that I recall her mentioning. Though we'd been there less than a minute, she was already deep into a reminiscence of one Henry Spry when Holmes raised a hand.

"If we may, Mrs. – "

"Spence," she replied. "Eula Spence. Widow of Mr. John Bennett Spence, formerly of London, gone these twenty years. He trod the boards as well. Who knows what heights he might have reached before his untimely passing? One of the greats, gentleman! Even from a young age, he was one of the greats! Thanks heavens we had set up this lodging house before his illness began, and before he departed. I can't count the times that – "

Holmes glanced at a nearby wall clock. "Our appointment with Mr. Singer is overdue," he said. "Might you direct us to him?"

"What? Oh, certainly. He wasn't feeling well, the poor lad, and came home early from the rehearsal to take a nap. I sent for the doctor – he didn't want me to, but I insisted. After the passing of my husband, Mr. Spence, I'm ever-so careful, you know. Gone twenty years! One never knows, does one? In any case, Mr. Singer said that when you arrived to please join him in his room. Upstairs, one floor. Middle door on the right."

We thanked her and she continued talking, but this time to herself as she turned and moved off toward a closed door beyond the foot of the stairs.

The house was very quiet, and the sound of the squeaking steps as we ascended seemed excessively loud. Upon reaching the first floor, we found a dim hallway stretching toward the back of the house. It was lit only by a window behind us, over the stairs we had just climbed and facing the street, and another at the far end. In between were just six closed doors, three on either side. From the overhead transoms, I could see that all the lights were out, except for our destination. We stepped to the middle door, as directed, and Holmes knocked. There was no answer.

A second knock resulted in the same non-response. Holmes, being who he was, had no compunction at reaching for the door knob and turning it. It was unlocked. He pushed it open and I involuntarily gave a small cough as the faint smell of smoke, unmistakably from a recent gunshot, wafted out.

Holmes glanced at me and then stepped inside. I joined him, pushing the door softly shut. Then I locked it with the key that was protruding from the keyhole on the inner side.

I knew that Holmes would prefer to examine the room first before others disturbed any clues, but I had a duty to perform as a physician. "I need to check him," I said. "There's a chance he's still alive."

"Step carefully," Holmes replied. Then, as an afterthought, he asked, "Do you think she'll bring tea?"

"Likely so." I walked carefully in a straight line to the narrow bed, where the body of a man was lying on his back. I knew that Holmes would be able to identify the marks of my footsteps as he sorted the various telling signs in the room, but I didn't want to add any more confusion than necessary to his task.

The room was illuminated by a gaslight on the wall near the door, and another above the bed. It was a humble space, and the fact that Singer had stayed here, instead of somewhere nicer, indicated to me that his stature in the theatrical community, despite his role as the leading man, had been rather small. There was a bed and small table holding an empty glass, and I leaned to sniff it. The scent was unmistakable. Nearby was an open wardrobe with several bureau drawers in the lower half, a small table suitable for eating, and two straight chairs beside it. There was a low bookshelf near the door, with just a couple of shelves filled with what had looked to be darkened and old volumes from many decades past. There were no windows, as the building was squeezed between two others of identical construction on each side. A small fireplace was on one wall, its chimney no doubt shared by the adjacent room farther from the stairs toward the rear of the building. The room was warm, but the small coal fire had gone out.

Beside the bed were a pair of patent leather shoes, apparently removed by the man when he lay down. He was on his back and a quilt was pulled up to his chest, with his arms lying relaxed on top. A pillow was under his head, and another lay across his upturned face, hiding it from us. The white linen of the top pillow was marred by a dark irregular stain, sloping down to a small darker indentation. In Holmes's company I had seen this before: A gun had been fired through the pillow, muffling the sound but blackening the pillow cover with a powder burn. I glanced at the man's chest. There was no movement. He was most certainly dead.

While Holmes stood on the other side of the bed, leaning over to watch carefully in the stance of a predatory bird, I carefully lifted the pillow to reveal the awful site underneath. The man's features were horribly marred by a bullet hole over his right eye. Death had certainly been instantaneous. From the lack of blood on the pillow beneath his head, the bullet had remained in his skull, no doubt ricocheting multiple times and doing massive damage to the brain. The right eye itself had been terribly expelled from its socket by the sudden expanding pressure of the entering projectile just above it. It was nearly unrecognizable, while the left eye stared into eternity, its surface having that peculiar and final flat film.

"How long?" Holmes asked softly.

The skin was cool. "Hard to tell, since the fire has gone out."

"That wasn't long ago," Holmes said. "The coals are still warm." I hadn't seen him examine them – but then, the sight of the body had taken much of my attention.

"Possibly an hour. Mrs. Spence or the doctor can confirm when they last saw him."

"Go down and seek her out – prevent her from coming in here, and have her send for the doctor. Tell her that Singer's condition has worsened – a fair assessment – but share nothing else."

I nodded and left him to his further examination of the room. Downstairs, Mrs. Spence was in fact completing the assembly for something approaching a high tea. She began to babble once again, something about a recent visit by the noted Thomas Weldon Anderson, and she was able to talk for far longer than I wanted when I was forced to interrupt her and ask that she send once more for the doctor.

"Dr. Honner?" she asked. "But aren't *you* a doctor?"

"I wish to consult with him about Mr. Singer."

"Oh – Isn't he getting better?"

"No. Is Dr. Honner very far?"

"Not far at all – just two houses up." She wiped her hands and pushed the tea makings back from the edge of the counter. "I'll be back as soon as I can."

I followed her to the hallway, noting that she had suddenly become very quiet. As she put on her coat, I went back upstairs, pausing halfway to look back and verify that she had left the house. I wondered if I'd just spoken to the murderer and then requested that she leave the premises.

I found Holmes in one of the chairs by a table. He looked up. "I've already checked – all of the other rooms on this floor are currently empty. Four appear to be completely untenanted, and the resident of the fifth hasn't been in since last night – the accumulated dust, though insignificant, is enough."

He nodded to a small and sturdy strongbox open on the table beside him. He was thumbing through a stack of letters, apparently retrieved from it.

"Singer was being threatened," he explained, waving one of them. "There are over two-dozen of these, stretching back several months, and all mailed to Singer in care of different theaters in different cities – no doubt wherever he was appearing at the time." He set the letters down on the table. "They're quite vague – simply demanding the return '*of what is mine*' or '*what you stole from me*', and promising punishment."

"He likely thought of asking for your help when the play moved to Eastbourne," I added. "After all – he was playing you on stage, so he may have taken the time to find out a bit about you, including that your 'retirement' is located nearby."

"Very possible."

"And the strongbox?" I asked.

"That tells its own tale," he said. "It has a very good lock – it took me nearly a half-a-minute to open it." I knew that he rarely went anywhere without his lock-picking tools. "Apparently it defeated the person who previously tried to get in – I wasn't the first to try. There were very fresh scratches on the lock, showing that someone recently tried to retrieve the box's contents – almost certainly right after the murder."

"Was there anything else in it besides the letters?"

"Yes. A number of bearer bonds and deeds for properties in the north which will need sorting when we have more time. The box was hidden in that drawer at the bottom of the wardrobe. The drawer's lock also had scratches in the keyhole – fresh ones, and that time the intruder was more successful, as the drawer was opened to reveal the box."

"It isn't very big – no more than eighteen inches long. Why didn't he – or she – simply carry it away after the murder?"

"Perhaps it was still too bulky, and the murderer was afraid it would be seen, or raise questions. Possibly the killer panicked and fled when the box wouldn't easily open, before obtaining what he came for. And I see you've jumped to the assumption that the person who sought the box and its contents was the murderer."

"I think it's a safe leap to make."

"I would tend to agree – provisionally."

I looked around. "Where are the keys – to the wardrobe and the box?"

"I made a quick search while you were downstairs. They aren't in any obvious locations, and they weren't in the Singer's pockets. They're likely hidden somewhere here in the room – he wouldn't have left them at the theatre."

"Are you satisfied that the dead man *is* Singer?"

"I think it's a safe assumption. He looks the part."

I glanced toward the body on the bed, the head now uncovered, while the blood-stained portion of the pillow that had been lying against the dead man's face was turned upward beside him. From this angle, without the terrible distraction of the bullet wound or the distended eyeball, I could see that there was indeed a strong resemblance to my friend. Singer was tall and lean, and the angularity of his skull, along with a strong jaw and high forehead, gave him quite the resemblance to a reclining Sherlock Holmes. He would have been a good choice to portray the detective on stage in Gillette's play.

"Has the doctor been summoned?" Holmes asked, interrupting my study.

"He has. I'm told he only lives two houses away, so he should be here soon. You haven't found the keys – did you discover anything else of interest?"

"Several things. You will have noticed that the empty glass on the table smells of medication – likely something given to Singer related to his sudden illness."

"Laudanum," I agreed.

Holmes continued. "I believe that the killer entered quietly and that Singer simply never woke up, probably due to the medication. The pillow was quickly placed over his head and the gun was fired. It's very unlikely that the killer then lifted the pillow to look at the dead man, or to verify that he was dead. The blood stains on the underside of the pillow are completely centered around the bullet hole in the pillow covering. There is no smearing, meaning that the pillow was left to lie where it had been during the murderous shot. Death was instantaneous, and there was no excessive bleeding. This fact might be of use to us.

"Other than our footprints, I've identified four other individuals who have been in this room of late: The dead man, as matched by the shoes beside his bed, and his other pairs in the wardrobe. A woman with small feet and a very short tread – clearly the landlady, Mrs. Spence. There is another who has walked around both sides of the bed – This was certainly the doctor – randomly dropping Trichinopoly cigar ashes, such as those produced by our friend Thorndyke. Then he tossed the stub of his cigar into the fireplace, overpitching the grate."

He reached into his pocket and removed one of the small glassine envelopes he always carried for the placement of evidence. "From the marks on the cigar's remains, this man's front right central incisor is shifted slightly ahead of the matching left tooth. Identifying him will be child's play. This man left ashes on the bedside table, probably when preparing the medication, and he seems to have been on both sides of the bed, back and forth, occasionally treading across the ashes he dropped – probably as he carried out his examination. When he arrives, we can confirm these facts."

"And the fourth person?"

"Almost certainly the murderer – for his curiously small footprints and right inward twist appear to have approached the bed directly from the door. He then went to the wardrobe, and nowhere else. Those footprints are the most recent, treading across all the others. The dead man and the landlady were here first, followed by the doctor, who treated Singer after Mrs. Spence's departure. Then the doctor left, having conveniently dropped ashes throughout the room, and sometime later the murderer arrived, leaving his footprints over the top of the other three. Possibly not since the Biblical Daniel scattered the ashes to trap the priests and diminish the dragon have ashes been so useful – they help to establish the order of what happened here."

I considered pointing out that he had also made use of ashes in a similar way just a decade or so before, when he'd used them to locate the hiding place of Professor Coram's estranged wife. But before I could speak, we both heard a subtle and nearly imperceptible noise, as if a door had shut somewhere in the big quiet house. Holmes glanced my way. "She's back with the doctor. Go and bring him up, but keep her downstairs. Let her think Singer is simply ill. I have an idea – quite a long-shot, but if it works . . . ."

I left the room and was halfway down the steps when I met a grizzled fat man carrying a doctor's bag on his way up. Just behind him trundled Mrs. Spence.

Introducing myself, I truthfully explained that Mr. Singer seemed to have taken a turn for the worse, and asked if Mrs. Spence would mind waiting downstairs while we carried out our medical examination. I could see that she wanted to continue upstairs with us, and to assert her rights as the landlady, but my firm expectation that she would comply with my request seemed to convince her, and she nodded and she exited the stage, muttering.

"I'm Dr. Honner," explained the man as he moved up the steps to where our eyes were at a level while offering his hand. He looked to be in his late sixties, with shaggy iron-gray hair and matching bushy eyebrows and beard. He was about five-and-a-half feet tall, and plump. As expected, the front of his suit had evidence of cigar ash spilled across it. "I'm not sure how he could have gotten worse." His voice was rough, and I soon determined that he had a habit of clearing his throat often. "He seemed to have nothing more than the beginnings of a head cold. He was rather stressed – opening night nerves, I gathered – so I gave him something to relax."

I didn't like to judge Dr. Honner's medical skills on such scanty evidence, but I had to consider that the young man had been prescribed a strong-enough dose of medication to sleep through his own murder. Additionally, the smell of liquor hanging about my fellow medico tended to bias my thinking quite a bit. I introduced myself and asked, "What did you give him?"

A quick look crossed his face, as if suddenly cautious because questions were being asked. Then, apparently recalling that I too was a physician, he replied, "A bit of laudanum mixed with water. He seemed to be a stressed," he repeated. "I thought it would be just the ticket."

To myself, I questioned whether it was just a "bit", and also the man's judgement and the efficacy of his treatment, as the actor, expecting visitors momentarily and then needing to be at the top of his game for his opening-night performance just a few hours later, probably hadn't wanted something that would put him to sleep to such an extent – so soundly that his murderer could enter the room unnoticed and carry out his fatal task.

By that point we were outside the door to Singer's room, and as Honner reached for the knob, I laid a hand on his arm. "I want to let you know, Doctor, that Singer is dead."

His eyes widened, and I felt his stance stiffen. "*Dead!*" he hissed, and I knew that he was wondering if his treatment had killed the actor. If I'd been the attending physician, I might have done the same, instantly recalling the prescribed medicine and wondering what factors I might have missed. I nodded but hurried to clarify.

"He's been murdered. You're the first to be informed, before we call the police."

"We?" he asked. "Who is 'we'?"

"Sherlock Holmes is inside. We discovered the body when we arrived to keep an appointment."

He nodded. "He mentioned that someone was stopping by." He glanced at the door. "Can I see him?"

I reached and opened the door, letting him precede me inside.

Holmes was standing by the wardrobe, holding one of Singer's suits. I assumed that he was looking for the missing keys, but I was to learn that I was incorrect. He was checking its size.

Dr. Honner glanced that way, but then he stepped to the bed and leaned over. I heard him gasp at what he saw.

Holmes hung the suit back in the wardrobe and turned toward the doctor. "What time did you see him?" he asked with any preamble.

"What?" Honner refocused his attention and turned our way. "What? About two hours ago."

"And we've been here for nearly half-an-hour," said. "The murderer was here between your departure and our arrival." I had Honner repeat what he'd told me concerning his summons and subsequent treatment.

"Did he give any indication what was causing him stress?" Holmes asked.

"Not a thing – but it's not unusual, you know. For these actors. They work themselves up into such states. I'm able to help a great many of them."

I could only imagine how many actors found themselves addicted to laudanum after being *helped* by Honner – but this wasn't the time to address that question.

"I have an idea," said Holmes, speaking more to himself than the two of us. "I noticed from the wires outside that Mrs. Spence has a telephone. I'm going to notify Inspector Bardle. In the meantime, could the two of you wrap up the body in the quilt?"

Then he slipped out of the room, leaving me and a very confused Eastbourne doctor. I started to explain that Holmes had his methods, which often only he initially understood, but the man raised a hand. "I've read your stories, Doctor. I once worked with a man of similar temperament – Dr. Bell in Edinburgh. I believe you know him as well. Men like him and Mr. Holmes have minds that race far ahead on faster tracks than the rest of us. I have no fears that what he's doing is for the overall good. I simply have one question: Why am I so immediately included in your councils? Why am I not a suspect as well?"

I indicated that we should begin wrapping Singer in his temporary shroud, and as we did so, I explained about the evidence of the cigar ash, and how Holmes had determined that another man had entered the room following the doctor's departure. Honner nodded. "Thank God I'm a cigar smoker, then," he said. "Something good has finally come of it."

At that moment Holmes returned and, seeing our progress, nodded. "I've taken time to quickly re-examine this floor now that I've identified the killer's footprints. He isn't the other tenant – that man's feet are much larger. The killer didn't go anywhere else on this floor except from the top of the stairs to this room, and then back again to depart."

"Do you think that Mrs. Spence let him in?"

Dr. Honner started to protest the lady's innocence, but Holmes raised a hand. "It seems that he was being very quiet. Some of his footsteps in the hall and here in the bedroom show that he walked on tiptoe, and he took care to fire the gun through the pillow. If the landlady had helped him, she could have told him that no one else was home besides Singer, and there would have been no need to be so careful.

He stepped to the wardrobe and turned to face us. "I managed to use the telephone without Mrs. Spence overhearing me. I spoke to the inspector, and he's in agreement with my plan. Place Mr. Singer's body under the bed, along with the bloody pillow, and re-make the bed to look as if it hasn't been used."

"To fool the killer if he returns for the strongbox?" I asked.

"No, simply to hide the body away for a while so that Mrs. Spence won't find him and summon the authorities, causing a distraction from our other plans."

"Which are?" I said with effort, as by then we'd placed the body on the floor and were pushing him underneath the bed.

"The killer didn't get what he wanted," said Holmes. He then summarized for the doctor the evidence of the strongbox and the papers within. "It's likely he's watching the house to see if he can get another chance – or to see if the body has been discovered. Instead, I intend to decoy him elsewhere."

As he spoke, Holmes began to change out of his own clothing and into one of the dead man's suits – the one that he'd been holding when we entered. Within two minutes, he had not only donned the new outfit, but seemed to have acquired a new personality as well.

"Of course I never met Mr. Singer," he explained, "or saw him in life, but I know the type. He looked to be in his thirties and, as an actor, he would have always projected a certain energy and attitude." Holmes then practiced strolling around the room with a vim and vigor that I hadn't seen from him in several years. I always thought of him as rather ageless – and he certainly seemed to be aging at a slower rate than me – but seeing him display this new vivacity, looking so much like the young man in his mid-twenties that I'd first met nearly a quarter-century earlier, reminded me of just how much time had passed.

"Conspicuously carrying the box, I shall make a show of departing for the theatre in time for my call, and with any luck I'll lure the killer to follow me into our trap."

I did not miss what he'd said.

"Your 'call'? Do you intend to take Singer's place on stage – *playing yourself?*"

He nodded. "If necessary – depending on how long it takes our killer to make his move."

"But Mr. Holmes," countered Honner, "what makes you think that you can fool the murderer into believing that Singer is still alive?"

Holmes explained how he'd determined that the pillow was never raised after the bullet was fired through it – and thus the killer hadn't confirmed Singer's death. "Or so it seems. We shall use that to our advantage. And if he does know somehow that Singer died, it will unnerve him to see the man walk out – and carrying the strong box that he killed to obtain."

"If he's watching," I said, "he will have seen the two of us arrive – and also Mrs. Spence go to summon Dr. Honner."

"But he won't know what any of that means. Two strangers entered – possibly tenants. A man with a doctor's bag – to treat the actor who didn't die after all. All he'll know for sure is that Singer – the man whom he thinks he killed – will depart for the theatre in just a few minutes, carrying the box that he'd kill for. Since I arrived as Sherlock Holmes and will leave as Brian Singer, that should be enough to fool him."

"But what's to stop him from shooting you in the street and taking the box?" asked the doctor.

"I will lure him," replied Holmes, "but I don't intend to let him catch me!"

Then, satisfied that the body was hidden and the room reasonably restored to normality, he ushered us quietly into the hall. Pulling out his nipper from his lock kit, he carefully inserted it through the keyhole and, using it to grasp the end of the key which was still in the lock, he turned it so that the room was locked from the inside. Entry, if attempted, would be that much more difficult.

And so it was that I was dispatched downstairs to keep Mrs. Spence, whom I found in the kitchen at the back of the house, distracted while Holmes would be let out of the front door by Dr. Honner, who would remain in the shadows. As I tried to hold her attention, the little landlady was clearly curious, as what was supposed to have been a simple visit by two middle-aged gentlemen to one of her lodgers had escalated into a summons for the neighboring doctor – his second visit of the day – followed by Holmes's use of her telephone, and then the conversation which she'd been unable to overhear. I vaguely informed her that Dr. Honner had given the actor additional medication to ready him for his performance, and that he was departing even as we spoke.

We heard the thump of the closing front door and I nodded. "Mr. Singer must have just left for the theatre. I should be going too. Thank you very much for your hospitality."

She glanced toward the tea tray, still in the process of elaborate assembly, with a look of disappointment. Without waiting for the chance of further conversation, I nodded and left the kitchen.

I feared that she might trail along behind me, but she remained where I'd left her, and I found Honner at the front door. Beside him, the curtain covering the small window beside the door was pulled slightly back, as if someone had been looking through it. He nodded and whispered, "Mr. Holmes set off with a brisk stride, and in mere seconds, a man revealed himself in the areaway across the street – his head popped up and he watched intently until Mr. Holmes reached the corner. Then he came out and set off down the street in the same direction."

501

I nodded. The bait was taken. Pulling on my own coat and hat, and also retrieving Holmes's Inverness and fore-and-aft cap from the stand, I indicated that we should depart. We slipped quietly outside, pulling the door shut without any noise.

I started to thank the doctor and say goodbye, but he held up a hand. "If you don't mind, I'd like to accompany you. I . . . I feel a bit of responsibility for my poor young patient."

He might have said more, but I simply nodded in agreement, and we set off for the theatre in silence.

Chapter III

Dr. Honner and I walked through several short streets, and I was always alert for signs of Holmes or the man who was following him – along with the possibility of sudden violence if the man tried to attack Holmes and steal the box from him. Yet we encountered nothing, not even other pedestrians on that cold January afternoon, and in just a few minutes we had reached the theatre.

I had seen it before during other trips to visit Holmes, but had paid little attention to it. Rather inauspicious, it might have been a long storefront. The street before it was narrow, and the building, possibly a hundred feet or so long, was only three stories. The upper floors were represented by plain uninteresting windows, and along the street were four or five entrances to small shops. At the center of the building was another door, this one to the theatre's box office. It was to this that we walked at a steady pace. We were thirty feet from reaching it when Honner whispered, "There. In the shop entrance two doors down on the left. It's the man who just followed Mr. Holmes."

In the dim evening light I couldn't see much, except that he was in some sort of cream-colored coat and that his bald head, looking much the same color as his outer garment and giving the illusion that they were all of one piece, was unprotected by a hat. I had the sense that he was tall, but I only had a glimpse, and then we had entered the theatre.

At that time, it was slightly over twenty years old, but the previous year, it had received quite a bit of attention in the form of new improvements and judiciously applied paint. Originally opened as the *Theatre and Royal Opera House*, in 1904 it received its new name, *The Royal Hippodrome Theatre*, as well as a new focus in the type of entertainment presented. I was sure that having a performance of Gillette's play in January, when the tourist season was at its ebb, was part of the management's new strategy to encourage visitors during the colder months of the year.

Inside, Dr. Honner seemed quite familiar with the layout, and he took me through the building and along several winding passages that seemed to double back on themselves until we reached a dim hallway containing a row of dressing rooms. He paused at the first on the right and knocked. "This would be Singer's," he explained. "He was the star, you see."

The door opened to a narrow gap, and then, when we were recognized, wider to allow our entry. Sherlock Holmes nodded as we passed and shut the door behind us. There were two other men in the room. One I recognized: Inspector Bardle of the Sussex Constabulary – a steady and solid man who watched the world with thoughtful, if bovinian, eyes.

The other man was introduced as Mr. Pilsbury, the theatrical company's manager. He had a most troubled look on his face. "We don't have an understudy," he complained. "The cast is already doubling some of the parts. I suppose that Hinkle, who plays Moriarty, might be persuaded to be Holmes, and Willis, who plays McTague, can take on Moriarty, but – Oh, that won't work! We'll have to cancel the show!"

"That won't be necessary," said Holmes. "I can take the lead."

This was met with silence – and a raised eyebrow on the part of the inspector. I myself had long maintained that the stage lost a fine actor when Holmes became a specialist in crime. More recently, I recalled the night before Old Baron Dowson was hanged, when Holmes and I had been summoned to his cell so that he could provide the final pieces that helped explain his motive for murder. After he'd extracted a promise to keep the truth from his granddaughter, he'd relaxed, and even praised Holmes, stating that what the law had gained when he became a consulting detective, the stage had lost.

"Mr. Holmes," said Pilsbury, apparently not quite sure how to respond, "do . . . do you think you could? The curtain rises in less than an hour. It's a long script, and Sherlock Holmes – that is, your character – is on stage for a substantial amount of time."

"I've seen the play before," said Holmes, "and I was an actor once, long ago. I perfected the trick then of quickly memorizing lines. I was in the Sasanoff Company twenty-five years ago. We only performed Shakespeare, and we frequently changed from play to play, with very little time to learn the next one."

"Then . . . then that would be exceptional!" cried Pilsbury. "The publicity will be wonderful. I'll just have time to notify the newspaper – "

"You misunderstand," Holmes said, cutting him off. "My participation must remain unknown. I will be playing the part of Brian Singer, who just happens to be portraying Sherlock Holmes. We hope to lure the killer into the theatre to obtain the strong box – apparently the motive for the murder. Hopefully he believes that I'm here – as Singer –

and he will be confused as to why the man he murdered is still among the living." He glanced toward me, and I nodded.

"A man was hiding across the street. He surfaced as soon as you left, and he's now across from the theatre, lurking in a doorway."

"Presumably," added the inspector, speaking for the first time, "he's more interested in the contents of the box you brought than in killing Singer for a second time – so he'll be back here where we'll set our trap, instead of trying to kill you while you're on stage, Mr. Holmes."

"But what will I tell the cast?" asked Pilsbury.

"Let them know that Singer is indisposed, and that I've agreed to step in. You can say my name is – "

"Presbury Roylott," I interrupted.

Holmes smiled. "Presbury Roylott – Exceptional! But whatever you do, don't announce the substitution to the audience."

It seemed a simple-enough plan, and Pilsbury went to inform the cast that there would be a change for the night. In the meantime, Bardle set about placing his plain-clothed officers in different spots in the theatre, each briefed on what to expect and whom to be watching for. Holmes used what time he had to make a quick but intense study of the script. However, he took a moment to discuss the matter when I brought him a cup of hot coffee.

"Did you find Singer's keys?" I asked. "When I went downstairs to meet Dr. Honner?"

Holmes nodded. "He'd made a small incision at the bottom of the bedspread and hidden them there. I've seen the same thing done at times where something small was hidden in the bottoms of window drapes – but that room had no windows, of course."

"I wonder what would have happened if the killer hadn't followed you here," I said. "After all, he was likely watching when he saw us enter – followed a short time by the doctor." I nodded to Holmes's coat and hat, lying on a nearby table where I'd left them. "You do cut a rather distinctive figure. Surely the killer would have been suspicious seeing us visit there."

"Ah, you perhaps give too much credit to our supposed fame," was the reply. "Why should the murderer suppose that we were there to visit Singer? There are other rooms for rent. We could have been there to see any one of those tenants, or to visit the landlady herself. The killer might have been aware that Singer was playing me, but he wouldn't necessarily know that he was actually *seeing* the real Sherlock Holmes when we arrived at the house."

Something else had been bothering me. "Holmes," I asked, "are you certain of the footprint evidence? It occurred to me that Dr. Honner says he saw the man across the street when you left the house – but I didn't.

And then, when we arrived at the theatre, it was him again who pointed out a man standing in a distant doorway and identified him. We only have his word that there *was* a man across the street from the house. Might Honner have been the killer after all? For some reason unknown to us, he may have been writing the threatening letters. He saw his chance today when summoned by Mrs. Spence. He tricked Singer into drinking the too-strong laudanum, and then he shot him. Afterwards, he tried to get into the strongbox and failed."

"And the other set of footprints?" asked Holmes with a smile. "The ones overlaying those of Honner and the rest?"

I realized that my theory, never very strong, was breaking down. "Perhaps he obtained another set of shoes to make fake footprints?" Even as I said it, I understood that it was ridiculous.

"You're right to question, Watson," said Holmes. "It never hurts to pull every thread. But in this case, I believe that the doctor's veracity can be accepted." He finished the last of his coffee. "No, the last set of footprints were real."

Then he went back to his studies. Soon he would need to apply makeup – to look like Brian Singer's version of looking like Sherlock Holmes. I excused myself and went to confer with the inspector.

"He's here," he whispered. "Based on the doctor's description, just such a man bought a ticket and entered ten minutes ago."

"Where is he now?"

Bardle looked suddenly sheepish. "We lost him when he came inside. He slipped backstage, and could be anywhere. But we believe that he'll head for the dressing room as soon as Mr. Holmes takes the stage – and that's when we'll have him."

There was nothing to do but wait for it. A search through the theatre might alert our prey long before we found him, spooking him into fleeing before we could take him. With the approach of the curtain, I had no choice but to take my own place, hidden behind some flats near stage right, not far from the entrance to the dressing room passage.

Long before I met Sherlock Holmes, I'd had some familiarization with the theatre. As a medical student in London of the 1870's, I became something of a stage-door lurker – not something I'm proud of, to be sure, but nevertheless a formative part of my young adulthood. As such, I was often backstage, so the inner workings of the theatre, and the off-stage behaviors of the actors and actresses, was no surprise to me. Of course, through my long association with Holmes, there had been many calls to theatres, ranging from interviews to the investigation of terrible and bloody murders.

I'd come to know a great many actors as well, so it was no curiosity when I'd been approached by William Gillette, the famed American performer, writer, and producer, about his interest in presenting a play about Sherlock Holmes. Sometime in the mid-1890's, unknown to me, Doyle had taken it upon himself to write a five-act play about my friend (and me, I presume), and had been in touch with the famed American producer, Frohman. The latter apparently didn't care much for Doyle's finished product, and suggested that William Gillette rewrite it – as well as play the lead.

Gillette was a handsome fellow, but he didn't look much like Holmes, whose likeness was so well captured in the illustrations by Sidney Paget in *The Strand.* (When Doyle and I first began publishing with the magazine in mid-1891, I was adamant that Holmes be correctly portrayed in the *Strand* illustrations. I had no such influence when the later American illustrator, Frederic Dorr Steele, began using Gillette's visage to represent Holmes in the American magazines.)

Gillette apparently did a revision of Doyle's play, but both works were lost in a San Francisco hotel fire in 1898, and Gillette began anew. That's when I first learned of the matter – when he wrote me a letter indicating that he was going to be in London and would like to meet. He arrived in May 1899 and we had lunch at the Langham. I didn't know until then what had been in the works for years, and that he'd already met with Doyle the week before, upon his arrival in the capital.

I read the play and was unhappy with several aspects. However, considering how much money I was offered, I was willing to set that aside. Of more concern was Holmes's possible reaction. After his return to London in the spring of 1894, he'd absolutely prohibited further publication of his adventures – and now a drama melding aspects of several of his cases was going to be premiered, not only getting some things incorrect, but worse – abandoning his pure reasoning approach to provide a romantic conclusion wherein his character and the leading lady are in an affectionate embrace, implying that he has abandoned all of his principles for her.

I should have known that Holmes was aware of the matter long before I told him, and curiously, he was indifferent. Or so he implied. At that time he was involved in a series of extremely complex affairs, and I believe that rather than waste energy or thought on combatting the play, he simply placed it into a separate box in his brain attic and hid it away.

Although the play premiered in the United States in the fall of '99, it didn't come to England until September 1901. Holmes and I were in the audience on opening night, although Holmes was well-disguised, and I went mostly unrecognized. Doyle was certainly willing to soak up the attention – a fact that I attribute to his interest a couple of years later in once again publishing more of my stories about Holmes.

Holmes and I rarely discussed the play. I believe that he didn't blame me too much, since so much of the initial preparation of it was accomplished without my knowledge. I didn't know for sure, but I was always fairly certain that he'd read the script – either to codify his thoughts on the matter, or simply because he had once been an actor. In any case, he intended to draw on what he'd previously seen on the stage and subsequently read in order to carry out his performance, and I wished him well, even as I shifted in my hiding spot, waiting for something to happen.

I was aware when the audience's rustling and conversation silenced and the play commenced. Holmes wasn't immediately on stage. The first of the four acts has a long scene involving the conspirators' discussion before Sherlock Holmes ever makes an appearance. After that, his appearances are intermittent but effective through the first half of the play. If the killer were to make his move, he'd need to do so during those times when Holmes was on stage and out of the dressing room – and unless he knew the play quite well, picking those times might be a matter of luck for him.

I heard the first act roll along, and then I was aware when Holmes took the stage. His voice was distinct and clear, and he spoke his lines with confidence. I dearly wished that I had the opportunity to be in the audience and see this unforgettable moment, but alas, my duty was elsewhere. I redoubled my efforts to perceive anything unusual in the dressing room hallway – and I didn't have long to wait.

There is always something going on backstage, as preparations for upcoming scenes are made, things used in old scenes are removed and sets are struck, and actors and technicians with time to kill move from here to there. But during a lull, I saw a movement from behind some stored flats – it was like a ghost hovering about a foot above the floor, moving quickly to the door of the star's dressing room. I realized that it was the killer's bare head and cream-colored coat had merged into a ghostly shape, while the floating illusion occurred due to the man's black pants legs and shoes underneath. Even as I comprehended what I'd seen, the man reached the star's dressing room and slipped inside. As I emerged from my hiding place, so did Bardle and four of his men.

Sometimes the capture of an insidious villain is memorable or dramatic. After "Killer" Evans shot me in the leg, Holmes whipped him across the head with his pistol. We found Grimesby Roylott dead from a snake-bite, with the vicious serpent coiled nightmarishly around his head. Rodger Baskerville had died after being swallowed into a Dartmoor mire – or so we had believed at the time. Lord Blackwood had managed to hang himself amongst the construction atop the Tower Bridge. And Fenton Cable, in attempting to electrocute both Holmes and me, was instead grounded himself in the pool of his last victim's blood and had been left a smoking husk, unable to fall until the current was turned off.

But other criminals were taken with a minimum of fuss. Such was the case for Dale Warriner, the man in the cream-colored coat. We opened the door to the dressing room to find him trying and failing to open the strongbox which Holmes had placed in an easily spotted location. He looked up and saw us blocking his escape, all with guns drawn, and with a sob he simply sagged to the floor, a beaten man. He wept quietly for the next couple of hours as we left him alone, with two officers close by on either side should he unexpectedly decide to do himself an injury.

Bardle and I had agreed that Holmes should be there when we questioned Warriner, who had provided his identity without any resistance. During his first respite from the performance, Holmes had slipped back to the dressing rooms and seen that his plan had succeeded. However, before he could do much more than get a look at Warriner, and be seen in return by the surprised and weeping fellow, he had to return to the stage – this time for the scene where he was visited in Baker Street by Professor Moriarty, stylistically dramatized from the true events as related in "The Final Problem".

Seeing as how the prisoner was well-guarded and subdued, I took my chance to edge my way into the theatre. In spite of the January off-season performance, the show was sold out, and I was only able to find a place standing along one of the side walls.

There was silence from the stage, but there was tension nevertheless, and I saw that everyone in the audience was tightly focused on Holmes as he moved with purpose from a listening pose to retrieve a revolver from a nearby table and then slip it into his dressing gown pocket. Afterwards, he seemed to relax, facing a door which slowly opened. A man walked through – tall, thin, and with a high shining dome above his eyes. He was dressed all in black, and even though the man was simply acting a part, he managed to convey the evil that had always exuded from Professor James Moriarty – curiously and incorrectly renamed "*Robert*" by Gillette for the play.

Moriarty and Holmes simply faced each for a moment, and someone in the audience hissed, while another gasped in apprehension at what might occur.

In a low voice, Moriarty stated, "It is a dangerous habit to finger loaded firearms in the pocket of one's dressing gown."

Holmes responded, his voice also low-pitched, but with unmistakable authority. "You'll be taken from here to the hospital if you keep that hand behind you."

Moriarty lowered the hand in question and grasped it with the other.

"In that case," said Holmes, taking the revolver from his dressing gown, "the table will do quite as well."

As he placed on the table beside him, Moriarty sidled a step forward. "You evidently don't know me."

Holmes nodded toward the revolver. "I think it quite evident that I do. Pray take a chair, Professor. I can spare you five minutes – if you have anything to say."

What followed was much the same conversation that I'd heard told to me that long-ago day in April 1891, when Holmes, his knuckles bleeding, had managed to sneak into my medical practice in order to enlist my aid in the affair that would terminate just days later atop the Reichenbach Falls.

I had an interest in the play as a whole, and which parts of the narrative still made me wince. My thoughts on the chap playing "Dr. Watson" are best left unrecorded. In general, I noticed which actors were more successful than others, but in truth, I was most interested in Holmes's performance. Of course I was in awe of his ability to perform the role so well, having only seen it once years before – at least that I was aware of – and also with just a couple of read-throughs, one just a few hours earlier.

He moved with the vitality of a man half his age, and under the lights he seemed to be an even more intense version of himself. I would not have missed that performance for the world.

He held the audience in the palm of his hand. When he played his famous trick with the cigar in the Stepney gas chamber, some in the audience applauded or cheered. And they cheered again, over the thunderous applause, after Holmes stated, "There is every reason – " to the actress playing Alice Faulkner before pulling her to him in an embrace just before the lights darkened and the curtain swung shut.

The curtain calls were met with great enthusiasm and cheers, and none more so than for the man playing Sherlock Holmes – whom the audience believed to be the unfortunate late actor, Brian Singer. When curtain finally came down, the cast were just as enthusiastic. I felt sorry for them when they learned that Holmes's performance was a one-time thing.

Finally Holmes and I were able to return to the dressing room, along with a beaming Mr. Pilsbury. Holmes sat down across from Dale Warriner and introduced himself. The man seemed to have no idea who Holmes was, and appeared to assume that he was another policeman. As Holmes succinctly laid out his observations as to how the murder was committed, almost as if he'd been there and watched it, Warriner's eyes widened, and he agreed.

Then Holmes finally removed the various letters, deeds, and bonds from an inner pocket.

"My bonds," Warriner said, his words slurred. I wasn't sure if he was unhealthy, or simply spent from a day that ran from murder to capture.

"How is that?" asked Holmes.

"Brian and I – we were half-brothers. His mother married my father when we were boys. He was always clever – much more than me. He was told to help me. To help take care of me. But he never did. He would smile and lie, and they would believe him, no matter what I said.

"We – my dad and me – had some lands in York. Family lands. My dad was always careful, and saved, and invested, and bought the bonds. It was all supposed to be mine, from my father, just as the lands had come down to him from his father. When Brian's mother died, he was nearly grown, and he felt no ties anymore, and he left to become an actor. Dad and me, we got by, but then he died too, and he passed the land to me. But there was something wrong. The lawyers said there was something wrong, but they couldn't make me understand, and just then Brian came back for a visit. He understood – something wrong about the way the documents were set up. He said he'd help, but then he took them and left, and the lawyers said there was nothing that I could do.

"Brian owned everything now – I don't know how – but I kept living there because I had nowhere else to go. Then I found out where he would be as an actor and wrote letters – telling him what he'd done was wrong – but he never wrote back. Finally I was running out of ways to pay the bills, and the lawyers were saying I would have to leave soon, so I decided to find Brian, and visit him, and make him give back what he stole."

"How did you get into the house today?" I asked. "Without being seen?"

"It was easy," Warriner replied, noticing me for the first time. "I'd watched for several days. Only one other person besides Brian and the old woman were living there. They came and went all the time. The front door was never locked – they would just open it to go in, and pull it shut to leave. I always followed Brian to the theatre and tried to work up the courage to speak to him, but I never could. Today he left the theatre and went back to the house early, and I decided that this was my chance. I was about to go in when the old lady walked out. She was back in just a few minutes with an old man – *You* – " He nodded to Doctor Honner. "That spooked me, and I hid until the old man had left again. Then I figured I'd best take my chance, so I slipped across the street and went in."

510

More tears were rolling down his face now, but he didn't bother to wipe them away. "It was dark inside, and so quiet. I didn't know where Brian was, but I figured it was upstairs. I went up, and there was only one room with a light on. I went to it and knocked on the door but there was no answer, so I looked in, and he was asleep on the bed.

"I went over, intending to wake him and ask him to give back what was mine, but there he was, and an anger welled in me like I'd never felt before. Everything thing he'd done to me since I was a boy was in it, along with feelings about what he'd taken from me – what he'd *stolen!* – and how bad my life had been since then. It was almost like I was watching someone else from an audience as I took out my old gun. I knew that the bang would call up the old lady, and I would lose my chance to search, so I put the pillow over his head and . . . and then I . . . ." He broke down sobbing and couldn't continue. But it didn't matter, as we already knew what happened after that.

Holmes stood and handed Bardle the packet of letters and papers, and then he his men shepherded Warriner from the room. Honner, shaking his head sadly, silently shook our hands and departed with them. The theatrical manager, Pilsbury, remained behind, looking pale and numb.

"I cannot . . . Life is so *desperate* sometimes," he said. "Why does fate play with us in such ways?"

I had heard Holmes, in some of his darker moods, ask the same question. I have never found an answer.

Holmes removed himself to the makeup table, where he sat and leaned forward in order to remove those additions and enhancements that had simply served to make him look more like himself.

"I thought it went well," he said, changing the subject. "The gas chamber scene wasn't as effective as Gillette's version, although in writing his script, he deviated quite a bit from the actual fact. Some of the actors were thrown by my timing – which is understandable – and they were all clearly curious about me, since they'd barely been introduced to 'Mr. Roylott' before the play began. One chaps eyes widened when he heard the name – no doubt one of your readers, Watson, who recognized the association." He finished his task and leaned back. "All in all, it was a tolerable experience."

"*Tolerable?*" asked Pilsbury. "Mr. Holmes, you were brilliant! I realize, sir, that you were playing yourself, so to speak, so your interpretation is bound to be the definitive one, but still, you were miles past whatever Mr. Gillette was ever able to convey. Certainly better than Brian Singer – God rest his soul. I know it's too much to ask, but would you be willing – ? I mean, is there any way that I might entice you . . . ?"

511

Holmes rose, turned, took a step forward, and offered his hand to the manager, who wordlessly took and shook it.

"No, thank you, sir," replied Holmes. "I am retired, and this curious detour back to the days of my theatrical youth is a very-much one-time thing. I do appreciate the unexpected though tragic opportunity, and also your faith in allowing me to assume the helm of your production."

"Mr. Holmes, based on what I saw tonight, I'm offering you a partnership! As an actor – "

"No, no, my decision is final. But again, thank you. Good evening."

I wished the manager the same as Holmes retrieved his coat and hat from where I'd earlier left them, and then we departed.

Outside, the temperature had dropped considerably, and only then did I recall that my automobile was still parked near Mrs. Spence's house, several streets away. Pulling my coat tighter, I said with a rueful smile, "Faces to the north, then, and quick march!"

Only later, when we'd driven halfway back to Holmes's villa (as he liked to call it), did he speak again, pulling us both from our various thoughts. "I suppose," he said, "that in some round-about way, your writings cannot be blamed for this occurrence."

"Hmm?"

"The murder would have occurred regardless. In fact, without the connection forged by way of your stories and Gillette's play, and the character portrayed by Singer, we might not have been involved at all."

I shook my head. "These questions of fate are too deep for me. It's late, and I'm hungry."

He was silent for a moment, and then he continued. "What I'm saying is that, in the great tapestry of events, your recording and publication of my cases has not been completely objectionable."

"Kind of you to say so."

"And," he added, "should you choose to do so again in the future, I would not be averse."

"It's likely up to Doyle," I said. "He may have lost interest again."

I sensed that he nodded. It wasn't until we'd rattled past The Gables and were approaching Holmes's farm that I spoke again. "I enjoyed seeing your performance, and I sense that you enjoyed being able to give it." I glanced toward him. "Happy Birthday, Holmes."

"Indeed," he replied. "Forgive me for saying so, but, in spite of the tragedy, it *was* a happy birthday." He shifted into his seat as I turned into his drive, noting that the front window was lit and there was every indication that something appetizing awaited us.

"I wonder," he added, "what tomorrow will bring?"

As it turned out, quite a lot . . . .

The Mediobogdum Sword

"This is intolerable," muttered Sherlock Holmes, standing and walking toward the high window. As he stood there, I knew that he would see nothing that would lessen his impatience.

I remained seated, watching him pace. Typically, he would seek calming solace from one of his pipes, but not today.

"Holmes," I said, attempting to gain his attention, but he was still lost in his own racing thoughts. "Holmes," I repeated, my tone more sharp. "You must be patient. This waiting will not last forever."

"But an entire day!" he snarled. "Wasted – and for what? All because of one man's stubbornness and stupidity."

I gestured around us. "At least it was a chance to think."

He looked at me as if I were mad, and then away, and back toward the window, as if a better answer was there. But it was no different than when he'd stood beneath it before, high on the wall, and it revealed nothing except whether it was day or night by the changes in the light.

Prison windows aren't meant to provide a pleasing prospect.

As we waited for time to pass, I recalled how, nearly a week before, Holmes and I had been summoned to Drigg, a remote village on the western coast. It had not been an easy place to reach – an understatement when considering the nightmarish travel we had faced. I could only imagine how isolated this spot would have been in the days before the railroads could even get us anywhere close.

Holmes had once saved the kidnapped child of the local Member of Parliament, in those years before I knew him, and it was this man who asked that Holmes journey so far north to such a remote location. This politician was an honorable man – a rare breed, as I was learning during my association with Holmes's investigations – and his brother was in a difficulty that, if allowed to proceed, would result in his death and a vast embarrassment for Her Majesty's Government. I doubt that Holmes was influenced by the latter, but he could not let a man die needlessly, and I agreed.

Thus, I was with him when we set out on an early train to Birmingham, and then Manchester – the two easiest legs of our journey. After that, things became more complex, and I have but vague and unpleasant memories of local trains of ever-devolving levels of comfort, and then rocking coaches and open carriages, before finally reaching our destination. With every mile that we traveled from London, I could only

513

ponder that at some point we would need to make the same journey back again.

The investigation, the specific details of which must remain secret until the passing of at least two men, led from Drigg to nearby Holmrook Hall, where we were assisted by the owner, who turned out to be a relative of one of Holmes's college friends – which was quite useful in giving us a base from which to plan our attack. From there, our quest culminated when we worked our way east one dark night, traveling nearly ten miles into the empty countryside. There, at the site of an ancient Roman fort, we confronted the man who had set these events in motion. He had hostages, but the bravery of a local lad, known only to us as Howe, gave Holmes the distraction he needed. The captives – including a number of children – were freed, and the responsible malefactor lost his footing, falling to a brutal death amongst the indifferent stones that had settled long ago along the barren fort walls.

We had returned to Holmrook and the Hall, where the children were reunited with frantic parents, and I knew that the inconvenience and discomfort of the journey had been worth every minute. Holmes – and dare I add myself as well – had made some fast friends in this region for the rest of our lives.

After the excitement of the night had passed and morning was upon us, I felt the call of sleep, but Holmes was still alert. I asked him: Was there something else about the case that remained unfinished?

"No," he shook his head. "Rather, it's something that one of the locals – Wilson – told me about the old fort while we were walking. A legend."

I smiled. "Holmes, I've known you now for over two years. If there is one man that I would say for certain is uninterested in legends, it is you."

His expression was weary but amused. "I would hope that you'd know better than that – no one is completely predictable. I maintain a healthy skepticism, but I don't disregard that I'm intelligent enough to realize what I don't know. It's true that most legends are exaggerated twistings of past events, too often with the played-up emphasis of some false supernatural aspect, but there is often a historical basis – some actual event – that was once true, leading to a story that perpetuates for centuries afterwards. Something solid for all the subsequent twaddle to catch and hangs onto in later years."

"And this fort – what legend do they tell about it?"

"That is was once visited by King Arthur and Merlin."

I raised an eyebrow, unaware that the legendary king had supposedly journeyed to this part of the island. I associated those tales to areas much further south. "I had no idea you had any interest in such stories," I remarked.

Holmes nodded, a new glint in his eyes. "But I do. As a boy, I read Sir Thomas Malory's records, and they fired my imagination. In those days, my family traveled quite a bit, in England and Scotland, and on the Continent as well. I was thrilled to find that my father had the same interest – which pleased me to no end, as we didn't have much else in common – and it was never too difficult to convince him to arrange our journeys by way of theorized Arthurian sites." He took a deep breath. "I propose that, after we get some rest, I do a bit of research, and then we return to the fort later today – if you're interested."

Considering how weary I currently felt, the idea held little interest. Still, I too had always had something of an interest in the legendary king, though apparently not to the surprising degree held by Holmes. Even in 1883, over two years after meeting him, I could still learn new things about him – and I had sensed that there truly had been something mysterious about the old fort that seemed to call for further investigation. I nodded my agreement, and we planned on meeting again that afternoon to make the return journey across the countryside. As I ascended to my room for some much-needed sleep, I realized that Holmes probably wouldn't rest at all, instead spending his time marshalling facts for this new investigation.

I awoke in early afternoon, much refreshed, and more intrigued by the idea of our plan than I had been earlier in the day. After finding something to eat in the Holmrook kitchen, I went to the front of the house where Holmes was waiting in a dog-cart.

I was glad that he'd arranged more convenient transportation on this return trip, as we'd had to walk part of the way to the fort the previous night in order to avoid discovery. As we wound our way through the small village and onto the narrow track leading east, Holmes informed me of what he'd discovered.

"I located Wilson, who talked more about the legends he'd referred to last night."

"I've never heard of this part of England being associated with the Arthurian legends," I said. "Cornwall seems to be where most of that business seem centered. Tintagel, for instance, where Arthur was born."

"And don't forget Dozmary Pool in Cornwall, where he supposedly received Excalibur from The Lady of the Lake. But other areas have claims as well. A replica of the Round Table hangs in the Great Hall in Winchester. And Glastonbury Tor and Abbey, in Somerset, is where Arthur died and was buried."

"That's right," I added. "And after Guinevere spent the rest of her life in prayer at the convent in Amesbury Abbey, in Wiltshire, her body was taken to Glastonbury by Lancelot and laid to rest with Arthur."

I looked at the wild landscape surrounding us as we made the slow passage toward the Hardknott Pass, where the old fort was located. Our horse pulled us at a steady pace past small land-holdings, sometimes close to the road behind high hedges, and in other cases set far back, barely visible against the high distant hills. One would only know to look for these dwellings by when a dirt track joined the road, sometimes only marked by a break in the stone walls built hundreds of years before – or longer. Holmes and I fell silent for a while, awed by the rugged countryside, and the sense of long-ago history that saturated the lands all around us. And as we traveled, things only became more lonely and remote. The wind seemed to be whispering something – a story too long in the telling for our quick passing to perceive.

Finally I broke the companionable silence.

"Arthur was supposed to have visited here?"

"So Wilson said. And I confirmed it with the local vicar as well. Curiously, it isn't something that the locals seem anxious to promote. As Wilson put it, 'We need have no truck will all those visitors and tourists such as one finds crawling the rocks of Tintagel. We will keep to our own ways.'"

"Can't say as I blame him. Still, it's a wonder that the academics haven't found it out."

"Probably just a matter of time."

"What is the connection?"

"One that I hadn't heard," replied Holmes. "Sadly, my own studies into the Arthurian legends has diminished as I've grown older, although I do have a notion to make further studies of it someday. I have a notion that proofs might be determined by a full examination of certain old English Charters. I'm sure that a deeper dive into this pool can uncover many more connections – the information just needs to be assembled and compared. For instance, there is the belief that Colchester is actually Camelot – or *Camulod* as some would call it. I've been able to visit there and ascertain – "

He was starting to wander far afield as his enthusiasm grew, and I reigned him back in to our forthcoming visit to the abandoned fort at Hardknott Pass.

He smiled. "It's a ten-mile drive, Watson, but I see your point. I could talk and talk and still not get to what I want to say. I must guard against this surprising enthusiasm I'm displaying. It could very well distract me from more important things.

"Now: About the fort at the river's bend, as Wilson called it. The local legend is that some years after Arthur's birth, attempts were made on his life. Rather like Mary and Joseph fleeing to Egypt with young baby Jesus,

Merlin took Arthur away in secret here – or rather near here, to Ravenglass, near the coast on the River Esk, just south of Drigg. There are still Roman ruins there to this day – a bathhouse, for instance. Then, it was an important Roman naval center, beginning in the Second Century A.D., and lasting for several hundred years."

"Ravenglass," I said. "That doesn't sound very Roman."

"Exactly what I commented to the vicar. He said that it was sometimes called *Clannoventa* in ancient times. Apparently Ravenglass is more of a corruption of a Welsh name for the Esk, *yr afon glas*, meaning '*blue or green river*'. It was here that Merlin and young Arthur were welcomed by the local King Derek. However, due to attacks that soon followed, Merlin was no longer accepted, and it was arranged that he could instead take his young ward east – to the fort where we're headed, located near a bend in the River Esk. Mediobogdum, it was called then. It was there that Merlin and Arthur stayed for several years, and where Merlin trained the young man for his future – to be the heir to three kingdoms. His reign would unite them, unifying much of Britain in a way never seen before – if one believes the legends."

"This training – that would have been based on Merlin's magic. And what he had learned living backward through time, as some legends aver."

Holmes shook his head. "That's the popular version. Other more-knowledgeable scholars theorize that Merlin was no wizard. Rather, he was an engineer of sorts – a former Roman soldier, or perhaps the son or grandson of a soldier, who was still here in Britain after the Romans had begun their retreat to the Continent. As you'll recall, their departure left a vacuum here that was soon filled by warring tribes and kingdoms of varying degrees – some civilized, and some barely above savagery. It is believed that Merlin, with his knowledge of engineering and science that he'd obtained by way of his Roman heritage and education, *seemed* to be a magician. From what I read long ago, before my Arthurian researches waned, this version of Merlin – the historical version – was a master of battle tactics, and also scientific methods that were advanced for that time as well. This was the man who had taken Arthur, the heir to three kingdoms, under his wing to raise."

"So there is no promise of magic here," I said as we drew closer to our destination. "Unlike Glastonbury, which is on a Ley Line and supposedly has connections to the unknown forces of the earth, this is just an old fort."

"Don't say it like that, Watson!" Holmes cried, a merry light in his eyes. "Aren't you usually the one telling me that there's more to life than cold scientific fact?" He gigged the horse a bit faster. "Here we have the chance to walk in the steps of one of my heroes."

"The former king?"

"The man of science who was thought to be a wizard!"

As we drew closer, we discussed that we were likely on the path of an old Roman road stretching between Ravenglass, running up the Eskdale Valley, and then on through the Hardknott and Wrynose Passes to other Roman forts at Ambleside and Kendal.

"Wilson pointed out that the remains of Mediobogdum are located on the flanks of the Hardknott Pass, with commanding views down Eskdale."

"We aren't far from Scafell Pike," I commented, and Holmes nodded.

"It's not more than two or three miles north. This would have been one of the links for troops to police the interior against the potentially hostile native population. They were never friendly or welcoming at the best of times, and as Rome's influence waned, it only became worse."

I looked around us. Now the hills on either side of the old road had risen quite a bit higher. "It's beautiful in a rough and rugged way – I expect the locals would never be happy anywhere else – but it must have been a bleak existence for the Roman soldiers, recruited from all over the world, who were posted here, far beyond the edge of civilization."

"Oh, I don't know. They were just ten miles from a bustling seaport. I expect that they found ways to entertain themselves, as soldiers do."

He glanced my way but, as a former soldier, I refused to rise to the bait. Instead, I said, "Wilson told all of this to you? An outsider? You made it sound as if they wish to keep their secrets here about their long-ago illustrious visitors."

"I believe that he could tell from my knowledgeable questions that I could be trusted."

"'Knowledgeable questions'? Does that mean that you questioned him first, in order for the topic to be broached? I had the impression that it was the other way around – that he simply started telling you about the locality during our walk up here last night."

"Let's just say that in my researches at the British Museum a few years ago when I lived in Montague Street and had more time on my hands, I came across certain documents that made references to this place. When we came here, I was pleased that I could renew my acquaintance with the topic." He looked at me. "Ah, Watson, I can see you have more questions. I'm afraid that I can't be more specific. My researches were communicated to the proper quarters at the time, and all I can say is that there is more of interest here than I can share – aspects that might have international implications should truths be revealed. Let us just enjoy a visit to a place of interest and leave it at that."

I nodded, puzzled, but knowing Holmes well enough by this point that I knew nothing else would be forthcoming. "At least that explains why you didn't ask Wilson or the vicar to come with us," I responded. "Locals such as they might have provided some useful insight."

Holmes nodded. "That's why."

Our conversation had been punctuated by long silences while we absorbed the stark beauty around us as we traveled further from the coast. Finally, before I realized it (as the location looked much like other areas around us) we reached a wider spot in the old road where Holmes pulled the horse to a stop. We had reached our destination.

"It looks different in daylight," I said, "and when approached on a cart instead of by foot."

Holmes nodded. The wind was steady and made a never-ceasing noise through the long grasses which grew all around us, stretching in varying colors to the distant hillsides. "I am not a fanciful man, as you can attest," he said, "but there is an unusual feeling about this place."

"I know what you mean," I said. "And yet, you related to me a version of Merlin that was not magical."

"True, but a visit by one man – even someone like Merlin with the reputation of being a wizard, and even if he stayed for several years – would not have had much influence over a place such as this with the feel of more ancient powers."

I laughed with surprise. "Holmes, we must get you out of London more often. You're beginning to sound more like Alton Peake with every minute."

He joined my amusement. Peake was a friend of ours who had known Holmes since he lived in Montague Street. Whereas Holmes set himself up as a consulting detective who refused any hint of a supernatural explanations during his investigations, Peake was the opposite – a consulting spiritualist of sorts who investigated events with possibly other-worldly connections. To be fair, he was open-minded and perfectly willing to accept rational solutions, but he also kept his mind open to additional interpretations.

"No fears there, my friend," replied Holmes. "I suspect that Peake would examine this site from a far different viewpoint. I simply mentioned it because certain areas, like Glastonbury or Stonehenge, seem to generate more legends and superstitions than others – and rightly so, as a visit to them seems to make their *outrè* nature quite obvious."

He tied the horse to a nearby post, obviously put there for the purpose long ago, and we began to climb the narrow rocky trail toward the hill where the fort was located.

"The parson was telling me that this site is much more ancient than when the Romans were here in the Second Century. He asserts that within the fort is a fairy *rath*, where the ghost of a former king, Eveling, holds court. There is some local division as to whether he was a ruler of men or elves. He showed me a volume, *Britannia*, by William Camden and published in 1607, which mentions this mysterious king." The wind seemed to pick up, and we continued our climb. "For those living here two-thousand or more years ago, belief in such a thing seems almost understandable."

Mediobogdum
Hardknott Roman Fort
The Fort at the River Bend

For those who have never visited such a site, it might be difficult to realize what one was seeing. When picturing a fort, one would expect to see walls of stone, or perhaps logs in the American frontier. This, being far older, was much diminished, and consisted simply of various low rock walls, delineating where outer and inner walls of the structure had been located. Long grass grew here and there, but in other places it was missing where footpaths had been permanently etched by curious visitors, moving between the obvious sites of interest: A taller pile of rocks providing a view, or a low spot with futile hints of possible openings into lower levels. All around us, sheep grazed, up and down the hillsides, and within the boundaries of the stones.

"It sometimes seems that legends are thicker across the British landscape than these blades of grass," Holmes said. "I have a college friend from Sussex – his name is Musgrave – who had a family riddle that was repeated for so many hundreds of years that it lost all meaning to them. And he once told me of another set of Musgraves from Edenhall, not all that far from here, just a few miles northeast of Penrith, who have owned an ornate Venetian goblet since the middle ages – they call it *The Luck of Edenhall*. Family legend says that sometime in the fourteenth century, the butler from the Edenhall branch – and trust me, the Musgraves have employed some unique butlers – came across a group of dancing fairies. They left this object lying in the grass, and the butler seized it and refused to return it. The fairies fled, but one called back that '*Whene'er this cup shall break or fall, then farewell the luck of Edenhall.*' Since then, the family has done whatever they could to make sure that the glass does not break."

I laughed and looked back and forth, unsuccessfully attempting to identify the fairy *rath*. Another question about King Arthur came to mind, something I'd recalled about the Castle Rock of Triermain located several miles to the northeast and its connection to Sir Walter Scott's Arthurian poem *The Bridal of Triermain*. But it died on my lips as a harsh voice suddenly came from the northwest, beyond the boundaries of the stone walls, where the ground dropped away toward the distant river.

"Stop!" the unseen man cried, apparently out of breath and getting closer. "You're under arrest!"

Two men climbed into our view, one a fellow in his mid-fifties, tall and dressed in outdoor work clothes, but of a quality favored by gentlemen, and the other a burly constable of approximately thirty years. It had been the older man who had called out, and he paused for a moment to catch his breath while the constable moved around behind us, as if to prevent our escape back to the road and our waiting dog-cart.

"And you are?" asked Holmes, his expression more amused than peeved.

"August Pitt-Rivers," was the man's reply. "I am the Inspector of Ancient Monuments."

Augustus Pitt-Rivers
Inspector of Ancient Monuments

I had never heard of such a title, and was inclined to laugh – an idea that was terminated when I considered the unsmiling constable standing nearby. Holmes, however, looked at the man with a sharpened gaze.

"I've heard of you," he said. "That's a new position – it was only created at the beginning of this year."

The man frowned and nodded. "That's correct – and many people wouldn't know that. I'm not surprised, however, that artifact thieves would know of me."

That rankled me. "Now hold on, sir! We are not thieves. What gives you cause for such an accusation?"

Pitt-Rivers' eyes narrowed. "We received a tip. It warned us you'd protest your innocence. Now come along – you're under arrest."

"On what authority?" replied Holmes, having lost any of the good humor that the encounter had initially created.

"On mine," rumbled the constable. He laid a hand gently upon his belted truncheon. "We can make it easy or difficult. Either way, it's back to Drigg with you. We don't take kindly to grave-robbers here."

Holmes glanced around this way and that, and I followed his gaze to where it settled – a patch of ground near one of the fort walls that appeared to have recently been disturbed.

"I assure you – " he said, but Pitt-Rivers interrupted him.

"Not now. You may make a statement in the fullness of time, where it can be properly recorded. Until then, I'd advise against resistance. You clearly aren't from around here, and you won't be difficult to locate should you choose to run."

The idea of fleeing was ridiculous, but so was the notion that we were in custody. I looked toward Holmes and could see that he was quite angry, but keeping his temper in check. He liked to see himself as an emotionless calculating machine, but he could become as outraged or angry as any man, and in those earlier days – he was still just twenty-nine then – the inner calm that he would have in later years following his return to London after his supposed death in '91 was still a number of years in the future.

It seemed that cooperation was the better path, and so we followed Pitt-Rivers down the steep slope toward the river, where a carriage was parked out of sight underneath a grove. When we were seated under the gaze of the constable, who tersely identified his name as Wood, Pitt-Rivers steered his horse back to the old Roman road, and then east a short distance to where we'd tied our dog-cart. He climbed down and attached our horse's rope to the rear of the larger carriage before resuming his seat and setting us in motion back toward the small village by the sea.

Attempts at conversation or questions went unanswered over the ten-mile route. Upon arrival at an inconspicuous building maintained for the local law enforcement authorities – apparently just the one officer we'd just met – we were led inside under the gaze of a few curious and morose locals, through a small outer office, and then into a dimly lit hallway beside a single barred cell. We were locked inside without another word of explanation or an offer to take our statements, as had been mentioned earlier. And there we stayed for the rest of the night and into the following day, receiving several acceptable meals slid through to us by Constable Wood, but not a scrap of information, or even conversation. Our demands to speak to counsel or send a message were ignored.

Holmes was becoming more impatient. "But an entire day! Wasted – and for what? All because of one man's stubbornness and stupidity."

"At least," I countered, "it was a chance to think." And it had been that. I had slept and pondered. Being in the military, as I had been not so many years before, taught a man patience, as the occasional minutes of deadly excitement were separated by days and weeks of tedium and monotony. Holmes could be patient as well – when it served a purpose. If he needed to wait all night without making a sound or motion in order to solve a mystery or capture a killer – as we had done not so long ago in a sinister bedroom connected to its neighbor by a small ventilator just large enough for a devilish beast to pass – then he was in his element. But to place him in this situation, deprived of purpose or information, was, as he had stated, intolerable.

Fortunately we would soon have answers.

We heard footsteps approaching from the front of the building. The door between the rear and front opened, flooding our cell with light. It was too soon after our breakfast for more food, so possibly this visit had another purpose.

The shadow in the doorway resolved into our captor, Augustus Pitt-Rivers, the official Inspector. Holmes had explained to me that the position was a new one, created for the protection of historic sites. "But as I recall," he added, "it was created for London – and not a two-thousand-year-old rock mound in the middle of nowhere. What is he doing here? And why have we fallen into his net?"

Now the man was in front of us. Even as we both moved to the bars to confront him, he was joined by Constable Wood, who wordlessly opened the cell door. Then he turned and departed, leaving us alone with Pitt-Rivers. His mouth was tight.

"It seems," he murmured, "that you have friends in high places, gentlemen. I'm instructed to trust you. In fact . . . ." He paused to swallow. ". . . You have been appointed special investigators. I have no authority over you. I am . . . my orders are to explain the situation, and allow you to do as you will." Clearly the admission galled him.

Holmes, however, was intrigued, his curiosity replacing the outrage at our having been held since the previous afternoon. "May we find someplace more comfortable before you discharge your duty? I'd prefer to smoke a pipe while I hear your story."

Pitt-Rivers nodded and led us out and into the front room. Constable Woods was gone, but our pipes and tobacco were there – along with our bags from the inn. Soon we had found chairs and the room was starting to fill with hazy smoke, and the tension thawed a bit as the Inspector of Ancient Monuments began to speak.

"I was appointed to my position early this year. I believe that it came about because of my interest in archeology, as well as my long experience in the military. I was in the service for a total of thirty-two years, although there were periods when I was on extended leave. I mustered out in '82, and I only saw action once – the Battle of Alma in '54. My strengths lie in teaching and organization. I have a strong background in archeological research, but I must admit that I mostly received this position as 'Inspector' because it was created by my son-in-law, John Lubbock, an anthropologist and parliamentarian. Yet, despite achieving my position because of this connection, I take my duties very seriously.

"And yet, there is much more to it than I initially imagined.

"I expected that I would be spending a great deal of time involved in the protection of British historic sites and ancient artifacts, but I have occasionally been – I suppose the word is *co-opted* – by other governmental agencies when necessary, and much more often than I would have believed. Such is the case now."

He drew on his pipe and then stated, "I understand that you have learned of the Arthurian connections to the fort."

We nodded, and like Holmes, I was wondering who had told Pitt-Rivers of this fact – Wilson or the parson. As if reading our mind, the man nodded. "I heard from both the minister and Wilson. The former admitted he'd spoken to you when I questioned him. The latter is working for me – he has been since my arrival a week ago – coincidentally about the same time you showed up. It was Wilson who became curious – well, concerned is the better description – when you were asking questions about Arthur's connection to Mediobogdum, Mr. Holmes, and he observed when you sought out Vicar Weems afterwards to ask more questions. When you traveled to the fort, we followed."

He shifted in his seat. "Apparently you both have some clout in London, gentlemen. Unknown to us, someone from Holmrook saw when we detained you yesterday and brought you back to the village. Word of your arrest was carried back there, and then messages were sent to London. Your friends there then notified me of your identities and new status."

As I tried to imagine who might have intervened on our behalf, Pitt-Rivers gave a small shrug. "I was unaware of your reputation, Mr. Holmes. I had no idea who either of you are, or what you came here to do – and quite successfully I'm told, in spite of the fact that it must remain a secret. When you were asking about Arthur and Mediobogdum, I only knew that two strangers were involving themselves in my business, and it's too critical to simply allow you to roam free when taking you into custody might have forced the issue and given us answers sooner rather than later."

"We need to know both the answers," interrupted Holmes, "and the questions. You have vaguely explained your interest in us, and why we were taken into custody. We still have no explanation as to what's going on."

Pitt-Rivers looked from one of us to the other. "What have you heard of King Anguish?" he said, seemingly veering into a completely new topic.

I widened my eyes, thinking that such a name sounded like something from *The Pilgrim's Progress* – Christian, Evangelist, Obstinate, and so on. Or perhaps more along the lines of *The Canterbury Tales*, with the Knight, the Wife of Bath, and the Pardoner. Such a name – *The King of Anguish* – didn't seem so unusual in that company.

But Holmes, who kept much more in his brain attic than he would ever admit, replied, "King Anguish is Ireland's equivalent to King Arthur. He was one of Arthur's early enemies, but Arthur defeated him, and Anguish acknowledged Arthur's supremacy." He leaned forward, setting his pipe aside. "How does this relate to Mediobogdum?"

Pitt-Rivers pursed his lips, as if considering how to respond. "You will have noticed – Wilson told you – that the people here are proud of their Arthurian connections, but they also have no wish to advertise them. These beliefs run deep, but are kept secret. Nothing but generalities are ever mentioned. But there are deeper legends and stories.

"You will have heard of Excalibur?" We both nodded. "There are varying origins of this aspect of the legend. Some say that the sword that Arthur pulled from the stone to show his true kingship was Excalibur, while the more common tale is that the famed sword was actually the one later given to Arthur by the Lady of the Lake."

"At Dozmary Pool," I murmured.

Pitt-Rivers nodded. "Exactly. And when Arthur died, some chronicles state that the famed sword was thrown back into the lake, but just before it hit the water, a woman's hand suddenly shot up, catching it, and then pulling it down and away from human sight for all time."

"But other accounts claim that it was buried with the dead king," countered Holmes.

"Correct. At Glastonbury. One historical account says that it was later dug up in the 1100's and given by Richard the Lion-Hearted to the King of Sicily as a gesture of good-will – although why he would do that . . . ? Others claim that it still resides with Arthur in his tomb."

"And I perceive that there must be some lesser-known story," added Holmes, "where it was buried *here* – or rather at the old Roman fort, Mediobogdum."

Pitt-Rivers looked impressed at the statement. Holmes waved a hand. "You wouldn't have mentioned it if the story wasn't leading to that point. But I am curious about King Anguish's connection to your narrative."

"The connection is that there is a revolutionary Irish group, the Sons of Condran, who have allied under the ancient reign of mythical King Anguish and are building strength to some sort of attempt to drive the British from their island. Somehow they learned of the obscure legend that Excalibur is buried at Mediobogdum – and they've decided to get it for

526

themselves as a symbol – a talisman of power. To give their cause a mystical legitimacy."

"And so you're here – "

"I'm here because of my position, and my military background, and because of certain skills that I've acquired in my past that make me useful right now – here, at this place."

"Do you think they have the sword already?" I asked.

Pitt-Rivers nodded.

"I saw a spot at the fort," added Holmes, "alongside one of the walls, that looked as if it had been recently dug up. We were . . . *interrupted* before I had a chance to examine it. Is that where you think the sword was recovered?"

"Possibly. We know that they found some kind of sword – although it certainly wasn't Excalibur, for such a thing assuredly does not truly exist. But any sword, with the weight of importance and legend and the supernatural attached to it, becomes a powerful tool for such a group as the revolutionaries forming under King Anguish's long-lost banner. And then, when you arrived with very pointed and intelligent questions – well, there was no question, at least in my mind at that time, that we must find a way to get some answers, before things progress further and we lose track of these men."

"Wilson told you why we initially went to the fort and Hardknott Pass. Didn't that satisfy your curiosity?"

"He knew some details, but couldn't establish the whole story – and that made me suspicious. And in any case, after your business there was apparently complete and successful, you continued to involve yourself – asking questions and paying a visit. The rising threat of these Sons of Condran is quite serious – I couldn't take any chances that you weren't both involved, and that your initial reason for being here wasn't just a ruse to get you into the area for whatever their next step will be."

He set down his pipe, which had long since gone out, and then turned up his hands, almost a gesture of surrender. "Since I've been here, I've learned – by way of what Wilson could overhear – that a sword was located and dug up, just two days ago, but that's all. Nothing else has come to light." His gaze focused on Holmes. "I have assurances from London that you can be useful, Mr. Holmes, and that you've been involved in affairs of this sort before – dealing with revolutionaries. I have no choice. Time is wasting, and the sword could already be on its way to Ireland. I leave the next move in your hands."

Holmes didn't nod or give any acknowledgement of the man's statement. Instead, he settled back in his chair, one hand curled around his pipe while the other drummed silently on a nearby table, and let his gaze focus on some distant scene. Pitt-Rivers looked at me, as if for some assurance that this was expected behavior. I nodded, and the inspector busied himself with repacking and lighting his pipe.

Finally Holmes spoke. "How well do you trust Wilson and the constable?"

"Just barely," was the reply. "I've found that I can rarely trust anyone. I only trust you because I've been ordered to do so." There was no malice tinging this statement. It was simply a fact.

Holmes nodded. "How much have you told either of them – about the sword and the Sons of Condran, and about Watson and me?"

"Nearly nothing. Wilson told me you were asking questions during your first trip to the fort, and that you had visited the vicar. I haven't seen him since – he comes and goes. And I simply used my authority to have the constable take you into custody, and then to have you released. He didn't need to know why."

"That may be helpful," Holmes replied. "There isn't much time, and Drigg is a small place. I'll need to work alone." He stood and nodded to our bags. "You checked us out of the inn?"

Pitt-Rivers nodded. "Last night. I searched your bags to see if you had any connection to the revolutionaries." He said it as a simple statement, with no implied apology.

Holmes looked at me. "Take our things and go to Holmrook Hall. They'll be happy to let you stay. No, wait –" He stopped himself. "As I recall, there's an inn very near there. Stay there – that will prevent any of those at the Hall from being too curious. I'll be in touch – probably this evening." Then he turned to Pitt-Rivers. "I'll be leaving town now, but I'll return later. Don't look for me. I'll get a message to you when I need your help. Watson – a word outside, please."

He picked up his bag and I did the same. Then, with a nod of dismissal toward the suddenly nonplussed Inspector of Ancient Monuments, he departed. I did the same, pulling the door shut behind me.

We walked a few hundred feet, ignored – as nearly as I could tell – by the few visitors up that early.

"I plan to leave and travel somewhere close where I can effect a disguise." He checked his watch. "There's a train heading north that leaves in a few minutes. I hope that I don't have to go as far as Egremont or even Whitehaven. In any case, I'll return as soon as possible and attempt to insinuate myself into the locals and see what I might learn."

"Holmes," I interrupted, "do you believe this fellow? He checked on us, and received marching orders from someone in London – or so he says – but we took him at his word as to his position and story."

"That is my first priority," replied my friend. "To check on this Pitt-Rivers fellow and see if he is who he says. I'll send a wire from the Drigg station before the train departs. If he isn't legitimate, he'll find that he's suddenly in a deeper game than he's prepared to play." Then he handed me his bag. "To the inn for you, then, and I'll be in touch as soon as I can – hopefully later today."

With that he turned and walked until the next intersection, where he turned west and then vanished from my sight.

I considered finding someone to drive me the mile or so to the inn located near Holmrook Hall, but in the end, following the night of incarceration, I decided to walk. While the day was darkening a bit with building clouds, I knew that any rain was unlikely for the next hour or so. Holmes and I always traveled light, so our bags were no great burden, and I had the two of them held symmetrically. And after being in the small cell since the previous day, a walk suited me quite well. Adjusting my grip on our bags, I set off to the east.

Drigg and Holmrook

It was a narrow track that wound between houses on either side while still in the village, but in five or ten minutes I had left most of those behind, and the landscape widened out around me, with the occasional small house set back from the road, and the grassy spaces in between dotted with preoccupied sheep, intent on feeding and indifferent to me. In the distance I could see the rising mountains, although I was sure that none were the famed Scafell Pike. As the road took gentle turns, I was uncertain as to which exact direction the ancient fort was located, although it was generally in the same direction in which I was heading. I tried to imagine

529

this area during the years when the Romans were here, those centuries before and after Christ when their influence was so profound. They established cities and towns throughout the island which were still in existence today, along with the roads connecting them. They had brought incredibly influential civilizing influences and knowledge that had remained to varying degrees even after they left Britain.

From the time that Julius Caesar set foot on our shores in 55 B.C. until Constantine III thoroughly withdrew the Roman Army in approximately 410 A.D. to defend the Continental Empire from encroaching Barbarians, the influence of the Romans on Britain was almost incalculable – and yet it was simply part of the land in which we lived. I once had an American friend visit London, and we discussed his country where, except for a few native structures of unknown age in the southwestern deserts, there were virtually no buildings more than a few hundred years old. This conversation had occurred after we had passed the massive Roman wall fragments near The Tower, simply standing there by the modern thoroughfare for current citizens to touch or ignore as they chose every day. The wall had been part of the original square-mile Londinium, and various pieces were easily found. It was quite routine to read that excavations for new roads, buildings, or extensions of the Underground frequently uncovered new Roman sites on a regular basis. Having such reminders of our ancient past so easily accessible had certainly helped shape our national character.

As I reached Holmrook, the road I walked tee'd into a thoroughfare alongside the River Irt, with a sign pointing to the right, south to Ravenglass. I turned left upon the track which I knew led to the Hall. However, after only a few hundred feet, I reached a snug little inn on my left, a couple of hundred feet before the drive that led to Holmrook Hall. I presented myself and requested two rooms and a sitting room, if available, explaining that my friend would be joining me later that day. I registered under my own name, but didn't provide Holmes's. Then, after I was shown upstairs and left the bags, I went back down and asked for some breakfast.

I was pleased to learn that the Holmrook Reading Room was located at the inn and, after my meal, I made an investigation of the small library's contents. I discovered several pamphlets and books related to local Roman history, including some further information specifically about the ancient fort.

I read that Mediobogdum, sometimes locally called "Hardknott Castle", was constructed from nearby stone, along with red sandstone and other materials such as non-native timber, that the soldiers would have transported up from the coast. It was laid out according to typical Roman-fort design, and one could still see evidence of granaries, administrative

530

offices, the temple, and residences. It was roughly square with a gate in each wall. Although long since vanished, a tower would have stood at each corner, and many of the soldiers had probably lived in tents pitched outside the walls. There was no evidence that a civilian settlement had grown up nearby, as Mediobogdum was probably close enough to Drigg and Ravenglass that none was required.

The fort, as well as many like it, had been necessary because many native Britons hadn't submitted easily to the invaders during that violent time. Mediobogdum had held five-hundred or so men, and its commanding location above the valley of the River Esk had guarded an important trade route stretching over one-hundred-and-fifty miles. It had been abandoned by the early 140's A.D., although no one knew exactly why. I went through all the relevant documents and books in the library's collection, but I could find no mention of any Arthurian connections.

Afterwards, with who-knew-how-many hours left until Holmes returned, I pulled down Dickens' *The Pickwick Papers* and found a comfortable chair. Although I had read it countless times, another visit with that peculiar club was just as pleasant as always. By late morning, I ordered a whisky, and then it was time for lunch. Afterwards, seeing that the rains had arrived, I climbed upstairs to my room for a nap. I slept for several hours, finding restoration after the mostly sleepless night in the Drigg cell. I was deciding whether to continue reading in the upstairs sitting room or move back downstairs to the chair I had occupied all morning when there was a knock, and the door to the hall opened.

I found myself facing a roughly dressed man, somewhat over six feet, although he slouched terribly. He was carrying a ragged carpet bag in his left hand. His hair was ragged and gray, and the gaunt thinness of his face was emphasized by prominent cheekbones. He had a ragged tuft of a goatee on his chin, and his shifty expression glanced up and away frequently from the tattered cap still on his head.

"Come sit by the fire," I said to Sherlock Holmes. "I see you were caught out in the rain without a proper coat."

"You sound like Mrs. Hudson," he said, straightening to his full height and removing the cap. "It's been a productive day," he added.

By the light of the small fire which I built up as he found his chair, I could see how he had darkened his cheeks to shadow them. He spit out a couple of wads of cloth, probably torn from a linen handkerchief, which he'd held in his mouth to emphasize the prominent cheek bones. Although his rough clothing had helped to establish his character, what mostly made him so convincing was simply that he seemed to *become* a different person. It was a gift and a skill that he regularly put to successful use.

"I went to Egremont," he explained, "where I found a wire waiting for me from London. Pitt-Rivers' *bona fides* are confirmed – as well as our brief to assist in the recovery of the sword, and to strike a blow against these Sons of Condran. I arranged with the Egremont police inspector to obtain his assistance. He has reserved several of his men, and they're waiting just north of Drigg for our rendezvous at dusk. He also helped me to assemble this quick disguise.

"Returning to Drigg, it wasn't difficult to learn who was new to town, and who had been associating with them. I managed to confer again with Pitt-Rivers, and he didn't have that information, although his man Wilson could have obtained it easily enough. That led us to suspect that Wilson is playing both sides. I had to be careful, since even in disguise, I was someone who hadn't been seen before, and if I ran into Wilson, he might suspect my true identity.

"By asking around as if I were expecting to meet up with a friend, I found where an Irishman, Billy O'Toomey, has been staying at The Queen Hotel, and meeting with a number of shady locals each night in the pub. Apparently Billy has been recruiting for something, although I couldn't find out exactly what. However, the owner, sensing a chance to gossip, told me that Billy meets with these men in the back of a room located off his main bar, and that at some point during these conversations, he shows them something wrapped in a cloth or blanket, approximately three feet in length."

"So the sword is still here," I noted.

Holmes nodded. "That's the most likely explanation. He generally holds court around eight o'clock – which is when Inspector Hodgson will carry out his raid – with our help."

The rest of the evening passed quickly. Holmes, back in his own clothing which he'd pulled from the carpet bag, joined me as we went downstairs for an early meal. Then, in spite of the rain, we set off on foot back to Drigg, deciding that slipping into town during the twilight drizzle and reaching our destination unseen was better than arriving openly in a cart.

As we walked, I related what I'd read about the old fort, while Holmes told me some of the other Arthurian legends in this part of the country, including the legendary king's last Battle of Mons Badonicus in Bathampton. "I was involved in an archeological investigation there," he added. "Before your time – and definitely a tale for which the world is not yet prepared." As we walked through the darkening drizzle, he shared it with me, and I had to agree. Hearing the details while passing along that same road which had carried Roman soldiers back-and-forth from Drigg

532

to Mediobogdum centuries earlier was enough to raise the hair on my neck. I almost expected to see us surrounded by Roman ghosts.

We paused at a church on our right before we entered the village proper. There, in the darkness, I was introduced to the inspector and his men. "They're gathering in the inn," explained Hodgson. "This is our lucky night – it seems that O'Toomey's recruiting by ones and twos has culminated with a big meeting. We should be able to snare him and find out who all the locals are as well."

"I doubt of the locals are worth anything," said Holmes. "They are little fish, fresh into the nets. But O'Toomey will be an important link back to the larger organization. He can give us names and information. But most important, we can get the sword before it has a chance to become a relic for them to rally around."

Hodgson informed us that he already had several other men in place around the inn. We only had to join them and then the raid could commence.

I've accompanied Holmes on many such skirmishes. Some went well, but some ended dreadfully horrible. The capture of Tré Bonfardin and his Soldiers of Cromwell was successful beyond measure. Conversely, the raid upon Conner Strickland's abominable breeding dens beside the Thames went terribly, tragically wrong, and the loss from that fire always tainted the value of preventing Strickland's vile scheme. In each case, for good or bad, the event was dramatic. In contrast, the taking of Billy O'Toomey and the recovery of the sword was almost anticlimactic.

The police entered the pub while covering all the entrances to prevent escapes. They flooded into the back room, taking Billy into custody while getting the names of all the men in attendance. It was no surprise to find Pitt-Rivers' local man, Wilson, there as part of the group, and it turned out that he was a semi-important figure within the revolutionary group's counsels. Later, when the Inspector of Ancient Monuments found out the truth, he rightly understood that hiring one of the enemy as his contact person was a professional *faux pas* that would stain his reputation.

O'Toomey was taken into custody and spirited away, back to the police station in Egremont. He would be in our custody, along with our companion for the journey, Pitt-Rivers, during the return to London the following day, where we three delivered him to Scotland Yard. Although I never knew the details, I understand that the information he provided to reduce his own punishment was instrumental in disbanding and incarcerating the Sons of Condran.

We left Pitt-Rivers with the prisoner at the Yard, and then we made the short journey by cab to another building near the British Museum, a non-descript house on the south side of Keppel Street, just off Russell

Square. The door was opened by a wizened little woman who seemed to recognize Holmes, her toothless mouth smiling happily and her head bobbing as she reached and pulled him inside. "She's deaf," said Holmes, turning his head toward me so she couldn't see his face.

She pulled me in as well, and then shut the door. After taking and hanging our coats and hats, she led us down a hall to the back of the house, and into a wide room that appeared to stretch the width of the building. There, behind a cluttered desk, was an ancient man who seemed more corpse than living flesh. But his face lit up as had the woman's, and he forced himself to his feet.

"Do you have it?" was his only greeting.

Holmes, who had carried the blanket-wrapped sword from Cumbria to London, laid the object on the desk before the man. He seemed to stop breathing, and I wondered if he had died while standing upright, somehow locked in place instead of falling. Then, defying expectation, he lurched himself into motion and pulled back the wrapped cloth, revealing the sword.

I hadn't seen it since we took it from O'Toomey the night before, and while it had been impressive in the dim light of the pub's back room, it was immaculate here in the sunshine from the wide south-facing windows. The rains of the previous day had vanished.

It was something over three feet in length, heavy, and extremely shiny. It had no nicks or scratches. It was all of a solid piece – point and blade and fullard on one side of the guard, and grip and pommel on the other. No doubt, two-thousand years earlier, the grip had been wrapped in leather windings to enable the wielder to better hold it, but that had long-since rotted away. Now, without any extraneous trappings, it was simply pure metal, nearly glowing with its own peculiar light.

Holmes looked me. "This is Aldbury Aston Lonsdale – the greatest Arthurian expert in the Kingdom. Probably the world."

The old man waved a hand at this statement and then lowered it to the blade. He hovered his hand back and forth along the length of it, then gently pressed a thumb against the edge. "Razor sharp," he murmured. "Still, after all this time."

He removed his hand and then looked up, speaking to one of us, and then the other. "Very few know of the legends that tell of Arthur and Merlin's stay at Mediobogdum. The Romans had already left by then. Merlin arrived in Drigg with the young and future king after attempts had been made on the boy's life. He was given permission to move to the fort, ten miles east. Merlin was no magician – he was an engineer, with Roman knowledge and skills. He set about fortifying the abandoned site, and also training Arthur for his future duties. All sorts of knowledge – mathematics,

534

engineering, geography, and – of course – warfare. And it was there that he gave him the sword. *This sword – Excalibur.*"

My breath caught. This was surely foolishness. Such a weapon was only legend. And yet, this man, according to Holmes, was the world's greatest Arthurian expert. But perhaps a lifetime of such expertise had clouded his old mind – he wanted to believe, so when an unusual sword was brought to him, he *did* believe. He saw what he wanted to see.

He seemed to read my mind. "You don't believe me," he said, holding my gaze. "Look at it. Any confirmation will prove it – this is a metal alloy that is unknown, as the oldest and least-known stories tell us. It came from a place beyond human knowledge."

"The Lady of the Lake," I whispered, and the old man frowned.

"Nonsense! Foolishness!" He worked his mouth, and then continued. "There was no lake, and no magical woman living in the bottom of it. The sword was fashioned from metal that fell from the sky – a meteorite! Several meteorites, actually. A Roman named Publius Varrus found them and learned how to smelt them. Initially, not knowing what else to do with them, he cast them in the shape of a small statue – which he called *The Lady of the Lake.*"

"How do you know this?" I asked. "You say it as if it's fact – but nothing definite is known of any of this – only varying and contradictive legends. Many parts of England all claim to have some Arthurian association."

"There are documents – all preserved and handed down. In my youth I traced them – read and copied them, and when I could, delivered them into the safekeeping of the Museum. They're still there . . . for those allowed to look."

"But why are they not revealed? If they are fact, they could change history."

"That's exactly why!" countered the old man. "There are secrets within these papers that, even today, could change *history*! Disunity and jealousy and resentment could grow and lead to civil war!"

"But surely after all this time – " I began, but Londsale raised a frail blue-veined hand. "Enough, Doctor. Greater minds than ours have made these decisions, and very long ago. I made the same arguments for public release of the papers when I was your age, but to no avail. I've since realized the wisdom of these strictures. You have just seen how the power of these ancient events and objects can be used. Objects with stories have power. The Sons of Condran are not the only group of that sort."

"You say it was made from meteorites by a Roman," interrupted Holmes. "How came it to Merlin's possession?"

535

"He was Varrus' descendant. Caius Merlyn Britannicus, to be more specific – with *Merlyn* spelled with a *Y*. His cousin was the ill-fated Uther Pendragon, father of Arthur. Merlyn took over the care and training of the young boy – and also provided him with the sword, which had since been refashioned from *The Lady of the Lake*."

"And now that it's been found," said Holmes, "it must be hidden."

"For now, young Mr. Holmes. For now. But – " And he looked with great intensity at each of us. " – they say that Arthur will come again. When he's most needed. And he'll need that sword. I trust that when the time comes, he'll receive it."

I expected Holmes to answer that with a trace of a sneer in his voice, but he was only serious. "We must trust those who will now be the sword's new guardians. One can only hope . . . ."

The old man nodded and laid both hands on the blade. "If only I could hold it, but I am too weak. Show it to me, Mr. Holmes. Before you wrap it up and take it away forever, show it to me."

Holmes nodded and reached for the plain-metal grip. Getting his fingers underneath, he wrapped both hands around the grip and slowly lifted it upright before his face. It glinted and shined in the light – and yet, it seemed to have a light of its own, from somewhere deep within. It was then that old man spoke – so softly that I doubt that Holmes, just across the desk, could hear. I could not look away.

"You see it, Doctor?" he whispered. "Of course you do! It *is* Excalibur – there is no doubt! Ah, that I have finally touched it! And you see, don't you? See it? It's held by a worthy man!"

I could only nod. I don't know if Lonsdale noticed me do so, for surely he was looking at the sword as well. I don't know how long we watched – no more than seconds. Then the spell was broken when Holmes lowered it back to the desk and re-wrapped it in the cloth.

There was nothing left to say. We thanked the old man for his time and left the way we'd come. Outside, I considered asking to see the sword one more time, but I realized that it would be foolish to reveal it on a city street. In any case, Holmes spoke first.

"Do you go back to Baker Street with our bags," he said. "I have a delivery to make, and then I'll join you shortly. Perhaps in a few hours, we might visit Simpsons? I feel like celebrating."

I nodded without speaking, my throat dry. I was strangely affected by what I'd seen. The sword hadn't looked so special the previous night, in the light of the pub, or subsequently in the upstairs sitting room of our inn, but today . . . .

In any case, Holmes didn't seem to be as impressed. But then, he wouldn't be. It took a great deal to impress him, and he would never admit

536

to something that smacked of anything beyond human comprehension –
certainly not an ancient sword that seemed to luminesce with its own inner
light and power.

I watched as he set off along Keppel Street, and then turned at Russell
Square toward Montague Street. I stood there for quite a while longer,
imagining him as he carried the artifact past his old rooms before turning
into the Museum, or perhaps continuing on to some anonymous building
in Whitehall. Possibly someday I'd know more of the sword's story.

I finally shook myself into motion and headed the other way, toward
the solid familiarity of Baker Street.

NOTES

The Inspector of Ancient Monuments

Lieutenant General Augustus Henry Lane Fox Pitt-Rivers (1827–1900) was an English officer in the British Army, ethnologist, and archaeologist. For most of his life, he was known as "Lane Fox", but he took the name "Pitt-Rivers" in 1880 upon inheriting a cousin's large estate. In 1882, he became the first British Inspector of Ancient Monuments, (a position created by his son-in-law, parliamentarian John Lubbock.) He was a strong advocate for archaeological methodology, although his position didn't give him a great deal of authority to protect historical sits on private land. His lifelong collection of historical objects led to the founding of The Pitt-Rivers Museum at the University of Oxford, and his collection from the area around Stonehenge forms the basis of The Salisbury Museum in Wiltshire.

Mediobogdum

For more information about Mediobogdum and the time that Merlin (or *Merlyn*) and Arthur stayed there, see the late Jack Whyte's *The Sorcerer Part I: The Fort at the River Bend*. Additional information about Merlin, Arthur, and the otherworldly origins of Excalibur can be found in his highly recommended *Camulod Chronicles* (also known as *A Dream of Eagles*):

- *The Burning Stone* (2018 – *Prequel*)
- *The Skystone* (1992 – Published in Great Britain as *War of the Celts*)
- *The Singing Sword* (1994 – Published in Great Britain as *The Round Table*)
- *The Eagles' Brood* (1994 – Published in Great Britain as *Merlyn*)
- *Uther* (2000 – Published in Great Britain as *Pendragon*)
- *The Saxon Shore* (1995 – Published in Great Britain as *Excalibur*)
- *The Sorcerer Part 1: The Fort at River's Bend* (1997 – Published in Great Britain as *The Boy King*)
- *The Sorcerer Part 2: Metamorphosis* (1997 – Published in Great Britain as *The Sorcerer*)
- *The Lance Thrower* (or *Clothar the Frank.* 2003 – Published in Great Britain as *Lancelot*)
- *The Eagle* (2004 – Published in Great Britain as *The Last Stand*)

About the Author

David Marcum plays *The Game* with deadly seriousness. He first discovered Sherlock Holmes in 1975 at the age of ten, and since that time, he has collected, read, and chronologicized literally thousands of traditional Holmes pastiches in the form of novels, short stories, radio and television episodes, movies and scripts, comics, fan-fiction, and unpublished manuscripts. He is the author of over 100 Sherlockian pastiches, some published in anthologies and magazines such as *The Strand*, and others collected in his own books, *The Papers of Sherlock Holmes, Sherlock Holmes and A Quantity of Debt, Sherlock Holmes – Tangled Skeins*, and *Sherlock Holmes and The Eye of Heka*. He has edited over 80 books, including several dozen traditional Sherlockian anthologies, such as the ongoing series *The MX Book of New Sherlock Holmes Stories*, which he created in 2015. This collection is now up to 39 volumes, with more in preparation.

He was responsible for bringing back August Derleth's Solar Pons for a new generation, first with his collection of authorized Pons stories, *The Papers of Solar Pons*, and then by editing the reissued authorized versions of the original Pons books, and then volumes of new Pons adventures. Most recently, he wrote *The Further Papers of Solar Pons*. He has also brought back the adventures of Dr. Thorndyke, and has plans for similar projects in the future. He has contributed numerous essays to various publications, and is a member of a number of Sherlockian groups and Scions. His irregular Sherlockian blog, *A Seventeen Step Program*, addresses various topics related to his favorite book friends (as his son used to call them when he was small), and can be found at:

http://17stepprogram.blogspot.com/

David is a member of numerous Sherlockian societies and the *Mystery Writers of America*, and he's the winner of the 2020 Wolfe Pack Pastiche Award and the 2023 Arthur Conan Doyle Award for Fiction for his Holmes pastiche "The Unintended Offenses". He is a licensed Civil Engineer, living in Tennessee with his wife and son. Since the age of nineteen, he has worn a deerstalker as his regular-and-only hat. In 2013, he and his deerstalker were finally able make his first trip-of-a-lifetime Holmes Pilgrimage to England, with return Pilgrimages in 2015 and 2016, where you may have spotted him. If you ever run into him and his deerstalker out and about, feel free to say hello!

Also by David Marcum
from MX Publishing

Traditional Canonical Holmes Adventures

Hardcover, Paperback, E-editions, and Audio

The Papers of Sherlock Holmes
"The Papers of Sherlock Holmes *by David Marcum contains nine intriguing mysteries . . . very much in the classic tradition . . . He writes well, too.*" – Roger Johnson, Editor, *The Sherlock Holmes Journal*, The Sherlock Holmes Society of London

"*Marcum offers nine clever pastiches.*"
– Steven Rothman, Editor, *The Baker Street Journal*

Sherlock Holmes and A Quantity of Debt
"*This is a welcome addendum to Sherlock lore that respectfully fleshes out Doyle's legendary crime-solving couple in the context of new escapades . . . .*" – Peter Roche, Examiner.com

"*David Marcum is known to Sherlockians as the author of two short story collections . . . In* Sherlock Holmes and A Quantity of Debt, *he demonstrates mastery of the longer form as well.*"
– Dan Andriacco, Sherlockian and Author of the Cody and McCabe Series

Sherlock Holmes – Tangled Skeins
(Included in Randall Stock's, 2015 Top Five Sherlock Holmes Books – Fiction)
"*Marcum's collection will appeal to those who like the traditional elements of the Holmes tales.*" – Randall Stock, BSI

"*There are good pastiche writers, there are great ones, and then there is David Marcum who ranks among the very best . . . I cannot recommend this book enough.*"
– Derrick Belanger, Author and Publisher of Belanger Books

541

Also by David Marcum
from MX Publishing

Traditional Canonical Holmes Adventures

Sherlock Holmes and The Eye of Heka

"Marcum could be today's greatest Sherlockian writer, and Conan Doyle himself would be proud of this story."
– *Lee Child* - New York Times *Bestselling Author*

"David Marcum is the reigning monarch of all things Sherlockian, and his latest long-form work, Sherlock Holmes and The eye of Heka, *showcases his utter mastery of Watson's narrative voice, while at the same time entertains and enthralls with his spot on descriptions of the characters and themes which animate the world of the Great Detective himself. No mere pastiche,* The Eye of Heka *is a robust and creative novel in its own right, not to be missed!"*
– *John Lescroart* - New York Times Bestselling Author

"Marcum assuredly handles multiple intriguing plots while plausibly adding emotional depth to Dr. Watson . . . Marcum expertly balances deduction and action as he more than meets the challenge of recreating the spirit and tone of Conan Doyle's originals. Sherlockians will clamor for a sequel"
– *Publishers Weekly* Starred Review

Also by David Marcum
from Belanger Books

The Papers of Solar Pons

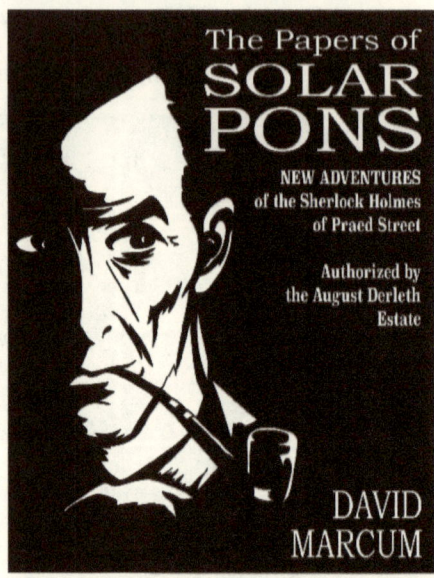

"*As a long-time admirer of the Praed Street sleuth,
I know no one better to chronicle his further exploits.*"
– Roger Johnson, Editor, *The Sherlock Holmes Journal* (Summer 2018),
The Sherlock Holmes Society of London

Introduction: A Word from Dr. Lyndon Parker
The Adventure of the Doctor's Box
The Park Lane Solution
The Poe Problem
The Singular Affair of the Blue Girl
The Plight of the American Driver
The Adventure of the Blood Doctor
The Additional Heirs
The Horror of St. Anne's Row
The Adventure of the Failed Fellowship
The Adventure of the Obrisset Snuffbox
The Folio Matter
The Affair of the Distasteful Society
*And Forewords by August Derleth, Roger Johnson, Peter Blau,
Bob Byrne, Tracy Adam Heron, Derrick Belanger, and David Marcum*

Edited by David Marcum
from MX Publishing
The MX Book of New Sherlock Holmes Stories
(MX Publishing, 2015-   )

"This is the finest volume of Sherlockian fiction I have ever read, and I have read, literally, thousands." – Philip K. Jones

"Beyond Impressive . . . This is a splendid venture for a great cause!"
– Roger Johnson, Editor, *The Sherlock Holmes Journal,*
The Sherlock Holmes Society of London

<u>In Preparation</u>
Further Untold Cases (Part XL – and XLI and XLII as well?)
. . . and more to come!

Edited by David Marcum
from MX Publishing
The MX Book of New Sherlock Holmes Stories
(MX Publishing, 2015-   )

<u>*Publishers Weekly*</u> says:

Part VI: *The traditional pastiche is alive and well . . . .*

Part VII: *Sherlockians eager for faithful-to-the-canon plots and characters will be delighted.*

Part VIII: *The imagination of the contributors in coming up
with variations on the volume's theme is matched by their ingenious resolutions.*

Part IX: *The 18 stories . . . will satisfy fans of Conan Doyle's
originals. Sherlockians will rejoice that more volumes are on the way.*

Part X: *. . . new Sherlock Holmes adventures of consistently high quality.*

Part XI: *. . . an essential volume for Sherlock Holmes fans.*

Part XII: *. . . continues to amaze with the number of high-quality pastiches.*

Part XIII: *. . . Amazingly, Marcum has found 22 superb pastiches . . .
his is more catnip for fans of stories faithful to Conan Doyle's original*

Part XIV: *. . . this standout anthology of 21 short stories written
in the spirit of Conan Doyle's originals.*

Part XV: *Stories pitting Sherlock Holmes against seemingly supernatural phenomena highlight
Marcum's 15th anthology of superior short pastiches.*

Part XVI: *Marcum has once again done fans of Conan Doyle's originals a service.*

Part XVII: *This is yet another impressive array of new but traditional Holmes stories.*

Part XVIII: *Sherlockians will again be grateful to Marcum and
MX for high-quality new Holmes tales.*

Part XIX: *Inventive plots and intriguing explorations of aspects of Dr. Watson's
life and beliefs lift the 24 pastiches in Marcum's impressive 19th Sherlock Holmes anthology*

Part XX: *Marcum's reserve of high-quality new Holmes exploits seems endless.*

Part XXI: *This is another must-have for Sherlockians.*

Part XXII: *Marcum's superlative 22nd Sherlock Holmes pastiche anthology features 21 short stories
that successfully emulate the spirit of Conan Doyle's originals while expanding on the canon's
tantalizing references to mysteries Dr. Watson never got around to chronicling.*

Part XXIII: *Marcum's well of talented authors able to mimic the
feel of The Canon seems bottomless.*

Part XXIV: *Marcum's expertise at selecting high-quality pastiches remains impressive.*

Part XXVIII: *All entries adhere to the spirit, language, and characterizations of
Conan Doyle's originals, evincing the deep pool of talent Marcum has access to.
Against the odds, this series remains strong, hundreds of stories in.*

Part XXXI: *. . . yet another stellar anthology of 21 short pastiches that
effectively mimic the originals . . . Marcum's diligent searches for high-quality
stories has again paid off for Sherlockians.*

Part XXXIV: *Mind-bending puzzles are the highlight of Marcum's fully satisfying 34th anthology,
which again demonstrates that multiple authors are capable of giving Sherlock Holmes and
Watson innovative mysteries to tackle while staying in character. Marcum's inventory of canonical
pastiches shows no signs of being exhausted any time soon.*

Edited by David Marcum
from MX Publishing
The MX Book of New Sherlock Holmes Stories
(MX Publishing, 2015-)

549

Edited by David Marcum
from Belanger Books

Sherlock Holmes: Before Baker Street

Sherlock Holmes and Doctor Watson:
The Early Adventures
Volumes I, II, and III

Edited by David Marcum
from Belanger Books

After the East Wind Blows:
WWI and Roaring Twenties Adventures
of Sherlock Holmes
Volumes I, II, and III

The Nefarious Villains
of Sherlock Holmes
Volumes I and II

Imagination Theatre's Sherlock Holmes

The Further Adventures of Sherlock Holmes:
The Complete Jim French Imagination Theatre Scripts

Edited by David Marcum
from Belanger Books

The Complete Solar Pons
by August Derleth

8-volume Paperback Edition

4-volume Hardcover Edition

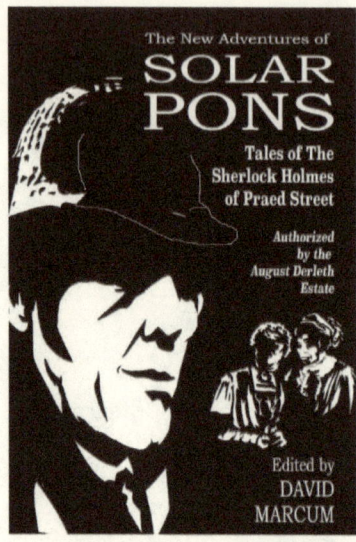

Edited by David Marcum
from MX Publishing

Sherlock Holmes in Montague Street
by Arthur Morrison
Sherlock Holmes's Early Investigations
Originally published as Martin Hewitt Adventures

Complete Hardcover Edition and Three-volume Paperback Edition

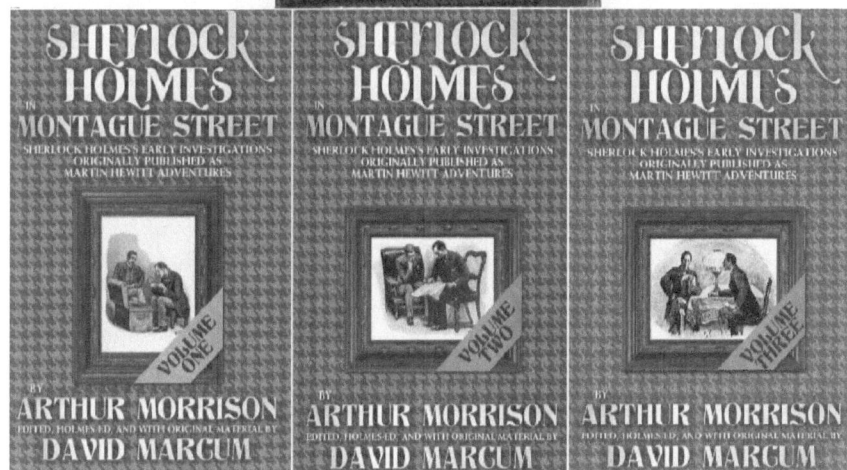

Edited by David Marcum
from MX Publishing

The Complete Dr. Thorndyke
by R. Austin Freeman
Volumes I-IX

Hardcover and Paperback

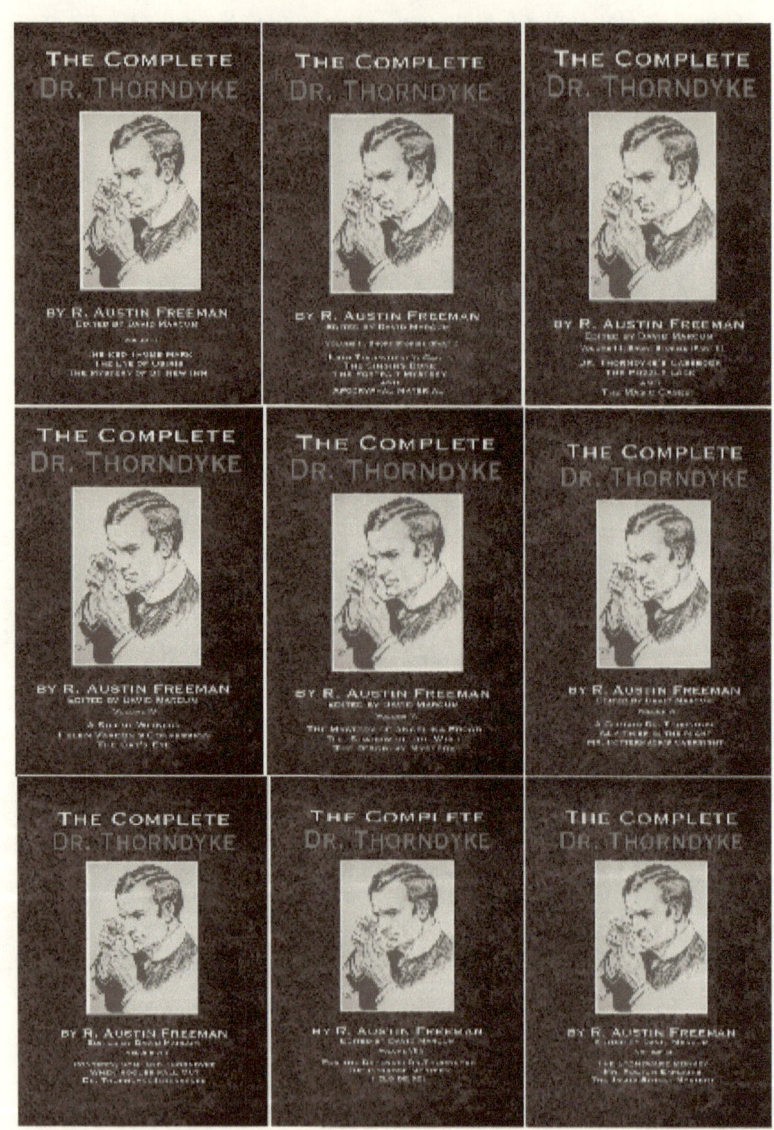

Edited by David Marcum
from MX Publishing

A Proof Reader's Adventures of Sherlock Holmes
by Nick Dunn-Meynell

Hardcover and Paperback

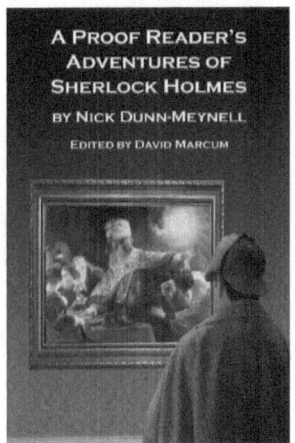

The Rediscovered Annals of Sherlock Holmes
Written by Terry Golledge
Curated by Niel Golledge

Hardcover and Paperback

Edited by David Marcum,
Derrick Belanger, and Sonia Fetherston
from Belanger Books

Sherlock Holmes is Everywhere!

MX Publishing

MX Publishing is the world's largest specialist Sherlock Holmes publisher, with over five-hundred titles and over two-hundred authors creating the latest in Sherlock Holmes fiction and non-fiction

The catalogue includes several award winning books, and over two-hundred-and-fifty have been converted into audio.

MX Publishing also has one of the largest communities of Holmes fans on Facebook, with regular contributions from dozens of authors.

www.mxpublishing.com

@mxpublishing on Facebook, Twitter and Instagram

www.ingramcontent.com/pod-product-compliance
Lightning Source LLC
Chambersburg PA
CBHW032254020726
47495CB00001B/99